INTO THE DARKNESS

Axe Druid Book Four

CHRISTOPHER JOHNS

MOUNTAINDALE
PRESS

CONTENTS

DEDICATION

I'd like to dedicate this book to my readers. Especially two little ones who helped me to realize that even when I'm writing a bunch of goofballs—those goofballs can be important too. Kayda and Tmont say "hi" guys. To those special people out there who these characters touch and resonate with, thank you for sticking around.

And last but certainly not least, my gratitude eternal to my family for understanding that my long hours at the keyboard or on my phone are important to me and others. Your patience is appreciated though I know it comes at a great personal cost to you. I love you.

ACKNOWLEDGMENTS

My sincerest gratitude and thanks to those who slog through these books in their raw, untamed glory. Those of you editors and beta readers who trim the jungles of my thoughts and navigate the depths of my mind—you guys are awesome. My only comfort at your loss of brain cells is that you seem to be as invested in Brindolla as I am.

With love, respect and absolute awe,
Chris.

GETTING CAUGHT UP

Hey guys, Zeke here. It's been a wild ride, and things have really been looking up for us, you know, the boys and me.

You all know how this happy adventure began, right? Let me remind you. Radiance, one of the nine gods of Brindolla, reached through the veil between her world and ours hoping that we could help her, and her siblings solve a little problem. A galactic baddie called War had come to try and take their planet.

He worked his way through the galaxies taking world after world with his war machine and adding to the fold. Constantly moving from one to another, but never skipping any he set his sights on.

And that was how we were going to help stop him from reaching our families and world, Earth. By giving them our aid, the Brindollan gods hold the line against him. We had volunteered—no matter how unwittingly—to hunt down the minions and generals that had arrived before the gods had known what was happening. Once we found them, we were to destroy them by any means available to us.

And oh, do we have the *means*. Sorry.

So, what do we do? We come to this huge world based on modern role-playing video games and start beating ass. We have stats, levels, magic, axes, more magic. *Bigger. Axes.* And lots of friends from this new world to assist us and sort us out.

Did we take our lumps? Hell yeah. Fighting a bone dragon? Cool as hell—scary as shit—but still cool. Watching helplessly as a kid was murdered in cold blood so that one of War's generals could banish us to the Fae Realm? Wasn't fucking cool. I was even "gifted" lycanthropy from our time there in the fae realm, and it's kind of screwed with the crew and me in a few ways since we came back. But the general, Rowan, died for that —nowhere near as painfully as we would have wanted, but he died. Just not before he sent our rogue friend, Balmur, to the Hells, though. It still kind of messes with me today.

Point is, we're here doing the thing, taking our lumps, taking names and kicking ass as best as we can. Thanks to some clever thinking, we even got our friend Balmur back from the Hells and managed to kill another General in the process. There are three of them left as far as we're aware of, so we have those goals, right? That was with the help of some friends we had made after liberating the high elves from the Children of Brindolla, a bunch of assholes who think we're the bad guys for coming to help defend their planet. It was a whole fiasco, let me tell you, and we'd had a bit of a scuffle when we first arrived at the high elf city. After proving we had Mother Nature's backing to help the planet, their leader Queen Silvannas, a former idol of Maebe's who had mistakenly decided to side against us, had her power stripped by Mother Nature and died. After that, we had a friend in power.

Silvannas' son King Telfino had done well in trusting my friends and me to investigate the goings-on in his kingdom. Those Seelie kidnappers and their Doffilnar accomplice never saw us coming.

What's that? What's a Doffilnarr? It's a highly dangerous

creature thought to have been hunted into extinction by the Fae. The Seelie must have found one because they had it pretending to be a dryad so it could lure victims into a portal to the Fae realm. They likely tortured them for information on how to get closer to their own equivalent of Mother Nature —Samir.

That was how Maebe, the Queen of the Unseelie Fae and my girlfriend, had assumed they may try to get the upper hand in their millennia-long feud for supremacy.

But now, my brothers and I have our sights set on the next leg of our quest to return order to this planet; and keep the galactic equivalent to a steaming bag of assholes away from Earth, our friends, and our families. The kingdom of the drow —dark elves covered in fantasy lore since well before I was a pup, and typically evil as hell.

What, y'all are having trouble with the boys? It's the fourth time I've told you lot the story, do I need to break 'em down again? Fine, fine. But you know what they look like, so I'm not doing that all over again. Needy.

Yohsuke - My brother from another mother who I served with in the Marines. Fast friends for a while now, he's my best friend, and he's a real O.G. gamer. You know what it is. He's our spell blade with a pact to a demon and an abomination elf as well. Half drow, half high elf, all angst.

Jaken - A goofy, surfer like gamer buddy of mine from home who recently had a darling little girl. Proud papa and powerful paladin of Radiance. His Fae-orc avatar is a little wild at times, but he's a super nice dude. Admit it, you like him.

Bokaj - One of my former coworkers at a local gym, guitarist and singer for a band and a lovely musician who finds time to school me in most games. He could be a bit catty and cold at times, but that's mainly because his avatar is an ice elf, and his distancing himself is so he can fling arrows like a young kid flings boogers. Let's not forget his kooky, tail-biting asshat Tmont, house cat, and his panther companion.

Balmur - Our Azer dwarf buddy, who is also a friend from the gym who I would sit and talk about the latest and greatest RPGs with when we weren't spotting lunks. Super awesome guy, though he can be a bit quiet at times. Useful trait as a rogue, as you would think.

James - Another buddy from the Marine Corps I met through Yoh. He's a New Yorker through and through, and he can be a confrontational guy at times, but he's working through all that. Meditation helps. He's more dragon than half-dragon, half-elven lately due to a bad trip on some black dragon magic. His wings are fucked up and weird, but we love our monk.

Muu - Jesus Christ. This guy is my roommate back home. Lovable, affable, and has NO idea when to shut up. His antics make his role as a fighter all the more reasonable because his mouth has a tendency to piss people off. Funny as he is, he's a damned fine addition to the team, and we're happy to have him as our dragon-kin dragoon. Green-scaled asshole that he can be.

We caught wind that they could have been affected either by the proximity of a minion, or a general. Their presence seemed to cause people, animals, and creatures, in general, to go completely insane, even attacking a city of dwarves with a small invasion force, which seemed pretty fucking unsound to me.

After our time in the city was at an end, we had decided to leave the high elves of T'agnolian Val, under the somewhat steady hand of their leader King Telfino, to their own devices in dealing with their newly discovered enemies, the Seelie Fae. They didn't have to deal with much really, just the "ambassadors" who had denied any and all involvement, despite the fact that evidence stated otherwise. We couldn't get them to swear to it, which was telling.

I had received word a day ago that Maebe may be coming back to the Prime Realm now that the spies had been ousted. But that didn't guarantee that the ones on her side had been found, or that there hadn't been some sort of attack. I was starting to get a little worried, but I didn't dare try to get ahold of her with Shadow Speak just in case she was fighting or busy. That could prove detrimental to her.

With the group back together and my lovely girlfriend on her way, it's time to follow some leads, track down the rest of these assholes, and get home for some more, less deadly gaming. You coming?

CHAPTER ONE

Fading light filtered in through the leaves and the branches of the trees above, the beams of pale brightness against the shaded forest where I laid in the dirt. Tired. Exhausted and mentally drained. I was even bloodied if the tickle above my forehead could be trusted.

"Again!" Yohsuke barked.

I sat up to see my tormentor seated against a tree twenty feet away in his customary dark cloak, his gray features, and the horns he had because of an accessory he wore, only slightly hidden. His bright, sickly yellow eyes shone with both mirth and frustration.

"Look, I know it's funny to beat on the werewolf, but can I at least rest long enough to not have to mentally beat the shit out of this asshole who keeps pressuring me to bite you guys?" I grumbled tiredly. I cast Regrowth on myself. It's a relatively cheap spell mana-wise and speeds my regeneration significantly.

"You know that we need to try and get all of our ducks in order, brother," Jaken, the one I could usually trust to intercede on my behalf, sounded apologetic as he helped me stand.

He wore his full battle-rattle of beautifully polished full-plate mithral armor with two swords on his hips, his half-Fae-half-orcish features obscured by shadows. Golden energy lit along my body, and my health leapt up to full.

"One more time, bud. Please?" His presence drifted away, but his voice remained strong and imploring. "Then we can go rest in the springs for a bit."

"Better be the last, I'm dirty as shit," I said with a growling tone to my voice. I closed my eyes and honed my will. Looking inward, I was starting to get a little better at calling to the beast that lived inside me, but even if he was tired of our bullshit and my tapping into his strength. *Our* strength.

Before, when I gave in to my lycanthropy, I would *feel* his presence within me, and he could talk back. Now? I was there with him. Inside some sort of cave, the core of my being, where he sat on a throne of bones and stone. Why? I don't know.

Maybe he has a flair for the dramatic that mirrored my own? Maybe he was a damned fine interior designer, and this was just his idea of feng shui—I tried not to judge. I mean, I had no sense of style and can barely dress myself, so who am I to talk mess?

Why do they insist on struggling against us? The lycan before me tilted his head. The manifestation of his spirit was that of a hulking hybrid wolfman. It was my fall back, the only one that I had taken since becoming a werewolf.

"They want us to get this ability under control, and so do I," I returned as I watched him.

He stood, all seven feet of muscle and hatred clearly visible in his features as he stepped toward me, a slight, cool breeze of death and rage ruffled the black and white fur along his frame.

That they do not fear you is the problem. He bared his teeth angrily as he looked down at me from where he stood. *We are alpha. The strongest of the pack. It is our right to lead. We took it from the other alpha. You claimed it, and yet you do not claim me. You refuse to do what must be done. You refuse to be hard and correct the issues in your pack. And worse still, you refuse to allow me to help you do so.*

"They're my friends!" I stepped close enough to look up at

him. "We're all learning together. And *I* am the alpha. The first time you took over, you ended up making me attack Jaken. The last time I acted alone with your strength, I ripped someone's fucking heart out in full monte fucking front and center and almost alienated them. This transformation isn't like my normal ones, and there's a fine line between you and me. I don't like that, and I *will* have more control over this."

That was truly the moment I knew there was hope for you, but now? He shook his head, with his eyes closed in recollection and then opened them, one eye glowed red with malice and the other blue and radiating power. *I do not know. You seek my strength, but you subconsciously limit yourself. Then you limit us further on purpose so that you do not harm your* precious *"friends."*

"Because if we kill them." I grabbed it by the fur on its chest and pulled it down to look me in the eyes, "Then I've murdered the people who stand the greatest chance of helping me home! People who know me best—my brothers. Our pack. So, instead of fighting me, and questioning me, give me your support, and we can move on. Then, when a real enemy comes, and we need to defend ourselves, you and I can fuck them up together. Okay? Because if I have to fight you, I will *fucking destroy you.* This is *my* body and my will."

The werewolf seemed to think it over before holding his massive clawed hand out to me. I went to take it, but he pulled it back and cold cocked me in the jaw, sending me onto my ass. I snarled and launched myself at him with a closed fist, but he stepped aside.

Stop limiting us. They are fighting to learn how to protect themselves from creatures like us. The malice gone from the red eye at that moment replaced by curiosity. *You are hurting our pack's chances of dominance by fighting at half strength. Let loose, so that they will learn and so that you will as well.*

I blinked, unaccustomed to the thoughtful nature of the request, but it made sense. Why he had decided to try and hit me, I wasn't sure, but I nodded and held my hand out. He clasped it and squeezed.

I opened my eyes and knew that I stood in my hybrid form. Everything around me was crisper. The scents of the people around me, sweat, and horrific body odor.

I looked to my left where the party rested from their own bouts with me and each other, "Muu. Take a damned shower, you smell like hot ass wiped with gym socks."

"Tell me how you really feel," he grumbled sullenly.

I looked to my newest opponent, Bokaj. "Look. New rule: I'm no longer limiting myself in my werewolf form. The wolf… really going to need to name him, seems to be under the impression that when I hold myself back, it limits your abilities to protect yourselves. He hinted that when I don't go for the kill, it leaves you unprepared. All of us unprepared."

"Sounds good to me." James hopped down from a tree, his dark-winged form outlined against the light filtering through the trees. "But it's weird to know that you've been holding yourself back when it seems like you keep getting your ass kicked."

I looked over at him and sighed. So, time to play.

Yohsuke groaned, "Enough jawing, get to it!" Then the fight was on.

Tmont, Bokaj's familiar and black-furred panther, barreled toward me as her master rained arrows toward my position, but I wasn't going to just take it.

I gripped the earth beneath my feet and *pushed* myself out of the way. One second I was there, and the next, I was out of Tmont's way and on the side of a tree with my claws digging into the bark as if it were wet ground. I grunted and leapt from the tree and sailed toward Bokaj. Rather than try to land on top of him like I had the last time we had sparred; I went toward the rear of his position. I wasn't as stealthy as I would have liked to be, but it was enough.

He must have guessed my trajectory and fired an arrow into where I should have landed—where my leg should have been. But rather than land fully on my feet, I threw my arm forward and executed a forward shoulder roll that I'd learned from the Marine Corps that moved my body just far enough out of the arrow's path that I only mildly felt the burn of the arrow's silver attachment. The bastard had taken to preparing his arrows with a tied-on silver wire. And I had no doubts that silvered arrowheads were in the immediate future.

As soon as I landed, I did the same thing as before and pushed myself toward him. He shot an arrow, and this time I dove headlong into a forward shoulder roll and kicked up as I twisted beneath him. I took a slice from the wire and he missed the worst of it, but I still caught him under the ribs and sent him ten feet into the air and climbing. Tmont slammed into my right flank, and rather than being moved, I simply gathered my breath and roared into the evening air, using Predator's Call.

The ability allowed me to try and instill fear in my opponents, freezing them in place. Several rings in the area glowed blue, but only Tmont stilled with a hiss.

I bunched the muscles in my legs before I launched myself skyward after my opponent. As I caught up to him, the bastard froze and the werewolf in me bayed and rejoiced.

End him! The voice echoed in my mind. It was almost enough to make me reach out with my jaws and bite.

But instead, I grasped him by the throat and twisted, throwing him down to the ground. There a sickening crunch as Bokaj hit the ground, his health shot down by about 30%. A broken bone symbol popped up under his health bar.

As I landed, I ensured that I did it with my claws inside his stomach cavity, trying to avoid any major organs.

"Sorry, buddy," my bass voice ground out of my throat, as I lifted him up, precious bits of red draining from his health bar. "But we need to be prepared."

"We do," I felt a burning down my back, a dark blade piercing the meat of my ribs painfully as Yohsuke's voice reached my ears' from over my shoulder.

"That's no fair," I snarled, throwing Bokaj over my shoulder at where I hoped Yohsuke would be.

"No such thing as a fair fight, and we will never let someone just have their way." Yoh growled. "Especially not with our friends. Let's push it."

I turned and tried to rush him, but he was on top of me in a second, and I was on the defensive immediately. His astral adaptor carved into my health bar like a hot knife through butter, and it was all I could do to return a single blow.

I tried to reach for my magic, but it wasn't responding.

We cannot use spells, but we can do other things. Limit yourself less! I know that you see this one as a litter-mate, but he is here to push you, too. Respond in kind.

I bunched my muscles like I was going to leap, then threw myself down onto the ground as Tmont freed herself from Predator's Call and came at my back. The large panther sailed through the air into Yohsuke, and the two of them became entangled briefly. I used that moment to leap onto both of them and tore at them both with my claws. I didn't make it far before a burning arrow found its way in between my shoulder blades, just out of my reach. Then I was done. They were on top of me, and I couldn't stand, the silver poisoning me more.

Eventually, they pulled the offending, ruined silver coin from my skin, and Jaken healed me.

You did well. The alpha within me stated, then was gone. Nothing further, just the sense of a job well done.

Time for a bath. Fuck this sparring shit.

———

The serenity of village life being as it was here lately in Sunrise washed over us. This was the place that we had begun our crazy new lives here on Brindolla. We had seen a lot of good done here lately, and that hot spring that had been given to us by the Primordial Water Elemental as a reward for killing the black dragon Riktolth and cleansing his influence from the ocean in doing so? *Sooooo nice.*

"This is the life." Jaken sighed as he settled his bulky naked body further into the heated water.

"You said it," I grumbled.

Typically, it's considered rude to stare at another naked dude. Me? I'd been in the Marine Corps. After boot camp, I'd probably seen more dudes' junk than most of the women I knew.

Yeah, yeah, laugh it up. It's okay. Who's the one dating a queen? That's what I thought. Sit down.

Jaken's figure looked like it was cut from the same cloth as some of the Greek Gods, so some people could be jealous, but whatever. His long fingers attempted to twirl his mustache into a handlebar as he observed the place lazily, but it was foiled. He was going for the handlebar-goatee combo, but it just wasn't working out in his favor.

"You sure this water isn't going to do anything negative to your fur, brother?" He raised a skeptical eyebrow my way.

I looked down at my beautiful, silky, raven-black fur with dots and specs of white throughout that mirrored the night sky and smiled. "Yeah."

As a kitsune, my fur was just as much a part of my skin as his was. It was just hair. Could I have taken human form at that moment? Sure. But I preferred this form most of the time. My tails floated freely behind me, all five of them. Unfortunately, I hadn't gained another one in the last seven fucking levels.

I'm not butthurt about that in the slightest. But hey—I got tails baby. And that's all that matters.

I sank into the water a little further and really let myself truly relax. It was a community bath house now. Everybody was allowed in, but it seemed at this moment that people wanted us to have this time alone to relax and recoup.

I opened my eyes to take in the place around us once more. The wooden walls were stained a darker color, beautifully done, but it was bright and warm. Very inviting. There were mage lights enchanted in sconces that offered a soft sort of light that played along the top of the water to give a shred of privacy from the view below. So gazing was a little difficult. Which was good. There were plants potted around the area that gave off delicate and soothing scents that mingled well. And there was a slight hint of steam to the room as well that opened up the pores. Before getting into the water, we had used a system similar in design to showers at the pools back on Earth.

You clean yourself off first, then come here to relax and soak. It was so nice.

The door opened and closed, the sound of others joining us reached my vulpine ears. The first to walk in was James and then Muu.

"Thought we would find you two here." Muu grinned and flashed his sharp teeth at us before charging into the water.

He cannonballed into the water and came up a second later. "Shallow! Don't jump, hurt my ass."

"What a stupid bastard." Yohsuke chuckled. "Don't splash all the water out, we need to relax while we still can!"

"Too busy relaxing to pay attention, sorry. What did you say?" Muu arched an eyebrow ridge in the other man's direction with his purple eyes sparkling mischievously.

Yohsuke rolled his eyes and flipped Muu off, he kept me humble most of the time.

"Tmont opted out of bath time," Bokaj advised as he sat himself on the edge of the water with his legs in it as his best bud Balmur stood nearby, observing the surroundings for what they were, and likely what they could be. His year and a half in the Hells had not been kind to him.

A small flash of light off his sweaty, tanned skin where part of the beard on the left side of his face was disfigured thanks to a nasty cut that had scarred over and claimed his left eye. It remained shut, but we had made a commission from Xiphyre and Thogan to see about getting him a magical eye similar to my arm.

I looked down at the green and purple piece of craftsmanship that had siphoned a whole level's worth of experience from me to act as if it were the limb I was born with. It moved and worked as a normal arm except for the fact that it was metal, and that was badass for the low price of a majority of my mana pool. I was *so* happy to have been using it so far, but I felt like I'd enjoy foiling people stabbing me with that bad boy just a wee bit more.

Balmur dropped into the water softly with a sigh of relief, "This is nice."

The seven of us sat there in the water just relaxing and enjoying the quiet for a short time before Balmur spoke once more, "You guys know what kind of eye I'll be getting? It was well before we left that you put the order in."

It had been, and it was likely that it would be finished soon. I had sent the order ahead using an item that Vilmas, the now-grandmaster enchanter who worked with my first *true* enchanting teacher Shellica Light Hand, had given me.

The item, a small raven, allowed me to send messages over long distances for a hundred MP anywhere in the plane of existence I'm currently in. Xiphyre hadn't made an eye like that before, but we had brought him some powerful components in the last weeks, and he was excited to try it. The little man worked fast, as he was a powerful enchanter. Easily stronger than Shellica and Vilmas combined, but I imagined he would take his time to ensure it was great.

"It's probably going to be very similar to what I have." I had been showing him my arm, as we had discussed commissioning the eye beforehand. He had seemed fine with it even if there was any sort of experience drain in order to activate it.

"I wonder if it will help you see in the dark?" Muu raised the question. "That would be really cool."

"We'll be underground, man—I can see underground already." Balmur frowned in thought. "Though with the eye you commissioned, I'm not sure what it will be able to do, or not do." He fell silent after that.

"Worry about all of that shit later." Bokaj clapped him on the shoulder, the dwarf flinched but calmed down instantly. It seemed he was starting to relax a little bit. "For now, we need to try and get our rogue here kitted out, and back into fighting shape before heading into the land down under."

"Australia?" Jaken raised an eyebrow questioningly with a slight grin.

"No man, the down below." Bokaj rolled his eyes.

"Speaker box!" I challenged. That one seemed to fly over his head; seemed like decent rap music went way over his head. Moving on.

"What do we call this place? Wasn't there a term that Farnik had used?" James rubbed his temples as if the massage would help him recall the name.

Balmur snapped his fingers and grinned. "The Great Below!"

"Terrible time for a dick joke, my man—but good try." Muu patted him on the shoulder affectionately.

"No, man." Balmur shrugged the hand away angrily. "That's what they had called it before. The name they used for it."

I had to admit, Balmur was having a rough go of things lately, especially where Muu was concerned. We were hoping that he would be able to perk back up, but we would be watching out for him.

"Balmur, bud, it was a joke!" Bokaj grinned at his friend with a look of concern. "You okay? That dick joke flew way over your head."

"Not hard when he's so short," Muu muttered with a devious grin, and Balmur rolled his eyes at the jest.

"Can't you boys keep your minds out of your pants?" A breathier voice sounded from outside.

A woman's head poked through the door, Vrawn, our orcish lady friend. Her green skin glowed a little in the warm mage light. Her fiery orange mohawk was artfully braided over the side of her head and swayed as she tilted her head, "Room for one more?"

I sighed, knowing what was coming and looked up to find my friends grinning wolfishly in my direction. Balmur looked completely lost but caught the general mood of our brotherly ribbing.

"Vrawn, we would be delighted to have you join us," Muu all but purred.

Using the telepathic earrings we had, I growled at the others, *You do realize that I can straight up merc you, right? I will curse the fuck out of your items.*

Balmur seemed to catch on to what was *truly* happening, because his smile deepened considerably before he turned to greet the woman in the doorway. "Hey there, I don't think we've met yet. I'm Balmur!"

He waded over to the side of the water closest to the door and held a hand out for her to shake.

She blinked at all of them, her eyes finding and holding mine for a moment. When I didn't offer any kind of resistance to her presence, Vrawn's large frame cleared the doorway, and *oh, my giddy great aunt, she was naked!*

Balmur, James, Jaken, and Yohsuke instantly gasped and looked away. All of them had some lady loves back home to whom they had pledged their undying love. Hell, Yohsuke was married as fuck—had been the majority of the time that I had known him, and his wife would straight-up fight Vrawn for this.

Worth it. *Got you, you fuckers.* I growled at them victoriously.

Now, I know what you're likely thinking. Either A) look at the orc lady, you putz. Or B) But Zeke, what about Maebe?

My lady Queen, in our budding relationship, had plainly said I was stupid for denying Vrawn's *very* forward attempts at getting my attention. To the point where she had asked if…the Great Below worked. Well, it does, and knowing how she felt, I wasn't going to be too terribly modest at this moment.

Of course, Option C) I'm going to describe her because y'all know what my brothers look like, and I told you I wasn't gonna. So there. Now, to treat you and me.

Vrawn was moving toward the water now, her confused eyes skirting over the men who were looking away from her, but then her eyes rested on me, and she smiled.

"Hi Vrawn, how was recruit training today?" Jaken craned his neck, still looking away.

Her voluptuous form displaced the water a little, but it was okay. Her muscled body, something that would make some of the male bodybuilders at home slightly jealous, moved well in the calm waters of the spring. Her broad shoulders were about head height for me when we were standing. So, she was taller than me by more than a little, but that didn't mean she wasn't womanly in the slightest. Her waist was narrow comparatively speaking to the rest of her body, and none of that muscle was remotely unsightly. If anything, she put most of the women I knew to shame in a lot of ways, physically.

Eventually, she reached the point where her assets were below water and sat next to me with a sigh, answering Jaken, "It went well, though I still do not know why you have me doing this 'incentive training,' or what it does for troop welfare."

She underwater? Yohsuke's query made me grin. I confirmed it, and he finally opened his eyes.

"It's meant to simultaneously break them down, strengthen them, and ensure that they listen to you without screwing up too much," Yohsuke explained. "When you do it to most of them at once, the others feel guilty for not being with the team, or for causing it. But it makes them sharper."

"Like honing a blade—you can't do that without whittling the metal away to carve to the cutting edge," James added on. "In the Marines, by the end of our training, usually when one of the recruits gets 'I.T.'d' the others join in as a show of solidarity."

Muu, Bokaj, and Balmur glanced askance at Yohsuke and I, the former taking pity and explaining, "It means 'incentive training,' basically that if you're stupid, you get destroyed with push-ups or some other inane exercise."

I looked at the other two Marines and grinned. "Those who suffer together, will endure together. They have to learn to embrace the suck."

"Well, I have noticed that they are much more capable when I use the stick and not the carrot." Vrawn frowned.

"Carrot comes later." Yohsuke waved at her as if bidding

her to perish the thought. "They aren't being punished for fucking up, so much as they are being punished for doing so too much, too often. Have you noticed other improvements?"

"It has only been two days, but they are *much* more disciplined and willing to work harder." As she spoke, I felt the large woman drifting closer and just resigned myself to what was coming.

"It took more than three months for us to earn our title. Thirteen weeks and going through hell. Between you and Zhavron—these guys are going to be badasses." James laughed. "Can you imagine ol' Zhav working with newbies?"

A few of us chuckled, I refrained though. "He's hard because they need him to be. I've seen the man work. Those recruits aren't getting the same treatment that we did, that's for damned sure."

Muu shivered and narrowed his eyes at the door. "He comes," he said in a display of odd clairvoyance, yet nothing happened.

"Fuck, usually when you talk about him, the devil fucking appears, this is bullshi—" Muu screeched as the water behind him exploded upward, and Yohsuke burst from the spot laughing wildly.

The rest of us laughed probably too hard, Vrawn joining in the good-natured revelry, and we relaxed even more.

"Do you know how long you will be staying before you leave?" Vrawn leaned down so that her heavily muscled shoulder leaned against the top of my arm, her bust resting on the side of my body.

I fought the urge to move away, my friends being close-by throwing me off a little more than it would have if we had been alone.

"I'm not sure yet. Xiphyre is working on a project for us with Thogan, and we need to try and find a way to get down into the Great Below," I looked over into her blue eyes. "You don't happen to know of an entrance, do you?"

She shook her head, forlornly. "I do not. My apologies. I

only ever hear rumors about raids in the outer lands of this continent. There are cities above ground across the sea if I recall correctly. There was something about them being able to create barriers of spell-woven glass to protect their cities from the light of day."

That was both impressive and depressing. We would have to spend gods knew how long at sea to get to drow that didn't seem to have anything to do with this case of drow craziness since the ocean separated them from Djurn Forge. No, we needed to find a way to get to the ones on this continent.

"Thank you for that, it'll be something to keep in mind for the future." I reached under the water, using her arm as a guide and held her hand. A friendly gesture that she seemed to take as a carrot in this instance.

"I've been trying to grill Vilmas when she has a minute between lessons and her dates with Rowland on what happened when the drow tried to invade." James sighed, leaning back against the edge of the ground where he sat. "She just keeps saying that they burst through the ground in the center of their city."

"They likely did. Drow aren't known for being diggers, as they have their cannon fodder do all that for them. A powerful spell caster could have blown a huge hole in the ground after it was dug to where it needed to be. Then boom"—Yohsuke punched the water before him, a geyser of water spouting from the spot—"they're in and wreaking havoc."

"You aren't suggesting we blow a hole into Djurn Forge, are you?" Balmur's skeptical look said it all for us.

"No," Jaken replied vehemently. "But there could be another way. What if we had Pebble take us through the ground?"

"It's something." I shrugged. "I mean, he is an earth elemental, so he can easily move through the ground. I don't know about taking all of us, though."

Bokaj slapped the ground at his side. "It's an option!"

"What about that rift with all the spiders?" The others

looked at me, clearly horrified at my question. "It makes sense. There's this huge chasm that these spiders live in beneath the jungle after we fought that asshole minion, Decay. That had been a really shitty time. It stands to reason that it would connect in some fashion to the Great Below."

"Yes, but the hollow of Brindolla's underground is a harsh place. Can you afford to wander aimlessly for who knows how long, blind, and out of your element?" Vrawn stretched langorously. "According to what you have said, there is a recent trail to follow from this Djurn Forge. It seems the best option."

"It does. But you know we aren't going to be able to do a raid on the drow without Farnik sending half the fucking city with us." Bokaj grunted, then looked at us all and continued with his thought, a soft smile on his face. "Especially if it's the drow who could be responsible for his wife's death. And any of them traipsing down there with us would be a beacon to any minions or generals of War."

"Maybe." Jaken frowned in thought. "Maebe has been traveling with us for a while and they don't seem to be wanting to hide from us, or any wiser to her being near us. And if they're surrounded by drow, isn't there a chance that one blip on the radar of possibly thousands of blips could go unnoticed?"

"That's a lot riding on a chance," Yohsuke grumbled quietly. "But we've taken bigger risks before. Still, I don't know how comfortable I am having people down there with us that haven't proven themselves team players. The seven of us? Yeah. Maebe too? Cool. But anyone other than that is just as much a liability to us as the unknown is."

That was...true. Unfortunately. Telling Farnik and the clan that they couldn't come along would be potentially devastating to them. Possibly even alienating them. Then again, the heat from the water and present company could be playing hell on my mind. Probably time to get out of the bath.

"We should discuss this more at length sometime... lader ohn." my eyelids drooped. The sweltering heat taking me slightly. The world swam. I dipped lower into the water.

I remembered, in my nearly unconscious state, someone lifting me almost effortlessly out of the water. I caught flashes of sight, sounds, and sensations. Soft skin. Murmured questions, and finally, green and orange blurs passed my eyes before I fell gently to sleep. Intense dreams of darkness coming alive at every turn and none of it the void I had trained with.

CHAPTER TWO

I woke up some time later looking at the wall of an unfamiliar room with the sound of rhythmic, but slightly obnoxious snoring behind me. The walls were wooden but the planks stood vertical rather than horizontally like the ones in Willem's tavern.

A heavy weight on my shoulder made it hard to move and I looked down to spy a large green forearm. I hadn't noticed before, but there were fine lines along them that looked like scars from something sharp. With little thought, I traced my fingertips along some of them carefully, wondering what had caused these injuries. The bordering-on-bestial snoring coming from behind me suddenly stopped, and the pressure on my shoulder eased a little.

Vrawn's face came into view with an inquisitive look, her voice groggy, "How are you feeling, right now?"

Before I responded, I took a mental inventory of myself. I was nude. Oh boy. I was tired, a little dehydrated, and warm, but not overly so.

"Okay, I think." I looked up at her. "What happened?"

She snuggled a bit closer, making me feel slightly more like the little spoon that I was at that moment.

"The others are under the impression that your fur in the hot spring caused you to overheat." Vrawn put her hand over my forehead, it felt cool to the touch, and it was nice, to be honest. "I am of a similar mind."

"So, you carried me here." I looked around to see what I could, but the austere conditions confirmed it. "To your room then?"

"I did," she replied simply.

"Thank you. I appreciate it." I was caught in a bit of a conundrum, though.

Do I stay? Or do I go, now? I was awake but tired. And she was awake, and I was still coming to grips with the fact that Maebe was weird in her way and was okay with Vrawn hitting on me. Something about Maebe being royalty had conditioned her to a different set of morals that seemed odd to my own. Deviant even. And with her Fae longevity, more so.

"As a reward for me carrying you all the way here, could you stay with me?" Vrawn asked softly, seemingly guessing at the thoughts in my head. "Queen Maebe has asked that when she is not here to care for you, I act in her place. I have no issue with this, do you?"

Stricken by her unusual lack of subtlety, I watched her for a moment before answering. "I'm not sure, honestly. Where I come from, it's normal for someone in a relationship to maintain that bond by not being with anyone else."

"Sure, not everyone's relationship is the same, and not everyone thinks that way, but it's still hard to get over that initial teaching and training. Does that make sense?"

"It does. There are people I know of, and entire cultures who think that way." Vrawn slid her arm over my shoulder, the weight of it suddenly gone. "If you would like to leave, I will not make you stay. I understand that these sorts of changes and differences in culture can be difficult to work thr—"

I cut her off with a hand on her leg. "Just put your arm back around me, and let's get some rest, okay?"

She sighed in relief and the weight of her arm returned, pulling me even closer to her. My heart thumped loudly in my chest, but somehow, it was nice to be held like this. Reassuring even.

Her willingness to accept that I had different thoughts and a moral difficulty because of the way I was raised, had solidified my staying. She had earned that, and had been willing to accept me for me.

You done with thinking my moment of enjoying being the little spoon is weird yet, or not? Because I kill shit in this story. Best believe. Yeah. You'd *better* recognize.

I settled into her and closed my eyes, her steady breathing pulling me into a deeper sense of an almost meditative state. Close to sleep, but just this side of it. Where dreams cannot find you, you're alert and aware, but also resting. I'd had naps like that, but this was something else.

I stayed like that for some time before Vrawn's fingers began to trace shapes through the fur of my chest, my mind falling deeper toward true sleep. It was…nice. Really nice.

"Zeke," A familiar voice whispered almost next to my ear, "time to wake up."

I growled deeply from the base of my chest. That was a fucked-up thing to say to someone who had just gotten to sleep.

"It's mid-morning, you sleepy thing, wake up!" a teasing voice insisted.

I turned, blinked my bleary eyes at the figure sitting in the chair, and realized that the snoring person still holding me was Vrawn, and in the chair, sat Maebe. A pleased smile graced her lips, and her vibrant green eyes sparkled in the low light filtering into the room.

"Hello, Zeke." Maebe's body disappeared, and I felt the cool wash of shadows that signaled her moving into the space between me and the wall. Vrawn snorted in her sleep but otherwise didn't wake up.

I lay there for a moment, overjoyed by the fact that the woman I loved was there in front of me. She wore a short, white dress that reminded me of a sundress on Earth, made of a thicker material, and some lace about the chest and shoulders. Her starry, night-colored skin making a stark and pleasantly shocking contrast to the clothing she wore. While the curves of the body beneath the dress were enticing, it was her face that I found most captivating. Her deep green eyes stared into mine, so close that I could smell her scent; like fresh morning snow and some kind of berry. Her black hair with multicolored highlights was pulled back into a ponytail, with just enough of it loose to frame her face. Her high cheekbones, almost razor-sharp, and her button nose were charming, her delicate chin met by a strong angular jaw and finally, a new smattering of starlit freckles that danced across her nose and cheeks.

She bit her pillowy lower lip. "I have missed you."

Words couldn't possibly describe the relief soaring through me in that moment of her being so close, safe, and sound. I pulled her against me and kissed her, as much of her as I could touch at that moment would never be enough.

The air soured slightly, the scent of copper filtering in. As I opened my eyes, I saw Maebe staring back. Lifelessly. Her once beautiful green eyes dull, mouth slack and blood slowly trickling from her lips. A gaping hole in her chest where her heart should be.

"No...no, no, no!" I tried to stop the bleeding, a torrent of new, fresh blood bubbling from the wound. But it just kept coming. The weight behind me shifted.

"You're not strong enough to protect her from us, little fox." Vrawn's voice but somehow not her voice whispered into my ear. "We're on to you now. And we have so many more *wonderful* plans to make you *wish* you had just left us to our own devices."

I whirled on the threat with a snarl and tried to slash at the creature holding me. Vrawn's face was slack, the eyes purely white. "Get used to losing those you care about."

"Wake up, Zeke!" An insistent voice urged me, as if underwater.

The eyes blinked at me once. "Nothing can save you now. Stay away and enjoy what little time you have left in this pathetic existence."

"Zeke!" Another call, a fleeting flurry of sensation along my chest and muzzle.

"We're going to kill you all, and while I don't know who you are," my voice was more beast-like growl than words. Flecks of spit flew from my jaws as I spoke, "I will find you, and I will make you *suffer* for this."

The possessed Vrawn grinned menacingly, and a sudden pinch and pull on both of my cheeks caught my attention.

The world around me faded, and I came back into focus in the same place. My clawed hands were stuck into the bed, and something warm and sticky was on my left hand.

"Zeke! What's wrong?" Vrawn hissed in pain. I blinked, the growl escaping my chest stopping as I realized I had dug my claws into Vrawn's shoulder.

I gently separated my claws from the wounds and cast Heal on her, the holes sealing and leaving not so much as a scratch, immediately.

"I am so sorry Vrawn, are you okay?" I searched her for other wounds, she was still nude and I cast all thoughts of vengeance away without a second thought while focusing on her.

"I could ask the same of you," her large hand cupped my cheek softly. "You were growling and snarling so ferociously, and I heard you threatening someone?"

"It was a really bad dream." I growled and sat up, casting my gaze about with no luck gleaning anything from the shadows. *You guys all okay?*

Fuck that, whatever it was, Bokaj spoke softly.

James grunted, and the others made similar noises. Didn't seem like something any of them had enjoyed, but they were okay.

"I don't know what it was, but I think the generals are onto us, they're trying to get us to leave them alone, and that isn't something we want to do—are you sure you're okay?"

She frowned. "I'm fine. Those wounds were nothing. If you don't want to talk about it, that's alright. But there is still quite some time before the sun rises, would you like to try and get some more sleep?"

I thought about it a moment. As angry and outraged as I was that something was able to infiltrate my dreams, I had definitely had worse nightmares in my time. Though... I shifted form to that of human so that I wouldn't accidentally gouge the poor woman again.

"We can try to get some more sleep." I went to turn over, but she stopped me.

"Sleep facing me. So that if you start to have a bad dream again, I can help you." She rubbed my shoulder comfortingly.

She had been doing a lot lately. Not just for me, though. She had been so kind. She'd come to help guard the village, befriended the painfully shy Vilmas, helped to protect Sunrise from the undead sent by a lich. Then she was training the recruits, helping us, and probably even more.

Vrawn was an admirable woman, thoughtful, kind, and beautiful to boot.

Her soft smile and intense eyes were so observant and full of curiosity.

"Thanks for always being so awesome, Vrawn." I took my hand and ran it gently up her neck until I cupped her cheek. "You've always been so kind. You're amazing."

"I simply am who I am. I do not think I'm 'awesome' or amazing. I just care for the people I care about." She flashed her dainty tusks in a wider smile. "I throw myself into the now so that I have no regrets—no *more* regrets, rather."

Her smile faltered, and it hurt a little. I knew why, as she had held her adoptive brother, who had fallen in a battle during some kind of war, as his life ebbed away. It had been beyond shitty for her. She had lost her station in the army she served with and all of her remaining family, except for her adoptive sister.

"Well, everyone seems to like you." I pulled her head closer so that she rested on my shoulder. "And you've done so much for everyone around you. I think you're amazing. And so do the others."

She nestled into my body a little more, her warm breath puffing against the skin of my throat. It tickled a little. She lifted her head back, breathing against the base of my jawline, sending a thrill down my spine.

"Hey, that tickles," I murmured against her forehead.

"This is nice." Vrawn sighed, her eyes opening to stare into mine.

"It is. Thank you again for taking care of me." I ran my fingers through her hair.

She closed her eyes once more in rapt enjoyment. While she was distracted, I leaned down to kiss her forehead. Just a soft brush of lips against her forehead. A reward of sorts.

As soon as my lips would've touched her skin, she lifted her chin and claimed my mouth with her own. At first, my heart skipped a beat, and I stiffened.

Vrawn broke the kiss first. "I'm sorry, I shouldn't have been so forward."

Her dejected composure was deeply saddening, and I couldn't help but feel responsible.

"I saw you dead in that dream, Vrawn." I whispered, fear and anger almost getting the better of me. "Mae too. That's why talking about it is a little rough."

I lifted her chin so that I could look her in the eyes. "I'm not going to let that happen to you, or Mae. Not so long as I draw breath, okay?"

She nodded, still looking uncertain of herself. The cold and confusing loneliness clouding me at that moment was almost unbearable. Mae wasn't here to help make us feel better, and I didn't know what to do right now to try and help Vrawn feel better, either. So, I kissed her back of my own volition. She had been kind. And I had permission. Besides, for now—this was as far as I wanted to go. And if the need arose, I would make that known. But I think at this moment, we both needed this sort of comfort.

Her lips weren't as soft as Maebe's, but the sensation wasn't unpleasant, and the feel of her tusks digging lightly into my lips was also different. Her hands found their way onto my back and kneaded the flesh there. It was nice. A deepening kiss that I halted, likely sooner than either of us wanted.

"Thank you, again." My breath mingled with hers as I murmured the words.

"Always." Her lips pressed against my chest, but she didn't push the issue. That gained a good deal of my respect.

Shortly after, Vrawn's snoring vibrated my chest a little. I couldn't help my smirk. My eyes closed into a blissfully blank sleep.

———

I woke up to several small kisses on my shoulder, smiling, I whispered, "That's a nice way to wake up. Good morning."

Vrawn's voice vibrated against my chest, "Good morning."

A scent of fresh snow, and night sky reached my nostrils and I breathed deeply. "Good morning, my Queen."

Maebe chuckled from her place in the darkened corner. "Good morning, my busy little champion."

Vrawn stiffened, and her breath caught in her throat. I put a hand on her shoulder. "My Lady Darkest, you grace us with your presence."

"Forget the formalities, my love." Mae was gone and then suddenly behind me, almost like the dream, and I felt the cool of her body against mine opposite the heat of Vrawn's large form.

"Hi Mae, I've missed you." It was hard to keep the jackhammer that was my heart from leaping from my chest. *This isn't a dream man; it's real. They're alive.*

"Hello, My Queen," Vrawn's voice sounded slightly uncertain, but she greeted Maebe, anyway.

"Vrawn, I will say this only once, and I want you to take it to heart," Maebe's voice took on a stern tone. "At this moment, you are my friend. In settings such as this when we are alone, or in company that I deem safe, you may call me Maebe, or Mae. I trust you to discern the times that have need for formality, if I do not tell you beforehand. Is this agreeable?"

"Why?" Vrawn's voice was still uncertain.

"Sit up, please," Mae ordered. I went to move, but she put a hand on me and kept me lying on the bed.

Vrawn obeyed, and I turned onto my back so I could watch them both. Maebe leaned up and then sat with her legs crossed easily, her small frame almost levitating in the shadows. Vrawn's bed was larger than mine had been in the tavern below.

"When we first met, you showed great respect to me, to Zeke, and yourself, by addressing something with me," Maebe began. "You had paid me the courtesy to state what you thought of as wrong, risking much to do so, proving that you could be trusted with someone important."

Maebe's hand was suddenly on my stomach. "He was my first friend. I have gained others, but none whom I trust to hold his, or my interests above their own. Not until I met you and learned where you were coming from. That is why I gave you my permission. That is why I trust you. Both of you."

"You do know that you can trust the party, right?" I raised an eyebrow at her. She just looked at me stoically. "We can address that later, then. Carry on."

Vrawn chuckled at that, her smile widening. "Thank you, M—Mae, I trust you as well. I have seen how you treat the villagers and the children. How you treat him. I am jealous at times, but he has come out of his shell a little, as you said he might."

The level of talking the two of them had been doing was beginning to dawn on me. And I had to admit; I was more than a little disturbed that Maebe had known I might eventually allow Vrawn to be more forward? Or that I myself might— let's just leave it there.

"The fact of the matter is that neither of you is what the other initially thought, nor are your motives." I offered. The women both looked at me, so I continued. "Vrawn was coming from a good place in trying to make sure you weren't just going to throw me aside when, or if, you got bored. Or I wasn't convenient for you and your power. And Maebe, you had to be sure that Vrawn wasn't using me as a way to get to you, to harm your throne or your power. Am I right?"

Then I added, "Or to hurt me."

Both of them nodded, and I did the same. "So what do we do now? With all this mutual trust?"

"We forge on." Vrawn stated. "Nothing has truly changed. I am here, as I will always be. I will support you both, and when Mae is not here, I am who will watch over you and ensure that you are taken care of on her behalf."

"No." Mae shook her head and put a hand on the other woman's shoulder. "You showed last night that you could be trusted to hold yourself in check when he was vulnerable. You are a part of this, now. You can do this for yourself, too."

"You were here," I stated flatly, my eyes narrowing slightly.

"I saw everything." she bowed her head. "I knew I could trust you both, but instinct is a hard thing to fight when you have lived as long as I have. I hope you will forgive me?"

I wasn't mad. Not really. I was happy she trusted us, but that dream had been so real. So very real. And the fact that she had seen my reaction to it and not stepped in hurt a little. But realistically, what could she have done? Nothing.

Stop being such a baby, Zeke. I ordered myself. *Handle your shit.*

"There's nothing to forgive," Vrawn answered before I could, but I could almost feel the hurt in her tone. "I trust that you had good reasoning for not coming to either of our aid when his nightmare turned violent."

Maebe nodded once, and I felt like their gaze held a conversation on a level of understanding I would likely never know.

Vrawn visibly relaxed and so did Maebe, then both women looked down at me, and I had to admit, the searching in their eyes left me with one question.

"You guys just had a whole life-altering conversation without me understanding any of it, didn't you?"

Their smiles, both so vastly different, said the same thing. They had.

"What's it mean, for me then?" A heavy, exaggerated sigh escaping my mouth. "Being the second, or is this third time that you both seem to have decided something all on your own without me, assuming that I will just go along with whatever your whim is?"

"That you belong to both of us now," Maebe's matter-of-fact tone surprised me.

"If you're alright with that?" Vrawn's voice wavered, worry within her tone and suddenly in the line and hold of her body. A slight quiver.

I could hardly help the gentle eye roll that was so hard to break. "If my queen and the lieutenant of the guard of Sunrise have spoken, I have to listen, right?" A wry smirk crossed my face. I would try this.

"Excellent." Maebe touched my chest to get my attention. "You need to eat and explain that nightmare to us. Preferably sooner rather than later. I have news for you as well. But the whole of my champions should be present."

"Your friends, Mae." I growled in a tone of warning. "Those guys like you. Okay? It's okay for you to call them your friends."

"But they have not invited me to be their friend." She shook her head. "I would not force that on them."

My mouth opened. Shut. I blinked several times, trying to force my thoughts to the fore and out of my mouth, but nothing came.

"I think you have broken him, Mae." Vrawn laughed out loud at the sight of me.

"I seem to have this effect on him at times." She looked

proud, and then disappeared into the shadows. She reappeared near the door. "Shall we go?"

Finally, my brain fired off, and my mouth worked again, "We most certainly will not! You get your ass back in this bed, young lady!"

Vrawn gasped audibly. A dark look passed over Maebe's face before she stepped back into the shadows and then sat on the bed.

"Yes?" Her voice was stoic, light, and held a note of indignation.

"You've been here all night, and haven't given me a single kiss." I sat up and moved so that I sat on the bed facing both of them. "You just had this conversation about trust and love, and emotions that I didn't entirely get, but the two of you seem to. And while I find the prospect of being with you both slightly alien, and daunting, I'm willing to give it a try, but gods dammit you better love me right now!"

Maebe's face had been covered slightly by the slowly retreating shadows in the room crept toward mine. Her intense eyes blazing and her face a blank mask.

Her face stopped in front of mine, mere inches away, before she spoke, "How I have missed you."

She grasped my head in her hands and pulled me close enough to kiss me, leaving me breathless after a moment, then stopping. My vision swam a second longer, and a warm grin split my face.

Mae wagged a finger and pointed behind me, Vrawn shyly came forward, and her bulky figure engulfed me, a kiss from behind.

Well damn. This could be much nicer, after all.

We went to breakfast a little while later than we had thought. Our minds clear, and our stomachs growling.

Hey, *hey*—let's be adults here, okay?

We sat with the others; all of their faces plastered with varying looks of grumpiness.

I had to ask, "You guys have a nightmare, too?"

They nodded, James pointing out the obvious, "It was way too personal, and they know we're here, now."

"But that does confirm one thing." Yohsuke growled. "They're scared. They want us to back off because they're afraid."

Jaken smacked the table, his face a mask of anger. "We find who this is, and they die. Period."

I looked at him, gauging his reaction against my nightmare. "They messed with your daughter, didn't they?"

He just nodded. And that was enough. The others had loved ones, wives, fiancées, or friends that had come forward bleeding. Broken. Dead or dying to beg them to stop. Then, the voice had come with a warning. To quit and accept our deaths.

"Fuck that." Bokaj spat. "We're going. As soon as we can."

"Balmur, it is good to see you again." Maebe cut in lightly, throwing all of us off our tirades.

The dwarf nodded to her. "Majesty. It's good to see you once more, as well." Balmur smiled and offered his hand to her. She took it and nodded back to him. "Thank you for taking such good care of our friends while I've been…interred."

I looked at her, smugly. "See what I mean?"

"He does not speak for all of them," she hissed.

"You've been traveling with us for how long, and you still don't see us as friends?" Bokaj raised an eyebrow. "Maebe, you wound us."

She blinked, the others watching her closely, before she spoke, "You all feel this way?"

The others nodded slowly, as if she were a little daft, and Yohsuke flipped her off. "You're family now, Maebe. You've treated my brother well, despite us trying to fuck with him. You're our friend. Period."

"I've seen that gesture tossed around amongst all of you, is it meant to be a sign of encouragement?" Maebe didn't turn her head, but I knew she was talking to me.

"It normally depends on the meaning of what is behind the gesture." My frown of disapproval made the other man drop his hand. "It ranges from very confrontational and insulting, to a friendly reminder that you've been stupid."

"I'm going to take this as the latter, and we will move on." Maebe raised herself to her full royal bearing. "If you would all, please, join me outside?"

We all looked a little confused, the guys looking to me and me having to just shrug and join the Fae queen as she walked toward the exit.

Do you seriously not know what's going on? Muu wondered at me through our earrings.

No clue, man. Sorry. I know that we did a lot over the past couple weeks, but she may just need to speak to us. I tried to remain hopeful, but we would only find out when she was ready to tell us.

The sun was on its way into the sky, still early enough in the day that only a few vendors were en route to the square to set up for the day's sales.

When all of us were outside, each of us fanning out a little from the others, Vrawn standing over my left shoulder with more bearing in her features than I could hope to have at that moment.

Maebe held her left hand aloft and gripped the sky. I watched in fascination as the shadows around us flitted toward us and built into a barrier similar to the one that had been our shelter most nights while she traveled with us.

"Now that we are alone and will not be disturbed, all of you, please kneel." She motioned for us to obey, then turned her gaze to Vrawn. "Vrawn, will you join me, please?"

The orc woman stepped around all of us, carefully avoiding breaking the ranks, and stood next to Maebe on her left. I looked to the others, all of them confused, but obeying at different speeds. Once all of us took a high knee on the ground, Maebe reached into her inventory and produced a sheathed sword.

The craftsmanship was much fairer than anything I had ever seen in my life, at home or here. The sheathe radiated beauty, the dark purple base with silvery filigree shaped like delicate leaves and stars. The hilt was simple, a crossguard shaped like icicles and a golden, wire-wrapped handle.

Maebe took the sheathe in her left hand and freed her blade; the midnight metal shimmered in the light, somehow, despite the matte black coloring. Then I realized that the shimmering light came from stars in the metal with diamonds, rubies, sapphires, topaz, and other small, precious stones. It didn't look like a practical weapon, but rather one of station. Ceremonial.

"As you all kneel, in observation of the power before you, I would ask that you think on your service to this crown, and my appreciation." Maebe handed the sheathe to Vrawn who held it reverently. "Your deeds have served the Unseelie Fae in ways that even I did not foresee. You have gained us a powerful ally, and though I have named you champions of my realm—of a new cause and era—that was given in name only."

She stood solemnly in front of Jaken, her sword resting on his left shoulder. "I stand now before Jaken, a paladin in service to a Light that I do not understand, but he has served my people well." She tapped each shoulder going over his head with the blade as she spoke, "I now Knight you in service to my crown and bid you rise, Sir Jaken. May you hold your station ever more and with the same commitment as you have before."

Maebe nodded to the newly named knight and turned to step toward James.

"I stand now before James, dragon of his own making, and monk trained, who has served my people well." She performed the same motion on James. "I now Knight you in service to my crown and bid you rise, Sir James. May you hold your station ever more and with the same commitment as you have before."

Moving to Bokaj, she stated, "I stand now before Bokaj, one of the finest rangers I have ever known, and a bard whose talent I find endearing. He has served my people well." Tap. Tap. "I now Knight you in service to my crown and bid you rise, Sir Bokaj. May you hold your station ever more and with the same commitment as you have before."

Step, step, step. Smart turn, then, "I stand now before Yohsuke, hated by demons and a spell blade of devastating skill whose own legend is becoming known. He has served my people well." She tapped his shoulders slowly. "I now Knight you in service to my crown and bid you rise, Sir Yohsuke. May you hold your station ever more and with the same commitment as you have before."

Muu was next. "I stand now before Muu, a fierce fighter and self-styled dragoon, the weakest in level, but strong of heart and drive to do better. He has served my people well. I now Knight you in service to my crown and bid you rise, Sir Muu. May you hold your station ever more and with the same commitment as you have before."

As Maebe stopped in front of Balmur, she knelt in front of him and lifted his chin to stare into his eyes a moment. She stood as she spoke, "Gaze upon me, Balmur, rogue."

Balmur's face was an unreadable mask at that moment, but he listened to her and looked up at her as she stood.

"Your sacrifice and service to my people was unwitting, brutal, and long. Your suffering was great. You hurt, and there is nothing that I can do, but I tell you that your service is most appreciated, and I gift you with this."

She reached into her inventory and pulled out a small package. "Please, after our business is concluded, open this and know that you are well loved, and I am elated at your return."

"Thank you, Your Majesty." Balmur bowed his head and spoke softly.

Maebe nodded once and began her speech. "I stand now before Balmur, a rogue, but possibly the noblest and honorable person I have met in my years as Queen of the Unseelie. He has served my people well. I now Knight you in service to my crown and bid you rise, Sir Balmur. May you hold your station ever more and with the same commitment as you have before."

Finally, she stepped in front of me, her feet probably shoulder width apart as she spoke. "I stand now before Zekiel, druid in service to Mother Nature and beloved friend. He has served my people well. I now Knight you in service to my crown and bid you rise, Sir Zekiel. May you hold your station ever more and with the same commitment as you have before."

Each of us stood, one by one, as we had been ordered. A thrill sailed through my body. A notification popped up into existence.

Congratulations!
You have been awarded the title of Knight among the Unseelie Fae. There are benefits to titles like these. Speak with the one who gave it to you to learn more!

Okay. Seemed a little self-explanatory, but whatever.

"As knights of my kingdom, the Unseelie Fae will see you and give you aid as befits those of your ranks. They may still resort to trickery in an effort to gain power from you somehow, so mind yourselves, but they *will* treat you with the respect due your station." Her voice took on a more guttural cast. "Should they not, you have my express permission to cut them down. But only if they would be a hindrance. I will know if you lie to me.

"With this, you will now have some of the power of a Fae. It may take time to manifest, some of you more attuned to us than others, but you will gain from this, I swear it. The Seelie will also take it upon themselves to thwart you in any way they see fit. Be careful."

I received a notification of her oath and dismissed it out of hand. I wondered what would happen, or what I might gain, but who knew when it would come about.

"Thank you, Your Majesty." Jaken smiled at her, his winning grin radiant even to me several feet away.

"Nothing has *truly* changed among us, you and I, other than elevating your station." Maebe looked a little bashful at that moment, so cute, but reached out and took her sheath from Vrawn to put her weapon away. "We are all still friends, and though I like the idea, it will take me time to become more used to it. To think of you all as such more swiftly and easily. Forgive me."

"We understand." Jaken put a comforting hand on her shoulder, and she put a hand over it gently with a smile in return. "Right, guys?"

"Maebe, what's that weapon called?" Muu pointed to the weapon just before the others could answer Jaken, and the blade was safely home in its sheath.

"This blade is called Morningstar, and she has been passed from Queen to Queen since the conception of my people eons ago."

"Is it a ceremonial sword?" I turned and glared, cutting Muu off.

"It is used for those occasions deemed necessary for ceremony, but it is just as capable a weapon as Magus Bane, or any other weapon you all hold." Maebe brought the weapon out once more for us to look at.

James was the first to speak after that, "Leave it to the Fae to make something so beautiful into something so deadly."

Maebe seemed to take that as a compliment because her smile widened. "Beauty is capable of many things, Sir James. Beauty inspires, creates, takes, and kills. As the Fae do. You would do well to remember this."

"Well, I'm hungry, who else is starving? Let's go eat, yeah?" I raised my eyebrows and ushered the others out of the dome that dissipated around us as we finished. "Food sounds good now that we aren't all stuck in our feelings, what's for breakfast?"

We piled inside to our table, Yoh having let the chef do all the cooking in his lessened mental state due to the dream he'd had. Chef brought out several steaming plates of food. Eggs, toast, ham, bacon, sausage, rolls, and fruit all piled high. The table was a little crowded, but we ate heartily as we went over the events for the day.

James was going to see if he could try and piece together a map of rumored locations that the drow had raided in recent history. One thing we agreed on during the meal was that with whoever it was out there contacting us knew what we were doing. With that knowledge there was no way we could bring the Dwarves in on it without their lives being put in jeopardy.

It was an unnecessary risk and too tempting to send a raiding party of in as well.

Jaken and Balmur would be going to see Thogan about his weapons and gear, and to see what else could be done for him. I would be going to find Xiphyre to see about Balmur's new eye, and Yohsuke would be getting our food stores stocked.

Bokaj would go to see what was new on the potion front, as we had given Nora the components procured in T'agnolian Val for her. Her husband could plant some, but we hoped she would be able to use them to make potions.

Kayda and Tmont would be allowed to hunt and scour the area for fun while we worked, and that was that. Well, Muu would likely do whatever the hell he wanted as he didn't have anything to really do for the group, speaking of.

"Why don't you go see if Kynin and Farrin have some pointers for you on leatherwork and crafting?" Muu shoveled food in his mouth but acknowledged my talking to him by looking at me. "Two bear-Kin crafters. Kynin is super friendly, her brother Farrin has a bit of a temper, but he can be cool. Their place is just off the square; you'll be able to find it."

"Awesome," he replied, just barely swallowing before eating more and looking over to Balmur. "You going to open that up, or what?"

Balmur blinked, held the package up, looked at Muu. "No."

"Fucking tease," Muu grumped.

Maebe laughed aloud, and when we all looked at her in surprise, she pointed to Balmur. "He was being funny. He's going to open it, right? Was that not sarcasm?"

"You're getting really good at this, Maebe." Balmur grinned as he tore into the package.

"We also need to talk about you saying 'fuck' for the first time a little while back," I added with a soft tone of teasing reprimand.

"Hold the fucking phone—Maebe dropped the F-bomb,

and you didn't say shit?" Yohsukes eyes shot open in surprise. He looked to Maebe. "Is that true? You said that?"

Maebe blushed, surprisingly, "Yes. I was upset."

The party high fived each other with whoops of laughter and cheers.

"Why are you like this?" Vrawn asked with concern. "It's a crass word."

"It's a crass word that we say *a lot*," Bokaj corrected her gently. "When someone curses with us, especially someone who has never done so before, it's a sign that they're comfortable with us."

"It's always nice to know when someone's comfortable with you," Balmur agreed as he pulled out a long, thick box roughly six inches wide, four thick and a foot and a half long.

Balmur lifted the lid and pulled out a wicked-looking dagger, the crimson blade flashing in the dull light in the tavern dining area.

Balmur had been admiring it when he stiffened.

"I must warn you he can be a little much at first when you don't feed him." Maebe put her hand out to ward anyone from touching the blade. "He is—"

Balmur interjected, never taking his eyes from the weapon in his hand. "Sentient. His name is Sorrow, and he craves blood."

"Well, does it do anything cool for you?" James peered over the dwarf's shoulder.

"It adds a plus sixteen to attacks against creatures with blood and will give me a portion of the damage I deal as added damage to my next strike, and it stacks up to three. And if I quench his thirst, he says he will reward me with a permanent stat boost of my choice."

A knowing smile curled on Maebe's face. "That will require quite the battle. Or rampage. But I wanted you to have him, as he was a good partner for me to have when I was young. Thank you again for your sacrifice. It is truly good for you to be here."

"Thank you." Balmur smiled and finished his water before standing. "Ready to head to the forge, Jaken?"

Jaken shoveled some more food into his mouth and nodded enthusiastically as he stood from his seat. The two of them left the room.

Yohsuke leaned back and smacked his stomach contentedly before standing. "Better go see about food to feed your fat asses. Send word when we're ready, yeah?"

The rest of us nodded to him before he walked away, merrily.

"I'd better see about finding where Xiphyre is then, got a new eye to see about. Maybe some good weapons and stuff too for Balmur? Who knows?" I stood up and began to walk away when Maebe stood and joined me with Vrawn. "I take it you two are coming along?"

"We were going to see how the children were doing, actually." Maebe took Vrawn by the hand and gave me a kiss on the cheek. "Send for us when you're done."

"I will." I watched the two of them walk off hand in hand before turning and walking off myself. I wasn't entirely sure where the diminutive Fae would be, so I cast Mental Message. "Yo, Xi! Where you at?"

A voice responded inside my mind thanks to the spell, "*Xiphyre*, fox. And I am currently putting the finishing touches on your order, but I needed a secluded spot. I am currently in the forest. I will fly back once I am able. This will cost you, well, you've already lost an arm, haven't you?"

I rolled my eyes, casting the spell once more. "How long?"

"Give me half an hour," his annoyance was obvious from the tone in his voice by now, so I left it at that. "I'll meet you at the forge when I finish."

What should I do for half an hour? I wondered to myself as I ate my food.

I decided to take a flight to check the forest around the village. The wall had been added onto to include the newest addition to the area, the baths, and so was larger now. Vilmas had assured it would be a simple thing to do, enchanting the new addition with Xiphyre's help.

The skies were nice today. The clouds in the air seemed to lazily float along, spaced sparsely and silver against the vast expanse of blue. I watched other birds in the area flutter and flit about as I scanned the world below me as an owl.

The thermals here were lovely beneath my feathers. I reached out to Kayda mentally and found that she had decided to take a nap in a tree in her smaller, parrot sized form that she had learned to take recently from a druid friend of ours among the high elves, Questis.

His companion Fern, who usually took the size of a house cat rather than the saber-tooth he was, could shrink at will as well. It was nice not to have to worry about having a twenty-foot-tall Storm Roc around, so having her shrink was truly a convenience.

Flying through the skies was lovely. After scouting the area for a little while, I figured I should head back down to the forge to wait for the tiny enchanter.

As I came to rest on the roof of the forge, Xiphyre stepped from the building.

"By the gods, if you're that bird and you've kept me waiting, Zeke, I'll have your feathers!" Xiphyre threatened menacingly.

I contemplated shitting on him, but decided against it, unfortunately.

I landed next to him and shifted into my fox-man form, "Why so grumpy, Xiphyre?"

"You have the *nerve* to interrupt my work to ask me to basically hurry along, and you're late yourself!" He fluttered dangerously close to my face.

"Woah, all I wanted to do was to see how you were coming."

The Ragalfr scowled. He looked like a pixie—decidedly not a pixie, because the proportions were different for the head. His matched his body, though his attitude was about dragon-sized.

He had punched me once and done some serious damage. Little fucker.

At about a foot and a half tall, violently green hair spiked in a mohawk of sorts, Xiphyre cut a very…punk rock kind of figure, and it was always interesting to see him out and about.

"You done admiring?" The little man growled; his fists balled.

"Looking good, man, I dig the shorts." I tried to make the complement as flattering as possible. His brown trousers fluttered in the downdraft of his tiny wings.

"Dig nothing, fox. Come, I must show you my work!" He seemed to forget the slight against him, so into the forge we went.

The inside of the place was as clean and organized as I had ever seen it, though on the multitude of racks and counters, there were new weapons made of new kinds of ores.

"Hail, Zeke!" A gravelly voice bellowed. I turned to see Thogan Swiftaxe, followed by his apprentice Rowland. "Finally come to visit, eh?"

Thogan was an odd-looking dwarf, skin craggy, and pitted like stone the color of midnight with diamonds sprinkled throughout it. Almost as if his oath of service to Maebe had made his body a mirror of her own. His head was bald, and he had a beard as dark as his skin. Golden eyes shimmered at me merrily while he offered his fist. I rapped his knuckles with my own and then did the same with Rowland.

Rowland was the owner of this fine establishment, and pretty tall for a dwarf, standing almost a full two inches taller than Thogan, his new master. His black beard was longer than it had ever been and looked as though there was a shine to it that I didn't recall either.

"Love what you've done with your beard, Rowland!" He waved it away halfheartedly. "And you guys know that we needed time to decompress after what happened."

Thogan nodded sagely and slapped my shoulder affectionately. "We know, lad. Cannae be dwarves if we donnae grief ye, aye?"

I smiled, and Rowland socked me in the shoulder lightly.

"Seriously, Rowland, you're looking pretty damned good!" I tried to see what other goodies he had woven into his beard, but he shoved me away playfully.

"Bah, is nae much. Thogan were kind 'nuff ta lend me a secret fer a softer beard. Normal lady dwarves like a gruff beard —like their men—but Vilmas be a true prize, and I be needin' ta show her I got class as well. Aye?"

"Nicely done then, Thogan." He simply grinned at us and motioned toward the forge area behind him.

We walked back into the area, and it was vastly different from before. The former forge had been taken completely out, and the old anvil replaced by a deep maroon-colored one, with a twin half a dozen feet away. The old wooden counters had been gutted and replaced by thinner stone slabs. Tools hung on hooks in their assumed proper places, and there was plenty of room to move and work in.

"What's the deal with all the new gear fellas?" I wandered around the space. It was warm, the forge on a constant low heat. And holy *fuck* the forge.

"Admire yer handiwork lad." Rowland clapped me on the shoulder. "First time seein' the Dragon's Maw Forge, be a bit much ta take in, but ye get 'customed.'"

True to the name, the forge had taken on the shape of a dragon's head with the Fire Primordial Elemental's flaming crown symbol in the middle of the top half that looked like a forehead. The sides that had once been flaps were now teeth and lips that could have been moving as I watched.

"This is incredible," I whispered in awe. I went to touch the forge and Rowland stopped me with a hand on my forearm.

"Careful lad, she be temperamental." I took his warning for the truth, and left it alone. "She's been doin' right fine work. Heats the metal perfectly, an' with Thogan here ta help—me shop's better'n ever!"

"I'm really happy for you, man." I rubbed my green and purple arm, the prosthetic having replacing the limb I'd for fucking up this very project. Well, not fucked up. It was better than I had ever planned. But that still had almost gotten me and my friends killed when I had enchanted it, though I had only lost my arm instead. And been unconscious for more than a day.

Look just don't ever try to work with a crazy-large ruby with flame-aspected mana, because unless you want to make a bomb, it's not a good idea. Okay?

But, rather than dwell on the past, I turned to Xiphyre. "Where's the eye?"

The Ragalfr grinned and flitted toward the forge, Rowland stepping over beside him with a long set of tongs. The dwarven smith almost lovingly touched the side of the forge and whispered something. The top rose a little bit, so that he could reach in with the tongs and pull a small object out easily.

Rowland brought it over and set it onto the closest maroon anvil. It was a small cherry-red object, with the orb portion looking the same as an eye would from any anatomy textbook. It was both simultaneously cool as hell, and really weird.

"Balmur!" Thogan called loudly.

A few seconds later, Balmur and Jaken bustled into the room. They both wore aprons and held different tools. Jaken held a small set of tongs and Balmur a small hammer.

Xiphyre flitted to the Azer dwarf and ushered him toward the still glowing appendage. "It requires a sacrifice, but I had something that would work thanks to Her Majesty."—he took the tongs from Jaken and lifted the still hot item from the anvil. He prodded it toward Balmur—"Hold open your eye, boy. The heat won't bother you."

I came over to stand next to Balmur as he obeyed, though a little nervously. The eye floated toward the socket in the tongs, and as soon as it was close, Xiphyre jabbed. He released simultaneously and suddenly fluttered behind my right shoulder.

"The fuck are you doin' you little coward?" I snorted when he smacked the back of my head for the insult.

Balmur groaned and blinked, his hands flying to his face.

Xiphyre howled, then shouted, "Don't take it out! If you do, there's no way to get it to stay again; you must work through the pain."

"You've dealt with worse, Balmur!" I encouraged my friend. Jaken and I both cast healing spells on him, but they did little. After a full three minutes of our friend hissing in pain, he finally managed to stand and turn a tear-stained face to us.

"That sucked," he whispered.

Xiphyre moved forward to sit on Balmur's shoulder. "But it will be worth it because my genius smiled on this item!"

He pulled out a small jar with a single eye in it and whipped the lid off. Before anyone could do anything, he had the eye up and out of it, presenting it to Balmur's new eye like some kind of priest making an offering.

A spectral mouth that looked vaguely like a demon's appeared a centimeter from the blank eye, reaching out with sharp teeth that plucked the offering from the air, devouring it like a cherry. Balmur's body went rigid for a heartbeat; he groaned some more as he rubbed his eyes. He looked around in a fugue state, then blinked as a tear fell from the new orb's home.

"You alright?" I closed the distance between us to look him over.

He nodded, a hand out to stop me from getting too close. "Yeah. The price for it was just a bit steep."

"What is it?" Rowland knelt next to the doubled-over man.

"I get to see how the owner of the eye died from their point of view." Balmur blinked again, and his vision seemed to clear. "This one ran afoul of Xiphyre and lost an eye in a bet. You're crazy, man."

The ragalfr grinned maniacally. "Have you noted the ability yet?"

"It absorbs ocular abilities?" Balmur's voice held curiosity and wonder. "That is so cool. But it can only have one at a time."

Xiphyre handed over the jar that he had held. "Hence this jar. It is a package deal. The component that was brought to me was a doffilnar's eye! With that, I was able to give it the ability to take one power of an eye that it consumes. But that is the problem—it *must* consume. Once a week should be fine, but it could depend. It will let you know when it hungers. As I am sure it likely did when it settled into its new home?"

Balmur nodded once, raising a hand to touch his face around the eye. I watched the item closely, moving just a little closer to him to see it more clearly. It now looked exactly like his other eye.

"Now, it won't inhibit any sight that you have naturally on your own. I understand dwarves can naturally see under the ground?" The dwarves all confirmed his question. "So, you will have an added bonus to your natural sight. Things like Zeke's True Sight, the ability to see the magic that some creatures have. Other things too, I would ask that you try to track what you get and let me know if you can. This is fascinating."

"Yup, will do. Thanks, Xiphyre." Balmur shook the little man's hand and turned to me. "Thanks for hooking me up like this. I hope it hasn't set you back too much."

I grimaced. It had. It had cost a good portion of the chunk I'd taken from Riktolth's hoard, and some from the others as well. I didn't want to talk too much in the area of prices, but cha-fucking-*ching* didn't describe it well enough. But, if it did what it was supposed to, then the item would be well worth the cost. Not to mention the fact that we could go back and collect more money if needed, a little Teleport and bam we had money in the bank.

"Ready for a drink tonight then lads?" Thogan raised his eyebrows, hopefully.

Balmur grasped his shoulder with a grin. "Some booze sounds really good. We'll see you tonight."

Oh. Great. Some of the biggest drinkers in the village

getting together to drink to whatever they wanted? This was going to get interesting.

But with Rowland being here…. "Hey Rowland, where's Mini?" Mini was a small fox kit that I had rescued, and in turn, became a constant companion to Rowland. Someone to help him cope with the PTSD of the attack on him by the thugs from the Children of Brindolla.

"She and Vilmas be thick as thieves now, though she does drop in an' check on me." The smith smiled wistfully. "Enjoys harassing Thogan and Xiphyre more than anything these days —does enjoy a nice cuddle and a meal with me, though."

"Sounds like she's having a great time then." I couldn't help the stirring of jealousy. I missed Coal; the flame wolf I had helped strengthen for the primordial flame. He had reached a high enough level to return home, and I couldn't be so selfish as to keep him from his life and family.

"What will you do now?" Jaken had come to stand next to me while thoughts of Coal flitted through my heart.

"I'll likely go see about finding Maebe and Vrawn. Maybe go for a longer flight. I'm not sure. But I do know that we're likely heading out tomorrow, so get what you need doing done. Yeah?"

Jaken nodded, then seemed as if he stared straight through me for a moment before pulling me in closer to him. "I know it feels weird being idle like this. But it's just helping us. It's okay to relax a little."

"The last time I relaxed and let things happen as they would, two of you almost died against that doffilnar." I still recalled seeing Jaken kneeling over Bokaj, who had died in the fight and was subsequently being brought back to the living by the paladin. As well, James hadn't been faring much better himself, barely hanging in there.

It was only when Telfino had stepped in and helped us that we had gained the ability to truly fight back. And now we had these damned nightmares coming to make things shittier.

"You had no way of knowing that it would take your

shape and have that much mana." Jaken actually shoved me when he spoke. "Don't dwell on it—learn from it. Then move on."

He very carefully made eye contact with me for this next one. "Because we have. We don't have the luxury for you to space out and think about what could have been, or what ifs. We need you here in the present. Okay?"

My frown wasn't from the disdain at being told to let go, but from wondering when Jaken had grown so wise. He'd always seemed to be able to make things better, but this was next-level insight.

"Yeah, you got it, Jaken." I put a thumb up, and he shook his head. "What?"

"You've been a little off since before then, too. I know you miss Coal, but we're all here, and he's home, now."

The others turned toward us, watching with interest. My cheeks burned a little but being called out like this in front of people I trusted wasn't so bad. Still hard to fight my initial urge to tell my friend to fuck off, though.

"I've known you for quite a while now, and I know that this isn't going to get through that thick skull of yours," Jaken punched me in the shoulder kind of hard. "I've seen you being rough on yourself from all of this. You take things too seriously at times, and you're always hardest on yourself. Sometimes it takes a little help for us to realize that we're being assholes to ourselves. Let it go. Seriously."

"I'll try," I stated with little ease. I'd always been this way. And it would likely not change overnight. But sulking wouldn't help, right?

Without waiting for him to start in again, I shapeshifted into my owl form and flitted outside.

I heard a call, but nothing after, and nothing through our earrings. It was time to find the ladies and forget my wounded pride for a heartbeat.

Watching the skies around me, something moved below the horizon line east of us and cruised toward the village at a steady pace. As I closed in from above, a large cart bustled along, pulled by a warthog.

The creature was larger than the cart it pulled, was red and gold, with large tusks jutting from its mouth capped with jagged silver spear points.

The cart moved on as I landed in front of it on a branch high above so I could watch more easily. A young-looking human child. No. As she came closer, noticeable signs of age like wrinkles on her golden-tanned skin and fine lines on her forehead and around her eyes sparked my interest. This was a halfling woman. I had seen a few of them in this world, and they were kind of popular in a tabletop game back home on Earth, but it was still so disorienting seeing them every time and not thinking of children.

She yawned, stretching in her seat at the helm of the cart. The bench looked a little worn, but it was a nice-looking cart for sure. She wore a pink dress with a black bodice beneath it that lifted her small chest a little higher and cupped her stomach and lower back tightly. It looked highly impractical.

"Well, Humphrey, seems we have a watcher up yonder!" The woman's southern drawl was surprising. The cart came to a slow halt, and Humphrey, the large warthog, eyed his surroundings warily. "Oh, it's up yonder Hum, don't worry. He's an owl. You probably won't be able to see him too well, on account of your eyes bein' all weird about looking up. But he's a looker!"

The halfling woman stood up and reached into a bag beside her; my heart pounded as her hand disappeared before pulling out a large vole. She held it aloft, "You hungry, fella?"

I turned my head to the side in confusion and ruffled my feathers anxiously.

"I don't blame ya for not wanting an easy meal 'round a stranger fella, but I got a way with animals, see? Pa always did say, 'Manly, if yer good to nature, nature'll be good to you. Ya hear?' And boy, I'd always holler 'yes pa!' And it ain't never led me wrong. So, I'll toss this here critter aside for you to have. If you want it? Well, you can have it."

She tossed the now-struggling animal off to the side of the cart, and it landed in a bush. Well, if she was good with nature, that was good enough for me, right?

I could almost reveal myself to someone like this, but now I had the village to think of.

The creature is going to run further if you aren't careful, the owl's instincts tutted. *If you want to be a believable predator, leaving a meal like that alone would be bad. Though an owl who hunts during daylight hours is odd enough. You might want to secure a different avian form for daylight hours.*

Won't that overwrite you? I returned as I dropped toward the bush.

I eyed the smiling—Manly, was it? She made no move to do anything other than watch me fly.

Only if the form you take is that of an owl or is stronger than the one you use, now. It is possible to have several different forms of the same type but upgrading them isn't a bad idea either. I notice that you don't have a rodent form, either. This is a folly on your part.

That's likely a fair thought from his perspective. Having more forms I could take would be nice, for different aspects I could use, and for the ability to blend in a little more, sometimes. It was only a benefit.

Still didn't mean I liked the voices in my head being pricks about it.

I'd have to see about what to do later on.

I dove into the bushes, *bank left, and extend your right claw in front of you.*

I did as the owl had instructed and burst from the bush with the vole clasped in my claws. It struggled, but I would likely let it go here in a minute.

As I cleared the foliage, a hand reached out and grasped me by the back of the neck.

"There we go!" Manly's voice reached my ears. "That's a

strange leg for a critter like yourself to have. Are you someone's pet?"

I struggled and flapped my wings, the vole forgotten in my grasp.

"Don't worry fella, I don't wanna hurt ya! I just want to look at that purty wing of yours!" She tried to make that last bit soothing, but I wasn't having it, and thrashing about was all I could do without giving away my natural form.

Now that she had captured me so easily, I wasn't sure I wanted to do that.

"Well, you must be important to somebody, because that's quite a serious piece o' hardware there. And there's even a bit obscuring information on it from someone else touching it." She turned me so that I stared into her molasses-colored eyes. "If you were a wild owl, I'd take you and see what you'd fetch at auction, but I ain't no thief. I might be out and about hunting for different things to add to my collection, but you're safe from me, little fella."

I screeched once, and she finally released me. I fluttered back toward a tree but left the area so that I could be out of her sight.

I listened carefully, the sound of the gigantic warthog snuffling the ground, pawing it then moving on. Toward the village. I didn't want to leave the others in the dark, nor did I want to lose the cart and the halfling driving it.

I shifted and cast Mental Message to Yohsuke since we were out of range for our earrings to be of use, "Cart inbound to the village. The enchantment should hold, but I'm following it. Not certain if hostile or not."

I shifted back and fluttered around to stay out of her sight, then behind the cart until I could land on it. Once on board, it was easy to see that the woman had no true plan moving forward. Her plodding gait forward seemed lax. And more than a little at the whim of Humphrey.

The large beast didn't stop much, grazing on the go, but he was sure-footed and seemed to have no issues pulling the cart.

You sure they're on their way toward us? Jaken said through our earrings.

The enchantment worked when I was in animal form, but it was one way. I couldn't respond to them. But what I could do was have Kayda act it out to them!

Kayda, go find the others! I called through our bond. She responded with an image of Jaken below her from her perch. *Good! Plop onto his shoulder and do as I tell you to do, okay?*

She obeyed, and the tops of the trees nearest the village came into view.

Nod at him. She did, and he seemed a little confused until she pecked his head and really got his attention before nodding exaggeratedly this time.

Oh! Smart man. Okay. How many are there? Tell Kayda to stomp on my shoulder for how many there are. I had her stomp once. *They a threat?*

I had her shrug for me, then nod once.

Uncertain then. Could they know about the village? Did they mention anything about it? Kayda swiped her head back and forth to say no, which I'm fairly certain would have looked hilarious because I knew she could just turn her head and say it. She'd been doing it since she was a chick.

Focus.

I'll gather the others and wait inside the gate. If they get too weird and shit goes south, let us know and start slinging spells. No chances. Jaken's voice was uncharacteristically angry, for once. I was a little worried.

Yohsuke interrupted, *why don't we just meet them outside the gates?*

Because that would give away that there's something around here to be interested in. James answered flatly. *You have a hard boss show up in any random location where no one should be, and you do what after you kill him or escape?*

Immediately start snooping, Balmur and Bokaj intoned together.

Exactly. Let the enchantment do what it is supposed to do, and then if anything happens, we can take care of the rest, Jaken finished.

The others seemed to be relatively okay with the plan, so we waited. Eventually, talismans began to crop up in places like the crooks of trees, in large holes, or buried in the roots of shrubs. Perched just above and slightly behind the lip of the white cart's roof Manly's former look of confident ease filtered out of the line of her body. Almost imperceptible at first, but the closer they came, the worse it seemed to get until Manly looked like she was about to vomit, and Humphrey stopped eating and chewing altogether.

The talismans had been a new touch that some of the kids had made to give a sense of unease. They weren't enchanted to really do anything. What Manly was feeling now was the influence from the wall. It went pretty far, I guess. As Vilmas grew in strength, she and Xiphyre had been able to add a little more power to the enchantment itself, increasing range and all of that good stuff. I was pretty impressed with the result.

Then came the gas—I hoped it was nervous gas coming from the huge animal, but hey, I'm not one to tell someone they can't be flatulent due to gender, man.

Seriously though, whoever that was smelled to high heavens, and I was surprised my feathers hadn't crisped, damn.

"Maybe we oughta get on, Humphrey," Manly grumbled below me. "This place ain't right. Somethin's wrong, buddy. Like somethin's tryin' to warn us away, you know it?"

We were about a dozen feet or so from the gates, the party and the guards standing on the walkway above them when Humphrey turned right and began to pull a little harder than he had before. A breeze hit us, coming westerly where I had settled. All of my friends watched as the cart turned, and I thought we were safe.

Humphrey stopped cold and whipped his head toward the wall, and his eyes narrowed. Fuck.

Why'd they stop man, what's up? Muu asked nervously.

I wasn't sure, but I looked down to see that, despite the discomfort and obvious sense of dread and evil around her, Manly got off the bench and knelt next to her friend.

"You caught on, buddy?" Looking ill didn't keep her from

excitedly leaning toward her partner, then grimacing as she tried to breathe through either her discomfort or the squealing gas that just erupted from Humphrey. "It was toward the breeze, right?"

Humphrey grunted and patted the ground before tossing his head toward the wall.

"Thanks, buddy." Manly scratched the giant pig's snout before standing and turning toward the gates. "If there's someone there, come on out! I mean no harm, just a fair lass seeking some trade!"

The guards seemed concerned and didn't know what to do while my friends looked ready to start lobbing spells and ass-kickings.

Time to see if we can't keep things under control, then. I shapeshifted on the bench that I had just dropped down onto.

"Well, you caught me, then. What can I do for you?" I did my best to sound unsurprised and unconcerned. I adopted an attempted foppish pose to appear relaxed as I lounged on the bench. My whole body went rigid as she spun, and her hand went to the bottom of the bodice. A knife appeared between my legs. "Strike one. Why do you bother me?"

"Who are you?" She narrowed her eyes; then her gaze fell on my right arm.

"A curious owl, Manly." I grinned, allowing the gesture to be simultaneously threatening and cool. Hopefully. I had never really been all that good at effecting confident faces. I was just too weird for it. "Last chance to answer me, Manly. You were kind to nature, so I will allow you a chance I do not give often— why have you come to my hunting grounds?"

"We came out this way looking for exotic animals and things to add to our collection and trade-off to high-end buyers," She replied with a sigh. "I'd be more inclined to believe you iff'n I hadn't been able to smell that there's at least three different scents o' food, a powerful body odor, and a freshly cooling pie upwind from us."

Jig's up y'all. She knows something is amiss. I told the others with our earrings.

"So, you know my given name." She stepped a little closer, her hand resting on the bolt that held her porcine friend in the straps for pulling the cart. "So, what's yours, mister curious owl?"

"I'm Zeke, and I'm afraid that we've reached a bit of an impasse." I sat up slowly, pulling the weapon that had embedded itself in the wood between my legs with my metal hand. I fiddled with the blade half interested in the craftsmanship, but mainly with how well she had thrown it. "You're somewhere that not a lot of people were able to come before. I can't know if you mean the people I care for harm or not, and since I can't know that for certain, I don't rightly know what to do with you."

"Well, I could give you my word, if you like?" She offered politely with raised eyebrows.

Not going to do much for me, I'm not Fae enough for tha—or am I? I thought back to the fact that I was a knight of the Unseelie Court now. Could I make her swear a binding agreement?

Maebe there, anyone? I asked the others, hopefully.

Nope. She heard a threat could be coming, so she went to the children immediately, Bokaj stated. I looked over to see that he had drawn an arrow and had a handful more in his hand that held his bow aloft. As if to grab them faster and deliver them priority to a certain halfling's center mass.

Couldn't argue with that. And I didn't have the time to deliberate any longer. She would get suspicious and either start questioning me, or a fight would break out.

Fuck.

"Swear to me on your power and upbringing what you like, but most importantly, that you aren't a threat. Do that, earnestly, and I will consider it." I hopped off the cart and slowly moved toward her. Humphrey eyed me closely but didn't move.

"I swear on my strength and my bow that I was raised not to

harm any what didn't mean to harm me first. So long as no one means me harm and don't attack me first, I will stay my hand, so I swear on my ma and pa's spirits as they rest in their grave together." She held her hand over her heart as she spoke, her face earnest. Humphrey grunted and tossed his head beside her. "Humphrey too, though if you have a compost heap, he may terrorize it a bit. Who could begrudge him that though, eh? Not I."

Her smile lit her face, and I eyed her warily. Then I got a notification, and it appeared that she had as well.

Warning!

You, as a knight to a queen of considerable power, have been given an oath, the consequences of which are incredibly dire. As someone who has received an oath, it is up to you to do what you can to see that the pledge-giver upholds their promise. Should you actively seek to harm this individual, they are unbound from their oath and allowed to protect themselves. The same goes for them if they break their vow. Congratulations!

"Well, that's different, but at least now you know I ain't lyin' to you." Her smile turned to a full grin. "So, can we get out of this uncomfortable place and get somewhere more…hospitable like? Humphrey gets real gassy when he's scared, and he's not been too shy about letting it all out. As you will likely be smelling right about now."

I looked at her in confusion before gasping and gagging. *Oh, my god!* I retched audibly. "Yea-ugh, let's."

I led her to the gate and opened the place up with my palm. The large doors opened slowly, and all of my friends except Balmur stood there waiting just inside.

"She's cool guys, but beware of the warthog, he just shit himself." Bokaj's face screwed up instantly, and he gagged. "Told you."

Balmur appeared next to her and grimaced. "That's rough." He stepped back into the shadows and moved away from us.

"So, who do I have the pleasure of greetin'?" Manly waved

to everyone as soon as we were fully inside. The gates had closed, and both of the visitors seemed to be in much better spirits.

"Well, we're from left to right—our left, sorry—Jaken, James, Yohsuke, Muu, Balmur, and Bokaj. You've met Zeke." Bokaj explained as he pointed to each of them. Kayda fluttered from Jaken's shoulder to mine, and I distinctly caught the halfling's eyes following her appraisingly.

"She's not for sale, and if anyone touches her, they pay." I said it mildly so that it wouldn't be construed as a threat. She seemed to take it in stride as she looked around some more. "Now, care to introduce yourself to the others?"

"Oh! Sorry 'bout that. New surroundings and whatnot." She stepped forward and put a hand onto her warthog's side and bowed a little. "Name's Manly Warbottom, trader and procurement specialist of wild and exotic animals. My journeys led me out this way in search of another set of animals to trade to the highest bidder. I appreciate your hospitality, and I'll be keeping this place a secret in exchange. I hope we can have a good working relationship."

"Well, that depends, but it sounds like whatever you told Zeke was enough to gain you entry to the village." Yohsuke eyed me, and I gave him the barest of nods to let him know that he was correct.

She swore an oath to me, and as a knight, it worked. So let's keep that in mind when we're talking to people, unless we want them to know what we are. The others took that information and nodded back.

"Any of you in the market for a pet?" She raised her eyebrows hopefully, and I had to admit, I was curious to see what she had.

"I am." Jaken stepped forward. I blinked at him, and he ignored me. "Let's clear out of here and go somewhere a little more business-friendly so that we can discuss?"

"Sounds fair to me, sir knight!" She grinned and turned to get up onto the cart as Jaken and the rest of us stiffened.

"How...how did you know that, Manly?" James stuttered for a second.

"Know what?" She looked from James to Jaken. "Oh! That he's a knight? Well, all that fancy armor sure makes him look like one, but if mister Zeke here is a knight, I figured y'all might be the same as him as his friends. Sure, look pretty strong as well, so that helps too."

She's not wrong. We do look strong as shit. Muu preened to the rest of us.

We eyed him steadily, but he wasn't taking it back.

What do you need a pet for, Jaken? Bokaj asked as we walked up the street toward the town square where things were bought and sold.

I don't—it's for our moping druid. He shot me a side-eye that anyone would have noticed a mile away.

I'm not moping, you ass. I'm sad that I lost a friend! There's a difference.

Yohsuke snorted audibly. *One that you* knew *would eventually be taken from you to return home in exchange for a huge sum of experience and favor from a being akin to an elemental god. Dude, it's cool to be sad for a bit, but it was a job. A quest. We have a job to do, and not only are you keeping yourself from relaxing and partially the rest of us, but you're oper- ating at less than full power.*

The others, James, Muu, Bokaj, and Balmur, had taken the chance to get behind the cart to watch it and also get away from the three of us left in front.

We understand that you feel that loss heavier because he was almost literally a part of you—and don't get me wrong, we liked him too—but he was always destined for something other than the life that we have at this moment. He was promised elsewhere. Yohsuke sighed and looked to Jaken.

You know he wouldn't want you to be this sad over him going home. You know for damned sure that if you spend valuable time, you could be training another familiar while mourning his loss. He would be sadder knowing you could have been able to defend yourself, and his other friends, better with another familiar, so that you could call on him once more some-

day. We all need to be at full strength, or on our way there. Jaken walked into the square. *So, if you won't get off your ass and procure something strong for yourself, I will, and you'll like it and love it and name it something cool as fuck—just like me.*

"What an ass," I murmured out loud and walked toward the central area.

The normal selling and hawking of wares came to a grinding halt when we broke through into the square. Children and families watched, excited at first to see us, but then truly curious at the sight of Humphrey and the cart he pulled.

As I gazed around to see that everyone was okay, when movement in my peripheral vision made me turn my head fully.

The shadows in one corner of the square coalesced, growing deeper and deeper until Maebe stepped out with Vrawn in tow. The orcish woman looked a little timid at first, stepping through shadows was a hard thing for someone with no training. Likely she had been terrified, but rather than let Maebe come here alone, she had sucked it up and joined her. Kudos.

Once she had seen the cart, though, Vrawn's features were purely business. This was the second in command of the guard, a former sergeant in her mother's army, and I dared to say, an incredibly strong woman. She would protect these people or die trying.

"My subjects, I felt the oath given to one of you, who took it?" Maebe looked at the others before I stepped forward and took a knee.

"I did, Your Majesty." I bowed my head, and her hand touched my shoulder.

"Lift your head, Sir Zekiel. You acted well as a Knight as the situation would have dictated." She eyed the newcomer with a frosty glare. "We can discuss this more later—we *will* discuss this more later. Rise."

I stood and took my place on her left side between her and Vrawn.

"You come to sell?" Maebe asked. Manly hopped onto the ground and walked over to stand before Maebe.

"I take it that you're who these people owe fealty to? Nice folks here, ma'am. And yes, I've come to obtain and sell a few rare creatures if I could, but then I stumbled on this place and mister knight over there. Had to come on in and say hello!" Manly's smile was well in place, and it seemed genuine to me.

"Is it normally okay for someone of no station to address a queen in that manner?" Vrawn growled as she stepped toward the other woman.

Manly blinked. "We don't really deal much with royalty where I'm from, but judging from her skin and features, I'd say she's a Fae Queen. Bit far from your throne, Majesty?"

The halfling woman put her hands on her hips and leaned forward to observe Maebe's features closer with a perfectly friendly expression on her face.

"Vrawn, stand down." I was having a hard time holding the woman back, but Maebe's command helped immensely. The veins in Vrawn's neck were popping out against her skin, and she looked ready to blow a gasket. Maebe turned her attention back to Manly. "I am a Fae Queen. And your intelligence is correct; I am indeed far from my throne. But I also care for these people as if they were my own. So, if something were to happen to them, any of them, I would be very distraught."

She leaned down so that her face was directly in front of Manly's, mere inches away. "I don't know what I might do to someone who harmed my subjects."

"Is that a threat, your Majesty?" The halflings tone, formerly sweet, took on a menacing edge.

"It is," Maebe's voice took on a similar tone. "But that is for everyone and anyone who thinks this place, or these people are to be taken advantage of."

The two of them stared at each other for a moment longer, then blinked and stood erect.

"Glad to know where everyone stands." Manly held her

hand out to shake, and Maebe didn't so much as glance at it. She took her hand back, and that was that.

"Come one, come all, and venture through my stall!" Manly called as she expertly pulled straps and buckles.

Portions of the cart fell to the ground on poles that made it look like a stall. There were eggs in nests, small cages, and bins with different creatures inside. Some were cute. Others grotesque and elaborately colored. But all of them seemed to be well taken care of.

People gathered around. The smaller items for animal care and capture that she had time to make on the road, Manly sold for a premium, but people seemed to eat them up no matter the cost. Though some grumbled about highway robbery. The prices seemed fair for the amount of labor involved, and though no one could afford the animals or eggs, there was nothing we could do. Though Jaken did peruse the items that she had available.

"What are these eggs right here?" Jaken's voice carried and I wandered over to see what he had found.

Manly, busy with someone else, glanced over and explained in an even, practiced sales tone, "I crossed the ocean a couple months back, returning from an expedition on Isla dar Ragmarrath. It's a large island just off the coast of the creature continent, where some of the more monstrous species of creatures are said to live. While I was there, I found several of these eggs. You'll notice that each of them has a different coloration that seems to match a different elemental type. I'm not sure why, or what they could be—but they were hard to come by and pretty expensive."

She finished the sale with the villager and turned to us. "What do you think? Care to purchase one?"

"How much is it?" Jaken picked one of them up, a green one, and held it close to his eyes to observe it closer.

"Hmm. I'd say I'd be willing to part with it for thirty-five thousand gold?" Her voice sounded hopeful, and Bokaj hopped in on it from there.

"I don't think so." The ranger sighed, exasperatedly. "If it were hatched, half-grown, and trained, I could see that hefty price tag. But for the egg itself that we can't guarantee will hatch anytime soon, that's way too much, and it sounds like you know it."

"If you think so." Manly looked contemplative for a moment. "I'd be willing to trade one for that bird that Zeke has in his possession."

I snorted. "Never going to happen." I eyed Jaken a second. "Those eggs are interesting for sure, but nothing and no one will ever be worth trading Kayda. Later man."

Fed up with the crap there, I walked off. Vrawn stayed to oversee the newcomer, but Maebe stepped away with me. The others stayed behind and looked at the wares, clearly knowing they could do as they pleased.

"Are you okay?" Maebe took my arm and pulled me close to look me in the eyes.

"Yes and no, more annoyed that she would even suggest trading Kayda for something else." I spat, my anger almost boiling over and red clouding my vision. "All she sees on my shoulder is gold. Not the creature that she is. Not our relationship, just money."

"I can understand how that would be upsetting," Maebe said. "But you do need to realize that rare it is for a stranger to see a relationship and understand it completely. Her perception is that you have a rare animal that would fetch a handsome fee at auction."

"I do, but I had already told her no. The fact that she doesn't respect boundaries enough to know that when I said no the first time, I meant it. Period. And something tells me that she's going to keep trying."

"She may, but you made it so that she wouldn't hurt anyone who doesn't try to hurt her first." She eyed down the streets and behind us. "That was good thinking getting her to swear, though you could have led her with the appropriate wording that you had desired. With the oath she gave, she can take anything from a threat to someone stumbling into her to mean that they were attacking her, then she would be able to attack them with impunity."

My heart fell. Fuck. I'd managed to fuck that up, too.

"Is there a way to fix it?" I eyed the streets as well; no one was around, surprisingly. Likely trying to look at all the odd creatures.

"No, but what you can do is get on her good side and get her out of here." Maebe reached between us and clasped my hand in her own. "You have worked hard for this place—all of you have—and her being here could threaten that."

"How would you suggest we do that?"

"She collects rare and valuable creatures? Offer to take her on an expedition to the Great Below with you, to protect her until she gets something, then part ways amicably," Maebe raised my hand in hers then began to squeeze it. "Then, who knows what may happen to her down there,"—she raised her eyes to mine— "but that will no longer be our problem."

I couldn't help but laugh. Was it slightly nervous? Sure. Was I a *little* afraid of her? Yup. But you could truly tell that playing the game was something bred into Maebe. You had to appreciate that.

"So. Why don't you go back to her to win her over, and I will go oversee the children. Tonight, as the others drink and party, we will make merry with this Manly and have her believe that we will assist her in gaining a valuable asset." Maebe pulled me down so that I was inches from her so she could whisper, "then we leave her high and dry in the shadows to fend for herself."

"I don't know about leaving her to die," I replied sourly, more so than I meant to.

"Her death is not guaranteed, my love, only that she will have to depend on herself to survive," Maebe explained patiently. "If we were to become separated, then we could hardly be held liable for her safety, could we?"

I growled as I considered her words, the equivalent to all the plotting that had been done against her as she had been on the throne. Plotting that her people had been involved in likely longer than any of my ancestors had even been alive. "I will do what I can."

I reached out and pulled her close to me, my body now human so that I could kiss her deeply before shifting back. "Be safe."

As I turned to move away and go back to the others and my duty, Maebe stopped me. Her eyes, so dark green as shadows crossed her face from the trees above that they could have been emeralds. Her face was somber, but somehow not.

"You have come far, Zeke. I acknowledge your strength and that of our friends." She clasped my hand once more and held it to her chest. I could feel her heartbeat beneath her night-sky skin. "Would that I could reward you with more for that."

That made me stop. "What are you trying to say?"

She blinked. "Nothing, for now, my heart. There is still much to do and more time to think upon things." Her gaze grew fiercer as she whispered, "I love you."

"And I, you." I bowed my head slightly as she went. I watched her saunter into the shadows of the wall next to us and disappear. "Weird."

I shook myself out and headed back into the square where a large crowd had gathered to watch Manly take a small creature no bigger than a fat chihuahua, that looked like a dog but had scales in place of fur and spines like a porcupine along its back, through a series of hoops and commands.

"Good girl!" She drawled at the little creature who looked happy enough, but it had eyes only for her as it moved about, dancing and leaping.

As soon as they were finished, the crowd clapped, and several young adults rushed forward with small pieces of meat and coins to offer for the show.

I had neglected to cast Nature's Voice earlier, but I did so now while she was distracted and moved to her cart to speak with the other animals.

"Hello everyone," I spoke softly.

There was a pause before someone inside answered, "Who's there? You speak to us?"

I saw a large head poke over the side of the cart, one that reminded me of some kind of iguana with black and white feathers on the side of its head that looked kind of like a mane.

"You speak to us?" The wizened voice rasped curiously. "How? Why?"

"I'm a druid, and I can speak many languages," I stated, leaning against the cart casually. "How are all of you treated? Do you eat well?"

"As well as can be expected of someone who takes you from your home," the reptile grumbled. "I am the eldest of all of her creatures, and no one wants to purchase me for that reason. The young know no better. And the ones she's captured lately have been by request it seems, because they don't stay with us long."

"I see." I took to looking him over. "She treats you well?"

"She doesn't beat us if that's what you're asking." An exotic-looking bird with a small beak and weirdly sized gray feathers hopped forward and tapped my metal finger curiously. "She's very patient with animals, and with a sale. But for other things, her patience wanes swiftly."

"Is she violent?"

"She is a great hunter," the reptile grunted, his forked tongue venturing forward to taste the air between us. "There aren't many things that she cannot catch when she puts her mind to it. She is learned and cunning. Many seek her skills, many test her. Few win. I have been with her many cycles, and I know this is truth. Better than I know my tail."

"Thank you, friends. Tell me, what are your names?" I pulled a small bit of jerky from my inventory and offered it to the reptile.

"I am Jarlenill," he flicked his tongue in the bird's direction. "She is Rilly."

"A pleasure to meet you both." I thought about taking the

birds form but with the way it looked, and how small it was, I'd be better off with a hawk, falcon, or even an eagle.

It seemed the show was over by now, Manly with her small show animal in tow, made her way toward the stand.

"You're back swift," she stated observantly. "Rethinkin' a purchase?"

I blinked. *You know what? Yeah.* I thought to myself. *Why not?*

"How much for the reptile?"

"Higgins?" Manly's nose crinkled for a second before she regained her composure. "He's pretty rare…hmm…I s'pose I could part with him for a thousand gold."

I smiled. "So rare that he's been with you for many cycles? I think his words were, 'the younglings have known no other life,' because he's the oldest creature you have? How about I take him off your hands for a quarter of that and free up some space for you?"

Manly shot the reptile a dirty look, so I thought it appropriate to soften the blow. "He says that you're an excellent hunter. And had nothing but nice things to say. Animals are typically like that, you know? Honest. I tend to believe them when I can."

She frowned, pulling a buckle on the side of the cart so that steps popped out, and she could climb up. The skepticism in her features while looking between us, narrowed eyes lingering on me as if she was clearly uncertain if she should believe me or not, almost made me chuckle.

"Ask him." I shrugged. "Ask all of them."

She turned to the animals, eyeing them critically, then grinned. "No. I got a better test. If he really spoke to you, then touch him."

I stuck my left hand into the cart without hesitation or even looking. The bird I had spoken to fluttered back up to where it had been perched before. Scaled skin met my palm, and a thrumming growl or purring vibration rumbled against me.

"Well. This is new then." Manly looked both taken aback and curious at the same time. She leaned forward and rested her upper body on the board. "Normally Higgins bites anyone who tries to touch him. Nasty infections come after that. One noble even lost a hand to it. That had been an interestin' few days in the local jail. But—shouldn't touch merchandise you weren't invited to."

I smiled, despite the fact that she made me want to hurl her off a cliff for being a risk to the village, yet her forwardness and drawl were a little endearing. And they were growing on me.

"I'll let you have him, hundred and fifty gold." She pointed from me to him. "But only because he seems to like you."

I withdrew the required amount, and twenty-five extra. "So that I can learn what he likes, and also so you don't take too much of a loss."

"Mighty nice of you, mister Zeke!" Her smile was infectious. "Well, Higgy, come on out and meet your new owner."

The cart rattled as Jarlenill shifted and shuffled out. His large head came out first, his muscled jaw and feathered mane coming out into the light. His first thick, green leg thumped out onto the ground, then the second, and he walked the rest of his long body out. From the tip of his nose to the end of his tail, he was about sixteen· feet long and probably weighed a good four hundred pounds. His body had a good, thick coating of muscle, and his head was a little more triangle-shaped than his mane let on. He looked fucking sick. I loved it.

I'd happily have him join me in a fight, but looking at him, I could just tell he was too old for combat. He probably had a few years of good life left in him but fighting the way we needed to would likely be the end of him.

I'd be happy to give him the rest of his days living freely.

"Thanks, Manly." I offered her my hand to shake.

She took it and shook it firmly. "Pleasure doin' business with ya'."

"You're coming to the tavern for drinks later, right?" I asked as I sat next to Jarlenill. He thumped my shoulder with his large head, my body listing to the side from the strength of it.

Her eyebrow raised. "You plannin' to drink?"

"A little bit. It's going to be my friends really throwing down." I grinned, thinking about all the shit they would get into. "But I wanted to apologize for being a jerk earlier. And let you know that just because you found this place, you aren't a bad person. Sunrise is a great place with great people. We're just protective."

"I understand wantin' to protect you and yours," she offered as she closed up shop. She stopped suddenly and turned with a bashful look on her face, her eyes downcast. "I'm real sorry 'bout buggin' you to sell me your familiar. I just see somethin' purty like her, and I gotta try. I meant no disrespect to you, or her. I know y'all been together for a while, I've seen the way she looks at you when she's on your shoulder. You got a good one there. Mighty fine."

The apology took me by surprise, especially since I was *just* saying something about it. "Uh, yeah. No worries. So, drinks later? Dinner too? We can talk business and the like as well. There's an inn not too far away, so we can set you up with a room if you need it?"

"Mighty kind of you, Zeke. Tell you what, I'll take you up on the drinks and food, but I prefer to sleep with my assets. Keeps us both safe, get my drift?" Her demeanor was significantly more relaxed than before.

"Sounds good to me." I shrugged. "You can have Humphrey pull it over by the tavern, so you don't have to go too far after drinking."

"Sounds good to me!"

I helped her finish putting her cart back to traveling condition, but once it was there, I led her toward the tavern with little difficulty. Vrawn following at a distance. She was distrustful, and I didn't blame her.

CHAPTER THREE

As everyone ate, we had a light conversation between the party and Manly, and finally, it happened.

The question that everyone had been waiting for.

"So, uh, Manly," Bokaj spoke haltingly for once, possibly uncertain of how to proceed. "Your name is interesting."

"That's how you wanna ask me then?" The halfling raised her eyebrow.

"I didn't mean any disrespect." My friend backpedaled, looking to us for help.

"You aren't the first, and you won't be the last to ask how I got my name." She took a swig of her drink, clapped it onto the table and stared into the sky. "My ma wanted a girl, in a mean sorta way. My pa? Well, he wanted a boy what could take over the family business. See, he was a hunter and tracker, a damn fine one to boot. Thought that only having a proper heir would work."

She grasped at her chest and I thought she might cry, but instead let out a loud and satisfying belch. "Well, the day came when they had me. Imagine my pa's poor heart breakin' but being reborn anew. See, ma wanted me to be a real lady, but pa had other plans. See, in my culture, it's the pa who names the children. So, as he picked me up, he dubbed me what he wanted me to be—Manly." She took another deep draft of her drink and sighed. "Now, ma was a good sport about it, truly she was. She'd put me in pretty dresses, read to me by firelight in the evenin's and took care to teach me proper manners. But pa, he'd take me from bed real early in the mornin' dress me in breeches and a tunic, and we would go hunt, practice trackin', and woodcraft."

She laughed then, small at first, then as she looked to remember more, she laughed harder. Finally, a moment went by and she quieted.

"Sorry, I remembered that time I went out practicin' in the new dress my ma gave me, she was so mad. But when I found that bandit camp for that nice man who asked pa, they were all so surprised." Her face grew somber. "Well, when they went and got arrested, their friends didn't take too kind to that. They heard about the little girl what found their friends in the pretty pink dress, and they went lookin'."

I felt I knew where this tale was going, but I let her continue. I wanted to know, and at the same time, I didn't want to take her chance at expression away. Who knew when she spoke to others? Especially about this.

"When they found us, pa had sent me out on a huntin' trail that day. He'd taught me all he knew, and I had even managed to pick up a bit more from the book learnin' ma had me doin'." She sniffed once. "Well, I found my quarry in a cave, it were a dire bear. I wasn't s'posed to kill it, no. Wasn't strong enough for that. But I could track it and knew how to stay outta sight, so those were my orders. It picked up a scent not too long after I found it, and when it began to track it, I followed. Led me all the way back to my farmstead home. See, dire bears'll eat anything really, ain't too picky. So, when he stumbled upon the farm, I got worried. Then I saw the blood. Everywhere. Everything was covered in it."

Manly's gaze grew distant but hard. "The folks lookin' for us had found ma while she'd been sloppin' the pigs. Pa got to her with his bow as they were harassin' her. They didn't stand a chance, but the tracks at the scene spoke different. They'd eventually got pa away from ma and had questioned 'im. Real tender like." She shivered but led on. "They must have held out a while because there was a scuffle. Best I could tell, ma got free somehow, took a sword, and ran her watcher through. Made it to pa as they ended their questions."

The small, sad smile on her face spoke louder than her whispered words, "Ma had a temper, rest assured. They paid. But not before they got her. Some of 'em, wounded, got away. They left their friends there, picked clean of coin and gear, took what they wanted from the farm, and left it as it were. Like they wanted to send a message"—she took a long draught of her drink, lines of booze spilling down her chin.—"Well, as that beast picked his choice of the bodies there, I dragged my ma and pa inside and gave 'em a real warriors funeral. Grabbed some clothes, all the arrows my pa had fletched and set out to find 'em."

"You found them, though—right?" Muu asked, a look of intense fascination on his scaled face.

Manly's face split as a feral grin spread, baring her teeth to all of us. "I did. Since then, I've done my best to always exemplify both my ma and pa's wishes for me. To be a good, lady hunter. And that's why I'm named Manly. Now, as for my surname, see Humphrey outside, with his wee bucket of slop and ale?"

I turned to look out the window by our table at the front and jumped as Humphrey belched loudly, spittle flying as he tucked back into his slop greedily.

"Well, he's got a real bad temper too, but I fight on him. Been my best friend since after I found my family's murderers. Been with me ever since. And since he's usually under my bottom, well, Warbottom seemed to come rather easy after that." Her grin was less fierce now, but a slightly haunted look had taken her eyes.

I almost let myself reach out to comfort her, somehow. To tell her things are better now, but I wasn't sure I could. My hand fell back into my lap and it stayed there.

It didn't really matter, because it was then that Thogan and Rowland crashed through the door to the tavern. Rowland had a huge barrel on his shoulder, and Thogan carried two.

"Willem! Put that swill away. Tonight, we all drink the good stuff!" The crowd cheered as the old paladin behind the bar rolled his eyes.

Thogan bellowed, "get me cups and glasses, for the lads and lasses!"

"Oh, no." I groaned.

"What?" Vrawn and Manly asked in unison before glancing from me, to each other, then back at me.

"They've already started rhyming," I sighed, settling into what would likely be a long night of booze and terrible, *terrible* decisions. And the hangover, oh god. "It's never a good sign when they rhyme before even touching a drink."

"Hope you got your drinking pants on, boys." Vrawn chuckled. "You'll need them if that's his special brand of booze in there."

It was after about three cups, but who could remember how many they'd had after two of Rowland's forge inspired ale that a moment of drunken clarity hit me.

I turned to Manly, who clapped as Thogan tried and failed to juggle a set of rocks that fell and clocked Rowland on his head.

"Manly," I slurred, very seriously. "Listen, hey, hey, lishten— you should come hunt with us for an entrance to the Great Dick!"

"That sounds like a proper fun time!" She guffawed, dropping the last rock onto Thogan's head.

"Thash not right. Great Below! Thash it. You should come with us, and we can help you get some new and weird creashers to shell." I blinked at her, all three of them, and pointed to her button nose. "You can prowl it out, and we keep you company!"

"Yeah? You reckon I should do that then?" She stood up on her chair, wobbling a little bit, looking *fantastic* a little taller. "We're going to the *GREAT BELOW!*"

She threw her head back, giggling like crazy and toppled onto the ground; from there came an *ooph*.

I tried to be concerned, but it was hysterical. Eventually, and probably more cups than I should have had, I found myself lifted bodily and taken to bed.

"Hey! You gotta buy me dinner first, man." I grumbled rudely. "I'm a classy broad. There's a line for this ride, and you are *way* too strong to ride it."

The soft comfort of bed reached me, and that sweet soft embrace of a dizzying slumber took me. I was too drunk to really dream that night. But I was minutely aware of a comforting presence.

———

I woke up to a wet sensation on my bare shoulder that made me smile. The room wasn't spinning too badly as I rolled over to see who or what had been kissing my shoulder.

I turned to find Jarlenill staring at me, his tongue flickered over my nose, and I yelped. "Fuck!"

I didn't even need to cast Nature's Voice to know what was on his mind, but I cast the spell anyway.

"Hungry, druid," he rumbled at me. The door was wide open, and someone shifted behind me.

"Wha's wring?" Vrawn asked tiredly as her large hand cupped my shoulder, and she looked over me. "What's he want?"

"Food," I answered. Maebe's small hand holding a leg of meat came into view from over my shoulder.

"Thank you," Jarlenill spoke around the large leg happily enough. He turned and slowly made his way out of the room and the door shut behind him. A small shadow creature having shut it and melted back into the void.

I rolled back over to find Maebe laying in Vrawn's arms, staring at me with hooded eyes. "Good morning, my love."

"Good morning," I returned and scooted closer. "Rest well?"

"After carrying you in, then Vrawn? Yes."

"That was you?" Vrawn whispered against the top of her head. "You're very strong."

"Thank you," the queen purred. "How are you?"

"I'm hungry," Vrawn grumbled, she lifted her free hand and ran it over my fur. "Good morning, Zeke."

"Good morning," my stomach gurgled angrily. "I suppose it's time to eat, yeah?"

"Yes. It would be a good idea to eat before we leave." Maebe sat up, throwing the covers from all three of us. She smiled as she crawled over me to get onto the floor where she brought shadows up her body from the floor to cleanse herself like a shower.

I stood and did the same. I was getting much, much better at it, by now. It only took about a minute, but the entire time, Vrawn stared openly.

"And that cleans you?" She brought herself to the edge of the bed, her clothes ruffled and wrinkled from a night sleeping in them.

"It does, but it doesn't do clothing," Maebe informed her as she walked closer. She sat on Vrawn's lap, looking up at the larger woman with a hand over her heart. "Take them off, and I will have Zeke clean you with his shadows."

"I don't know." Vrawn narrowed her eyes skeptically, but Maebe pressed.

"Do you trust me?" She looked over toward me, "Do you trust us both?"

Vrawn didn't hesitate this time. "Yes."

Maebe placed her hands on either side of Vrawn's face and knelt in her lap, "Then stand, and let us care for you."

Maebe leaned forward and softly pressed her lips against the other woman's. Vrawn reacted the same way I would have, and soon they parted.

Hey. Monkey brain. Yeah, I'm talking to you. Got a little hot in here. You okay? You need a walk? Yeah, I know, me neither. Shall we?

"Okay." Vrawn stood with Maebe in her arms and gently deposited her onto the bed so that she could undress.

I wasn't going to stare outright, so instead, I looked to Maebe. The queen sat on the bed with nothing on and just watched. She saw me staring at her and winked with a sly grin. Oh man. I really did like this woman.

Vrawn pressed herself, surprisingly soft, against my shoulder. "Will you help clean me?"

You know what? I may be a fox but inside my head? The cartoon wolf with the mallet came out, and suddenly, I heard whistling and all kinds of birds. What was my name again?

"Hello, nurse," I whispered out loud. Vrawn raised an eyebrow, but I shook my head. "Yes, I'll help you clean up. Don't worry. It'll be a little foreign, possibly even a little cool at first, but you're completely safe."

She nodded once, her bearing masking any emotion or uncertainty that could have been going through her mind at that moment.

I reached my will into the shadows and called it to my hands, the nebula of darkness wringing my fingertips cool against my skin. I touched her shoulders, lightly caressing down her arms so that the shadows cascaded down her, eating the sweat and debris from the previous day. Shadows fell over her scarred, green flesh like water, her first reaction to shiver, but then I focused on cleaning, and she leaned back against me.

"This is…nice," She whispered breathlessly, her voice rumbling through the back of her body into my chest. It was comforting.

Admittedly, I took my time. Could I blame it on the fact that she was basically a giant? Sure. Could I blame it on her muscled figure being difficult to navigate? Yup.

But I'm not going to lie to you like that. I was enjoying myself. And I didn't want this closeness or the newness of it to go away so soon.

After a while, the three of us left the room and went to breakfast. We walked out to furtive glances and my snickering friends.

"Look who's finally up?" Muu teased, his gaze flicking from me to the two ladies, and his eyebrow ridges waggled wildly. That was saying something. "Look, man, are you going to start a harem, or not?"

"Hell no." I growled at him. "I'm not going to deal with all that."

Two hands clamped onto my shoulders, both Maebe and Vrawn reaching for me. "Two is enough. More than enough." I gave each one a light peck on the hand. "I'm happy with who I have. These two, my babies, Kayda, Coal, and all of you fuckers? Heart's full up. No more room."

"Yeah, yeah, mushy stuff and all that." Yohsuke sighed behind me. "Sit down, let's get you fed and get the plan going."

While we ate a delicious breakfast of hotcakes, sausage, and eggs, we spoke about what was to come, and I filled the others in on the game plan.

"We're going to take Manly with us to the Great Below." I finished the plan telepathically through our earrings. *When she finds an animal or something, we can leave her if we decide she's a threat; that way she's out of our hair and away from the village, and our oath is upheld. I may not be too okay with it, but if it keeps these guys safe, I can deal with it. You guys?*

"She going to provide her own food?" Yohsuke raised an eyebrow.

"I think that would be something she could do as a hunter and procurer of fine animals, but we can discuss it on the road. Not like she's hurting for money." James added demurely with a half-stifled yawn.

"True, and we need her out of here." Jaken smiled behind me and opened his arms, "Mornin' Manly!"

"Oh, Jaken, not so loudly, if you please," the halfling woman said, then groaned, she looked as though she might be ill at that moment.

"You sit here, and I'll get you some food and a root." Yohsuke sighed as he stood and moved toward the kitchen. He came back a few minutes later with a loaded plate of food, a glass, and a special root on the tray.

"Chew the root," Muu offered it from the tray, careful to keep his voice low. "It helps dull the headache and the hangover a bit."

She took it gratefully and popped the whole thing into her mouth before spitting it out a second later into her hand. "Nasty."

"It is, but it helps." I chewed on my own. Now, I've never tasted gym socks and ass before, but with this thing in my mouth, I may have preferred that taste.

She chewed it for a minute longer, then spit it into a napkin to toss away later, then tucked into her own food. "Mmm, this is so good!" She spoke between bites. "So, we're still headin' to the Great Below, right?"

"You are still welcome to join us, if you like?" I tossed her a roll from the center of the table. She grabbed it and nodded appreciatively.

"You good to pay your way on chow?" Yohsuke had begun to gather plates to take back to the kitchen.

"I'll join you, if you don't mind it. I can kick up some fresh game as well, so you don't need to purchase as much. If this was one of your doin', I'd love to have a fresh meal!" Had to give it to her. She could be endearing.

"Nice of you to offer." Yoh nodded to the rest of us, "seconds anyone?"

Muu's arm shot up so fast it was a miracle he hadn't flown from his seat.

"Fat lizard piece o' shit," the gray elf's good-natured grumbling made Muu grin more.

"Well, it's really only going to be a matter of finding a way to get into where we're going for now." I turned to James. "Any luck finding anything out?"

The dragon-elf shook his head, but it was Manly who spoke, "Y'all need a way in? There's rumor of one northwest of here, on the other side of the mountains, 'bout a day or so outside of Lindyburg. Out that way toward the capital of the nation, Zephyth."

"Can you take us there?" James asked excitedly, his excitement making his deformed wings flare a bit, walloping Jaken and making the Paladin curse softly. "Sorry."

"Well, access to it is kind of restricted." Manly pulled out a pipe, a long and dainty affair. She tapped the item into another handkerchief, pocketed that one and pulled some tobacco out of her inventory to pack it. "Y'all mind?"

We shook our heads, and she nodded her thanks as she struck a wooden match and took a couple starting puffs to light the tobacco properly.

With a sigh of pleasure, she turned back to us. "There's a guild called Nimran's Flame in the capital that controls it in the name of the king and their own interests. Now, the king don't have exclusive rights to it, but the guild has been known to let folks in from time to time if the coin is right."

"So, if we can get orders from either one, we're in?" Muu offered for the sake of clarity.

"Reckon so." Her brow furrowed in thought, a double gout of smoke bursting forth from her nostrils like a dragon. "The guild are religious types, though. So y'all will have to be okay with them spoutin' at you a bit."

Muu's ridged brows raised. "Do you know which one?"

I looked at him oddly, but before I could say anything, Manly answered, "I think it was...Yerlila, the Shade?"

"The shade?" Jaken looked like his curiosity was piqued.

I had to admit, mine was.

"Do you want a lesson in religion, or to get things in order and be on our way?" James said, then huffed.

"Religion please." Muu raised a hand once more.

Manly, being a good sport, patted his leg. "You sir, can ride with me on my cart, and I'll teach you what I know. But we can get a move on if you like. Did y'all give him your gift already?"

"Gift?" I raised my eyes to my friends, and Manly thumped the table.

"I never was all that good at keepin' secrets, my apologies y'all." The halfling woman held her hands up as if to defend herself, and the others just smiled.

"We all pitched in and bought one of the eggs." Jaken reached into his lap beneath the table and pulled out the object in question.

You seem to have a stronger connection with all of the other elements, so we thought that we would see to it that wind was included this way. Yohsuke spoke through our earrings. *Let's make sure we keep what we can do on the hush. We don't know her that well.*

"Yeah." Muu grinned. "So, make like a duck and hatch it already."

"How?" I took the egg into my hands. It was maybe the size of a football, ovular and slightly warm against my palms.

"Well, creatures like this with elemental affinities are rare, so ain't much that's known, but I reckon if you were to match the element of the egg in your hands for a bit, it may hatch." Manly took a long, final puff on her pipe before adding a small drop of water from a glass to it, then sliding it into her pocket in a handkerchief. "What're you plannin' to do with Higgins?"

I'd thought about that as I was dressing. He needed to be somewhere he was safe, and with people who would care for him. But with something to do.

"Vrawn, would you care for Jarlenill while we're away?" I turned to her as I spoke, and she seemed confused. "The large reptile who woke us this morning?"

"Does he need that much care?" The large reptile seemed to gather that we were speaking of him, his thumping steps trailing our way.

"Just feed him twice a day, and he will be fine." Manly smiled as she reached down to stroke his massive shoulder. "He ain't a picky eater neither, so if you get him some greens, fruits, meat, he'll have it all."

"Thank you, Manly." I bowed a head to her. That information was valuable. "I'll leave money for food, and I'll talk to him about what is expected of him so that he isn't too much trouble."

"If he will promise to behave, I will care for him." Vrawn looked decided. Maebe reached out and grasped Vrawn's hand beneath the table and whispered something against her shoulder that made the other woman relax markedly.

"You're leaving, and the green one is going to care for me?" Jarlenill's eyelids flicked shut, then open again.

"Yes, and I would like to ask a very important favor of you." I took a deep breath, collecting my thoughts before speaking again. "Please, don't bite anyone unless you feel there is danger, and you will know when there is, as you seem smart. Please, be good to the children, some of them may be afraid of you at first, but the braver ones won't take long to find you and want to play with you."

"I have never cared for strangers touching me." Jarlenill hissed.

"Don't think of them as strangers. The people who live here will love you and treat you like family if you will let them. Especially Vrawn, the green one, who will be kind enough to watch over you for me while I'm away, so long as you will behave."

"What am I? A nestling?" His forked tongue scented the air for a heartbeat. "Behave. Feh. Fine. I will be fed, and I will defend the small ones. But I do not care to be climbed on as if I were a tree. I may swat them if they irritate me."

His large, whip-like tail slapped the ground with a loud crunch. Oh fuck. If that thing were to hit a kid full force… "How about you don't swat the kids, and I may be able to get a live rodent thrown into your meal plan every so often?"

His head bobbed up and down. "I find this agreeable."

I turned to Vrawn. "He's promised to behave and not whip

the children with his tail when they irritate him in exchange for a live meal every so often."

"I believe that can be arranged." Vrawn nodded her head once, but it was Maebe who stood and stalked over toward the reptile.

"Translate to him for me," Maebe ordered me softly. She knelt down next to where I sat so that she was about eye to eye with Jarlenill and spoke, "If I find out that any of my children have been harmed by you, in any way that wasn't meant to save one of them from greater harm, I will kill you myself."

As she spoke, the temperature around us dropped lower, dangerously so, and the shadows deepened while I spoke for her.

"I have lived long enough to know that no matter what I say, she will not trust me, nor do I care. But since the nestlings are important, I will do what I can for them. See that the live food comes, and they will not be punished for their coming insolence." His tongue flicked almost dismissively. "And I will not bite any but those who deserve it."

I was honestly a little stunned that he had seemed disinterested in Maebe's threat, if not downright standoffish against her.

"What did he say?" She asked, a small hand on my shoulder squeezing lightly.

"That if live food was coming, they wouldn't be punished for their coming insolence." I put a hand out to ward Maebe away from the creature, but she didn't move.

"He bargains well," she raised an eyebrow and nodded to herself. "Then we are set to leave."

Vrawn stood and walked over to Jarlenill and thumped his head with her great hand. The reptile hissed but made no move to bite her. She walked us outside, and all of us moved toward Manly's cart and gathered around.

"There's a path over the mountains I've used that's about a day's hard ride west of here if I'm mappin' things correctly." Manly patted Humphrey so that the large swine would wake up.

"We can get there tomorrow afternoon or the day after if we push ourselves."

"We go at a moderate pace," Yohsuke stated, eyeing all of us as if we might disagree, we didn't just because this was how he had been in the Marines as well. "Zeke, you have Kayda on overwatch, Bokaj, and Tmont can scout, and the rest of us will move with the cart. Zeke, I want you focused on trying to get that egg hatched. However, you gotta do it, you do it. Capiche?"

"Aye corporal." I rolled my eyes to give him shit, but it was a solid plan. And I was curious as to what was in the egg.

James laughed at my joke, and everyone set to gathering themselves up for what they would need. Maebe and Vrawn were speaking to each other, so I gave them some space. After a minute, I felt something tugging at my sleeve and turned to see the shadows at my feet, pulling me and Maebe smiling at me.

I walked over to the two of them. "Hello."

"Hello, yourself." Vrawn pouted at first, her sullen look leaving as quickly as it came. "I'm sad you both will be leaving so soon, but I want you to know that I'm going to do my best to watch over things while you're gone and that I will miss you."

"I'll miss you, too." Maebe kissed Vrawn's knuckles as she stared into her eyes. "Until we meet again, I leave you with the children."

Vrawn leaned forward and kissed the other woman on the forehead. "They'll be fine. But they will miss you."

Maebe looked sad, so I reached over and took her hand. "You'll be back to see them as soon as you can. The only reason you wanted to come in the first place was so that we could introduce you to the drow and hopefully keep them from being brought into the Fae realm power struggle."

"It is for good reason that I go." Maebe nodded, more to herself than anyone else with a stoic look of self-contemplation.

"It is," Vrawn agreed, then turned her beautiful blue-eyed gaze on me. "I will miss you, too."

I couldn't help the boyish grin that came to my face as I reached out and pulled her closer to me. I shifted into my human form mid-pull and pressed my lips to her own in a rough kiss that stole both of our breaths away.

When we parted, I murmured, "I'll miss you too. Stay strong and be safe."

There were no words after that. No tears, though my heart pounded, and I yearned to stay just one day longer, we were off.

CHAPTER FOUR

We watched the mountainous stone through the trees, our pace a manageable one, as we wound our way through the forest westward.

"I still can't believe y'all got them fancy mounts from whistles." Manly beamed again at Thor, the kirin I rode on snorting majestically under her watchful gaze.

"We all got really lucky in this." Jaken smiled from his own mount. We were trying not to talk too much about ourselves just yet.

"So, religion time, yes?" Manly leaned back on her bench as Muu nodded excitedly. "What gods are you aware of?"

"Uh, well, Radiance, Fainne, kind of, and um, Mother Nature." Muu's ridged brow furrowed in thought.

"That's a start, though it is surprising that you don't know more of the nine." Manly's eyes flitted about our surroundings. "First, Mother Nature is *akin* to a god, she's not actually one. She's the embodiment of the will of this plane of existence, the very planet we are on. Some other realms have the same kinds of beings, though they're not gods, they're mighty powerful and ain't to be trifled with. Lady Radiance, well, she be the one what brought light to the world, and her brothers and sisters assisted her in making life."

Jaken rose up beside us on his summoned battle charger to add, "She's worshipped by a lot of folks, especially humans because they say she gave them birth from the soil and water of the realm, then breathed intelligence into them."

"'Preciate that, Sir Jaken." Manly grinned.

"Jaken, please," the paladin insisted.

Manly nodded, then turned her eyes to the front. "Fainne be the god of the dwarves, smiths, and crafters. Most with the talent to make, owe some sort of praise to him, and worship through their makin's and followin' o' his Way."

"Makes sense with what I had heard before. Cool." Muu nodded as if he were mentally checking off boxes.

"After him comes Uk'Beth, god of war and warriors." She chuckled to herself. "You wanna take a wild guess as to who may worship him?"

Muu didn't even hesitate. "Melee fighters and those who owe their victories to physical prowess alone."

Seeing the odd looks on the woman's face, mine, and Jaken's, he added quickly, "When she said the name, I remembered something from Zhavron, he mentioned an orcish god I thought by that name."

"Well, that's absolutely correct, good ears, Muu." Manly thumped his arm amicably. "Well then, this next one be one I know you'll hear of soon. Nimran, god of compassion and storms. I don't know how the guild of zealots got their name, considering they're a bunch of people with various backgrounds, near as I can tell, but they're not to be trifled with, either."

"Why?" I couldn't help the question. Kayda was above and ahead of us. The skies clear, and the forest quiet.

"Well, that's on account o' their treatment o' their god's will. See to them, compassion means that they kill anything that gets in the way o' protectin' the weak." She frowned. "Sometimes, even the weak themselves if it means others suffer less. They hoard power and money to gather strength, and seein' as they're the ones what found the dungeon, they offered to let the king and his folks use it if they could be given premium rights to it and be left alone to 'worship' as they see fit."

"And I'm guessing that they have been allowed?" Jaken said, then growled. "Like, if we try to get in there without permission, we could start a war or something?"

Manly nodded. "Nobody dares to face the storm o' their wrath, not even the king and queen. They'll rise up to defend it, don't you fret."

Muu frowned slightly. "I see." Then he frowned. "Wait, I thought you said they worshiped Yerlila?"

"They worship both Nimran and Yerlila," Manly explained patiently. "They hold to Nimran's love o' his sister—weird one, that one, got a sister complex—and while they offer protection to the weak, they make regular sacrifices o' those they deem 'too weak' to the Shade. Yerlila is the Goddess of Death. That's part o' what they ultimately do when they 'protect the weak' and it's not s'posed to be all that pleasant."

"And what's this about a dungeon?" James asked, curiously.

"Oh!" Manly fidgeted excitedly. "There's a dungeon they're said to rule over'n share with the capital occasionally. Rumor has it that it goes deep enough to butt up against our destination. Might be a good idea to check into gettin' in there. I don't know of too many easy places to get to that go into the Great Below, and none of 'em less than a few days from the capital, so it'd likely be worth the trip there to get into the place."

A knock on my shoulder grabbed my attention and I turned to see Yoh staring angrily at me. "What?"

He rolled his eyes. "Get that egg *hatched*, Zeke."

I sighed and checked my spell inventory and noted that I had not one single wind spell, except for my wind elemental form. I could do that first, but I would need to come up with a more permanent solution.

I called the egg into my hand from my inventory, fell back to the absolute rear of the party before shifting into my wind elemental form. It was hard to hold the egg, seeing as though I didn't really have any kind of hands, but I concentrated on sending my magic into the egg in my…grip?

At contact, the green along the shell thrummed to life with luminous energy. For the duration of my shift, I was able to keep the lights on, as it were. But afterward, I would have to wait until the cooldown was over to do it again.

That was a completely inefficient way of doing it.

I dug out my messenger raven and sent my question to Xiphyre. "Hey, Xiphyre, I have an issue with an egg that I'm trying to hatch. It needs elemental energy, specifically wind, that I don't really have any spells for. Would there be a way to convert normal mana into wind-aspected mana with an enchantment?"

The raven figurine in my grasp came to life, the green wings moving, then a spectral purple raven fluttered into the air and toward the village as fast as it could.

After about ten minutes, a fluttering sensation in my hand, and the raven settled in my grasp.

"It is, it's not too advanced either, so you don't have to worry about blowing anything up with your negligence," he ribbed.

… haha, you little bastard. Ha. Ha.

"All you'll need to do is have the proper intent and a good engraving for wind. A catalyst might help, too because the conversion could get tricky. A component with a decent attachment to the element would be a good idea as well, but to keep it simple, it is possible." He completed his statement, and the raven was still once more.

So, then I could do it. It was just going to take some leg work. Sounded good to me!

I pulled out the blanket that I slept with on the road and made myself a makeshift egg carrier so that the object would sit in the center of my chest so that my hands were free.

Thinking on it, I decided that a good component would be necessary for this and I had to find one. If I recalled correctly from my lessons with Shellica, quartz, emerald, amethyst, and opals held strong affinities for the air element.

I shifted through my inventory as best as I could, not finding anything of value until, eureka! I pulled out a mid-sized chunk of opal roughly the size of a quarter and about an eighth of an inch at its thickest.

I took out a bag and slowly carved into the opal with the nail of my metallic hand easily over a small handkerchief that I had picked up in town for these occasions. It only took a couple minutes; precious molecules of the gem powder escaping into the air as we rode, but I did the best I could.

I reached back into my inventory in search of some sort of glove, or gauntlet. Metal would be best. Nada. Damn it.

Anyone got a metal glove or something they aren't using, and that is not *enchanted already?* I broadcasted to the others. *Better quality metal appreciated.*

I looked about as the others sorted through their inventories, then Yohsuke replied, *Got a metal one here, iron. Also, Muu, get something shitty, like a snack out of yours. We don't want Manly to know we can speak this way.*

I glanced toward Muu and saw him pull out a small notebook and quill and begin to take notes on what she was saying.

Well, that's one way to do it. I snickered.

I have one, left-handed mithril, James offered.

Better than what I have, Bokaj said, then grunted. Muu and Balmur were quiet.

Jaken answered next, *same here.*

James rode back, and slyly handed the item to me.

"Why did you have this?" I frowned at him.

"I picked it up a while back, wondering if it could be used as a weapon, but before you could enchant it, I got my two other ones so I figured I'd just hang onto it. Just until Balmur or Jaken start cranking out things of Granda's level, I think I'm good with these ones, for now." He clapped me on the shoulder with a grin and rode off on his long, Chinese golden dragon.

Monks and their awesome shit. My Kirin, Thor, was amazing in his own rights.

But back into enchanting for now. We can drool over my mount later.

Thinking back to the mark on my chest that symbolized my connection to the element of wind, gifted to me by the Primordial Wind Elemental, I frowned. I didn't want to go with the tornado that I now had on my chest around the spell pentagram.

I called out to the others, "I'm going to go to the bathroom for a second, I'll catch up!"

Manly looked back at me. "Should we stop?"

Muu snorted. "I live with him, terrible idea with the smells that can escape him. Slowing down would be nice but stopping could kill us all."

Their chuckling at my expense was alright, but the others frowned at me askance. I shook my head and waved them away so I could focus a moment.

But the old one would likely work. "Hey Thor, would you mind stopping for a moment?"

"As you wish, druid." Thor stopped just long enough for me to take my mana and use it to engrave a pattern of lines, thick in the center and thinner at the ends that chased each other in a never-ending circle.

I hopped off his back and went behind a tree to act like I was doing my business, then realized I was still out of my depth here, and if I fucked this up, our goose was cooked. I hopped back onto Thor with a bitter scowl.

"Thank you, Thor, you can catch us up to the others, buddy." The mythical steed snorted and dug his claws and hooves into the ground before driving us forward swiftly to catch up to the others.

I set about gathering my will and intent before I began to question the design. Was it too simple? Was I overthinking it? Fuck. Was there going to need to be...yeah. There would. Because Xiphyre had mentioned the catalyst.

"We planning on taking a break for a second, any time soon?" I asked Manly as she continued to speak to Muu.

"Why's that? We only been on the road a couple hours," she drawled and stretched.

Fuck. That was fair. Uh. I mean, I guess I could wait and formulate the right pattern that I wanted, right?

"You know what? I thought I had to go to the bathroom, but it turns out it was just gas." I smiled placatingly, shrugging as I continued, "I was asking just in case I need to stop and move things about or stand to get things going, you know?"

"Ol' Humphrey gets like that too, Zeke, so no harm there." Her snorted laughter almost made me join her. If it hadn't been for the lie, I might have.

So, until we broke for lunch, I would be taking wind elemental form to try and keep this egg alive and get it ready to hatch. Which I did. It wasn't hard, really. I just tied the makeshift egg holder to Thor's saddle and did the best I could, the others did their best to distract Manly while I rode in the rear to try and feed the egg mana as an elemental.

While we rode, Kayda relayed what she saw—nothing—and the others did the same. There was fuck all around us. And that gave me a decent amount of time to contemplate how I wanted to do the glove.

When we did finally stop, I made like I had to go to the shitter again and had the others watch Manly. I don't know why I didn't want her to see me enchanting, but I just didn't. I didn't fully trust her, but if she saw my elemental form, I would just try to play it off as an ability I had. Enchanting seemed like so much more of a personal and dangerous thing in her company.

Once I was far enough away from them, I began the process of engraving the circle around the symbol with it taking up the center of it.

Inside the circle, I placed arrows that show all things leading toward the center flowing inward from the points of the star, contained by a circle outside. So, basically, it was a standard pentagram with arrows shooting inward and touching the middle, where the wind symbol was trapped inside.

I made sure that both my ring, Mage's Well, and my mana were completely topped up before continuing.

Once they were, which didn't take long at all, I gathered my will and intent before sending pure mana into the item.

The idea was for the gauntlet to take mana that it was fed and release it into the object it touched gently at a steady rate as wind aspected mana.

As I reached the halfway point, I sprinkled a good amount of powdered opal over the it then filled it until my instincts told me to stop. Took a surprising 1,103 MP. I had eight hundred myself, and the ring gave me an added five hundred.

But the prize was all that mattered, for now.

North Wind's Breath

Mana fed through this gauntlet by the wearer converts to wind aspected mana at a ratio of three to one (3 to 1) when touching an item. This conversion is per second.

The gentle caress of the wind in your hand, breathing life into...whatever you touch.

Gauntlet made by master smith Siff Villy and enchanted by adept enchanter Zekiel Erebos.

I snorted at the description, but it was what it was. I found my way back to the others without issue and just in time to get something to eat. I touched the egg in my little carrier, and activated the glove, carefully feeding the egg wind aspected mana.

The drain wasn't actually all that bad, to be honest. After every five seconds, I recovered the mana lost and could keep going at a constant rate. My hand got sweaty in the gauntlet, sure, but that was worthwhile. The constant drain on my mana was irritating, but, hey, it had to hatch at some point.

Muu took over the driving for the second half of the day under the halfling's instructions. Manly was off on foot to hunt for some food after we stopped just before dusk. Bokaj went with her, taking Tmont in his hood and a promise to be mindful.

While they were gone, we spoke amongst ourselves.

"So, how are we all feeling about her?" I kept my voice low just in case. I wasn't sure if she could talk to animals as well, but it wouldn't hurt to be cautious.

"She's pretty cool. And informative," Muu piped up with a half-raised hand. "She's been very kind, and she seems straight-forward."

"She does," James looked around us carefully before contin-uing. "It just seems too good to be true. She's got a shrewd eye for business, sure, but I don't know. She seems off like she's hiding something."

"She probably didn't tell us her full back story. And that's okay, right?" Jaken sat back with a contemplative frown. "I mean, we haven't been the most forthcoming, either."

"And she's really knowledgeable on things a hunter might not normally know." Yohsuke said, then grunted. We looked over toward him and he scowled. "The religion shit? Seems a bit too in-depth for my liking."

"Dude, some people know about all sorts of gods they don't worship." Muu waved his worries away while rolling his eyes. "Zeke and I used to have discussions about them in length."

"Hail the All-Father, Odin." I grunted, then my smile turned to a frown. "I want to trust her. I want to let her prove that she's cool so that we don't have to be shitty to her. But until then? Eyes on a swivel and ears to the ground."

The others nodded, and we went about our business until the two rangers, because while she called herself a hunter, she was actually a ranger like Bokaj came back with a brace of three rabbits. The clearing was roughly large enough to fit all of us and still give us about twenty-five feet of open space all around before the trees began.

Yohsuke took the carcasses to clean, skin, and dress while Manly opened the back of the cart up and then unhooked Humphrey from the front to let him free to graze and stretch.

She walked around the back and pulled out more than a dozen large food dishes and began to fill them with foods of various sorts. Then she laid the seed on top of a large stool that she collected with several bars out and around the top of it, slightly lower.

"Come on out now, y'all!" She hollered. "Supper time!"

Several smaller and larger animals of all shapes and varieties exited the cart. Each of them went to a bowl and waited. Manly gave a shrill whistle before they dug into their food greedily. The sounds of snarling and chewing reminded me of some of the pets I'd had growing up. It was incredibly endearing.

"You have all of them incredibly well trained." I stood next to Manly as she watched over her wares.

"Takes patience and know-how." She smiled. A bass growl broke her concentration, and her gaze snapped to one of the dog-like creatures that had scales and a lizard-like tail. "Shiva, you raise your voice near me again, and you don't eat tomorrow."

The large creature, Shiva, stopped growling at another animal and continued her meal in silence.

"Now, y'all mind and eat up, so I can feed the others when you finish." She took out her pipe, packed it with fresh tobacco, and lit it with a match. Which she pocketed after putting it out.

"There are more animals?" I wondered aloud, my jaw slack.

"Where do you put them?" Muu began to walk around the cart.

"Lady has her secrets, but I suppose y'all magic folk would know somethin' about dimensional enchanting?" She puffed her pipe excitedly, a mischievous glint in her eyes. "I had a strong one work on my cart here. Holds many different kinds of animals safely, and only weighs as much as a normal cart, to boot."

"That's amazing!" Jaken's awed voice took me by surprise as he touched the large wooden contraption, a look of confusion on his face. "There's no description, though."

"Wouldn't be a good idea to advertise I have money, would it?" Manly shook her head exaggeratedly. "Nope. So that be hidden well. Alright, you're done? Get on then."

The animals bounded back into the cart's rear, and Manly pressed a hand against the inside lip of the opening and touched something before stepping back and whistling shrilly once more. Several kinds of reptiles came out, none of them looking particularly well, so I reached down and cast Regrowth on each of them in turn.

They were grateful as they munched on their leafy food that Manly placed in the bowls for each of them, along with some freshly cut fruit that reminded me of bananas.

"Y'all mind this next one, hear?" Manly warned. "She's real dangerous."

After the other animals all moved back into their mobile home, Manly had a long serpent slither from the back, her deep purple scales mesmerizing as she moved in the evening light.

"You're beautiful." I admired her from a distance, but when I spoke, she turned her head toward me, curiously scenting the air with her tongue.

"Thank you." She wound her way toward me, her head arching up to stare me in the eyes. "It hass been sso long, ssince a friendly vissitor could undersstand me."

"You've spoken to many people?" I tilted my head to the side, and she mimicked the gesture.

"I have, there are many like you where I come from." She moved a little closer, giving me a clearer view of these small tendrils on top of her nose no larger than a pencil lead.

"That's close enough for her to get, Master Zeke," Manly cautioned. "She's a vorpal viper. Potent venom and strikes that are almost too fast to follow unless you have a high enough dexterity."

"You aren't planning to attack me, are you?" I murmured sweetly. "That would put a terrible damper on our being able to talk."

"Why would I attack ssomeone sso sssweet as you?" The viper swayed slightly left and right, as if unsteady.

"They have a habit of hunting larger prey," Manly continued to warn.

My friends took note of what was going on and sidled closer in case shit hit the fan.

"It appears that your captor doesn't trust you." I lifted a hand to motion toward Manly, and the viper eyed me suspiciously. "I take it you gave her cause not to?"

"I am in a land far from home, with none of my friendss, and none of my family." She stated with more than a little bitterness in her tone. "But I alsso am hungry. Sso very hungry."

"Then let's get you fed." I smiled as she lunged. Or I thought she lunged. Everyone gasped, me included as the viper just butted her head against my shoulder.

"Thanks, druid," she muttered before turning toward Manly, who stood with her hand in her breast pocket and a surprised look on her face.

Manly moved in jerky motions as she reached into the cart and pulled out a large rabbit. The viper slithered over close to it, and much the same as it had with me, the head blurred and instead of tapping the rabbit, the jaws flared, and teeth sank into the rodent's flesh with a soft thud.

I watched as she flexed the top of her head, likely working her venom glands as the rabbit struggled less and less. Manly released the rabbit, and the viper let it go as well.

"Do you mind if I sit with you while you eat?" I asked the serpent, almost having forgotten the egg in my gauntleted palm.

She turned on me. "You will not touch my food?"

"I promise I won't, I was just going to sit you in my lap for a little bit and enjoy your company, if that's okay?"

The slitted eyes blinked once. "I don't ssee the harm."

Yes! A new form, here I come! I sat down near the food, all the while making sure that I held onto the unhatched egg carefully, and she slithered over my lap easily. Her coiling and contracting muscles felt weird, but it was alright as each loop also hit the ground before she folded over my lap.

The others watched my shenanigans quietly, so I snapped at them, "Don't you guys have shit to do?"

She might suspect I'm a druid, but I cannot pass up this form. Please, someone run interference.

"So, Manly, what other goodies you have hidden away in there?" Muu asked with genuine interest.

"Well, after Ulla here, there's Frederick," Manly frowned. "He's a rare one, and his temper ain't somethin' to trifle with. So, when I call him out here, please don't approach him or make any hostile motions."

We nodded, and I was content to just sit there with the serpent on my lap. She wasn't heavy, and as I fed mana to the egg, I stroked her scales with my metal hand. It was almost relaxing. Granted, she was a potentially dangerous viper. Looking at the rabbit she was gorging herself on, I changed that assessment to deadly.

After a couple minutes I had her form, and she was most of the way finished with working the meal into her unhinged jaws. The feet being the only thing left sticking out from her heavily fanged mouth.

Manly touched another portion of the cart and then stepped slowly away from it with a large sack in hand.

One large, hairy fist rocketed out of the cart and clamped onto the roof, then the full figure swung out of it. A six-foot-tall gorilla with green fur, beady black eyes, and bulging muscles that made Muu look dainty, sat on the roof staring at us.

"Uh, that's a gorilla?" James walked closer to me, the serpent in my lap turning her attention toward him, uneasily.

"He's a variety of them, yes," Manly advised. "Terran gorillas are wildly territorial. I've known Frederick since he was a baby. Won him in a card game a long time ago, and though people seem to like the idea of him bein' somethin' they could hunt or somethin', I just can't bring myself to sell him. He's a friend, I think, after all this time."

And that went a long way toward upping my respect for her. Almost enough to try and sort out a way for her to not be a threat to us and the village. I would have to continue to watch.

"He seems pretty calm right now." I put my arms beneath the serpent in my lap. "I'm going to help you back into the cart, so don't move too much, okay?"

"Frederick, come to me!" Manly ordered, gently. She held out the sack in her hand, and he seemed interested for a moment. Taking a few steps away from the cart so that he could get closer; the halfling backed away at a steady pace, and he followed as he sniffed the air before him.

I put Ulla near the cart door and the fur on my neck waved as puffs of hot air pooped against the back of my neck instantly.

"Don't you do it, Freddy!" Manly barked viciously, order and anger seeping into her tone. "He's only helping Ulla! You get back here and eat your supper."

Another gust of hot air hit the back of my neck. "But he's too close to it. If he goes in, I have to hurt him."

There was a pause. "Please give me a reason. I'm so bored."

I turned after watching Ulla slither into the cart safely, slowly. Manly walking over and speaking to me in hushed tones, "Don't be lookin' him in the eyes, Zeke. He gets real fired up when anyone does it. Broke a lady's arm for it a few weeks ago. I don't think he meant to, but he takes it as a sign of challenge."

"From the sounds of it, he wants a fight." I felt bad for the big guy. "He's bored. How often does he get to come out and exercise? I'm not trying to be rude; I promise. I'm just wondering."

"I try to let him out every so often if we're in a secluded enough area where he can roam without getting into trouble." She frowned as she noticed the tension in his body. "That was a few weeks ago when he met that lady out for a stroll."

"I see." the others moved in my peripheral vision and Frederick saw the same things. Rather than wait, I turned and addressed him, carefully looking at his chin area. "Hey there, tall, green, and mean. How you doin'?"

He flinched as if struck. "You speak?"

"Why does everyone ask me that?" I grumped under my breath. "I do. And I heard what you said. You spoiling for some exercise?"

"I want to fight. Something. Anything." He bared his large fangs at me.

Up close, his fur looked really odd. As if it were grass or some kind of flower in places, and he smelled really good for some reason.

"I get that, and I'm half inclined to let you join us for a bout of fun. But if you want, maybe let's go for a run or something? Just gallop around a little bit to burn some of that energy off?" His heavy brow lowered considerably as he sat back.

"You would do that?" He scratched his chest, then his back absently. "You aren't scared?"

"Why would I be scared of you?" I blinked at the odd sincerity of his question. "You're big, and likely really strong. But I'm strong too and so are my friends. And you don't seem to hate anything, you're just bored. That doesn't make you bad or scary. Just need to have your energy redirected. It's not your fault that you come off intimidating to some folks."

He snorted and beat the ground with his hands excitedly, before looking over to Manly who seemed anxious. "She will never allow it."

"It doesn't hurt to ask, and if you promise her not to hurt anyone anymore, she may allow it." I turned to Manly and spoke softly, "Frederick would like to stay out and play with us for a bit. Would that be okay? If he promised not to hurt anyone, would that work for you?"

"I'm not worried about him, I'm worried about you lot." Manly snorted. "He's strong, and the only reason I can deal with him is because we respect each other."

"Do you promise not to hurt anyone, Frederick?" I asked the gorilla with my eyebrows raised.

"I promise not to kill any of you," he grinned with his teeth bared again. When I didn't blink, he added, "Fine. I promise not to hurt anyone on purpose, unless they go into my cart. Then they are fair game. And I will crush them."

I shook my head, exasperated that he was so smart, but I repeated his promise to Manly, and she seemed to mull it over.

"He sleeps in his cart tonight, but he can stay out, for now." She sounded like a worried mother. Before I could tell him, she added, "And tonight is only a trial! If he's not gonna behave, he can't do it again, am I understood?"

Why did I feel like I was about to be scolded by someone less than half my height?

"Yeah, we promise." I looked back to my friends. "Fred's gonna come and play with us. Anyone else up for a game of tag?"

"Got any rules?" Muu asked as he limbered himself up.

"Yeah, no attack spells, no weapons. It's just an all-out game of tag." I scratched my head a bit. "Utility spells are okay. Let's keep it close to camp, though, yeah?"

"This should be fun!" Bokaj grinned. "T', you better be fuckin' good at hiding. And stay out of my hood!"

The panther snuffed at him before scampering into the wooded area around us.

"Well, at least we know who's not it." Muu chuckled as the cat disappeared. "But how do we know who's it?"

"We decide before everyone else runs off?" Yohsuke smirked as the dragon-Kin opened his mouth, then closed it. "But once you're tagged, you come back here so we know who's out. Sound good?"

Kayda circled around the area above us, her massive form casting a shadow over us in the dying light.

"And none of that cheating bullshit," James added hurriedly. I tried to give him the, "Who, Me?" look, and it didn't work at all. "The bird stays out of it, or she stays in your collar."

Kayda, babe, we're going to be playing a game of tag, but I want you not to tell me. Can you watch the camp while we play? If you see anything suspicious, tell us. I felt her tilt her head at my request.

Play? She asked in return. I saw what she meant as she sent me a memory of us both flying together, then another of her torturing Muu with the little girl in the square by tickling him.

Tomorrow, I promise. I just need to find a better bird form that's built sturdier and stronger.

She took that news well, and she aggressively agreed to watch over the camp and the surrounding area and then cut off contact.

"Alright, she's got the camp on lock." I looked over toward Maebe, who frowned at us. "You going to play?"

"Play?" She asked, oddly echoing my companion. "What is this game? Why do you do it? What purpose does it serve?"

I had heard that question before, and I knew how to answer it, as well.

"A game, like children play. It's called tag,' and you play it by chasing your friends." I gave Muu and James a look, and Muu tagged James and sprinted away. The other man gave chase. "We teach it to children to teach them skills. To help them become cleverer at defeating opponents, tracking skills, and to become faster in a safe manner. That way, if something is hunting them, they can get away. Some of the meaning may have been lost over time, but it's still there."

"So, why are you all doing it now?" She frowned a bit more and motioned toward Frederick. "And with him, as well?"

"Because if we don't include him, he could be trouble at some point if he gets too bored," Yohsuke answered before I could, having likely heard my conversation with Manly. "If we're going to travel with each other, these animals need to know us, and we need to be able to trust that they won't try to kill us."

"So, then, this is a way for you to safely train your abilities, play, and build a rapport with each other?" Her brows narrowed. "This is new."

"You want to play with us, your Majesty?" Jaken stood next to her and offered her his fist. "It'll be fun and good training."

"So, the person who is 'it' touches someone, and they return to camp?" She asked as she returned Jaken's fist bump.

"In a nutshell, yeah." Muu gasped as he jogged back over.

Frederick seemed enthused by this game. "We used to play this game long before I was separated from my troop as a baby. What are the rules? No attacking?"

"And stay close to camp," I added as he thumped the ground excitedly.

"I will do this, tag," Maebe announced.

"Awesome!" Muu grinned and looked to the rest of us. "Since it's her first time, one of us should be it, right? It's only fair."

That seemed reasonable. The rest of us looked back and forth at each other and held our fists out in an age-old, timeless tradition of decision making.

Rock, paper, scissors.

"Rock...paper..." We spoke, and before any of us could do anything else, a voice speared through our minds.

Rock! Muu shouted.

We were all so confused that some of the others, Jaken, James, and Balmur actually chose rock.

"You cheeky fuck!" I growled as he took his paper and covered the other three. The only ones to beat him were Yoh, me, and Bokaj tied with him.

"You boys won't get anywhere doin' that. Here." Manly came over with a handful of twigs and offered them to us. "The shortest one has to be the seeker."

"Does this mean you'll be joining us?" Jaken cocked his head to the side and smiled hopefully. "We could always use one more."

"Sweet of you to ask, but I'll be needing to tend the animals a wee bit before we head to sleep." She nodded to the sticks.

"Shit. I'll ref then, since I need to be sure that dinner is cooked right." Yoh backed out and turned to the cooking fire and adjusted the rabbit meat and veggies.

The rest of us shrugged and drew lots. In the end, it was James cursing vehemently as he held up the short stick.

"Y'all got to the count of fifty, then I come running." He closed his eyes and took a breath.

"Dude, that's hide and seek," Muu corrected with an incredulous look on his face.

"Fifty. Forty-nine. Forty-eight." Then he counted down as all Marines remembered from boot camp. A skill that many poor souls learned that drill instructors had mastered—speed countdowns.

A thrill ran through my nerves, and I moved toward the opposite side of the camp as I gingerly put the egg into my inventory. The others scattered as well, and we were off. The first thing I did was shapeshift into my hare form and bolted into the underbrush. I shifted back into fox-man and used Nature's Path to touch a tree to move from it to another tree about a hundred feet away, up toward the top where I waited quietly.

Once I was in the tree, I pulled the egg back out and held it in the gauntlet. The whole process was odd as I still funneled my mana into the egg, but it moved with me regardless. It was a small mana cost at 30 MP, but the constant funneling meant that it was a little longer than normal getting back to full MP.

After what felt like a long time, I decided to cast Life Sense, another small mana cost that allowed me to do exactly as the name stated. Little blips of life appeared as if on a radar screen in my mind. All of them gray, so they weren't hostile, though one was green, and it was almost directly beneath me.

My heart pounded as I cast my eyes about, wildly. But it was only Balmur moving beneath me in the fading light. He shifted through the shadows with ease, then turned invisible. I could still see him thanks to my True Sight, but he was hazy even then.

This was going to be fun. I heard shouting, so James must have found someone. A crack and manic laughter, likely from Muu as he sprinted away. Then cursing. Did I dare move closer to try and get a look?

If you said no, you're in the wrong here.

Leaving my hiding spot in the tree by using Nature's Path to travel just a little further closer to the camp was a great idea, as I had phased out in time to see Muu walking dejectedly back toward the campfire. Yohsuke laughing and teasing him a bit.

"He came out of nowhere!" Muu retorted loudly to one of Yoh's jokes. "Fucker moves like lightning, and I'm not talking FF-thirteen man."

"Dinner will be done soon, so sit down and shut up." Yoh sighed. "Pay attention, though. May learn something."

I decided it may be a good idea to put the egg into my collar for a bit so I could focus and have my hands free. I shifted into my owl form, carefully skirting trees and branches to keep me and my green, metal-armed beacon hidden. Swift, but surprisingly heavy movement, like footfalls and branches being gripped and moved violently to my left drew my attention to Frederick who eyed me curiously as he moved from tree to tree.

Then I noticed James hot on his trail, *damnable gorilla brought him straight to me!*

I plummeted to the ground and shifted into my fox form in a bush before taking my new vorpal viper form. Being a snake was weird. I could somewhat make out shapes, but most of what I "saw" was infrared heat. I could sort of sense that they were in the area through scent and heat signatures.

Frederick weaved and dodged the monk to the best of his ability, but the gorilla just wasn't built for speed.

It was irritating that I couldn't see all the details, but the reds and oranges moved in the sea of blues and greens well enough that I saw when James tapped the gorilla on the head and danced away laughing.

Frederick beat his chest in frustration, then moved toward James and his exposed back. I tensed up to try and do something, and help if needed, but I saw the orange of Frederick's hand smack James's ass as if to say, "Good game."

What a weird animal.

It took a little longer for him to find Bokaj, the ranger growing bored and moving.

Then he was on my trail, his nose working overtime.

"Come on out, Zeke." James cautiously moved through the trees and brush as quietly as he could.

I was still in my viper form so I could see him moving, the warmth of his body lit like a beacon. He left the area, and I stayed completely still.

It was another ten minutes before a cry like thunder sounded from above, and James called over our earrings, *Hey, I think we have company.*

Yeah, right, you just want us to come out so you can tag us. Jaken snorted.

An explosion rang out east of my position, close enough to set my ears ringing.

Moving west toward the camp! There's five of them, and they're armed to the teeth! Balmur called to us. *They spotted me somehow and cast a fireball, but I was able to evade them.*

Move on the eastern portion of the camp. Stay out of sight if you can. Muu and I are already waiting, Yohsuke ordered through the earrings.

I shifted into my fox form and moved that way, quickly, but cautiously. It was so much better being able to see what was actually going on in real-time. Kayda worked on trying to get a better eye on things but had trouble due to how these guys moved. They weren't too amateurish and stuck close to the trees. Likely why it took her so long to see them.

I came upon a group of five men huddled close together, all of them dressed in thick leather armor except for the two in front. Those wore cloth and plate armor. Then I began to see others separating from the trees. Fuck. There had to be a dozen more, at least.

I got eyes on at least twenty of them, Bokaj stated, startling me slightly. I glanced to my right and saw Tmont's eyes glowing from the underbrush.

James added to that. *At least ten more moving in on the western side. A couple of their levels look to be in the late teens and lower level than us.*

I heard swearing in the center of the camp. *Alright boys, time to see what's going on.* Yohsuke sighed heavily. *Zeke, Bokaj, and Balmur—you lot stay outside the perimeter. Let them surround us. Once we know what's going on, you fuck up as many of them as you can on our signal. Everyone else, come in.*

"There are more of them coming from the trees to the north," the man in cloth spoke. He looked like he could have been a mage of some sort, but he wasn't all that old. Maybe in his twenties or so. Looked young with his longish dark hair.

"Good," the armored one spoke, his deep voice took on a more commanding tone. "All of you fan out. Surround the camp, and don't let them leave. That bounty is as good as ours. And remember—we want them alive. So, don't kill them."

That was a good bit of information for our use. But the bounty? I remembered Jaken saying something about Lindyburg looking for us, but why? Anyone could have killed those guards they sent after Pharazulla.

My thoughts had distracted me enough to allow one of the leather-covered soldiers to get within inches of my position, so I stood statue-still until he was passed me. I released my held breath and shifted slowly until I faced their backs.

Level 19

Not too terrible. Significantly lower than us, but there were thirty of them and counting.

"No sense trying to hide when you have us surrounded," Muu called tiredly. "Come on out and let's chat. No one needs to die."

Oh man, maybe don't lead with the stick, buddy. I crawled forward a little more so that I could see more of what was going on in the camp.

The armored man snorted, then he motioned and his people stepped into the clearing. Several of the ones on my side held back as others moved in. The ones in the rear took out bows and strung them swiftly, nocking arrows onto the strings and loosely taking up fighting stances.

"Well, that's mighty kind of you to say, mister," the apparent leader drawled sarcastically. "There's supposed to be more of you, where are they? They hiding like the murderous, thieving cowards they are?"

"We don't know who you are, or why you're here." Yohsuke hadn't even stood from the cooking fire. He checked the bottom of the rabbit meat and flipped the one in the center before switching it out to place it in the best heat. "But you can still walk away from this."

"Why don't you all go ahead and just do this the easy way, right?" One of the others standing next to the leader groaned with sarcasm dripping from his voice, "No one wants to just save themselves a beating, come quietly."

"Now now, Shepherd, it's alright." The older man comforted the other before turning toward my friends once more. "You're wanted for crimes against the Governess of Lindyburg, to include theft, murder, and evasion. If you come peaceably, I can try and put in a good word for you. If not? Well, we get paid, bruised or not."

Jaken walked into the circle past a couple of the fighters with a smile on his face and continued toward the center.

They stepped back and raised their weapons out of instinct, and I tensed. If they moved to attack him, every one of them here would die. Badly.

They didn't attack, but they looked visibly shaken.

"Seems they may have some higher levels in their group, we should move with caution." The cloth wearer, likely the caster, advised the leader from where he hid.

They're starting to get a little wary of us, James mentioned as he walked calmly into the center from the south. *We need to make sure that they're all eyes on us.*

"So, you don't plan to walk away?" James called. "We don't want to fight. And we didn't do anything that you're accusing us of. We don't want any trouble."

"Then all you need to do is come with us and let the Governess know what your side of the story is." He spread his hands and stepped forward magnanimously. "She's a fair woman. All she wants is justice."

"And all we want is to be left alone," Jaken called back. "Ours is a mission from the gods. You're interfering. Please. Leave us to our pursuits."

"Oh great, some other kind of zealot," one of the fighters near the leader grumbled. Then he looked to the leader. "That cart is bothering me, though. What's inside?"

"Why don't you take a group of three and go check it out but be careful." The leader ordered. His men took another step forward, the one he had given orders to marched over along the line of men and collected three others to go with him.

"Wouldn't recommend that," James said, then growled as he turned to keep these in sight.

This wasn't going to be good. Something shifted inside me, the werewolf looking out.

Soon. These ones would make excellent additions to the pack. Specifically, the young one in the robes. I can smell him. The deep rumble in my mind was appreciative as I fought to control my eyes.

You have no place in this fight, wolf. My friends are in danger. I growled back. The small group was closer to the cart now.

Did you so swiftly forget that promise you made me? If you do not use my strength now, I will never come to your aid again.

I snorted softly as I shifted into my fox-man form. I wasn't worried.

I would see all of your friends die. And if you think I won't sabotage you in any way that I can, you are dead wrong. The wolf was silent. Almost contemplative. *I wonder which of them will fall first because of your inaction. Will it be the green one? The gray one? Or the mate?*

Fine! But we're brutal and efficient. No turning anyone or I swear I will swallow silver just to spite you. Got it?

A flash of muted light in my mind saw me back in the throne room standing across from the werewolf. *We fight together. Come.*

I was back just in time to watch as the cart door burst open wide. Three arrows burst from the lead fighter's head before

Manly barreled out, rolling to the ground onto a knee and firing another arrow at someone in her sights. Frederick leapt from the tree line into the other three nearby and began walloping them with his huge fists.

Now! Jaken, Yohsuke, and James shouted, and the fight was on.

I took my werewolf form and crossed the distance between me and the unsuspecting mage in a single leap, my strength, and dexterity carrying me far enough to clock him in the back of the head hard enough to knock him prone.

He did not stand back up.

The sound of arrows flooded my heightened hearing, and I turned my sights on the bowmen. I dipped my shoulder and sprinted into the one on my left.

"*Oof!*" He grunted as I shoved him bodily against the tree behind him and sunk my claws into his throat.

More! The wolf roared, *bleed them all!*

I fought him back and just finished the man in my grip by cracking his head against the tree brutally, his HP falling to zero.

I turned in time to see Balmur materialize between two of the bowmen and slice through their bowstrings. The bows snapped up, catching the one on his right in the chin, knocking him unconscious and the other in the shin. Balmur decided to take that one with a blade to the temple and moved on before the corpse could even hit the ground.

We respect that one, the wolf growled even as I thought the same. Could he read my mind?

Would you shut the hell up? I fired back, and it just chuckled.

Arrows flew into the men who had the rest of my friends surrounded, coming from Manly and Bokaj. The bounty hunters fell right and left and didn't seem to be doing all that well. They had stupidly decided to group together and fight against Muu, Jaken, and now James.

The three of them fought savagely, red aura radiating from Jaken as he took the enmity of those around him and Muu assisting him with his spear. James waltzed through the fighters around him with his ki surrounding his fists, and now feet, as he struck with impeccable timing and cruelty.

Limbs snapped; people shrieked in pain. Lightning flashed from above us where Kayda dropped through the air, and a man next to Yohsuke froze solid, a look of terror on his face. The spell blade slashed through it and moved on.

This could have been avoided if they had just listened. Though, maybe we ought to take a trip to Lindyburg to clear ourselves of this.

"Surround them again!" The armored figure ordered loudly as he tried to corral his people. There were maybe a dozen of them still standing and uninjured, though they looked ready to run. "Do not lose your composure!"

Frederick was losing his fucking mind. He bellowed at all comers, picked one man up over his head and threw the guy onto his buddy's sword, then taking a spear that one of them had dropped. He launched it into another man ten feet away before turning toward the cart once more.

Someone get that asshole before he rallies them, Yohsuke said like a bark to us.

The fight was going poorly for them, and the archers slowly stopped firing arrows to try and regroup around the leader.

That won't do, I growled as I stalked into the light. They were distracted, so I used their ineptitude to my advantage and plowed into them like a freight train of teeth and hatred.

I slapped one of the archers out of my way with a backhand that left thin claw marks across his features and pulled the leader toward me by the throat.

Bite him! Claim their alpha as your own, the wolf howled. *Think of how much safer the pack would be if we would just add to our numbers!*

I blinked, a low growl trickling from my chest as I stared into the man's eyes. To his credit, he didn't look terrified, but I could tell they hadn't been prepared.

"We will leave." He swallowed heavily, sweat beading on his forehead, his body shaking in my fist. An arrow dug into my lower back, a couple percentage points of my HP bar fell away, then came back as it left my flesh and fell against my ankle.

"We gave you that chance." My tongue lolled out of the side of my mouth, drool and spittle hit my chest, and I *wanted* to bite him.

Take his throat in your jaws and clamp down. Let the gift flow from you into him. This is what the alpha does. This is as it should be!

It was harder to fight the beast in me back with prey this tantalizingly close. The scent of his fear, *all* of their fear wafted into my nostrils, and the drool came faster. I swallowed hard as I fought myself.

We are the predator. We are the ones who should be feared. Their numbers could be our numbers. Take them. You could rule!

"I don't want to rule," I snapped. "I want to protect my friends!"

I looked up at the man in my clawed hand and saw his confusion.

"And you're making that harder." My fist moved before I could even begin to comprehend what I was doing. I punched him in the nose, grabbed his head in both hands after I let go of his throat, and snapped his neck in one fluid motion.

I turned to find that all but one of the archers had been slain by Yohsuke, Manly, and Muu.

"I got him," Balmur called, Tmont springing from nowhere and dragging the man screaming and kicking to the ground before she went for his throat. A second later, he was quiet.

"What's up with the werewolf form, man?" Muu asked, the others seemed uncertain, as well. Manly had an arrow drawn and aimed at my chest.

"If I didn't use it, he would have sabotaged my attempts to protect you guys." I began the process of mentally separating myself from the power of the beast and reverted to my fox-man form.

"You can drop that arrow now, Manly." Yohsuke settled his gaze on her angrily. "He's not a danger to anyone, now."

"He snapped a man's neck with his bare hands!" She only lowered the weapon a fraction.

"And you put three arrows in a man's eyes from two paces away," Jaken retorted with an eyebrow raised. "We've all killed people tonight. It was a necessity. Grim, though it was."

"Loot 'em." James patted me on the shoulder and nodded toward the mage I had knocked out.

I walked toward him with Yohsuke pulling up beside me after a second. "Hey man, you good?"

"You guys always ask me that after I take werewolf form." My gaze wandered the area to be sure we were good before continuing. "I'm a fucking werewolf, man. No. I'm not good. But I've got it under control, no matter how badly he seems to want me to turn someone."

Yohsuke grasped my arm lightly and pulled me to a stop, lowering his voice so we would not be overheard, "Do we need to try and find some kind of cure?"

I knew this was coming from a good place. I knew he cared. I knew that he was only trying to help. But I still wanted to lash out. I couldn't tell you why. Summon Celestial aside, we had options to get rid of my lycanthropy, but that particular spell was kind of emergency only use.

Could it have been anger at the beast howling at me to take a life, even now? Could it have been that I was close to turning that leader into a snack pack? Probably that one, actually.

"No man, I'm good. It gives us an edge, and despite the thing being an asshole, he does care about the pack." I glanced over at the mage. "We need to get him bound and possibly gagged before he gets to waking up. He could be trouble."

"Why don't we kill him then and be done with it?" Yohsuke asked with a shrug, his astral adaptor igniting readily.

"Because we aren't murder hobos, damnit." I shoved him lightly as I stepped toward the kid. "We need information and he may have some."

CHAPTER FIVE

Other than money, okay weapons and armor, and some really shitty travel rations, the bounty hunters had very little of value on them. No enchanted items at all, and there were no orders or anything. After Balmur collected a couple eyes he thought might be useful, I used the shadows to get rid of the evidence, the hungry void eager to take them away.

Maebe had come out of hiding while we were eating, looking especially victorious.

"None of you could find me," she purred happily as she sat next to me. "I am the queen of this game."

We glanced at ourselves, at her, and then back before most of us broke into fits of laughter. She was unfazed, used to us finding her funny.

The kid woke up after we had eaten our dinner and looked around as if in a haze.

"Bokaj, you want to talk to him?" Jaken motioned toward our captive guest.

"Sure." Bokaj sat in front of the kid with his legs crossed. We had taken the precaution of binding his hands and searching him. All we found on his person was a small book.

Bokaj tapped the kid with his last Silencing Arrow, a projectile that played hell on a caster's ability to use spells. It silenced you and cut off the flow of mana.

"This arrow will not only silence you, but it will hurt like fuck if you try anything funny, okay?" This kid was silent, stoic even. "Now, why were you all here?"

He just stared at Bokaj in defiance, not answering his question.

"Come on kid, your friends are all dead, and we don't really want to have to kill anyone else tonight, right guys?" He glanced back at all of us, and when he got to me, he winked.

I smiled, working desperately to make it look as bloodthirsty as I could, feeling like I would rather be doing anything else at that moment. "I do."

Again, the kid was silent. His eyes unfocused.

"This is getting us nowhere." James groaned as he threw his hands into the air and stood to pace. "We know why they came —to die. They had no idea what the hell they were doing and were hopelessly outmatched. They didn't even give all that good of experience!"

"You take that back!" The kid spat vehemently as he struggled against the bonds.

James stepped past all of us to kneel in front of the kid so that his eyes were level with our captive's, "They thought that numbers would be enough against innocent men, and when we gave them three chances to run after seeing they were outmatched, they refused."

So, the old spite bit, eh?

"Yeah, I mean, he didn't really last all that long once I got my hands on him." I yawned lazily. "Snapped his neck after I knocked you out; again—wasn't hard to do, kid."

Tears ran down his face, and I was beginning to feel bad for him, but then he spat in James's face and shouted, "We got the wrong information! It wasn't Captain Kelly's fault! He was a good man and then you *monsters* killed my friends, like animals. You'll pay. You'll all pay!"

Bokaj reached out and touched his shoulder, his voice sooth-ing, "Listen kid, we don't want to hurt you. And we didn't want to hurt them. All we want to do is go about our business. You know how that is, right?"

A dazed look fell over the kid's face for a moment, then his vision sharpened, and he nodded, "Yeah, but that's not gonna happen now. You all are wanted criminals."

"Wanted for what?" Bokaj must have charmed him because he stared at the ice elf even as Yohsuke asked the question.

The kid looked to Bokaj, who nodded for him to speak. "Stealing from the Governess, murder, evasion of justice and murder of the Governess' guards. Lindyburg wants y'all bad."

"But we had nothing to do with any of that." Muu blinked before looking at the rest of us. "I mean, right? All we did was leave. Pharazulla came with us, but we had no idea that she stole anything, and she mind-fucked Zeke into killing those guards. It wasn't his fault. Fuck, she made him try to kill all of us, too."

Balmur touched Bokaj on the shoulder. "You left that one out, man."

"Sorry." Bokaj looked back at the kid. "Who sent you?"

"The Governess put out a contract." He shrugged in his bindings. "Once we got wind of the price, we came to collect."

The more he spoke, the more the kid began to look lucid. He was beginning to float back to the top of whatever it had been keeping him calm.

"You charmed me." He blinked as if waking up to stare almost through Bokaj, then his face went beet red, and he opened his mouth, lurching forward.

An arrow sprouted from his throat that rocked his whole body back, and flame erupted from his neck in a geyser ten feet high.

"What the fuck?!" Bokaj grunted as he fell backward away from the show. I cast Void Shield in front of him to take the falling flames, 203 MP draining from me instantly.

I turned back to see everyone staring at Manly, who still had the bow in hand with an arrow drawn and her pipe in her teeth, as if ready to keep firing.

"What the hell was that, Manly?" Jaken was the first to stand and move her way.

She planted the arrowhead in the ground between her legs and lifted her chin, even as she puffed on her pipe. She expelled the smoke hurriedly and turned her eyes to Maebe. "Queen Maebe, I swear to you, here and now, what that boy had been about to do would have put all of you, needlessly, in danger. I ended it."

Maebe blinked and looked to the rest of us. "She speaks the truth, or at least believes what she says to be true."

That went a long way toward clearing her with me. She had saved my friends. Fought with us. Tried to be nice. And had knowingly risked herself to swear to Maebe, who could murder her easily for lying to her.

I stood and marched over to her, looking her dead in her eyes before offering my hand. "Thanks for that."

She eyed me hard. "You won't turn me into a werewolf, will you?"

I blinked, she snorted and took my hand. "I'm teasin'. But it would've been nice to know." She looked to the others. "I'll be beddin' down for the evenin'. Thanks to the lot of you for the assistance in the fight, and for playin' with Frederick. I don't think I've seen him have so much fun in years."

"He speared a guy in the chest." Muu spread his hands wide. "He's welcome to play any time he fuckin' wants!"

We laughed at him, despite that, he insisted he was serious.

James looked at the book after Balmur checked it for traps. It was just a bunch of complex formulae that the monk just couldn't comprehend. Looking at it, it seemed vaguely familiar to me, but it just hurt after a while to look at it.

"Those are spells," Balmur confirmed after taking a glance at it. James and I looked at each other, then back at him, and he continued. "Yeah, this one right here is for Fireball. And the page after that is for some kind of Lightning Step?"

"How do you know that?" I tried to look at what he claimed were spells, but all I saw was a headache coming, so I stopped.

"It could have something to do with the fact that my magic is actually arcane based, where yours is a gift from nature." He half-heartedly shrugged as he turned another page.

He looked it over more seriously and seemed to forget that we were standing there as he went to his bedroll over next to Bokaj and Tmont.

"Guess that solves who gets the book." James shrugged. He patted my shoulder, then went to take his place near his bedroll.

I went and sat down next to Maebe, her back was to me, but she turned as soon as I was there. While I went through the experience notifications, I saw that it had been enough to almost put me up to level 38. I was *so* close.

I guess fighting so low-leveled a group with a bunch of higher-level folks yielded expectedly little returns.

"You seem bothered," the statement was sudden, but not unexpected. She knew me too damned well by now.

I pulled on my new gauntlet and then got out the egg so that I could feed it wind mana as I thought.

"The werewolf wants me to start turning people. And he's been more and more insistent and somehow—right? I don't know what the hell is wrong with me that I'm not just ignoring him, but it's getting rough dealing with it."

She leaned against me, her weight a comfort, and spoke softly, "Why did you choose to fight as a werewolf when you could have not transformed and saved yourself the trouble?"

"Because I promised to use it the next time we fought something," she blinked at me, and I knew where her thoughts went. "No, I didn't promise to turn someone."

She nodded and stroked my tails absentmindedly. "You have brought so many of your powers under control. You have been gifted strength and power from the elementals. Won my affections and saved your friends countless times. This creature dwells within you and is *part* of you. Tell me, do you know what would happen if you were to crush it?"

"Kill it?" My eyebrows shot up as I stared down at her open-mouthed.

"Crush it," she corrected. "When I was a young queen, there were those who thought themselves more powerful than I, though I was the chosen heiress, they felt they had a rightful claim. They came to me in search of my throne and found only strength and my will. When they challenged me, I took each one in stride, and right after each, I made them bow. It sounds as though you need to bring this creature to heel."

I settled against her, finally feeling a measure of peace within myself. The next time we weren't balls deep in now-enemy territory, I was going to have to have a serious heart to heart with the werewolf in me.

*I look forward to it...*it growled within my mind, then it was silent.

Cold dew settled over me as I woke, almost as if a frost had fallen in the night. I opened my eyes to the clearing, but there was blood everywhere. My friends' corpses, mangled and torn apart, scattered everywhere.

Claw marks slashed the ground, deep grooves scored into the cold earth, and I wasn't sure what to expect. Was this the wolf's fantasy? Was this another of those nightmares?

"Hello?" I called warily, my body falling into a crouch even though I had no weapons to protect myself with.

Whispered phrases in multiple languages assaulted my ears, some of the ones I could make out babbling about the end that was inevitably coming being so much less gruesome than this.

I snarled and turned to scour the trees, finding nothing. Finally, I stopped moving and as soon as I blinked, all my friends stood as one and surged forward to converge on me.

I gasped noisily and launched myself out of the bedroll, drenched in sweat and breathing heavily. Between my gasped and ragged breaths, I explained the situation to Maebe. I turned to find my brothers very much alive but struggling through their nightmares, as well.

Throughout the next day, we traveled slowly and cautiously with Kayda keeping an eye out for any more visitors, flying through the trees in her smaller form so she could see easier. When we stopped for any reason, we had lookouts posted, and that night, we posted a guard. Maebe put up a shadow barrier around the camp as we ate so that we wouldn't be disturbed.

"I would say that we should train you in more of the shadow spells, but I do not think that wise with present company." Maebe sighed as she looked over at Manly, who puffed on her pipe on the back of her cart.

"You don't trust her," I stated, her look at me confirmed it. "I don't blame you. But you do have to admit; she's been helpful."

"Yes, a snake is helpful when it eats the rats and mice in the granary, but never when it bites the farmer," her voice was light, but there was a hint of anger in it. "Something is wrong. I do not know what it is, but I do not like it."

"I can believe that." I still had the gauntlet on my hand as I fed mana to the egg. I'd been doing it all day, and there was still no real activity from within. I felt the little creature, the heartbeat was much, much stronger than before, but there was no movement. "I think those bounty hunters had a lot to do with what's going on in Lindyburg, or what happened after we met you and before you came to this plane. And the sooner we get that taken care of, the better, but we need to move on."

"Yes, this is true, and the sooner you get this all taken care of, the better, as you said." She frowned deeply before shaking her head. "Having to defend yourself from random attackers would never do." I nodded. "Come. Let us rest for the evening."

I figured I would try to feed mana to the egg while I was asleep, it was a conscious thing so far, but I could feed mana around me as naturally as breathing now, so it would only be a matter of slight focus as I slept. I'd try it.

"If you fail to keep doing it, I will do so for you when you fall too deeply to slumber," Maebe assured me. I closed my eyes and began to work through meditative breathing cycles and funneling mana slowly.

As I dreamt of flying with Kayda, I felt the pull of mana through my hand. Excellent. It was working.

The skies were dark, but they were more like home than anything I had come to know in recent times. She swirled around me; her form larger than it had ever been. Her feathers almost as large as my body. As she soared about me, the steadily darkening skies seeming to come closer and condense, I felt her love.

Wake.

I opened my eyes with a startled gasp and reached toward the sky, the dawn light stretched across it.

"You dreamt?" Maebe's soothing voice reached me from my right. She watched me curiously, the shadows around her legs deeper than the deepest black that I had ever seen.

"Yeah, it was a weird one this time." I glanced around, and the others were still asleep or meditating except for Yohsuke. "Nowhere near as bad as before, but still odd."

"Come, we must speak." Maebe stood and beckoned for me to join her.

I looked over to my brother, and he seemed to gather that we would be stepping out as he mouthed, *be safe,* then tapped his earring.

I nodded once, cradling the egg as I stood and joined my queen. She led us through the trees, the dawn light just beginning to truly shine on the world around us until she came to a hollow tree.

She stopped and touched it, uncertainty on her face.

"What's wrong?" I closed the distance between us to stand next to her.

"Why do you assume that something is wrong?" She frowned as she turned to face me. Her features looked as lovely as they always did. Her black, multi-colored, highlighted hair shimmering in the light.

"Because normally when someone you love says 'we must speak or talk' that means something is wrong," I tried to soften the statement for both of us, but the words still sounded jaded even to me.

Her face lit up as she shook her head. "I simply wanted an excuse to speak with you away from the others. I am not unhappy."

The relief was almost immeasurable, and a weight shifted from my shoulders. "Oh, okay then. What's up?"

"I was happy to see that you reached for the shadows when that boy unleashed that flame spell." She grasped my hand, and the stars along the back of it seemed to glow brighter at the contact. "That shows that you are more comfortable with your powers. But I wanted to ask you something."

"You are always free to ask me anything you want, Mae." I smiled at her, leaning closer to kiss her forehead.

Her eyes, green fire in the morning light, searched my face a moment, "Are you happy with me? Truly happy?"

I blinked, a little blindsided by the question and the uncertainty in her tone. I tried to think back to all of our dealings. Had I not been paying enough attention to her? Affection?

"Of course, I am, Mae." I took my hand from hers and lifted her face with it so I could look at her properly. "You know I love you, right? I know we may not have the chance to say it all the time, and that lately things have been more than a little distracting, but I'm wild about you."

"And I, you." She frowned. "Something I said last night, about things being done sooner rather than later, made me think as I watched you sleeping, and it has me feeling things I would not normally feel."

Realization dawned on me. "This is about me possibly going home someday."

Her small, sad smile said it all. I pulled her closer, her breath warm against my chest. "I have tried not to think on it too much. But as time passes, I find myself wondering what it will be like to lose you. To lose all of my friends. The man I love."

"I'm sorry, Mae. I wish I could say that I know for sure what will happen, but I don't." I tried to think of the right words. Anything. The strain of it on my heart and my mind making me lose control of my mana flow, my mana draining faster and faster into the egg still in my hand. I took a breath.

"I don't want you to stay," Maebe blurted, and I froze. She looked up into my eyes, suddenly very serious. "If you can go home, I want you to. I want to be certain that all of your hard work pays off and that you can be with your son. I would not steal his father from him. And I would not steal that joy from you."

Again, I was at a loss. I knew for certain that she was being kind and considerate in this. Her love of children and me bleeding into one another.

"Does this mean that you want to end things?" My voice was soft, as I tried to mask the hurt.

Her fist connected with my stomach lightly, surprising me. "No."

She reached up and pulled me down so that I could see the myriad emotions playing over her features. "I love you. And I want to spend this time that we have left together. Every moment is precious, and I would share them with you. And Vrawn."

I couldn't help the snort of laughter that escaped me. "And Vrawn." I shook my head. "You know that she very well may kick my ass if she finds out that you were crying because of me."

"It would do you well to train with her. I know that you have seen her fight but watching her with those undead was top notch." Maebe grinned.

"I bet it was." I smiled back, and suddenly she kissed me. Pressing her lips and body as close to mine as she could, and all of my air was gone. Once more, my mana control was gone, and a wild stream of mana funneled into the egg as our lips mingled.

"You know, I've meant to ask you something else." She cast her eyes down when a sound caught my attention.

Crack, snicht, crunch

I looked down, spiderwebbed cracks formed along the scaled shell of this egg.

I brought it up so that our eyes were almost level with it. Of course, Maebe had to levitate so that she could see properly.

A small nose pushed through, a tiny sharp bump on the nose to help crack the shell. Brown eyes peeked out from within, and as I went to help the creature out, Maebe swatted my hand away.

"I read a book on hatchling creatures," she hissed, her eyes still on the hatchling. "If they do not get out of the egg on their own, they may not develop properly. You could hurt it."

I sighed and said a soft prayer for the little thing as it fought for freedom. Strands of viscous fluid stuck to the little creature as it clicked and opened its jaws. A sharp intake of air, and a soft croaking sound emanated from the eggshell. A wee piece of it lifted as the creature within looked about almost cautiously.

The slitted brown eyes fell on me before more excited croaking and small claws reaching out of it, the shell crumbling in on itself as the little thing tried to escape.

Alert!

A Gust Raptor hatchling has imprinted upon you. Would you like to take it as your familiar?

Yes/No?

My friends had bought her for just this reason, right? Though Gust Raptor was pretty fucking amazing for a species. I wonder what it did? I accepted and read over the next alert.

Alert!

You have accepted the Gust Raptor hatchling as your familiar, would you like to name it?

Yes/No?

I could feel the mental bond already formed between us, her mind was a flicker against mine, but it was inquisitive and sharp. She needed a good, strong name. A name that would strike fear into the hearts of many.

"I think I'll call you Bea," I announced, proudly naming her after a famous gunnery sergeant of Marines, beloved actress and one of my favorite funny people. She wriggled her body in my hand, trying to look around her. Her mind quieted at the name, and she growled hungrily. "Yup. All we need now is a couple of old ladies and some cheesecake, and all the ladies are here."

"She is beautiful," Maebe whispered. Both Bea and I looked up to see her staring in wonder.

"Do you want to hold her?" I asked as I offered her to Maebe with a hopeful smile. I was here without any sort of pocket bacon, so I would need to look for something for her to eat. "I need to find her something to munch on."

The queen didn't hesitate in the slightest to take the hatchling from my hands, cooing to her and rocking her as if she were a child. I sent mental images of Maebe and attached the feelings of safety and security to her. Feelings of love. That settled the hatchling for a moment.

I cast Life Sense, and there was nothing in the immediate range of the spell, so I reached my awareness out into the shadows around us as the sun rose higher. I felt motion up in the north of where we were, a small creature, a baby rabbit, and sighed. It would have to do.

I hardened my heart and reminded myself that all creatures needed to eat and that soon enough, Bea would be able to do this on her own. For now, I would hunt for her.

I reached out with my mind and cast Nether Transport (Minor) on the rabbit, bringing it into my outstretched hand in a ball of solid shadows.

"I'm sorry little friend, but my baby needs to feed." I came over to Bea and held the terrified creature out to her, her inquisitive head tilts looked so cute just before her jaws opened wide. Sharp, small teeth coated her jaws, and she snatched the struggling creature from my fingers greedily. She barely chewed, settling with rocking her head back to open her throat and swallow the morsel mostly whole.

"Fuck, that's cool." I groaned with feeling. I remembered Kayda being pretty brutal as a baby as well, that thought brought her attention to me. Our bond opening slightly as she stirred from sleep.

"We should get back to the camp before Kayda figures out what we have here and starts to tear the forest apart to get to us." I grinned at Maebe, and she nodded back just as excitedly before we took off back toward camp.

Maebe stroked her gray scales while we walked, the small lines of light green that seemed to flow over her body like a representation of wind breaking over her was so beautiful I almost tripped trying to take more of her in.

When we arrived, the others had begun to move about the camp and clean for our trip out that day.

"Welcome back," Yohsuke called from his place by the cooking fire. He glanced up and saw us then smiled, "Congratulations. The hell is that thing?"

"This is Bea," Maebe announced proudly. "She is the gift that you all bestowed upon Zeke. Come and see her."

The queen toted the little raptor like she was a proud mama showing her newborn child to her closest friends and relatives. I was proud, but at the same time, an emotion I never thought would clench my chest quite so tight as it did, found its way into my mind and heart—longing.

Did I want this with her? She had told me that she was happy with me. That my time here with her was good, but she wanted me to go home. I wanted to take her seriously. And I wanted to have my son in my life and be a huge part of his.

My mouth went dry, and it was a fight for the rest of the world not to fall away from me at that moment as I thought about my little boy. My fists clenched, droplets of blood dribbling down my left hand, grounding me in my mission here. This was as much for him as anyone else on Earth. He was my reason back home, even if I had reasons to fight here, as well. I tried to swallow past the cotton mouth I had and took a few steadying breaths.

Now, I might never know what this would be like with Maebe. What was I going to do? Fuck. *Damn it!*

I shook my head and opened my eyes, grateful that my friends and Maebe were distracted by the scaled bundle in Maebe's arms.

By now, the others had gathered around, and Kayda was truly awake, having opted to sleep in her full, twenty-feet-tall normal form, she hopped closer to take a look. I stepped in front of her, she craned her neck to see past me, and I put a hand on her plumage.

"Wait, dearest," I spoke soothingly as I blocked her path. "Let them come to you. I know that you wanna see, but remember what happened when you came at Coal too fast?"

She blinked and looked around for her lost brother and I sighed, the loss still fresh. Kayda, me, and the whole party had grown attached, so when he had been called home, there had been a good deal of sadness.

Scared? Kayda quested, our bond fully opened now. She sent me an image of Coal cowering behind me.

"That's right, baby. She could be scared, and we don't want that." I ran both my hands over her thick feathers soothingly. "We have to take this slow and do it properly so that she gets used to you. So, you stay here, and I'll get you some food while you wait."

Food! She spread her wings and shuffled her feathers noisily as she waited.

"Yo, Yoh!" I called to my brother, who turned my way. "Can I get some chow for tiny here?" I thumbed my nose and shoved the thumb toward Kayda, who pecked at me playfully.

"Yup!" He reached into his inventory and pulled out a massive haunch of meat, ribs still within it, and offered it to me. It was heavy to him, but with my significantly higher strength, it was light as hell for me. I tossed the large morsel up for Kayda, who caught it deftly and bent her head to put the item between her talons to begin pecking it apart gleefully. Ripping muscle and the sound of her clicking beak accompanied me over to the others.

"Coochie coo." Muu tickled Bea's slightly distended stomach as she watched him lazily. "Doesn't move much does she? What even is she?"

"That be a gust raptor hatchling," Manly yawned as she joined us. Today she wore a baby blue dress with small frills and a white bodice around the waist. "Travel in pods of five to seven normally, and they're damned right mean, at times. That was a lucky egg."

"Yes, it was, and I feel like she will be a fine addition to the team." I watched as Muu stopped paying her enough mind that she was able to nip his finger.

"Ouch!" He grumbled and pulled his hand away. "Okay, evil baby, has an attitude. Got it."

Maebe tickled the top of the little thing's head as she struggled, and the others seemed to get their fill of her before Maebe, and I took Bea over to Kayda.

The obscenely large bird stared down at the newborn with apparent wonder in her gaze. Sharp eyes transfixed.

"Kayda, this is Bea." I ran my hand through the elder beast's feathers as she inched closer slowly. She was being careful. "There's a good older sister, yeah. Gentle now."

Kayda was close enough for the small creature to be able to reach out with her tiny, still-forming claws and grab her beak. The large bird took it in stride, cooing softly. It was when Bea began to try and nibble on her beak that Kayda pulled back.

She looked down to her feet at the remains of her meal and began to pick meat from the bones to ferry up to her little sister. *Food*, she cooed as she fed the little one, who gobbled things up as swiftly as they were given to her.

Maebe laughed at the exchange and held her still while they bonded, so I decided it was time to speak to Bea at length about what was what. I went through each individual party member and how I felt about them. I attached a name to each image and made sure that she was getting the idea before moving to the next.

When I came to Kayda, I included memories of her fighting so that the little biter didn't get any bad ideas about trying to eat her. Watching Kayda fight seemed to make her want to move because she struggled mightily in Maebe's arms.

Then I focused on Maebe. That was a quick process because Bea picked up on my feelings while she was in the egg. How, I wasn't quite sure, but it could have been the mana that I fed to her. Or the fact that Maebe had been there when I was holding her.

Either way, the little creature seemed quite attached to Maebe already.

We ate a hearty breakfast, then saddled up for the day head into the mountain pass that we were a few miles from. Thor, the Kirin I had as a mount, acted interested in Bea until she tried to bite his nose.

"I will allow her to ride if you promise she will not bite me." He posed with his eyes locked on mine. I smiled and nodded before he acquiesced to me riding him. I held the little monster close, and we traveled on.

When we stopped for lunch that afternoon, on a large enough outcropping of rock, I let Bea down so that she could stretch her legs a little. She hadn't earned enough experience to have a status screen, so how much could she do?

How often has that phrase been uttered, and your mind immediately goes to all the things that are about to go wrong? A lot? Every time? Every time for me, too.

Her first steps were adorable. She held herself up, wobbling a little, then tried to step and lost her balance immediately, tottered to the side, and fell to the stone ground with a light thud and a few chuckled, "awws," from everyone around.

Another five minutes of practice and more than a little prodding from Kayda, and she was up and taking measured steps. Then she was trotting about two minutes later.

"She learns so quickly!" Maebe spoke with pride as she

watched the little raptor hatchling trot around her legs in tighter and tighter circles.

"Anyone else feel like they just gave a shark legs?" Muu quipped as Bea bit at the air, her mouth hanging open as she sprinted. "I feel like I'm watching Jaws on Ice."

I tried to grab her after a second, but she juked to my left, and I fell forward, barely stopping myself from falling onto my face with a grin of embarrassment.

I got the image from her that she found that entertaining as she sprinted and hopped around the place, venturing dangerously close to the edge as she moved.

"You've gotta be shitting me," I grumbled, standing back up to go and get her. *Bea, come here, we have to go.*

Through our bond, her exhilaration at running, of being so fast and so close to the wind was just overwhelming at first. I didn't think she was doing it on purpose, but that didn't mean that I was going to allow it, now.

"Bea Arthur, you get your scaly ass over here!" I barked loudly. She ignored me as she sped off closer to the side of the outcropping. "You little fucker."

The others were standing now, Balmur, especially, as he was fast enough to catch her without trying, thanks to his insanely high dexterity. I waved them away; I had to do this on my own.

I marched into the center of the outcropping, waiting for her to pass, then willed my shadow to stretch toward her path, then poured intent and mana into it.

As soon as she saw it there, she leapt off the ground, flying over it, but as her shadow touched it, her body froze.

Shade's Prison – Caster takes his shadow and spreads it in a certain direction in order to trap another creature for a short period of time. Cost: 57 MP. Duration: 30 seconds. Cooldown: 1 minute.

I stepped closer to where she had landed on her face, not hard enough to hurt her, but hard enough to let her know that what she had done hadn't been smart.

I pulled her into my arms, breaking the spell, and spoke

directly through our link. *I am the one in charge here. You will obey me. You could have hurt yourself, and that will not do. Do you understand?*

Her head tilted to the side in confusion, but she understood that if I had wanted to, I could have let her get hurt. I sent her the thought of her flying over the side of the outcropping, and she didn't like that either.

Then you will listen to me. Come along. Kayda reached out through our bond and probed for information. She soon understood my reasoning and fluttered off to scout.

It was going to be a long trip if I couldn't make Bea listen.

CHAPTER SIX

Our cautious trek up the mountainside trail with Manly talking to us and inquiring about us was a little tense. Not just because of the last couple times we had been in these mountains having resulted in attacks that had almost resulted in one of us dying, but because we still weren't sure how to take our guest.

And because we expected to be attacked, what with all the nightmares we seemed to be infrequently having between all of us. One or two of us hit every night or two. It sucked.

After the end of the second day on this mountain trail, the next portion of our journey was in sight. We could just make out the lights coming from the capital as the sun fell in the western sky.

"What's the capital city like?" James wondered aloud as we looked for a place to spend the night.

The wind this high up really wore us down, though Bea seemed to like it just fine. Her tongue flopped and flapped out of the side of her mouth and waggled wildly as she let the wind buffet her full on.

"Well, there's lots o' folks there," Manly began as she glanced around to help answer. Humphrey had a thing against the wind as well, she had said. Smelling him over the last few days, I knew what it was. He needed a bath. "Lots o' nice ones, and ones what ain't so nice, but the majority of 'em don't care for outsiders. It's a mostly human city, and after the high elves slapped their greatest wizards down some time ago, they truly don't care for elves. Dwarves do okay, and gnomes and halflings'll be alright. Beast-kin are a real sore spot. There're some there who still ply their trade in *managin'* them. Don't rightly care for that, but I can't stop 'em."

So human form for me and disguises or outright hiding for the rest of you guys, I grumbled to the others.

Could you make us rings so that we can just blend in? Yohsuke looked about as he walked ahead.

I could give it a shot at the very least, I thought to myself, then the same to the others.

"Found something!" Muu called as we walked toward a cavern off the trail by about a good twenty feet. "Looks like a good place to call it for the night. You think?"

I shrugged. I had long since put Bea into my collar, her struggling to be free grated on my nerves. Kayda still scouted above, but even with her large size, the wind tossed her about as well. I called her down, and we piled into the cave to inspect things. The cave went back forty-five feet, so plenty of room for us to get in, and lay everything out nicely.

We checked for false walls and traps to be safe, then ate a good meal and chatted a little more about the city before Manly decided to speak to us a little more seriously.

"Now, I reckon we're close enough to talk about somethin'," she broached as she puffed on her pipe lightly, leaning against Humphrey. "I couldn't help but overhear that fella what was leadin' that band o' miscreants sayin' that y'all had been accused of some things—mighty unlikely that you did 'em, I reckon—but a lady does try to learn more of her travelin' partners after such talk."

Should we tell her? Muu yawned quietly and listened through the earrings. The others glanced about and nodded to each other.

I blinked, wondering how much we should tell her when Bokaj cleared his throat. "We had needed someone to teach me how to do some things when we met this bard, Pharazulla."

"She's pretty famous 'round where I came from!" Manly smacked her thigh and leaned forward. "Was she as purty as the old men seem to think?"

"She was pretty." Muu shrugged as he piled more food into his mouth.

"She was, and she was also unavailable to join us when we first met her," Bokaj continued. "We saved her life that night, and she still said no. So, we packed up in the morning and decided to head on. Well, a little way outside the gate, there she was and packed to travel. So, we didn't think much of it."

"Now, that does seem odd," Manly scratched her head, then motioned for him to continue. "Well, did she teach you anythin'? What happened? The lot of you look like somethin's eaten at you."

I suppose the jig is up, and she does seem cool. Bokaj sighed. *I vote we tell her the truth, at least about the guards.*

The other members of the party agreed, and Bokaj continued the telling. "Until some guards came with orders to bring her and anyone she was traveling with back to Lindyburg."

Manly nodded as he spoke. "Didn't mention anything to you?"

We're this far in and having someone knowing that we weren't in cahoots with her would be nice, Muu reasoned. He went to speak but stopped when Yohsuke threw a stick into the fire.

"Nope, she just cast a spell on Zeke that made him cast a spell that killed them, then turned him against us trying to get rid of us," Yohsuke muttered angrily. That last bit was still a bit of an embarrassing thought even now.

"He had no control over what he did, she mind fucked him, and he had no choice," Bokaj insisted. "We're innocent."

"Then why not go make that apparent to the Governess at Lindyburg?" Manly swatted at Humphrey, who had just farted.

"That's fucking rank, man." I groaned as I shifted from the blast zone behind him.

"Sorry, Zeke, y'all were sayin'?" Manly raised her eyebrows before packing a little more tobacco into her pipe, the first time I had seen her do so.

She seems pretty insistent. James scowled from where he sat around the other side of the fire.

Jaken shrugged. *Wouldn't you be if someone was telling you such a juicy story?*

"If we go back now, it takes us away from our mission, and with the way Pharazulla works, there's more than likely been more crimes she could have committed and tried to attach us to, to make sure she gets off scot-free." Bokaj stood up and began to pace. "We have to move on. It's the only way forward."

"I see." Manly smiled, genuinely happy with what she had heard. "Y'all seem like real nice folk. I'm sure that you're inno-cent." She yawned and stretched before patting her companion. "I'll be heading to bed then. Y'all be safe now, and I'll see you, soon."

"Night Manly," Muu and Jaken called as we got ready for bed ourselves.

Think we did the right thing? Balmur gestured quietly after her as we sat around the fire still.

No one answered, because all of us were lost to the weight of our inadvertent sins. Especially me. Did I feel guilty? Hell yeah, even knowing it wasn't my fault. That's why we had our rings now.

As Maebe and I lay together, Bea in the collar and Kayda asleep near the front of the cave. I smiled despite the gravity of the revelations that had been revealed earlier. It had been a decent couple days all things considered. Muu was on watch, and James sat near him. The two of them were having a lively debate about which game of a series was better. Muu swore it was nine, and James was of the opinion it was seven.

I closed my eyes and breathed in Mae's scent before I drifted to sleep.

I had to have only just closed my eyes and drifted off when a whispered word reached my ears, "*Her.*"

I opened my eyes in time to see someone stalking toward Maebe, and I before she levitated from our bedroll and held out her palms.

"Who are you, and how did you get behind us?" She spoke loudly and with authority.

"Sorry, Majesty, but you're a threat we don't have time for." The figure held a hand to his mouth, then a shrill whistle, and a beam of light struck Maebe in the back, and she disappeared from in front of me with a shimmer and a growl.

I was out of bed instantly with crimson deep in my vision and I *knew* I had transformed into my werewolf form. I looked to my right, seeing that there was a human man in his mid-thirties with a bald head and days-old stubble. He was thin but looked wiry and held a staff out before him.

Mage Level 43

I went for him without thinking, he had done something to my love! I snarled and leapt before a wall of muscle slapped into my side with a large object in hand. Then searing burning fell over my body as a net was cast over me. Even as I snarled in rage, I tried to reach out to the others, but nothing happened, and no one responded.

"It's alright, werewolf," the human man tried to calm me with a soothing tone. "I didn't hurt her; all I did was send her home for a few days. Costly spell, but worth it not to die, don't you think?"

The burning from the net didn't die down at all, but the rage in my eyes began to wane as pain took hold.

"That's much better," a husky female voice from where the behemoth had struck me reached my ears. "You know, that rage of yours is something. You would have made a damned fine berserker."

"Don't tease the bounty, Bonnie," the mage tutted. "And

you can put that hammer of yours away, for now. The others are all bound and silenced, he's the last one, and I don't think he will be too much trouble with that silver all over him."

"You should know better by now than to think lightly of a captured foe, Nicolas," another female voice drawled from behind him. "What about that last guy we captured outside Billindale who clubbed you over the head before one of us could stop him? You know, when you decided to monologue in front of him. I think it was about the futility of his trying to escape?"

"It was once, Dawn." The mage huffed, the sound of wood tapping the ground reached my ears. "I've been better about it since then, have I not?"

"Sure, once he passes out, load him into the cart with the others, Bonnie," the voice ordered casually. "Now, where is that fighter? Nick is usually so readily available."

Lightning flashed, and a cry of thunder rang out around us, Kayda's anger fueling mine briefly before our bond snapped shut.

"He's outside trying to tame the bird; you know how he is with animals." Bonnie smiled as she leaned over me. I could just barely make out her horned figure before she spoke again. "And here I thought that birds were your thing, Dawn."

I snarled and tried to grab at her, do anything, but the net was weighted, and my strength fled faster and faster with my health.

Colors and shadows ran together and I could no longer differentiate between the real people and their shadowy doubles and triples. Eyes dropping dangerously I tried to stand and fight only to fall one last time.

———

I woke up to motion, the sensation of being jostled about like so much cargo in a cage-like structure. I groaned, the burning of the silver hadn't quite healed yet, but I could feel it nearby.

Looking at the bars of the cage, there was silver wire wrapped around each one and soldered on there. It would be painful to touch, but I coul—

"Don't be thinkin' of tryin' to bust out, Zeke," Manly sat in a chair just outside the bars, her southern drawl was much less pronounced, now.

"Where are we, and why did you betray us like this?" I growled. I didn't dare move closer to the bars themselves, or I would risk hurting myself. "What happened to Maebe?! And your accent, are you really who you say you are?"

"It's not a betrayal getting close to a bounty." She shrugged, her face still pleasant and kind. "I'm Manly Warbottom, as sure as you're my quarry. I knew that there was something off about y'all, but I couldn't quite put my finger on it. Still can't. But don't worry, your queen is likely safe in her lands in the Fae. See, Nicolas is quite the spell slinger, and being a wizard, he knows all sorts of magic to use against creatures from other realms. All he had to do was send her home. She's going to be there for at least a week our time—plenty of time for us to get you to Lindyburg to prove your innocence, and for us to be on our way."

"If you think we're innocent, why take us there at all?" I spat; it was hard to control my emotions. "Why not work with those other bounty hunters to capture us?"

"'Cause they had stepped out of line, and I'm gonna need to discuss the terms of the contract with the Governess." The halfling growled, shaking her head sadly, a frown taking over her face. "She should never have sent someone to compete for the contract once I had taken it. But, Manly Warbottom gets her bounties, yessiree. Now," she came closer to the edge of the bars, remaining carefully outside my reach. "I know that you and your friends are tight-knit, so I'll let you know right now that they're safe, and as long as y'all behave, it'll stay that way. I gave my word, and I mean to keep it."

"What proof do I have of that?" Crestfallen that I hadn't

thought of my friends, or Kayda sooner. "Where's Kayda? She's not hurt, is she?"

"She's on the mend. Nick, another one of my pals, isn't always the most conscious of his meetin's with animals. Loves 'em. He truly does. But he gets too excited, and sometimes they get hurt." Red clouded my vision, and she leaned back. "As for the evidence, well, you're wearin' it. We know that you're all smart people, and though these cages are designed to hold powerful creatures, you still have your inventories. Hell, soon as Kayda's feelin' shipshape, I'll let her come in here to be with you. Now, be warned, the cages are warded somethin' fierce against magic used on them from the inside, so any spells you try are just going to rebound on you."

"What if we double the contract fee?" I offered, more out of desperation than I was willing to admit.

"I don't renege on my contracts, mister." Manly squared her shoulders. "Not even for people I believe are innocent. And especially not the ones I like."

She stood and walked toward the door before she stopped, turning back to look me in the eyes. "I am sorry, Zeke. I wish that we had met under better circumstances, but this is just business. Nothin' personal."

With that, she was gone, and I was left to my own devices.

First thing I did was try to melt one of the bars with flame-aspected mana. That was stupid. The red mana soaked into the metal, then coursed out of it and back into me, sapping 250 HP from me and draining my mana completely in recompense. Looking around, the floor was made of the same sort of metal as the bars.

It was large enough that I could lay down comfortably, but not large enough for me to fully stand. There was a pallet off to my right to sleep on, but nothing else.

I thought about summoning Magus Bane then and there to bust out of here, but the others would be in danger if I couldn't get to them in time. They had been higher levels than us. Not the first time we had faced those odds, but we had never done it one on one in this kind of situation.

How would we get out of this? I mean, realistically speaking, yeah, we could go and just prove our innocence. It wasn't that big of a deal, but it was just really inconvenient and potentially dangerous. What if no one believed us? What if they tried to throw us in prison? What if everything she had told us had been a lie?

And we had fallen for all of it so easily. What the fuck were we going to do?

We would likely have to slaughter half the city in order to escape, and that was just…more than we probably wanted to do to be free. Granted, yeah, we were at the point where all that kept us from going home was a few more of War's generals. Three, if I recalled correctly. What was some time as fugitives?

Uh, fucking detrimental, that's what. I growled at myself. And what's worse, I couldn't harm a hair on Manly's head without breaking my word. She hadn't hurt us first, not purposely. And I think that was what would keep the word from being broken. Especially, since I hadn't gotten any notifications that she had broken her vow.

And besides, did I even want to hurt her? She had been cool to us, and this was, after all, just business, right? She was doing the best she could to survive. But I wondered how they had laid that trap…

The goddamn cart we were inside. They laid in wait and set their trap perfectly.

Especially since she had a wizard at her beck and call. I found myself wondering if he was an enchanter, because if he was, there was no telling what kind of traps could be in this place.

Which made breaking out not only risky, but stupid because navigating a pocket dimension, or series of them would be tricky. I reached for my magic and tried to focus on Teleport, receiving a sharp stab of agony in my mind shortly before my mana drained away completely with a healthy chunk of my HP bar. Teleporting out wasn't an option, either.

We could break free when we got out of her grasp. Or go to trial.

I tried the earrings, *Can anyone hear me?*

I waited for a while and nothing. Could be the cage acting up, but it could also be the cart itself interfering.

So, with nothing but time on my hands and an enclosed space to work with, I let Bea out for a time to stretch her legs and work with her.

It was slow going at first as I had little to no food to give her as treats. Maybe Manly would give me extra food for her? She didn't seem to have any issues with animals, maybe she wouldn't mind helping with her?

Didn't mean I was going to let the time pass without being productive, even if I couldn't get her out much and feed her.

After an hour of us playing and building a decent rapport with each other, I brought her back into the collar so I could focus on my spell work.

I'd put this off long enough, and it was time to buckle down. The first thing I did was focus on my healing spells. The focus was to restore health. Was there a way to harness that healing power and use it with new elements?

Only one way to find out then, I grumbled. I sat in the center of the cell as best I could and meditated.

The first thing I did was take the base spell I wanted to tinker with, Regrowth.

The spell allowed me to regenerate my health faster by 6 HP per second for thirty seconds, per casting. It was a druidic spell I learned early on, not bad at all, but thanks to a reward from the Primordial Water Elemental, it had more than doubled in potency. All of us had received a boost to water, healing, or frost type magics thanks to our quest on her behalf. Hell, even Maebe.

Thinking about her made my heart pound as I prayed that she truly was fine.

I took that spell and mentally put it into the flaming forge in my heart, where I envisioned my Flame Tinkering ability. The last time I had done this, I had forged a couple of spells, one being Phoenix Burst, and the other a holy blade spell called Falfyre. Here's hoping I struck gold again.

I stoked the flames, precious mana sinking into the spell, and hammered into it with my flame aspect. The nature spell was more stubborn than the holy spell, Purify, that I had used to create Phoenix Burst, so it was much harder and mentally taxing.

I poured my mana into the act and refocused my efforts, forming my intent and will into what I hoped would be enough.

"You seem focused, do you always meditate so fiercely?" A slightly familiar voice almost broke my concentration, but I ignored her. Just a little more.

I funneled the mana in faster and took a deep breath. There, done.

Renewing Flames – Flame invigorates the recipient's body and heals them for 30 HP instantly, and 8 HP per second for a short time. Duration: 30 seconds. Cost: 45 MP. Cooldown: 5 seconds.

Excellent. I addressed my new guest, "Not always, but a little bit of meditation keeps the hunger and boredom at bay, right?" I opened my eyes and saw a woman staring intently from just outside the bars. I recognized her outline instantly. "You must be Bonnie, right?"

She smiled, her fanged features taking a pleasant turn. She looked like a demon, complete with horns and tail, her skin a teal color, and her eyes a vibrant gold. Her ruby-red pouty lips flared into a larger grin as she noticed me sizing her up, but I didn't think she was used to someone looking for her to be formidable. She was lean in all the right places like one of those ladies in the gym who lifted purely for physique, strong arms, and legs with well-toned muscles. Her jawline was strong, eyebrows done perfectly, and her silvery hair thrown wildly behind her horns that stuck out from her forehead and curved up and back a little.

"Enjoying the show?" She gave me a cocky grin, and I smiled in kind.

"I would love something to eat if you have anything?" I tried sweetly, my relatively low charisma had better work for me, or I'd be miserable.

"My question first," she purred. Her eyes narrowed as she leaned on something. I looked and saw that it was a large wooden hammer with spikes nailed and banded together on one side. "Please."

"Yeah, as far as views go in the present? Absolutely stunning." I struggled to keep my biting sarcasm in check. "Unfortunately, I'm taken and happily so, so… looking is all that's gonna happen, lady."

"Tha's fine," another voice added as they walked through the door, male this time.

I looked over to see as a stout figure, a dwarf walked into the room carrying a tray of food.

"Ye weren't s'posed ta be with the bounties, Bonnie, ye know tha'." He stood next to her and scowled at her softly. He looked to me. "Best no' ta get any ideas, lad. This one may look 'n talk sweet, but she be a demon."

"Half Demon, Nick, you know that." She pouted as if he had ruined her fun but turned her eyes on me. "Mom was a demon; dad was a priest. Quite the scandal in both realms, but people seem to love me for my own quirks."

"My dad left when I was a kid." I gave her a little something to show I cared, a little. But it was the dwarf I had eyes for.

His armor was well kept and polished to perfection, and his fiery red beard had one section braided intricately over his slightly portly belly, with the majority of the rest fanned out behind it. His head was shiny and bald, likely polished as well, but it was his tanned skin that was odd to me. The other dwarves didn't usually have that feature.

"I heard you're the one who roughed up my Kayda." I

growled, coming close to the cage despite the burning silver wires.

The dwarf looked down, abashed. "Well, see, uh, ahem...," he stammered, and finally, Bonnie took pity on him with a roll of her eyes.

"Hill dwarves love animals, and his family is a bunch of druids back home, so animals were always about, but he... what was it your parents had said, Nick?" She looked over at the dwarf who looked abashed and smacked his shoulder lightly.

"Oh? What, me folks? They said I weren't 'compatible' with the magics o' nature. Animals never seemed ta like me either I s'pose." He scratched his head, frowning. "Had a heavy hand, I reckon. I didnae mean ta hurt her, lad. I swear on me beard. Now, ye may travel with a dwarf, but I be tellin' ye, ta swear on yer beard—"

I interrupted politely, "Is a very serious thing to do." I believed him and, as a show of that faith, muttered, "The hammer falls."

I dismissed the notification that his word gave me, mentioning that as a knight of the Unseelie realm, oaths gave me a measure of security over someone. So, if he broke his, I would receive some sort of recompense.

He looked shocked, Bonnie had to sock him again, the tray in his grip almost tumbling out. He caught it and looked at me with new eyes as he finished, "An' rises again. Well, this changes everthin'."

"What's it change?" Bonnie leaned closer to him curiously.

"Means we know he be likely innocent." The dwarf smacked Bonnie excitedly, and she just smiled back. "Only kin be knowin' our phrases an' be brave enough ta say 'em ta a dwarf proper as he did! He's a righ' proper follower o' the Way, I reckon! Who's yer clan, lad?"

"Mugfist." I smiled. I was proud to have been adopted by the group of surly, battle-hardened assholes. Defenders of their city and their people. "And I follow the Way."

"Respect from Clan Glennybrook, out of the Kuhn Plain

Hills." He bowed at his waist and pulled a latch on the bottom half of the cage, and a slit large enough for a tray opened. "This here be for ye, but I'll be gettin' ye more. I can nae do much, but I be a humble chef. And I'll feed ye proper, aye?"

"That sounds nice, Nick." I grabbed the plate. "I have a request, though, if you'll hear me out?"

"I will nae let ye out lad, tha' be more than any o' us will likely do." He shook his head forlornly. "We hold ta a code, much the same as I do the Way."

"I thought not, but I would settle for some extra meat so that I can feed my familiar." I took my food and set it aside for now.

"Oh, I be takin' real proper care o' her, Manly were insistent on it, though she be doin' the feedin' herself." He bashfully smiled and nodded to himself.

"Thank you, but I meant the one I have with me, now, she's a baby, so I can't let you get too hands-on, but I'll introduce you if you'll agree to bring extra food?" He looked uncertain. "I swear on my clan name that I will not lie to you in this, Nick. Also, the others, Jaken, the Fae-orc, and Balmur, the Azer dwarf, are clan as well. The others are close family to me, and that makes them important to the clan. I would hope that you would see that they're treated well?"

Warning!

You as both a Knight of the Unseelie Court and a member of a dwarven clan have given your word. While a broken oath will have dire consequences in either realm, failing to keep your word in this will have extremely dire consequences. If you fail to uphold your word as a Knight, your court's honor will be besmirched, and your title in jeopardy. If you break your oath as a member of a clan, your clan can turn against you, or exile you.

Be careful.

Fuck me. I hadn't had any real thoughts of breaking my

word before, but goddamn. So, this Fae thing was a double-edged blade, and it could easily be held at my throat, too.

He nodded fiercely, but Bonnie answered, "We may work a little underhanded at times, and get into some hairy situations, but we always treat our bounties with respect. You abide by our rules and our expectations of you, and we won't harm a hair on you or anyone else's heads." She smiled, and this one seemed genuine, too. "I don't have a beard to swear on, so I don't know if you'll believe me, but Manly is insistent that we treat people with respect."

Fuck. These guys were making it harder and harder to want to destroy them. They hadn't harmed anyone on purpose, and they seemed genuinely cool.

"Sounds like a good policy to have." I gave them a genuine wry smile, my mood lifting a little despite the situation.

"It's one we all signed on for when Manly and Dawn recruited us." Bonnie gripped her hammer and lifted it easily before standing. "I'll get out of your way, Nick. Do be careful, though. This one's got some rage in him."

"Aye, aye." The dwarf waved her off, took out a little notepad, and a sheet of parchment. "What kind o' food ye be needin'?"

"Meat," I stated simply. "Lots of meat. If you have anything living, like rodents, that would do nicely."

"Manly keeps the live feed, but I'm sure she'd be willin' ta part with some." He scowled as he took notes.

"I'd be happy to pay for it," I offered, more out of respect for their coffers than anything.

"She may just go for tha'," he nodded and finished up. "Ye eat tha' an' I'll be bringin' ye some more from me personal stores until we get tha' sorted, aye? Looks like we forgot a bucket for yer, uh, business. I'll be bringing' ye one o' them too."

"Okay." I waited until he was gone and analyzed the food that was there. Meat and potatoes with what looked like some vegetables and a cold glass of milk.

I cast Purify on everything, but the base mana cost of the spell likely meant that either they hadn't touched the food, or the stuff they had used wasn't very potent.

I ate what was there swiftly and cleaned the plate with the shadows at my command. I'd be working with them as well, as there was no sense in wasting time.

I focused on shaping the shadows around me until Nick came back. Weird name for a dwarf, if you asked me. Must be a hill dwarf kind of thing.

"Alright. I've got ye a bucket, and some more food. Fare earlier was shite, but this ought ta be good, eh?" He smiled and approached the cage, then frowned as he eyed me, seriously. "I open this here door, ye stay put, aye? I do nae wanna tussle with ye, lad. Ye seem a good sort, but I'll be defendin' meself if'n I has ta."

"I'll stay still." I nodded and folded my legs beneath me. From the looks of him, I'd say that I'd have a bit of a hard time in a straight fight, given his level was equal to the mages from earlier. The silver on the bars wouldn't help me, either.

He took me at my word and opened the door to the cell by flicking his wrist and motioning something I couldn't quite make out, then a small *shink*, and the door was open.

Nick took the bucket and set it inside, I nodded my head. "Thank you." Then he set the other food and a bag with blood on the bottom on the floor, just inside the cage out of the way of the door.

My eyes widened a bit at the blood, but he shut the door and explained as he did so, "Tha' be the meat I promised. Figured if it were fer a wee beastie, getting' 'em used ta blood would be a good idea, nutritious fer 'em."

"That's very thoughtful of you." I smiled at his tone and had to laugh. "So it was all true, right? Being raised with druids?"

He thumped his armored chest. "Aye. Proud o' me people, I be."

"Well then, as promised, I'll introduce you to Bea." He

looked to be extremely interested in seeing her. "Uh, just let me eat this food first."

He nodded enthusiastically as he pulled a long pipe out of his inventory and packed it full of tobacco while I cast Purify over it. I turned my eyes up to see him looking at me with knowing eyes, but he paid me no mind.

I ate quickly and deposited the treats into my inventory before releasing Bea, again.

She burst into a run as soon as she was out and looked for food, eyes landing on the blood on the floor. She bolted straight at it, lapping it off the floor greedily.

I called her attention to me, but Nick spoke first, "Wow! What is she?"

He leaned closer to the cage and eyed her with apparent wonder in his eyes.

"She's a gust raptor hatchling." I pulled out a piece of meat, and her attention was instantly on me. She sprinted at me, but I put a hand out to stop her, she skidded to a halt, tapping my hand with her nose excitedly.

Damn, she was so cute.

"She be a real cute one," Nick muttered with awe, he smiled around the mouthpiece to his pipe as smoke filtered out of it.

"You want to give her a treat?" I offered him a slice of the meat.

He waved it away with a shake of his head. "Do nae wanna harm her, lad. I appreciate the offer."

"I'm not worried about you." I smiled at him and threw the meat in my hand toward the dwarf. He snatched it out of the air, and Bea's attention was on him and him alone. Well, really the meat in his hand.

She eyed me when I attempted to get her attention mentally, turned her head toward him, then back to the meat. Her questioning thoughts brushed mine, and I pointed toward Nick, *You be easy, and he will feed you that. Do not bite him.*

She ran full tilt toward the cage and smacked into it with a thump that made me groan. She was stunned, laying on the ground frozen, blinking dazedly, so I cast Regrowth on her to help out.

Nick was standing above her with concern on his features. "Oh no! Ye a'right, lassie?"

She shook her head and tried to climb to her feet. The process was slow, but she did it.

"I'm going to coach you through this, okay?" I told Nick, and he listened intently. "Follow my instructions, and you can learn to be gentle with animals."

"A'right." He looked to be concentrating as he stared intently at Bea.

"First thing, is relax," I spoke softly, so that Bea would relax, too. "Animals can sense when you're tense, and that makes them tense. It's a predator-prey kind of thing."

I watched as he took two deep, calming breaths, and his body visibly relaxed.

I smiled and slid closer, at least as close as the silver would comfortably allow me, "Excellent. Now, take the back of your hand and slowly present it to her so that she can get your scent. This is important for her comfort and for her to be able to identify you by your scent."

He did as he was told and slowly offered her the back of his hand. I sent her an order to sniff him, *just* to sniff him.

She did so, but her eyes were still on the meat in his other hand.

"Okay, now, show her the meat, and before you give it to her..." I raised my voice slightly, changing the pitch to a lighter and more playful tone. "Reward her with a praising voice like this, and say something like, 'good girl,' okay?"

He blinked at me, the absurdity of my behavior clear on his face. I raised my eyebrows and pointed to her, Bea's eyes on the meat, her mouth open and reaching but being stopped by the bars.

Her nostrils flared and he did too, so he cleared his throat and adopted a funny praise voice, "Tha's a good lass!" He brought the meat over in his hand and flashed it in front of her, the blood of it dripping slightly onto the floor. He offered it to her. "Easy now, there's a good lass."

I commanded her to take the meat gently, and she wasn't sure how to do that, so I showed her a memory of Kayda gingerly taking food scraps from my hand, and some of the boys as well.

She thought it tame, beneath her, but she did it anyway after I growled at her through our connection.

She stuck her snout out of the bars and gently snatched the meat from his fingertips without biting him.

"Well done!" I clapped, and Bea's tail swatted the air behind her. She chirruped happily, a slight barking sound to it, and pranced around the cage.

"That were remarkable!" Nick clapped his hands and leaned back, obviously delighted. "Reckon I'll be bringin' her a mess o' food ta be her friend, the wee beastie."

"She would appreciate that, and so would I." I chuckled. "You know, I believe you guys don't mean any harm by this. And I appreciate you being so forthcoming. If there's anything I can do to make this all a bit easier, I'd be happy to help."

"Mighty kind o' ye, master Zeke." He nodded and winked as he took a puff of his forgotten pipe. "We'll be keepin' yer kindness in mind, do nae fret, but we're professionals, lad. Been at this game for quite some time."

I nodded, a little deflated, but Nick rapped the bars softly. "Ye mind if I work with ye, though? With the bein' gentle with the animals? Never had one nae bite me afore. Were nice."

I had to laugh. "Yeah. You come on in here, and I'll help you learn. If Manly will let us borrow some of her animals, I can help you even more."

"I'll talk ta her this eve, thank ye!" He hurried out of the room; the tray of food forgotten and left me to feed Bea. She was happy to eat some more and then nap in my lap as if it were her nest. For a while, it would be.

At regulated times, Nick would return with food and light conversation, then disappear for a while until the next meal.

The food was good, and I purified it all. It didn't matter that they seemed cool—I wasn't going to just give up on testing to be safe.

That night, I slept alright. Bea out with me for company as she snored noisily next to my face.

CHAPTER SEVEN

Shortly after my agreement with Nick, Manly brought Kayda into the room with me, chained to the wall where she could get to me, but not close enough to try and get to the door. The next couple of days were spent in a similar pattern as the first. In the mornings, I would do push-ups and sit-ups so that I wasn't losing too much of an edge physically. After that, it was meditation and spell creation. I had managed to blend fire and shadow together to create some interesting attack spells.

Black Flame – Caster ignites the target's shadow and burns them for a small amount of damage over time. Range: Touch. Cost: 123 MP. Duration: 15 seconds. Cooldown: 30 seconds.

Nether Implosion – Cast a ball of pure void energy at enemies that expands to a 60-foot radius, then implodes on impact. Range: 120 feet. Cost: 150 MP. Cooldown: 1 minute.

After that, I would work with Manly and Nick in trying to get the fighter to be less of a brute with animals. It was slow going at times, and he was a little thick when it came to larger beasts. But he was learning, and that was what was important.

"No, no!" I corrected as the ham-handed dwarf went to pick up a stubborn weasel. "You have to respect the animals as much as they have to respect you. There are times a heavy hand will work for you, but that's only if you have the rapport built up and sparingly. Offer him some kindness and a treat with a soft and reassuring tone. Go."

Nick took a steadying breath and reached out with his palm down, I'd taught him that earlier on as well with smaller animals. Bea was one thing, but a lot of other smaller animals felt the same way.

"Come now, wee fella," Nick tittered at the weasel from a foot or so away. "I got ye a nice wee snack here, an' I be meanin' ye no harm, aye?"

The weasel glanced up, then at me, uncertainty in his eyes, and I shrugged. I had promised not to interfere with my druidic abilities so that Nick could learn properly. He snuck forward a bit as Nick smiled and reassured him sweetly until, finally, he'd heard enough and bolted up onto the shocked dwarf's shoulder and chittered crazily until his treat came.

"Well, ain't that somethin'?" Manly clapped with a grin on her face. "That was some right nice animal handlin' there, Nick! Soon enough, I may be able to leave some of the critters to your care."

I laughed at his shocked expression, and we carried on the lesson for a little longer, then I would be left to my own devices until mealtimes. Bonnie stopped in rarely, I think it was because I was a little less entertaining than the others, but she did stop in to say hi and see if she could tease me a bit. It was harmless, and the company appreciated at times.

It was the third day, and right now was my "free time." Cramped as it was, I could actually sleep without fear of the nightmares in here. I wasn't sure if it was the extraplanar area, but I was grateful for it.

I was currently working on another new spell incorporating my shadow magic.

I was busy taking the base of my Heal spell and trying

something with my Regrowth spell as well as adding shadow around both, like a cool blanket, building them up. Mana siphoned from my pool at a rapid pace, then began to dip into Mage's Well.

My heart began to pound rapidly as I began to tighten the tendrils of darkness tighter around the two ideals to give them shape and form as one. I pushed the doubt eating at my nerves aside as I felt the spell form. 1,497 MP later, I had an interesting new spell.

Void's Respite – Temporarily heals a single target for 60 HP until that amount of HP is healed. Then if the target is in shadow or darkness, they regenerate 6 HP per second for a short time. Duration: 30 seconds. Cost: 83 MP. Range: 60 feet. Cooldown: 30 seconds.

Warning: If HP is not recovered fully before the duration of the spell ends, the target loses that temporary HP regardless of how much they have. Be careful.

I had heard about abilities like this before in games at home, but I'd never seen one, here. That was interesting as hell. I was curious to try it out on someone. If I used it in conjunction with Heal, or even Renewing Flames, it would be well within the time limit, and they would be fine. And the added regeneration if we were in shadow and darkness?

Hello, nighttime heals!

I couldn't help the smile on my face despite the mana headache I had. The figure who walked through the door to my compartment in the cart made my smile fade a little.

I hadn't seen her before, and she looked like she was the serious type.

Her armor was silver, with a tree and moon-shaped crest embossed on the front, silhouetted against a field of stars over her lithe, kitsune figure. I had seen other kitsune in the Fae realm, but not here. It was interesting.

Her fur was auburn in color, with white that ran from the base of her throat down to meet her armor and slide below. Her eyes were hazel, her features no less vulpine than my own, but she only had one tail.

"Well met, Zekiel Erebos," she spoke softly, and I recognized the voice as the one they called Dawn.

"Well met, Dawn," I returned, and eyed her as she crossed the room to stand before my cage.

"We have not yet had the pleasure of speaking, and you know my name? I am Dawnstar of Simioln." She took the stool behind her and moved it easily to the front of the cage where she could sit and see me at eye level. "Though my companions state that you and your friends are a force for good, they have yet to be able to provide any evidence of this to me."

"I don't see why we should have to, considering that we've been hunted down like common criminals for a crime we didn't knowingly commit," I grumped, and she just stared at me. "So, what is it that I can do for you?"

"It is what I can do for *you*, master Erebos, that brings me here today." She finally blinked and noticed me staring at the symbol on her chest once more. "This is my goddess's banner, her name is Seraestar, goddess of cosmos and magic, and it is she whom we owe our spell-craft and abilities where magic is concerned."

File that away for later. Out loud, I asked, "and I take it that you wearing her banner means that you are something of a cleric or paladin of hers?"

She nodded her head once, not speaking, but smiling in affirmation. "Back to my original statement, I am here to assist you and your friends, if you would allow me."

"How, exactly, do you plan to do so?" It was difficult to hold back my anger. Helping us would have been leaving us the hell alone.

"I have a spell that will force you to tell the truth, anyone within the radius of it really, and you can use it to confirm your story," she looked like she had more to say, so I stayed quiet. "But that means you will not be able to lie. Obviously."

I blinked, more than a little confused. "Isn't that the point of a truth spell?"

"It is, but there is nothing that you can hide from this spell." She seemed concerned, her features drawn.

Then it dawned on me—no the pun wasn't intended—. "You know."

She nodded once. "I know. My Lady told me that our saviors had come to being in our realms."

I couldn't contain my excitement. "Then you know that we're here for a reason! That this is a waste of time, and that we're innocent."

Her composure slipped, anger bursting forth. "Do you not think I know that? The laws are what they are for a reason! I am *bound* by my oath to my goddess to see that justice is done in all ways that I can see it be done. I cannot turn a blind eye, even if the gods favor you." She growled to herself and reigned her emotions back in. "We are taking you there to prove your innocence if that is the case. My offering this service is to help you in providing evidence! There is nothing more I can do aside from that."

I'd be lying if I said I wasn't salty, but it was necessary. She was bound by her oath. And they needed to flee before Maebe got here. Word or not, she would likely kill them for sending her home without her say.

That sent a shiver down my spine, I would hate to be them.

"Thank you. If that's all you can do, then so be it." I sighed. "I appreciate it."

"You are welcome." She held her head higher. "Your companions say that it was you that this Pharazulla chose to mind control into doing her bidding?"

"It was," I answered honestly.

"We are a few hours outside the city," her lids closed, and she muttered a few words, with accompanying gestures. "I have cast the spell, neither of us can lie to each other, now. I cannot use it again for two hours. Let us begin."

"How can I be sure you're telling me the truth?"

"I don't care enough to tell you a lie, not that I would, anyway." She blinked and smiled sweetly.

"Alright, I get that the truth hurts, but damn, no need for the hostility." I grumbled. "Fine. Ask what you will, but I'm going to ask you some things, too."

"Good." She steepled her fingers before her. "Where are you from?"

I fought to say Sunrise Village, but I opened my mouth and couldn't, the air was sucked from my lungs. "You are learning that not even misdirections will work in this zone. Fae truths will do you no good here."

I growled; my voice having returned. "Fine. I'm from Earth. Where are you from?"

"None of your concern." She smiled sweetly, "I've already told you. It's not my fault if you don't remember."

I gasped. "How is it that you could dodge the question, and I couldn't?"

"I've told you where I was from, and you do not have to answer the questions presented to you. Misdirection will not work, but you do not need to speak if you do not want to." Her smile grew ever larger. "For now, let us dispense with that. It is imperative that you know your mind before we go to your trial. Were you truly ensorcelled and made to attack those men outside of your own free will?"

I blinked, damn. She was getting right into it. "Yes, Pharazulla cast some kind of spell over me that made me attack those men and my friends." I closed my eyes as I searched myself. "But with the way it was done, it was as if I *wanted* to do those things for her."

"Why?" She cocked her head to the side.

"I don't know." I would have said because of the spell, but the one with influence over me now wouldn't allow me. "I had been so used to people seeking us out and attacking us, hurting the people that I cared for, that I had assumed that these men would have done the same. If I had truly thought that they meant us harm, I would feel no guilt about destroying them.

But her spell took that reasoning from me, and I know for damn sure I would never attack my friends in cold blood like that."

She frowned deeply. "That could be taken many ways in a trial. I would be careful how you answer those questions."

"How? You literally made it so that I can't lie or tell half-truths." It was harder to deal with my anger at having to confront the fact that I had become so callous that I could kill someone for doing their damned jobs. Spell or not, if I were to look in the mirror at that moment, I would see a monster.

"You did not need to add all of that. You explained it to me, you found the heart of it, now you can use that. It is not a lie or half-truth to say, 'I thought they could mean us harm, and her interference stole my judgment' it is the truth. The rest was calculated and unneeded."

"Fine." I growled. "Why are you with these people?"

"I like them, and they have a worthy mission for one as blessed as I." She stated matter-of-factly. "Why were you helping Pharazulla?"

"We weren't. She was helping us. We went to her to seek bardic training for a friend, and when she originally refused, we were going to move on." I frowned. "Then the next day, she shows up to help, and we accepted her with open arms."

"Without suspicion?"

"No." I shook my head, still frowning. "I suspected she was on the run from something or someone because someone had been trying to kill her in her room the night when we first spoke to her. I had assumed it was a jilted lover, I think, but the exact reasoning escapes me."

She smiled and clapped her hands. "Very good! Using deductive reasoning helps as well, and the killer thing, leave that, too."

And on we went for half an hour before she left me with a bow and not another word.

Nick brought in one more good meal, with nary a word as well, and I was left to my own devices.

Time to buck up and see what was going to go with the Governess.

When we arrived at the location where we were to stop, Manly came and collected us one by one. Bokaj, Jaken, and James had been brought out before me. As I walked into the open air for the first time in days, I truly appreciated how beautiful and magical this environment was, even with the stench of Lindyburg around it. I had taken my human form, Dawn as well it seemed, her long auburn hair tied into a tight bun. Her features seemed decidedly stern for a human, but that was likely for a cleric. Or was she a paladin? I still didn't know.

The city hadn't changed much since we had last been here, the high wall of the Governess's home protected by guards who looked even more active today. More than a score of them stood lining the pathway inside as if begging us to fuck about and do something wrong. They weren't close enough for me to see their levels, but that was fine.

I'd wager they weren't all that high anyway.

The moat around the wall had since been added to; wooden, metal-capped spikes randomly placed around the place. The wall was covered in murals of roses and flowers, but some of the flowers looked a bit like skulls. This was not how I remembered it. Shit was about to get weird.

The others were brought out one by one as well, and none of us had manacles on, much to the lead guard's chagrin.

"These prisoners should be bound." He grimaced at Manly as if she were garbage, she just eyed him stoically back.

Kayda had fluttered out and landed on my shoulder, she had been fine, as Nick had said, and she was looking a little plumper in her parrot-sized form.

We all still cool with these guys? Everyone okay? I asked the others.

Yohsuke responded first. *Nick's cooking was pretty good. We even traded recipes. The poor bastard ain't getting my famous jambalaya recipe, though.*

They treated me well, Nick even took a shine to Tmont while we were holed up. Bokaj stretched, and some of the guards put their hands on their weapons as a precaution. *Although, Bonnie kicked the shit out of me at cards. Lost about fifty gold to her. Fucking crazy.*

The others looked to be alright, though not as talkative, except Jaken, who spoke out loud, "Thanks, Manly. I know that you guys are good folks. Let's get this over with."

Manly, who had been about to tear into the guard in front of her, her face an angry mask flipped a switch. "See? They ain't gonna run, no way. Shut your gob and take us to the Governess. Now."

That last bit had been a barked order as the others in the group gathered around us.

It was Bonnie, scantily clad and bubbly, Nicolas, tired and irritated, Manly at the fore guiding us and Dawn and Nick in the rear.

As we walked through the guards, their contempt became even more evident.

Guard Lvl 15

Guard Lvl 16

These guards weren't the highest level, I didn't think, which likely meant that the governess would have the best around her.

Once over the actual moat itself and into the walls, the yard was immaculately cared for, with trees and shrubs of all sorts inside. More guards were stationed in the inner walls, and as we walked through, they hissed and booed openly.

"They really don't seem to like you guys," Muu observed aloud with a dispassionate glance at the rest of us.

"Us?" Balmur eyed him uncertainly. "I wasn't even there, why not you, too?"

Muu grinned. "Because, bitch, I'm adorable." He flicked his hand over his shoulder, tossing his hair, and the rest of us laughed. Bonnie snorted, and Nick chuckled openly.

"Professionalism, you two, if you would," Dawn's clipped

tone bit at Bonnie and Nick, but as I looked over my shoulder at her, she too had a smile on her lips.

We walked into this small castle of a building, entering through the front door and going through a long hallway covered in portraits of what I took to be a long line of governors. Men and women of all ages in various modes of dress.

The hall was nice, and a maroon carpet led us into a long ballroom with guards lined up along the wall. The closer we came to the platform at the end, more of them had their weapons bared.

"We have come to deliver our bounties, ma'am," Manly announced proudly. "The Braves o' the Thorn always get their marks."

I snorted and Nick smacked my arm lightly. "I suggested tha', lad. Show some respect, aye?"

"Sorry, Nick," I grumbled in return.

A figure stood from a chair behind the platform, a rotund woman with a severe face, beady eyes, and a formidable group of chins. Her clothes were black, like funeral garb, and her face angry.

"You seem to be awfully chummy with criminals," she observed, her voice deep and attempting to sound more authoritative.

Side point, lemme explain. You ever meet one of those people who somehow ends up being in charge, and you can just *see* it going to their head? Then, when they talk, they have to constantly try and remind everyone that they're better?

Yeah this was her. Back to the show!

"These are good people, Governess Belltree, and I think that you will find that their innocence is evident and their involvement circumstantial," Dawn strode forward to stand next to Manly as she spoke. "They have been nothing but honorable, and as a humble servant of—"

A large bag of coins smacked onto the floor in front of them.

The woman, I assumed she was the Governess, raised a

dismissive hand. "Your presence is no longer required. You may leave."

Dawn growled softly, and Manly put a hand on the other woman's hip before speaking, "Thank ya for yer patronage. We would be delighted to stay and offer our assistance with the dispensation of justice. It is, after all, what my friend here was about to offer as a humble servant of Seraestar."

"If you wish to bear witness, so be it. You may step aside." She waved them aside and the group left us. "The trial of the accused begins now; all of you are accused of aiding a known criminal in evasion of the authority of this city, murder, obstruction, evasion, and use of *magic*."

That last was hissed, and the guards around us growled like savage dogs.

"How do the accused plead?" She raised her chins as if daring us to defy her.

"Not guilty, your honor." Bokaj stepped forward with his hands to his sides, showing her his palms. "If you would allow us, we can explain everything."

"How do I know that you will speak the truth?" She tilted her head sarcastically, almost as if it had been planned.

"I can provide the truth, your ladyship." Dawn strode forward once more. "With the use of a simple ability that my goddess has allowed me, I can force people to speak the truth."

I was worried then about the others, *you guys gonna be okay with this?*

She did the same thing with all of us, we're ready, Jaken answered, *she's thinking, pay attention.*

"Magic is not welcome here," the governess growled.

"It is not *magic*; it is divine providence." Dawn lifted her chin in return.

"My providence is the only one that matters here." The larger woman spat before turning her glare back at us. "Speak, or I will pass judgment."

"We didn't know that she had done anything wrong when she approached us as we were leaving." Bokaj hurried to fill her in. "When we had gone to her to request that she train me in the ways of the bard, we found someone had been about to kill her in her room. When she came to us the next day, we had assumed she was fleeing someone trying to kill her."

"And when my brothers came to seek her out for justice?" Shouted a guard who stepped out of the line to our left, he looked young and untested.

"Silence!" Belltree howled, and the guard looked cowed. "I am asking the questions!" Her glare turned to us. "Who was it who cast the spell that slew my guards."

"Pharazulla." I stepped forward, my friends trying to stop me, but I shoved them aside. "She used her magic to take away my reasoning and caused those men to die!"

"I was unaware that she had the capability to use fire magic, and through someone else's hand, Killian!" She barked, and another guard, older and more trained, stepped forward and knelt at her side. "Tell the court what it was that you saw."

"I watched from a distance as our suspect whispered something to the man there, who is a kitsune, and he then cast some sort of fire spell that killed our men. Then she gave him a command, and he attacked the others and another known subject to this court, Zhavron. I made my escape before they had the chance to kill me, as well."

The large woman tapped him comfortingly on the shoulder, and he visibly cringed.

"Is this true?" She allowed her voice to sound almost sweet.

"Yes, but as I had said, her magic robbed me of my reasoning and made me cast that spell, and then she made me attack my brothers," I reasoned. The others stepped closer to me in solidarity.

"Magic among us is a great sin, and what she stole from me is more precious than anything." Tears of rage gathered in her eyes. "You helped her escape. You killed my guard. You allowed her to escape you. You are all useless. And you are all *guilty.*"

"That's bullshit, and you know it!" Muu shouted, and the guards stepped forward.

"You had no intention of seeing justice done here this day!" Dawn's voice rang out over the din of the armored guard surrounding us. "You only wanted to punish someone for your failings! Didn't you?"

A small tingle ran along my skin, like ants crawling all over me, and then it was gone.

Governess Belltree rose up on her feet and tottered forward, her massive body now fully visible, and she growled victoriously. "I have no intention of allowing magic users to go free, and someone must pay for the crimes against me!" Confused for a moment, she stared blankly at us, her jowls shaking.

"You had no intention of letting them go if they proved their innocence, did you?" Manly asked, stepping closer to the guards who now stood between everyone and the platform.

"Never!" Spittle flew from her great maw as she laughed evilly. "I will rid this world of them, and their cursed magic. The only justice they will know is *death*."

Get ready for a brawl boys, Balmur warned. *They're moving on us from the rear.*

"Braves of the Thorn!" Dawn roared, all motion ceased. Her fist was raised high above her head, "To me! To see justice done!"

Nick's eyes rolled, and Bonnie began to laugh and move about.

"Seize them all!"

The fight was on.

Move toward the door, Yohsuke ordered.

The governess was still shrieking on her podium. *Someone shut her the hell up!* Bokaj growled.

Want me to kill her? Balmur asked sweetly.

"No!" I shouted out loud, before thinking. *If we kill her, then we're no better than she is. No better than the minions and generals of War.*

Fine. She can live. Balmur grumbled as he began to sweep his daggers over kneecaps and thighs.

Better try not to kill any of the guards to keep things safe, Jaken advised.

Manly had ducked under a guard that I push-kicked away from me and grinned at us. "Well boys, reckon we're in for it."

"Yeah." Bokaj grunted and fired an arrow into the guards that had gotten ballsy enough to group together and move on us.

"Let's get back to the cart then." I grunted as I socked a guard in the nose and tripped him on his way back. "I can probably get us out of here."

"Works fo' me!" Nick called as he took the brunt end of a wooden spear and smacked guards in the face as if it were a machine gun. "This is the exercise I been needin'!"

A crowd of guards shouted lewd comments, "Demon bitch." Bonnie threw two guards into the air and her hammer rocketed toward them.

"Don't kill 'em, Bon!" Manly called, as she shot arrows into people's legs and arms with sniper-like accuracy. "Reckon y'all can keep up?"

I grinned at the challenge, and we worked our way toward the doors with Jaken and Muu taking the front. The Braves moved through the guards like wrecking balls, except for Nicolas, who seemed content to join us and freeze the occasional person solid.

"Do you see how I move my hands in this manner, Balmur? The motions are very important to wizards," the human smiled as he gave his lesson.

Balmur, more than a foot away and weaving through projectiles and short swords, snorted. "Do I look like I have time to pay attention"—he ducked under a sword and jabbed his blade into the guard's foot—"to your hands?"

"Yes." He blinked, nonplussed, "combat is an excellent place to learn."

Muu laughed, and I had to admit, it was funny. One guard got too close, and I decided it was time to let loose.

I took my ursolon form and used Predator's Call. The guards in front of us froze in fright, several more backing away from me.

"That's a scary lookin' bear," Manly commented as she slammed her knee into one of the female guards' junk, her cry of pain turning into a gasp.

I used the backs of my paws to swipe the frozen guards out of our way, and we were into the hallway in seconds.

I charged the guards in front of us with Muu and Jaken covering our exit, and they fled full tilt, knocking into each other in their hurry to escape the gigantic beast pursuing them.

I immediately took two spears to my shoulders as I cleared the doorway and roared, my health falling by 14% total.

Guards Lvl 23

That explained the damage I'd taken, the metal digging into the bones of my shoulders painfully as I roared my displeasure.

Muu took his hammer and bashed the guard on my right in the stomach and sent him careening into a group behind him. He reached back, yanking the spear from my body, and threw it so that it pierced the wall next to an archer's head and stayed there. I lost another percentage of HP but was alright.

The other guard twisted his spear with a roar, 20 HP drained from my health bar, and he called, "Kill this thing!"

"Not a nice thing to say at all!" Bonnie took her hammer and cracked him in the head, his body crumpling and the spear breaking. I shifted, the weapon still hanging from my fox-man arm, grating the bone.

"Thanks," I grunted and yanked the weapon from my arm, casting Renewing Flames on myself. My HP climbed slowly, and the wound started to knit back together.

"Oh, happy to help a big teddy bear." Bonnie beamed, and Balmur was there just in time to swipe a spear out of the air behind her. "Better get to the cart."

Fighting our way there was intense, and since I needed to conserve mana to get us out of there, spells weren't the best idea, so Magus Bane got to come out and play. I used the less deadly, if only marginally, hammer side of the weapon to bat some of the guard's legs from beneath them as arrows rained down around us. Jaken popped over toward me as a volley would have caught me in the shoulder and deflected them with his shield, an excited grin on his face.

"Hurry it up!" He called and sprinted forward between two fallen guards, then broke right to save a man that had fallen due to friendly fire. He had heard something and rushed off back behind me, but I had to beat down another spear-wielding guard to keep from being gored.

The majority of us were at the cart in seconds, Jaken lagging behind with Dawn in his grasp as she refused to leave many grievously injured behind since we wouldn't be killing them.

When we were all there, I took count. Our seven, wait, it was nine with Tmont and Kayda, and their five put us at fourteen people. Good. I was good.

"I'm going to teleport us, so hold onto each other and the cart!" The others grasped hands, shoulders, and the wood of the cart before I picked the location of our teleportation and loosed the spell. The world around us lurched, and I felt a sharp sensation of agony in my abdomen. I grunted and gritted my teeth as we landed in the cave we had been in three days ago.

The lance shaft in my stomach still vibrated, and I staggered.

"That's some fine spellwork master Ze—that's a spear!" Nicolas gasped. "Oh, that's no good. Dawn! We've got a bleeder."

Here in the cool darkness of the cave we had been captured in, I took my metallic hand and broke the shaft protruding from my stomach before I slid it slowly out of the wound from my back.

Muu was kind enough to give me a thick piece of leather to bite down on as Jaken, Dawn, and I cast multiple healing spells on me. The agony receded, and I was able to think again.

"Thank you." I sighed and put my hand over where the hole had been.

"No problem." Manly grinned, then looked bashful. "Oh! You meant the healin'!"

"Thanks for standing up to her with us as well." Jaken offered the small woman his hand, and she took it. "We would've been in a tighter spot, I think."

"Nah, ye would've been fine." Nick chortled. "Those guards were but sacks o' grain. Were only so hard cause we weren't tryin' ta kill 'em!"

"Even more cause for justice to be done," Dawn spoke, and all of us turned to look at her, her gaze burning. "The crown must hear of her wrongdoings. Manly, we must do the right thing."

"Aye." Manly sighed heavily. "She was mighty rude, too, I reckon. Plus, ain't right to be afeared o' magic. Not at all. But do we really need to go all the way to the capital?"

Dawn gazed at her and said nothing, but the other woman knew. "Alright then, to the capital it is! Only noon now, if we travel swiftly, we can be to the capital in…three days."

She hesitated, and eyed us nervously, meaning she was worried about Maebe. She should be worried. But, I figured I would help them.

"I'll talk to her." I offered, holding a hand out to stop anyone interrupting. "She is a queen, first and foremost. Her word once given is law, and I've never known her to break it. We will speak about it."

"Good idea, but I don't think moving this evening is a good idea," Yohsuke advised as he looked around us. "Not that they would be anything more than a nuisance, but they'll have search parties out, most likely, and other bounty hunters like yourselves. We should bunker down and plan for now."

"Sounds good to me." Bonnie yawned lazily. "That was a good little stretch, but I'm hungry and a little tired."

She walked toward the rear of the cart and peeked out at us. "Wake me for dinner?"

Manly held up a hand as affirmation, and Bonnie scampered off.

I left the others and walked to a thickly shadowed section of the rock outside and activated Shadow Speak.

Maebe's form became immediately visible, and she crossed over to me to look me over.

"Where have you been?" She asked, the emotion thick in her voice. "It has been hours here, and I did not know if you were alive or dead. I tried to contact you, but it didn't work. I thought you were dead so many times."

"It's okay, Mae." I hushed her softly and touched the shadows with my hand. I had been working with them so much it was almost a physical thing. "Things have been happening, and I was somewhere I couldn't use communication magic."

"I will kill those traitors!" She seethed, her features screwing up in anger, her fists clenched. "They sent me here against my will, how *dare* they. When I find them, I will tear out their hearts and freeze them as I should have—"

"No, you won't," I interrupted her, and she looked at me harshly. "They were doing their jobs, and they didn't hurt any of us on purpose. They're bounty hunters who had taken the bounty before they knew us. They've treated us with respect and dignity, and they just helped us get away from the governess who wanted us dead. They're on the run now, too."

"Why would they do such a thing?" She seemed confused but didn't automatically come at me with questions or accusations. I liked that.

"They're good people, and they have a code that they follow. Once they learned that we were truly innocent, they offered to help us clear our names." I turned to ensure we were truly alone, we were. "I wanted to kill them too, but they proved they meant no harm when the governess tried to have us killed after finding out it was because of Pharazulla that I killed those men. She wants to do away with magic completely, and she's going to kill people to do it."

"What will you do, now?" She put a shadowed hand on my cheek, the coolness of it grounding me more than I thought I had needed.

"We're going to hole up here for the night, then go to the capital to report her, and try to get permission to get into the dungeon, I think." I blinked at her. "The entry is in the mountains somewhere, but if we try to go in without permission, we would just be attacked by unknown odds. How about you? How has home been?"

"It has been home. I have been trying to reach you since I got here. The time limit of the spell they used is waning, and soon I will be able to return to you all." She frowned, then sighed. "And I will have no choice but to allow this to pass. For now. But if they ever cross me again, I will kill them all. You have my word."

I blinked at the notification that I received that showed her vow and nodded. "Okay. I'll be sure to let them know."

"You do that." She growled, her shadowy figure stepping closer to me. "I am glad that you are safe and unharmed. I love you. I will come to you soon."

She brought her lips against mine and dissipated against me with what sounded like a sigh. My lips still tingled a little where the shadow had touched.

I returned to the others and passed on the news. The Braves outside the cart were relieved that they were safe, unworried about crossing her or us in the future. Then we plotted.

"It'll take about three days to get to the capital at a good clip, and now that the lot of you know about all of us, there's no need to travel slow." Manly winked as the two chefs compared notes over the cooking fire.

Balmur was off with Nicolas discussing magic and who the hell knows what, while the rest of us planned.

Dawn was meditating, and the others were preoccupied with dinner, so I was with Manly, Muu, James, and Jaken.

"Well, since you guys know we're cool, and we know that you're cool, why not see about having Zeke acquire the animal forms of those that you have in your possession?" James asked Manly.

She frowned. "That don't hurt 'em, does it?"

I shook my head, but it was Muu who answered for me, "I've seen it hurt him, when they bite him."

"Did Ulla bite you?" She seemed concerned, but I just laughed.

"No. I got her form from holding her while she ate, which you should try sometime, she seemed to really enjoy it." I stretched but pursued the thought. "It would be really helpful to acquire a few new forms. Or at least one more."

Manly eyed me knowingly. "You want Frederick's?"

"Yes, ma'am." I grinned happily.

She frowned. "Only if he agrees, and I'll see you pay for it too!"

Ever the shrewd businesswoman. I grunted.

"Manly, money is not important in this." Dawn groaned as she opened her eyes and blinked at the halfling woman.

"It may not be to you, but it is to me. He eats a lot, and I need to feed him." She reasoned with a shrug as if she couldn't help it.

"I'll give you a hundred gold for it."

Dawn gasped, and Nick sputtered as Yoh whipped the food away from his face.

"Deal!" Manly held her hand out, and I shook it.

"Why on earth would you pay so much to have that form?" Dawn wondered at me.

"Because it's worth it." I shrugged, trying to decide how to continue. "Manly may be shrewd with her coin and have an eye for business, but I know animals. His abilities would suit the party well. A small price to pay for an advantage."

I gave her the hundred gold, and she went to call for the Terran gorilla. He stomped out of the cart and eyed all of us as he passed everyone.

He stopped at Muu and touched his armor and snorted before beating his hands on the ground. Muu smiled in return. "Good to see you, too, Freddy."

"He is fun to play with." Fred sniffed a bit and scratched his ass.

"When did you play with him?" I narrowed my eyes, slightly confused.

"I roam where I want in the cart, I found his cage, and we played many games." He pointed at Muu, then made a funny face by crossing his eyes and puffing his cheeks out. Muu tried to do the same thing and failed miserably.

Frederick laughed, his grunts and excited motions making Muu laugh too. "Take it he's telling you about our games? He fucking cheats, man."

I ignored the only slightly indignant dragon-kin and looked to Frederick. "I wanted to see about taking your form, see, I'm a druid, and that's a thing I can do."

He came over and looked closely at me. "If I do this thing, will you play with me, too?"

I nodded, and he threw his arms into the air and spinning in celebration before looking back at me. "What do you need?"

"To touch you for a couple minutes or to fight you—oof!" He clocked me right in my solar plexus and laid me out flat.

The others were moving instantly, and I held a hand up so I could wheeze, "It's okay, it's cool. We're playing. Ouch."

"Don't hurt him, but it's okay to play rough," Manly sounded genuinely worried, but I couldn't tell if she was talking to the gorilla or me.

I sat up, and Frederick offered me a hand up. I took it, and he launched me into the air behind him. As I flew ass over teakettle, I shifted into my owl form and banked hard so I wouldn't hit the wall.

I dropped toward the ground as the sound of scuffling feet came my direction and shifted to fox-form and bolted underneath Frederick as he leapt at me. He hit the ground, and rolled, but I was already up and in my fox-man form to box with him.

We punched at each other for more than a minute, both of us getting winded and me having to dodge in and out of his range as he came at me.

Finally, I ducked one punch and took another to the gut, and he tossed me with it. I skidded back and growled as I stepped forward, the rumbling low in my throat.

I had the form by now, so why not use it?

I shifted and my body grew until I stared back at the gorilla before me, his face twisting in joy, then play as he galloped forward.

We clashed with an audible smack and much grunting as each of us sought to get a headlock.

A rumbling voice reached out into my mind, *backhand him, then use his arm to throw him.*

This must have been the gorilla's instincts. *He is fighting for dominance. He has yet to find someone who can lead him. Show him that you can lead.*

I grunted and took my metallic right arm and backhanded Frederick across the left side of his face. When his right arm soared into my vision, I slid so my body was facing slightly away, and hip-tossed him over my head. He landed on his back in a heap, and I beat my chest over his head before I booped his nose and skittered away laughing and whooping.

I shifted in time to see him stand. "Thanks for that."

He nodded. "That was fun, we must do it again, soon."

I walked over to him and offered him my hand and he took it in his, gingerly. Then his grip tightened, and I was airborne again.

"Goddamnit!" I cursed as I watched him hoot all the way back to the cart. I landed on my feet this time. "I'll get that little bastard."

Manly laughed out loud at the display, and we returned to waiting for dinner in companionable silence. Bokaj and Manly played a card game she had offered to teach him.

It looked simple, but I've never been one for card games outside Go Fish.

Dinner was great, and after that, we all laid down to go to sleep. The day's events having taken a toll on all of us.

Manly took watch, and James sat across from her, and the two of them spoke quietly. Kayda took her natural form and I slept against her that evening.

CHAPTER EIGHT

The next morning, I woke up to bickering. Nick and Yohsuke were arguing about what to make.

"Nah man, eggs and bacon are the way to go." Yohsuke pointed to his ingredients.

Nick pointed at his. "Biscuits 'n gravy be a good start ta anyone's day, lad."

"Boys," I grunted tiredly as I smacked my lips. "Both sound amazing. Breakfast is the most important meal of the day. So, it needs to be badass, yeah?"

The two of them scowled at me, looked down at the ingredients, then looked at each other and shrugged.

"Competition it is." Yohsuke smiled as he began breaking eggs.

"What's the prize?" Nick began to work on his own. "Loser cooks dinner?"

"Sounds good to me!" Yohsuke laughed and patted the dwarf's shoulder as the two of them worked together, then he paused and amended, "Loser cooks dinner that the winner chooses."

I snorted at the two of them and wandered outside to find a

good spot to relieve myself. I found it, did the business I needed, and then started back before an idea occurred to me.

I'm going to go for a flight and see if I can't check the trail before we get on the move, I warned the others.

Be safe, and take Kayda along too, Yohsuke advised.

I called the bird to me and had her take her parrot-sized form, and we soared into the skies. The world below us was empty for the most part, nothing of true interest so far, and as we headed east, not a damned thing came either. It was some time before we crossed a little closer to Lindyburg, and we could see that there were people leaving and fanning out in small parties. None of them seemed to be heading toward our current location.

As we watched from above, two riders galloped east in light gear. Looked like messengers. If we swooped down there and killed them now, someone from the city might see us.

Kayda, follow them, but be careful and hide sometimes, so they don't see you, I ordered.

Follow, she confirmed and took off.

I flew back to the mountain as fast as I could and found the others after shifting. "We may have problems y'all."

"What's up?" James asked as he stood from his trance-like meditation.

"Messengers from Lindyburg are headed east, and there are search parties out combing the land for us as we speak." I took a drink of water. "Kayda is following the riders."

"Good." Manly had her pipe out and puffed thoughtfully. "You saw them how long ago?"

"Hadn't kept track of time." I picked up a plate of food and began to scarf it down as fast as my Marine recruit training had taught me to.

"This is something that we can work to our advantage, maybe," Jaken mumbled, the rest of us turned our gaze to him. "Well these guys wouldn't give a missive from their leader by word of mouth, right? It's going to be some kind of written note."

My eyes narrowed at him, what was he trying to get at here?

"So, instead of trying to kill them, we get the letter and switch it to something that would support what we have to say to the king," Jaken concluded with a flourishing bow. "No one would possibly see that coming."

"That's good." Yohsuke gave him a fist bump as he bit into the biscuits and gravy. He closed his eyes and groaned. "Yeah, you win man. I got dinner."

Nick chuckled and almost spat his food out, "Ack! Forgot Bonnie!" He set his plate aside and sprinted toward the cart muttering, "She's gonna whack me good, I know she will…"

We turned our sights back toward the present, and Yohsuke took over. "So, tonight we have a stealth mission. To try and make this happen, we make sure that we get there roughly the same time and then we make sure we go see the king."

"How're y'all gonna get their copy, though?" Manly asked, she packed her bedroll tightly into a waterproof bag.

"Zeke and Balmur will fly there under cover of darkness and make the switch," James interjected.

"What if they have it in their inventory?" Dawn asked as she finished her own plate of food.

"They likely won't," James replied with a shrug. "In a lot of…scenarios I've seen in days past, messengers usually carry their message on their person so that if one of them should fall, or both of them, a passerby who finds it will see the attached note and get it to the proper recipient. Or not. But it's all we've got, so it's best just to try."

Yohsuke clapped him on the shoulder and added, "Failing that, they can make a judgment call and decide what to do from there."

That wasn't any pressure on either of us, not really. They would die easily if we deemed it so, but was that what we really wanted at this point?

Bonnie came out with a languorous stretch that left little to the imagination what kind of curves she had under the plain clothes she wore. She took her plate and began to wolf down her food with gusto.

I fed Bea and had her run beside us as we traveled to stretch her legs. To keep her near me, I had a tether of shadow attached to hers from Thor's. The Kirin was irritated because he thought that she would slow him down but was pleasantly surprised to see that not only could she match his pace, she was able to stay just ahead of him for more than an hour.

She was quite impressive.

"She's adorable," Bonnie's voice drifted over from the cart, where she sat watching Bea running. "She gonna get much bigger than that?"

"Yeah," Manly explained from her seat. "Gust raptors are large for something that's meant to be so streamlined; they're built for speed. It's really not outside the realm of possibility that she could be a faster mount than even the one you're on."

That was interesting to learn, though I had had the idea, generally, as soon as she was born. Still, nice to know.

That day we ate our lunch on the backs of our mounts. Bea tried to jump up and grab at the pieces of meat that I had been preparing to throw her. The little dickens.

While in the cart, I'd had a lot of time to spend contemplating enchantments, and there were some I wanted to try soon. Possible spell combinations I wanted to do. I was really interested to see if I could make a shadow holy blade, like a dark version of Falfyre. That would be cool.

There was nothing I could do on Thor's back, so I just rode and took in the sights. Kept tabs on the messengers through Kayda and eyed our surroundings some more.

It was an easy day, for the most part. Boring, at times. So, I spent time sharing my memories with Bea, as well. Letting her learn more about our fighting styles and how we worked together as a team. I had much more to work with, now, than I had with Kayda.

Bea was excited to try her hand at combat. She would hop

and flail her little legs as if kicking at enemies, and it was adorable.

As the sky grew dark, the others made camp while Balmur and I prepared for our stealth mission.

Then it occurred to me. "What the hell do we write? And how?"

"Oh!" Nicolas came forward and waved his hands. "I know! I have a spell designed for this very thing!"

"But Zeke can only carry one person in his collar," Balmur explained, throwing a thumb in my direction.

"Yer a druid, righ'?" Nick motioned to me from where he rested and let Yoh do the preparations for dinner. I nodded, and he shrugged. "Do ye know the spell Polymorph? Me da used it all the time to get us about quick."

"You keep your faculties while transformed?" I asked. It hadn't said anything in the spell description. Just that it changed the target's shape for half an hour.

He nodded, and I looked over to the wizard with a smile. "Welcome to the operation then, Nicolas."

"Please, call me Nic, I know it will be confusing with the two of us here, but still, it will be pleasant and easier." He patted my shoulder softly and turned to Balmur, "Short lesson before dinner? You've come a long way."

"Lesson?" Bokaj looked up, excitedly. "What lesson?"

"Magic man." Balmur grinned, his scarred visage looking a little intimidating. "When I picked up that book the other day from that wizard we put down, I unlocked a class with my high intelligence, mana use, and the proper item. I'm training to pick up wizardry."

Yohsuke, Bokaj, and I floundered, our mouths gaping.

Finally, I recovered. "But, why?"

"Yeah, man, you straight up kick and *redirect* arrows and shit as a rogue," Muu included and stood to walk closer. "You can actually move through shadows and stab anybody you want. Why?"

"Having magic was the only thing that truly kept my mind

from being completely broken." He threw his hand out and motioned with his fingers moving deftly.

A small dome of redirected light burst into existence.

"I would hide in this little dome for eight hours and sleep and watch as my tormentors, and their pets couldn't get to me." Balmur frowned. "Ever since then, I've been more than fascinated, and I've sought more magic out. Now that I'm stronger and faster, I can focus a little more on magical learning."

A heaviness settled over my heart, and I frowned, nodding. "Hey, bud. No worries. We'll help you out. Okay? Tell you what, I'll talk to Maebe and see if she will teach you shadow magic with me."

Balmur's haunted gaze lifted to my face. "I'd like that."

"Cool." Yohsuke spat, and we looked over in surprise. "Remember those vials that Archemillian had before we fought Melvaren?"

I blinked. "You knew about those?"

"Yes, you stupid bitch, me and Bokaj were the only ones who did, though." He growled at me then collected himself. "Those were vials of infected blood that Balmur had inside him from being in the Hells for so long. If we don't do something for him, he breaks them."

"So what? That just means it's wasted," James snorted. "How is that a big deal?"

"It means that when they break, that blood makes a demonic version of our friend, and that demon will seek him out to possess his true body," Yohsuke sighed audibly. "With how strong he was in the negotiation circle, think about what a demonic, emotionless killer would do to get to Balmur? Then imagine the killing spree it would go on to ensure he was strong enough to take control of his body."

Fuuuuuuuck, I groaned to myself.

"So, in having that asswipe help us get him back, he took some serious leverage to use against us," Yoh grumbled. The Braves looked confused, so he looked at them. "I can explain this over dinner. No worries. What does he want us to do?"

QUEST ALERT!

Demon's Day Out – The newly promoted arch-demon known to you as Archemillian, has tasked you with finding a demon who escaped his clutches into the Prime Realm. All he has to give you is the hint that a powerful human summoned it.

Reward: Destruction of the three vials of deeply tainted blood.

Failure: A demonic copy of a dear friend that will hunt him until one or the other is destroyed.

Do you accept? Yes? / No?

"Fucking asshole." I spat and stood to pace. "We have no goddamn choice; we can't let that thing run rampant up here. And we sure as SHIT can't put people at risk because we failed to act, *again*. We have to go to the capital and get permission to go into the damned dungeon, tattle on Belltree, somehow manage to get into the Great Below, and visit the drow to investigate them and their motives. And now we have to worry about a goddamn demon Balmur? What the fuck do we do?"

"Accept it," Jaken ordered, and we all looked at him, me, especially, after my rant. "We go on our path as we have been, and we just keep a lookout for demonic activity."

He had that whole paladin look about him, and Dawn was right there next to him with a similarly righteous cast to her stance.

"We will also keep an eye out," she stated, but Manly stopped her with a hand on her stomach.

"For a small fee, o'course." She grinned around her pipe as her animals ate behind her near the cart.

"With as much as she thinks with her purse, it's a miracle she doesn't charge a fee to talk to her." James snorted.

"I charge a consultation fee, James, don't you fret now, hear?" The halfling smiled and chuckled as he let his head fall into his hand.

"Fine, whatever." Jaken tossed her a bag of coins and

grunted, "Keep an eye out and kill it if you can. We'll even share the quest with you."

"I accepted and shared it." True to his word, another notification popped into view, and I accepted the quest.

"Let's eat and get going." I sat down and began to get what I thought I might need ready. "Kayda's getting hungry."

"Can't have that," Yohsuke mocked me, and I shot him a glare. "Shut up, you know I'm teasing."

"She will shit on you." Muu shook his head. "Twenty-foot-tall bird has to have a big-ass turd."

"Let's focus on food, aye?" Nick grunted as he lit his pipe.

An hour later, and we were ready to move toward our target. Well, almost.

Balmur grunted and growled in pain, gasping at having to sacrifice yet another eye to his magical one for the second time this week.

"Normal eyes not cutting it as much?" I grasped his shoulder, and he grimaced at the contact.

"The magic that it holds on to eats the normal eyes faster than if I use the magical one itself." His explanation came just before he wiped his face off with a rag. "Let's get going."

I took Balmur into the collar around my neck and left Bea with Manly and my friends to chill.

"You ready, Nic?" I turned to the wizard, who looked himself over, patting his body as if checking to see if everything was there.

"Yes, quite." He shook out his shoulders and prepared himself. "Wait, what will I be exactly? And must we do this tonight?"

"I was going to make you a hawk or something." I shrugged, it would be the easiest, right? "And to be honest, they may expect something closer to their target. If we do it now, we cut down the risk of running into a patrol coming out to meet them and thwarting us. Or them being on guard."

"That is very astute reasoning, very well. Hmm, learning to fly could take too long." His face contorted in thought. "Better go with a rat, something large enough that you won't kill me in your claws but won't accidentally drop me to my death."

I blinked, suddenly finding it hard to swallow. "How about a garden snake so I can carry you in both claws and you'll be safe?"

"Excellent suggestion, my boy." He seemed happy, and I had him sit on a pack so he would be safe from the others' feet.

I focused on the animal I wanted him to become and cast Polymorph. A hundred mana drained from my reserves, and a puff of smoke briefly obscured the wizard and then blew away. In his place was a small, green snake about two feet long.

"I'll lift him up if you want to grab him on your way up," Bokaj offered as he carefully lifted the snake.

I nodded once, told Bea, *Behave!* And then shifted into my owl form. I snatched the snake up with both claws as I passed above them. The weight felt weird, but once he had the good sense to wrap himself around my leg, it was alright.

I checked Kayda's location in my mind, noting her position on my map, and began the trip to her. Luckily, we had been going in the same direction, so I only needed to cast the spell once more to see our journey to a close. I found Kayda sitting in the grass watching her prey about a hundred and fifty feet away; she was still small, so the grass mostly masked her presence.

I landed and shifted, dismissing the spell on the wizard and summoning Balmur from my collar just after. Kayda rapped the gem with her beak and filtered in with a small flex of my will. Taking a look at the messengers, one sat up, awake, and the other was asleep on the opposite side of their dying fire. The warm air around us swirling and luckily slithering away due west so that we were downwind from them.

"How you wanna play it, Balmur?" I whispered for Nic's sake. "You're the sneaky one here."

He rolled his eyes at me, "Really?" I shrugged, and he just shook his head. "You both stay here, and I'll go see what I can see. If I can nab it, I will, and I'll bring it back here to you guys."

"I'll be ready to step in if it gets heavy." I took a step back and took my saber-tooth cat form and crouched in the grass.

"It is so unsettling that your eyes glimmer like that." Nic shivered and took a knee beside me. I bumped his leg with my shoulder to let him know to be quiet. "Sorry."

I glanced over at him and sighed softly, then turned my sights back toward Balmur as he snuck forward cautiously. His knees were bent, and he stepped slowly moving as if he were on one of those fast-moving floors in the airport. There was no sway to his step, no bob as he stealthily made his way forward.

He was in his element. Then he sank into the ground and disappeared before his body came back into view out of the shadow of the one who was awake. Balmur's shape blurred a little bit, and his hands flashed this way and that. After ten minutes of watching him work, he made his way toward us.

Once he was close enough to whisper, so we both knew what was going on, he said, "Nothing on that one," he shrugged his shoulders and sat down. "Guess we wait until they switch out."

"No." I had shifted back from my animal form as soon as he was close. "That guy's going to sleep here in a couple minutes. Follow me."

I shifted back into my saber-tooth form and padded softly toward the messenger who was still awake, far enough away that he wouldn't hear me. Walking in a circle around him so that I could position myself directly behind him, where I shifted into my fox-man form and slowly drifted forward.

Once I was in position, I let my body relax, standing almost directly behind and above him. I had trained in this technique while I was in the Marine Corps, a very simple technique called a blood choke. My right arm shot forward, under his chin around his throat, where my bicep and forearm pressed against the carotid arteries on each side of his neck. I locked the choke in by cradling my right hand in my left and gripping tightly.

He flailed a little, but I pulled him back and held the choke until he stopped moving, and then a moment after that to ensure that he was out and would stay out.

We won't have too terribly long, I mentally told Balmur.

Already on it, came his reply as I slowly laid the guy down on his bedroll, pillow under his head. *Got it.*

I waved Nic over and he took the folded square of parchment with wax in the center. I was completely unsurprised to see that the governess had her seal as a rose. How bland.

"You need to open it?" Balmur readied a blade. Through his earring, he added, *I hope this thing at the capitol doesn't take too long. Whatever it is behind all this is weird. Could it be a general?*

It's possible, I confirmed, then aired my own thoughts, *What if the asshole who sent us those dreams is behind this and is messing with a powerful enough figure to cause strife in the kingdom, so we get distracted?*

We didn't have the time to continue the conversation, because Nic moved next to us after having had his eyes shut for a long moment.

Nic shook his head, took the parchment in one hand and a green quill in the other. He opened his book and muttered quietly and motioned over the two of them. After a second, the quill dissolved into the parchment, and it glowed green, then dulled and looked as if it had never changed.

"It is done." Nic passed it back to Balmur, who then methodically put the message where it had been before.

As soon as he was with us once more, we moved away to watch them. Twenty minutes later, the messenger that I had choked out started awake, holding his throat. Fuck, I knew I should have cast a heal on him! Too late, now. His gaze swung about before he stood, and moved around his friend and woke him up. They exchanged words quickly, and the one still laying down pulled the message out. They looked it over and decided that it was good, but they were both up, for now.

"Mission accomplished," I sent ahead to the party with my raven figure as we observed the two messengers. "We'll be back soon."

They looked around the camp, and rather than waiting to

see what they would do if they found our tracks, I touched both of the others and cast Teleport.

We landed back at the camp with several weapons pointed our way.

"Hey, chill the fuck out." I growled, more than a little tired, then saw that the bird had just now made it to Jaken. "We did it, now leave us be so we can get some sleep."

The others grunted and just left us alone, I went to where I had laid out my bedroll, let Kayda out and collected a slumbering Bea from Manly.

"She's a handful," the halfling griped half-heartedly as she handed the sleeping hatchling to me. "I don't envy you."

I nodded to her and went back to my bedroll. I put Bea into the collar to be safe and laid down. I don't know why I was suddenly just so irritated. Was it because I could have fucked that up? Tipped them off?

Damn it. I just didn't know. I needed to start thinking more.

I closed my eyes and fell into a fitful slumber. My dreams evaded me, something nagging at the edge of my consciousness that kept me from resting completely.

I woke up just before dawn, groggy, pissed off, and wanting to do some damage to something. So, I turned that thought inward and began meditating over a new spell.

I took Purify and my Shadow Tinkering ability and swallowed the spell to weave it into the shadows. The radiant light of it seemed to dissolve the shadows as they touched it, so I stopped before wasting any more mana.

300 MP just gone, like that. I stood and looked about, Kayda watched over me curiously.

Mad? She tilted her head and hopped forward. I didn't know how to respond, so she smacked me with her wing, *Hunt.*

She sent imagery of her prowling the skies, the thermals lifting her higher and higher as she searched the skies for prey.

Okay. I touched her cheek, then turned to my friends. James was awake, and Bokaj was strumming a song I recognized as a restful one to some of the others.

"I'm going for a flight. Be back in a bit." I hopped into the air and took off as an owl before they could respond, the wind beneath my wings helping minutely to clear my head.

Kayda shrunk to her smaller size, and I caught up to her as soon as I could. She was much more adept at catching thermals than I was. We coasted for a while, the light peeking over the horizon line and shedding gold and orange over the land in waves.

Pretty, Kayda thought at me. And I had to agree with her. Motion caught my eye below us, and my sight synced with Kayda's as she thought *Prey!*

As we dove together, I saw what it was that we were set upon. It was an adult eagle, and Kayda grew as she plummeted. Her full height and wingspan easily dwarfing his. She caught him easily, gripping his wings and upper body before diving toward the ground faster than I had ever seen her do so. As soon as she was in range, with me right behind her, she let go of the eagle, and it crashed into the earth.

The snap of its wing audible from my position. She wheeled around quickly and set upon him, her talons penetrating the flesh, making the severely hurt creature cry out in pain.

I shifted and stepped forward, ready to heal it and send her off, but she screeched at me *No!*

"Kayda, we have plenty of food at the camp, baby. Let him go." I tried to reason with her, but she gripped tighter.

And for the first time in so long, she truly spoke through our connection in a way that she hadn't before.

We are kings of the sky, father. We rule. We hunt, and those who do not fly as high as we do are our prey. She sent me visions of her flying before I could when she was smaller and had to worry about these kinds of things. *We hunt. We kill. We survive.*

I stepped closer, and she thrust her beak out at me to make me stop. *You worry what prey thinks when you need to worry about what hunts above you. This is Nature's way. And you are druid. Mother's chosen. You are special but refuse to be the predator.*

It stung, coming from her more than *anyone*. But she wasn't done.

She stood to her full height in front of me, and her wings spread as far as they would reach, her head high. *Take your place with me, father. Let us take our place together.*

Is this a dream? Kayda turned her head to the side and eyed me as if I were crazy. "How am I supposed to do this? Any of this? How am I supposed to know what isn't being orchestrated by some unseen puppet master pulling strings?"

By believing in yourself and in those around you. Kayda supplied with another spreading of her wings. *We who hunt, we who are strong decide what our reality is. The true question is if you are strong enough to decide if you are capable of this reality.*

Her argument was sound, and it was likely that, coupled with the fact that this was the most that I had ever heard her say at once, made me think that she right. She was absolutely right.

If I was going to be a monster, I was going to be a good one.

That eagle, this symbol of freedom and strength in my homeland, would become the symbol of my genesis. My new beginning.

Our new beginning, I corrected myself and summoned Bea from the collar and sat her on the ground, nudging her awake.

Blood? The thought and scent hit me, and I knew what needed to be done.

I stepped forward again, and instead of Kayda stopping me, she lifted the still-living bird of prey closer to me, and I lashed out with my metallic right arm, ripping through the breast to find the heart, the last dregs of the bird's health draining to nothingness.

I pulled the now-still organ from the wound and took a bite, the blood dripping down my jaw. I tossed the rest to Bea, who munched on it happily. Kayda watched over her, and then eyed me.

Proud, warmth filled our bond, my chest, and my heart. She pressed her head against mine and tousled my fur.

"Since when have you been able to speak so well?" I took her head into my hands so I could look her in the eyes.

A while, a mischievous glint filled her gaze.

"Then why haven't you?"

Didn't want to, she took her wings and buffeted me before turning to the carcass in her grasp, tearing bits of the meat off for Bea and me. I gathered mine and put them into my inventory. After she was finished, we flew back.

Since I had technically fought the eagle by killing it, I had taken his form, and flying back was a trip. It was so much heavier than that of my owl's. Powerful. Each movement of my wings carried me faster, and I wanted to push myself.

So, I did. Kayda and I made it back to the camp in half the time it had taken us to reach our hunting grounds.

I landed with her and shifted into my fox-man form, the others watching us carefully.

"You okay, buddy?" Muu asked cautiously stepped closer to Kayda and me.

Uncle Goblin! She ruffled her feathers, and watched him as I smiled. "Yeah, man, why?"

"You're kind of covered in blood, and so is Kayda." James pointed out from his seat.

I lifted my hand to my chin and chest, my fingertips coming away with slightly congealed blood.

"Oh, Kayda and I went hunting, which reminds me." I pulled the meat out and slapped it into Yohsuke's hand. "This is breakfast food."

"What is it?" Jaken called, as I walked away toward where my gear was.

I called over my shoulder without looking, "Eagle meat. Pretty tough, but it's good. Nothing like chicken."

I ordered the shadows around my feet to clean me and my clothes absently as I surveyed my gear. It needed cleaning too. I sent more shadows to do the work, then packed my things and turned back to the others. Kayda preened herself, and Bea nosed at the grass, some of the blood coming away on the ground. The group still watched me.

"What?" I raised an eyebrow in question.

"Just… you seem different, bud." Muu frowned, the finer scales of his forehead creased in worry. "I should know I live with you. Usually, you're only like this if you're upset or angry. You okay?"

That was the question, wasn't it? The one final thing I tried to pack away and ignore that I couldn't anymore. No. I wasn't. I had been working so hard, and it was never going to be good enough. I had so many things I couldn't control acting against me. Against us. Couple that with the fact that even though I was blessed by Mother Nature—hell even the elementals!—and we had to worry about some nut job who hated magic standing in the way of our mission. As well as this dream-giving creature, whatever the fuck it was? No. No, I wasn't okay.

My chest rose and fell in heaves as my adrenaline spiked, and the desire to hurt something rose in me. The werewolf in me stirred, and that pissed me off even more.

"Take a knee, Zeke." Yohsuke was suddenly closer than I thought he had been, and it startled me. He looked concerned and put a hand on my shoulder softly. "Take a knee with me. Let's work it through."

Use this anger, the werewolf whispered through my being. My muscles bulged and cramped painfully as I fought him. *We can turn many of them before the paladin and cleric turn against us. Then we can overwhelm them. Act! Do it now!*

Kayda's mind brushed against mine, suddenly cool and reassuring, *We are the predators. That voice is a part of you. Claim it. Claim yourself, and we can become what we were meant to.*

What was I meant to be? I blinked, the rage welling in the core of my being spilling toward my mind. I could see the werewolf gaining strength steadily.

You are meant to be the alpha! And we will rule all! The images flooding my mind made me groan, falling to a knee with a vision that left me absolutely shaken to my core. "Fuck."

Hundreds of werewolves flooded around Sunrise then began heading toward the mountain and Lindyburg on the other side. We would turn the city and move through this world like a plague. A wave of bloodlust so thick it was like I was in an ocean of crimson, that crashed against me relentlessly.

I began my breathing cycles to try and regain my mind, my will, and control once more. Breathing in and out, in, holding the breath then out once more. Cleansing my mind.

Submit to me! The wolf howled urgently, the rage returning and welling up faster inside me than it had before.

Father, Kayda's voice urged me to come back. *Remember, you are more now. You are the predator.*

Something in me snapped. One second I was struggling against the rage in me, then it was mine. It had always been mine. And the wolf knew that. I was cold. So terribly cold.

I blinked, and suddenly, I was there with him, staring at him as he launched himself from his throne. But it wasn't his. It was mine. All of this was mine.

I caught him by the throat and growled, "You're nothing to me. You *are* me. And I am you. We are one. But you will *never* gain control over me."

I took the shadows around us and willed them to coalesce around me, shivering up my body, then over him as he struggled to free himself from my clutches. The shadows pulled him into me, and as he came closer, I leaned in and *consumed* him. Bent him to my will and strapped him to the wall of my being.

This beastly fragment of my soul. My monstrosity. My power.

We were now, finally, one.

And as the shadows returned to the reaches of the cave inside my body, I claimed my throne. What had always been mine.

I blinked, and I was back, taking a knee with my brother. And for the first time since I had been bitten and my emotions ran high, the red was gone. I was free.

"You okay?" Yohsuke muttered with his hand still on my shoulder.

"Finally." The wolf had been showing me what *it* had wanted. But also, what I had wanted in a way. It was time to share that. "We need to talk. Just our party."

He nodded and looked pointedly at the others before we walked away from the camp. We were in sight, out of earshot that I was aware of, but I looked over at Balmur.

Think you can summon that little hut to cover us? He looked confused for a moment. *I need this to stay between us.*

"Okay." He held his hand out and cast the spell, the opaque light-bending dome covering us if only a little snuggly.

"What's going on man," Jaken asked, a look of concern plastered onto his features.

"You were kind of out of it there for a second and seemed to be going through something." James touched my chest as if to see if I would break.

"It was a little something." I grunted and flicked his hand aside. "Kayda said something to me this morning that made a lot of sense—we keep concerning ourselves with the thoughts of prey when we should concern ourselves with our needs."

"That's what I've been *saying*!" Yohsuke threw his hands up in exasperation. "Leave it to fuckin' chicken wings to get through that thick damned skull of yours."

I cut him an annoyed glance, and he just flipped me off, and I continued when he was done, "I think we need to go about this differently. We try the kingdom first and see if they do anything, and if they do cool..."

I left them with a pregnant silence, and Muu was the one who picked up my thought. "And if they don't, we do?"

"What the fuck are we going to do?" Bokaj looked confused. "A king doesn't do something about *his* people, so we go in there and what, murder the people in charge?"

I blinked at him, staring him in the eyes steadily. I watched the realization dawn over Bokaj's face, he seemed to almost crumple in on himself with it. His shoulders slumped, and he shook his head. "Dude, I'm cool with a lot of things, but that's… that's a lot."

"After all the blood we've shed here, can you honestly say you want to leave that crazy bitch behind to fuck with the mages that keep this world strong?" I challenged as I turned to stare each of them in the eye. "If magic fails here, that means War will be able to get in and fuck things up on Brindolla and come to our world, anyway."

"And if we leave her at our six, she can still gun for us," James added contemplatively. "I don't like it. But it's not the wrong kind of thought."

"How would it be any different from killing a minion or general?" I reasoned, pointing at Balmur. "They may not belong to War, but that doesn't mean that he won't capitalize on them. He was tortured at a general's bidding. Do you want that for your families if we fail to do the hard shit while we're here?"

They said nothing, their gazes cast down at the ground. Some in thought. Some for other reasons.

"I don't." I growled, my fists clenched. "This world made me out to be a monster. This lycanthropy was forced on me, and now I'm a beast. Well, fine. I'm done concerning myself with that. I am the beast. I am the monster, and my prey is out there. I know you fuckers are with me, so let's do what we can, where we can, and be what we were meant to be."

"The only thing monstrous about you is your fucking mouth, man." Balmur shouted back at me. "You think we haven't thought these things?"

I stared at him, a little surprised at his outburst, his face contorted in anger and pain.

"I have," he continued as he stepped forward. "I have to fight my urges all the same as you do. So, don't you *dare* come at me with that monster shit. I know what I had to do to survive."

"Hey man, no one was saying anything negative about you," Bokaj tried to calm his best friend down. "At least I don't think so. Right? Zeke?"

I blinked, shaken out of my stupor, "I was only pointing out that we were going to have to do some hard shit, still." I waved a hand in front of his face slowly so he would look up at me. "Seriously, Balmur, you aren't a monster. What they did to you would have broken a lesser person. And you came out stronger. You're a fucking beast."

"We might have some rough edges and hard parts about all of us," Jaken interjected, calmingly touching my shoulder, but looking each of us in the eyes as he spoke. "We have the blessings of the gods, and even the elementals. Lives depend on us. Billions of them presently, but future generations, as well. Our cause is righteous, no matter how we have to overcome the obstacles in our way, we will. Together."

We all stood in solemn silence to contemplate what the paladin had laid on us. Heavy as it was, he wasn't wrong. We were capable of great things. All of us.

Balmur narrowed his eyes at me and stepped forward to pull me into a tight hug. "Sorry. That's a bit of a sore subject for me."

"Rightfully so." Muu clapped him on the shoulder affectionately. "If I were half as ugly as you are, I'd be mad, too."

Muu, ever wonderful at comedic relief, took a shot to the junk from the dwarf that saw him crumple to the ground.

"I do feel better now, though." Balmur smiled cruelly and walked out of the dome, popping it on his way out.

Muu laid there in a fetal position while the rest of us just shook our heads. Jaken went to heal him but stopped.

"That was a little poorly timed, bud," the paladin patted his shoulder and walked toward the camp.

So, what's up with this sudden shift in perspective that we've been waiting for? Yohsuke grabbed my arm and pulled me away.

I finally got control of the werewolf. I don't know what it means yet, but it happened while I was taking a knee, I frowned. *Did I really fuck that all up?*

Kind of, yeah, he shook his head slowly. *We've had that kind of thought process going on for a minute. That was the point of the training so hard. Getting our asses into gear to face whatever came next, be it minion or general. Or civilian. It's good to know you're finally fully on board with the program, but damn, man.*

I shrugged, speaking out loud again, "You know I've been on my own fucking program since day one, brother."

He smirked, "That OFP shit stops, now. Though, I guess the whole predator and prey shit is different for you, huh? Either way, we need to be sure we have a good plan in place before we get to the king. And I agree, by the way, about Lindyburg. We can't leave her alone."

"I'm glad to know that I have you to rely on if shit has to get all chaotic," I muttered darkly.

"Hey." Yoh hit me as hard as he could in the shoulder. It didn't do much at all, but it caught and held my attention. "None of that shit. Understand? We work together. We're a team. This little argument doesn't end that."

"Yeah," I sighed, hating that he was right. "I got it. Let's get some food, and I'll try and dig myself out of this shitty hole I seem to have fallen into this morning."

"Fucking, soars with eagles ass, druid, piece o' shit," Yohsuke teased as we walked back toward the group together.

There was a tension I wasn't used to in the air that made things a little terse between all of us, furtive glances toward Balmur and me now and again showing that what had happened between the two of us hadn't been so easily set aside. Other than that, breakfast came and went with no other incidents.

As we rode on that day, the sun fought its way through thick clouds that looked to be nearing storm level thickness. Kayda was fascinated by them and wanted me to come fly with her among the charged clouds, but I politely declined.

Nicolas and Balmur road together inside the cart, so there was no chance of me having more of any sort of reconciliation with him in our travel time. Granted, he had said things were okay, and they seemed that way, but it wasn't in me to leave it alone without really making sure things were alright.

So, time for the next best thing.

I moved over toward Manly. "Hey, Manly, can you tell us a little about the city? Last time we had spoken about the dungeon, you mentioned Nimran's Flame, but nothing about the capital."

"Zephyth?" She blinked and frowned. "Big city, like that? You don't wanna know about that place."

"You know we do." Muu elbowed her playfully, gently displacing her from her spot by about six inches.

She glanced at him as she sidled back to her place and sighed theatrically. "Well, I s'pose I could tell you a little bit." Her eyes wandered the road for a second, no one in sight.

"The place is huge, much bigger than Lindyburg, I reckon 'bout three times as big?" She scratched her head, then continued, "Big place with a lot o' human folk, halflings and some gnomes thrown in. Like I said before, they don't rightly like reminders o' their peoples' failed attempts at magical dominance. So there ain't many elven or beast-kin folk about. They're fair with their trade, got a lot o' high-quality craftin' and magic items there, so if you be in the market for 'em, get 'em there."

"The people themselves be good folk for the most part. They got crime, same as any other place, but the thieves guild and whatnot be within the city as well, so even the thievin' gets regulated. Bounty board there be good business too, if not a little harsh at times, but it's work."

"What about the monarchy?" Muu leaned forward closer to her.

I stayed close, wasn't going to pass up on this info, and even James had wandered closer to listen in.

"Well, I don't rightly know too much 'bout them as I tried to steer myself clear o' the royalty and nobility, as a lady. But I do hear that the king and queen be good folk, as well. Got a young'un to boot. A little princess. The queen, if memory serves, was from the continent of beasts, the place I found them eggs y'all were lookin' at."

"That's wild!" I whispered in awe. "Is she some kind of beast?"

"Did you not hear her just say they have issues with beast-kin?" James said from the other side of the cart.

"Shut up, dick." I growled.

"Boys, listen here, I don't know much about the royals, but I do know…." at this Manly dropped her voice so that we had to ride closer to hear her. "That the nobility ain't folk to cross. So, if you have business with the crown, get it done quick-like. Aye?"

"Sounds good to me." Yohsuke joined us. "Having one royal with us constantly is bad enough. Who needs more?"

I knew he was teasing because he had already tossed the finger my way, and I rolled my eyes.

We continued on for the rest of the day, speaking about little things, nothing terribly important, but it was nice conversation. The weather continued overhead and passed us by heading southwest with the wind. Kayda was disappointed, but that was to be expected.

When we stopped for dinner that night, the guys decided it was time to break our hiatus from training.

"Maybe the exercise will be good for everyone, and we can stop bickering so fucking much." Jaken eyed all of us, and my cheeks burned in shame.

"If y'all are gonna have a bout o' sparrin' maybe have Nick and Bonnie join in?" Manly suggested as her wares came out of the cart to eat their dinners. "Frederick would like to, but after last time, I'm afraid he'd get too banged up tryin' to best Zeke."

"That's not a bad idea." Yohsuke's eyebrows lifted at the thought. "Give us a little bit of a break from each other and we can spread our skills around and maybe learn something new."

"I'd be happy to play with all of you." Bonnie bounced over to us and looked around hopefully.

I blinked and looked at the others, the same thought crossing my mind as theirs. "Not it!"

James touched his nose last and swore mightily as he walked

into the field with the demon-touched fighter. We didn't even really know what the hell her class was, though she had said something about "berserker" that I recalled.

"What are the rules?" James called to Bonnie as he stretched and limbered himself up.

"What rules?" Bonnie tilted her head and then charged forward with her hammer flying behind her as if it weighed nothing.

James laughed and sped forward to meet her, his fist leading. She swung her hammer around toward his midsection, her feet barely on the ground. If it connected, the strike should have had little to no power behind it, but James bent backward, and the weapon missed him by a hair.

But rather than readjust and find another opening, Bonnie just held on and let the momentum of her weapon's swing carry her forward so that she could drive her left knee into the monk's side.

"Oof!" He grunted and landed three feet away on his side, his health having been dropped to 94%.

"That was a good one." Bonnie smiled as she bounced forward once more, her hammer lifting ominously.

James was up and in motion this time much faster than he had moved before, likely using his Haste ability. His movements were incredibly fast, and Bonnie had to step back and move her body this way and that to dodge some of the blows, but a good majority of the light taps landed. The damage was adding up when her hammer fell like a pro-golfer's club and clipped James in the shoulder with a sickening crunch.

"Damn it!" James growled, and his wings spread behind him as he began to course his ki into his hands. The two fought back and forth for another couple minutes before Bonnie started to get a little more serious. She began to rely less on her hammer and more on her hands and feet, then when James was recovering, she would move in with the blunt end of the weapon to try and seal the deal.

James waited until just the right moment and executed a

perfect spinning back kick that made the former martial artist in me glow with pride, his foot catching Bonnie right across her chin. Her head snapped back, her long hair waving with it.

"Oh no," Nick grunted, a look of panic growing on his face. "He should nae ha' done tha.' Lads, a couple o' ye may wanna get in there, or James is gonna be a scaly pancake in a moment."

"Is she that bad?" Balmur muttered before a howl of unabashed outrage shattered the air.

My gaze shot over to where the two of them had been sparring, and the woman had left her hammer on the ground and was stomping toward James.

"Tha' hammer is her crutch, lads. She drops that, she means business." He shoved Jaken and me forward. "Go, or he may well die."

I nodded to Jaken, his shield and sword at the ready, and then I cast Aspect of the Ursolon, pulling out Magus Bane as we rushed forward. My body grew larger, and my fur slightly shaggier as I moved, muscles bulging and growing denser as my strength increased ten points temporarily, and my attack power boosted with it.

Bonnie roared as she bolted toward James, who dodged as swiftly as he could, he didn't have time to go from one martial form to another as he should have to channel his ki to greater effect.

I turned my axe so that the hammer portion was forward and activated Wind Scythe, throwing the weapon forward. It smacked into her back with an audible thud and the sound of a smack, but she just kept moving, and her health only dropped by like, 5%.

She was enraged, similar to my Feral Rage ability when I was in animal form and could take heavy damage.

"She's taking half damage," I warned Jaken, who clapped his sword against his shield, glowing red as he did.

"Hey, Bonnie! Come and get the metal guy," Jaken taunted her, but her attention was on James.

I'll go run interference, and you get her attention then. I pressed the breath from my body and sprinted forward to my weapon where it laid behind the frightening figure. Her tail flipped back and forth like a cat's over top of it, and that gave me an idea.

I collected my fallen weapon and yanked on her tail as hard as I could, her left arm came back and I just barely caught it in time to keep it from clocking me in the side of the face. The momentum from her attack helped me to twist my axe and keep the limb pinned, her glowing red eyes turned to me.

"Hey, Bon. How's thi*iings?*" She planted her feet beneath her body and threw her left arm forward with me still on it. I scrambled for any kind of purchase I could get but found none.

Get the fuck over here, damn it! I howled to Jaken as I sailed through the air.

Bonnie hopped forward into a crouch and pulled her right arm back into a haymaker where I looked to be falling toward. Her savage grin filled with even more crazed delight as I came closer.

Kong! Jaken's shield flew into her as if thrown from some kind of Avenger and then lifted itself and began to batter her as Jaken came in with his great sword drawn. He hopped into the air and snatched my body close, and we landed together.

"Thanks." The sound of fleshy knuckles cracking into the metal shield was all we could hear for a second.

"Got any ideas?" James was suddenly next to us, his lip bloodied, and he looked haggard.

"We could let her go and try to just subdue her." Jaken shrugged as he peeked over the lip to watch the woman beat on his shield. "How do you come out of your rage ability like that, Zeke?"

"Usually when combat is over." A fist came up under the shield headed our way, but the metal object cracked her on the back of the wrist, and she was back at it again.

"We could let the shield take the majority of the damage." James looked hopeful. "Like letting a cat play with a toy until it gets bored or tired."

"She's gonna figure ye out, lads," Nick called. "Gonna have ta not hit her, or let her hit you, for a minute. So like tag, but don't get whacked. Hahaha!"

I blinked at the hill dwarf and thought of a few colorful things I'd like to say to him before a sound caught my attention. I looked back to see Bonnie grunting and straining as she was dragged around by the shield as it tried to escape her clutches.

Better get a move on. The other two sighed, but an idea occurred to me. *Keep her distracted and away from me. I can trap her.*

I thought of using Shade's Prison, but the duration was thirty seconds and the cool down a minute. It wouldn't work.

But I could possibly enchant something that would. I pulled out a platinum coin; it would serve. On the front of it was a simple design of some figure I didn't recognize, but on the back was a smooth surface.

I engraved a small birdcage into it, lifting my eyes in time to see my two friends hooting and calling at Bonnie as she tried to get around the shield.

I smiled and turned my attention back to my work. I took my will and intent, then fed shadow-aspected mana into the coin. It took some concentration, but I was rewarded with a nice little prize.

Trickster's Coin
Holds target (anyone who isn't the owner) in place with a cage made by their own shadow for a short time.
Duration: 2 minutes, or until the cage is broken.
Coin enchanted by Adept enchanter Zekiel Erebos.

"Okay, guys, I'm read—" A fist that felt like it had been attached to a fifty-caliber machine gun whacked the side of my face, thoroughly ringing my bell. I flew head over tails six feet away and landed on my ass.

Well, that restarted the fucking minute. Shit. I glanced over to see three swimming Bonnies crouching and moving in my direction.

I took the coin in my hand and just fell onto my back, and

as soon as she was on top of me, my vision cleared, and her mouth was wide open, a snarl of feral anger escaping her lips. I grunted and acted as though I was going to hit her in the face, and she grabbed my open hand and the coin.

She froze then, the red glow in her eyes deepening markedly, and I heard her grunt. The muscles in her body bulging and the veins popping against the skin as she struggled and failed to move.

For an item that had cost me 569 MP, that should hold her for at least a little bit.

I slid myself out from beneath her crouched form and dusted myself off, casting Heal on myself. Jaken was taking care of James, so I wasn't too worried about him.

After a minute and forty-five seconds, Bonnie burst the cage, then fell to the ground unmoving as all of us watched her.

"Shit," Jaken grunted, and I moved with him a heartbeat later. We were casting heals on her so fast that we barely noticed she was snoring. I picked up the saliva-covered coin that had fallen from her mouth and put it into my pocket. That was a good item to hold onto.

"She gets like this when she comes out of her rage without killing people," Nick explained as he lifted her from the ground carefully. "Poor thing loses control for the first bit 'til someone dies, then regains herself a bit more at a time."

"Hitting her in the face does that?" James asked with concern.

"Aye." Nick nodded and carried her into the back of the cart. Appearing again a few minutes later. "She'll be out at least an hour."

"Where the fuck was the warning on that!" I rolled my eyes and Nick looked at me bashfully. "Some friend you are, almost getting us killed and shit. Dinner better be fucking amazing."

We ate dinner, which was pretty damn awesome, Nick taking food to Bonnie when it was done. She was a little embarrassed by her outburst and didn't want to come out right yet, he had informed us. Couldn't blame her, but damn she had been strong.

A shiver raced down my spine as the sun fell from the sky for the day, the shadows taking the land in their umber embrace.

Then her smooth voice greeted me, "I am here."

I smiled, Maebe had returned to this realm, and as I turned to the voice, I saw a more perfect shadowed representation of her as she stood in the moon and starlight.

"Hello, my love." I climbed to my feet and stepped toward her. "Where did you come through? I'll come to you."

"No need." She held her shadowed hand out to mine, and I took it, reveling in how soft the shadows felt against my skin.

"What do you mean, 'no need?' How will you get here?" I blinked at her, and the shadows around her dissipated and left the real one standing there. "How?"

"Teaching you has given me a better understanding of these things myself." She smiled at me, her eyes sparkling in the little light we had. "I have missed you."

"I missed you too." I took human form and kissed her greedily. She laughed against my lips and pulled me closer still. "Sorry about the lack of communication over the last couple days."

She shook her head. "I needed time to myself to find something, and I have it now."

I tried to pull back to look at her, but she stopped me with a tighter hug. "I have something for you," she whispered against my neck; her voice wavering with uncertainty.

"What's that?" I lifted her chin to look at me, and her features were uncertain too. "What's wrong?"

"I am nervous." She frowned, her nose crinkled, and her brow furrowed in thought. "I do not like it."

"I can't imagine that you would." I hugged her shoulders tightly and kissed the top of her head. "What is it you wanted to give me?"

She glanced around the camp, most of the people there not having noticed us, except for Kayda, who watched attentively.

"Can we go somewhere we can be alone together?" Her hand was in mine and pulling before I even said anything.

Going for a walk, I'll be okay. Nearby, and what not. I broadcast to the others, and they all grunted back. Muu was asleep, so nothing from him.

We walked for a little bit, well out of sight of the camp, but still close enough that we could sprint back to help if anything happened.

"Let's have a seat." I offered as we slowed our pace.

We sat together, staring up at the dark expanse above us.

"Do you remember much about how things had gone with Samir in my realm?" She was quiet after that, and I had to think on it for a minute, until she added, "Specifically with the Blood Rite?"

"Oh!" I frowned as I tried to recall. "That I would never be able to be your successor, right?"

"Exactly." Maebe nodded. "You will never come to power should anything happen to me because you survived the rite."

"I don't know that I would do well leading the Unseelie without you around anyway." I laughed nervously, uncertain as to why she was bringing that up after so long.

"You cannot lead my people without me," she insisted.

"Yeah, Mae, I get it." I frowned, a little hurt that she would just be shoving this in my face like that. I had never wanted to rule her people. I just wanted her.

I wanted her.

I turned to see her radiant face in the moonlight, she held a small box in her hand that she held out in front of her as if presenting it to me before kneeling beside me.

"I can't have you forever," she began softly, her sad voice wavered a little as she continued, "but what I have with you, I want to be properly had. I love you, Zekiel Erebos, will you be my king?"

To say that I was shocked would be the understatement of the century.

What do I say? All I could do was let my mouth open and close as I stared at the item she had presented to me. The small ring held a line of black stones with smaller bright white, red, green, sapphire, and other colored stones inside.

"It was my grandmother's," Maebe spoke, likely filling the silence so that I would have time to come to grips with her question, though a contemplative and slightly concerned look filled her eyes.

"It's beautiful." The emotion ripping through my heart at that moment was unreal. Did I deserve this? Knowing I'd be leaving? Did *she* deserve that? I had to know. "Why?"

A glistening tear fell from her right eye, leaving a slight trail down her cheek. "Why not? I will have little to nothing left when you leave. I do not expect to find this kind of thing again, so instead of never knowing, or asking myself what may have been—I will live in these moments with you, and our friends."

I blinked, and she was buried in my chest with my arms around her for support. My body had reacted on its own, pulling her close enough to where I could whisper my heart to her.

"I don't know what it will mean to do this, and we will definitely be discussing that, but yes. I'll marry you, Mae."

I lifted the ring from the box, and before I could put it on, Maebe took it from me.

"There's a process, and I have to be the one to put it on your finger," she explained as her eyes met mine. "It may be odd, but please, allow me to put it on you. It is enchanted, and when you wear it, it will bind us together. No matter where you are, I will know, and vice versa. Is that alright?"

Thinking about it, that wasn't too bad at all. It was an insurance policy really, because if we could find each other, that would be good, right?

"Is there anything I have to do?" I asked, not uncertain but nervous, anyway. This was a big thing. "What about a ring for you?"

"We need a witness." She frowned against the light. "And another ring will not be a worry."

"I know someone I would trust to see this through." I closed my eyes and sent a telepathic thought to my friends. *Yohsuke, can you come here a minute?*

Give me a minute, you needy bastard, he grumbled back.

It was a couple minutes later when he walked over to join us, his angry gaze casting about in the darkness, "Where you at?"

"Oh, forgive me, I forgot." She squeezed my hand before waving her other one allowing the darkness to fall away from us. "I did not wish for us to be disturbed again; it was vexing not being able to tell you how I felt previously with all the interruptions."

Ten feet away, still searching for us was Yohsuke. I whistled softly, and he turned around swiftly.

"Oh, there you are, and hi Maebe, how you doin'?" Yohsuke asked as he sat down next to us. "What's up?"

"We need a witness." I patted him on the shoulder, and he looked down into Maebe's hand.

His eyes widened, and he looked to me and then back to her. "Are you sure, man?"

I nodded. "Yeah, I am."

He then looked to Maebe. "And you seem to be as well, but is this really okay?"

Maebe's suddenly shy smile seemed so cute at that moment before she looked at Yohsuke and nodded her head once, but she held a hand up so that she might have a moment to think before he spoke again.

"As you may have been able to see, I am …in love with your brother." She hesitated, unsure how to continue. "He is a light to the darkness in me, and in him, his presence, his friendship, and in this relationship, I have known solace. Joy and wonder in ways I was unaware existed or were even open to me. I want to be with him always. And I know that with his duties to this world, his own, and his duty as a father, he will be forced to leave me, eventually."

Yohsuke no longer looked skeptical, but he listened to her quietly.

"I do not wish to stand in his way of returning home, in fact, that is my desire. That he returns to his son, that all of you return to your home should you wish it and continue to live happily." Her voice quivered, and she frowned, wiping her eyes before continuing, "But while all of you are here, I wish to experience this love with him in every way that I know how to. This is one of those ways. I wish to bind the two of us in marriage."

"And we needed a witness, I wanted that to be you, if you're okay with that?" I raised an eyebrow, and he shook his head.

"Always getting us into some crazy shit," he muttered half angrily, half exasperatedly. "The others deserve to be here for you too man, we're all in this together. I'll go get them, and then we can do this."

Maebe and I sat there as Yoh went and began to gather the others. Even the Braves came to join us, some of them bleary-eyed like Nick and Nic, but they were here. "As witnesses of the Realm," Maebe had explained, though she watched all of them distrustfully at first.

"Now, I can witness." Yoh smiled as Maebe and I stood. "You two have vows?"

She looked at me, her eyes wide in a panic. "What are these vows? Is it like a wedding contract?"

"They're meant to express intent and a promise from one partner to the other as a show of commitment," Balmur informed her politely, then grinned. "I've been working on mine for my fiancée for a long time. I miss her."

I reached out and put a hand on his shoulder. "We're going to get you back there, and it's going to happen. You'll get your happily ever after, bud."

He ducked his head, and then a tug on my hand drew my

attention, looking over to see Yoh motioning to my soon-to-be wife.

"I have some thoughts I would be willing to share. If you would all hear them?" Maebe looked at the others uncertain, her stoic demeanor cracking slightly.

"We're already here, ain't we?" Manly's voice only *sounded* sour as she stood there in her nightgown and a light jacket that covered the rest of her. She was grinning ear to ear as soon as she found out Maebe was here, and she was invited to an impromptu royal wedding.

"You are." Maebe eyed the little woman a moment, the others remaining respectfully quiet. "Zekiel, I have known you only a short time, but in that time, I have known you to be kind, thoughtful, patient, intelligent, cunning, and ruthless. I have come to know the spectrum of your character and have found that within that essence of you is a light that I wish to have within myself. We may not have long together in this world, in these realms, and your calling is elsewhere, but I would spend what precious time I can with you and our friends. I promise to love you as deeply as I can, and to have no regrets in this life, hoping to see you again."

She grasped my hand gently in her own and held it as she looked into my eyes. "If you will have me?"

"Zeke." Yohsuke put a hand on my shoulder and nodded toward Maebe. "Do you have anything you would like to say?"

"Yes." I gave him a quick reassuring smile and nodded once as he stepped back. "Maebe, you have been a mystery to me as long as I have known you. You are the single strongest person I have ever met, and simultaneously the most wonderstruck. So in awe of all the world around you that when others see it, they see a little of that wonder, too. I want to experience that with you for as long as my time in this world will allow me. I would be honored to have you, if you will have me?"

"I will, until the end of time, my heart is yours." Maebe leaned over, her eyes filled with tears of joy. I held out my hand, and she slid the ring over it onto the ring finger of my left hand.

"With this ring, we are bound, our hearts and souls will never be alone again."

As we came together in a hug, kissing each other passionately, my heart skipped a beat. I heard and felt Maebe's breath catch at the same time as my own did. Her eyes widened with mine, and I felt a burning in the pit of my stomach and an itch inside my head.

"Mae, is this supposed to be happening?" My voice sounded breathless, because it was. It hurt so badly, and as I stared into her eyes, I realized that she had known on some level that this might happen. The tears in her eyes stemming from worry.

"It will be over soon," she whispered against me. My friends' voices were all around us, but they were growing ever softer.

Then my heart rebounded, and I was stronger than I had ever felt before. There was no longer space in me left to fill, or take up, because just Maebe was there. Right there. Touching my hand and staring at me as if it were the first time that she had ever seen me. At that moment, I was doing the same. I could feel the cool and dark of her being in mine.

Everything about her was intoxicating. Where her hand touched mine was an anchor, and I could have floated away in that very second.

"This is weird," I whispered.

"This too shall pass." She pulled me closer, the press of her body lining my own with warmth and magic that spread through my being like air. "Though I wish it would last forever."

"I do too." Her scent was all over me, and I reveled in it more than I cared to ever say. I noted that my friends were smirking, then Yohsuke waved them away.

"May want to...uh... get a room, you two." He tried to sound authoritative, but it seemed like what he was witnessing had freaked him out a little. He walked off, joined by the Braves.

Bonnie watched a little longer, but I pulled my attention from Maebe for a single second to raise a wall of shadows around us in a dome. Same as I had witnessed Maebe do so many times before.

"Party poopers," Bonnie grumbled as she stalked away.

A press of lips against the side of my neck brought me back to the moment. "Thank you," my now-wife whispered. "You are king now. Let me hold you tonight, my King."

And she did. For that night, we stayed in the darkness, separated from the world around us, and I had never felt so in touch with the light as I did in those precious moments.

CHAPTER NINE

My shadow dome had faded at some point in the night. But I could honestly say that I have never been quite so angry to see the sunlight. Fiery bastard.

Maebe purred as her fingernails trailed down my chest, a matching ring on her finger. "Good morning, my King."

"Good morning, my Queen," I mumbled back, throwing a hand up to ward off the light.

"Good morning to the king and queen," a breathier voice purred from above our heads. I looked up to see Bonnie there with plates of food offered out to us.

I sighed. If she was going to tease us about this, the others were going to be unbearable.

"Thanks, Bonnie." I groaned as I went to stand, my hips and legs were killing me.

Obviously, from sleeping off of the bedroll.

"Your Majesties," Bonnie's voice was light, *almost* deferential as she bowed her head. She looked back up and caught my eye with a wink. I was naked.

A cloth of shadow whipped from mine on the ground and covered my nudity.

"No fun." She left our plates on the ground and scampered away, almost skipping.

"That one is odd," Maebe's voice brought me back to myself. I turned to find her wearing a yellow sundress with a thick, black belt that sat over her hips and dipped on one side. "Are you ready to be with our friends once more? Or would you like to sit together a little longer?"

"I think it would be good to see our friends and sit together." I rushed her and lifted her into my arms. She giggled and kissed my forehead.

I got dressed swiftly, putting my armor on even more deftly than usual. We joined the others, and it was quiet at first. Eerily so, then a smile crept onto Muu's scaly mug.

The party stood, stepping over until they stood about a foot from both of us and knelt down onto one knee.

They spoke in unison, "Hail the Queen and her King of the Unseelie Fae. Long may they reign." They each looked up with shit-eating grins.

My eyes widened, my gaze whipping over to Maebe, who blinked, confusion on her face, then she looked to me. "This is sarcasm, correct? They are not truly wishing us well, just teasing us?"

The others laughed and came forward with hugs and soft-spoken words of congratulations and affection. By the end, I'd had the fur on my head ruffled so much I thought it would fall out.

Maebe looked to be truly enjoying herself, her grin was wide as she traded words with each of them.

"We're happy for you both." James returned to his place around the cooking fire. "And we didn't even have time to get you anything."

"And I swear if any of you start calling me 'king' or any of that shit, we will scrap."

Muu, being the shit he was, had a mouthful of food when he put a hand to his reptilian ear. "What? I couldn't hear you; your kingliness was deafening."

"You sonofa—" I growled and began to rise from my seat, he smiled and made ready, but Maebe stopped me.

"It is only right that they do." She shook her head. "In certain company, it's imperative that they do, so that our position is secure. We come from a place of power, where perceptions of that power are important in maintaining it."

"I get that, but these are my brothers. They're family." I looked at each of them. "I know we shit on each other, and we play, but I would throw my life on the line for any of them. They're my equal. They're my friends."

They each smiled, even Balmur, who I still needed to really apologize to.

"So, I guess if it's all the same, I'd have them treat me the same unless they have to?" I looked to each of them, and they nodded in turn.

"You may be a king, but there's only *one* true king," Bokaj stated with seriousness in his gaze.

"Who is this king?" Maebe's eyes widened with wonder.

I knew where Bokaj was going with it. "Elvis, baby."

Bokaj strummed his guitar dramatically, doing his best Elvis impersonation. "Thank you very much."

The Earthlings laughed, while the others seemed a little confused. Eventually, I had to explain to Maebe that the king had been an exceptionally gifted musician on my world who had many of the people there smitten.

"He sounds a very gifted bard," she nodded to herself. However she had to understand it.

"What's the plan for today? We want to get there a day later than the messengers?" Bokaj asked as he put his instrument away. "Or do we want to get there the same time and look suspicious?"

"Why not get there at the same time and be there for an unannounced diplomatic greeting from visiting royalty?" Jaken looked pointedly at Maebe and I. "We could get their permission to possibly use the dungeon as well, because that should go deep enough to get us close to the Great Below, right?"

"That is unlikely, but it will help, I'm certain," Dawn interjected. "The truth may be enough to spark their interest, but letting nobility into their dungeon? Possibly not."

"But royalty to a guild?" Manly mused. "They come bearing a big enough tithe, they could let them use their dungeon."

"It's worth a shot." Yohsuke flipped some more bacon as I let Bea out to play with Kayda. I fed her some of the bacon and scraps of meat from the eagle we had killed. She was looking a little plump. We would need to level her up soon so she could really start growing.

"We're going to need to go hunting for Bea soon," I muttered as I watched her chase after Kayda, the older of the two swatting her playfully with her wings.

"Sounds like a good idea," Balmur whispered behind me, making me jump. "Come on, man. We need to chat."

I stood and followed him as we walked away from the camp. Once we were far enough away, he cast his hands out, and his own little dome popped up around us.

"Look, Balmur, I really wanted to apologize for the way I had spoken the other day. You went through a lot, and there was no reason for that." I hung my head, ashamed. "It was insensitive."

"It wasn't." He thumped my chest. "It was from the heart and from the hip. All you were doing was trying to prove a point, and you weren't wrong. I survived, and that's all that matters. You guys came for me. You all did. And all I want to do is move on. So, I'm doing that. I've taken up the wizard class, and I'm going to study magic. And I want to have you help me if you want?"

I grinned at him and pulled him into a massive hug, "I'd be honored to, bud." I smacked my forehead. "Shit, let me go ask Maebe about the shadow magic thing!"

I turned to go out, and Balmur stopped me. "Seriously, Zeke. Thanks. I owe you guys my life."

I blinked, taking in the look of haunted shame on his face

before I punched his shoulder affectionately. "None of that. You would've done the same."

Before he could try and deny it, or make things worse for either of us, I stepped out of the dome.

"Hey, Mae!" I blinked as the light hit my eyes, and she was suddenly just there in front of me, "Woah!"

"You called, my love?" Her smiling face and green eyes stared up at me expectantly.

"Uh, yeah." How the hell had she gotten here so fast? "Would you be opposed to Balmur learning shadow magic with us?"

"Not in the slightest." She turned to regard the dwarf next to me. "You received a blessing from the shadow elemental, correct?"

He nodded. "I did. They made it so that I could pass through shadows easier and farther than before. I also got something called Shadow Friend?"

"That should be enough to allow you to manipulate shadows." She thought for a moment, her hand raising to her chin contemplatively. "I think that we should also approach Yohsuke about training as well. It will be good for you to have others to test yourself with."

"Yeah, that would be great!" I thought about all the fun we had when we were trying to learn new video games together.

"Thanks, both of you." Balmur smiled and melted into the shadows, popping up within the group, scaring the shit out of Muu.

Maebe was beaming, her smile from ear to ear.

"How did you get over here so fast?" I was concerned, but mostly curious.

"The rings." She held her hand up, the finger with her own copy of the ring I wore waggling. "If we focus on it, we can feel the general state of being the other is in. I could feel that you wanted me, so I came to you."

"That's really fucking cool." I frowned as I raised the item to my eyes, but no matter how much I concentrated, I couldn't see the stats of it. "Is there any reason why I can't see the stats on this?"

"Because they aren't needed, you can *feel* them." She held her hand out, and I took it without thinking. "The rings bind us together, not just as a form of contract that is marriage, but to the soul. Have you noticed that you feel differently?"

"I feel...*whole* right now." I narrowed my eyes, my eyebrows drawing together in thought as I searched myself. "I also get more of a read on your emotions, I think."

"And do you feel like you know where I am when I am not next to you?" Maebe stopped, letting go of my hand and pointed forward. "Walk that way and see if you can feel where I am."

I did as she asked and closed my eyes. I focused on the ring, and I felt it pulse in time with the rhythm of my heartbeat, then I felt a pull to my right when I thought about Maebe. I opened my eyes, and there she was, ten feet away to my right.

"Wow," I whispered, and held the item up to my eyes. "What else can they do?"

"After a while or so, we will eventually be able to send each other thoughts." She meshed her fingers with mine and we continued forward. "Other than that, my grandmother never told me. Though I have noticed that your magic concerning shadows is much more instinctual. I do not yet know whether that is due to the magic of our bond, or confidence on your part. We will know soon."

"How soon?" I kissed her hand as we came into the camp.

"We will train while we move." The evil grin on her face signaling a really shitty, productive day. "The others will begin their training this evening when the shadows are deepest."

"Lucky bastards," I muttered and got a smack on my ass from the playful Fae queen for my insolence.

The others had begun to pack things up, and I found Kayda defending our plates from little Bea.

Thank you, sweetheart, I called to her. She ruffled her feathers and swatted the little raptor away once more. "We're going into a mainly human kingdom, and they take issue with a lot of non-humans for shit their ancestors did. Do we know how we're going to hide the fact that the majority of us aren't human?"

"I thought items would be a good idea," I suggested readily while Yohsuke kicked dirt onto the fire to snuff it. "I can enchant some items to make you guys look human if I can get the enchantment right."

I thought about the quality of material I might need before reaching into my inventory for a ring of decent make and material. Gold band, simple and effective.

I was honestly at a loss as to how to engrave the ring to make it so that it would support my enchantment, so I just decided to wing it and engrave the word "human" in cursive so that it flowed well. Once that was finished, I gathered my will and intent before I would normally begin funneling my mana into the item, but Maebe stopped me.

"Allow me to cast a glamour onto it, it is similar to casting a spell, correct?" Her hand was over the ring already, but I stopped her in turn.

"It is, but it isn't." I took her hand, then began to explain, "When someone else casts the spell, normally I understand the concept of what they would be adding, like Jaken with his holy damage and whatnot. I understand what glamour is meant to do, but not necessarily how it works."

"It is meant to bend the light with a shield of magic around the caster that gives them the appearance of something they are not," her voice was studious and direct as she explained. "A thin barrier of mana reflects, refracts, bends, and molds to the body to give it the almost perfect appearance of what the caster wishes someone else to see."

James blinked at her slowly. "So then, how you look right now is covered in glamour?"

"Yes." Maebe frowned a second then decided against what she had thought of, likely bending the light to some degree and letting them see her in some way. "Fae do this almost constantly to the point that their glamour is instinctual. It changes with their whim and dependent on who they are with. Pay close attention to me."

I stepped back and watched with the others as her body slowly morphed. First, her ears dulled and shifted before our eyes until they were very human, then her angular features and the shapes of her eyes became significantly more rounded than they had been. Her nose rounded a little more and the bright green of her eyes seemed to be deeply enhanced.

"Having one feature, typically the eyes, draw attention from the rest of your features will further assist in ensuring that any imperfections in your glamour are somewhat unnoticed." She waved her hands in front of us and motioned to herself. "I also stay very close to what I have to work with. I do not change my height, or much of anything else."

"That's amazing!" Muu stepped closer to look at her. "How does it work with your shadow, though?"

"Well, I *am* the Queen of the Umber and Frozen Wastes." Maebe grinned. "But, I admit, it is also a bit of glamour. Younger Fae have issues with that level of control, I am centuries old—I do not."

"So then why don't you just glamour all of us?" Yoh asked politely for once.

"Because the second I lose even the most minute detail, or one of you says or does something to contradict the glamour, then it will fade and leave us visible." Her explanation seemed sound, though it was shitty.

I pointed to the ring I had engraved. "With her intent being an almost perfect glamour, and my intent being for it to be human, we should be able to make sure that you guys are good, but we might need to fine-tune it. Let's try the first one on Muu, I think his will be the hardest."

"Then maybe work on something easier first so that we can perfect it?" Maebe offered with a raised eyebrow that was *so* cute.

"God, I love you," I hissed, and I heard someone gag.

"Jesus, fuck, get on with it already!" Yohsuke swore a few

more times for good measure. "You fuckers weren't exactly quiet last night, and although I don't need to sleep, it's hard to meditate through that shit."

"On it!" I barked, more than a little embarrassed.

Together, Maebe and I cast her spell, my intent, her expertise, and will into the ring while I attempted to meld them all. It shattered in my hand, blowing away to dust.

"You have got to be shitting me," I grumbled angrily while reaching into my inventory for a finer ring, the materials used to make it much better this time.

We went through the same process this time, and the ring turned to dust, again.

"Fuck!" I growled, then I turned on Maebe. "How much mana are you putting into that spell?"

"Only as much as I use," She shrugged, then began to calculate. "I think about, roughly six hundred mana?"

"Ding ding!" I breathed a sigh of relief; glad it wasn't something I had done. "Do you *have* to use that much mana if all you're doing is passing along the concept? Because I'm adding mana as well, and that's not going so hot."

"I use as much mana as is necessary to significantly hide myself, but if you require I use less, then I can do so," she looked a little shy for a moment. "I'm sorry for making you do so much extra work."

I waved it off, "You didn't know, and all you were doing was what you know to do, it's understandable. Let's get to work, yeah?"

She nodded, a look of pure focus on her face as I dug out the next ring. This time, it worked. And exceedingly well, in fact.

Fae's Band of Glamour
Allows the wearer to use a small mana sacrifice to appear as something they are not until the spell is dismissed or the ring taken off. Cost: 1/4th of wearer's mana. Warning! Certain creatures and people may be

able to see through this illusion with natural abilities or spells.

"That's badass!" I tossed the ring to Yohsuke, who deftly caught it to observe.

"A fourth of my MP could be bad in a fight." He frowned as he tried to choose which ring to take off, before finally just picking one and putting the new one on.

He focused for a second with his eyes closed, then loosed a held breath and allowed his hood to fall down. He looked human, with a deep tan, and his eyes were slightly less yellow and browner and a little brighter than normal. His features were much the same as they had been, but his ears were more rounded. Except for his horns, he was human.

"I'll take the horns off if needed, but the added look is still dope, so fuck everyone else." He looked pleased with himself and smiled at me. "All is forgiven, vassal."

Maebe froze, and I put a hand on her shoulder. "It's a joke, brother to brother. Something we have been saying to each other for years."

She let out a breath and nodded, Yoh ignored her. He wasn't about to change for anyone. That was just who he was.

"Do the Braves need any?" I called to Manly and company with a huge, shit-eating grin firmly in place. "I'll give you a good discount!"

"The Braves'll be fine, Zeke." Manly's eyes glinted with mirth. "Ours is a hard-fought reputation. We're all set. Thank you, though! Mighty kind of you, I reckon."

"Suit yourselves." I laughed as I turned back to Maebe. "Let's get the rest of these done then, eh?"

She nodded, and we got back to work. Eventually, we were able to perfect it and get each of them a ring that made them appear human. James, with his wings and Muu with his tail, would have to wear cloaks because even with Maebe's perfected control, the materials we had just wouldn't allow for that much depth of power, but that was fine.

When we moved out, Maebe and I began to practice my

work with shadows. And so far, it did seem more instinct than it had been. It hurt me less to use them over prolonged periods.

Granted, if you focus on anything for hours straight, it gives you a mother of a headache.

Speaking of headaches, seeing Balmur's interest in magic reminded me of a certain little dwarf who had been gifted serious power by the Primordial Earth Elemental.

When we took a quick break from traveling for a bite, I decided to see about calling for some aid with the Flame Primordial. He and I had a good rapport so far, and it would be something that might be up his alley.

I closed my eyes and tried to focus on the tattoo of the flame that he had given me before calling, *Primordial Flame? Can you hear me?*

A warmth pressed against my chest, and the presence of the flame was there.

I am here. It is strange for you to seek me, little flame.

It is, I envisioned myself nodding, it was weird, so I stopped. *I wanted to know if you had need of a mage, blessed by your hand?*

There was silence, then, *I have you.*

I smiled, his trust was nice, but I knew we all needed to be stronger for what was to come. Just me wouldn't cut it.

I have a friend, an azer dwarf, who is beginning his tutelage as a wizard, and he could likely use some love. I frowned, how was I going to manage this one? *If there were some way that we could prove to you that he's worthy, would that be okay?*

I will confer with the other Primordials. There is much that I do not know of our offerings, but that you have been the only one to have earned our trust in the prime realm.

Before the crackling flames receded, I offered, *The Earth Primordial has gifted a dwarven child named Fainnir his support at the request of the god Fainne. His power is amazing, and I know firsthand how awesome your element can be.*

There was a longer pause followed by intense heat, the crackling voice searing along my mind, *This is news, a child of dwarves with earth magic, I see. And there are still trying times ahead, I am sure. Let me think on this, and I will be in touch after I have spoken to my brothers and sister.*

The heat left me, and I felt cold, and more comfortable for it. It would have to work.

I didn't want to say anything to Balmur just yet, but if it worked, I could see about bridging the gap for some of the others, perhaps.

It could take a few quests, but that was much better than being hogtied and shipped to a city for a crime we hadn't really wanted any part of.

Quests for rewards? We could do that.

We ate lunch and moved on, more training with Maebe and the shadows around us, with Kayda scouting the area ahead for us.

She sent me images of farmlands protected by a low wall, and farmers working the fields. The majority of them were human, but the ones who weren't were orcish.

"We should probably appear human soon, we have farmers about an hour out from here," I warned the others, then took my human form. It was a little easier on the riding.

The others did the same. Each of them assuming human forms close to their current looks. The mounts would attract attention since it seemed that they were somehow reflections of those who rode them. Normal looking humans riding wicked-looking mounts and things like that seemed a little farfetched, and we would rather have erred on the side of caution, so we began to travel on foot shortly after.

Farmers eyed us from a distance, some of the children venturing closer to see the newcomers, but the majority of them just went about their work when they gathered we weren't an immediate threat.

It was another few hours before we came into sight of the city walls. At the pace we were moving, we could probably have made it to the city gates by late evening. So, we skipped dinner and kept trucking along.

The houses that I could make out from the road were well

built and functional. The barns that stood close by, stout, likely to keep the winds at bay.

As the light of day fell in the western sky, we were in line to get into the city. Things were moving slowly, no matter what the people seemed to be trying to get through with, their goods, their belongings, and sometimes even their persons were subject to extensive searching and questioning. Then there was paperwork to be done for the declaration.

All of it was tedious, and the guards looked to be enjoying making the process last as long as they possibly could. Looking around, it was easy to see why they might.

"Reckon I know what they're hoping to do," Manly growled angrily. "See that inn yonder? I'd put coin on them being on the docket, more 'customers' they send to the inn the more coin they grease their hands with."

"Is that illegal?" Jaken eyed the group of guards as they *thoroughly* inspected a man's fruit cart.

"Prolly not," Nick said sourly as he watched. "More'n likely tha' the guard sergeant had his hand greased too so tha' the guard captain 'n the crown donae find out."

"Because complaints go through the sergeant." James snorted, his arms crossed in contempt.

It was the elderly couple in front of us that pissed me off the most. Not them, mind you, but the way the guards treated them.

"State your business," the eldest guard, and the fattest, droned on in a bored tone. His green and white checkered uniform looked slovenly, and his stubble signaled he hadn't shaved in days. He wasn't even looking at them as he eyed the sun setting. The motherfucker.

"We've come to see our grandchildren and our sister," the little old lady's head shook as she spoke.

"Anything to declare?" The guard droned again.

The couple looked at each other in confusion, before the man answered, "No?"

"Stand by for a search of your person." The guard nodded

to the two goons waiting over to the right side of the gates. As soon as they were there, one drew a sword and kept it loose in hand as the other began to pat the two of them down.

As having been trained to do this sort of thing before, the guy was professional about it. Simple, no excess movements, but he wasn't exactly gentle about it.

The man was first, and he was visibly shaken. The older woman was next, and to the guy's credit, he was markedly gentler. He even put a hand on her shoulder and whispered, "My apologies, ma'am, just protocol."

It had sounded sincere, but the smirk on the head guard's face said it all.

"Sorry, folks, gates close at sundown!" His smile made me want to rip his fucking throat out. "Come back in the morning to get in."

"But we can't afford to stay at the inn," the old man scowled, if he had been younger, it may have been something, but right now, the guard just laughed.

"Not my problem, old-timer." He turned, then stopped as the old man muttered something that made me grin. "You got something to say to me? Huh?"

He paced forward, his features contorting in anger, his left hand falling to the hilt of his sword.

Jaken stepped forward until he looked over all three of them, growling. "Didn't anyone ever teach you to respect your elders?"

"You threatening a guard?" The fat thing jiggled his chins threateningly.

I snorted. "Ugly *and* stupid."

"Seems we have a group of people who don't want to get into the city." One of the younger guards came forward to try and salvage things. "That or they want to spend a night in the city jail?"

"Sure thing, sweetheart." Muu fluttered his eyes at the guard and puckered his weird-looking human lips in a kiss. "But I have to warn you, I'm not a cheap date, so if you're going to try and take me out, you're gonna have to work for it."

The guard went to draw his sword, but Bokaj stepped over with his winningest smile, and put his hand around the guard's to stop him. "Hey, woah, let's just ease it back here, right? Look, you've had a long shift, we've been traveling for days. We're all a little on edge. Here's a gold coin for you. Have a couple rounds on me tonight."

The guards scowled at all of us, but they let go of their blades and turned to walk away.

The elderly couple turned, defeated looks on their faces. "Thank you for your kindness, strangers."

"We're sorry that they were like that, even though we can't help it, there's no excuse for it." Jaken smiled reassuringly and put a hand on each of them. "You both must be tired. Why don't you come with us for a meal?"

"That would be nice, but we should really find somewhere to stay for the night," the man grumbled with his brow furrowed.

"Well, the drinks may have been on me tonight, but your meal and board"—Bokaj grinned, producing a small coin purse with a wink and a flourish—. "Is on the guards."

The old man stuttered for a moment, but his wife took it with a grateful smile. "Thank you, young man."

"Always happy to help." Bokaj smiled reassuringly as he led us toward the inn.

We sat with the couple and ordered whatever food was available. There weren't many large tables around, so we scooted a couple together, which didn't seem to bother the wait staff any. Bokaj went to see about the rooms for the night and came back a few minutes later.

"Luckily they have three rooms available." He glanced over to the elderly folks with a kind smile. "You two took the fourth, and the Braves I think are staying in their cart, right?"

Manly nodded, and the others did the same, so he looked back to the others. "Zeke and Mae get one, me and Balmur in another, and I know that James and Yohsuke are cool together. Jaken, who you want to bunk with man?"

"He can bunk with us." Yohsuke winked at the happy paladin. "We know what we need to do tomorrow, right?"

"Hope that guard doesn't realize he was hoodwinked?" Balmur offered helpfully before taking a sip of his drink, grimacing. "Oh, that may as well be piss."

"Specialty of the house, I'm afraid," a young waitress said tiredly as she joined us. "Your food will be out soon. Can I get you something *actually* worth drinking?"

I blinked; she was a good one. "Yes, please."

She bowed her head once and moved away, swatting the hand of what I hoped wasn't an off-duty guard away from her ass as she walked by without so much as a glance his way.

"Seems like the guard here want to get dead." I watched as the guard lifted his tankard to his lips and leered after her, waiting for her to come back.

A hand touched my shoulder and I glanced at Maebe. "She seems capable. Do not act unless you think it absolutely necessary, but if you do kill him, make it look like he started it."

Yup! I know, right? My wife, everybody. Isn't she just the best homicidal Fae you ever did meet? I know I feel that way. Back to it.

"Where are you youngsters headed?" The older woman asked as our food was brought out to us. "Oh! I'm sorry, you helped us, and we haven't even told you our names. I'm Lillian, and this old codger is Mic."

"Codger, she says." Mic snorted and winked at us. "She's older than I am."

She smacked him on the arm, and he just laughed and held up three fingers. It made me and a couple of the others laugh as well. Bokaj introduced us, then the Braves. Mic and Lillian seemed to know who they were and spent the majority of the meal having the group regal them with some of their wilier bounties.

I took the chance to look around the place while we ate.

There were a couple of bulkier men, likely the inn's protectors since it was outside the city wall.

How much you want to bet this place has a secret entrance to the city in it somewhere? Muu interrupted my thoughts, looking about furtively as I had been.

You know there is, it's flush with the fucking wall, man. I looked over to Yohsuke, who winked and pointed to the cellar door behind the bar area.

"Hey!" The waitress's annoyance reached us; her aggravation turned on the guard whose lap she now struggled in.

"Come on, Terra, you know I'd treat you right, I don't care that you're nobody inside the city." The guard, a beefy man who looked like he could bench a tank, tried to grope the feisty young woman as she continued to beat on his chest to no avail.

The enforcers in the corner stood, but the light hand on my shoulder as Maebe moved around us quickly kept me seated and the enforcers paused. Terra's hand rose and fell, slapping the brute across the face, making him angry enough that his hand rose. And it stayed there in Maebe's crushing grip, giving the young waitress time to stand and move slightly away.

At first, he seemed confused, the enforcers watched in the same mode of thought. But when he looked over into the fury that was Maebe's being, he must have seen something the rest of us didn't because the puddle forming in his lap spilled down to the floor around his ankles.

Maebe's voice was almost cold enough to make the man see his own breath as she sweetly whispered, "If you ever even think of touching a woman in the same manner again, the Unseelie will find you, and no matter where you look, you will see their red eyes staring at you from the shadows, waiting for you to stumble as you run."

She leaned forward, her head tilting as she did so, and stopped a mere inch away from him and uttered a single word that made the fur on the back of my neck stand on end, "Curse."

The man paled and began to buck and foam at the mouth

as he struggled to remove his hand from her grasp, but the sweetly smiling queen only held tighter. When he stopped moving, the candles in the room dimmed significantly before flaring to life once more, and she let go of him. He slumped to the floor into the puddle of his own making and stayed there.

The queen collected the frightened girl. "Do not fear me, child." Her slim hand caressed the girl's face, removing the dirty blonde hair from her eyes. "If a man ever treats you this way again, speak this."

Maebe leaned forward and whispered something into her ear that made the girl shiver and look at her in disbelief.

"And you'll come? You can do that?" Her eyes grew larger as the smaller woman nodded once, then leaned forward to give her a kiss on the forehead. "Thank you."

"Go and clean yourself, child." Maebe reached into her pocket, palming something that she handed to the girl and shooed her away.

The queen returned to the table, all eyes in the room on her or the unconscious man on the ground before one of the enforcers thought it safe enough to drag the asshat out of the room and to bring a bucket of water and a mop.

"And you said to make it look like an accident." I snickered, her green-eyed gaze turning on me.

"He will merely wish he was dead, but if he does what I told him not to, well..." She looked pointedly at one of the shadowed corners across from us, where a pair of crimson eyes blinked into existence, stared at me, then were gone.

"You are *terrifying*." I shivered, and she grinned wolfishly as if she knew. She did.

"We will begin to practice as soon as your meals are finished," She advised, looking me, Yoh and Balmur fully in the eyes as she spoke. "Enjoy yourselves now, but not too much."

She stood and walked outside as if nothing had happened. I finished my food swiftly, as did Yohsuke. Balmur had been done before us, eating fast had been a habit he picked up in the Hells.

He had just waited there for us, watching the room around us observantly, his eyes never really stopping for too long.

It was a habit that we had noted almost immediately, but it was times like this that we really noticed it. He lifted out his jar with three eyes in it and took a deep breath before lifting out a small organ to sacrifice. He stiffened and grunted as the eye was consumed, and he relived the demise of the poor bastard he'd taken it off of.

"Bounty hunters?" I asked quietly, and he nodded once. I left it at that.

We walked out the door, into the cool darkness of the night and began to look for Maebe. I focused on the ring, and it pulsed, leading me toward the far side of the building.

Once we were near, a dome of shadows that was almost indistinguishable against the trees and night sky appeared before us. I stepped through the dome with the others staying outside because they weren't certain.

"It's okay guys, you can come in." I poked my head out and motioned to the others to come inside.

They looked at each other, shrugged, and then stepped through with a shiver.

"It gets easier once you get used to it," I comforted them knowingly.

"Enough." Maebe calmly stated, her voice taking on an instructor's cadence. "We waste time. Zeke, call the shadows to you."

I focused on the shadows around me, expecting them to come to me as easily as they had been lately, and they didn't. *What the hell?*

"Yes, I am fighting you for control of them, and only you." She motioned to Yoh and Balmur. "They know very little of manipulating the nether, and you know only a little more. You, though, need to exercise those muscles and train harder. They will go through the same steps that you did."

She walked the two of them through working their will and intent of summoning the shadows to them. Balmur seemed to be having trouble with it, his reasoning being that his magic allowed him to move *through* the ink-black substance. Once he began to treat it like an entity rather than an inanimate object, he started to have more luck, moving it in little spurts.

Yohsuke was able to call it to him within the first hour, seeming to grasp the necessary mindset fairly quickly. Shadows came to him soon in waves, and he was beginning to have fun with it.

"Excellent, Yohsuke," Maebe purred proudly. "Keep focusing Balmur, you are doing well."

I struggled to pull a wisp of shadow to me with a grunt, and I just knew the veins in my neck were visible. "Zeke, your focus is good, but your will needs work. You try too hard to order the shadows to you, to bend them to what you want."

I released the pent-up breath I hadn't realized I was holding, and the oxygen to my brain eased the throbbing in my mind. I let my brain relax and reached forth, and out like I was one with the shadows.

I became them as my consciousness melded with them. I could feel Maebe in them as well, her control tenuous because she allowed it to be. So, I focused on calling a little of my mind and the shadows with it to me as if I were gathering myself.

I had my eyes closed, so I couldn't see anything, but I focused on bringing the element as old as time into my left hand that I held palm up at my waist.

As soon as I felt the build-up there, I cast my mind back out like a net and brought in a little more. And more. Until I had a tennis-ball-sized orb in my hand.

"I am proud of this," Maebe's voice whispered into my ear. "Release it, and start again, this time, with your eyes open. Again!"

We practiced for another two hours. Both of my friends receiving the shadow version of Elemental Tinkering and became further blessed by the void. Both of them, impressive feats in their own rights, but to have earned them without the same sacrifice of their vitality as I had given was a little galling.

Oh well, I was happy to know they had new weapons to fight with.

As we left the dome, I summoned all the shadows in the area around me to my hand and compacted them, my mana trickling away steadily. I packed it tighter and tighter until it was the size of a basketball, then threw it at Maebe. She grinned and stopped it with her hand.

"You are learning quickly, this will be the next game that you and I play while you work on gathering shadows to you." She crushed the ball between her hands and the shadows returned to the world. "No more, you need to rest now."

"Yes ma'am." I saluted, my hand snapping down to my side, then I pitched forward and fell onto my face.

I looked down to see shadows pooling around my foot. I looked over to Maebe, and she smiled but shook her head.

Then I looked over to my friends, and both of them smirked and bumped fists.

And so, the games began.

As we made our way into the inn, we pulled more juvenile pranks on each other before a sharp stinging sensation erupted on my ass.

Turning and looking back, Maebe held three long strands of shadow in her fist with a look of mild annoyance. "I thought I said no more?"

The other two rubbed their asses as well, and we headed up to our rooms for the evening.

CHAPTER TEN

We woke in the morning to the sound of hooves and whinnying and people speaking to each other. We grabbed a bite to eat down in the inn's dining area before walking into the rising sunlight.

The crowds had gathered at the gates to wait until they would open. A set of guards exited from a door built into them, and the larger ones began to swing inward.

"Alright, folks!" Called one of the men, "Don't worry, we'll get you all in nice and quick. Just be patient, and you'll be admitted."

"We should go over there," James grumbled sleepily. "Anyone check in on the elderly couple?"

"I looked into the room for them a few minutes after waking up and getting dressed. The room was completely empty." Jaken scratched his face absently. "Didn't look like it had been slept in at all."

That's weird.. "Did anyone see them go into their room?"

The others shook their heads, so we walked outside and into the crowd. The guards at the gate this morning only stopped people they weren't familiar with or who looked to present a threat. There weren't many it seemed.

They stopped us, as we were a large, armed group of people. Couldn't blame them.

"We're here to check the boards for any new marks what need huntin' down." Manly kindly smiled at the guard who had questioned us. "Braves o' the Thorn, at your service, my friend."

The guard's eyes widened, and he mouthed the words he'd heard and turned excitedly to his friend who held a logbook. He snatched the book and quill out of his friend's hands and passed it to Manly.

"Ahem, if each of you would sign this, please?" He looked hopeful.

"This ain't the same page he was writin' on," Manly said with a grin.

The guard glanced around, people were starting to take notice. "It's, uh… for me, ma'am."

Manly signed it and passed it to the rest of her friends who happily did so as well.

"These ones with you all, ma'am?" The guard looked us over, with another hopeful smile.

"Sure are," Nick answered for Manly. "Braves recruits."

Yohsuke bristled at being called a recruit, and James just smiled sardonically.

I was ambivalent about it—whatever helped us get in.

"I'll have you all sign it as well, then. Just to be safe. Here you go!"

He thrust the book into each of our faces and we signed where he pointed. He seemed like a good kid if not a little high strung.

"You got any suggestions on where we might find lodging and a good drink tonight, friend?" Bonnie smiled at the starstruck boy.

He stammered at first, then cleared his throat and said, "The

Wandering Swallow has some of the best ale in the city, and it's near the castle, so only folks what can afford it go there. They have large rooms and baths. Go straight from here, three streets in take a right, then a left at the next intersection, and keep going until you see the castle. It's along the water, so you'll see it."

"Thank you." Bonnie stepped closer and brushed a hand along his flushed cheek. "You'll be there, right? Don't tell anyone else we're here quite yet. Maybe we'll have a story for you to tell?"

Oh, this poor fucking kid.

He nodded violently, I thought I heard his brain hit his helmet, then he ushered us through with a grin.

"One of these days, Bonnie you'll find a man who makes you want to settle down." Manly chuckled at her friend.

Bonnie turned a seductive gaze toward the other woman, then winked. "I have to try looking, don't I?"

I snorted, and the others chuckled at her as well. Walking through the city so early was a little bit of a pain so close to the gate, but by the time we needed to make our turn, we had broken from the crowds and worked into the more urban area.

This portion of the city was okay. There was money here, and that was obvious, but there was nothing really here but food stalls and children who looked to need a bath and a few good meals. They begged, pleading for food and money, their clothes torn, muddied, and sometimes too small.

Maebe took my hand as we walked on and I felt her heart breaking, through our new bond, as she saw some of the children.

"Don't worry, love." I comforted her. "We will get ourselves set up with a room, then we can wander before seeing the king, or after. But first, we get lodging out of the way."

"Why don't you guys just go to the guard and get it over with?" Balmur wondered.

"Because they may try to attack us if they find out what we are exactly," I answered carefully in a low tone. "At least with the royals themselves, they may listen to reason."

More children stared out at us from the alleys and shadows near doorframes, pitiful looking and poorly clothed.

"If they approach us, I will not be able to tell them no," she whispered, her hands rubbing her arms as she went. "The iron here is already making me uncomfortable. Please, do not make me deny them."

"I won't unless it gets too bad." I kissed her forehead, and we moved on. Walking silently before I had to ask. "You know, in some of the Fae lore where I come from, the Fae steal children, some to replace with changelings, others just outright. Why?"

She thought for a moment. "Changelings are fickle things, but if you can bind them to you, they make excellent spies. Those children who are taken are usually assimilated by the changeling sent there. Meaning they become one being. They aren't harmed, and very rarely do they ever hate their lives. They have the strength and resilience of the Fae and retain autonomy when they are awake."

"And the other thing, I asked?" I blinked, keeping my voice low as I glanced about us.

"The others, at least from the Unseelie perspective, are taken, and given what they would never have in the Prime Realm," there was a sadness in her tone as she explained. "As I said, not all Fae can have children, but most of my kind love them fiercely. They are taken and made Fae, if they wish, and given the love and adoration they deserve. These children… these little ones deserve so much more."

"They aren't harmed? Even if they want to return home?" I tried to keep the judgment from my tone, but it crept in, anyway.

"Oftentimes, they are given back with gifts." Maebe took a coin from her pocket and chucked it into the lap of a small child sitting to the side of the street. The girl looked around wildly to see if it was a trap, then snatched it up and skittered away.

"Those gifts vary, some monetary, some magical, some with

a Fae creature who serves as a guardian until they are strong enough to protect themselves," there were tears in her eyes as she stopped herself from doing more.

"What would need to be done to see some of these kids taken care of?" Jaken asked from behind us, startling me out of my own thoughts on the matter.

"First, finding Fae royalty, or nobility, who could stand to be around this much iron for an extended time." Maebe scooted closer still. "And one powerful enough to take them to our realm. Someone like me, or someone who would rival my strength. All of them. All of them could go if someone strong enough were here."

It was hard to follow at first, but as we walked by a house, I noticed the nails in the walls. They were everywhere—iron was everywhere. And she was right here in it.

"What about an extremely powerful Fae who owes their loyalty to you?" James offered, and I looked about angrily. Who the fuck else was listening in?

Those two were it. Good.

"They would need to be highly intelligent and magically gifted," she frowned as she thought. "I know of one, but I do not know that she would be interested in ferrying them across to my realm."

"Let's get to the inn, and we can talk more." Jaken said as more and more people filled the streets.

It took us about an hour and a half of walking to get to the point we could see the castle, a large, copper-looking affair that turning green with time loomed in the distance.

Bokaj asked around, and someone pointed us to this building with vibrant green walls, a dark roof, and sign out front embossed with a large swallow on it that held a small fish in its beak. How cute.

Bird? Kayda landed on my shoulder in her smaller form and eyed the signage.

"It is a bird, not as pretty as you, though." I reached up and stroked her feathers affectionately.

Bokaj went in first to ensure they had rooms available, which they did. He got each of the others a room for themselves at six gold apiece, a steep price, but it included dinner and bathing. Mae and I got our own room at eight gold, but there were two tubs in this one and a slightly larger bed.

While we were there, we hatched a plan to help put Maebe at ease and help the children.

"Would it be smart to ask the crown before we just send the Fae in to take care of these kids?" Balmur sat on the floor near the door as we spoke in one of the rooms we had procured.

"What kind of noble is going to willingly agree to have the waifs of his kingdom relinquished to the Fae?" Muu, tapping his foot because there was almost no space for us all to move in the private dining room we had crammed into.

"None." Bokaj shrugged, frowning. "If they let these kids rot like this, they don't have the infrastructure to take care of them, or they don't care."

"And if we act before we know, we could turn the whole city against us." Maebe's hand tightened on mine as I aired my worries. "So, I think we should wait until we know more about what's going on."

Jaken growled, his teeth grinding a little. "They're suffering now."

"And another few hours to a day at most." Yohsuke put a hand on his shoulder to calm him. "Look, man I know that you're gung-ho about this kind of thing. Maebe too. And I've got little brothers and sisters too, so I know how you feel about wanting all of these kids to be safe."

He looked at the rest of us, his eyes resting on Maebe. "We have to do this smart. But we may not have to wait too much longer after finding out."

He closed his eyes in thought, the rest of us watching to see what he came up with, but it was Balmur who surprised us.

"We get the Fae ready before we go talk to the royals," he glanced at Maebe. "You know any Fae who are adept with portals?"

"Many, but they need an anchor. Something that would create a natural rupture in the veil." She frowned, her finger tapping her jaw. "We could try and find something to use as one. A mushroom circle, or a stone henge?"

"Can Zeke make something?" Muu proposed and shrugged as I stared at him. "He's made some really amazing things so far, and he's not even at master level in enchanting. He could do this if he has access to the proper materials, right?"

"I might be able to, but I wouldn't really know how or feel comfortable doing so." I sighed, wishing I was better at this. "I'm not good enough, I don't think. And other than blood, I don't think there would be a powerful enough component to use that would attract the Fae we needed."

"What about that spell that Nicolas used?" Maebe's gaze flashed. "He was able to forcibly send me back to the Fae realm. Could he pull something here?"

"I guess what I don't understand is why you don't just open a portal like you have been?" Yohsuke looked confused. "If you're strong enough to open the door for yourself, letting some Fae you trust through wouldn't be that big of an issue."

"Because when I come through, I forcibly tear through the veil and come here," Maebe explained patiently, using her hands to show what she meant. "Doing so taxes me greatly, and if I am simply returning home, it would be fine. My strength recovers faster there. Here? It returns slower. Much slower. And it would leave me vulnerable."

"Okay." I frowned, then smiled. "So then, we need to weaken the veil."

"That's what I'm sayin'!" Jaken threw his hands in the air excitedly, accidentally elbowing Muu. "Sorry, man."

"It's cool, just my face, no worries." He rolled his eyes before looking at me. "What's the play?"

"I make the items, but I design them in a way that they only weaken the veil so that way whoever does the tearing doesn't get weakened too much." I grimaced. "I'm not sure what kind of materials to use."

After a few minutes of quiet thought, Maebe sighed heavily, looking at my arm, then the others. "I want this. And it gives me an opportunity to teach Zeke more of the Fae." She stood slowly. "I am going to call in another favor from Xiphyre."

"But, Mae." I stood with her, the two of us perilously close to being *too* close. This room really was too small. "I can do it; it shouldn't be too hard—"

"Like last time you were out of your depth?" She shot back, Yoh and Muu nodding in agreement. "He can teach you. He can help you understand, but he will be doing this. Better that I keep all of you safe and help those children than keep another two favors to lord over him for another few centuries."

It was hard to argue that logic, though I was curious about the things she had to teach me.

"We will leave soon," she nodded to the others and looked to me, "Please, join me in our room for a moment."

I nodded to the others, and we left, opening the door narrowly and slipping into the main dining area of the inn. It was beautifully and expensively decorated with all-wood fittings. After walking up the stairs, we took a left, and our room was at the end of the hall on the left side. Once inside, the bed made the room a little smaller since it was bigger, but it would do.

"Sit on the bed, and I will explain." Maebe waved to the tan comforter that felt so thick beneath me as I sat.

She wove her hands in front of her and shadows so thick I thought they were night, filtered into the air around us. They meshed together at the top, and the sound of the world around us fell away as if I had water in my ear.

I hated it instantly.

"Now, what I am about to teach you is referred to as the Calling." I blinked at her and she continued, obviously aware I would be confused, "The Calling is simple. It is what a powerful Fae does to call a lesser Fae to them, no matter where they are. It is how I summoned Xiphyre to begin with."

I nodded because what she said tracked with some things I

had heard before, but I didn't know fully the gravity of it. Not yet.

"When you call a Fae, you must use their true name, or they will not hear you."

That gave me pause. "Wait, I know that true names are important to your kind, but how is it that you can hear when people say your name, but others don't?"

Her smile was that of an encouraging teacher, "Think. Why could that be?"

"It can't be because you are *actually* using your true name, could it?" I frowned, and her smile deepened. "But that's crazy! That means anyone could use that against you."

"They cannot, because while one holds the crown, their true name becomes their power." she frowned as she thought of a way to explain it. "You told me once of a title you had earned, 'Marine?'"

I nodded for her once, my chest puffing up a little despite my usually relaxed nature toward my service.

"Think of the name becoming my title." She waved her hands, and a crown of ice and shadows appeared in her grasp. She tilted it onto her head and eyed me. "As I wear the crown, my name becomes me and more. It can never be taken, because I own all aspects of it, as it was gifted to me. When the next to take the throne does so, they will assume full control over their true name as I have."

"But what about once you abdicate the throne?" She looked at me in surprise. "Yeah, I'm literate. I like big words."

She laughed then; a throaty rumble that made me smile in return.

"You never fail to surprise me, husband." Her green eyes sparkled as she said the word again under her breath, "Husband. I do so love the way that feels. But yes. After we abdicate the throne, our name stays the same. The crown cuts the tie of the name from us, and we are whole with it. It is difficult to explain."

I smiled back at her from the bed. "Thank you for trying. So, the Calling, how do you do it?"

"You speak the true name of the Fae you wish to summon, and they are called to you." She gestured toward the room before her, where there was a little room. "It is simple, really, and I will show you now. But I cannot betray Xiphyre's confidence. He is much too powerful to have as an enemy."

I raised my eyebrows, and shrugged. "Too useful as well."

"You are learning to think as a Fae royal. Excellently said." She made a motion, and a globe of darkness covered my head, obscuring my view and hearing for a second, I panicked, then it was gone. "There, it is done."

"How long does it take?" I asked curiously as I watched the air around us.

"Not too long." Maebe joined me on the bed, her hand clasping my own. "After that, I will teach you to do it."

"I don't know if I want to summon anything like that if it could be potentially devastating to your power." I frowned as the scent of ozone and nickels pervaded the room, and a rent in the air burst open, and Xiphyre shot out. Naked.

"This had better be g—Majesty." The Ragalfr knelt in front of us and looked up, his serene features taking on a look of shock. "Those rings!"

His supplication forgotten as he fluttered close enough, "I made these several centuries ago for…your grandmother on her wedding day."

His eyes shot back up to Maebe's face, her countenance controlled and observant.

"You…" His eyes shot back to me, then back to her. "With him…? Majesty, this is quite the scandal if I may say so myself. The court will be beside themselves!"

Maebe's hand shot out and grasped the winged man by his throat, pulling him close to her face so that she could snarl at him. "They will find out when *I* am ready for them to. Until then, you will make something for me. Call it another debt cashed in."

Maebe released him, and he righted himself mid-fall.

"What can I make for the Queen and her King?" He bowed as if he actually cared. The little shit.

"You will make either an item or a series of items that will assist in weakening the veil between this realm, and the Fae." He gave her an odd look, but she continued. "If it can be portable, that would be best. But I want you to teach Zeke how to do it, as well. He needs the training."

"He does." Xiphyre shrugged. "If it will get rid of one of the favors I owe you, fine. It will be hard, though. The item that I will need has to be the highest quality, so it must be Thogan who makes it. The components...three different samples of Unseelie Fae blood, and two of blood from people of this realm."

He landed on the ground and paced, then stopped and closed his eyes. "Thogan? It's Xiphyre, shut up and stop what you're doing. I don't care if you're making mead, I said stop!"

I leaned toward Maebe, whispering to her as I watched the scene in front of me, "Is he always like this?" She nodded. "When is he going to put pants on?"

"I heard that!" The little man snapped.

———

While Xiphyre prepared for his enchanting, Thogan was hard at work on the item he had requested. It was painfully simple, according to the Fae, so it shouldn't take more than a few hours, but we would see how that went. As for the components, Rowland had offered his own blood as a component, and one of the children would likely have to suffice otherwise.

It had taken some use of my raven messenger, but it made things much easier for us, being able to speak almost directly.

Xiphyre would use some of his own blood, and Mae offered hers at the time of enchantment. Blood was a powerful thing and though he owed her, Xiphyre was crafty. Giving him access to it could prove dangerous. The final vial Maebe filled with a small creature she summoned with a word muttered so low that not even I could hear it.

We met with the others, and then we were off. I guessed that during this time of day, most people who held jobs were at them, because the area nearing the castle was pretty deserted. The castle, made of stone and glass in small chunks that looked worn but the higher additions looked to be made of copper like I had seen from a distance. The side that faced the ocean was green from oxidation like the Statue of Liberty. It was cool to see that those same kinds of scientific changes and reactions took place here.

There was a moat around the castle, more than thirty feet wide, and the land it was on seemed to be connected by a bridge over the water, and maybe some other contraptions under the water. Perhaps it was like a vessel? If the city was attacked, the royals and those in the castle could go out to sea and coordinate an attack by the water?

Observations about the area aside, making our way toward the castle in human form had proven to be very easy, though it proved a little more difficult than we thought to get through the guards, even with the Braves' help. They tagged along for this leg of the journey to give their accounting of what had happened in Lindyburg as well.

"The king and queen don't have time for every person in the realm who cries foul of their local governors, we would need good proof, and even then, it would have to go through the proper channels to ensure it isn't tripe." The human guard, to his credit, seemed like he knew what he was talking about.

His scarred features and burly build even lent him a little more credibility than the half dozen others around him. But it was just his bad luck that he happened across us.

Maebe was fed up. She was tired of this city. She was tired of the iron. And she sure as *shit* was tired of being told no.

"You will take us to the king and queen, now, human." She smiled sweetly as she growled at him, throwing me off.

"You say that as if you aren't one yourself," the guard

narrowed his eyes at us. "You all here under false pretenses? Or are you like some of the others who try to pretend they're important when they don't get their way?"

"I think you can drop the act, My Queen." Yohsuke sighed and knelt on the ground where he stood.

The others did the same, except for me. I stood at her side, on her right hand, just behind her shoulder. It was weird, but I would have to get used to it.

Maebe waved her hand, and the majority of her glamour fell away. Her yellow sundress turning into a form-fitting, black silken affair with bits of yellow near the hips that peeked out. Pale, ice blue accents flared out along her chest and neck to highlight the ebony of her skin, even with the starlit freckles. On her head sat her crown of ice and shadow.

"May I introduce the Queen of Dark and Cold, She Who Whispers Death to Her Foes, Queen Maebe. Ruler of the Unseelie Fae, and visitor to the king and queen of this realm," I did my best to keep my voice emotionless as if I were narrating a video back home. My inflection was important, but my bearing was necessary. "It would be best if you led us to your rulers. I doubt they want you keeping visiting royalty waiting."

The guard motioned to the others to bow deeply, then stood. "Raplie, three sharps and a long, please."

The thinnest man with a horn on his left hip pulled a string deftly and raised it to his lips. He blew three sharp bursts of noise, then one long one that lasted ten seconds. The head guard clapped the younger man on the shoulder, then motioned that we follow him.

Smooth talking, man, Yohsuke teased. *Good thing master sergeant was always a stickler for news voice, huh?*

Video, video, video, I groaned back. Yoh had been privy to more than a couple of our lectures on the importance of videography from one of the senior Marines in my office who had gone to Syracuse for it. The dude was amazing, and I learned a lot from him, but *damn* did he have a hard-on for video.

I pushed the thought from my mind and paid attention to our surroundings. We walked over the moat, the water giving me the creeps as I glanced down and saw motion under the lightly lapping waves. Not going into *that* water without a damned fine reason. No sir. Not this fox.

Once we were back on land, we entered a large hall, this was easily another thirty feet wide, the large ebon-wood doors opened wide. The interior was simplistic, the masonry on the side decorated with murals of sweeping tides carved into the walls. It was what was in those tides that I found equally as intimidating as those outside.

There were murder holes lining the stone walls and guards spaced every twenty feet as we walked through.

Muu, shield arm to the left of Maebe, walk a little in front of her and out of her immediate reach. Jaken, you take the right side and do the same. Shit gets heavy, you two crush in and guard Maebe.

They stepped forward with no argument, shields out and ready just in case.

"Not a necessary precaution," the guard leading us advised amicably. "Those murder holes are only armed in times of war and for training purposes."

We remained quiet, letting our silence speak as to our belief in that statement. He sighed and continued on. After a moment or so, he had us enter a room with lavish couches, servants who looked bored until we walked in, and a small table in the center. Once we were in and seated, they busied themselves pouring wine, water, and other refreshments as the guard went to fill in whoever it was that he answered to.

It was a good half an hour before anyone came to collect us, but the man who did looked respectable. His armor was simple, covered in a tabard of a shark fighting what looked like some kind of octopus in seafoam green and gray. He wore a neatly trimmed blond goatee with a smartly curled handlebar mustache. His gray eyes sparkled in the light of the room, and his perfectly coiffed blond hair had gray near the sideburns.

The guy was definitely silver fox material.

"Good day, all of you, I am Jay Renald." He bowed low at his waist and lifted his head to speak. "My humblest apologies, Queen Maebe, on your heinous wait. The king and queen are receiving a report currently, but they have asked that you be introduced to them without delay. If you would, please, follow me?"

"We would be delighted." Maebe's smile looked to be forced, and it showed on his face that he knew.

He stood and backed out of the doorway, allowing us to stand and have Jaken leave the room first to ensure it was safe. After that was me, then Maebe, then the others, with Muu bringing up the rear.

For the next leg of the journey, the halls were much more constricted, about six feet wide at the most, and there was only a set of guards at the beginning of the hall and another set at the end of it. Each of them were armed to the teeth. Swords on each hip, belt knives, shields on the walls behind them that looked great as decoration and as if they could take a beating, and they all held halberds.

Guard Lvl 30

That wasn't bad at all. These must have been the guards that Zhavron had been talking about when he referred to ours. How he thought they would be better than these guys. If that was the case, Sunrise was in good hands indeed.

We walked through both the hall and the guards unmolested, which was good. Starting a fight with these guys would have sucked if all of them joined in. Dodged that bullet.

Through the doors was a truly spectacular sight to behold. I wasn't one for the ocean, but with a view like this? I'd give it a shot.

The entire back wall was open to the water, serene crystal waters lapped at the edge of the stone floor. Pillars supported the room, but they looked like they could have been made of pure sand like someone had made the entire structure to be a sandcastle.

Inside, the room itself was open to the light from the

noonday sun flooding in from the side windows and the rear wall. Carpeted flooring in the center gave way to what looked like tan stone.

To the left of us as we entered, was a raised set of steps leading to three thrones, and before them was a couple that looked vaguely familiar.

"And as you can see, Your Excellencies, if the city guard are allowed to continue this grievous injustice to our people, this dire dereliction of duty, our people will suffer." The older gentleman spoke. His clothes were much, *much* finer than they had been, but that was the old man who had been at the gates. And next to him was his wife. Or was she really his wife?

"Thank you, Pilth," the man in the center throne rumbled, his baritone voice sturdy, but somehow full of kind regard. "And Virrity, your report?"

"Just that a serious ass-kicking be issued to the city guard, Your Majesty." The old man looked like he was about to shit himself, but the woman seemed uncaring. "They think that their time on and off shift is their own and not that of the city's. Some of them care not for the subjects, the reputation of our city, nor even the reputation of the guard. Why, if it hadn't been for the Fae Queen who just walked into the door over there and her entourage, a girl may have been sullied by one of those brutes."

The woman in the left throne leaned forward, it was hard to make out her features from this far, but her soft voice carried, "How do you mean?"

"Had his greasy mitts almost all the way up her blouse at one point, and when she made to defend herself and her honor, he made to hit her back." The old woman took the can in her hand and thumped it onto the ground, making me jump a little. "But Queen Maebe of the Unseelie put a stop to that. Cursed the boy. Likely scared him into priesthood."

She cackled maniacally at that and turned to look over at us before continuing, "That is all of our findings, Majesties. If it pleases you, we would stay and welcome your guests with you? I am certain they would have no issue assuring you that our claims are just and fair."

Jay took that as his time to motion us forward. Maebe led the way of course, and the knight announced us, "My King, Queen, and Princess, it is with profound honor that I introduce to you, Queen Maebe, leader of the Unseelie Fae, the Coldest Night, her entourage and the Braves of the Thorn."

The King stood, followed by his wife and their daughter, striding down the steps with practiced ease, the king smiling as he greeted my wife. "Queen Maebe, a pleasant and unexpected surprise!"

"Indeed." Maebe smiled and curtsied at him. He came up short and bowed back, his wife and daughter mimicking Maebe's greeting.

The king was a man in his mid to late forties with greying hair and a short beard. He was a little flabby about the midsection but was tall and muscular still, his greenish-blue eyes sharp as they took us all in.

"Please, it has likely been centuries since you cared for human politicking, I am Abioye Westwind." He motioned to his wife, then his daughter, "My wife, and Queen, Chareen West-wind, and our daughter Princess Villeroa. We welcome you to Zephyth."

The Queen Chareen was young, possibly even our age, in her twenties, well-muscled, but on the thin side and had long, silver hair. Her black, swallow-tailed eyes flitted to each face, as if memorizing each individual. The pint-sized princess was an adorable mix of her mother and father. She had white hair with the same thin eyes as her mother, but with her father's blue coloration and was a little chunk. Like I said, adorable. She looked like she couldn't be too much older than my son. Maybe around seven or eight?

"As your knight so aptly introduced, I am Queen Maebe, and those are the Braves of the Thorn, likely someone that you know of in passing?" The king nodded, and his daughter was instantly switched on where she had looked to merely be suffering through the day. She paid more attention now that there seemed to be something worthy of her time. "The rest are Knights of the Unseelie, and this one is my husband, King Zekiel."

Oh, that was going to take some fucking getting used to.

"The honor is ours," Queen Chareen spoke and nodded her head once. "Tell me, please, is it true what Lady Virrity reported?"

"All of it is truth, so I swear by my power and title." Damn, she was pulling out all the stops!

The queen gasped at the notification she received from the oath, and I was happy to see the outrage on her face.

"If I might add, Your Majesty," Bokaj held up his hand and leaned out so that he could be seen and heard clearer. "The guards made it a point to be as rude and condescending as possible, and to ensure that everyone knew that they didn't care... except for one, and he was the one who handled her patting down, ma'am."

"I see." Her jaw clenched, and she glanced over to Jay. "Sir Renald?"

"Once this is through, My Queen, I swear to you that I shall *personally* see to the reformation of the city guard and that it soars beyond your expectations." He bowed slightly at his waist and stood proud after.

"Thank you, my good knight." The king smiled and looked back at Maebe. "To what do we owe this pleasure?"

"It seems that my knights ran afoul of the Governess of Lindyburg when they were taken advantage of by a powerful bard who stole something from her," Maebe began, but the king raised a hand for her to pause.

"Lindyburg, you say? We received a strange missive from her concerning a conquest against magic." He turned to his wife, who handed him the note. "Ah, yes. 'These filthy magic users corrupt our people and sway their minds with their deceitful ways and demon-begotten powers...' it goes on for some time then titters off into madness and talk of hunts and genocide. We have little to no mages of note among our kind here, Queen Maebe, for the fact that many among the fair-folk and neighboring lands see human magicians as budding evils."

"They hold your past against you," Yohsuke spoke, drawing attention, then averting his gaze.

"Quite," the king sighed. "We have military might, and trade with enchanters for some magical items, but we are vulnerable without magic. To be truthful, being rid of the abilities in others would give us protection from those who have it and would seek to use it against us."

Queen Chareen's gaze hardened, and her face became a mask. Their daughter, Villeroa simply stepped away, moving toward the back wall where the sparkling waters refracted rainbows and shimmering light along the high ceiling of the room. She swayed next to the water on her own, and Renald joined her to point out things in the water as she giggled.

"That is a difficult stance to take." Maebe's eyebrows raised in surprise, but otherwise, her face was stoic. I could feel the emotions through our budding connection, though. Fury. Anger. And something I didn't know she could feel—fear.

"We would do only what we had to, but what choice do we have?" Chareen stepped closer to her husband so that she could hold his hand. "No mages will work for us outside of mercenaries, and bloodlines with magic in them were wiped out long ago. Before even the eldest of our citizens were born, magic was stolen from us by those who thought us inept because of people who decided they would play at being gods."

Move away droplet. A cool sensation entered my thoughts as Maebe spoke again, drowning her out. *We need to speak, now.*

I blinked and looked to the others. *I'm good right now, but I'm going to go over here by the water and talk to the Primordial Water Elemental.*

Everything alright? Muu bumped my shoulder with his to catch my eye.

I don't know. I answered, honestly. I stepped away from the group of them with a bow. "Forgive me, Majesties, I feel a little out of sorts. Some fresh air may do me good."

"My most heartfelt apologies!" Queen Chareen frowned before clapping loudly. Two servants separated themselves from behind the thrones. "Fetch the guest tables, fine food, and drink for our guests, set up near the water. Go. Please, friend, go and wait by the water with Renald and the princess."

I bowed, and they nodded as if to dismiss me and did as I said I would. *Yes, Water Prime, what can I do for you?*

The others are still in deliberations, but I refuse to allow them to beat me in this, her voice lapped against my mind.

I guess I don't understand then, beat you in what? If it's about letting us earn some power, we would appreciate the opportunity—I began hopefully, but she cut me off.

Not just you and your friends, droplet, the world. As I stared at the ocean, I saw the water take a definition I hadn't seen before. Like it was as living and breathing a being as I was. *A threat to magic has come to realization.*

Well, I hardly believe that one crazy governess in a city a few days from here is a true threat to magic. I snorted at the idea of that blathering loon being a realistic threat. Even if there was currently talk of it mere yards away.

No, droplet, not just her. The serene waves grew choppy in front of me. *There are rumblings that the generals and minions are plotting to target those who use magic and kill them. Those with magic are targets and those without are vulnerable.*

Shit. I turned my mind back to the conversation at hand. *What do you need of me? Of us? The others will agree to help you, I'm certain.*

I am of the mind that we have the ability to step in and assist in protecting our world even further, and it was my dirty brother who started it.

If that meant what I thought it did, then something was about to get magical.

I sense potential around you, and as my brother did before me, I will also relinquish a gift for the changing times. Droplet, assist me. Find the one who holds the potential around you. Do this, and I will continue to vouch for you with the others.

QUEST ALERT!

Wet Behind The Ears – The Primordial Water Elemental has requested you help her find the person near you with a potential affinity for water magic.

Reward: Assisted representation with the other elemental Primordials as they debate further involvement in the affairs of mortals.

Failure: Loss of trust and potential favor with the Water Primordial.

Will you accept? Yes? / No?

I shared it with the others immediately, all of them stopping and looking toward me as I accepted it.

They looked around at each other, the servants who came in to set up food and drinks on tables they had brought into the room. The tables were small, and the food smelled really good. But my mind was on how the fuck we were going to do this?

Maebe and the other royals glanced my way. "King Zekiel, what is wrong?"

"What if I were to offer your people a way to fix that?" I blinked, fighting to come up with a reasonable explanation for what I was talking about as they openly stared at me in fascinated horror.

"My husband, as well as some of the other knights in my company, have odd bonds with higher beings. Mother Nature, myself, the gods, and even the elementals themselves." Maebe blinked at me. "I take it you mean the last of them?"

I nodded, then did the kingly thing and opened my damned mouth to speak for myself, "Someone here has caught the Water Elemental Primordial's attention. She's asked if we would help facilitate a test of sorts to see who among you has the potential she seeks."

"And what would this mean?" The king stepped forward and motioned to his daughter to come to his side, brushing her back behind him to his wife, who clasped her shoulders. "To whom would we owe fealty for this 'gift?'"

"No one," I shrugged and held a hand out to the water. "You have the biggest supply of water anyone with water-based magic could ever want, and you were just complaining that you don't have the magic you need to appropriately defend yourselves. Rather than weakening the world around you by killing those who have what you so sorely lack, you could reach out and take your lives back."

He seemed unconvinced, so I added with probably more venom than I should have, "Rather than taking another step down a path of hate and discontent in the shadows of your ancestors, do something worthwhile. Take magic and make life with it. Be among the first to become whole new beings." The king's eyes bulged, and he looked ready to fight. "Seize this opportunity to claim power your ancestors abused! Walk away from the past, having learned from it and help your people prosper!"

The servants had stopped what they were doing, some of them fearful, and the footsteps of metal-clad guards came into the room from where we had entered. One of the guards stepped in and eyed me.

"This gift is offered freely, then?" The king narrowed his eyes at me, then turned to look at the ocean.

"Power always has a price, and as I learned from a hero early on in life, 'with great power, comes great responsibility,'" I stepped closer to him, and Abioye didn't budge. "There is always a price for power, but the elementals want to help. We don't want anyone to die for their natural abilities any more than you want your people to perish for the mistakes of your forefathers. Stand with us in this, and you will gain much."

The others in my party moved to stand with me, some of them looking at the king comfortingly. Others, Yohsuke, scowling but remaining quiet.

"Then, we can try." He raised his head and regarded the servants. "All of you finish what you are doing, then come back so that we can administer the test. And yes, Filten, you as well, my boy, come here."

The guard in the door looked uncomfortable but marched forward to stand closer to Sir Renald.

"How do we administer this test?" Chareen stepped closer quietly as she watched things being set up.

How would you like them to do this, my watery Lady? I questioned the Water Prime.

No answer. Thinking back to my lessons with Maebe, Balmur, and Yohsuke, I had an idea, though.

I held my hand out and willed the shadows in the farthest corner to come to me. The inky darkness slithered across the floor and rushed into my hand excitedly.

"We see who it decides that it likes." I shrugged. Honestly, it was the best way to do this that I was aware of.

We waited patiently as the servants finished setting up, then they gathered and sat on their knees on the floor until they were needed. Very rough way to sit, but if they were used to it, who was I to judge?

"It may be a good idea to have everyone gather along the missing wall nearest the water so that we can do this." I frowned. There were twenty people, including the royalty and the guard. This was going to be fun.

"Why not have those of us who are familiar with magic spread out and watch over the others and offer advice," Yohsuke offered as he began to assist in lining everyone up about a foot and a half apart from each other so we could see between them. "Maybe have our king and queen assist the royalty?"

"That is an excellent idea." King Abioye smiled as he looked toward Maebe and his wife. "It will be difficult then?"

"It is magic, my love." Chareen smiled at the older man affectionately. "It is wiliest and elusive when you want it."

That gave me pause. "Queen Chareen, you know much about magic?"

She shook her head, "Only that it can be tricky. There were

people in my homeland, shamans and spirit warriors who used magic, but always at great personal cost. The magic was taxing and terribly ineffective if you sought it out. Some of our best mages were those who had never wanted it to begin with."

"Where are you from?" It was hard to hide my curiosity, which never failed to get me into trouble back home.

"I am from the continent of beasts, my people came here not more than ten years ago," she informed me with a rigid back and turned her sights back to the ocean in front of her.

"My Queen does not normally care to speak of her homeland." Abioye put a comforting hand on her shoulder. "It makes her terribly homesick. Should we begin?"

I nodded and took a steadying breath. Using my chest, I spoke loudly as I explained the process of calling to the element before them.

"Clear your mind and focus on what the water in front of you looks like. What it sounds like. Let its scent fill your nose and mind. Envision what the water before you means to you and what you know of it." My voice boomed as I called to them. "Close your eyes, and see it in your mind and then will it to come to you."

All of us watched as they began to do so. The king and queen were closest to the throne, with the princess standing behind her mother as she had been ordered, watching things with interest.

Ten minutes after we started, one of the servants pitched backward with a nosebleed and another crumpled to the floor.

"Don't lock your knees!" I heard James bark at some of them. "Keep focusing."

I looked over at the water in front of everyone, and there was nothing. I turned, watching the Braves pick at some of the food on the tables with interest, so I called to them, "Hey, why don't you guys get over here and try some of this out?"

"Am no good wit' magic, lad," Nick answered as he popped a small sandwich into his mouth and grimaced. "That were sour."

Manly bit into an apple and smiled, "Dawn and I aren't the types to have elemental magic, I tried my hand at magery and never liked it."

I looked at Dawn, and she pointed to the crest on her arm with a small, knowing smile. Bonnie sauntered over and began to try and do what the others were doing, then gave up after a moment. Nicolas, well, he just appeared disinterested as a rule.

"Magic is amazing, but elemental magic is just so... base." He shook his head as he motioned in the air with his hands. "I prefer magic that bends reality to my will, thank you."

"Would you fuckers just try so that we can be safe?!" Muu howled from the other end of the hall, and they all hurriedly got up to comply. Though Manly looked like she was about to walk down there and shove an arrow up his ass.

I turned back and noticed that a few more of the servants and Renald had given up. The king was drenched in sweat and looked to be growing pale. Then I saw a flicker of motion in front of the queen. Villeroa had wandered over and was pointing at the water in front of her mother.

The king began clapping as a section the size of a small fishbowl rose out of the water with a very colorful fish in it and separated from the waves.

"So pretty, momma," the little girl spoke for the first time since we had gotten here, wonder evident in her voice. Then I noticed that it wasn't the queen who was raising the water, but the princess.

CONGRATULATIONS!

Quest completed - Wet Behind The Ears – The Primordial Water Elemental has requested you help her find the person near you with a potential affinity for water magic.

Reward: Assisted representation with the other elemental Primordials as they debate further involvement in the affairs of mortals.

Damn.

CHAPTER ELEVEN

She is the one I will give my strength to first, droplet. I felt the cool of the water in my mind, and it felt like somehow, she watched the little girl.

Her parents watched her in stunned silence, and the others in the room were pleased to see her interacting with the water as well.

But she's a child! I tried to reason with her, but she wasn't having it.

As was the dwarven boy who is now an earth mage, She retorted, and I couldn't argue with her logic. *Do as you did for the dwarven child and show her how to summon her elemental companion.*

I growled audibly, and the people around me looked worried, but I just ignored them.

"Princess Villeroa?" The child looked over at me, her blue eyes sparkling with joy in the light. "I've been asked to show you how to summon a friend. Please, join me?"

I walked to the side of the wall area and checked over the side where I saw a thin embankment that I dropped down onto deftly.

I reached up, and the girl glanced at her parents for permission, they were too stunned to say or do anything, and she just happily took my hand and hopped down with my help.

"What I want you to do, is touch the water and call out to the Primordial Water Elemental." Thinking back to Fainnir, I added, "There's no right or wrong way to do it. All you have to do is just *know* that she will hear you. Okay? Okay. Go ahead now."

She looked me over cautiously, then reached down into the water and concentrated, before mumbling, "Hello, my Lady. I'm doing as you asked."

"You do so wonderfully, child." A voice coming from the water before her spoke. The creature that stood on the water looked like a watery version of the little girl in front of it, but with a lot less detail, no eyes, and a mouth that seemed to work well.

"What's your name?" Villeroa's voice squeaked out softly, as if she weren't used to speaking.

"I can be called many things, child," the water elemental spoke softly, her watery hand rising to brush a stray white lock of hair from her face. "But what you call me will seal our bond. What will you call me?"

"Zygnal!" The little girl giggled.

"What does that mean, princess?" My curiosity peaked.

"It means beautiful in my mother tongue," Chareen's voice coming from next to my head spooked me. She knelt on the floor above us.

"She is," Villeroa insisted.

"Thank you, child." Zygnal bowed her head. "Our pact is sealed. I will protect you and grow with you. Please, take good care of me, and I will do the same for you."

"So, who will it be that teaches her magic?" The king wondered aloud.

"I will teach her some." Zygnal looked up. "I will explain the basics to her, and the prime will teach her as she sees fit. There is no one more qualified to teach her."

"And this is supposed to help us?" The king sighed tiredly,

his eyes closed, and he looked older at that moment. "One seven-year-old water mage?"

"What if I were to offer you assistance with your homeless child population?" Both the Zephyth royals eyed Maebe with suspicion. "If you will allow me to summon my people, we will offer them homes, love, and strength. Your streets will be cleaner, your child crime and death rates will plummet, and in return, I will offer you an alliance."

"What do you gain?" The queen eyed Maebe further. I helped Villeroa up onto the floor above us. Zygnal popped up as well.

"Followers, power, and being able to know those children are taken care of," I answered for her. "Her decision in this was influenced by me."

I had offered her a chance to appear callous and cold to protect her reputation. Hopefully, she took it.

"I would allow those who wish to return to your service to do so stronger and as capable warriors and mages." Maebe smiled. "You will have to promise them something to return to, mind you, but I give you my word that if you agree to this, I will see them returned to you."

"And what will you do in the meantime while we are still defenseless?" King Abioye waved toward the table of cooling food.

We joined our hosts at the table while I racked my brain on how we could do this. The Fae wouldn't be able to come here and survive with all the iron. And then the Unseelie would be at risk without fighters there.

"What if we were to give you exclusive rights to the Braves of the Thorn as mercenaries purely for defense of the city?" Manly picked up a little finger sandwich to look it over. "Provided, we would need to discuss a retainer, then pay, but we would give you a discount on account of our support of this goal, and your people."

Nick also slapped the table excitedly. "Me family too! They been wantin' to travel and branch out from the groves. If ye promise 'em a wee bit o' land, ye could have a mess o' druids willin' to help yer kinfolk. Maybe take on apprentices if they find any what can?"

The king and queen looked at each other with uncertainty, Villeroa surprising them by saying, "Mother, father, please do this."

They looked to her in confusion, the king responding first, "Sweet child, this is much to think over. Lives are at stake with this."

"Lives are at stake anyway!" She whined. "I've seen them, Renald showed me! They need help."

The Queen's gaze shot to Sir Renald, who nodded once. "What is the meaning of this, Renald?"

"During the princess's tutoring time, I, as her ethics instructor, took it upon myself to show her the disparity between her status and those without. In order for her to understand the lives that would be affected, should she think selfishly." The man looked at the princess affectionately. "Never have I been so proud. She understood right away and spent her allowance and even some of mine to ensure that each one we came across ate that day. The kingdom is in excellent hands."

"Please, we don't have the infas-infrare—." The princess paused, frowning.

"Infrastructure, Highness," Renald offered patiently.

"Yes, thanks Sir Jay," she beamed at him, and he sputtered at her use of his given name. "We don't have the infrastructure to take care of them and ensure everyone else is taken care of. This will make it so they are taken care of, and we have a really nice ally."

The king and queen were at a loss, on the one hand, their daughter had just outed them to strangers who could likely take this information and lead a rebellion or attack that could destroy them. Then on the other, they had to worry about whether we were sincere in our offers or not.

"If she is to rule someday, the Unseelie Fae would be happy

to have an alliance with her." Maebe couldn't take her eyes off the girl who smiled winningly at her.

The king sighed and put his head in his hands, then ran his fingers through his hair as he sat up.

"If you will take the children and some of the younger teens, train them and potentially bring them back, we will allow you to take them." He took his wife's hand and continued, "Also, if you will enter into a mutual protectorate with us, we will offer you the orphans in our orphanages."

"What do they stand to gain upon their return, should they decide to do so?" Maebe's fingers formed a steeple in front of her.

"For those who choose to take the warrior route, fast-tracked candidacy for officer positions in our army, special consideration for knight training and a competitive wage," my eyebrows raised as Queen Chareen offered this. "Those who acquire magical abilities will be treated well, depending on the strength of their abilities, they will be given titles and rank as we can create them for a new mage corps."

"And what of the Braves' offers?" Manly interjected as she leaned forward.

"We will honor negotiations between both the Braves of the Thorn and your people," the king motioned to Renald. "See to it that you speak to Nick here and get a messenger to his people so that they might send an able negotiator and example of what they can offer us."

"There be an example sittin' next to Queen Maebe right there, your Majesty." Nick motioned to me excitedly. "King Zekiel be a druid, an' quite a strong one if I can say it."

I chuckled at his forthcoming nature. Goofy asshole.

"If this is true, can you explain what we would have to gain from such a deal?" The king's eyes fell on me, and he looked me over, likely on instinct.

"I can't speak to his family's strength, but with druids, our magic is tied to nature itself," I explained, opting to stand and move away from the table as I did so. "We can shapeshift into animal forms, use battle magic, and also some healing spells. It just depends on what kind of choices the individual made."

"I take it you stood so that you could give us a demonstration?" Queen Chareen smiled as she took a bite of something that looked creamy, like a potato salad.

I nodded. "Yes, please allow me to show you some of it."

I took my Ursolon form, my body growing suitably, my massive bulk filling the area. I sniffed at the world around me, then shifted into my fox form, then into my saber tooth form.

"Oh my!" The queen gasped aloud. "And he has abilities with magic as well?"

I glanced at my friends, and Bokaj spoke up, "He does. He's capable of doing a whole slew of things that Mother Nature allows. He's quite adept. But, speaking of adept, we had one more minuscule favor to ask of you, your Majesties. If you will pay us mind one more time?"

"What is it you require?" The king narrowed his eyes almost on instinct, but his queen took his hand and pointed toward their daughter. She played with the little elemental shooting water from her hands into the ocean as if it were the most natural thing in the world.

His tone changed, "How can we be of assistance?"

"We're trying to find a way into the Great Below, and we'd heard that there's a chance that your dungeon could get us there," Bokaj began, but the queen stopped him.

"If it's entry to the dungeon that you want, we can allow you entry to the top floors." She looked to her daughter, then back. "Anything beyond that is outside our control and into the Nimran's Flame's territory, they control the whole thing. My husband can draw up the necessary paperwork this evening, and then we can have it to you tomorrow."

"Thank you, Highness." Bokaj bowed his head and looked to see that I had shifted back. "Zeke, care to show them a little magic?"

"It would be best if I didn't." I smiled. "I don't want to hurt anyone. But, as King of the Unseelie, I do know some shadow magic. I could show you a little more of that if you wanted?"

They delighted in me showing them how I could control the shadows for a little bit. By the time we were ready to leave, it was later in the afternoon.

"To reiterate, the children who wish to go, may go—we will not force anyone. Those who desire to return will do so, and to boons from the kingdom, correct?" Maebe spoke to the other two royals, who nodded solemnly. "And tomorrow, we will return for a missive saying we are to be allowed entry into the dungeon so that we can attempt to gain entry into the Great Below."

"Yes. And as you have been more than charitable to our people and us. We will also write a letter of recommendation to the Flame, informing them that you have proven yourselves capable." The king strode forward and held a hand out to each of us, shaking our hands in turn. "When do you start?"

"Sooner, the better." Maebe smiled excitedly. The king and queen blanched and looked to each other. "Thank you for your hospitality, King Abioye, and Queen Chareen. It was enlightening to meet you both. Princess Villeroa, study hard. and play hard. Your heart and mind in unison will make you an excellent ruler in this mortal realm."

With a nod and friendly dismissal, we were on our way back to our lodging with Sir Renald as a chaperone of sorts.

"Sir Renald," Muu began, but the knight cut him off.

"Jay, please." He encouraged with a good-natured smile. "Around court, among unpleasant company, perhaps, but here? Jay will do fine."

"How do we get the children to come?" I cast my eyes about casually. There was a child or group of them on almost every street corner, begging or looking for marks. They needed help.

"You can leave that to me." Maebe grinned wolfishly. "I will gather them. We must first check on Xiphyre. He should have our supplies ready by now."

"We've only been gone a couple hours at best." Balmur

looked confused. "How could he have gotten things put together in that short of a time?"

"Because of all the things that he is...." Maebe pointed toward the inn we were staying at, a flash of light burst from the window of our room as a small crowd gathered below on the street. "Lazy is not one of them."

We pushed our way through the building crowd, made our way up to our room, and Maebe and I went in while the others went to see about food downstairs.

I walked in first, catching a broken flying piece of chalk careening toward my face, "Nice to see you too, Xiphyre." I greeted the frantic Ragalfr.

He flitted around the room, making different drawings of runes, symbols, and pentagrams of varying sizes and complexity.

"Shut up, boy!" He screeched, flitting here and there. "Better yet, send a message to Thogan and see if he has finished my item!"

I rolled my eyes and did as he said to shut him up. I pulled out my messaging raven and fed it a hundred mana to speak to Thogan.

"Hey Thogan, it's Zeke, Xiphyre asked me to check and see if the item he asked you to build is done?" I completed the sentence, and a spectral copy of the figure in my hand flew through the wall toward the village where the blacksmith was.

A few minutes of silence, other than Xiphyre's manic mutterings, and a dull *shunk* sounded in front of the little man.

"Ah, ha!" He cried, holding up a golden-stemmed, platinum lidded mushroom. It held different sized, crudely cut gems in the gold stem and imbedded in the top was a set of rings in slots that appeared to be silver that jutted out at similar angles.

I saw motion in my palm and heard Thogan's hearty reply of, "Sure is!"

"Excellent craftsmanship as always, the rocky thing knows how to work" Xiphyre smirked, then pointed to Maebe and I. "The two of you can wait on the bed. Do not move, and do not touch any of the symbols. I need the door open, though. It's symbolic of the system I'm creating."

We carefully made our way over to the bed, then sat with a sigh. Xiphyre winged it over to the runes and ensured all of them were good, then narrowed his eyes at us. "Better thought, Queen Maebe, please cover yourself and the king in a veil of shadows so that the magic of your various items doesn't interfere."

She blinked, and a small, thin film of shadows passed over us both as Xiphyre centered himself over a central pentagram.

He sat the item in the center and mumbled into the air. As the words fled his mouth, the runes in the room glowed with power, green in color. Then he began making precise motions and gestures with his hands. More of the symbols on the room glowed, giving off a purple light.

Now he swayed, not just a portion of his body, but the whole of it. His wings didn't even move as he shifted through the air in a pattern as well.

His voice grew louder, sweat building on his brow and chest as he barked three words in a language my mind couldn't even comprehend.

He dropped to the ground weakly, pricked his finger, and added his own drop of blood. "Now you, My Queen."

Maebe left her place beside me, bit her finger, so a small droplet of blood touched the top. Xiphyre pulled a small bowl out of his inventory and added another drop. "Now for the prime plane creatures."

Two more vials containing a single droplet of blood popped into existence before Xiphyre, and he smiled tiredly. "Good, Rowland and his daughter are so helpful."

He dripped them into place, and the symbols on the walls were *sucked* onto the outside of the mushroom. It rattled for a second, glowing radioactively, then plopped onto the ground.

"How do you keep getting items delivered to you?" I asked incredulously.

"It's a box I tied to my being. If it fits, I gets." Xiphyre grinned at me, spreading his arms wide.

"That's convenient," I observed with more than a little hope in my voice.

"Also expensive and time-consuming," he added pointedly. "Your thinning of the veil is there, Majesty, all you need to do is cast the spell, and it will be much less taxing for you."

"Consider the debt you owe me decreased once more, Xiphyre." Maebe lifted the item high to eye it in the light streaming through the room. "Tonight, I will summon the children, for now, I will bargain with my mother."

"Your mom?" I almost audibly gulped.

"Yes, my mother." She smiled nervously, then turned toward the dazed Ragalfr. "Thank you, Xiphyre. You may go back to Thogan if you so wish."

"Thank you, My Queen." He stood, yawned, and scratched his stomach before fading from view.

"Why is he so weird?" I wondered to no one in particular.

"He has been so since he was merely a babe, newly crowned one," a strange, melodic voice answered.

I turned to find a woman of similar height and build to Maebe, staring at me from the shadows. My lovely wife must have contacted her with Shadow Speak.

"Mother, my husband's name is Zekiel," Maebe spoke with a tone of exasperation. "Zekiel, this is my mother, Eiran'a, former Queen of the Unseelie Court and first of her name."

"A pleasure to meet you, your Highness." I bowed slightly at the waist.

"Indeed," she replied dismissively. "Why have you called, daughter?"

"I require your assistance," Maebe began and made to explain before the other woman cut her off.

"No request? I run your kingdom in your stead while you galivant about the prime realm with these 'champions' of yours, while you haven't increased your power base whatsoever—"

"Mother!" Maebe barked, her fists clenched at her side and a growl growing in her throat.

"Eiran'a, you haven't seen the things I have," I spoke in a respectful, but reproachful tone as I put a hand on Maebe's shoulder. "If you would let her finish her thought, you would know that her task for you is worthwhile."

The room was colder now, I could see my breath and Maebe's puffed out as well.

I pulled shadows around us and fed a little of my flame aspected mana into it, and the shadows became warmer.

"I need you to collect the children we will be bringing from this realm to our own." the shadow covered woman made to speak but Maebe held up a hand to stop her. "There will be dozens, if not hundreds, mother. You will do this as it pleases me, and our people will thrive. I have an item to assist me in holding the tear open longer, but someone needs to collect them."

"Very well, My Queen." Eiran'a bowed her head. "I will gather the Unseelie, and we will prepare swiftly."

The shadows dissipated, and the temperature returned to normal. I relinquished my control over the shadows, and they fled us.

"That was clever thinking," Maebe whispered as she sat on the bed.

"Thank you." I put a hand on her shoulder. "Hey, fuck her. She doesn't know what you've done for your people. But I do wonder what you meant by 'our people will flourish'?"

"Being near mortals makes the Fae more fertile," Mae stated quietly, seeing the confusion on my face made her explain more. "Specifically, children. Something about their juvenile life essence makes the cosmos, or whatever it is responsible for our conception rate, confuse us for them, and we can conceive more readily sometimes."

"So, having this many children in one place in the Fae Realm could mean a baby boom." I frowned, then smiled. "So our people will be able to experience life for themselves!"

She looked at me in shock. "What? I have something on my face? The heated shadows didn't singe my fur, did they? Damn it."

I tried to get a glance at myself, but she stood on the bed and held my face. "This is the first time you've claimed the Unseelie as ours since you became king."

I blinked. I hadn't really thought about it that way. "Well, when your mom was being a dick, I kind of just had to react, and that must have put things into perspective."

"She wasn't necessarily wrong though, Zeke," she frowned to herself in thought.

"Yeah, she was." She frowned deeper at my insistence. "Your ice magic is stronger than before, and you've knighted seven people for your realm. You've brought alliances to fruition with two kingdoms in a realm where your people have little control, and you're about to send a bunch of fertilizer over to your people so that they can have the joy of both raising children and possibly having their own. You're *killing* it."

A puff of warmth against my neck, and she was there, her face held against me in a tight hug. She was silent for a moment longer, then, quietly, "Thank you."

"Of course." I rubbed her back softly before pulling away. "I've gotta support my queen, right?"

She smiled, her perfect white teeth flashing in the light. "Let's go eat with the others, then I will summon the children."

We headed downstairs and joined the others at the table.

"I take it things went well?" Muu munched on a plate of some kind of fried vegetables as he spoke.

"Goddamn, man—manners!" James growled as he shoved the other man's shoulder disgustedly.

"Yes, Muu, things went well. After dinner, we will summon the children to us. We will need nature for this, somewhere without too much iron." Maebe sat and thought for a moment.

"Jay, is there a beach somewhere?" I waited politely as more food was brought to the table.

"There is, and it isn't too far from the castle grounds." He thought for a moment. "Though there are homes near the area where there could be iron."

"We will figure out a way," Yohsuke resolved as we tucked into our food.

"How do you plan to lure the children?" Balmur looked around quietly, as more and more people piled into the dining room of the inn.

"The Fae are adept at this, but there are some among us who are even more so," Maebe explained. "I plan to call to them as I did Xiphyre, and have them entice the children to come and be well cared for."

"None of them unwilling, I'm certain?" Jaken arched an eyebrow at her.

"The Seelie Fae do that, their lies as sweet as their fake beauty," Maebe spat, then collected herself. "We offer the children love, power, and security."

"In return, you get fertility," I added, and the others looked up. "As well as children to spoil, and potential members of the court, do they change?"

"Into Fae?" Maebe smiled knowingly. "Yes, eventually. But this is only after centuries of your prime years. And usually only in minor ways. They might become minor Fae creatures, or be reborn as true Fae. The ones who are blooded as you were, Zeke, become something different based on the blood offered."

"So, no one is getting kidnapped." Jaken nodded his head and sighed in relief.

"You have seen me go to great lengths to protect the children of Sunrise, is it so out of the norm for me to want to ensure that these children are also cared for, Jaken?" Maebe looked a little hurt at his obvious relief. "Do you truly think me some sort of monster who would prey on them?"

The paladin looked stunned into silence, unable to speak, so Bokaj did, "I think it was more in keeping with his duties as a Paladin for Radiance and a father himself. Children are precious to all of us, and this is all outside of our realm of expertise. I think Radiance loves the kids and all but being a father could've been playing up a part of his relief."

Maebe stared hard at both of them before speaking solemnly, "I, Maebe, ruler of the Unseelie Fae swear on behalf of my people and do hereby bind all Unseelie by my will and word, that not a hair on any of the children obtained from this city by my people will be harmed outside combat, training, and needed lessons by the Unseelie. If this should prove to have been a lie, I, Maebe, Queen of the Unseelie, and rightful ruler of my realm, offer my life as forfeit should it be so proven. Is this amenable to you, Sir Jaken, Paladin of Her Light?"

Jaken's shocked face was enough for her at that moment, but he cleared his throat and stood before pacing over to stand in front of her. He knelt and took her hand in his before bowing his head.

"I, Jaken Warmecht, Paladin in service to the goddess Radiance and Knight of the Unseelie Fae swear by my power and name, that I meant you no harm by my questions. I accept your vow, only in that you had given it." He raised his head, a serious glint in his hazel eyes. "I swear to you that I only had the best at heart Queen Maebe. Thank you for your trust in me. I hope you will never think that faith misplaced."

Maebe lifted him, physically lifted him, to his feet and patted his arm. "You have learned well, Jaken. I am proud. Please, let us continue our meal as friends."

"Thanks, Maebe." He grinned his usual grin, and went back to his food, tucking into it with zeal.

The rest of the meal went without issue. The food was okay, not necessarily anything to write home about, but it was serviceable.

Once we were finished and dusk shone in the west, we set out to find the beach in our human disguises except for Muu. He figured that something like him would attract attention, and we needed that for now. Any children we found along the way, we stopped and spoke to briefly, telling them to find the youngest of them so that they could come with us and be taken somewhere safe. A few listened, some ran off to find others, and those who were alone followed us.

One little boy seemed completely smitten with Maebe, the queen carrying him as if he were a prince and the most precious thing in the world. A couple children ran around Muu, giggling and laughing as he teased them and swung his stubby tail with great effort after. They cried out in amusement at his expense.

Yohsuke grumpily handed out food to the little waifs who asked for something. His grumpy nature was really just a front, he wanted these kids to be happy almost as much as Maebe did. His own family at home being why. He liked kids. Said he hated them, called them shitty, but gods help anyone who hurt a kid in front of him.

The others and I brought up the fore guard, ensuring people were out of the way, while Jay and Jaken brought up the rear to make sure the kids didn't get taken or abused on our way.

It took a little while longer than it had to get to the castle, but eventually, we made it to the beach. Just before true darkness.

The beach was long and thin, the water not even a hundred yards from the nearest homes. The water gently lapped at the shoreline as people went on about their lives. Some of them stopped to watch this large procession of children with strangers walking through, but as none of them were their kids, they left well enough alone.

Which was why they were in this damned mess in the first place.

As they came, they gathered around in the cold. I frowned, looking for any nearby trees, and finding one, I took my axe out and made for it. I felled the palm in three strokes with Magus Bane, casting Regrowth on it immediately after so that Mother Nature wouldn't strike me down. It was for a good cause.

Bokaj and I cut pieces of the tree, and I dried it out with shadow magic, eating the moisture inside easily. We made three bonfires so that the poorly clothed children would be warm as Maebe prepared.

"Zeke, I will now teach you how to Call a Fae creature." She brought up a dome of shadows while Muu, Bokaj, and Balmur entertained the children. "I will give you one of my most trusted creatures, as he has been with me since I was but a child."

"Why would you do that?" I asked, concern taking over. "He's your oldest partner, he belongs with you."

"Because a king in truth would have brought his own subjects to call," Maebe spoke softly, but I could tell it was her trying to soften the blow to my pride. "And I give him to you because I trust him. There may be other Fae who wish you to know their true names and others who will hate you for who you are. He will not care, because he is loyal."

Fair enough. "What do I do?"

"Focus your mind on bringing him to you and speak his name. There will be a mana draw, and it may be steep the first time you do so. Once he learns to trust you, it will cost less and less as you summon him." She held up a hand, and her tone shifted to one of warning. "But beware, if you summon him carelessly, he can choose to harm you. Or make the price to summon him so high that it will hurt you to do so. Be cautious. Be honest. But most importantly, be cautious."

"You said cautious twice, my love."

She whipped her head back to me from where she had turned to look at the children. "Because it is important!"

"What's the name you want me to use?" I asked with a patient sigh.

"He is called…Milnolian." A cold shiver run through me, as she said the name and knew I would likely never forget it. "Summon him, and I will summon my own."

A shadowy partition separated us as she issued her order.

I cleared my mind and focused on summoning the creature whose name was "Milnolian."

A mana headache occurred almost instantly, my nose

bleeding as some of my health fled my body. My mana reserves and my ring, Mage's Well, were both completely drained, and my health had gone down by two hundred points.

"Fuck me," I groaned as I stumbled.

"Who are you to perform the Calling?" A formless, owner-less voice whispered harshly in front of me. "Why do I sense my queen?"

"I am Zekiel Erebos, and Queen Maebe has entrusted your true name to me." I collected myself, wishing I had some mana to cast any healing spell on myself at that moment. "I am King of the Unseelie Fae. I called you for a reason; we need your help."

The sound of a deep breath in, as if it were trying to find a scent, reached my ears before the voice returned, "I cannot smell the lie. Well, *my King,* why have you summoned me, and how may I be of assistance to you?"

"Maebe needs our help to round up the homeless children of this city in hopes that they will choose to go to the Fae realm for a better life, until such a time as they wish to return here and serve their kingdom." Finally, my mana reserves had a splash of mana in them, and I cast Regrowth on myself. "Or they decide that they're better off in the Fae realm."

"Ah, children." The voice chuckled; the whispering deepened as it spoke. "Yes, she has always had a weakness for the little ones."

"You imply that she is weak?" I growled.

"You imply that you can threaten me, *King?*" I tumbled back. "If it will aid her, then I will assist you."

"Thank you," I muttered, glad that was over.

Shimmering golden eyes opened in front of me, slits in the center of them, and a tiger of black and gray stalked from inky depths toward me.

My adrenaline spiked as the whiskers twitched. "Do you find this shape I take…frightening?"

Remembering that Maebe had said to be honest and that

the creature had already said it couldn't smell the lie, I opted for the truth, and deflection.

"You may want to take a form that children would find either fascinating or comforting." I wrangled my quickly beating heart into submission with some breathing exercises. "Also, what can I call you?"

He cocked his head to the side, his gait thrown a little, and his whiskers twitched again. "Cleverly done. The Queen calls me 'servant,' but what you would call me, I do not know. I do not know you. I do not trust you."

"That's fine." I shrugged, and he halted, eyeing me curiously. "Look, I can gain your trust as I have Maebe's. I've never meant her any harm, and she was the one who asked me to be her king. I didn't ask for any of this, just her love. By choice. She chose to give you to me because you were loyal, and you wouldn't care who I was. If I have to earn your trust, so be it."

The skin of his nose crinkled as he took a deep breath. Blink. Once, twice and a third time before exhaling.

"No lies," I spoke before he could.

"Call me Servant," the creature stated finally, shadows melting from it until it was a medium-sized dog that looked like a husky. "It's alright, Majesty. I won't eat your chosen king, though I do find the iron in the area taxing."

I frowned, and the partition fell; Maebe stood with more than a dozen creatures of varying friendly shapes and sizes standing behind her, shadows and ice wreathing her hands.

"Glad to hear, Servant." Maebe nodded curtly to the creature, and he did a flawless bow as a dog. I was a little jealous.

Several of those creatures behind the queen circled me, their eyes glowed different shades. Some red, green, blue, and brown while others were a milky white. They all looked to be creatures of shadow or ice.

"This kitsune is the King?" One of them asked excitedly, and my skin burst into goosebumps as I looked at the shadowy figure. "This is the first time this has ever happened! And don't expect that disguise to fool everyone, child. Us old ones can spot a kitsune in human form easily."

I growled, tired of all the showing and speculation. The creature seemed more excited by my irritation. I called all of the shadows that I could to me, the swirling mass of my anger igniting as I added flame aspected mana into it.

"None of you had better give the Queen any trouble." I tried to come off as more menacing than my dwindling mana made me feel.

"Oh, you are adorable, new King." One of the larger creatures, a bird the size of a small child chuckled. "Queen Maebe, you may tell him my true name. I find him interesting."

Maebe snorted, I shot her a look, and she motioned to my hand knowingly. I allowed my magic to die down, and the creatures turned their attention to Maebe.

"Go and find all of the children in the city who are not wanted and tell them that they are welcome in the Fae realm. Bring them to me, and I will speak to them." Maebe raised her voice so that they would all hear the seriousness in her tone. "You will be kind, approachable, and honest. Protect the children, and do not fail me. Go!"

All of the creatures moved except one, and I sighed, "Her orders are my own, Servant—go."

He nodded once and bolted off into the night.

"You did well," Maebe assured me, taking my hand and pulled me into her. "He will learn to trust you, as you hadn't lied to him."

"What would he have done if I had lied to him?"

She turned her head and smiled at me. "He would have eaten you."

"I thought you had said that being cautious was the most important thing?!" I threw my other hand up as she giggled.

"It was—be cautious not to lie to him." She kissed my cheek and pulled the mushroom out of her inventory, sitting it on the ground. "Better that the thinning between the realms begins sooner, rather than later."

We waited for more than four hours as the Fae creatures ventured into the city to collect as many children as they could, and came back to the beach to deposit them before going back in.

After the fourth hour, two cloaked figures and Jay came to where we were and waited with us for another hour. Queen Chareen and her daughter were both tired, but they would be here to see the children off.

Finally, after the fifth hour of waiting, the Fae creatures returned, bowing their heads. "It is done, Majesties," Servant reported.

"Thank you all for your help." Maebe nodded her head once. "If you would wait, you can return to the Fae realm with the children. I must speak to them before I open the tear."

The Fae creatures fanned out among the children, nuzzling the ones who were sleeping near the still-burning bonfires awake. Some of them looked frightened. Others hungry and tired.

"Good night, all of you," Queen Maebe called to them all. I could hear the Fae throughout the large crowd repeating her greeting. "I am Queen Maebe, ruler of the Unseelie Fae, creatures like the ones who brought you here to me this evening. I have an offer I would like to make all of you—come and be loved among my people."

One of the older girls in the crowd began to sob, one of the younger boys near her began to try and calm her.

"Servant," Maebe whispered. The creature bolted forward and listened. "Find out what happened to her. Herd her to the side if needed so that I may speak to her."

I nodded, and he was off. The boy went with the girl and followed the Fae off to the side.

"By that, I mean that you will be well fed, cared for, taught, trained and given all that can be given in the name purely of our adoration," Maebe called, and again the Fae echoed. "There is nothing to fear. None of the Unseelie will harm you. We will teach you, coach you, and help you learn to defend yourself. We will help you, however we can, but I do have but one caveat."

The children listened silently, their full attention on her, but I could tell some of the more jaded among them—the elders—appeared to have been expecting this tidbit of information.

"Should you choose to return here, you will be given station, power, and pay, by order of the crown for any service you can give to the country," she called and left it at that. The crowd of children whispered among themselves, the noise growing to a dull roar.

Finally, Chareen and Villeroa stepped forth and cast back their hoods. The crowd gasped, and they all knelt there in the sand.

"Children of Zephyth!" Chareen called out, raising her hands. "Know that Queen Maebe speaks the truth. We are not abandoning you! You are not unwanted! Our hearts break, and we weep that we cannot care for you properly, as you deserve! Should you choose to return, you will be given all that this country can give to you in your service."

Villeroa called out, "Zygnal!" The water behind her crashed, and the elemental surged out of the water.

"Today, my daughter came into power that all of you have a chance to earn with the Fae," Chareen explained. "Those of you who return here may do so with the promise of stature, power, and surety! We need your help. We need you, now more than ever, and Queen Maebe offers you a chance to become something greater than your current lives."

"Beggin' yer forgiveness, Highness," One of the small girls near the front looked horrified, but her curiosity had gotten the better of her at that moment. "Never mind."

"No, little one," Maebe encouraged. "Please, speak your mind. Go on."

She seemed scared, so I slowly made my way forward, where I knelt next to her and whispered softly, "No one will hurt you, child. I swear it by Mother Nature. Ask what you like."

"Can I ask you?" She looked near tears, so I nodded. "What if we don't wanna come back?"

I patted her head gently, and she sniffed, "She wants to know what would happen if they choose not to return."

Maebe looked to Chareen, ensuring that the woman hadn't planned to answer before doing so herself, "Then you will be welcome among my people until the end of your days. And you would be able to count yourself among my court."

The whispers had turned into full out cries of joy and happiness then. Some of the older kids seemed to be wary of the offer, but hopeful, I thought.

The Fae had joined Maebe, who turned and began to cast her spell complete with gestures, eccentric words, and gathering darkness. Children cried, their fear winning over, and I turned to help the others calm them.

I turned back in time to see Maebe grip the sky with her hands and *tear* reality in two. A rift of light and darkness opening and several figures walking through.

"Time to come along children!" I called, motioning toward the rift. Some of them were scared, but the older children lifted the younger ones and led them toward the rift. Maebe stood at the side of the opening, sweat on her brow, but she didn't look nearly as tired as she might have.

Next to her stood her mother, Eiran'a, in her full glory. She wore a form-fitting, ice-white dress complete with ice crystals that dangled from a collar around her throat. Her hair was stark white, and she made no attempt to appear less beautiful than she was. Her skin was the same dark tone as her daughter's, but she looked so different from Maebe that I would definitely not be confusing the two.

As I approached, Maebe saw her opportunity to get away. "If you will forgive me, mother, I have a child to see to."

I watched as my wife moved toward the girl, and they spoke in soft, muted tones as Maebe raised the shadows around them.

"You make her weak, mortal," Eiran'a's voice crept forward icily. I rolled my eyes, then turned to face her.

"Hello, mommy dearest," I tried not to be sarcastic, her blank face giving me no indication my snark would reach her. "And aside from marrying someone who would merely use her for her power and station—how is that?"

"She could have moved on the new Seelie Court if it hadn't been for her dalliance here in the mortal realm," she commented dryly as she looked haughtily over the children who passed not twenty feet from us into the Fae realm.

"Yeah, and there would be some new threat to your power almost immediately." I observed my nails as if in disinterest. "Specifically, the threat of the Dofilnarr who seem to be working with the Seelie."

Her gaze shot to mine. "You you will mind your tongue, kitsune. You know nothing of the threats to our realm."

"No, I don't." I smiled sincerely. "But I'm learning. And not only am I learning, but I'm helping her as well. Did you know that she now has two alliances with kingdoms in this realm?"

The queen said and did nothing, so I continued, "These fine humans here, that have so nicely volunteered to help you all be a little more fertile—yeah, I know about that—and give you something to do and children to spoil and love." Her shoulders tensed and she seemed displeased, so I did what I always did when confronted by something that could easily kill me.

I was a raging smart ass.

"And let's not forget that she even managed to gain an alliance with the high elves' new king. Something you lost, and she found again."

She was inches from me then, the rage in her features should have made me piss my pants, but it was much too cold for that. "If I were you, I would never speak to me that way again, mortal."

"Yeah, and if I were you, I would find a better way to spend my time than judging the one creature in the world who seems to love a frigid bitch like you," I said back, growling and shoving my own face forward angrily. "She loves you and her people. She's working herself sick over here trying to ensure that all of the people she loves are taken care of, first and foremost her people."

"Then why in all the realms did she choose *you* as king?" The former queen said, her tone spitting venomously.

"Because I love him, mother," Maebe's voice greeted us before her arms wrapped around my shoulders protectively. "For the same reason that you married father."

"Do not speak of that…that…fine." Eiran'a stood erect and held her head high. "If you refuse to learn from my mistakes, so be it. You will understand why I gave my heart to the Frozen Depths soon, child. Far be it from me to attempt to spare you that suffering."

As she turned to leave, she halted and graced me with an icy glare. "No matter where you go, mortal, I can find you. Remember that."

"Yeah, and when you want to have dinner with us, I'll bring dessert." She looked confused, and honestly, I was too. I shook my head and growled at myself. "Look, I don't want you and I to hate each other. I love Maebe. I will care for your people as best as I can. I've not lied to her about any of my intentions— ever. The least you can do is support her, even if you hate me."

Eiran'a blinked at me before regarding her daughter. "I will always support her. As she did so for me. My daughter is all I hold dear other than my people. For someone who thinks that I 'hate' him, you are surprisingly calm."

She turned back toward us and stepped forward until she invaded my personal space once more. "I do not hate you, Zekiel. I hate what you represent, and the pain my daughter will experience once your time here is at an end. I wish you both happiness, all of the happiness I had before the end. Fare thee well, Zekiel."

Eiran'a glanced at Maebe, a soft, sad look in her eyes then left without another word.

A sigh of relief escaped my lips, "That wasn't so bad. All things said and done, I kind of like your mom."

Maebe smacked my arm lightly. "We can discuss that later. I

sent Servant to collect one more thing, then the portal will close."

"What did you send him to collect?" I stared at her with a pointedly worried look on my face.

"Just some trash," Maebe replied flippantly.

Three minutes later, Servant, in his original tiger form, dragged a screaming man onto the beach by his leg.

"What the fuck is that, Mae?" I cried as I bounded toward the two of them.

An impossibly strong hand gripped my arm and pulled me back onto my ass, my legs flying into the air.

"As I said," her voice a harsher tone reserved for anger. "Trash."

Servant dragged the man over to us, then sat with the leg still in his mouth before dropping it onto the ground and putting a paw on the man's back.

"This is the lie that you followed, Servant?" Maebe tilted her head as I climbed back to my feet next to her.

"This one *reeks* of lies, but his is the same scent on the girl." Servant eyed the man hungrily.

"Come here, child." Maebe waved to the girl, who looked to be in her mid to late teens. "Do not fear, he cannot harm either of you."

I frowned and noticed that the boy who was there had to help her walk forward, he looked to be younger than her by a few years as well, so maybe around ten to twelve? Kids looked different here than they did at home.

"Is he the one who harmed her?" Maebe squatted down to be at eye level with the boy, who nodded erratically. "I see. Tell Servant what his favorite lie was. What did he promise you both?"

"He would always promise that he would care for us and love us," the girl whispered. Her pale, milky eyes unseeing as she looked ahead.

"He said he was an alchemist," the boy sniffled. "Said that

he could give us a good life if we would help him with his work. Then we would be rich!"

The horror of what these two had been through dawned in my mind, and I wanted to murder the sonofabitch right there. Right then.

My rage made my vision turn red for the first time in a while, but the voice of the wolf was gone. I was responsible for this.

Then I got to thinking. If his experiments had been on her eyes, then maybe I could fix this. Better to try and get help, though.

Jaken, I need you over here, buddy. Balmur, you too. I called to those two and held a hand up to get their attention. Within seconds they were there.

"You needed us?" Balmur asked with an eyebrow raised as he took in the scene.

"You more so in a second." I patted the fire dwarf affectionately on the shoulder, and he shrugged. "Jaken, you have anything that can cure organs?"

"Not really specifically, but I have that buff spell that protects us from adverse effects." he held his hand out like he was going to cast it and I waved it off.

"We're going to try to help you, but I'm going to need to touch your face." The girl drew in a ragged breath and watched us.

I looked to Jaken, "Can you pray and kind of enforce a holy spell for me?" He nodded, and I put a hand on each side of the girl's face. "I don't know if this will work, but I'm going to try to heal you, okay?"

She nodded tears in her eyes once more. Jaken touched my shoulder as he began to pray, "Lady of the Rising Sun, whose Light brings joy and righteousness to the land, I ask of you…"

I tuned him out as I focused on holding the spell Purify for a full thirty seconds, then used Vulpine Casting to halve the spell cost to 800 MP.

Warmth flooded me, spreading from my shoulder where Jaken touched, into my chest, then to my hands. Finally, as I released the spell, the warmth flared through me and into the girl's head.

She glowed a vibrant orange for a moment, then blinked a few times, dark tears fleeing from the corners of her eyes. "I can see…" She looked at her hands, then the boy who wept openly in joy. "Seamus? Oh, Seamus, it is you!"

"Go now into the portal, little ones," Maebe whispered, her voice sweet and cheerful.

The man at our feet cried out again, and I grimaced. "Balmur, you want to mete out a little eye for an eye justice?"

The dwarf frowned, blinking as he pointed from the girl to the man on the ground and smacked his head, "Shit, and here I had forgotten!"

He leaned down and flipped the balding, skinny man onto his back as he struggled for all he was worth.

"Balmur." Maebe touched his shoulder lightly. "Do not kill him."

It had been an order, and I would help see it through. "Jaken, you uh…may wanna go away buddy."

The paladin nodded stoically and moved away from us as Maebe erected a shadow barrier and grinned, "You may begin."

It took only seconds for us to finish our grim retribution, I made sure I healed him, and he would live. He wouldn't see, but he would live.

"Servant." Maebe stroked the Fae creature as she eyed the man. "Take him into the Fae with you and have my mother add this one to my collection. Also, take the girl to her as well. My mother will appreciate her as she should be."

The tiger nodded eagerly, then turned to me. "You aren't half bad as a king, call me again."

He not-so-gently grabbed the unconscious man by his leg and trotted off through the tear. Maebe took her place next to it and grasped the sky once more to slam it shut with an audible groan of effort. Then she collected the mushroom and put it into her inventory.

Jay had counted two hundred and thirty-seven babies, children, and teens that had gone through the rift. And of that amount, nearly sixty had sworn to return once they were strong enough. That had been a decent payoff, right?

Balmur had fed one of the man's eyes to his own and was excited to see that when a normal eye was fed to it as upkeep, the magical effect was still safe. That was great to know.

The queen and her daughter thanked us for our service to the kingdom and opted to go home with news that we would be by in the early morning to collect our paperwork for the dungeon.

We walked back to the inn a little weary, but with a lightness to our steps that I felt was much needed. We had saved lives tonight. Granted one asshole was *definitely* going to get his, but those kids? Those kids were in good hands now.

That was what mattered to me.

CHAPTER TWELVE

The following afternoon we were on our way back to the castle to gather our documentation to get into the dungeon.

We didn't even make it to the gates when the king, queen, and their daughter met us at the bridge to their castle. Their finery was forgotten, they wore normal clothes, and they had nothing but smiles.

"Two hundred and thirty-seven, with sixty oaths to return." The king grinned broadly. "Several of them expressed interest in magic. But it was all thanks to your offer. So, here are your papers, your letters of introduction, and our gratitude."

"Should any of you need more, please, do not hesitate to ask, and if the Unseelie Court has need, we will rise to assist you." Queen Chareen bowed her head once, then nudged her daughter, who hung back shyly.

"Come out, water mage," Zygnal ordered patiently from the water nearby. "Speak to them as is expected of a princess. If you are to have any chance at proper magic, you will need to overcome your shy nature."

The girl regarded the direction the voice had come from sourly and marched out from behind her mother.

"Thank you, lords and Queen Maebe, for helping our kingdom, and our people," she spoke measuredly as if she had practiced quite a bit. "And thank you, King Zekiel, for helping introduce me to Zygnal. That was very nice of you."

"Was that so hard, child?" Zygnal's voice bubbled our way from the water, and the princess shot a murderous glare her way.

"You are welcome, Princess Villeroa." I bowed my head, and Maebe just smiled. "Good day to you all, and should you need us, Zygnal will have a way to reach me. That, or whisper my lovely wife's name. She will know who you are then."

Maebe smiled larger than before, and we turned to leave.

"I forgot; we going to be on our own?" Yohsuke smacked my arm as we walked through the city toward the gates. "Or will we be taking the Braves as well?"

"The Braves offered to meet us at the gates while you were getting some more supplies this morning," Jaken supplied as he observed his surroundings. "Jay requested that they show him something on his way there."

As we continued on our way, I noticed more and more of the royal Zephyth guard on the streets.

"I wonder what's going on?" James grumbled as we watched the goings-on.

From the looks of things and the royal family's avulsion to how things had been run according to reports, I'd have said it was a good house cleaning. But I had been wrong before.

Once we made it through the gate, under the watchful eyes of more Zephyth royal guards, a crowd gathering around something beside the inn we had stayed at before entering drew our attention. I had yet to see our new friends, and that concerned me a little, my frown evident to anyone who might glance my way.

A sharp whistle pierced the air, and I glanced toward the wall itself and caught a glimpse of Manly waving to us behind her cart, "Y'all are missin' a show!"

I looked at the others, Yoh, Maebe, and James shrugged; the others were already on their way to the spectacle.

We arrived, having to push past a couple of the locals, but once we got there, the sight was worth the hassle and confusion.

Seven of the guards, dressed like the ones who had been on gate duty when we arrived, were in stockades, little racks that held the hands and head of prisoners in an awkward, almost bent over manner. That way it was nearly impossible for them to rest or be comfortable. In addition to the guards, a normal-looking man in finer clothing with a balding pate was also detained.

In front of them, was a single stake with leather draped over it, but the man in the center of the ring was the real sight to see as he spoke to the crowd, "These people you see before you had deemed it fit to forestall entry into the city, and thereby mistreat the people, our guests, and the reputation of Zephyth to any and all comers and goers for monetary gain." It took me a second to realize who it was, the guard who had searched the elderly couple before us. "By royal decree, they are to be held in the stocks for all to see for seven days, fed bread, and water once a day, and lose all worldly possessions. They took much from the fair people of this city, of this country, and it is their turn to pay."

"You were there with us!" Spat the fat guard that had been the loudest when we'd tried to get in, the obvious leader.

The guard nodded stoically. "I was, and my punishment is even more severe, as I had known it was wrong and been too afraid to stand up for myself."

He wore a simple off-white shirt, cotton pants, and worn black boots. Outside his armor, he looked to still have a decent build, and considerably younger than he had before. He made his way to kneel in front of a stake in the ground that was taller than he was kneeling and tied his hands together with a piece of leather.

"What's he doing?" Muu asked, but I couldn't take my eyes away from the man.

"He prepares himself for his punishment," Jay's voice startled me. I turned to see him standing between me and Yohsuke with a somber look on his face. "This is a part of my duties that I do not enjoy. All of you, please, do not interfere in this."

He stepped forward, and doffed his armor, his clothes underneath were simple, and unadorned. His somberness reached the crowd, too curious and concerned to even whisper as he went about his business.

Once his chest piece was off, he rolled his shoulders and neck as he sat it down, then looked to the crowd.

"Some of you are familiar with who I am.' He spread his arms wide. "To those of you who are not, I am Sir Jay Renald, Knight of His Majesty's realm, head of His Majesty's Guard and ethics tutor to the princess. This latest title, I hold in high regard, as it is my firmest belief that we, as a people, should hold ourselves responsible in all things."

He pointed to the man kneeling at the stake. "When questioned about the goings-on at this gate, this young guard was honest and forthcoming. He advised me, under oath, that he simply followed the orders of those to whom he had been trained to follow. That in all things, he attempted to never harm anyone when in the course of his duties. And that when he had spoken ill of those who had been corroborating this farce of order and duty, he had been threatened and blackmailed into silence."

A shiver of something akin to dread began at one end of the crowd and moved like wildfire to the other, landing in the pit of my stomach. How many people were experiencing the same? Elsewhere in this world, and possibly at home on Earth? How similar to situations I had almost been in? Where 'I was only following orders', was used to transfer the guilt and blame for one's actions to another, higher power? It was too real.

"Tell me, guard Fents, do you have naught else to say that can save you from this? Stand, turn, and address me, boy." The guard turned, his face tear-stained, but he held his composure. "Is there anything you wish to proclaim?"

With a heavy sigh that made my heart sink, he looked down, then back up and shook his head. "No, sir. I were wrong. I should've made it clear that this were wrong and gone to the proper folks when the chain of command had proven to be rusted." He lifted his bound hands and wiped the tears away from his face before squaring his shoulders. "My only hope be that I can make amends to the ones what got hurt by their actions… and my inaction."

I found myself nodding without thought in agreement with what he said.

Jay did the same, nodding, he stepped forward until he was almost chest to chest with the guard. In armor, Jay had been a little bulkier than he was now, but he was still tall. At least a couple inches taller than this guy, but their musculatures were night and day.

"We who serve, wear the manacles and shackles of our duties." He reached into his inventory and pulled out a pair of silver cuffs that he presented first to Fents, then to the crowd. "We, who are bound, bind ourselves to the greater cause, in hopes that those who are bound with us will help to pull those who cannot serve into the light of righteousness. These are cuffs of honor, duty, and selfless love."

Jay brought out a knife and sliced the bonds off of Fents' wrists, to the other man's shock, but continued to speak, "It was not you, who failed young Fents, it was these people. These guards and this corrupt innkeep."

As the crowd stirred once more, some excited at the prospect that the young man would be absolved of his crimes, others in confusion. The show wasn't over yet.

"It was these people who failed you and led you astray." Jay held his hands up for silence, then sighed heavily. "And it was I who allowed it. As head of his Majesty's guard, it was my duty to ensure that all of those who serve under me felt that they could come to me in times of need. And you did not. It was my duty to ensure that those who cared for this city were strong, and without corruption. I did not. And as I see you, ready to face this public punishment for something that could have been avoided, I cannot allow you to do so. Quartermaster Vinciswalla."

A large man carrying a cat o' nine tails stepped into the group of people from inside the inn. His hulking form covered head to toe in armor that looked more like lead than steel, his footsteps almost heavy enough to shake the ground with each footfall. He wore a helm that covered his face, but I could see a glint underneath it.

"Yes, Sir Renald?" A deep baritone voice ground out with a metal tint to it.

"Please, how many lashes was young Fents to receive?" Sir Renald asked as he placed the shackles he had used to show the crowd what he was saying around his wrists, locking them in place and handing the key to the quartermaster.

"By order of the crown, he was to receive ten lashes, and by your order, three more in lieu of stripping him of pay, previous earnings, and possessions," the quartermaster turned to eye the young guard as he spoke, pulling his weapon taught. "Sir."

"Very well." Sir Renald ducked his head once and smiled at the man. "Aim well, my friend."

The quartermaster didn't do anything other than step into position as the knight turned to the guard with a soft smile, speaking low so that the humans around us wouldn't be able to hear. Luckily, I wasn't human.

"Your punishment will come, but if you would be so kind, kneel here at the stake in front of me. I want you to see the consequences that can come with both action and inaction first-hand. And that it comes of all ranks, stations, and ability levels." He turned back to the quartermaster. "Thirteen lashes for the boy's penance."

The knight knelt down in front of the stake with the chain between the cuffs held by the stake as Fents knelt on the other side. The quartermaster brought his massive arm back and deftly whipped it forward, the weapon arching cleanly across his back, slicing cloth and flesh alike with a small spray of blood.

Renald took the blow silently, but it was Fents who tensed, then teared up. The entire time Renald just watched him, whispering that it was okay, it was his fault. The only time he ever raised his voice was when Fents made to block one of the blows. Renald took the strike and shoved the guard back in front of him.

After the thirteenth lash, we let out our breath, I was angry, but I understood. Leadership had a price. Some people weren't willing to pay that price. Others were. My boy Renald was.

"That is not all, Fents." Renald gasped.

I focused over his head, and his health bar appeared. He was at around 55% right now, but he was bleeding, too. And that whip was gnarly. "Your turn, you take the whip, and you give me seven more. One for each of the men in those stocks who are under my command."

Fents shook his head, "No, Sir Renald, please. No more. You more than paid for all of th—"

"I did not ask your opinion, Fents!" Renald barked, surprising us all. "I gave you an order, and if you would defy me even now, then I truly have failed this city."

Fents looked horrified but stood as the quartermaster lumbered over to drag him to his spot. He shoved the whip into Fents' hands and gestured to Renald. "You do it right, and I don't throttle you and make you do it again. Understand? Nod if you do."

The guard nodded after a moment, took a steadying breath and called out, "I'm gonna start now!"

Renald just stared ahead intently at the first man on his left. "This one is for you."

Seven lashes, well-delivered by Fents who feared to upset either of the other men involved and Renald's health teetered at a measly 7% and falling.

Dawn and Jaken both moved in to help the other man stand, healing him a little as soon as they touched him.

"Thank you both for waiting as long as you did, I realize

that it may have been hard on you," he slurred tiredly, his eyes fluttering.

"The show's over, you lot!" The quartermaster called loudly, chasing off some of the crowd before turning to Fents. "Go home, guard. Your next tour of duty is the squire training grounds tomorrow morning at dawn."

Fents was stunned, his mouth agape, eyes wide, and stumbling to find the words to say anything.

"Dismissed, squire-to-be," The quartermaster growled, and the guard hustled away. After ensuring no one else was around but us, he turned to Jay. "You alright, my friend?"

"I'll be okay, Jenrie." Jay grunted as we continued to heal him. The guy had a good amount of health. "You're as delicate as ever, old friend."

"I've never been one to shirk my duties for a friend, Jay, you know that." I heard the teasing tone behind the helmet. "If you lot will entrust him to me, I'll see to it that he gets back to the castle."

"Good idea," Manly added, making me look toward her. "Bonnie, Nic, and Nick are gonna be headin' to see Nick's family and bring some of 'em here to start negotiatin' with the king an' queen."

"Will they be okay?" James looked to all of us, then blushed as Bonnie put a gentle hand on his shoulder.

"You tell me?" She smiled as she pulled him closer to her. "Will we be okay, James?"

"Nope, you guys should be alright!" He stuttered, and she let him go.

"It'll be a swift thing." Nic smiled as he pointed to Manly and Dawn, "The two of you be safe."

"Thanks for all the lessons, Nic." Balmur smiled over at the human wizard.

"Happy to have someone who finally understands the finer things in life!" He grinned, then wagged a finger. "You be sure to contemplate your spells as you work on them and remember —you have the tools to change them as surely as you do yourself. Focus, and persevere. Also, don't worry about that magic hating fool, we will see that she falls. Trust in the Braves."

Balmur nodded as the other man tapped his two companions on the shoulder, and they were gone from sight instantly.

"Was that…" I blinked, slack-jawed, and pointing.

"Teleport." Balmur smacked my stomach with the back of his hand. "It's a higher-level caster spell, sure, but for a wizard? It's not all that hard to figure out. He's been able to cast that for a while."

"That's really cool, man." I frowned, then grinned. "So, you really found your thing with magic?"

"I'm good at killing up close, but with magic…." He shrugged his shoulders and just spread his arms with a smile. "I have so much more control over this than I did before. I don't like losing control the way I do, it's just what happens, but with my magic, I have ultimate control over the outcome."

"Provided nothing goes wrong." Muu clapped the other man on the shoulder and nodded toward the road. "Let's get to getting before it gets too late. We got some ass to try and kick."

I frowned at Muu, normally so flippant and goofy, being serious for once.

"I look forward to seeing what you are capable of with your magics, Balmur." Maebe offered him a thumb up that made her look weird.

Balmur just laughed, and we began getting ourselves sorted out. Muu would ride with Manly, the others would ride on mounts while Dawn was in the cart, and I would fly with Kayda for a little bit, then train with the others with shadows at dinner.

I took my eagle form, spread my wings, and lifted off after Kayda. I would leave Bea in my collar until I could earn her some experience to help her level up.

Flying like this with Kayda, though, was still so very unreal. She loved it, as we chased each other from cloud to cloud on the breezes and thermals. Rising and falling at a whim, true hunters, and rulers of the skies.

They've stopped father, Kayda's mind touched mine, and I

looked below, seeing that her observation was correct. Had it been that long already?

Does this mean you plan to talk more often, little one? I teased her as we dropped from the sky.

Not if you keep that up, she slapped me with her wing as she dipped through my path.

I chuckled and spread my wings to slow my descent. Once I was ready to land, I shifted into my fox-man form and dropped to the ground.

"I'll never not be jealous of that shit." Muu sighed as the others gathered around the cooking fire. "I mean, yeah, I can jump really fucking high, but you can *fly*, dude."

"It's amazing," I agreed, "I'll never get used to it if I'm being completely honest."

"Well, druid abilities aside, come on, let's get some practice in." Balmur clapped me on the shoulder and waved to Yohsuke. "Yoh, you okay to let the food go?"

"So long as someone can stir the soup as it cooks, yeah." Yohsuke glanced over at Manly, who waved him away with a wordless nod.

This evening, we practiced sensing movement through the shadows. Something I was already familiar with, but there was a knack to it. Balmur was more adept at this than even I was, and it was easy to tell why. He had to be intimately aware of where the shadows around him were, and the depth of them, so that he could move through them to better effect.

We spent an hour trying to pinpoint where Maebe moved through the shadows inside her practice dome. It was fun for a while, but soon she began to use shadow doppelgängers that felt and moved like a real being.

After dinner, Maebe gave me some more one on one practice with moving and adjusting the shadows with her causing it to resist my will.

Finally, I'd snapped and growled. The low rumble in my chest made my blood race, and my mind sharpen a little bit. That minute flex in concentration allowed me to take in another two feet of shadows before Maebe's resistance grew more oppressive than before.

"Husband," she whispered into my ear, her hands on my shoulder and around my waist. "Your anger can sharpen your mind, yes, but when you let it rule you, it can be detrimental to your observational skills."

I blinked, not having noticed the crimson in my vision, then began to take note of the jagged lances of darkness pointed at me.

"Sorry, dear." A sigh escaped my lips, and I waved the weapons away.

"Do not be sorry." Maebe comforted me with a gentle press of lips against the side of my head. "I have come to notice that even though you say that you have assimilated the manifestation of the werewolf inside you, your anger still holds sway over you. Why?"

"I guess it kind of always has." I shrugged as if I wasn't sure how else to answer. Or if there even was another answer.

Tap tap on my left hand, her tapping her ring against mine made me smile sadly.

"I was never really the happiest person at home." I raised my hands and added another barrier of shadows designed to stop noise around us to help keep our conversation private. "Life was rough, and I know that other people had it worse, but my anger has always been there for me. It helped me get through a lot of tough times. Kept me company. Got me through school, boot camp, the fleet. Even though no one ever really got to see the angry side of me because I hid it behind a mask of smiles and humor, my anger allowed me the strength I needed to survive and thrive."

"So, it is a source of comfort for you then." Her touch was gone, but I felt her presence still near me. "I can understand that it is how I feel about the darkness. It is alright to take comfort in something when it is of no consequence, or when it serves a purpose, but those other times may be more easily navigated by simply turning to cleverness. If you had simply taken your awareness and probed for weaknesses in my own, you would have found places to draw from."

"Thank you." I flexed my will and crushed my own barrier, sending the shadows into the ground. I pressed my awareness against her and it was flawless.

"You are unhappy that I criticized you." Her observation drew my attention to where she stood. "I did not mean to upset you, Zeke."

I couldn't help the small smile on my face. "It's okay. I guess I've kind of known for a while that my anger makes me a liability at times. Not just the lycanthropy, but my actual rage, that is mine. It feels good like you said. I have to get used to operating cold. Calculating."

"It would be helpful, yes, but I think I have a solution to offer if you would hear it?" I glanced at her, then nodded so she would continue. "What if you were to hone your anger into a weapon that you used while you were at your most cunning?"

I blinked at her in confusion. "Uh, come again?"

She frowned, then tried again. "Instead of letting your anger take control, you call upon it when you need it most. For instance, your spell Falfyre. It is expensive to cast in some cases, but it is worthwhile. Destructive, deadly, and highly effective."

"I mean, I just did that, didn't I?" My eyebrows furrowed in concentration, thinking back on it.

"Yes and no." Maebe took her hands and spread them in front of her, the shadows above us allowing moonlight into the dome and light into the area. "Think of yourself as this portion of light."

She brought a thick band of darkness in around it until there was a six-inch circle, me, and then the rest of the light around it.

"The outer band of light is your awareness of the world around you." She motioned to what she spoke about. "As you act and think normally, it is clear, as you can see. When you allow your anger to take you, your perception of the world around you changes."

The light in the center was the same, but the light around it dimmed considerably, and I could see spears of darker black entering toward my position in the center.

"If you were to use your anger in a constructive, and more cunning way, it would allow you to plan for some of the consequences and avoid them while focusing your rage instead of letting it go."

This time the spears came, but the circle of light that represented me began to move about in the moonlight and avoid the dangers within, then a beam of darkness shot from me into the void, and then the circle was gone.

"Do you understand what I am saying, now?" She watched me patiently.

"I think so, but I don't even know where to begin trying to do that." I scratched my head in thought.

"Making that mistake was a start, and from there, you learn to channel it in more and more brutal and cunning ways." Maebe smiled and released her dome. "For now, we can retire for the night. I am sure all this training has made you quite tired."

I kissed her on the cheek, and we went to bed. She took my watch without asking and I slept through the night. I woke up to her meditating for once and kissed her on the head. It was nice watching her smile as I showed her affection in her equivalent to sleep.

"Good morning, beautiful." Her green eyes fluttered open and turned to me.

"Good morning, handsome." Her return was smooth, but she looked tired.

"What's wrong?" I tried to look her over, but she wouldn't let me.

"Sometimes, the more powerful Fae have 'dreams' in their meditative trances." She began to explain but halted distractedly.

"And you had one." I finished for her. "Guessing from your

reaction, it must not have gone over well. Want to talk about it?"

"It was a dream concerning my mother," she frowned some more. "I do not think I do. Let me digest this and I may be able to express it."

"Okay, I'm here for you, you know?" She smiled and patted my hand. "Good. Let's get ready to go and then eat, yeah?"

"Yes. Let's." She nodded once, and I had to ask.

"It wasn't something like my dream, right?" I couldn't keep the concern from my tone. "The one that I had when I was in Sunrise?"

She stiffened. "Was someone you loved dead in it as well?"

"You." I could feel my eyes losing focus as I remembered the gruesome details of the night.

She grasped my biceps, pulling me toward her as she stared into my eyes. "It was you. You were dead, and my mother had been taken over."

"And your mother warned you not to help us?"

Maebe glanced away. "She warned me to kill you to protect the children."

I was enraged. How could those *assholes* do this? To *her*?! Of all people.

I growled openly. "Your eyes are red, my love. Rein it in."

I didn't want to. I wanted to find this monster and make them pay. I wanted it so much more than anything.

Waves of cooling air pressed against me, my chest going numb bit by bit. I glanced down to see Maebe blowing on me, the ripples of my shirt moving out as she did so.

It went a long way toward reminding me of what I needed to do. I needed to bottle this up, like a bottle of diet pop and Mentos. Then, I'd shake it just before this asshole came in, and I'd be *unloading* that on them.

I took a breath and released the anger I had for now.

"Thank you, dearest," I muttered against her forehead. "I'll keep my rage in check for now."

Her teeth flashed in the morning light. "You're learning. Good."

"Let's make sure things are good and go get food." I led her over to the others as they began to gather their things.

"You get food for us, and I'll pack up our bedroll." I tousled her hair lovingly, and she chuckled.

Clean up was swift, I put the folded and rolled item into my inventory. Then I cast Regrowth on the ground so that there was no trace of us using the place as a camp. Even where the fire had been before.

"That's a good thing to be able to do, Zeke!" Manly informed me, even as she subconsciously did the same thing I was doing with her pipe into a handkerchief. "Though why the fire?"

"Pretty much the same reason that you do it. I'd say, Manly," Yohsuke observed, and pointed to her hands. "Covering our tracks, like you do with your tobacco and trash."

"That's what that is?" She looked at her hand in surprise. "I just did it 'cause it was somethin' pa did."

"Some people with special training, where we learned some of our own military skills, do that to avoid detection," James added helpfully.

"Yup!" I nodded. "Honestly, I thought that you had known about it, so I never said anything about it. It makes sense for a tracker not to want to be found. Senseless for a creature or mark to be able to find you by carelessly leftover trash."

"That's likely the right of it," Dawn said as she looked over her friend's shoulder curiously. "I always thought it a peculiar quirk, but I never questioned it because you seemed so certain of it."

We ate a hearty breakfast after that, and then we were on our way.

"Should only be a day out from where we be currently!" Manly belted to us as we rode.

I had decided to let Bea out to stretch her legs, her lively moving tethered to Thor once more so she wouldn't run too far away.

She screeched and rampaged within the confines of her shadow lead, angry with me for having to keep her within the collar for so long. But around so many people? And as untrained and temperamental as she could be?

Yeah, not a good idea. Especially when no one else in the city had magical abilities. Honestly, I wasn't sure how much of that I believed—the whole world was full to the brim of magic, how could no one in the city have access to it?

I absentmindedly tossed a chunk of meat toward Bea as she moved alongside us, she hopped up to catch it, but it was just outside what she would be able to grab. Then her eyes glowed slightly, and she found solid footing in the air, as if stepping off of the wind itself, and caught the chunk mid-flight.

"Woah!" I couldn't hide the amazement in my voice.

"That was impressive!" Muu called from the front of the cart. "What is she again, some kind of anime monster? Holy shit."

I did the same thing again just to be sure it hadn't been a fluke, and sure enough, she was able to step off the air once more.

"That is too interesting." James's voice popped over my shoulder. I looked back to see the monk eyeing her with obvious fascination.

"I'm not going to give her too much more, but I want to see how this plays out and see what kind of drawbacks or cooldowns this could have," I explained to him and no one else in particular. "It'll be interesting to see how she can use that in a fight."

We broke for lunch, the mountain range looming over us maybe another hour or so from the base of it, where a large crack began to form. I could see it from this distance and when I noticed it was when Manly confirmed it. "That's where it'll be."

"Looks a little intimidating." Jaken shuddered. "Sure that's it?"

"Aye." Manly smiled ferociously. "I killed three of my parents' murderers there. Reckon they'd been tryin' to get into the dungeon."

"Good shit, Manly." Yohsuke held his fist out for her to rap her knuckles against. "Let's be cautious going in there then. Quick lunch, enjoy the light, and then we go on."

He passed out some sausages that he grilled swiftly on a small fire I made for him. We ate with Bea out, I fed her chunks of meat, but she was ravenously hungry and had made for my food more than once.

Kayda eventually grew tired of it and smacked her away with her wing.

Little sister, you must be patient! The giant bird sternly growled at Bea, who eyed her reproachfully. *Father feeds us as we need it. I know you are small and understand only hunger and boredom, for now, but you will soon learn to fight and grow larger. Patience is needed for any warrior, and our father is dense at times, so we must be more patient still.*

"I heard that you feathered shit!" I harrumphed at her, and all she did was blink at me, then bow her head in acknowledgment. "Now, see here you...you...*Stop looking at me like that goddammit!*"

Kayda glanced knowingly at Bea, who seemed to get that she was being mean to me, from what she was feeling.

She trotted over to me, to coo at me a little bit while rubbing her snout across my hand, affectionately.

"See? Someone appreciates me!" I took the rest of my sausage and let her have it.

And that is how you play him to get more food. Kayda preened as Bea strutted around the camp with her head and tail held high.

...Did I just get played by a fucking pigeon and a lizard? Oh, hell no.

"Dude, what the fuck is going on over there?" Yohsuke threw his hands up as Kayda gave him the "feed me" eyes.

"I think they've adapted and have learned how to play me," I responded in feigned shock.

Yoh shrugged and tossed a whole sausage toward Kayda, only for Bea to hop straight up into the air to catch it herself.

"Ha!" I barked at the betrayed bird. "That's what you get!"

Bea still strutted as Kayda remarked, *Well played, little sister.*

Well played indeed. I'd need to be watching her until she was old enough to know better. For now, back in the collar she would go. We needed to at least attempt to make nice with the people controlling the entrance to the dungeon.

CHAPTER THIRTEEN

"You have got to be kidding," Jaken said, his voice a low growl.

I understood his trepidation—the entrance to the dungeon wasn't a gate, it was a fortress.

Along the sides of the walls in the crack stood tall stone walls that appeared to have been carved into them.

Dozens of men lined each side, looking lazily interested in us, but didn't seem to bother moving too quickly to halt our approach. They had bows, crossbows, and spears situated along the tops of the walls. Swords on their belts of varying sizes and values dangled into view where they stood on the walls.

"That's not good at all." James spat as he eyed the walls.

"And neither is the group of people moving toward us," Yohsuke warned as we continued forward.

"Wasn't like this when I came through before," Manly observed, a small grin gracing her lips as she spoke. "Though, I reckon my prey didn't quite make it this far."

"Just be calm, and don't make any sudden movements toward your weapons," Dawn advised from where she walked beside us, her eyes were cast forward, confidence oozing out of her. "Whomever among you carries the orders and introduction from the king, have it ready."

Jaken pulled the paperwork out and just loosely held onto it as we moved forward.

Manly started things off for us as soon as we were closer. "Howdy y'all!" Her southern drawl was back in full tilt.

"Hullo!" Called a man in an accent that sounded almost Russian, or Slavic. "What can we do for all of you and your giant animals?"

"Well, we came to see about this fine group o' people usin' yer facilities on behalf of King Westwind and the crown of Zephyth." Jaken held the papers out as Manly spoke.

He took the papers and scanned them, then opened the letter of introduction, reading it much more carefully.

"'For service to the crown,'" he muttered once, then handed back the papers. "You can enter the dungeon, but you must wait until tomorrow. Do you know how far down you plan to delve?"

"How far down does it go?" Yohsuke asked in return. The man tried to see under his hood, but he must not have seen anything because he stood back up with a shrug.

"Twenty floors beginning at level two for enemies." He explained carefully as he eyed all of us. "Each floor becomes progressively more difficult, with a waypoint every three floors where a group can rest without fear of enemies. For whatever reason, monsters stay away from those locations. After the twentieth floor, is Nimran's Flame territory, and I am afraid you are not tempered for service. Unless you wish to be?"

"I don't think anyone here has room to serve any other gods, friend." Jaken winked, and the man glared at him critically.

"Then you will likely find being admitted to lower levels more impossible," the man replied bluntly.

"How many more levels are there after twenty?" Muu broached politely.

"That is classified." the man shrugged noncommittally.

This peon don't know shit. James snorted to the rest of us.

Let's just play the nice guys so that we can get in there and get this show on the road, Yohsuke said to us, then told the man. "We can camp out here, tonight, so we will just go ahead and set up camp and come back in the morning, thanks."

"You are welcome." He waved to us lazily. "In the morning, you ask for Yani. He will admit your party to the dungeon, and have you sign the waivers."

"Waivers?" I raised an eyebrow, and the man just chuckled morbidly and moved along with his pals.

"This is gonna get sordid, but how about we camp *away* from where these guys can see us, so we don't have to try and explain ourselves to them?" Jaken asked as we moved away.

"We nervous about tomorrow?" Balmur asked to no one in particular.

"Hell no." I could hear the grin in Yohsuke's voice as he spoke. "This is probably going to be a cakewalk. It's going to be getting into the lower levels, then the Great Below that will be the crappy part."

"Why don't we just have Bokaj charm our way into the place?" The rest of us glanced at Muu, his face serious. "What? He has that mind control shit he can use. All he has to do is get a big wig to agree, or someone to sneak us in. Right?"

I blinked. The others blinked. We blinked at each other. It was an audible smorgasbord of eyelids clapping together in confusion. Then Maebe broke that silence. "It could work."

Yeah, it could! The other party members converged on the poor fighter affectionately, his cry of, "Oh god, yasss all the hugs, bring it in," resounding through the air.

He came out of the group loving looking disheveled and like he needed an adult. Maebe seemed confused, but she accepted that it was just something we were going to do regardless, and that won her brownie points.

"And on that note, I think we'll be needin' ta head off back to Zephyth." Manly grinned at us, winking at Muu as he frowned. "We've got us a contract to write up and money to make. But should you ever need us, call on the Braves. We got your back, friends."

Muu shook his head. "You better get your tiny ass over here and hug me." He growled and stalked toward her with a smile that made Manly snort. "How am I supposed to get my religion lessons without my little buddy?"

"Ya keep callin' me little, and I'll be sure to make certain ya meet the gods sooner rather than later, Scales." She slapped him on his shoulder as he lifted her effortlessly into a bear hug.

"Aww, someone's being a little short with me cause she's sad." Muu cackled as she slapped him fully across his face, and I heard a snort of laughter from behind him. Dawn was damned near in tears from that.

"I do not think that I have ever seen, nor heard anyone be so bold as to call her those things to her face, and they haven't either died or been turned into a moving target for her bow!" She snorted again as Humphrey, likely jealous, snuffed the ground and brought the cart closer to Muu and cried out loudly.

"Aww, I'll miss you too, porky." Muu set Manly down and patted the porcine companion. Humphrey snorted and nudged his hand with his tusks. "No, I don't have any more food, you ate it all on the way here! Now get away from me, you're too cute, but you smell."

Humphrey snorted and bit his hand. "Ow!" Then he trotted off without looking back.

"It was good to meet all of you, stay safe, and may Seraestar's love and guidance be with you," Dawn nodded her head once to us and climbed onto the front of the cart to wait for Manly.

"Don't be strangers now, hear?" Manly warned us, and we all nodded our goodbyes. Maebe was quiet, but Manly turned and curtsied. "A true pleasure to be an acquaintance, your Majesty. I truly am sorry things weren't better between us."

"I do not find you nearly as worrisome as I once did, Manly Warbottom, go forth into your new ventures knowing that the

Unseelie will not hunt you." Maebe smiled as the other woman looked more than a little worried. "I mean you well, child. Go now, and good luck."

The cart, and the two people on it, were off into the distance soon after leaving us to make what we would for a camp.

Maebe erected the shadow barrier, and we ate as soon as food was prepared.

"Tomorrow, when the fighting begins, we leave things to you and Bea," Yohsuke explained as we chowed down on some steaks and potatoes with light garnish. It was really nice. "At least for a little while. Her leveling is kind of paramount at this moment."

"Right on." I nodded. The others were quiet, for once, as we ate. "I wonder what we will be facing in there."

"A lot. Twenty floors are no joke, even if they are low level." Muu scratched his head a bit, then continued, "I think we should go in carefully. More so than ever but have teams like you guys do in the Marines. What was it called again, James?"

"Fire teams," the other dragon answered readily. "That's not half bad. Make sure that we know who we stick with just in case. What do you guys think, traditional split?"

"What is this, 'traditional split?'" Maebe looked worried.

"That would mean that each group has a tank, a healer, and two damage dealers," I answered as I cleaned my plate. "So that would leave you and me together because that makes an even eight and leaves us with two slots."

"We aren't splitting the fucking party." Yoh growled, his face a mask of anger. "Do you all not remember what happened last time we did? Those goblins could have killed us."

"It does seem stupid to split the party even if we aren't going to *actually* split up," Balmur observed as he held his new weapon from Maebe, Sorrow in hand looking it over. "What do we know about what we're heading into?"

"Drow elves are..." I began, trying to find the right words, but James interjected.

"Evil as shit, chaotic, and will backstab you in a heartbeat if they even *think* they will get ahead for it." I glanced over to see him reading from notes that he had in a book before looking up to say, "but they aren't completely like the ones that we have at home in our... media."

"How do you mean?" My brows rose curiously.

"They don't worship a spider goddess; their Queen is the spider." He frowned as he read more, "'Lo, there I gazed upon her legs and she at me, for where I saw a queen of pure fearsome power, she saw only a fly come to her web.' The passage goes on to describe her as pretty terrifying. And definitely spider lady."

Huh. That would be interesting.

Tiny druid. A rumbling call through my mind made my chest itch. The primordial Earth Element was reaching out.

"Hold on guys, one of the elements is talking to me." the others blinked and shrugged. Seemed common lately.

I turned my thoughts inward and responded, "Yes, Unmovable One?"

A deep rumble like an earthquake grated against me. *I see you have learned flattery. I have news. You will be our herald in times to come of a new age of magic, but first, all elements must be represented.*

"Okay, so that leaves fire and air, right? This is great, thank you for trusting us!" I was overjoyed to know that we could count on these hugely powerful beings to assist us.

Yes, and no, since the earth, water, air, and fire are no longer the only living elements, you will need to find one for light as well.

Light?! "When..." I frowned, my brows creasing deeply.

When you gave presence to the void, its opposite came into being as well, and now it seeks a champion as we all do, the elemental spoke. *The champion for shadow is there with you now, for she is their most loved.*

Well, at least that was good to know. So, three. Then we could just find someone with a good affinity! Excellent.

The others are...fickle about giving their blessing to mortals, but they are willing to set aside their past experiences for the good of all.

"Why doesn't fire just pick me?" I blinked at the blackened

dome above our heads. "He's already blessed me, as many of the others have."

A warmth washed over me, and I could feel the heat of the eternal flame on me. *You are indeed who I would choose, little flame, for I adore your spirit mightily. But your ties to the others weaken my ability to fully enkindle you and bring your heart to true flame. The same can be said for the others in your party, such as my dwarven child. I require someone else, forgive me.*

Gooseflesh, weird with fur, but it was okay, covered the back of my neck. "I'm honored, Great Flame."

Find our champions, as you have the others, and I will bless you and that new child of yours, druid. The air primordial whispered through my mind.

QUEST ALERT!

Elemental Recruitment Specialist – The primordial elements of fire, wind, and light search for their champions and have requested that you track down suitable candidates.

Reward: Suitable blessings from the elementals assisted, per champion found.

Failure: Potential loss in elemental aid.

Do you accept? Yes? / No?

I accepted and shared it with my brothers; they went through it as I listened to the earth prime.

I have one more request of you, tiny druid, and if you will humor me, I will bless you and yours greatly.

"What can I do for you?" I asked, now more curious and power-hungry than I had felt in a while.

My champion, Fainnir, and his friend 'Pebble.' The earth prime rumbled with a grating chuckle at the name and I grinned. *I would like you to take them with you on this expedition. I think they will be of service to you.*

"Is that okay?" I blinked rapidly. "He's still a kid!"

Child or not, tiny druid, he walks with the strength of the earth, and you will be nestled in his element; the elemental chastised me gently.

Bring him and help him to come into his power. Do this, and he will be able to assist you in things you do not yet know you need.

"Is that a quest?" I asked aloud and tried to keep an eye open for a notification.

It is a request, as I will not force you to decide on whether to take another life into your hands on a highly important mission. He gained a lot of respect from me at that moment. *But his people coddle him, and he cannot grow in the company he is in properly. He needs you, tiny druid. He needs a mentor who understands the elemental ways but will not force him to contain his strength without reason, or out of ignorance.*

I sighed. *That makes sense, Z.* I thought to myself, my left hand tapping on my metallic arm. *The kid was a little badass, and he was an adult now by dwarven tradition.*

You will find him among the monks who took in your friend. He is not weak, but they are not familiar with what he should do to proceed in his training, and that stifles his growth.

"Yeah, I think we can do that. Thank you for entrusting him to us." The pressure of their individual minds left, which eased my mind.

I glanced at the others. "We're going to have one more with us, and I think it's time that we let the dwarves know that you're back, Balmur."

"Oh, they've known, man." Balmur grinned at me, "I've been talking to them magically ever since we got back. They want to have us back for a feast so that we can tell our tales and that Farnik can skin you for not telling him all was well sooner."

My eyes widened, and my heart sank. I was going to have to fight the old fucker, and he was gonna beat my ass.

"I'm teasing, he understands that we've been busy, but asked that we do come back soon—they miss us." A slight smile crept over his face as he said it, and I had to admit things were simpler around the dwarves.

"Who's the extra body?" Yohsuke eyes narrowed my way.

"I'd guess it's Fainnir," Muu stated in a surprisingly knowing tone that made me look at him questioningly. "You mentioned 'one more' and the dwarves after talking to the elemental Primordials. Seemed to make the most logical sense."

"Who's that?" Yoh asked once more, looking a little more irritated.

"He's the only Elemental Earth Mage, and the only dwarven mage in recent memory," Muu explained, flashing the other man a large grin. "He's a good kid. Well, man now."

"He any good in a fight?" James smiled hopefully.

"He will be because he is training with all of you." Maebe made her presence known. We glanced over to her, and she nodded at me. "Go collect this dwarf, I am eager to meet him."

"Why?" Yohsuke frowned, then looked at me. "Are we seriously entertaining this?"

"Yeah, it was a request from someone who could possibly give us more power, or at least chances to earn it, and we will be underground—straight up his alley." I crossed the distance between the two of us and lowered my voice. "The earth primordial said that he could be useful, and that he needs training. If mages are to continue to flourish here, we need powerful mages on our side. Before and after we leave."

"So long as he can pull his weight, fine." Yohsuke shrugged after a moment in thought. "But no one else. It's bad enough that we will have Maebe, but her presence serves a known purpose."

"Thank you, Yohsuke." Maebe purred from over my left shoulder, her fierce green eyes lighting up as she watched him realize she was there. "Come, you and Balmur will train while Zeke goes to collect this Fainnir."

I kissed her on her shoulder and focused on the monastery where James had spent the first few weeks of his time in Brindolla, then before I loosed the spell, I looked over to James. "You wanna come with? He's at the monastery, you wanna see Elder Leo?"

"Sure, man, that's super cool of you!" He came over to me, and I tapped his shoulder before casting Teleport.

The jump through space was less disorienting than it

usually was as I blinked and took in my surroundings. Even in the fading light, the valley the monastery inhabited was gorgeous.

We stood outside the halls carved into the walls of the valley that resembled catacombs. The large valley floor was home to huts and small buildings throughout. Looking out toward the valley, on our left side, was the section of the valley that served as the monks' training grounds. Enemies, creatures of differing types and levels, ventured forth from an underground source of mana every new dawn. It wasn't a dungeon, per the Monks telling, but a blessing from their deity. A place they could channel their monastic abilities safely and learn to combat the darkness.

The place was quiet as dusk faded, kids and families returning to their homes and dinners after a day of doing… whatever it was they did there. I glanced back toward the monastery proper, and it seemed a little more quiet than normal, as well. There were monks outside, sure, but they appeared subdued.

A rolling crack of stone and a shout of triumph reached my ears, and James took off toward the training grounds. A huge boulder lifted from the side of the valley wall and sped toward the ground.

"Fuck." I spat and moved, casting Aspect of the Hare as I sprinted.

My legs stretched, and my ears lengthened. My dense muscles grew leaner and longer, but I moved faster than I would without the spell.

I hopped twice and then on the third I launched myself over the large fenced in area, small creatures moved en masse toward the entrance to where they sprang from, in fear, as the boulder bounced causing other large sections of stone and rubble to break free as well.

You get anyone in the area away from it, I'll get the kid! James called to me as he rocketed forward.

I whipped my head toward where the rubble fell, three

monks were in the area. I might be able to make it to two of them, shit. Focus!

I exhaled forcefully, took a deep breath, and bounded forward, snatching the first man up by his arm and throwing him to safety as gently as I could manage. I grabbed the other monk around the midsection in a sort of flying tackle, a large chunk of debris cracking into my right leg, just on the inside of my knee. I tried to put pressure on it so that I could make a mad dash for the final figure, but the leg gave out on me.

A boulder the size of a Buick careened toward the still, meditating figure. "Look out! Move!" I roared.

I pushed my will out into my shadow and the darkness around me to forge a line between us. Just before my improvised rope could connect, the boulder crashed into the figure, then split into several pieces from the weight of it.

"Well, tha' dinae go as planned, did it, lads?" A stout figure walked toward me with an angry-looking James hot on his heels. "Zeke! So glad ta see ya again!"

I ignored the voice behind me and made my way toward the boulder that had crushed the monk and started to try and push the stone away when a voice called out, "Leave me to my meditation, Zeke!"

I blinked, Elder Leo? I poked my head around and spied the elderly halfling who still sat serenely in a meditative trance. Well, he could whip my ass, and he wasn't even so much as scratched, so I left him be. I turned to address the boy.

Fainnir, because this could only be him, he looked like an almost eleven-year-old kid, but stoutly built and with the beginnings of some good muscle on him, likely from his father, Granite. His unruly mop of brown locks was a little slick with moisture and...were those *whiskers* on his chin?

"Fainnir, well met—what the hell are you doing bringing down the mountain like that?" I advanced on him and he stood still while I came closer. "You could have hurt any of those monks, or yourself!"

"They all be swifter'n me by more'n half, Zeke." The boy

spread his hands out. "An' Elder Leo be right as rain. Aside, Pebble be up there fixin' the integrity o' the mountain as we speak. Tha's why the boulder fell, I had things in hand."

"And since when do you speak so well?" I growled as I leaned closer so that I could look him directly in the eyes, I reached out and tugged gently on one of his little whiskers. He yelped. "You think because you're closer to true adulthood that I won't bend you over and spank you here and now, mage or not?"

"That will not be necessary, tiny druid." Pebble grew out of the ground, now slightly larger than Fainnir, but still the same roughly humanoid shape as he had been. His diamond gaze passed my way, and his misshapen mouth smiled. "I have been teaching him to be a little less harsh sounding in his dialect. I am glad to see that my work has been noted."

"I talk fine, ye pile a rubble." Fainnir growled, then smiled. "Did ye get it all fixed up, then?"

"Yes, Fainnir, I did," Pebble turned to address him. "Did you uphold your end?"

The dwarf scratched his head. "I just cannae seem to get it figured. I try an' reach into the earth with me mind, but when I do it, all that happens is shakes."

"It will come easier with time." Pebble turned back to me. "Why have you come, tiny druid? Has father asked you to intercede on our behalf and see to Fainnir's training?"

He closed his eyes, a little bit of the luminosity behind the diamonds in his face bleeding away. I knew he was checking in, so there was no need to answer.

"You will be in better hands with Zeke, than you are here, young Fainnir." Elder Leo sighed sadly. "Zeke, James, it is lovely to see the two of you once more. How fares the rest of the group?"

I turned to see the bald, elderly looking Halfling smiling at us, his simple, light robes colored orange without sleeves. His hands were folded in front of him, on top of the red sash across his left shoulder and hanging down to his right hip. His feet had simple black slippers covering them, and the brightest thing about him was his smile and storm-gray eyes.

It had been a while, but he didn't look to have changed in the slightest. Monks and their tempered bodies, or souls, or what have you. It was weird. I found myself wondering when James would become basically immortal, but then again—it wouldn't really be needed.

"While he's distracted, Leo, they're good, and it's *King* Zeke now." My gaze whipped to a grinning James, while the other two looked awe-struck.

"Ye be a king now, Zeke?" Fainnir whispered, then he looked over to Leo. "Ain't never met a king afore, Leo, what do we do?"

Leo glanced from James to me and smiled knowingly. "Judging from his reaction to being outed like this, I would say nothing."

"Thank you, Leo." I sighed in relief, then put my hand out for him to shake. A firm practiced squeeze later, and he let go, "Everything been alright here on your end of things?"

"It's alright, my boy, go on and collect your things from the guest quarters." Elder Leo kind of shoved Fainnir toward the monastery, then looked to us as the dwarf sprinted away, with Pebble lumbering behind him. "Things have gone well; we have informants among the populace here and there that feed us what intelligence they can in secret. I hear more than you might think, and I am happy to know that you were able to assist the people of Zephyth."

I blinked, trying to keep my surprise contained, making him grin. "I told you, we have our ways. Also, I hear tell of a Fae who travels among you?"

"Zeke's wife, and also Queen of the Unseelie Fae, Maebe." As he said her name, goosebumps covered the nape of my neck, and her awareness shifted onto us.

"Hello, my love," I whispered into the deepening twilight, which took hold of the sky in the west over the mountain-enclosed valley.

Her affection warmed me, and then her attention was gone.

Elder Leo's eyes widened in shock. "My informants mentioned nothing of the Queen herself coming to the Prime realm."

"We don't like to advertise it if we don't have to," I explained with a wry smile, the memories of her exploring and experiencing life here in child-like wonder. "It kind of ruins her fun if everyone is all stuffy and whatnot around her. Reminds her too much of home. Though there have been quite a few times where we have to, and it gets a bit out of control."

The halfling man snorted and slapped his knee as his chuckle turned into a full-on belly laugh. "Oh, you boys, and the crazy things you get into. A Fae Queen! And this one here is more dragon than elf it seems!"

Now it was James' turn to look bashful, ha! "Yeah, he ran afoul of some strange magic in a book, no big deal."

He eyed me dangerously, and I just flipped him off.

"Well, I am glad that things are still going well for you all, tell me; what will you do next?" Elder Leo waved us toward the monastery as well, we turned and made a leisurely stroll toward it.

"We have plans to get into the Great Below so we can try and hunt down the drow," James stated as we walked, then I took over.

"What he means to say is that we heard a rumor that the drow have recently begun behaving oddly, and we wanted to be sure that it wasn't a general or some kind of minion driving them to act that way." I smacked him on the arm, and he shrugged. "You know it's not some hunting expedition, man. And then, taking Mae there to meet them and whatnot as well. It's two-fold."

"They will be hunting you." James and I whipped our heads around to stare at the older monk as he stopped to look at us gravely, before speaking again, "The drow elves do not take kindly to inter-lopers, and they care less still for elves of other varieties. Their queen is a harsh and terrible creature who drives them to madness on her own. I doubt that there will be something there that does not belong, but it would be wise to investigate regardless. You will need to be careful, and do not take anything for granted down there."

We walked on in contemplative silence. I had known it was possible there would be things down there that would seek us out, but the whole of the drow people? That was going to be rough with seven crazy-ass outsiders, a Fae Queen with some serious firepower, a bird, panther, and a baby raptor with no idea what not to try to eat.

"Have you any idea where else you might go to seek out the enemies of Brindolla?" Elder Leo nodded his head to a disciple as we passed, and the young man took off at a sprint.

"Not really, no, but I think it would be a good idea to search the world," James shot a glance at me as I finished that thought. "Think about it, they have a whole world to corrupt—why would they all stay on one continent?"

"Ah, you speak of the continent of beasts. To the east?" Elder Leo grinned as he spoke, nodding sagely and clapping his hands. "We have no information collectors there, and I have been wondering if it would be possible to get some. If you were to go, I would appreciate some insight as to whether the network needs spread so far...."

James scratched his head. "I mean, sure, that'd be fine, I guess. Is travel to that continent all that common?"

"Takes about a month and a half or two months by sea to get there at times, but there are those who make the journey regularly." We had entered into the front halls of the monastery now. We stopped outside so that we could speak without interrupting the meditating monks inside. "All you have to do is find the right place to start!"

"Got any suggestions?" I said as he watched the sky serenely.

"How should I know; I've never sailed on the seas before." His face, when he got to say that, was priceless, as he was genuine, but his grin said he had known I would ask, and he wanted me to think for myself.

"So, I guess that means we scour the east coast until we find someone to take us there safely," I added that last bit hastily. Didn't want some yutz who didn't know what he was doing, taking us into all that unknown territory. Over water and whatnot.

I shivered at the thought of it.

After that, we spent a good fifteen to twenty minutes bull-shitting and filling in Elder Leo on some of the highlights of our forays into the annals of Brindollan history. All the cool things we had done, killed, fixed, and royally screwed up.

It was during the story about how we had been trying to get Kayda to stop with the storm magic before having to go to the jungle in the south that Fainnir returned. He looked flushed and a little out of breath.

"I take it that they haven't beaten cardio into your body yet, then?" I grinned as I spoke. I hated running too. At least at home, anyway.

"Well, there's only so much we can do in a week, and given his stout stature, it gets a little harder." Elder Leo observed good-naturedly.

"Dwarves donnae run, we fight our foes head-on." The young dwarf held his head up high as he touched the haft of the axe he had at his side.

"Oh, sweet summer child." I patted his head, taking in the youthful stubbornness in his demeanor. "You're a mage of the earth. Granted, you can move stone and manipulate it, but you aren't made of it."

"I be made from metal, Zeke, ye be know'n tha', yer kin yerself, ye ought not be sayin' daft things like tha'." He looked a little deflated.

"Ancestrally, yes." I cuffed his arm affectionately. "Look, Fainnir, I'm teasing you. You're gonna need tough skin if you come to fight with the rest of us, okay? Jaken, Muu, and I will be looking out for you, don't you doubt that. The others will protect you too, but you've got some respect to earn. Okay?"

"Aye, tha' be expected, an' I be welcomin' it." Fainnir thumped his fist to his chest three times as if to say bring it.

"I leave you alone for barely a moment, and already you lose yourself to your dialect. Please have some decorum, Fainnir," Pebble's rumbling reproach caught the boy off guard, and he jumped.

James snorted, and I just shook my head. "Thanks for everything you do, Elder Leo, and thanks for looking out for our friends, here."

"I am always happy to serve this world." Elder Leo jabbed his right fist into his left hand, then bowed as he held them forward a little. "My friends, good luck on your journey, and Fainnir—be careful."

The dwarf nodded once, and both he and James bowed respectfully. I did the same, my arms at my sides, bending at the waist, but keeping my eyes on him. Once we all stood upright, I touched Fainnir and James on their shoulders and cast Teleport to get us back to the party.

CHAPTER FOURTEEN

I blinked as we appeared about twenty feet from the dome of shadows Maebe was obscuring the others with.

"Zeke, you forgot Pebble!" James groaned, and I winced.

"Oh, no need to worry." Fainnir smiled as he wove his fingers together in front of him and pressed out, the joints cracking. His old dialect shifting like Pebble had wanted. "I can summon 'im anywhere. Watch."

Fainnir waggled his fingers over the ground, stomping once and raising his voice as he spoke, "Pebble, attend your master!"

"You did always have a flair for the dramatic, Fainnir," Pebble spoke dryly from behind us. "Thank you for attempting to sound clearer in your speech."

"Woah, Pebble, dwarves aren't stupid for speaking the way they do," James defended the young mage.

"It is not that they sound 'stupid' as you put it, but that other elementals may not understand him through his dialect, and therefore may not do what he wishes them to do." Pebble held out an oddly shaped arm. "He could ask for one thing, and they could misunderstand and end up killing him, or getting someone hurt who would otherwise be saved by him working on how he presents his desires through audible noise. It is not meant to insult the dwarves, nor make others feel poorly—it is to save his life."

"I've never really heard speaking referred to like that." I laughed out loud and stared at the elemental. "Let's go introduce you to everyone."

"Where?" Fainnir glanced around.

It was Pebble who pointed toward the dome. "There are several creatures of varying sizes over there, but I cannot see them. Why is this, tiny druid?"

"First of all, call me Zeke, Pebble, and second…." I pointed to the barrier, though I knew they couldn't see it. "That would be magic. My lovely wife and I can control and manipulate shadows. This allows us to be hidden from outsiders and keep us safe."

"How did you know they were there?" James asked, then stared at the elemental's legs, still connected to the ground. "You can feel them through the earth, can't you?"

He nodded once and tromped toward the dome. I reached out with my mind and created a hole large enough for all of us to walk through.

The others watched us in idle curiosity, Muu was the first to speak, "Hey there, Pebble, where's that fleshy lump usually attached to you?"

"He be right here!" Fainnir flew at the dragon-kin with a grin on his face and his arms out wide. "Ye get uglier every time I look at ye!"

"Well, I'd imagine looking at people's chins all the time doesn't help," Muu shot back as he pulled the dwarf into a great big hug. "How have you been? How's the family and clan?"

"Well, they were nae—*not*—pleased with me having to come topside, but they understand that I have to grow in me own way. Though it took a mean bit o' convincin' to be allowed me leave from the city." He shrugged and scratched himself on the leg.

"I'm pretty new to all of this meself, so, whatever ye can do, I'd be appreciatin' it."

"Well, this must be Fainnir, then." Yohsuke wandered over to us and looked over the smaller beings before him. "So, you're the earth mage that Zeke and Muu have been gushing about?"

"He is the only one, but why would they 'gush' over him?" Pebble sounded confused as he glanced at the rest of us. "Oh! That was a turn of phrase, correct?"

I nodded, then spoke to the others, "Guys, as Yoh pointed out, this is Fainnir. Fainnir, these are my brothers. Yohsuke, the guy in front of you, James, and Muu, our two dragons, Balmur the dwarf you've likely heard about, and Bokaj, the guy in the back with the kitty. Jaken, of Clan Mugfist, you likely saw around when you went to meet Muu, but he's the big Fae-orc in armor." I flinched as Kayda's mind brushed against mine. "Also, this is my first familiar, Kayda, she's really very gentle, so you don't need to worry about her hurting you. And this is my wife, Queen Maebe, Mistress of the Void and Chilling Winds."

Maebe's teeth flashed in the low light as her smiling form stepped closer. "That was a new reference and title, husband."

Her purr over that last word was so nice, but Fainnir pulled me out of my desire—literally, as he pulled me down by my arm to whisper, "What do I do when addressin' a Queen?"

I glanced over to see Maebe, uncertainty on her face, begin to raise her hand in protest when I spoke, "Well, Fainnir, what you do with royalty is give them deference, and show respect. To someone of Queen Maebe's station, a bow at the waist would be a good way to show respect when she comes into your presence or you into hers. While those who don't serve her might bow, those who do serve her would kneel. So, you would bow."

He looked a little flustered for a moment, but Maebe stayed her hand and allowed me to go through the motions of showing him how to bow properly. He had his arms at his side, then bowed his head down entirely too low.

"Fainnir, son of Granite and Natholdi, he of Clan Light-hand and friend of my husband and my friends, raise your head and know that I welcome you into my presence, child." Fainnir raised his head, his eyebrows furrowed and shrugged.

"Thank ye, m'lady." He smiled good-naturedly as she returned his easy appreciation.

"None of that. You may call me Maebe in this company, and this company only. Is that something I can trust you to do?" She raised an eyebrow at the young dwarf, who nodded enthusiastically.

"Good." Yohsuke clapped his hands together as he regarded Fainnir. "So, kid, what can you do, and have you eaten?"

"I can do magic, an' I can fight with me hands an' axe!" The weapon he had mentioned was in his hands almost instantly, and he swung it around excitedly.

"Hey—woah!" Jaken hopped forward in time to catch the offending weapon in a gauntleted-hand and pulled him back a bit. "Easy on the friendly fire, buddy."

"Ah, sorry." Cheeks flushed red, the bashful dwarf put his weapon away swiftly, his stomach rumbling. "Aye, I could use a nibble."

Yoh went and grabbed some food off his skillet and put it on an extra plate. "Here you go."

While Fainnir wolfed down his chow, the rest of us waited patiently. Maebe pulled me aside to whisper into my ear.

"You did well, teaching him like that." Her breath brushed against the side of my neck, and it sent thrills down my spine. "He should know how to treat royalty, and I almost stopped you. I am sorry."

"Don't worry about it." I brushed her hand with my own, lightly caressing her fingers before continuing, "I know how being constantly treated like an outsider and too special, ruins your fun here at times. It's okay."

Her lips feathered against my neck. "I love you." I pulled her into a hug and gave her a peck on the lips.

"Later, we can be more affectionate," I grumbled into her forehead and brought myself to step away so that I could join the others. I felt her hand on my back and knew I would be keeping my word.

"What level are you, Fainnir?" Muu's loud question startled us. The dwarf stopped chewing and glanced from the dragon-kin to the rest of us. "I only ask because I can't see it, no matter how hard I focus."

"That is because the elemental Primordials are protecting him with anonymity," Pebble explained before the boy could respond. "It isn't rare for people to have items that hide their level, but he is still very new to all of this. This newness means that he could be easily manipulated and taken control of—or murdered. If you wish them to know, Fainnir, you may tell them. But do not share your status screen."

"Well, I be knowin' *that* bit of it, that be a very intimate thing." He grumbled before taking a bite and chewing slowly. His head swiveled around as he looked for spies and finally, he stated, "I be level four."

"That's not terrible, and you're still young yet, so there's no reason to be bashful or shy about it." Jaken put a comforting hand on Fainnir's shoulder and smiled encouragingly. "Don't worry, we have your back. And Zeke will be teaching you how to help control your elemental magics, so you're in good hands."

"I will assist as well." Maebe raised her chin high as if daring any of us to tell her no. "I am quite adept at shadow magics, and that is one of the newest elements. I am certain that there is not too much of a difference."

"Adept?" Balmur snorted, the others looked at him, and he just laughed harder. "If you're an adept, we have to be less than beginners. Your mastery of shadows and use of the void and ice is so insane that to call you anything less than a master or grandmaster level mage with those kinds of magic would be equivalent to a death sentence for anyone who doubts you."

"I am truly glad that you are with us again, my friend, and it is my privilege to teach you all that I know." Maebe sauntered over and lifted him bodily into a hug that made the man grunt in what sounded like pain.

"Speaking of, what kind of combat capabilities do the two of you have?" James cleaned his weapons, the blades of his fist weapons almost dyed red with gore from previous fights, but he watched Fainnir and Pebble in interest.

"Well, I can usually have Pebble do a little bit o' fightin' for me, while I take a more 'hands-off' approach to things with some minor earth spells," Fainnir explained, then pulled out a tiny pipe, his eyes lighting up as he did so.

"Hey, woah, woah!" I scrambled toward him, snatching the object out of his hands, and he regarded me strangely. "The hells do you think you're doing?"

"Having a pipe o' larder moss to settle me stomach and mind, Zeke, it's something most dwarves do." He blinked at me, and I growled.

"Most dwarves aren't you!" I fought the urge to crush his property. "Do your parents know that you do this shit?"

"They encourage it," Muu spoke up. I turned a cold eye his way, but he didn't back down. "Something about the moss that they smoke allows them to digest things more quickly and energize their body faster. It's weird, I tried it, and it didn't do anything for me, but they encourage him to do it. Leave him be, besides, he's an adult now by dwarven standards."

My teeth grated against each other as I mulled it over. If it wasn't harmful, who was I to stop him from doing something his own parents encouraged? As a father, I could respect that other parents would parent their child how they pleased. I could only hope that they would have the courage to keep my son from doing something harmful to himself or others the way I had tried just now.

I held the item out to him. "Sorry, Fainnir, I didn't know."

"Ignorance be something tha' happens when no one asks what they need be askin', Zeke." He patted my hand and nodded sagely. "Ye been clan but a little while, and ye have nae spent time with dwarves en masse for long. Maybe a week or so at the most? Our ways be new to ye, and I'll nae be the one to hold it against ye. Aye?"

"You make my life hard, Fainnir," Pebble grumbled but was mostly ignored.

"Did you understand what he just said?" Maebe whispered with awe as she watched Fainnir light his pipe and puff on it merrily.

"I did, and it was very wise and kind." I smiled at her then the kid, and we went about our night.

———

We woke up the next morning well-rested and ready to rock. Our breakfast was hearty, our camp spotless thanks to Pebble and Fainnir's magic coupled with my own Druidic powers, and it looked like Nimran's Flame was expecting us. Pebble had been ordered into the ground by Fainnir for a little bit, at least until we got into the dungeon, and he could summon him again so that no unnecessary attention was brought onto us by the strange creature.

As we came into view, the group that had been waiting for us began to look us over.

"More than there were yesterday, but that's alright." Yani sniffed as he looked us over and walked around all of us. It made me a little uncomfortable, but if I wanted to, and with Maebe and the others' help, I could kill him, and we could storm the place. I relaxed a little more after that thought.

"If you return, you will pay us a total of twenty percent of the loot you earn in the dungeon, and the crown ten percent rather than the full twenty that it normally is," Yani explained in a bored, but matter-of-fact tone. "If you do not and you lie to us, we will know, and you will be slaughtered on sight if you try to return."

"And what if we die?" Bokaj eyed the walls for the third time since we had arrived.

"We loot your corpses, and all will be well anyway." One of

the men who was with the group smiled, until Yani backhanded him in the face, sending him sprawling to the ground.

"Weakness is a curse we have been striving to cure this land of for generations, your deaths will be a cleansing if you were to fall, but we will not seek to harm you unless you start something we must finish; I swear this by our gods." His eyes widened at the notification he had likely received, and he just dismissed it. "Ah, let us see you into the dungeon then, yes?"

We walked on into murder alley, my eyes wandering over the archers and spearman who watched us almost casually with their weapons at a mild ready.

"What can you tell us about the dungeon?" I asked as we moved further in, shadows deepened as the crack in the mountainside looked higher and higher.

"Nothing, that is our rule, and over this way, you will sign a waiver." Yani motioned to a table set up outside of a large metal door. There were smooth stones on top of papers, eight of them. "Janic, go and get another waiver from the locker, be swift."

One of the other men who had been with the group, a younger-looking man with blond hair, sprinted away to our left into a room. A moment later, he returned and slapped the paper onto the table with a similar stone.

"How are we supposed to sign these waivers without ink and quill?" Yohsuke asked, knowing full well that James had one in his inventory.

"These waivers are signed by blood, as some of the men and women who come to this place do not know their letters well enough to sign their names." A sense of unease settled over us, and I could almost feel the others tensing. "I know what you are thinking, 'but Yani, blood is a very precious thing to be spilled so lightly.' These stones seal and dry the blood so that it can never be used in anything other than this contract. Besides, it is really only so that your family cannot come seeking petty revenge because you were too weak to succeed."

I blinked at the man in front of us. What an ass. But he did have a point, and it did seem to be a sound judgment call.

I tapped the stone on top of the paper before anyone moved.

Security Stone

Dries any blood that touches any paperwork this stone rests upon, rendering it utterly useless in any matters unrelated to the dispensation of the terms agreed upon. Limit of one stone per page, per marking.

Stone enchanted by grandmaster enchanter T'lovic Missanderiyt

I nodded to the others and muttered, "Stones are legit."

I looked over the waiver; it seemed to be standard. The party of the first could not be held liable in the event of the untimely death of the second party by any and all would be prosecutors or pursuant of justice. That the second party will pay any taxes on any monetary gains inside the dungeon should they return to the dungeon entrance, and anything undeclared upon return will result in a merciless slaughter for compensation.

I glanced over in time to see that the others had jabbed their fingers with a dagger that we passed among ourselves. Once it was my turn, I wiped the blood off on my pant leg, then pricked my left thumb before pressing it onto the X on the page. The blood instantly dried a dull brown, dehydrated to the touch upon inspection, and then Yani had it in hand.

"Ouch!" Fainnir grumbled as I saw him raise his right hand from the axe on his hip. "Ne'er thought the first blood on me axe would be me own."

I couldn't help the wry smile that split my face at his grumbling, then patted his shoulder. "Well, you could've used this dagger, but don't worry, little brother, you'll have your chance to split some skulls. No worries."

Yani lifted his hands and made flicking motions to the two men on either side of him. They took out daggers, making our group immediately eye them as dangerous. "Do not worry, it is part of the process."

The two men stood on either side of the doors and slid their weapons across a palm, touching the door, then stepping away swiftly. The doors flew open, cracking into the mountainside with a crash that made rubble and dust fall from the stone above.

"You may enter now, and remember if you are going to die, die well." Yani grinned evilly as we stalked by. The now-lit entrance was stone covered in bronze. The scent of drying blood hit me, and I knew that this was a place of death.

The fuckers wouldn't be letting anyone out unless there was no risk to them—if they actually let anyone out.

After the last of us were in, the doors slammed shut once more, and darkness took over our sight. The dwarves would be fine; they could see underground, and what was a mountain, but heavy-ass ground? The elves and I had darkvision, but it was limited greatly at sixty feet, and it only made things look like they might in dim light.

"Light incoming," Balmur said with a grunt so that we could shield our eyes. A second later, dim light glowed in front of us.

"For this first one, we're all going to hang back and let Zeke and Bea do the majority of the killing so that she will be able to level," Yohsuke explained. "Fainnir, since you're level four, these first few floors will be where you start to get an idea for how we operate as a party, and you can learn what to do from us. I take it you know how to use that axe?"

"As well as I be know'n how to walk." The dwarf pulled his weapon out and readied it.

"Good, Zeke, unleash the beast." I snorted at his pun and let Bea out of the collar around my throat.

As soon as the hatchling was out and on her feet, she turned to us and immediately began to search for food. She halted in front of Fainnir, eyeing him curiously. She looked from his face to his hand, then back to his face before calling out to him.

"What's she be wantin'?" Fainnir mumbled his question and backed a step away.

"Food." Yohsuke sighed.

I touched her mind with mine, and I realized why. She thought that he was Nick, and when she saw the other dwarf, she usually got treats and pets. Now, there were no treats and no pets, and she was upset. Was the feeder and petter broken? Was he angered?

"It's okay, baby," I called to her softly. "It's time to hunt, then he can pet you. But we have to hunt first, okay?"

She seemed to take heart in this, as I mentally called to Kayda, *Sit on Jaken's shoulder and watch our backs, okay?*

As father pleases. Do not allow my sister to become too hurt. She squawked and shrunk as she hopped onto Jaken's shoulder, dancing as she turned to watch our backs.

"Time to go and play, Bea," I encouraged her, moving forward with her.

These tunnels were large enough that three of us could easily fit side by side in them, but it was me and her out front with Fainnir behind.

"Oh!" Fainnir snapped his fingers and tapped the ground with his foot. "Pebble, I summon you to my side."

The elemental separated himself from the wall quietly. "I feel many presences up ahead, small ones."

"Thanks for the heads-up, Pebble." I nodded at the elemental, then returned my sights to the fore. The walls and floor still had a brown tint to them, but the ball of floating light thirty feet ahead of the party allowed us to see very well. Balmur was getting pretty damned good at his magic.

The first thing that we came across was a large beetle the size of a chihuahua. Bugs. It *had* to be bugs.

Beetle Level 1

Mind you, I don't really care for bugs, but I'm not a huge fan of small things that can give me diseases that wreck my life.

I shuddered and began to go through how to proceed with Bea when I realized she was already on top of the beetle.

Chomping at it with her teeth didn't work, so she slapped it with her tail like it was an over-sized hockey puck, sending it careening into a wall. It smacked into it, the wings coming out to steady it before she was on *top* of it, snatching off the bug's wings.

I didn't know if bugs could hiss or not, but this thing sure as hell sounded like it was, and she didn't give one single fuck. They landed with a thud, and she dug her nose under the beetle's side, scoring a strike to her snout, but she lifted her head, sending the bug onto its back where she stomped a triumphant foot onto its exposed, softer underbelly.

She clacked her teeth in victory before sinking the exaggeratedly long talon on her foot into it, the beetle's health bar falling from 50% to zero in a blink.

"What the hell was that?" I grumbled. I hadn't needed to tell her anything. She was a natural-born predator, and all she needed to do was be set free.

She got enough experience from her kill, a measly three points, that I could finally see her stats.

Name: Bea Arthur
Race: Gust Raptor (Hatchling)
Level: 1
Strength: 2
Dexterity: 10
Constitution: 3
Intelligence: 4
Wisdom: 1
Charisma: 3
Unspent Attribute Points: 0

Well then, I know a certain little raptor whose constitution is getting added to at second level. Then I projected my pride to her. She'd only taken a couple points of damage from the beetle, so we moved on.

This portion of the dungeon was fairly easy to make it

through like one might think. It had a beetle, or ant every now and then, and the path was almost linear in design. The ants were an issue, as they were also larger than normal ants and were much stronger than her, so she had to creatively use her speed to confuse them, then whittle down their health. Watching her move put me at ease. At level one, she was fast; at higher levels, she was going to be a fucking wrecking ball with teeth and an attitude.

And boy, did she know it.

After each kill, she gave a shrill chirp, or bark of challenge into the darkness ahead of us before we would move on. Muu was to pick up any shells that were salvageable so that we could maybe make something with them or use them as components. Materials were important to gamers.

"She's gonna get her ass whooped by something eventually." Yohsuke snickered behind me.

"Yeah, she is, but man, can she move or what?" I agreed, adding that last bit proudly.

"Hell yeah, she can, she's god's gift to speed. Looks like something is up ahead." He nodded toward our path. "Go check it out."

Bea was close to leveling up anyway, so it wouldn't hurt. We walked into a larger room, roughly the size of a classroom back on Earth, and waited until the others joined us. Once all of us were inside, a wall of solid stone dropped from the ceiling to keep us from escaping.

"Boss room?" Muu asked excitedly as he glanced at the others. "Any takers?"

"We know what it is, where is the boss?" James growled.

Bea sniffed at the air, casting her eyes up into the darkness above us.

"Balmur, light that darkness up, if you would?" I pointed to the ceiling, already sending my awareness forth and finding what I thought I would.

"Happily." The globe of light shot up into the dark and illuminated a spider the size of a Rottweiler with venomous fangs and many eyes descending from a large hole in the ceiling.

The rear four legs held the web behind it for stability, and the fore four began to reach down toward Bea.

Sinisper Level 3

"This thing will be too much for her on her own, Fainnir, you're in too." The young dwarf stepped around me as I said his name, his axe in hand. I caught him on the shoulder before he could go too far in. "Weapon and magic, let her distract the spider while you attack."

He nodded stoically before turning back toward their foe and stepping closer.

Bea, I want you to distract the spider, but don't get too close. Let Fainnir do the work. She didn't acknowledge me at all, so I growled. "Hey, scaly, you better fucking listen to me."

She turned her head back just enough to side-eye me and waved her tail as she readied to pounce.

"Oh, for fuck's sake." I stepped forward, but two sets of hands grabbed my shoulders.

Jaken and Yoh both had me and pulled me back, Jaken whispering, "Let her learn the hard way."

"I'm gonna beat her ass, is what I'm gonna do." I grumbled but let them go. There was going to be a time when she would have to learn to listen to me. May as well be now.

"Pebble, you stay out of it," Fainnir called back.

The elemental said nothing, but I got the idea that he would do as he was told until he felt it time to step in. I was of the same mindset.

"Mind the fangs, you two," Muu called, like a parent calling to his children. "They're sharp and have venom. Okay, I love you, have a good time at school!"

"Why are you this way?" Maebe asked Muu with genuine concern in her voice.

Muu responded, very matter of fact, "Making others laugh gives me existential validation," There was a slight pause, then, "And because I didn't get my first kiss until I was eighteen."

I didn't get the chance to even go in on that weirdness before the spider made its move, hissing, and its fangs flashed forward toward Bea's throat, and the raptor hopped above its head and bounded over it. A slap of her tail brought its attention to her while Fainnir used the opening to summon a spire of stone from beneath its thorax, goring it a little.

Ichor splattered the retreating spell and floor beneath the spider and took 10% of its health with it. Sinisper screeched loudly, spitting a globule of something dark-colored and phlegm-like in appearance at the young mage, but a wall of thin stone rose in time to stop the gross projectile.

"Pebble!" Fainnir howled. "Ye'll nae do tha' again!"

"If you say so, master," Pebble replied in stony stoicism.

"Good save," I muttered to the elemental, but he remained quiet.

The spider's hissing brought my attention back to the fight, Kayda calling out in support as Bea flitted between the creature's legs causing it to fall. She bit at one of them savagely, tearing through a section of chitinous joint and pulling little of the meat away, stripping a few points of HP from it and a little of its mobility.

Not enough to really put it in a bind, but enough to slow it a little.

A leg whipped out and cut through the air just behind Bea, then in front of her, and she used her little air step maneuver to get around it. Two more stone spikes poked into the spider's gut, and it reared before turning and sending a line of web beneath it that caught Fainnir on the foot.

"Wha—" he began but grunted halfway through the question.

The spider greedily pulled him forward, swatting at Bea from where she worried at another leg. I cast Renewing Flames on her before she crashed into the wall behind her. That kept her from serious injury, the regeneration on the spell acting as a buffer for the damage she took, like a small shield. She took more than half her full HP bar, but it was recovering swiftly.

And she was pissed. The spider's dripping fangs shivered delightedly over Fainnir's prone form, then it tried to bite him.

"No!" He sputtered, a hand up in front of him to deflect the blow, but the fangs clanged off his skin, now encrusted in stones. Stone Skin! Clever kid.

He whipped his axe up into the spider's throat and exposed underparts, savaging it while growling in wordless rage. His left hand whipped out to the side, and after several motions and a flick of his wrist, a large spiral of stone drilled into the creature's head, taking the majority of the red in the HP bar with it.

A final chop of his axe saw the creature dead, crashing on top of him.

The dwarf grunted and tried to get the corpse off him, but to no avail.

"Suppose we can help them out now that the threat is dead." Yohsuke said playfully. Muu and Jaken stepped over and easily tossed the spider's body off Fainnir, who was covered in ichor and other gore-like bits.

"Good work." I helped him stand and patted his back. "Stand still."

I sent shadows crawling over him to wick away the disgusting battle residue. He panicked a little when it went over his face, throwing his hands up to check the few growing hairs on his chin. His sigh of relief when he found all was in order was too funny.

"Well, obviously, you know what needs to be fixed, right?" I asked him as he finished looking over himself.

"Fight better." He grunted, but I shook my head and grabbed his shirt, jerking him closer to me.

I pointed to Pebble. "You need to fight smarter and not hold yourself back by cutting out one of the most powerful tools at your disposal."

"I be a dwarf!" The boy howled indignantly. "We don't let no one do no fightin' for us!"

"And while you are here training with me and my brothers —my wife and my precious familiars—you *will* fight to the fullest extent of your capability!" I snarled into his face. "I will not have you, the first Earth Mage, champion of Fainne and the Primordial Earth Elemental, slacking off and doing as you please. I promised I would protect and train you, but you make it harder when you refuse to protect yourself."

"Zeke!" Muu called, rushing over to shove me away from Fainnir. "He's only a—he's still learning, man. Cut him some slack."

"Either he's a child, and needs to be taught valuable lessons on proper ways to handle situations, or he is an adult, who will learn because if he doesn't, he will die." James stepped between us, his gaze cast down at Fainnir. "Look, Fainnir, you're the only one who can do the things you do with your element. Fighting the way you wanted almost put you in a really bad situation."

"But I got out of it!" Fainnir implored softly, pleadingly as if he needed us to see that.

"But what happens if you run out of mana?" Bokaj grabbed his shoulder softly. "What if you'd been knocked unconscious? There are too many 'what if's' not to take advantage of the surest thing you have—your partner."

Pebble stepped forward, his misshapen hand on Fainnir's shoulder, "They are right, my friend. There is wisdom to be gained from knowing that no matter where you go or what you face, you are no longer the keeper and maker of your fate. I am bound to you, too."

"But I don't want you to get hurt, too," the young dwarf's voice was barely a whisper. "You're my friend. I need to protect you."

"I am your friend, and I will die to protect you," Pebble gently corrected. "These ones are here to protect and train you, and the Druid—Zeke—knows well what it means to use all his strength. His bond with his familiars is even stronger than our own. They are a part of him. To lose one is to lose part of himself. He meant well."

"I did." I let the anger I had within me flow out with a breath. "Look, Fainnir, I'm a huge part of who you are now—

I'm your first oath. I know that you are destined for greatness, but I need you to listen to us and learn from us so that you can achieve it and not die."

"He will." Maebe stepped forward, her eyes on the boy. "Come with me, child. I have much to show you. If you will all wait here?"

The rest of us nodded and let her walk away with Fainnir, Pebble hobbling along after them.

While they were gone, I turned my sights on my unruly familiar. She had begun to dig through the spider's corpse, the sickening squelching sound of tearing meat and hurried gobbling reaching us from more than twelve feet away.

"And you!" I barked, pulling on my bond with her so that she would step out from the corpse. I stepped around the floor boss until I stood directly in front of the hole, she had carved into it and where she currently dug. "Come here. Now!"

She continued to dig into the body, ignoring my order completely. I centered myself, so I wouldn't act in anger, then took a deep breath, sending the shadows at my feet snaking toward hers until I had them connected like a leash. I tugged once, and she resisted, mindlessly digging for something.

"Bea Arthur!" I snapped. She paused for a heartbeat, then began to dig again with doubled fury. I shook my head, "Fine."

I brought the leash of shadows into my hands and *yanked*. The little raptor screeched as she flew through the air into my grasp. I held her wriggling body while something brown reflected the light in her jaws. I reached into her mouth, her teeth grating against the metal of my right hand as we fought for the item.

"Bea, I command you, release!" I spat the words on instinct, her mind blanked for a moment, and her mouth slackened enough for me to retrieve her prize.

It was a small, brown crystal of some sort, roughly the size of a thimble and still dripping blood. Once it was in my grasp and my attention was off her, she began to struggle and snap at the item, so I willed her back into my collar, but she wouldn't go.

Finally, I'd had enough and put her onto the ground.

It calls to her, Kayda finally explained, fluttering to my shoulder to observe it. Kayda's closeness to the object making the raptor hatchling go mad. Barking, calling, and trying to jump up and snatch it out of my hand. *I do not know why, but she wants it badly.*

"No duh." I grumbled and threw the item into my inventory. She immediately stopped acting the way she had been but threw me hateful glares here and there. "Hey, you listen to me, and I may let you have whatever it is so long as it's safe."

"What is it?" Yoh called over.

"Some kind of crystal, no stats came up when I touched it." I sighed and began to go through Bea's level up. Her dexterity went up by one with her natural point, no surprise. I put two of her points into constitution and then the last one into strength. That would do her for now. Looking at her, she looked a little fatter, which given that she had gorged herself on spider meat, wasn't too great of a surprise.

"Think it could be some kind of boss crystal?" Jaken walked over and glanced from me to Bea. "There are plenty of games that have bosses in dungeons drop rewards that could be used as components or power-ups."

"Maybe, Maebe might know, so we could ask her whenever she comes back," James finished speaking, and I looked toward the door that we had entered when coming in here. It was open now, and I could make out Maebe and Fainnir against the shadows.

They seemed to be discussing something serious, so I left them alone.

"Found the door," Muu called from the other side of the room.

A small doorway with a symbol of a spider on it barred our exit from this portion of the dungeon. There was nothing else on it, but that didn't mean we just sat there idly looking at it with our thumbs up our butts.

"Open, says me," Balmur joked. The rest of us looked at him, but he was still laughing from finding himself so funny that he didn't care.

"Maybe try touching it?" James offered his hand, reaching toward the barrier. His palm touched it, and nothing happened. Huh.

"What about that crystal?" Yohsuke shrugged. "There wasn't anything like a key, I checked."

"And I had an eye out, too." Balmur lifted his jar of eyes, which now included two human eyes and one of the spider's several.

Jaken gagged. "Oh, gross."

I rolled my eyes and took the crystal out, the blood on it had dried a little bit. I glanced from it, to the door, then held it out until it was almost touching, then a blur of teeth snapped it out of my hand. Flecks of the blood landing on the door and the symbol. The door shifted a little, but the thing that took all of my energy was Bea. She had the crystal in her mouth and began to jerk her head back like she was swallowing.

"Are you fucking serious?" I spat, more in exasperation than anger. "What is your deal, Bea?"

She finished swallowing before I got to her, then started to strut around the room, her head bobbing forward like she was the queen of the roost.

ALERT!

Your familiar has found and consumed a monster crystal. This has resulted in there being a Mutation to her abilities.

Venom Claw – The creature that obtains this ability through consuming the crystal can envenom their main means of attack for a small mana cost. Cost: 20 MP. Duration: 30 seconds. Cooldown: 1 minute.

Do you accept? Yes? / No?

"Get the hell out of here, man," I grumbled. "Jaken called

it, that was a monster crystal, and I guess consuming them can result in mutations. So, we may be able to find something down here for Tmont, too, Bokaj."

"Hear that T'?" Bokaj excitedly pulled his cat out of his hood, her meowing at him bitter and slightly mutinous as he swung her around. "We might get you something cool."

I turned back to see Yohsuke throw his hand inside the wounds of the spider and come away bloody. He walked over to the door and smeared the blood over the symbol on the door, and it raised all the way.

"Clever way to get through," I observed, the gamer in me screaming about how amazing this was. I accepted the mutation and watched as the talons on the larger toes on Bea's feet darkened and turned brown. "That's fucking cool."

She eyed me haughtily, her tail flicking back and forth making me growl at her. "Don't you look at me in that tone of voice, young lady. I'll still beat your ass if you don't learn to listen to me!"

She sniffed but came over to me and nuzzled my knee lovingly. I could feel her pressing against my mind and opened our connection.

Father stupid. She teased, but I could feel both her tolerance and love for me in the thought.

"You make it real hard not to be angry at you, you little shit." I reached down and picked her up, letting her lick my nose. "Stop that, I'm mad at you right now."

She rumbled in her throat; it sounded decidedly like laughter. I sighed, and she rubbed her nose against my cheek. "Dumb lizard."

"We are ready to move on," Maebe announced as she walked back into the room with a bashful Fainnir in tow.

She stopped, and the dwarf stepped forward. "You were right." He looked up at us. "I'll listen to wha' ye say, an' I'll learn proper, because the lot o' ye are trustin' me with yer lives, and me people are trustin' me with their future."

Maebe put a gentle hand on the young dwarf's shoulder.

"Well done, Fainnir. You should be proud to serve as a leader. Leaders can do what?"

"Admit their faults an' seek guidance when it is available," he stated as if coached repeatedly.

"Lead on then, Fainnir." James waved him forward. They walked off, and I stayed back, letting the others go so I could talk to Maebe.

All I did was glance her way when she spoke, "He took what you said in anger to heart."

"I didn't mean to be so harsh." I frowned, feeling like an asshole.

"I know that, and the others know that." Maebe took my hand and had me wait inside the entrance. "But he needed a gentle hand. Luckily, I was able to help him understand that he is a leader, and that much is expected from him, because it is. And that we will be hard on him so that he knows how to comport himself on his own."

"I can sense the 'but' in there." I sighed.

"But from this point on, I need for you to be the king I will be training you to be." Her hand squeezed mine. "You are not just a mentor anymore, you are a ruler of the Unseelie Fae, and one of the only people in all the realms to have the blessings of the elements. You have to be the best example of all. You will be nothing less than that, do I make myself clear?"

I rose to my full height as I looked down at her, not like I was trying to intimidate her, but because I wanted to be that man. To be that person she needed me to be. To be the person my friends and Fainnir needed.

The kind of person they could rely on.

"Yes, my love," I said quietly.

Her hands cupped my cheeks and forced my gaze to her own, her green eyes shining in the dim light that floated ahead of us.

"I did not mean for that to sound so harsh, but cruel is the life of a ruler at times." She frowned, concern taking over her features. "And much the same as in my own life, I left you with little choice."

A wry grin split my face, and I shifted into my human form, as I pulled her close, I said, "I did say yes. I knew I wanted you. And if this is a price that I have to pay to have you, I pay it gladly."

We shared a tender moment together, there in the damp darkness of the dungeon then joined our friends.

They arched their eyebrows at me in my human form, but I ignored them. I stepped next to Fainnir and Pebble.

"Alright, you two, the experience is limited in here regardless, so we're going to have you go in with Bea anyway, ready?" I looked down at them, and they looked confused.

"Who are you, human?" Pebble asked with concern. "When did you—oh. Zeke. That was you?"

I had shifted into my fox-man form while he had been speaking and waited patiently. "Are we ready to proceed?"

"Aye." Fainnir looked forward and held himself upright, carefully scanning the distance. "Pebble, scan ahead an' report to me."

The elemental melted into the ground with a nod and left us there alone.

"You know, Fainnir, I was harsh, and I would like to apologize." I put a hand on his shoulder gently.

"It were only words, Zeke." He shrugged my hand off easily. "I know'd things'd be different. But I failed to realize that me position was so important. Ain't a normal dwarf no more, so I can't be approachin' things as a normal dwarf."

"You're special," I agreed. "That difference will cost you much, but you are also a legend in the making. Never forget who you are, and forge ahead."

He nodded, but I wasn't done. "You have a new Way now, Fainnir. And it is along that path, *your* path, that your people will find a measure of safety and salvation."

I saw his grip tighten on his weapon, tears streaming from his eyes. "That be a lot to put on a dwarf's shoulders."

Pebble returned then, his diamond eyes searching, and my lips quirked at the timing. "Yeah, it is. I guess it's a good thing that you have friends to help you bear that burden."

Pebble nudged his master and gave a lopsided grin of support. Fainnir sniffed and ran a hand under his nose.

"There are several groupings of creatures up ahead, small, not quite the size of the bugs from before," Pebble reported and turned, stepping in front of the earth mage.

"Then we march on, ye'll take the lead an' majority o' the physical attacks as I work on damagin' and defeatin' our foes," he glanced at me. "Zeke, I don't know what ye be wantin' Bea to do, but please, keep her away from Pebble. My earth magics won't harm him, but they will her."

"Excellent strategy, Earth Mage Fainnir," I congratulated him, softly. "I will do as you ask. For this floor, these are your calls. If you have questions, ask. Let's see what you've got."

He nodded once and grunted. "Let's go cautiously, Pebble."

I watched them stalk off, Jaken taking lead for the rest of us, letting the rest of them go before I did with Maebe.

"Well done." She grasped my hand and pulled me forward behind the others.

"Contact!" James hollered back to us, and I hurried forward.

When I made it to the front, the view opened up. Fainnir, Pebble, and Bea worked well together.

Bea went in first, collected the creatures that were nearby, and led them to Pebble. Pebble raised a stone partition that kept them near him, and Fainnir used his earth spells to whittle them down while Bea harried them at the rear.

It was an ingenious plan, and highly respectable. Once the violence was truly at an end, I checked on the group. Nothing more serious than a bite wound on Bea's leg, but she was fine once Jaken healed her.

The creatures were rats, but not the gigantic kind I had expected, but they looked a little on the malnourished side.

"Well done, all of you." I couldn't help the smile that spread across my face. "Excellent teamwork."

Fainnir nodded and made a motion to Pebble, who sank into the ground and went forth once more.

So the second floor went, the group would work together to bring the rats together into a trap, then dispatch them as swiftly as they could. They usually did this with minimal need for healing and with as much communication as what Fainnir deemed necessary. I would pass along Bea's observations, which typically were to kill more, and they would adjust where it was needed.

The boss of this area was interesting.

Hamelin's Weasel Level 4

The large weasel stood nearly as large a pony, slick gray fur and beady red eyes watched us as we entered the room. The amount of us that came in seemed to intimidate it a little bit. It cowered back toward a large burrow it'd made in a pile of rubble and stone.

"Pebble, I think we can make this work in one go." Fainnir squinted at the pile of rubble and our surroundings. "Check for an exit, and close both it and the entry off. I'll be takin' care o' the rest."

Pebble shrank into the ground at his feet and was gone for only a second before he was back and lifted his arms. Stone shot out of the earth in front of the entry, sealing it just enough that we could see a little of what was going on inside.

Fainnir stepped forward with a sigh and a look of resignation on his features before lifting his own hands and muttering a string of words under his breath.

Shrieking squeaks and hissed pain met our ears as he motioned into the air. Blood leaked from the slight sighting space we could see at the entry, the floor growing slick with it. Though *we* couldn't really see what was going on inside due to the dark and the motion, Fainnir could, and a swift casting of Life Sense showed me that the creature was dead.

I was really going to need to make use of more of my spells.

Bea seemed only a little interested in the body, but that was more for the fact that she had worked up a strong hunger and wanted a snack. Otherwise, she didn't seem to dig for anything in it once it was gone.

I took my hand and ran it through the blood of the weasel and slathered it over the image on the door to the next floor. They had said that every three floors there was a room to rest. It had only felt like we had been in here a couple of hours, we could make it through this place quickly if we pushed ourselves.

Then again, if we were tired and got careless, that was how people got hurt. We could afford to gauge our progress and go from the rest area if that was the case.

Something's up with Fainnir, guys, Muu stated through our earrings.

I blinked over at him, and Jaken responded, *Yeah. He's not taking this kind of use of his powers well, I don't think.*

What are you all talking about? I snorted in disbelief. *He's killing it! He's a fucking rockstar right now. And Pebble and Bea are right there with him!*

Muu shook his head. *I think we need to dig into this a little deeper when we can afford to, he looks...morose.*

James nodded. *Different from the kid I met last night, that's for certain. I think we should observe a bit longer, then call it and rest for a bit at the safe area while we try and sort him out if he needs it.*

I nodded, not really getting what the big deal was. He was a fucking earth-wielding wrecking ball, and now that he was using all the tools he had available to him, he was so much stronger than before.

We walked down a narrow path that wound down until it touched on the next floor, and immediately, the whole dynamic of the dungeon changed. There was air here, fresh and flowing freely. The ground was covered in grass taller than my ankles, and the room we entered was large and roomy. There appeared to be alcoves somewhat along the walls spaced out in irregular intervals with some trees and bushes scattered here and there.

"Could this be the rest area?" Balmur whistled softly.

I took it upon myself to cast Life Sense once more and wasn't surprised to see my friends surrounding me when the little blips lit up on my minimap. What *did* freak me out was the more than twenty red blips that had us surrounded.

"Uh, guys. We're kind of surrounded," I warned the others. "Twenty of 'em. Anyone want to take a guess as to what the theme of this place could be?"

Yohsuke growled and looked like he was beginning to puzzle it together. "I got it, I think. The first floor was bugs and a spider. The second floor had rats and a weasel. If it follows some kind of system, then whatever we fight here, the predator is the boss."

"Sounds reasonable," Muu muttered and looked around. "I mean, it's only level three for these enemies, so not all that much to be worried about, right?"

"They are beneath the ground." Pebble had knelt down and touched the earth beneath him. "But they seem to be content to stay where they are, for now."

"How many o' them be there, Pebble?" Fainnir glanced around and knelt next to his elemental friend. "Can ye tell what they are?"

"Twenty-four creatures in the immediate area and some of them are deeper down." Pebble put his other hand on the ground. "I do not know what they are, but I can go down and lure them up to you if you want me to?"

"Let's try something else first." Fainnir looked to me. "Could you have Bea sprint straight toward where some of the creatures are to see if they react to pressure?"

I thought about it for a moment, then decided that she was going to do what she wanted, anyway. I may as well try and get her used to the idea that I could help and at least steer her in ways I needed her to go.

I touched her mind with mine and we made a plan. All she had to do was sprint twenty feet out, turn and book it back our way. That was all.

I had her wait until we were all ready, then she took off at a trot.

"They're moving toward her, and the farther away she is, the faster they're going to move, get her back." Pebble, his normally placid tone replaced by panic, shouted, "Now!"

I mentally shouted for her to kick it into overdrive, and Bea was a blur as she sped off toward the far wall with long lines of over-turning topsoil forming behind her. She kicked off the wall and was on her way back. She juked left as a pair of long, wickedly curved claws reached out of the ground toward her. The earth gave way beneath her feet, and she sprung off the air as a creature gave chase, flying from the dirt and into the air behind her and closing.

Suddenly, Kayda was there, snatching the beast out of the air and screeching her sovereignty to the world around her. She flapped her way toward us, tossing the creature so that I caught it deftly and wished I hadn't. It was covered in dirt, smelled like shit, and urine, and was trying to claw me even though I was easily capable of killing the animal.

Mole Level 3

"If that's a mole, my magic won't be very effective against it." Fainnir looked distraught for a moment, and I could finally see what the others were talking about.

"Don't worry, buddy." I smiled comfortingly at the dwarf. "We can take care of these guys."

I looked at the others, some of them grinning, James looked bored and Jaken like he wasn't sure what to do.

"Balmur and Yoh, you two and I will use our shadow magic to reach into the holes and pull them out." I looked to the melee fighters. "You guys will kill what we pull out. Bokaj, anything jumps out at my babies—"

"Fill it full of arrows, got it." Bokaj took out his bow and sent an arrow soaring through the air and into the head of a mole that had latched onto Kayda's leg. "Hey, Tmont, time to play."

The cat yowled angrily as he shook her from her place in his hood. Once she hit the ground, she was growing and moving toward the action.

"Alright, boys, let's get to it." I drew the shadows on my side of the area toward me, then regarded Fainnir. "Fainnir, you protect yourself and the familiars. I'm counting on you."

"Aye!" The dwarf barked and set his feet in grim determination and marched forward with Pebble at his side.

I cleared my mind and fed the shadow infused mana in my hands toward the ground and into the earth itself, confining it to the holes that were growing around the dodging Bea.

Motion on one end of it made me yank whatever I had touched to the surface and reel it in like a fishing rod. A sniffing mole careened toward me, only to be cut in half by Jaken, who waited at my side.

"I've got your back, man." He widened his stance and readied himself for the next mammal projectile.

It took about fifteen minutes of us searching and yanking the little bastards out of the ground, screaming and shrieking.

We rested for a moment, trying to decide what the next thing we would be fighting might be, but Muu pushed us on.

"There's really no telling until we go into the boss room and find out, but let's check the area first, I am curious about these alcoves." Muu checked the one closest to the floor boss's door, but it came up empty.

Kayda, go fly the remainder of the room and see what is in the alcoves along the wall? She looked up at me and spread her wings. *I'll take a look, too.*

I leapt into the air and shifted into my owl form, opting that stealth would be better for this mission.

Glancing into each alcove, there was nothing of interest; still, it would be a good idea to keep our eyes peeled so that nothing surprised us, and we didn't miss out on any loot.

Speaking of loot, it was time to move on so that I could put a few things together for our newest member. Huh, here pretty soon, we would likely have to come up with a group name. Kind of like the Braves did.

Maybe we would have to have that discussion while we were resting.

We walked into the boss room, finding that it was much the same as the room before it. Lush and wooded, brisk even, but what was interesting to me was the large fox the size of a Great Dane sitting in the middle of the room.

His silver fur and blue eyes were beautiful.

"Wonder what's in here," Fainnir muttered as he scanned the brush, and Pebble stepped forward.

"It is there in the middle of the room, but how can I not see it? Are your eyes broken, too?" Pebble comically reached up and tapped on his diamond eyes. I glanced at the others, and they looked just as puzzled.

"It's invisible," I stated, then added. "This is a foe that will be rather tricky. If you want, I can make it visible to you with an ability I have, but once I do that, combat will likely start. What would you like to do, Fainnir? You're in charge for this one."

He thought for a moment, frowning from racking his mind at the situation presented.

"Can ye reason with it?" He tried politely, his eyes searching my face for some kind of reaction.

"I suppose I can try, what would you like me to say?" I cast Nature's Voice while he took inventory of his idea.

"That we only need enough blood to open the next door, an' that we don' wanna fight," he said. "If ye can convince him o' that, we can move on without much bloodshed."

I didn't see the harm in asking, and I could tell that something was going on with him.

"Hello, stranger," I spoke to the fox, and his eyes whipped to mine curiously. "Yes, I can both see you, and I speak your tongue. You know how we need to get out of here, right? To move on to the next floor?"

"You have to kill me." He rumbled, standing from his spot in the center of the room and wandering toward me. "I understand the human common tongue well enough, and the small one does not wish to kill me. I can feel the truth of it."

"How do you know that we have to kill you?" My curiosity took the reins of the conversation as he came to stand closer to me. "All we've needed so far is the blood of the creature to pass through."

He blinked lazily. "Yes, of the slain," he tilted his head and took a glance at my tails. "You seem strong and well-loved by our kind. I know that I will perish here, but the small one need not dirty his hand and stain his soul more than he has already."

"Tell me how you know, please." I was definitely going to need to talk to Fainnir after this.

"Because all creatures of the dungeon know their roles within these walls, our destiny is to either kill or be killed." He glanced at Fainnir. "I have slain my share of men and women, and I have been slain by many. But none with his compassion. This is the first that any have stopped to see about trying to find a less gruesome way through."

I nodded, understanding at last, that's why he took a shine to the kid. *Good for you, kid.*

"He says that the only way through is for him to die." I sighed as I watched the hope die in Fainnir's face a little. "But he said that you are the only person who has ever tried to find another way."

"If I be the only one, then how does he know that it won't work?" He asked, a little of the light returning to his gaze.

I explained what the fox had told me, the creature watching Fainnir with interest.

"Then there is no hope of doing this without bloodshed." He gritted his teeth and took his axe angrily into his hands.

"Do not allow him to do this thing, druid." The fox pleaded. "If you will end me, swiftly, I will tell you of a treasure on the floors to come."

"I'm listening." I put a hand out to Fainnir as I spoke, signaling for him to stop.

"There are false walls on the lower floors, I have heard rumors from the people who pass through here of traps and false walls that hide treasures. Some hidden by panels, others by magic. You can see through magic, so you may be able to find some of them."

"That's excellent information, thank you." I thought about how best to proceed from here. What would happen would be unpleasant, but necessary, and despite the necessity—Fainnir would likely still pay the price for it even if I did the dirty work.

"Would you like to thank him before the...unpleasantness has to begin?" The fox seemed thrown by the question but nodded once.

He dropped the invisibility and looked over at the young dwarf, dipping his head in gratitude.

"He wanted to say thanks for trying to be kind," I offered to Fainnir on his behalf. "He's also given us some information in return for your kindness, but in order to move on, what must be done, must be done."

Even as the words left my mouth, my heart dropped into the pit of my stomach. Fainnir approached the fox slowly and held out a hand palm down so that the fox could scent it. With a gentle caress of his tongue, the fox stood and looked to me, then wandered behind a tree to wait.

I stood straighter, Fainnir watching me with apprehension. "I should be goin' ta do the deed, then."

"Not this time Fainnir." I put my hand on his shoulder and looked down at him. "He's asked that I do it. He says that you're a good person, and he knows what it would take for you to cross that threshold. I agree, and we will talk about it more in a little bit; I swear on all my power and soul, that we are going to sit down and we will discuss this."

Leaving him to deal with his own notifications, I turned my back on the others who surrounded Fainnir with kind and gentle words while Maebe joined me in walking to the waiting fox.

I glanced up at his name.

Garden's Guardian Level 5

"Well, friend, it's time." I took out Magus Bane and

prepared myself, mentally, and emotionally for what needed to be done. "Any requests?"

"When I am gone, I would ask that the young one have my pelt. It may not be much, but I hope it will serve him and remind him that sacrifices are made by choices and that we can choose to be different as he did this day."

That hit me kind of hard. This was necessary. This growing darkness I was walking into with my friends, how deep was I willing to go to protect those I held dear?

I shook my head, determined to make this creature's sacrifice worthwhile. "Goodbye, friend. Rest well."

I growled as I cast Falfyre, then whipped the blade into the creature's jaw, through the mouth, and into the brain, killing it instantly.

I allowed the blood to cover my hand and made my way straight to the door behind where we had walked. The door opened with little noise, and I turned back around.

Muu, come here. I ordered softly.

The dragon-kin came over, and I gave him his bloody project, and he went to work.

While Muu worked, I looked at Maebe. "I'm kind of out of my element, here."

"How do you mean?" Her head tilted to the left quizzically.

"Fainnir, one second he's gung-ho about all of this, and now he's… not." I frowned, trying to put the words together so that I could get my point across.

"You have told him he is a child, you have told him he is an adult, and he has just found out—likely for the first time in full realization—that he will be the measurement against whom all of those who follow his path are measured against." Maebe pointed toward the group through the trees where they stood speaking to the object of this discussion. "Not only has he not had the chance to fully find out who he is as a person, he now has to become someone that there is no standard for among his people. He is alone, Zeke. And he is trying to find out who he is in all of this while meeting our expectations and having us find him lacking as well."

My already heavy heart felt ready to drop through my feet. This was the price of change. This was the cost that he had to pay for something that he had never asked for. And here I was, making it harder. I was so busy trying to teach him, strictly teach him, that I hadn't taken the time to become the mentor that he needed. And I had claimed to know him.

I let my head fall back so that I could focus on just breathing, rather than wallowing and berating myself for my failures. I could flog myself later. Right now, Fainnir needed me.

"Thank you, Mae," I whispered hoarsely as I stepped toward the tree line.

She grabbed my arm, pulling me back. "What do you mean to do?"

"I'm going to apologize," I explained. "And I'm going to go make sure that he knows that from here on out, I'm his mentor and not his instructor."

"You can be both, Zeke." Maebe let go of my hand, and I waited for her to speak again. "You can be there for him and still let him know that you will see him prepared for this. The two are not mutually exclusive. You will need to be firm, but fair. Understanding and demanding. You, as a king, must know your people and their capabilities so that you may use them to full effect. These ones are not statistics, I know, but they can be a learning tool for you as well. Go."

I nodded once, mouthing, "Thank you," to her, then marched over to the others. Jaken heard me coming and tapped James to get him to move. I wasn't stopping for any of them.

I walked straight up to Fainnir and lifted the dwarf into my arms for a bear hug. Several of his bones popped, and he grunted from the strength of it.

"Wha' be wrong?" He grunted as I squeezed.

"I'm sorry that at every turn today, I have failed you." I sighed deeply and set him down on the ground. "I've failed to notice things about you, I've failed to teach you properly, and I failed as a mentor. I know that things are hard for you, but I hadn't fully grasped it until now. And I will never be able to make up for that."

"Yer doin' yer best." He shook his head.

"I was being no better than some of the 'leaders' who failed me." Thinking back to some of them made my vision go crimson for a second, but I snapped out of it quickly. I had a mistake to fix, and I wasn't them. "I owe not only you, better than that, but myself too."

I glanced at my friends, Yohsuke and James nodded sagely. They knew about bad leadership, too.

"So, you and I are going to sit down, and we are going to figure out the best way to make this all work for you so that you can thrive." I thumped him on both shoulders. "And we are going to have some long, and hard discussions on ethics, and use of violence. How to make the hard choices in hard situations."

"I know how to do that." He frowned, but sighed, his dialect surfacing. "But, uh, I'll be listenin' hard. I know all of ye mean yer best, and ye'll see me through. Yer me clan for now."

"That's high praise," Muu called, as he walked over to us and raised his eyebrow ridges, the scales skittering over each other. "That means we need a name."

"Get out of my head." James snorted.

"It's been on my mind too." Yohsuke held a hand up with a lopsided grin.

"Can we at least get to safety before we start batting around group name ideas?" I raised my eyebrow tiredly at the others.

"You have much to discuss, and the time we are here will be better spent learning both on the go and by cautiously progress-ing," Maebe spoke to us all. "I think with all of the discussion needed and the adjustment to constant combat for Fainnir, Pebble, and Bea, a longer rest would be advised."

The others went to protest, but Balmur interrupted, "We're underground. We rest when we're tired, we do everything at our own pace down here. We have a timeline, but if we go too fast, we risk recklessness, and we can't have that." He nodded toward Fainnir. "We all had to adjust to fighting like this, and even as genius as he's been handling it, we can't afford a mistake because any of us is tired or drained."

"This group of wayward adventurers could have used your wisdom on many of their journeys, Balmur." Maebe placed a hand on the fire dwarf's shoulder with a smile. "It is good to have you here again, my friend."

"Forever glad to be back." His smile seemed a little sad, and that would be needing addressing as well. But when he was ready.

"I'm all done over there; I may need to have some help to get the leather properly taken care of so that it's usable." Muu wiped his hands on a rag. "Tanning it and whatnot. Maybe you can make an item that can simulate the aging process and chemical processes."

"We can try for that." I nodded thoughtfully. I wasn't sure I could, but I would try.

"Let's get to the rest area and set up camp then," Yohsuke called to us. "Come on!"

We all gathered ourselves and moved through the door and down a steeply declining grade to a set of stairs that seemed to even out. They were large stairs, about four feet long and a foot and a half wide with only a six-inch-tall step-down.

It took about ten minutes of constant downward movement to get to the area we were headed to.

The room, or rather the luxurious grotto, the walls covered in lichen and mushrooms lit with a bioluminescent glow that made seeing very easy. It was much larger than I thought it would be, easily fifty yards squared. The air was crisp and clear, there were trees with fruit growing on them and a small waterfall leading from the wall to a pond in the far corner.

"How the hell is this possible?" Jaken whispered as we all took in the sights.

"The one dungeon that I was aware of within the Unseelie lands had similar rooms within, but it was significantly more difficult to reach those." Maebe moved into the area. "Then again, the Fae are much stronger than the beings of this realm naturally, so things are harder by default."

"Does that mean you can give us some more information on dungeons?" Yohsuke grimaced as he set up the cooking utensils.

"There are differences in all dungeons based on where you are and in what realm." the Fae Queen ventured closer to the water and stared at it. "The one where I had gone into had been one of the dead and frozen, as it was well within the north of my territory. Inside, we found many precious things made of ice and magic. That was where my mother found Winterheart, if I recall."

"We've been in one before, with the goblins, remember?" James scratched his neck and stretched his wings slowly.

"I have heard this place described in your stories, tell me— was there a door like the one we crossed to come here?" Maebe asked curiously, though she kept her eyes on the water.

"No, it was just a hole in the ground that led us down into a series of tunnels," Bokaj offered as he pulled out his instrument.

"Then all that could have been was a lair, common among burrowing monsters like goblins." Maebe closed her eyes as if to recall something. "Entrances to dungeons are concealed and sealed so that only the blood of those who may enter can open them. If they were left open, creatures would escape and slaughter those around them."

"If that's the case, how are they sealed like that? Who does it?" Jaken asked as he began the process of taking his armor off.

"The gods of your realm, I would imagine." Maebe frowned, then shook her head. "I do not remember having read anything about their creation, but I do know that their existence is so that the people of the realm can grow without needing to kill each other. At least here. In my realm, they are places of great and terrible power that help us fight one another. It gives the realm entertainment."

Muu looked confused, but Jaken waved him off. "I'll fill you in more, later."

"So, dungeons are places to accrue power, sometimes magic items and whatnot, right?" I asked as I tried to fit my head around it.

To be blunt, this was nothing new, not really. In most games, dungeons were something to be crawled through and conquered. But each one was respectively different from the last.

"Yes, as well as resources. Some places within these tunnels and floors may have items, materials, and other things to collect that you should keep an eye out for." She peered closer at the waterfall. "Zeke, I cannot tell, and Balmur, you may want to look as well, but something beyond that water is bothering me."

I raised an eyebrow and looked over at Bokaj, motioning to the water. He looked confused for a moment before grunting. "Oh!"

He held a hand out and cast Watery Path on myself and Balmur. I stepped out onto the water as if it were solid ground. I tried looking into the water as it cascaded down the stone, but it was too hard to see.

"Hey Fainnir, you wanna make us a shelf to split the water about six feet up?" I called back to the dwarf, who hurried over toward the water. Then into it, falling in with a yelp of surprise.

He didn't come back up right away, so I bolted toward him and reached into the water to pull him up and out of it. He may have been young, but he was heavy. Stocky dwarves can be like that. All that compact muscle and extra-large livers for all the booze they consumed.

"Looks like we will be teaching you how to swim too," I heard Muu mutter as Fainnir sputtered and coughed up water.

Fainnir cleared his lungs and held out his right hand. He grabbed the air and yanked it back. A shifting of stone and a grating sound rang out behind me.

I smiled at the boy and ruffled his soaked brown hair. "Go sit by the fire for a bit after you get yourself dried off. Ask Maebe to help you get rid of the water."

He nodded silently, and awkwardly stood to slosh toward her.

I turned and walked back out onto the water and checked over the wall. Maebe had been right; there was something glittering in the stone. It was an odd color that I couldn't place, a reddish hue, maybe? But that didn't mean it was all that rare, right? We were only three point five floors into this place.

I touched it, then looked over at Pebble. "Hey, can you tell us what this is?"

He glanced from me to Fainnir, who made a shooing motion as Maebe used shadows to wick away the water.

"I can try." He sank into the ground and disappeared for a few moments before returning with a chunk of the metal in his hand. "I don't know what it is, but I can bring you more if you like."

"How big is the vein?" I asked cautiously.

"It is not large compared to the veins of ore and materials that I saw below us." He seemed to think for a moment then shrugged. "Roughly a hundredth of the size of some of those."

"That could be anything, but can you get to them?" Jaken frowned and called from the water's edge, but Pebble shook his head.

"No, there is a barrier between the 'floors.'" Pebble pointed up. "I can venture up, but not down. There are some poor-quality stones and gems in the area, but they are hardly worth the effort to retrieve them.'

"Then just what you can retrieve from here is fine, thank you, Pebble." I smiled at the elemental, then walked back toward the shore of the small pond.

"Let's rest and get our thoughts together before we have that discussion, eh Fainnir?" I called over to him, and he looked relieved as he sat near the fire and Yohsuke.

CHAPTER FIFTEEN

We sat in silence while I collected my thoughts, and the others went about whatever they might. Finally, I felt I knew how I wanted to approach this.

"Fainnir, Maebe and Yoh, if you three could join me over by the water?" I stood and stepped over to the water to sit down again, waiting for those I had verbally tapped to join me. While I waited, I sent a thought to the others, *I understand you all care, but you will all have many chances to impart wisdom and insight as we travel. For now, this is something that we need to do to gauge how Fainnir needs to be trained and how he can be his best self moving forward. He isn't us, and he hasn't had to deal with the evils we have up to this point. Please, let us find out what we will, and we can all discuss it later.*

The others turned toward me, and almost as if on cue, nodded once together. Chills ran down my spine, and I closed my eyes and focused on controlling my nerves. I cared about this kid, this young man, and I wanted him to be better off than we had been. Than I had ever been.

My paternal instincts kicked in hard, and it was a bitch to beat back. I missed my son, and here I was with someone else's kid. Shit.

As Maebe sat to the left of me, Yohsuke sat down on the opposite side of her on my right. Finally, Fainnir trudged over to sit in front of us. Trepidation in each of his movements. Pebble joined him but was content to just stand at his back for the time being.

"First of all, relax." Yohsuke beat me to the punch, gently reaching out and tapping the ground in front of us to get the dwarf's attention. Fainnir glanced up shyly and looked at us. "I think I speak for everyone when I say that there isn't one swinging dick, or uh... lady here who isn't proud as hell to have you with us. And from what I saw out there? We're all damned proud of you, Fainnir, and I've only known you for a short time. Listen to what we have to say with an open mind and an open heart—know that this is how we want to help you and that we care. Okay?"

Fainnir seemed to take heart in what my brother had so gruffly put. But that was Yoh, gruff, blunt and in your face. But the bastard had a heart of pure gold, and I'd fight at his side through hell and high water.

Thanks, brother. His slight nod let me know he had heard me, and I regarded Fainnir. "Like my brother said, we are all thrilled to have you with us. And as I said earlier—I am at fault. I should be asking you how you want to fight. I am probably the *furthest* thing from a traditional druid, yet I gripe at you for thinking like a normal dwarf. That's hardly fair of me. So, what I would like to ask you, is what do *you* want to do, Fainnir?"

He looked stricken at the question, blinking and looking down into his hands in contemplative silence.

"Your people are warriors of ferocious tenacity and honorable almost to a fault, Fainnir." His head whipped up, indignant horror on his features, but I stopped him with a raised palm. "I'm not saying that like it's a bad thing that they are such amazing warriors, or that they hold to their ways and their Way so fervently. I am proud to be counted among them, same as you. And though I have to make... horrible decisions at times as to how to proceed forward, I try to think like the dwarves I know when I can.

"Seeing you back there, realizing that you had so thoughtfully tried to avoid true bloodshed opened my eyes to how you may feel. To how your sense of honor and ideas of honorable combat may come into play." His gaze was downcast again, and I knew that I had struck a nerve. "Your entire life, you learned that to face your foe in honorable combat was the epitome of what it meant to be a dwarf. That anything less than that was dishonorable and sometimes seen as murder, perhaps?"

His gaze drifted up, though his head hung low. "Aye."

"Why do you think that is?" He looked confused, so I added to the question a bit. "Why did you feel like some of the things we did today weren't right? Before you speak, I want you to know that you are not to lie because you think we might grow angry or be insulted by your answer. Okay?"

He nodded as he thought, finally sighing and raising his head to speak to us, "It were because what we did was too easy. We didn't give them a chance to fight. We came in killin' from the moment we set foot in this place, and they stood no chance. Now, when I went in to fight that spider, I thought that a fair fight, I wanted to gauge me own strength, but I failed. I could'a died. If I'd been on me own, I would'a died."

When none of us said anything, he continued on, "The rats stood no chance. Just rounded 'em up like cattle to slaughter. And those moles? Just murdered."

"Okay." I nodded and narrowed my eyes at him. "Do you think you could've fought those moles on your own?"—he stammered a bit, not sure how to really answer, so I pressed on— "What about me? Do you think you could fight me and win? How about Yohsuke?"

Fainnir seemed thoroughly flustered with my questions, so I smacked the ground, "Speak!"

"No!" He howled, tears streaming from his eyes, at long last. "No! A thousand times, no! I'd have died out there, an' ye be knowin' it!"

I growled. "That's right! That is exactly right." I lowered my voice to a harsh whisper. "You would have died. If those rats had half a chance against you, they would have swarmed you, and you likely would have died. If those moles had come at you more than one at a time, you would have died. If you were to face any of us, we would kill you. Why do you think I ask you these questions, Fainnir?"

He sniffed and ran his arm over his face, hiccuping once, then again before answering, "I don' know."

I pressed on. "You do, but you don't want to admit it to yourself."

More tears fell as he sat in contemplation, Yohsuke reached out through our earrings. *I don't know man, I don't think he's getting it.*

I shook my head, and we waited. When Fainnir's tears abated a little, I asked again, "Why do you think I asked you these questions, Fainnir?"

"To show me that I'm weak." He looked to be on the verge of tears again.

"No, to show you where your truest strength is." I leaned forward and flicked him on his forehead. He grunted, and his hands covered the smarting area. "The way you handled those rats was nothing short of beautiful, skillful, and efficient. Now, I tell you that all these things would probably kill you because if you went into the fight thinking to give them the chance to kill you—they would take it and run."

"But that's the honorable thing to do!" He insisted with a confused expression I was growing accustomed to seeing on his face.

"No, it's the stupid thing to do." He frowned and looked damned-near mutinous. "Those moles would have worn you down and killed you. That fox could have torn you apart if it hadn't been for Pebble. Or your good heart. It's okay to want to give things a chance in certain circumstances, but I can guarantee you that any foe in here is likely to kill you and feel nothing but joy by it. And it would be because you thought that they would be honorable, too."

Yohsuke picked up from where I left off. "There are different kinds of honorable combat out there. You can refuse to use the same dirty tricks as your opponent. You can wait until they're healed and everything else, sure, but these creatures are all put here to devour you. The majority of them would sooner see you dead than give you time to heal or to rest. Their whole existence is to end yours. Now, outside in the sunlight, do whatever you think best, more power to you. But down here? We have to play for keeps."

"What they say, while somewhat confusing, is true." Maebe allowed, eyeing Yoh and I before looking to Fainnir. "Some people and creatures are as honorable as you may think but when it comes to your survival, honor is an ideal that could get you killed. Especially in the company of those without it. We will show you some of the times and places where it is fine to hold to your beliefs in this 'honorable combat' and when survival is king. What we need for you to do is trust that we do these things for a reason and that it is best to use your head."

"Well, if that be the case, then how come ye were so happy when all I was doin' was killin' things like the rats?" Fainnir scratched his head a bit.

"Because, Fainnir, that shows that you have the ability to see the situation at hand and do what mages do when the odds are against them—plan." I smiled at him as I tapped my head. "A mage such as yourself can grow in many ways, and you *will* get stronger. In any other circumstances against those odds, that would have been a grueling battle, but you were able to use the tools you had. With a little know-how you will use them to devastating effect. It wasn't cruel—it was smart. Your mind is and always will be your strongest weapon. If you take the time to prepare for a fight, you will be so much better off."

He seemed taken aback by what I said but a little happier as he thought it over, then I added, "And that leads me to what I wanted to say to you."

He looked apprehensive again, but I smiled sadly. "That fox sensed the good in you. And I think it's there, too. With what we do, we've all been forced to do terrible things, some of us more than others. Those hard choices we had to make were forced to make or were taken on by the thought of necessity tainted us. Made us different. Changed the way we think and see the world around us."

He looked more distressed now, good. "But that doesn't mean that we're bad people. There will be times in your life where you have to make those hard choices, and when those times arise, I hope that you have the same strength of character and the same conviction to do what you believe is right as you did today. I am beyond proud of you, Fainnir. And I know that Natholdi and Granite would be, too."

"Some of those choices would be fightin' smarter. Like I did earlier then?" He scratched his chin thoughtfully.

"You catch on quick, kid." Yohsuke grinned and clapped him on the shoulder.

"Much more quickly than a certain druid that we all know." Maebe raised her eyebrows and looked pointedly at me. Fainnir laughed out loud, and I thought I heard a rumble from Pebble too.

I shook my head and did my best Dangerfield. "No respect, no respect at all." I eyed Fainnir once more and sighed. "To show you how much I appreciate you using your head, and trying to do what is asked of you, I am going to enchant some items for you. Some, I will take requests on, some I will not. But I will make them today. Before we open that vortex of fun, do you have any questions?"

He thought, and thought hard before nodding. "Did ye still want to know how I be wantin' to fight?"

I could have snapped my own fucking neck at that moment. "Yes."

"I wanna fight like a dwarf, and I wanna fight like you, Uncle Zeke." I blinked at the name. "If it be alright to call ye that, sir."

A roar of laughter burst from my mouth. It took me a minute or so to fully be able to breathe, and he looked a little worried. "Yeah, buddy. You can call me Uncle Zeke. Hell, you can call us all uncle if you want. So long as you call Maebe, 'Auntie Maebe.'"

"He will call me what?" Maebe rounded on me, and her playful ire pointed at me.

"Run, boy! Save yours—" I tried to call out and ward him away, but Maebe dove on top of me and dug her fingers into my sides, underarms, and neck, eliciting a screech of both terror and pained laughter from me. When I had almost soiled myself, she lost interest and turned her sights on the dwarven boy who now stood with Muu as a barrier.

"Oh, hell no, kid. She's coming for you." Muu tried to pry him off his leg and out in front of him. "She can go through me like a fuckin' ghost. I don't want *any* of that shit."

"Is it not a'right for me to call ye tha' Maebe?" Fainnir squirmed behind Muu's back nervously.

Maebe eyed him critically before gracing him with a small grin. "Fine, but the second you let it go to your head, I revoke the right. Do you understand me?"

"Yes." He nodded wildly as her eyes narrowed, and she gestured for him to continue, "Auntie Maebe?"

"Good boy." She tousled his hair playfully and went on her way toward the darker side of the room. "Come to me, Balmur. We begin one on one training today."

Balmur stood excitedly and rushed over until he stood alone with her in a dome of shadows.

I took a steadying breath, trying to get the urge to continue laughing out of my system, as I waved Fainnir to my side.

"So, you want to fight like me?" He nodded, and I couldn't fight the grin on my face. "That means a healthy mix of magic and martial skill. You ready for that?"

"Since the day I were born!" The dwarf said proudly. Then he stopped his growling and scratched his head bashfully. "Well, the martial skill, aye. Magic still be new."

"You use it pretty well, but you don't use it as instinctively as the rest of us just yet, so that will take some time." I frowned as I looked over his clothing and gear. His clothes were plain. He wore a simple pair of boots and a belt with a loop for the haft of his double-headed axe. "You need some good, quality mage armor, but sturdier stuff, too."

"Well, a lot o' dwarves wear plate mail, though me da don't wear any at all," Fainnir offered helpfully.

"Magic users sometimes have to use complex motions and move their arms to cast spells, so bulky armor that is hard to move in could be a detriment to you." I frowned and peered through my inventory. I didn't have any squishy gear with me. Shit. I called loudly to the others, "Anyone have any un-enchanted robes or anything that I can give to the squish here?"

"Squish?" The dwarf's head tilted to the side in confusion at me.

"It's an affectionate term for a spellcaster because they normally get squished early in fights if they don't plan appropriately," Yohsuke explained as he checked his inventory, then shook his head. "Nada."

Jaken held out a cloak that was a muddy brown color. "This is all I have, think it could work?" I shrugged and took it off his hands with a nod of gratitude.

"All I have is pants, I would hold off on some truly amazing gear though, Z'," Bokaj called over as he strummed his guitar-like instrument. "Who knows what kind of gear we could come across while we're here."

That was a good point. So, then, maybe something that would help him to blend in a little better? Or be better defensively? How the hell was I supposed to enchant cloth items?

I took out my raven and used it to send my question to Shellica. "Hey, Shitty Granny, it's Zeke. I'm having a bit of a problem here, and I wanted to know how to enchant cloth items, like say a cloak or something? It's for Fainnir."

The spectral copy of the little bird flitted away from us into the stone and was gone. For the minute I had, I pulled out some items I knew how to enchant and set them onto the ground in front of me. That's when the raven shifted again in my hand, signaling a response from the recipient of the initial message.

"You stupid lad," she cackled knowingly. "All you need to do is make your mana into a thread, basically the same concept as engraving, and then you weave it into the item. You're skilled enough now that you should be able to manage it without screwing up over much. Give the raven to the boy so I can talk to him."

I grinned at the sound of her voice and handed the item to Fainnir. "Shellica wants to talk to you. Focus on the raven, feed it a hundred mana, and then speak to it. She will get the message. Go away so I can focus. And do *not* lose that item."

He bobbed his head and swiftly bustled away, jabbering at the item almost as soon as he was standing.

Then I set about the items I was comfortable with. My materials were good, well-made, and cared for. Perfect for what I had in mind.

First thing I did was make him a caster's best friend, a Ring of Storing. Simple fare holds a single spell to be unleashed at the caster's will with no current cost to their mana reserves. The cost came out at the initial casting so that it would be stored. Easily done and for a pitiable amount of mana that was hardly worth mentioning.

After that, I made a Ring of Defense that gave the wearer a plus fifteen to defense. After that, I made one that I hadn't made before that I was really proud of.

The thought behind it had been similar to a ring I had made for James that gave him the ability to cast Stone Skin. But this time, I wanted to give Fainnir a little added *umph* to that spell, so I had the impossibly hard facets of diamonds in mind when I engraved and enchanted the ring.

Diamond Crust

Wearer can use this ring to cast the spell Diamond Skin, twice per day without a mana cost. Duration: 1 minute.

Charges return the next dawn.

Sometimes all you have to do to see something shine is polish it, or in this case, wear this ring.

Diamond ring made by master smith Kelty Binson and enchanted by adept enchanter Zekiel Erebos.

That leveled me up by one level, putting me to level 41 as an enchanter. Awesome! Three rings down, one more to go. Rather than making him a normal ring, I decided to try and get a mana storing ring going for him, but no matter what I did, the rings failed. Thinking about it, it was likely just too hard for my current level. Oh well.

Instead of going for spell storing again or anything, I wanted to give him another "oh shit" button that he could use to get himself out of trouble. The main source of said trouble being enemies that got too close. Kind of like a magical panic button. Except this one blasted the offending party away from them.

Danger Zone

A flex of will with this ring held up will send a blast of force at whatever is in front of this ring, sending it away. Cost: 15 MP.

Aptly named for the place where whatever unde-sired presence is before the wearer deems they should not be.

Diamond ring made by master smith Vren Slet and enchanted by Adept enchanter Zekiel Erebos.

I chuckled at the name and just set it on the ground before me. Now for an earring. I decided to give him a boost to the powers of his perception, so for a small mana cost, he could see farther with the earrings I made him. It was really interesting to do, and I liked this aspect of enchanting. I would be working on it some more while we were down here, trying different things here and there, maybe. See what worked best.

The last thing I took care of while I was here doing this was the cloak. I took a gander at it, trying to figure out how I would weave my mana through it and make it do what I wanted. I tried on a sock and let it fail over and over until I got a feel for it. It seemed doable.

So, I put myself to work and trickled mana into the item like I would if I were sewing. I made a little chameleon on the inside of the hood. Next, I grabbed some dirt, leaves, and water from the surrounding area, then focused my intent on what I needed the item to do when the hood was up. I wanted it to help the wearer blend into their surroundings. As I infused the mana I had threaded into the hood with my power, I sprinkled the components I had collected over it, and they disappeared as they usually did. This time, I felt the shifting and imbued magic changing the properties of the item.

"That's wicked," I muttered as it stilled, then the information populated in front of my eyes.

Chameleon's Cloak

When the wearer dons the hood of this item, they become significantly harder to see. Does not assist against creatures with sight enhancing abilities and the ability to sense magic.

Wearer beware: just because you may be harder to see, does not mean that you are harder to smell or hear.

Cloak woven by craftsman seamstress Ilona Nileth and enchanted by Adept enchanter Zekiel Erebos.

I smiled at my work and put the bundle together so that I could hand it all over to Fainnir as soon as he was done talking to Shellica.

It was roughly an hour before he was finished, and when he was back, he was sniffling, but happy.

"She said to thank ye for lettin' me use yer magic item," Fainnir said happily, his accent returning full tilt. "She also had me tell me ma where I was, and who I be with. They said to thank ye proper for takin' me in like ye have. And to listen to ye."

"Solid advice." I raised my eyebrows and nodded sagely. "Here, let's trade."

I offered him the bundle in my hands, and he happily returned my raven. I pocketed it and watched as he excitedly put each item on and admired them on his person.

He turned to me, his cloak freshly in place and put it up over his face, not the hood, his arm. Like a kid playing at Dracula. "Ye can't see me now, can ye?"

His chuckle was adorable, really, but he needed to learn, so I told him, "I can see you perfectly. I have true sight. But also, the hood has to be up for it to work. You really should read the item descriptions first."

His cheeks flushed a bit, reddening, and he smiled, "Thanks."

A thought occurred to me as he held out his axe to me. That was a gift from his father, a birthright, and I wasn't sure I wanted to mess with that.

Another firing of the synapses in my gray matter led me down a different path. I had an axe that could steal mana, why not give him one that could act as both a melee weapon and a staff?

I had some talented crafters here with me, but was it possible? I would have to speak with the experts.

I waved him away for a second. "Not if I don't have to, that was a gift from your father. I wouldn't sully it if I can help it. But you still have that bandolier of throwing knives, right?"

He nodded and dug into his inventory, pulling them out. I smiled and took them. These I had enchanted for accuracy, so they were good enough, for now.

"How good are you with them?" He sputtered, and I tossed them to him. "I think I just saw Balmur leave the shadow dome. Ask him if he will help you learn to throw them."

I pulled the raven from my pocket as the dwarf scampered off to do as bidden and sent a message to Vilmas.

"Hey Vilmas, I hope all has been well," I began, then continued, "I have a question. Have you ever heard of a melee weapon that acts as a staff? Or some kind of amplifier for magic? I was thinking of making something for Fainnir, like an axe that will amplify his power or something."

A few minutes later she replied, "No, I can't say that I have. It is an interesting idea in theory, but in practice, it could be difficult to see through. You might try with master Xiphyre? The materials you would need for that would need to be able to handle a large amount of power, and… I'll think on it more and see what I can sort out. Try Lady Shellica or master Xiphyre. Also, Vrawn misses you both. Talk to her, please. Be safe!"

Shit, I swore vehemently inside my head. *Of course, I would forget to talk to her with all the bullshit going on around us. Okay. I'll talk to her soon.*

Next on the list of things to do was get in touch with Xiphyre. "How's my favorite Ragalfr doing today?" I said, expecting a witty comeback. "I wanted to know if you had ever heard of someone trying to make a melee weapon a magic amplifier, kind of like a wizard's staff?"

Barking laughter rang out when the raven returned. "That's the most idiotically absurd idea I think I've ever heard!" His chortling died out. "Oh, I would call you stupid, but I quite like your ignorance. Melee weapon 'like a wizard's staff' what a crock. Let me guess, you were thinking of making an axe that would do something like amplify spell output or strength, is that it?"

I blinked at what sounded like a high level of joyful conde-scension in his tone, my cheeks burned fiercely as I responded with a hundred more mana. "Yeah. No need to be an ass about it."

I barely even got the chance to respond when a bird that looked similar to the raven I had just sent soared from the stone above my head and landed on my shoulder. Xiphyre's voice filtered from it into my ear, "I send this to you so that you might know that my reaction was as it was because I have never had someone ask me such ignorant things and had them be so bril-liant. This would be a wonderful idea—deadly if it works—and expensive. The materials used would all need to be extremely porous to magic, both ambient and infused. I will speak with Thogan, Vilmas, and this 'Shellica' of whom she dotes excessively on and try to draft a blueprint."

That was…actually nice of him? I kind of regretted what I had said.

My raven returned, and Xiphyre's smug voice came from the open beak, "Well, if I weren't your favorite Ragalfr, I wouldn't speak to you so."

"Oh, you little shit!" I spat, and the bird on my shoulder flapped away swiftly.

Closing my eyes, I took a moment to gather myself mentally and then released the pent-up air in my lungs. This was going to be a long journey.

While Balmur went through the process of teaching his protégé the subtle art of flinging bladed weapons, I approached the others.

"Before you go into the whole shebang." Yohsuke held up a hand. "They heard everything. And I also told them a little about what we could do to help him grow a little quicker."

"What's that?" I pulled the shadows around us toward me with a flex of will and then let them go, needing to do something with my mind in that moment.

"I think we should split the party," James stated. I looked from him to the others who nodded grimly.

"I thought that was a no go," I sputtered.

"It was, but then I got to thinking—they aren't going to level nearly as fast as we did at their level if the experience they get is being constantly poached by us," Yohsuke explained. "I looked into it, well really I looked into the party settings and saw that things could be done differently. All of us are in a party, except Maebe. If we break it down to just you and Fainnir, then he stands a chance at getting some more experience, and we can power level both him and Bea. Which, by the way, you should let her out, now. She needs to socialize."

I nodded, that was fair. I tapped the stone on my collar, and the slumbering hatchling filtered out onto the ground. She opened her eyes for a moment, glanced around, and when she saw there was nothing to kill or eat, decided sleep was better.

"Okay, so what does that mean?" I looked to the others and opened my status screen, then went into the party features.

I never really liked tinkering with it. One, because it was fine that we were all in the party together. Two, because the information was so minimalistic that it was painful. All it had were the names of the members. The coolest thing it did was give me a live feed of everyone's health bars above their heads and in the upper left-hand corner of my vision if I focused on it really hard. Kind of gave me a headache, so I didn't do it that often.

There was the option to leave the party. "Leave the party, and then send an invite to Fainnir." Muu made a shooing motion, and I shot him a glare.

"Why not just have Fainnir leave the party and be on his own, that way, he gets all the experience he needs." I tried to reason, but their stoney faces said enough. "It's for Bea, too, right."

"Don't worry, man, we'll still be right there with you, it'll just be a little different." Bokaj tried to reassure me. "Besides, we will still have our earrings and everything."

"Okay then, before we leave here, I'll do that." I sighed and prepared myself for that, but decided I needed a distraction. "So, group name?"

"Do we need one?" James rolled his eyes and snorted as Muu and Bokaj nodded vigorously. "Fine, what would you suggest?"

Bokaj blurted out, "Bad Company!"

I chuckled at that. "Dude, we want to be liked here—no one is going to know that 'bad' is meant to be seen as good."

"Knights of the Fae Table?" He offered again, and the rest of us groaned. "This is going to be hard, isn't it?"

"That's what she said." I laughed as he flipped me off, then offered, "What about 'The Outsiders?'"

"That's taken bud, great movie though." Muu nodded and

waved a finger at me. "Matt Dillon really shined in that one. And I am totally not okay being known as a greaser."

"No one is going to be a greaser." I shot him a dirty look, and he just grinned. "I just figured it would be a good idea since everyone seems to view us as outsiders to this realm. Interlopers."

"Because naming ourselves, 'Outsiders' calls attention to us, man." Balmur joined us and gave me the *duh* look, making my cheeks burn a bit. "But something that could work is Storm Company?"

Bokaj looked at him oddly. "Explain your reasoning."

Balmur blinked, then grinned and pointed to Kayda. "We have the storm with us here. Bea is an incarnation of the wind. Bokaj and Maebe are the cold, and I bring the heat. Jaken has divine fury, and we have two types of dragons with us, while Yoh and Maebe bring the darkness too." He pointed at me last. "Not to mention, we have the only being that we know of in existence to be blessed by both Mother Nature and all of the elements except one. We are the storm."

"I'm not mad about that at all." Jaken looked surprised and nodded slowly out of respect.

"I am honored that you see me as a member of your party." Maebe smiled at the Azer dwarf's reckoning. "And it does seem appropriate to the party as a whole as opposed to some of you."

"All in favor?" Balmur posed the question, and everyone's faces lit up as the whole of the party raised their hands. "That's decided then. So, what's up with Fainnir? No, no, you keep throwing those knives, man. I want you to hit the target at least five times before you take a break."

The younger dwarf nodded excitedly and paced back toward the line in the dirt that Balmur had drawn for him. He eyed the simple bullseye twenty paces away and flung his arm forward and loosed a knife. It sailed through the air, whirling beautifully and twirled three times before hitting the center. Fainnir howled in delight.

He looked to us excitedly, but Balmur simply pointed to the

target. I hadn't noticed before, but as both Fainnir and I looked, the blade thumped to the ground.

The others chuckled good-naturedly at the boy's distress, Balmur took pity and joined him once more. He gave him pointers while we watched, then came back to us. Fainnir threw the blade again, and this time, it hit the outer ring, but it stayed.

Good shit.

Balmur joined us, and this time, Yohsuke spoke, "Zeke had the right idea. We figure out a way that combat works best for him—using all the tools he has and tricks we can teach him—so he can stay alive."

"And the others we have to find?" Jaken took the time to eye me as we began dishing food out to each other. It smelled great.

"We do what we can. Until we have leads, there's really nothing to do except try and approach each elemental and find out what they can feel." I shrugged, going with my best thought toward it. "When I was in proximity to Villeroa and Fainnir, was when the elementals took note of the kids, so I need to be in the area. How close, I couldn't say. But it's our safest bet, I guess."

"Sounds good," James said around his food. He glanced up and shrugged as I eyed him. "What? Not killing those things made me hungry."

"You suck, James," Muu teased, and the two began playfully shoving each other.

"Yohsuke," Maebe spoke from beside me. "Come, it is time for your training."

The two of them moved away, and Maebe erected another dome so they could practice undisturbed.

"Well, that means it's our turn." Jaken grinned at Muu. "Practice bout?"

"You know it!" Muu hopped easily to his feet and greedily plowed through the rest of his meal. "What weapons?"

I left the others to their own devices as I watched over Fainnir. His form as Balmur corrected him gently improved swiftly. Soon enough, he was able to at least hit the target every time. After five sets of five hits on the target, Balmur let him rest and eat some food.

He munched happily, admiring his handiwork with his throwing knives. The scores on the tree signaling his growth and improvement. The kid was a sponge, and he was eager to learn everything after we had laid out what we thought for him. Good.

"While you're eating, I want you to listen to me, carefully," I spoke from behind him. He rocked back and forth, trying to turn to look at me. "Stay there. I want you to face the tree and the walls and really *listen*."

He nodded and ate, then pointed to his ear.

"When you summon your magic, I imagine it feels very natural for you," I began, and he nodded again. "In that natural kind of feeling, you have to be careful not to grow stale, or become complacent. In our training, I want to have you meditate before we move on and before we sleep. During that meditation, I will take you through exercises designed to strengthen your bond with the earth. And with Pebble, hopefully."

"His bond with me will grow according to our time spent together and the quality of it," Pebble spooked me as he spoke behind my left ear.

"Holy *fuck*, Pebble!" I snarled as I whirled on him. "Warn me when you're behind me, damn it!"

"Maybe you should become more attuned to the earth as well, Zeke?" His face was as blank as it usually was, but I suddenly the urge to hit him battled against my will. "Besides, the meditation practice is one that father recommends, as well."

It took me a moment longer than I was comfortable with to realize that he meant the Primordial Earth Elemental.

"Finished eating, Uncle Zeke!" Fainnir called excitedly. He turned and smiled at his friend. "Nice work, Pebble."

I frowned and turned to where Fainnir motioned with an exaggerated nod. A pile of chunks the same color as the ore that he had been tasked to gather earlier sat on the ground by the water.

"Thank you, there is more, but to take it all would deplete the vein and leave the stone around it compromised." Pebble sank into the ground, but stopped at the waist. "I will rest, now."

"Good work, you've earned that and more." I nodded at the elemental, and he just ignored me. I moved toward Fainnir, and we chose a spot near the tree for our meditation.

I taught him how to breathe with his tongue touching the back of his top teeth, letting his exhale out, breathing in for a four-count, then holding it for a count of five. Exhale and repeat. Anything more was just complicated.

It took him a while to truly grasp the concept, but by the time an hour had passed, he was able to sit still comfortably breathing. I was happy enough with that. We could introduce more when we were getting ready to move on.

"Good work." I patted his arm. "Now, tell me about your powers. What can you do?"

He blinked at me and pulled up his status screen before reading some things to me.

"Stone Heart lets me control the earth a little better, Elemental Tinkerin' for Earth lets me fiddle with spells an' makin' them." He put his sausage-like finger up to the screen. "An' last, I have somethin' called Elemental Call. I think that's what lets me summon Pebble."

"You *think*?" My eyes narrowed at him as I asked, and he gulped. "Or you know? Have you read it?"

He looked down bashfully as I sighed heavily. "Read it to me."

"Elemental Call," his reading voice was uncertain, so he continued slowly. "The earth mage can call his elemental partner to his side an' release them home at will."—he stopped and grinned triumphantly— "See? I knew I were right!"

I made a continuing motion with my hands and stared at him pointedly.

He cleared his throat and continued, "Based on the level of the mage, the elemental who responds could be stronger than the previously summoned one." He seemed worried as he said that last bit, his eyes flicking to Pebble.

Silence between us grew as I continued to eye the dwarf, trying to decide if my instincts were correct or not. Finally, I decided to just say what I thought.

"You knew that, didn't you?" More of a statement than I had meant it to be, but it was out there now. Looming over him.

"Aye." He lifted his chin proudly, stepping between Pebble and me.

"Didn't you say that you grow together? And Pebble said something about being bound to you." I blinked in confusion.

"We do grow together," Pebble spoke from behind Fainnir. "But he worries that if he were to summon another in my place, that I would be gone forever."

"If you're bound to him, and he summons another elemental, what happens?"

"I do not know for certain," Pebble admitted, "I could ask my father, but it would be better to do it once and find out."

"I don't want to lose Pebble," Fainnir said, then harrumphed stubbornly.

"But you don't know that you will lose him, and besides, are you even strong enough to summon another elemental yet? *Are* there stronger elementals?"

"Yes, Zeke, there are." Pebble raised himself from the ground. "I can tell I will not rest much for now, so allow me to explain. My brothers and sisters are vastly stronger than I am. I am a minor elemental. As we grow older, some of us become stronger, but I never will."

"How do ye know tha'?" Fainnir challenged with his hands on his hips.

"Because I am one of my father's first children." Pebble shrugged as if it were common knowledge. "I can imagine that the Water Primordial has also positioned one of her eldest children to teach her champion. We are the teachers, and knowledge-able in our elements. That is why we have come to you. We are not nearly as suited to combat and battle as our siblings would be. And that is why I believe it likely that you will still be able to summon me, specifically. You will have much to learn, and only I or one of the others amongst my generation could teach you."

I rubbed my forehead for a heartbeat, then sighed. "Okay. That's actually really useful information, but my question stands for Fainnir; can you even summon another elemental, right now?"

"I don' know." He frowned deeply, looked to Pebble, who nodded at him. Fainnir closed his eyes and spoke loudly. "Bones of the world and element of my peoples' body, answer my call; rise from your slumber and walk beside your new master. Protect me and mine, serve as my shield and axe."

A tremor shook my body as the dwarf lifted his hands in front of him. Beads of sweat formed on his brow and trickled down his face, but he held fast. Finally, the rumbling stopped, and nothing happened.

"Doesn't look like you are quite ready yet," Pebble observed out loud. "But you are close. Your enunciation was flawless. I am proud of you, Fainnir."

Fainnir looked a little pale and plopped onto the ground. "I be mighty tired, Uncle Zeke. I think I be nappin' here for a bit." As soon as the last word cleared his mouth, he fell back with a crash and began snoring loudly.

I blinked at him with a grin forming on my face. "Watch over him, Pebble."

"Always," The little elemental responded almost happily.

The others eyed me critically, but when I gave them a wave, they just smiled and returned to their various doings. Jaken and Balmur looked to be talking over some designs for items they wanted to make. James and Muu were sparring off near the water across from the tree where Fainnir slept. Bokaj strummed on his instrument and sang a wordless tune as Tmont slept behind him, her body moving with his in time with her breathing.

A few moments after that, Yohsuke hobbled out of the dome, his leg bloodied. I cast Void's Respite and Renewing Flames on him immediately, his flesh knitting back together easily.

He sighed with relief. "Thanks, man."

"What the fuck happened?" I glanced toward the dome and saw that nothing had changed.

"She had me fighting a shadow monster with nothing but shadow magic. Didn't really work all that well after a while." He shrugged. "I'm getting better, but I'm not that good yet."

"That seems a little advanced, doesn't it?"

"Not really, no." Yohsuke sighed and reached into the air. A swathe of shadows burst from the ground and rose to his hand, forming a scythe. "We have this power because we're strong enough to use it. Shadows are ours to command. But the drow elves thrive in the darkness too, and they've lived there exclusively. We need every advantage."

I nodded and marveled at his use of the void before I entered the dome myself.

"Hello, husband," Maebe's voice greeted me with no point of origin.

"Hello, wife," I returned and called the shadows to me. They obeyed and began to coat my flesh, like armor that conformed to my skin. Once it was solidified, I pressed, tugged, and pulled it until it looked like a death knight's armor. Spikes on the shoulders and elbows that could impale my enemies. Slight ones on my knees for the same, and the plates were cruelly ridged so that if anything grabbed me, they would realize it was a bad idea. I hoped.

Dreadnaught Armor – A compression of the void around your flesh has increased your defense by 20 for a short time. Cost: 127 MP. Duration: 3 minutes.

"Most impressive," Maebe's voice echoed around me. Then

I saw red eyes on the far side of the dome and knew the fight was on. "I hope that you can create other spells so swiftly."

I spent some time healing my injuries after I had been mauled by the gigantic shadowy abomination. Its claws like pitchfork tines and covered in frost that sapped my strength with each successful strike. I hadn't been able to kill it, but I'd injured it a few times.

It was a start.

"Thank you, hon." I grunted as I cast Renewing Flames once more, the warmth of the healing magic doing more than enough to make me feel like myself again.

"You did well, not nearly so well as Balmur, but you did well." Maebe stepped from the shadows and swayed toward me. "Tell me, how did things go with Fainnir?"

"They went pretty good. He's got a little more of an understanding of meditation, and I will use that to assist him in connecting to the earth like you taught me with the shadows."

"A wonderful plan." She sat down next to me, her hand on my thigh. "I have been watching you with him. You have improved in a short time in your dealings. I ask that you keep improving."

"I hope to do my best always." I shifted into my human form and pulled her close. "I have a promise to keep."

She raised an eyebrow, and I snarled playfully as I lifted her into my lap. She laughed, and we spent the rest of our time together at play. After a while, slumber found me, and rest came at last.

CHAPTER SIXTEEN

"Get that axe up!" I called as Fainnir stepped into the trees. This was the first floor we were trying today as our own party, but he seemed to be in brighter spirits than yesterday.

Bea screeched at their opponents to try and get their attention. The wolves growling at them seemed torn, they didn't want to attack Pebble since he was made of stone, and that hurt, but trying to attack the hatchling proved almost as fruitless.

That left Fainnir as their outlet of bloodlust and anger. The wolves, only level four each, moved in groups of three. The dwarven mage had been able to surprise one of them and killed it almost instantly. The other two were trying and failing to circle him. It was going to be fun for him to try and work out how to get through this.

Maybe not for him, but it would be for me. He wasn't in any real danger, we would heal him, but that was it. Anyone could heal, but it helped me be able to really watch over them.

"Pebble, you move in when the left one charges. Grab him and hold him still." Fainnir's back shifted like he was going to lunge at the one on the right, and as he had predicted, the wolf on the left had tried to capitalize on his carelessness. Pebble touched the ground and stone rose to protect Fainnir's left flank, the wolf crashed into it with a meaty *thunk*, then the little elemental bustled forward to grasp the stunned creature.

Fainnir dipped back with his axe and exposed his left side to the wolf. The beast lunged forward with its slavering jaws held open wide, snarling and bit into the flesh of his arm. Fainnir grunted and bashed the creature on the temple with the pommel of the axe in his hand. Bea hopped onto the wolf's back and began slicing through flesh like it was papier-mâché. The creature released its prey and tried to buck her off.

Fainnir's axe flashed and cleaved the wolf's head in half, then he began his grim work on the wolf in Pebble's arms. Honestly speaking, I only had one complaint, and judging from the wound on his arm, I knew that he had an idea of what it might be.

"The next time you offer up your arm as a Scooby snack, I'm not going to heal you." I sighed dramatically as I cast Renewing Flames on him. The wounds closed as the flames swept over his body.

"What is that?" Maebe turned beside me and stared at me intently. "This 'Scooby snack' you speak of?"

I smacked myself in the forehead with my palm. "Sorry, it's a different way of saying a dog treat. Meaning, he shouldn't be careless and act as though he has a healer with him constantly."

The dwarf nodded bashfully but took the criticism much better than he would have the previous day.

"What way do you think you could improve what you just did?" Balmur surprised me as he moved past me.

"Uh, I don' know?" Fainnir stated lamely after thinking for a moment. "I got the drop on the first one, but that left the last two."

"Okay, that's good, but let me ask—does Pebble know that same earth spike spell?" Balmur asked, to which Fainnir nodded. "Then why not have him cast it on one, and you attack the other?"

"Because I might give away the plan," Fainnir reasoned. "Dwarves ain't the most stea—most dwarves, I mean—ain't the stealthiest sorts."

"You don't need to be stealthy; you need to be cunning." Balmur tutted and pointed at the younger dwarf. "You're already forgetting some of your best tools right now. What are you wearing?"

Fainnir looked down at his new cloak. "This."

"Put the hood up." I growled. He did so, and his outline blurred significantly. I could still see him perfectly, but it was like he had faded a little.

"And where are your throwing knives?" Balmur asked with an edge of rebuke in his tone.

"Me inventory…" Fainnir looked abashed, and Balmur took pity on him.

"Now, knowing what you have at your disposal, what could you do to make things easier and more efficient?" The elder dwarf led Fainnir hopefully.

"I can be puttin' me hood up and having Pebble cast the spell while I use the knives and me axe if it be helping?"

I clapped, and Balmur gave Fainnir a thumbs up. He was learning, slowly, but he was doing it.

"Think of it like this," I said, the young man watched me intently for a moment. "You have to come up with a style of fighting all your own, so holding to normal dwarven convention isn't going to produce the results you're looking for. Think outside the box."

Fainnir used the time after that to reflect then went at it harder than ever.

After the next few groups of mobs, he was finally beginning to get the system of it down. He would attack at the same time Pebble did, Bea would launch herself at the last one to distract it, while Fainnir dispatched the wounded one. Then all three of them would converge on the final wolf.

The last group—what we had thought to be the last group —had been a little trickier. It had been a group of five. The wolves sat inside a small set of bushes around a corpse that they were in the process of picking clean. Bloodied leather armor and bone scattered in the area, and there was gore on their muzzles as they eyed the area.

Before we even allowed Fainnir to go into the pre-battle phase, we had him join us a good distance from the wolves so he could explain what he would do.

"I need to kill two of them in one go, so Pebble and I will both cast Earth Spear on the biggest two. From there, Bea will serve as bait, and we can try at least one more before my mana runs dry." He eyed the area the wolves were in for a moment, then grinned. "I'll have a good plan after that."

Before any of us could stop him and ask what he had planned, he was off toward the wolves with Bea in tow and Pebble sinking into the ground.

A moment later, yelping and snarls burst the quiet like a balloon popping, and a storm of growling and baying moved toward us.

Three of the wolves chased a fleeing Bea from the brush, and a fourth hobbled out with a severely wounded rear left leg. For once, I didn't see Fainnir. But I saw that his health was fine. So, I waited.

Suddenly the rear wolf crumpled with a screaming whine, and Fainnir appeared, taking his hood down and shouting at the wolves, "Come and get me, ye mangy blankets!"

Two of the wolves broke from chasing Bea, who squawked indignantly at her pursuer and bore down on Fainnir.

The younger dwarf hollered, "Now!" And a wall of stone six inches thick burst from the ground in front of him. He pressed his hands to it, and a lance-like protrusion of stone grew from it spearing the lead wolf and goring the other's right shoulder.

"Fuck, yes!" Muu howled in delight.

"Let him kill them in peace, man," James whispered harshly. "See? You pulled that one over there away from Bea."

Bea noticed that the wolf was no longer behind her and that

it was springing at us. Dumb, if you asked me, but hey—dungeon wolf was an idiot.

She did not take kindly to that. Bea wouldn't be able to turn sharply enough to get back to us, so she leapt into the air and bounded *off the air* like she had when she walked on it. This little thing was amazing! Her path was now right behind the wolf, and she gained on it swiftly. Before it reached us, she jumped and latched onto its back, driving her envenomed talons into the flesh and tearing as harshly as she could with squawks of barked outrage.

Fainnir stepped around his barrier and kicked the wolf in the injured shoulder, pushing it to the ground in front of the earthen spear. He grasped the wall with both hands and pulled the heavy construct on top of the beast, killing it instantly.

Bea leveled up again, and surprisingly, so did I. That put me to level 38! *Woohoo.* I'd take care of her first, though. She got a natural point to her intelligence, taking that to five, and I put the rest of her points into strength, putting that to six.

For my own stats, I added one point to dexterity, and four to constitution, making my stats look like so.

Name: Zekiel Erebos
Race: Kitsune (Celestial)
Level: 38
Strength: 55
Dexterity: 50
Constitution: 49
Intelligence: 85
Wisdom: 45
Charisma: 19
Unspent Attribute Points: 0

That was a good feeling. Still magic heavy, sure, but it was expected. My spells and animal forms were important. No new abilities, but I did suddenly have an awareness of the work around me that I hadn't felt before. Weird.

"Fainnir, did you level up?" I called to the heavily breathing dwarf.

"Aye!" I looked over to see that he had collapsed onto the ground, his chest heaving up and down as he tried to catch his breath.

"Go ahead and put your points where you need them, then. We're here if you have questions or need advice." I tried to recall correctly whether people here got the same as the animals or if they got less. I thought it was less. "How many points do you get per level, Fainnir?"

His head whipped around and he stared at me as though I were daft. "I get two to spend by me self, and a single point tha' goes where it will."

"Sorry if that's a weird question." I backpedaled a little, *need to throw suspicion*. "See, when Muu got to level five, he got more points than the rest of us to spend on weapon proficiencies. Oh, damn, did I not make that clear?"

He blinked and fiddled with his status screen and smiled when he got to the screen he desired, "Looks like I get two on account of my Dwarven Proficiency. But it looks like it'll only work if it's used for axes."

I glanced at Balmur, who shrugged and fiddled with his own status screen. "Doesn't look like I have it."

"Might be because your people are more proficient with different kinds of weapons, cousin." Fainnir shrugged as he sat up. "Do your people pass down weapons as a rite of passage?"

Balmur shook his head. "Not that I can recall, no."

"That could be why then," I offered. That was some deep meta gaming though. Fuck.

"I got the axe proficiency, though. That extra point will hold until I level up some more, right?" Fainnir looked a little worried.

"It makes sense that it would because you met the prerequisite to keep it," Yohsuke explained. "Next time you level, you'll likely be able to pump it up to second level and get a weapon ability as well. Those can be pretty useful."

"Thank ye!" He looked happy, and it made me smile. He was getting his wish, alright.

"Why don't you sit and see if there's anything new about your class, any spells or abilities you may have gained while Zeke and Balmur go check the area for hidden chambers?" Yohsuke winked at the smiling Fainnir, who nodded and began navigating again. "Muu, I want you skinning these wolves while they're gone. This time I want you to do it as quickly as possible. When Fainnir is done, he can help you."

Muu grunted and offered a half-assed salute that James playfully kicked him for.

Balmur nodded to me and we made our way around the room with little trouble. There was a tree that caught my attention, the bark of it was really nice, and the leaves made noise as a slight breeze ruffled the branches.

And before you ask—yes. There's a breeze down here. I couldn't tell you why, but each individual floor felt more and more like it was its own ecosystem or world. All the elements were here, hell the rooms were even well-lit thanks to the lichen that grew on the roof, providing light that was a shade off from natural sunlight. I wanted to collect some, but I didn't know if it was possible.

Yo, Bokaj. Come check this tree out, man. I called through our earrings; his woodworking craft might assist him in identifying the wood for us.

Where you at? He returned. Looking around, this portion of the room was as much the same as the rest of the room, and I didn't really know.

I marked it on the map for you, Balmur replied and turned to me with a smile. "A simple spell that Nic taught me. See, since it's not attached to a quest, it would normally be hard to do things like that. But, with this spell, so long as someone is in the same party as you, you can share locations on your map with them."

"That's fucking sick, man." I had to look surprised because, in no small way, I was. "We might need to see if there are ways to make a combat application for that spell."

A moment later, Tmont and Bokaj worked their way through the bushes to our location.

"Huh." The woodworking ranger began looking over the tree in ways I wasn't even sure why. "Well, it does look weird. I won't know what it is until I cut it down and work with it for a bit. Let me go see if I can get ol' Jaken to help me chop this bad boy down while you guys keep looking."

I shook my head and called Fainnir to us, and when he joined us, I told him, "Watch how I do this."

He nodded enthusiastically, then I turned to my work. I spread my feet wide at shoulder's length apart and brought Magus Bane into my hands, then brought it behind my shoulder like a batter at the plate. I swung the bat and activated Cleave as metal met the wood, and the chop sank deeply into the tree. Two more strikes with all my strength saw the tree felled and I turned to see an awestruck Fainnir marveling at me.

"It's all in the hips," I nodded to him, and he mouthed the words reverently and took his own axe out to begin training. I snorted then turned back to a grinning Balmur.

Balmur and I nodded and went back onto our trail. While we walked, I had something to say to the other man that I needed to talk about.

"You know, Balmur, we went through a lot to get you back, man, and though I may have said at some points that I was glad to have you back, that doesn't quite cut it." He was quiet, looking ahead as we moved, but he didn't look uncomfortable or anything, so I continued, "I'm excited to have you here. And I'm happy that we were able to get to you. I just wish it had been sooner. We all do."

"I know that, because I wish you had as well," Balmur's soft voice took on a jaded edge that was gone just as quickly as it had come. "The only things that kept me strong in there were my memories of home and my fiancée, my Gatsby, magic, and the hope that you guys were coming. That last one waned at times, I won't lie to you about that. There were times I wanted to die, but when they came close, I would think about you all and how I needed to be there for the team."

I nodded. There were times I had those same thoughts, though they hadn't saved me from the things that he had gone through.

"They would torture me for hours a day," he added quietly. "Hours on end and they would laugh while they did it."

I glanced over next to him and saw that his left eye was starting to pale a little and lose its coloring. "Not to be rude, but is it time to feed your eye again?"

He blinked and nodded, reaching for his jar of…snackrifices to the eye. He pulled one of the specimen's out and held it by the optic nerve in front of his left eye. A spectral set of jaws leapt out of it, and the eye was gone. His eye's color returning even though he grimaced and began to sweat a bit uncomfortably. He took a moment to collect himself, and I stood by in silence as he paid his price.

"Thank you." He glanced left and right before we continued on. "It was hard."

"No doubt," I put a hand on his shoulder and spoke softly. "You know, you can leave the hard things to us for a while, right?"

"I know." He smiled up at me, and I let my hand fall away. "It helps. Being in the thick of things at times. Distracts me, like the magic I'm mastering does. Though, I didn't know that the gods would send someone to replace me so soon after I was gone."

I halted us in the grass for a moment in shock, "That's not what happened, man. Muu coming was always meant to happen, but he got home and crashed later than the rest of us did. I swear."

He dismissed the notification that my oath had given him. "Then that's what it was. I don't not like him, you know, Muu? He's fun to be around, and more than a little crazy. I kept that thought to myself because in my heart I knew it wasn't his fault, but I still couldn't shake the fact that it just felt like maybe…I'd been replaced? Like someone had counted me, out and I had no say, y'know?"

"I can't possibly know." I shook my head, a little bit of defeat and guilt settling on my chest. "I wasn't there with you. But if you ever want to talk about it, I'll listen. We all would. And I know that with us pushing him to get stronger faster, Muu took a lot of our shit in stride, especially from Bokaj. We weren't going to give up on you."

I looked over at him. A soft tongue of air rustled his black and purple beard, and a single tear fell from his good eye.

"We never will," I added quietly, I worried for a second that he hadn't heard, but he nodded and whipped his arm across his cheek, and the evidence of our moment together was lost.

We took our time, and twenty minutes later finished the room. Other than that one tree, there was nothing else in the place of note.

We returned to the others and reported in. I was happy to hear that Fainnir had a new ability.

"Earth Shards, lets the caster throw a small spike of earth at a target that will shatter on impact." Fainnir read aloud. "It has a much smaller mana cost than me Earthen Spears, and it will be a good replacement when all me daggers be spent!"

"You try it yet?" He shook his head, so I pointed to a tree and ordered, "Cast the spell then, Fainnir. Let's see what you got."

He took a steadying breath and cast his spell, his hand whipping forward and the shard thudding into the ground two feet in front of him, shattering like broken glass.

"You have to focus on the shard coming from your hand and treating it like a throwing knife," I stepped over and cast Winter's Blade as I swept my hand out and launched the sword-like spell of ice into the tree where it burst apart a heartbeat later. The tree was hurt, so I cast Regrowth on it. The wood repaired instantly, and the bark did too. It also seemed to grow a little healthier from my Druidic touch. Cool.

Fainnir closed his eyes and cast the spell once more. It didn't quite hit the tree, but it was much closer.

"We can work on that, but that doesn't mean that you forget about the rest of the tools you have, hear me?" I wagged my finger at him menacingly. "You use those knives when you need to conserve mana, and you have your axe."

"Yessir!" The dwarf gave me a smart little salute, and I growled at the others behind me.

"Who the fuck taught him that?" The others just grinned back and pointed at Fainnir.

"I learned that some of ye were in a thing called the 'Marines' from Uncle James, and when Muu did that, it seemed like a weird salute, but it be meanin' respect, right?"

I floundered for a moment, trying to find the right words to say when Yohsuke interrupted, "In a way, yeah. The way you meant it conveyed respect and agreement to the order given to you, but Muu? Not so much. You can do it sarcastically too. Better to do it sparingly, right?"

Fainnir looked around in wonder, "S'complicated."

I snorted and muttered, "Yeah, it is, kid. Yeah, it is. Let's go see what else is going on with this plot."

Fainnir looked worried. "Ain't no one here be plottin' on me uncle, aye?!"

The others howled with laughter, and Muu ushered Fainnir aside as we moved toward the boss room of the floor. I heard a bewildered, "ooooh," and Fainnir was quiet once more.

Once we were inside the room, the door slammed shut behind us, and the light above us grew silvery in color, casting a bright light over the cave-like walls and a slumbering figure the size of an SUV in the center of the room.

What was the saying? Let sleeping bears lie? Bokaj offered as we stared at the snoring creature.

I blinked, oh no. What had that fool just begun?

Well, this is going to be a grizzly situation. Muu snorted at his own joke.

I smacked his arm lightly. *You forgot to paws for effect.*

"Would you three stupid assholes shut up?" Yohsuke asked out loud, making the bear snort and sniff a little.

"Uh oh, he's waking up, Fainnir bear your arms!" Muu cackled as the others groaned audibly.

Ursula the Bear level 7

"This is seriously an unbearable time for this kind of humor," I shot back and whistled as the creature stood to his full height. "Dicks, Fainnir may not be koala-fied for this fight."

"Bear with me!" Fainnir surprised us all and cast Earthen Spear in unison with Pebble, goring the beast's front two paws in a single strike.

It roared in rage, and red coated his body, prompting Fainnir to yell, "Bea, run distraction!"

She gave a little barking hiss at me after I had given my mental order for her to obey him and ran through the bear's legs. It tried to reach down for her and through his legs, tottering precariously.

"Oh look, a yogi bear." Muu howled with laughter, and Jaken snorted.

"I hate to be the bearer of bad news," James said, working himself in, "But this could get uglier than Zeke. We need to pay attention."

"You're right." I tried to stop giggling enough to take a full breath that didn't hurt my aching sides. "You're right. We really need to stick our claws into this situation and get straight to the honey here."

"Oh, that was lame." Muu slapped my arm.

"No need to be so polar about it," Balmur interrupted and sent the two of us into a laughing fit that saw us on our asses. A blast of frozen air washed over both of us, I glanced back and found Maebe staring coldly down at us.

"Ope." Muu and I both stood and coughed into our hands. I released a trickle of flame aspected mana into the air to warm everything. I offered a hand to Muu in front of my body. "Put'er there, boo-boo."

"Sure thing, Yogi." He grinned. "No pic-a-nic jokes, though. Otherwise, our ranger may have to try and arrest you."

We had been distracted enough that Fainnir's implementing his own plan had flown under the radar. There were spiked traps all over the floor from Pebble, and Fainnir threw his knives at the bear's head to distract it. Bea launched herself off a back wall and landed on the bear's shoulder. She dug her envenomed claws in and passed poison into him, but it did next to nothing. The bear reached up and flicked her off his shoulder, and she careened toward the wall.

I cast Renewing Flames on her and watched the damage pile on. The regen was enough to keep her from being incapacitated, but she was severely shaken and dazed. I cast Regrowth on her just to be safe, and her health climbed up. I turned my gaze back to Fainnir. He had run out of his throwing knives and was now on his axe.

"Fainnir, one well-placed shot can ruin an enemy," Yohsuke called out. "Think of a place that will do the most damage or make it so that your opponent will do what you want them to."

The line of Fainnir's body went rigid as the new information was presented to him. He reached up and pulled his cowl forward and moved as cautiously as he dared.

The bear, having realized that his opponent was gone, glowed a deeper red, and it roared in the direction it had last seen Fainnir. The dwarf's form froze, and I thought he had been feared, and I might have to step in, but I waited. The bear crashed back down onto all fours, the pain seeming to be dulled, and Pebble waved his arms in front of him to try and get his attention.

That didn't work, the bear scented the air, and the great head turned slowly in Fainnir's direction from only ten paces away. The cloak's hood fell from a blast of hot breath as the bear caught the dwarf's scent, his eyes growing wide in glee. Then Fainnir's hand was in motion, arm moving like a pitcher's in a major league game. A single Earth Shard flashed forward in the pale light and hit the bear's snout.

Some of us groaned audibly, but the stone shrapnel from the spell flew in all directions, including the beast's eyes.

It reared and called out in pain, blood flowing freely from the wounds. Fainnir and Pebble both bolted forward. Pebble's arm shifted and turned into a spike that he thrust into the side of the bear's knee savagely, and Fainnir's axe flashed twice from behind the other leg near the hamstring. The bear crashed down onto the ground, and suddenly, I *knew* Bea was coming for him. Her call was deceptive, from more than twenty feet away, the bear's paws left its face to slash at the air in her direction, but she had used her ability to leap off the air and into the space above it. She attacked the back of the bear's neck savagely, latching on with her fangs as tightly as she could and shredding with her legs and foreclaws. A keening, whining growl tore from her throat as she shook her head and yanked to and fro.

The bear tried in vain to reach up and rid himself of the nuisance on his back but failed. And fell after Pebble and Fainnir really went to town on his legs.

Finally, the bear tried to drag itself forward, snuffing and growling as it swung its paws back and forth.

"End it, Fainnir. However you have to," Bokaj called to the dwarf.

"Ye fought well, Mister Bear!" Fainnir shouted, and the bear turned toward him. "Die well!"

Rather than going for the kill himself, he had opened up a path for Pebble to spring forward and crash into the bear's right eye with his morphed arm.

One final roar of agony echoed throughout the cave-like room and then silence. I watched, pride blooming in my chest, as Fainnir knelt next to the bear's head and said a soft word. I heard it, the small prayer to Fainne that this creature's end of his walk along the Way had been truly worthwhile. That it had fought well and had earned a place on the Mountain.

As he stood, all of us nodded to him, Maebe taking it on herself to say, "Congratulations, nephew. You have grown swiftly. Continue this growth, and you will soon surpass what limits you think you have."

Fainnir looked proud, but sort of deflated, and he used his hand to sop up the blood for the door. As he began to pass me, I reached out and stopped him with a hand on his shoulder. "This feeling of loss, this hurt you feel at having to bring this creature down—never forget it. It never gets easier. There will be times when you feel your heart hardening to death, and that you may be more comfortable with it. Don't. Let. It. Seriously, let it pass through you as you experience it, and don't dwell, but don't let it consume you either."

He frowned and sniffed, before nodding. "Aye."

I turned back in time to see Bea take a running leap for the spot that Muu had just cleared as he cleaned the pelt from the meat.

"God damn it!" I shouted, "Another one? At least let one of us help you, fuck."

She growled as I joined her, but I just tossed her away from the hole and clawed my way through the meat of the corpse. The squelching, hot mess of it was loud as hell, and I worked my way well up to my shoulder and a little beyond before feeling something solid clinking against my nail.

"The things I do for you familiars." I snarled and dug a little deeper into the beast's carcass. I grasped the item and yanked it as hard as I could.

The squat, hard crystal came free with one final gout of blood and viscera to which I heard Fainnir retch.

"Is this what you want, you greedy thing?" I glared down at Bea, and she eyed the crystal hungrily, licking her lips and clicking her teeth loudly.

"Fine, here." I tossed it down into her wide-open gullet, and she swallowed it happily.

ALERT!

Your familiar has found and consumed a monster crystal. This has resulted in there being a mutation to her abilities.

Ursine Power – The consumer of this crystal gains no added ability, but rather ability points to strength and constitution in exchange for a slight decrease in dexterity.

+3 strength, +4 constitution, -2 dexterity.

Do you accept? Yes? / No?

Oh man, that was actually a pretty decent trade, considering. But I figured I would ask her, "You okay with that, Bea?"

She chirped and gnashed her teeth happily and began to lap the blood on the ground, bits of gore and meat being gobbled up too.

I selected yes, and she stilled. Her streamlined figure beefed up considerably. Her form growing until she stood with her head to almost hip height on me. She had been about to my knee before, but now? Damn. The muscles in her body looked to be larger as well, including her legs and tail, too.

She took a tentative step forward, then another before breaking into a trot around the bear. Her mind touched mine, *Slow.*

"You chose this, Bea." I grinned. The added stats were nice. Really nice. "We can get you back up to speed when you level up again. So, fight hard and smart. Understand?"

Slow! She cried again, the scowl making me laugh as she glared at the offending legs beneath her as if they would suddenly move faster. She ran into a wall and fell to the floor, irritated at the world.

This is going to be fun. I sighed to myself as the others chuckled at her misfortune. *Where the hell were these things when Kayda was a baby? They could have helped a ton.*

Maebe had stern words for Muu and I, and even more stern words for me after that. Needless to say, that I was sufficiently cowed into not fucking about too much more when there was a serious fight going on.

"It is not only above your station as a mentor but also as a king, you would do well to realize that your actions and the tone you set are easily picked up by your young protege." She let me cool and think that one through for a while, but I understood what she meant.

And that was how things went from there on for the next few levels, resting once more but not practicing as much due to the increasing difficulty and actual need for rest. Sure, things got exciting. We found a few hidden chambers with surprises and loot that was nice. But nothing really out of the norm, or what one might not expect out of a dungeon.

There were no more crystals that we could find, at least none that Bea was interested in pointing out to me.

Oh well. Onward to more fun. We passed through the next door, leaving this floor and heading into the unknown that was the next.

CHAPTER SEVENTEEN

Both Fainnir and Bea leveled up a few times already on the floors above us, proving to be much more interesting if a little dull at times. But this last floor of the dungeon that we had worked our way through had taken the cake.

A floor full of worms as long as anacondas that regenerated unless set on fire. Don't think the movie, think factual. Like, thirteen feet, hundreds of pounds and like to eat dirt, but also flesh with rows of teeth designed to mush stone and bubbly, bulbous bodies that gave me the worst chills.

That had been interesting to say the least, and on a couple of occasions, we'd had to step in to help our little gladiators survive. More things had also been coming directly for us, so we took them as they came.

Bea and Fainnir grew by four levels since leaving the fourth floor, and experience seemed to be boosted for them.

I wasn't certain how Fainnir had managed his points, but I knew that it was going to be his job to sort that out for himself. We could only make suggestions since, in this world's cultures, sharing your status screen was an extremely intimate thing. What I could and had been affecting was Bea. Since the Ursine

Power crystal had taken effect, I had had to pump points back into dexterity so she would shut up about being slow. The boost to strength and constitution had been well worth it. Her other stats improved as well, all except charisma. I didn't need her to be cute. I needed her to kill, which she was proving to be quite adept at. Looking at her status screen this last time around showed some promising results, though.

Name: Bea Arthur
Race: Gust Raptor (Juvenile)
Level: 7
Strength: 10
Dexterity: 15
Constitution: 11
Intelligence: 10
Wisdom: 4
Charisma: 3
Unspent Attribute Points: 0

I wasn't sure what the change from hatchling to juvenile meant for her, but I guessed that time would tell. Like I had said, she'd been pulling her weight well.

Each of the previous floors were easier, sure, but for floors eleven and twelve, we had begun to have to step in a little more as the creatures grew steadily in strength and size. And in cunning.

But even as I say that Fainnir had proved himself well enough that we only offered help when he asked now, unless it was too dangerous. Still, his understanding of his role and the things he had to do in order to survive had improved dramatically, and his tactical mind was almost stunning. He was clever, quick to plan, and his nerves seemed to dissipate when he was faced with a fight. I couldn't tell you if that was the surefire cockiness of youth, genetics, or what, but the kid had balls. And he wasn't afraid of much after that.

I had to admit, I was damned proud of how far he'd come.

"So, as soon as we're all rested, we head down into the thirteenth floor, but something's been bothering me," I said, and the others glanced up.

"Is it the serious lack of humanoid enemies?" Muu huffed from where he sat tanning a hide that we had collected from one of the previous floors. I'd taken a large, flat stone and imbued it with the ability to assist the tanning process. I'd used what he told me of the tanning process, concentrating the heat of a fire to act as heat from the sun, then amplifying it a bit to work faster. It took the majority of our last rest together to really get it down, but the item was useful, at least. It wasn't instant by any means, but it would work, for now.

"Yeah, that's been bothering me too." Yohsuke frowned and eyed our surroundings. "A dungeon with cunning creatures? Sure. I'll buy that. But one with no humanoids whatsoever? Not going to go for it. I think we're coming up on some, and it's not going to be cool."

"We'll need to be cautious," Balmur spoke as he worked in his spellbook.

I glanced over to the dome of shadows where James worked with Fainnir on his meditation techniques while Maebe guided him through extending his consciousness into the earth around him. The concept was the same as me pushing mine into the shadows, and Pebble was there to let him know if it was working. He had made great strides toward getting the hang of it. Even Pebble was impressed.

On some of the floors, we had been able to find some more metal. This time, metal we were used to dealing with and that Jaken knew how to work with. So, some like copper, iron, mithril, and other semi-precious metals like silver and gold.

Before he had joined them, I'd had Pebble build us a makeshift forge, a simple construct that I could use to heat the metal that Jaken worked. He had lugged out his portable anvil and went about beating the metal into submission after we had formed ingots out of it. With my ability to superheat metal by adding mana to it, I was pleased to see that the results worked well.

And I wasn't really worried about enchanting because it was my mana in the item, to begin with. Nothing to worry about. If someone else were doing the enchanting, I'd worry.

After a good couple hours of work from Jaken, with me heating the metal, we had the beginnings of a decent axe head. Bokaj took measurements from Fainnir earlier and we had his axe on standby to act as a model for the shape and feel. Bokaj would make the haft from a portion of the special tree we had found earlier, and Muu would provide the leather grip for it from his own work.

After the third hour of hammering, Jaken quenched the axe head in oil that we had in a bucket. The sizzling popping echoed into the chamber around us, and a small bit of flame bubbled to the top of it. While the metal cooled, I looked at the haft to see if I could add anything to it.

"This wood is really weird." Bokaj scratched his head after he handed me his work. The finished product was beautiful. The slight curvature of the haft where the axe head we had designed would fit had been executed flawlessly. It was smoothly sanded, the finish applied with a dark lacquer to protect the wood that had a sort of matte brown to it which didn't reflect the light Balmur had given us to work with overhead. I loved it.

"Why do you say it's weird?" I held the wood up to my eye, but since it wasn't part of an item yet, I had no idea what it was or the type of wood it had been made from.

"Because it's ridiculously magic absorbent—" he held up his hands when I glared at him. "I meant to tell you sooner, but honestly, it's taken me this long to figure out. This is the first item I had the chance to make with it that I could bring out its full potential, and even that I'm not certain of. I'd love to get some to Sarah to see what she could do with it. I have the heartwood and all so that she can work it, I'm not that good yet."

"How can you tell that it's magic absorbent?" I kept trying to see if the wood would show me its secrets to no avail.

"A test we do." He took the wood and closed his eyes. "We touch it with our mana, and if the mana disappears, it has absorbed, and if it just bounces off, it isn't. Simple, I know, but there's really no other way that I'm aware of."

"Okay, cool." I relaxed a little. I found it odd that it had been in a dungeon we found a tree like this, and on such an early floor, too. And how had I known it was worthwhile? Maybe it was time to have a chat with Momma Nature and see what she had baking for us in the oven? "I really appreciate your hard work, man, thank you."

"Happy to oblige, and you know…." he paused for a second as he pulled a small hunk of the wood out of his pocket, no bigger than a fifty-cent piece, but as wide as it was long. "If you wanted, Balmur and I could try to come up with a design for a ring made of it and see what it can do as an accessory. If it absorbs magic really well, maybe you could come up with something interesting for someone in the group?"

"That's a great idea man." I smiled at him, getting more than a little excited at the prospect. "I used to love watching videos of people making rings at home. Let me know if you need any help, okay?"

He nodded and left me with a grin and a reminder to come get him when we were ready to fully attach the head of the axe.

I took my mana and pressed a familiar image of a certain popular hammer into the haft of the axe, then fed it mana with the intent that whenever willed, the weapon—the haft and everything attached—would return to the wielder's hand. To keep the weapon more streamlined and augmenting the strength of the haft in case it had to take a blow, I decided to use some fairy iron shavings because it played well with magic and was just pretty amazing.

It took a whopping 759 MP to enchant the haft by itself, and even the enchantment wouldn't show since the item wasn't fully formed. This was going to be tricky. It was interesting because I knew that the enchantment had taken. I could feel it, and I could see it in the green engraved hammer where the leather would cover.

I blinked and shrugged, motioning to Muu to come over with his glue and leather strips.

"This should be fun, as I've never really done this before," he grumbled as I held the haft out toward him. "Is that Mjolnir?"

"Yup!" I grinned at him as he snorted and slowly wound tan leather strips around the bottom of the haft. It was a process, that was for certain. We made sure to cover a decent portion of it, at least enough to make sure that if Fainnir decided to hold it in both hands, he'd be able to comfortably. We made sure there was a small nail that we hammered in to keep it firm in conjunction with the glue.

After that was finished, I set the haft in my lap and began to go through the process of engraving the axe head itself. The double-headed axe head looked fantastic, almost like it could have been wings that flared up as far as they did down, the tops almost meeting. It almost looked like one solid cutting edge. Beautiful work.

Rather than only engraving one side or doing a shallow engraving on both, I decided I would push the engraving all the way through to the other side so that it would look perfectly the same. That had taken about 506 MP, but it would be worth it.

"Yo, Jaken, you still have that obsidian?" I called over to the paladin as he cleaned up his makeshift forge.

"Yeah!" He reached into his inventory and pulled out a large chunk of it, something that was almost as large as his head. "How much you need?"

"Maybe a quarter of that?" He grinned and tossed it onto the ground, took his hammer, and tapped it until roughly a quarter of the bulk lay in chunks on the ground before tossing them to me. "Awesome. Thank you."

"Happy to help." He flashed his tusks and went back to work.

I took a clean handkerchief and began the process of

grinding it into powder and smaller chunks as best as I could with my metallic claws. I found that I could crush some of the smaller pieces if I squeezed hard enough, which helped a lot. By the time I was finished, I had long since recovered all my mana and focused my intent and will.

I pulled the mana from my mana pool, mentally taking it through the channels of my body up to where the elemental tattoos resided on my skin. I circled the mana around the diamond-colored mountain that represented my blessing from the Primordial Earth Elemental. Then I brought it back down through my arms and into the axe head. I wanted the earth to have the same elemental affinity as the wielder, and that would require that I use the magic I had available to me for it.

Rather than waiting until the halfway mark to add the obsidian component, as I might normally, I started a quarter of the way into my mana infusion, sprinkling it at a slow and steady rate. I couldn't have told you why I did it, but it felt necessary as if I had been inspired to do so.

More than a thousand mana later, the process was finished, and I still had no idea what I had made. However, the engraving was beautiful. Winding paths of black obsidian formed mountains on both sides with small lines leading to each other and out onto the cutting edge like the veins of precious metal in the stone of the world.

I looked over the work and figured it was good before hailing Bokaj and the others. "It's time, guys. Let's see what we've made."

Before putting the axe head on, Bokaj quickly measured the width of the hole in the head and how deep it would sit, then took a saw and made a cut into the top of the haft where the head would attach.

"What'd you do that for?" Jaken's worry and frown made me smirk as his head poked over the smaller man's shoulder to see better.

"It's to place the shim that will help hold the axe head in place." Bokaj attached the axe head, liked what he saw, and pulled it back off before pulling out some wood glue, and began applying it to the outside of the haft and replaced the head. Once that was done, he took a small wedge of the same wood and slathered it in wood glue as well, before slipping it most of the way into the slit he had made. "Well, if the head of this thing wasn't so damned badass, I could get a mallet in there to set the shim."

"Here, see if this will work," Balmur offered Bokaj a small hammer that he used for his crafting.

Bokaj took it with a smile and a nod before tapping the shim fully into place. A little still stuck out, but that was okay. We heated that with Balmur's touch and sanded it down before Bokaj had Muu take some strips of black leather and applied them around the head of the axe in the center. Nails went in to keep the leather, still and an X-shaped pattern saw the head fully seated and firmly placed.

When they finished, a muted *pop* and flash of light emanated from the weapon, and I lifted it from Muu's hands.

Behemoth

+ 16 to attacks, +13 bonus damage to earth aspected spells

Added Effect: Returns to the wielder's hand when summoned up to three miles apart.

When crashing stone lays low the land and chasms split the skin of the world, the creature who stares out of his nest of stone and bones sees only you, wielder, and pray you be worthy.

Axe created by adept smith Jaken Warmecht and craftsman woodworker Bokaj and enchanted by adept enchanter Zekiel Erebos.

"That just boosted my woodworking up to level 32," Bokaj whispered in wonder. "It had been at level 29."

Jaken grinned. "That's awesome, man! It put me up by one, but that's still nothing to sneeze at. Level 43 smithing, yes!"

I smiled at my friends, deciding that we should collaborate more like this. "Put me up to level 45 enchanting as well."

A rumble of earth under my feet sent me tumbling onto my ass, and Pebble reared out of the ground.

"You have been summoned." He reached out toward me with his misshapen hand and tapped my shoulder.

"What?" I grunted, and as soon as I blinked, my surroundings had changed.

I stood in a large, brightly lit cavern, carved of stone all around. Dark, almost jet-black stone with shocks of metals and gems shot through. Veins of diamond, mithril, sapphire, ruby, iron, jade, and other precious metals and jewels stood out in stark relief against the backdrop of earth.

Tiny druid... A rumbling pressure grated against my mind, not unpleasantly, really. Like having tectonic plates grinding against each other inside the ol' brain housing group.

"Stoneheart, Keeper of the Magics of Earth and Stone," I greeted him formally but glanced about hoping I would catch a glimpse of his corporeal form in his realm. The other elemental primes that I had met had been so vastly different from each other. Fire, a wall of burning flame, kind of lame really, but it had been intimidating as shit, let me tell you. And water had been human though her age had been fluid, first an old woman, then a lovely lady, a girl, and a baby. Each of their realms had been as different as those who reigned over them.

A small fissure in the stone opened before me, wider and wider until a gargantuan version of Pebble stepped through. Jet-black stone made up his body with visible veins of gold, platinum, and precious gemstones plainly visible throughout his form. He was magnificent.

I wanted to thank you in person for taking my champion in and being so diligent with him. All of you. Though I do not watch at all times, my child, 'Pebble' as he has been dubbed, reports to me the goings-on he deems worthy of my attention.

"I'm glad to help a friend." I smiled up at the twenty-foot tall creature, who knelt so that he could regard me closer. Earth had always been supportive and kind to me and our cause, and I would always appreciate that about him.

Friend…yes. He raised a hand and brought it crashing down into the ground, shattering the limb less than five feet from me, and I jumped damned near out of my skin, but I stayed still. *You do not fear me, or reprisal for taking power from me.*

The shattered limb now looked more like a hand made of platinum, significantly smaller so that he could put it onto my shoulder.

"I didn't mean to take from you, Great One, only that your strength may shine onto your champion and through his weapon." Had that been what I had done by cycling the mana around that mark?

Pebble confirms this even now, as he holds this weapon in his grip. It is a magnificent weapon, and I am proud to have my child wield it.

"It's far from the best thing that we could give him, we had an idea for a staff and axe combination that I thought might be a good fit for him when he understands his power a little more." The elemental was silent, so I thought to explain. "It would really just be an axe that amplifies his natural magic that he gains through you, kind of like what I did, but *way* better."

The platinum hand on my shoulder grasped me almost-painfully tight. *You would do all of this for him?*

"How many times have you and your brothers and sisters stepped into the gap for my friends and me?" I couldn't help the grin on my face as I patted his hand. "You give us power and respect where sometimes we hadn't earned it. And when we do earn it, the rewards are great. But like I said, I'm helping out my friends—that includes you. If I may be so bold?"

Friends. I am proud of the work you have done, but it is not quite complete. The grating in my mind took on a pleasant tone, softening greatly. *Tell Fainnir and my child to hold the weapon together, and strike it against the stone wall nearest the largest cap. There you will find further assistance in making this weapon greater, friend druid.*

"Please, my friends call me Zeke." He stood and loomed over me, his mouth attempting the word without sound first.

Zeke. Do this, friend Zeke, and continue to guard over my champion, and I will be happier all the more to reward you and those you hold dear.

There was a great rumbling and trembling that felt like the world itself was about to split in two that stopped after a moment. *A show of good faith and my support. The mountain nearest your village holds greater quality veins of ore and gems. Enjoy.*

"Thank you, Great One, Shaker of the Ground." I bowed my head, not being able to help the boyish grin I still had on my face.

Friends. Call me, Gorumbal. My head whipped up, and my eyes opened wide. *Fainnir is ready to summon my stronger children. Tell him to have faith, and he will be cared for. Goodbye, friend Zeke. May your path be wide to fit all those who walk with you, and the mountain you tread accepting. Be stronger than the stone.*

I blinked once more and opened my eyes in the cavern that we had been in with my friends staring at me.

"You cool?" Yohsuke asked worriedly as he glanced over me.

"Never better." I glanced over at Pebble, who seemed to regard me differently. "Go get Fainnir."

"Yes, stone friend." Pebble tottered away quickly as I stood and scanned the area.

This place was weird, it was full of fungi. Large, hulking mushrooms and patches of smaller ones growing from the bottom of them grew all around us. The stone walls weren't really slick, but it was a little damp and cool, but not musty like you might expect.

I found the "cap" I had to be looking for. A large mushroom that looked like a golden crown on a scepter of white and silver patches. Smaller red and green ones surrounded it on all sides, and the stone wall was visible. Good.

Pebble dragged a confused looking Fainnir behind him, and when the dwarf laid eyes on Behemoth, his eyes widened.

"What's that?" He squeaked in awe.

"This is the beginning of a gift, but I have other news first." The others had gathered around as well, so I spoke to everyone as I continued, "First, there has been a shift in the world, and the Earth primordial has sent a lot of love to the mountain near the village. It's going to be a material rich site if we want to cash in on it, so we need to get word to the others. Maebe, you want to send the message to Vrawn and Vilmas?"

"I would be delighted to after this is all concluded and before our next lesson." Maebe took the raven from my hand, and I looked to Fainnir, but her voice stopped me, "You may want to speak to her as well."

I turned back to her, accepting that I might sound like an ass at this moment, "I know, and I would like to, but this needs to happen now. I'll try later."

She nodded, a little less accepting than I had hoped, but I needed to focus and turned back to Fainnir.

"Your patron has stated that it's time to summon one of his stronger children." I could see the trepidation on his face as he looked over to Pebble. "He has asked that you have faith. I don't know what that means exactly, but he's never steered me wrong, and I trust him. You should too."

Before Fainnir could say anything, I held Behemoth out to both of them. "Both of you are to take this weapon and strike the stone here behind me. Do it together."

Fainnir held the weapon with reverence and took it in his left hand as he turned to Pebble. "Back to back?"

Pebble shrugged and put his back to Fainnir's once they were closer to the wall and put his nubby hand on the item.

"One. Two. Three!" Fainnir and Pebble reached out and struck the wall with Behemoth. A clang of metal against stone, and then nothing.

"Maybe we need to whack it again?" Fainnir wondered out loud as he pulled the weapon back to do so.

"Patience, young one," A voice tumbled through the air. We looked around, and a cracking sound and a shift shook us. All who stood fell to their knees and witnessed the sundering of the earthen wall next to the kingly cap.

A pair of large, glowing-crimson eyes blinked at us from the crevice. It reminded me of the axe's description, and that had me a little worried.

The sound of something large scenting the air reached me as a great horned head breached the tear in the stone.

"I am not so easily moved as I would have been centuries past," the figure stated, the deep baritone of it sounded like a landslide.

The eyes glared only at Fainnir as the second half of the creature, easily the same size as Gorumbal or larger came through and moved past us. His dense muscular arms made the ground quake even more with each heavy step, and his chest and back rippled with the same powerful strength.

A bestial snout topped by a deep black nose and heavy scarring along the ridge of it scented the air once more before Fainnir, the red eyes almost blocked by the thick black horns jutting six feet from the skull like the horns of a bull, blinked curiously at the diminutive form before him. While I appreciated the size of this monster, I noted small, oddly-spaced growths sprouting from them that looked like bone-like protrusions and his deep royal purple fur covered in dirt.

This was a magnificent beast.

"Ah, so you are the one that the whispers seem to hold in high regard," the hot breath roiled from his mouth, almost like a dense fog that seemed to encompass all of us.

Behemoth level 76

There were rows of buffs under his name and health bar that trailed off until I realized that he was speaking again.

"…yourself worthy, child?"

Fainnir, stared up from his rump with his weapon almost forgotten in his hand at his side, his mouth opening, then shutting in silence.

"How long has it been since I have eaten, I wonder?" Drops of saliva flecked the ground as thick bands of the liquid dribbled from the sides of the behemoth's mouth. "All of these morsels to take as recompense for my wasted time."

My friends and I readied for an attack, my preparation being to cast Aspect of the Ursolon and readying Magus Bane.

The behemoth's large head shifted, only a little, with teeth bared and eyes wandering slowly over all of us.

Stone shook once more, and it felt like the roof of the place would fall to crush us.

"No!" Fainnir barked and stood, his knees quivered, and his teeth chattered. I could see a wet spot having started on his thigh. I couldn't blame him. "I…if ye feel ye've wasted yer time, then ye can have me! They got nothin' to do with it!"

The behemoth's head ducked down swiftly until a single, glowing red globe stared widely into the dwarf's face from a foot away. "You would stand, coward? I see no threat here. Time to eat."

The beast raised a paw and began to move away, toward me, his jaws opening wide with teeth shining against the light.

"I would fight!" Fainnir roared and stamped his foot. "Pebble, to me!"

Earthen Spears erupted in front of the behemoth and snapped the creature's mouth shut.

Fainnir leapt forward, Behemoth flashing toward and scored a small slash against the beast's hide.

"Fainnir, stop!" Pebble cried and burst from the ground with his arms outstretched to fend off a blow.

"Yes!" The creature growled triumphantly, he tossed his head the air, and I had to dive to the side to avoid being gored. "Yes, puny dwarf. Reach into the bowels of your soul, face your foes as you just have, and all will kneel to your might!"

Fainnir, still not realizing that things—at least for now—seemed to have calmed down, was still trying to march forward to attack the beast.

"I'll die fendin' ye off, ye long-horned shoe!" He howled, and Pebble pushed him back again. "Get out of ma way ye pesky boot rock, I gotta protect me kin!"

Yohsuke threw a small stone at the dwarf's chest, and it knocked a little of his bluster aside. "Would you pay attention?"

The dwarf blinked and roared again, his new axe held high as he charged forward. "*Storm Company!*"

"Oh, that sounds badass!" Jaken hooted just before the behemoth roared so loudly and violently that Fainnir flew into a growth of mushrooms across the room only to land in a pile of spores and pain. His health had dropped by 90%, and he was sorely dazed.

Jaken, Bokaj, and I all buffeted the dwarf with healing energy and turned our sights back on the monster. Muu sidled over to stand between Fainnir and the behemoth.

"The weapon, Zeke!" Pebble called as he raced toward Fainnir. "Give him the axe!"

"I will collect it myself." The behemoth snorted and attempted to collect the axe, but his horns kept stopping him as they gouged large slits into the soft ground. "You, scaled one. Give the weapon to me."

"You gonna eat me?" Muu asked in retort, and I fought the urge to scream at him.

"Could you stop me?" The red eyes blinked at him, and Muu thought for a moment.

"No, but I'm really stringy, and I would probably give you gas." He shrugged and stepped forward to snatch the weapon off the ground then offered it to the monster.

The large head whipped forward and collected the item without severing the arm attached to it. Though the horns had come very close to goring him where he stood.

With the weapon in his toothy maw, the behemoth sat for a moment, closed his eyes in concentration, and hummed deeply from his throat.

After a few minutes, he spat the item onto the ground, saliva splattering the ground as it landed. He licked his chops then began to back into the crevice his entry had made until only his head was visible.

"When he awakens, tell him this. You are worthy so long as you stand for your own righteous cause, and so long as the earth holds you in high regard. Do not forget who you are, what you stand for, or run from the battles you must face, and my bite will be yours. Grow strong."

He blinked at us, a low growl trickling from his throat. "The dungeon senses my presence and attempts to ensnare me. Be careful moving on. Good luck."

His bulky head pulled into the darkness, his horns snaking in behind him, and a rumbling pressure sealed the stone.

"That was seriously some S.E. type shit, man," Yohsuke spoke with a hint of reverence in his tone, but his skin was pale.

"Yeah, it was, I wonder how much the gods took from the worlds they glimpsed from in our culture?" The thought of it forced a chill down my spine and shivered, as Jaken and I bustled toward Fainnir. He was whole and hale, but unconscious.

"He is with father," Pebble stated, sinking into the ground. "Keep him safe."

I glanced over at Muu, who shoved me away, and I went to collect Behemoth.

As soon as I touched it, I noted the differences in it.

Behemoth's Claw

+ 16 to attacks, +13 bonus damage to earth aspected spells

Added Effects: Returns to the wielder's hand when summoned up to three miles apart.

Blessing of the Behemoth – Randomly adds damage to attacks or a certain debuff to attacked foes. Any wielder deemed unworthy risks detrimental debuffs upon use.

When crashing stone lays low the land and chasms split the skin of the world, the creature who stares out of his nest of stone and bones sees only you, wielder, and pray you be worthy.

Axe created by adept smith Jaken Warmecht and craftsman woodworker Bokaj and enchanted by adept enchanter Zekiel Erebos.

"Well, shit." I whistled and tossed the weapon to Muu.

He caught it deftly and shouted, "Why the fuck wasn't this made for me?!"

"Because you suck?" Bokaj smirked, and Muu just narrowed his eyes at the elf. "Mainly because this wasn't expected."

"That's true. I mean, who the fuck would have thought that behemoths would exist here?" Yohsuke still had a note of wonder in his voice but had begun to sit in a meditative position. Maebe had been teaching him and Balmur how to press their awareness into the shadows.

"Who's up for a scrap?" I called, and Bokaj winked at me. The aspect spell I'd cast beginning to fade and allowed it.

I adjusted my neck, and he and I went to town on each other.

What better way to address the nervous energy that had been coursing through us? Could we have taken him? Not without everything we had and Maebe helping us. Even then, I couldn't hide the fact that I thought one of us would have gone down. And that was something I wasn't willing to deal with right away.

———

Fainnir, finally awake and ready to rock after we had spoken to him, was ridiculously excited to move on as the rest of us ate our breakfast.

"I feel as though I could wrestle a bear!" The younger dwarf snarled joyfully, his axe in hand.

The others turned their gazes to me, even Maebe, expectantly, but I just smiled and let the kid have his fun.

"Hey—*hey*—pay attention, damn it!" Yohsuke said, his voice a bark as he clomped too close to the cooking fire and almost put it out before the toast was done. "I'll have Zeke sit on you if you don't pull your head out of your ass."

"Sorry, Uncle Yoh." Fainnir hung his head a little, moving away from the fire a bit.

"You going to summon the stronger elemental, so you're fighting fit, or what?" Fainnir glanced at me and sighed at my question. "You're ready. Do it. Have some faith."

Fainnir glanced at Pebble, and the small elemental simply nodded once. "Pebble, go home."

Pebble's body fell apart in a pile of rubble that sifted into the ground and disappeared like cotton candy in water.

Fainnir closed his eyes and dispensing with the dramatic phrasing and gestures, stomped his foot three times on the ground, and raised his voice, "Warriors of stone with hearts of steel, come to my voice and make my enemies kneel. I summon you forth and bind you to me, let us form the pact!"

Shifting stone and slight tremors alerted us to a presence, a larger, almost seven-foot-tall stone golem that made Pebble look like a toddler. Craggy stones with veins of iron, steel, and copper flashed in the light of the flames as it moved to stand before Fainnir.

"Thank you for coming, are you willing to partner with me and be my defender?" Fainnir asked politely.

Ruby protrusions that looked like eyes stared blankly as the creature raised its left hand, and it was actually a hand, until it was palm up and presented to Fainnir.

"Blood from my body to seal the pact." Fainnir took a belt knife and slit his left palm open with an audible hiss, his HP bar sinking a little as he did so. He placed his palm on the elementals and spoke again, "Blood to stone, stone to stone, and stone to blood, again. You and I are bound, and with the binding, I name you Grav."

Under the eyes, the rubies shining now with some kind of animated life, a mouth formed, weird and slit-like in creation, and the creature spoke, "I serve, Master."

We watched, rapt as the veins of metal in the elemental's body glowed, burning where they were but trickles of the material traveled up the body and down the arm until molten metal reached Fainnir's hand. The metal coursed over his flesh, his grunt of tolerance evident as it settled and cooled, having taken half his health.

Being an elemental mage was looking to be a little more brutal than I had expected.

Blinking at the exchange, I cast Regrowth on the kid then moved to stand next to the newly-named Grav, so I could see the marking on his hand that stopped and faded just above the wrist. It was a swirling mass of gray, black, and copper that reminded me of a glove, but as I touched Fainnir's arm, it felt pliable like his actual skin. There was a circle in the middle of the back of his hand where it was just his normal skin color, though.

"There, it be done." He clapped his hands together, taking a moment to grow accustomed to the new addition to his hands. "Now, to try this. Pebble!"

Grav shrank into the ground, and Pebble sprouted from the spot he had vacated, looking the same as he had before.

"I am pleased to see that it worked," Pebble observed aloud as he glanced to Fainnir's hand. "The bonding worked. Excellent. And the summoning costs minimal mana?"

"Just like the big guy said," Fainnir confirmed, leaving me a question.

"What do you mean, 'minimal mana?'" I asked, stepping closer.

"Once the pact is formed, I can shift between elemental partners at will for a mana cost equivalent to me intelligence divided by the number of partners I have." He scratched his head and sighed. "I don' pretend to know all the math, never was all tha' good at it, but the stronger I get, the more intelligence I gain, right? So, I get smarter and stronger, and pay the price to summon stronger elementals."

"That's cool and all, but what's with the metal glove?" James lifted Fainnir's left hand and tapped to with his knuckles.

Pebble raised his hand. "That's the living metal." Pebble motioned to the mixture of steel, iron, and copper. "These metals are the weakest of the elementals other than just pure stone like me, but the living metal acts as a catalyst to the summoning. It will change as he summons more powerful members of my family. But this shows that he was able to summon a shield."

"That sure as hell wasn't a shield," Bokaj interjected. "That was a golem."

"Not a golem, golems are weak and made of clay or flesh." Pebble said, scorn heavy in his tone. "This summoning was for a shield it is a classification of the Warrior Caste of elementals. The weakest among them, but still very much stronger than I. They are not the brightest, as you may have noticed."

I heard a chuckle, but I didn't know—or care—who it had come from.

"Well, this is a very interesting turn of events, and it's super nice getting to know the intricacies of the Elemental Caste system, but we have to move on," Yohsuke butted in and began the process of putting out the fire and handing out the toast that he had made. Nice and crisp with a good helping of butter and some cinnamon and sugar on it. Lovely. "Let's go."

We swiftly packed up our things and moved on from the room, Pebble leaving us so that Grav could be there for Fainnir. I allowed Bea to come out of the collar, and she stayed near me for the time being.

As we wound deeper down into the earth, the light from the lichen above us grew dimmer, and dimmer, until eventually, we had to stop and have Balmur cast his light spell, but even that seemed to be too dim.

"Let me see if I can't make something, give me a second." I closed my eyes, then rebuffed myself. This was a teachable moment. "Fainnir, come here. I'm going to explain the process of making new spells to you, okay?"

He nodded enthusiastically, so I closed my eyes and began my process.

"First, I ensure that I have a spell or intent in mind for what I want. In this case, I want to create a spell that makes light that I can control. I have an ability called Fox Fire that allows me to control a type of fire that sticks to a target and exposes hidden creatures and objects by lining them in the flames. Cool, I know. But I want that control and aspects of it."

I focused my mind and thought of the forge inside my head

that allowed me to create things with my tinkering abilities. I stoked the flames with my mana and added Fox Fire as the base, explaining the process to Fainnir as I went.

"Next, I want to ensure that my intent is on being able to fully control where the flames go and how much light they give. So, I will 'hammer' that intent into it as I channel more mana into the spell. Now, I also have tinkering with shadows, so I will also add a little shadow manipulation and push the shadows away to expose more to the flames."

I finished the spell by focusing more on it being malleable to my whims. I wanted to be able to shape it freely as I would. Finally, another touch of shadow magic and I had a new spell that had cost me roughly 566 MP to make.

Exposing Flames – Caster wills malleable light into existence that allows him to see a great deal, both in plain sight and that of what would be hidden. Cost: 87 MP. Duration: 1 hour (or until dismissed.) Range: 600 feet.

"Guard your eyes, everyone." I had no way of knowing how bright it would be until I cast the spell. Once I did, I could see the glaring light even behind my eyelids. I lowered the intensity of it with a thought and a small trickle of mana until it was bearable. Manipulating it, other than moving it, cost a couple points of mana, but at my level, that was perfectly fine. Once I fully adjusted, I could see that the stairs and this section of the tunnel down seemed to have been dug out by crude tools of some sort. Widened and made taller to support taller travelers. That was odd.

"Let's go," Jaken whispered, and we set out once more.

Fainnir walked beside me, Grav underground and Bea on my right with the others behind us as a rear guard. Maebe was closer than normal, but that was to be expected because her presence was calming.

And I hoped that mine was the same for her. Then again, she was more at home here than anyone, so… I was just being a whiner.

"When we get to the next rest area, we need to sit down and touch base. With each other and Vrawn," I spoke quietly so she would hear me, and she nodded. "I know that you've spoken to her, but I feel bad."

We had come to the entrance to the floor by the time I finished speaking.

"Kill the lights," Balmur surprisingly ordered. I dimmed mine until it was almost translucent, then snuffed it out entirely. "Fainnir, you're on, be careful."

I could see nothing, but I heard his excited breathing as he pressed the door to the next floor open.

Dark corridors of the same kind of roughly worked earth greeted us, tunnels dug out by something that smelled musty.

A whispered, "Grav, where are the enemies?" Fainnir, it sounded like he was just ahead of me.

I could feel Bea's uncertainty, she didn't care for not being able to see.

"All around," the simple elemental replied. "Close. Far."

"He really isn't bright, is he?" Muu harrumphed sarcastically, earning a smack from someone. "Hey!"

"Shut up!" James whispered hoarsely. "Let's go."

Fainnir led first behind Grav, and off we went into the tunnels. It wasn't too long before we found the makers of these tunnels, and I was definitely interested as I hadn't seen any in this world so far—kobolds.

Not quite lizardfolk—more like an adjacent cousin?—who were roughly the same size as goblins, their mouths more beak-like with sharp teeth and lither forms than their taller lizard cousins. In the lore back home, kobolds were related to dragons, and depending on the color of their scaly hides, you could kind of tell the type of dragon they were likely serving. These ones were copper-colored. And even more surprising was their level.

Kobold Miner Level 18

We were on the thirteenth floor, so they should only be level 13. Something was wrong.

I tapped Fainnir on the shoulder and gave him the hand

signal to freeze before addressing the others, *We got trouble y'all. These guys are level eighteen.*

Shit! Jaken growled. *You think the dungeon may have tried to adjust the levels after the behemoth invaded? To try and keep from being taken over?*

It's possible, but we really won't be able to tell unless we learn more about dungeons in general, and we got shit to do. Yohsuke paused for a moment before coming to a decision. *Muu, you're still a lower level, you join their party, and Zeke'll be your healer. The two of you will have a more active role to play in the fighting if need be, but Fainnir needs to at least try. Should be easier with Grav there, but who knows. Play it smart.*

I thumped my chest and sent Muu an invite, which he readily accepted. I could see his health bar in the corner of my vision, where I focused. It was a good feeling.

"Okay, Fainnir, we move on as scheduled. Muu and I are going to be taking a more active role in this, so don't worry too much." I let him take that in before I laid the heavy on him. "But this is still you learning, so I want you to do your best and not take stupid chances just because you know we will step in, okay?"

"I'll be wary," Fainnir shrugged to loosen his shoulder muscles a little and brought Behemoth's Claw out of his belt loop and into his hand. "Kobolds are a crafty sort what burrow into our tunnels from time to time. We shoo 'em off, but they need cullin sometimes, and this time they're nae livin' creatures, but creations. May their gods or creator show them mercy. I won't."

The first fight came seconds later, Fainnir and Grav both attacking with Earthen Spears that came from the top and bottom of the tunnel like gnashing teeth and pierced the whole way through the little creature, his stone pickaxe clattering to the ground from his grasp. The spikes stayed, but the noise attracted others, so I cast a softer version of Exposing Flames.

Two more scrambled through the sides, one of them taking a throwing knife to the shoulder that made it cry out, "Grafh!"

"Grav!" Fainnir snarled and pressed forward. The large elemental backhanded the injured one snapping its beaked head to the side and shaving about 15% of its HP off. The uninjured one charged Fainnir with pickaxe raised and a battle cry on its tongue.

Fainnir pointed behind it and bellowed, "Snake!"

The kobold simply snarled and tried to plant the pick of its weapon into the dwarf's noggin. He parried the strike with his axe, then kicked the kobold in the stomach at the same time a metallic-bladed limb slashed through the kobold's right arm and sent the limb arcing into the air with a reptilian screech of agony.

Fainnir capitalized on the distraction and buried his axe into the creature's skull. He went to look for the other, but Muu stood over it with his short spear freshly bloodied. "Good job, Fainnir. Very nicely done."

"Good job with the trying to distract him too, but maybe do it before they're trying to pick your brain?" Bokaj suggested teasingly, and the dwarf snorted.

"Game time—game faces," Yohsuke reminded us. Maebe stayed quiet, which was unusual, but then again, we were focusing, and she needed to be sure we could handle our shit.

The next few fights went roughly the same way, though Fainnir was doing better each time. He would score a strike and rebuff the first attacker with his axe by throwing it, then cast Earthen Spears with Grav to kill one of the kobolds, then summon his weapon to his hand after the second was engaged with Grav. If he didn't kill it fast enough, Muu would end it.

Eventually, we came to a large room where I cast Life Sense. I regretted it almost immediately. There were at least twenty-five of them within range of my spell, and that wasn't nearly the extent of the room.

I snagged Fainnir by the collar of his cloak and hauled him away from the door.

Houston, we got a problem. I growled to the others, explaining what I had found. *There's no way we go in here without it being a blood bath and putting Fainnir at risk.*

Let him know what's going on after we back up a little way, and he can decide how to proceed, Balmur suggested. *He knows roughly what all of us are capable of, so he should be able to reason with the tools at his disposal.*

That was a really good idea, so it was what we did. Moving back toward the entrance a little, as stealthily as we could, was easier said than done. Dodging corpses and ensuring we didn't make as much noise as we had been, felt like we were trying to take all the water we had put into a tub back out with a spoon. It was highly likely that we would be walking into a shit show, and we were the main attraction.

"Well, Fainnir, time to shine." Jaken nodded to the young dwarf, and the rest of us gathered around. "Zeke?"

"Right, Fainnir, we're leaving the planning for this up to you. Everything from the approach to what we do—you will dictate." He looked ready to balk at the idea, but I gave him a hard stare and raised a single finger. "I will brook no argument from you. You are well aware of the things we're capable of from us giving you examples and fighting with you and sparring in front of you. If you have questions, just ask. Also, you can figure out the layout of that room easier than almost any of us could."

"Right." He closed his eyes for a moment in thought, and we left him to his own devices for it. This was a lot to pile on his plate, but then again, how old had I been when the Marines had put those corporal chevrons on my collar and told me to lead? He needed to be ready and to adapt.

We all did.

"Pebble." Grav sank into the ground, replaced by the smaller elemental a heartbeat later. "I need you to go to the south of our position and mark out the dimensions and layout of the room where all the kobolds are. Stealth is key. Go."

Pebble sank into the ground as he tottered toward the room and left us in silence. Ten minutes later, the elemental returned and gave us a rough, three-dimensional map of the room. "The room is a mining pit, and we are at the bottom that reaches approximately two hundred and thirty-five feet up into the air, is one hundred and two feet wide at the center and another eighty-five feet longer east to west." His nubs moved inside the outer walls, and floors of stone were added onto them, signifying what looked like landings or stories in the room. "There are floors with crude ladders and landings that lead down to lower chambers. They're mining."

He pointed to several small, well, pebbles, on the map. "These are the kobolds, they seem to gravitate toward low-burning fires and where the food is. Roaming kobolds that are slightly larger have whips and short swords for some reason and wander from group to group. A majority of them slumber right now, but some are awake and on guard duties."

"Damn, Pebble!" Yohsuke and James whistled low in unison before Yoh continued, "Wish we had more of that on our side."

"We do, Zeke just can't travel through stone." Muu shrugged, and my cheeks burned. "He's not hard enough.'

Fainnir softly cleared his throat before I could roughly explain the intricacies of traveling beneath the ground to the scaly piece of shit, making me stop before my rant could begin. Our party dissolved and we all received a party invitation from Fainnir, which we accepted.

"I think I have an idea, do any of you have any poison?"

CHAPTER EIGHTEEN

Gotta hand it to the kid, man. That was some solid planning, Balmur told the rest of us through his earring as he got himself into position.

It was a multi-tiered plan that had been very well thought out for something roughly twenty minutes in the works and constructed on the fly.

I don't care for the fact that two of us have to stay out of the room while the rest of you are working in there, Muu said, his grumpy mind-voice petulant as he stood in his spot outside the entrance to the room. Maebe was hiding both him and Jaken, where they stood on the sides of the room, cloaked in shadows. It was their job to stop any of them from running away.

Yohsuke sighed. *I get it, and when this is over and we move on, you can play more, but right now, we have a job to do. So put your big boy tie on and lace up your shit-kicking boots.*

I almost snorted at my brother's joke, but I was more concerned about getting to my own position. I was up on top of the highest tier of the room as an owl with Kayda in her parrot-sized form right beside me. For this first phase of Fainnir's plan, Operation Tummy Tantrum, as we had affectionately dubbed it, the sneakier party members would go to where the food was kept and enact a little hell on it. By way of poison, of course. Those few vials that Nora had given us would be great, not to mention the fact that I had some of my own that I had been more than happy to give. And would be more than happy to give in the future.

We found, after James had brought it up, that my vorpal viper form could use venom the same as the normal one could and that in order to use it, it cost mana. For a single use, it had been roughly a hundred mana a shot. So that meant I had eight "bites" worth of venom before my mana would need to replenish. Cool right? I know, I'm just an idiot.

I had spent five minutes filling vials that Balmur had invested in while we were still in the high elves' city of T'agnolian Val. He hadn't said why he had them, but I figured it could have had something to do with wanting to start collecting poisons or venom to augment his fighting.

Each of us had one of the vials and would go about our duties and communicate when we were done. We didn't want the venom going into the food itself, but the water that was located by the food. There was a bell by each little station and a kobold cook who stirred a pot of soup, with a large basin of water with a ladle and dozens of earthen cups scattered about.

I used the shadows to obscure my fox form and stepped as cautiously as I could toward the water. The small kobold yawned tiredly and smacked his lips before trying the soup. He must have liked it because he helped himself to a bowl that he ate greedily with distrustful gaze cast all about the room. I shifted into my fox-man form, then upended a quarter of the vial into the basin and moved on.

Then a bell rang. And another. And another.

It's not an alarm! Bokaj called to us, my heart racing. *They're waking everyone up for the day. Be careful, operation is still on.*

Several angry mutters in a language I didn't understand echoed, and several of the newly awakened figures trudged past me to get to the water. One of them had even been so kind as to stir it for me before it helped itself to a big gulp of it. A small fistfight broke out, and there was shouting and bickering galore as they fought over the next drink.

We went about our phase of the mission swiftly from there, some of the little creatures falling ill sooner than we had anticipated. The watered-down venom making them sweat and grow thirstier it seemed. After another ten minutes of skulking in the low light, the next phase could begin, and for that, we had to let Fainnir and Pebble take it.

As time passed, I noticed that some of the bottom section of the pit became a little less focused. Not like I was having trouble seeing, but that the ground grew softer. Fainnir had come up with the idea that quicksand would be useful, and while he couldn't really cast that spell himself, Pebble could make it naturally. All it took was a little know-how, and the little elemental had a lot of that going on. Four large sections of the ground grew unstable one at a time and stilled as Pebble worked.

Phase three, Bokaj muttered. *Balmur, you okay with this? You know we can have someone else do it.*

It's okay, bud. I'm really the best suited for it, I just worry that Yohsuke won't be able to keep up. I could almost hear the smile in Balmur's voice at ribbing the other man.

Keep up? Yohsuke shot back with a snort. *Fool, I was bred for this. See if you can kill as many as I do with my spell sniping.*

I'm rolling my eyes at both of you, Jaken admonished them, but I could tell by the note of dread in his tone that he was worried. *Be careful. Remember, we can drop them off the top, and they will likely die.*

I raised an eyebrow. *Top is where Bokaj and I will be playing, Jaken.* I told the paladin in a matter-of-fact tone. *And we will see who has the most bodies to his name. Muu, if you would have Fainnir count us off, I'll release the scaly beast and Kayda, and we can begin the culling.*

There was a slight pause, then, *Go!*

So much for a countdown, I chuckled dryly and set Bea loose with orders to stick close to Kayda and to create mayhem.

Kayda grew significantly larger, and off she went buffeting the kobolds with her wings and screeching as she moved about the floor. I took out Storm Caller and cast Aspect of the Hare. I grew lighter, my muscles lengthening in my legs and a little of my strength leaving me for it, but that was okay. I activated feather axe and bounded forward.

My axe cleaved through kobolds who scattered and tried to form any kind of defense against us that they could, but the venom won out and sapped their strength. This operation was brutal and efficient, and I was exceptionally proud of Fainnir for it. Though, I knew that he would likely think of this for some time to come as a victory that cost him much personally.

I cleared my thoughts just in time to shift out of the way of a cracking whip from one of the larger kobold overseers on this level.

Kobold Overseer Level 20

His muscular body easily dwarfed the skinny, almost-malnourished forms of his staff, but what stuck out to me were his eyes; they seemed a little more intelligent than the others that I had seen in here. As if this wasn't just your run of the mill kobold. And I know what you're thinking, 'But Zeke, it's not a run of the mill kobold, it's an overseer, it has to be more intelligent, right?'

Not always, and there had been a specific lack of intellect in the creatures in this place since we got here, the fox being the major exception. This thing seemed like it could be on par with that fox, and that worried me a little. Each floor seemed to feed off a theme, right? What was the theme to this one?

The overseer interrupted my worries once more by trying to whip me with that long cord of leather and metal. Rather than just ducking it, I let the whip wrap around my metallic arm and yanked the creature toward me. It caught on to the tactic and released the whip, the item's handle whacking me in the snout for my efforts. He took out his short sword and prepared for a fight.

A blur of green anger leapt over his left shoulder, gashing it on the neck with a clawed foot, and I activated Charge to cover the distance between us instantly. I slammed my great axe into his stomach, a charge of electricity jolting through him and throwing him over the ledge, his cry of fear echoing throughout the pit.

"STORM COMPANY!" I roared into the depths, the thought of the group working together like this under a single banner and badass name had chills running down my spine and a fresh surge of adrenaline running through me.

"YEAH!" I heard one of my friends cry out, then another worldless cry of assent. Two more and finally, Fainnir, as he sprinted into the room and stood in the center of the quicksand pits.

"Ye'll all die here! Come and get what ye can!" His axe was out, spittle flew from his lips, and he raised his hand. "Grav!"

The larger elemental burst from the ground and went to work slaughtering kobolds with its arms mutated into blades of metal. It roared wordlessly, likely feeding off Fainnir's rage and desire to end this fight swiftly.

I couldn't help the overwhelming urge to return the same energy the others were putting out. I saw Bokaj and Tmont begin moving toward the lower levels and decided it was time to move on from where I was.

Ten minutes of down and dirty fighting later, Storm Caller and I covered in gore and blood from head to toe, we stood at the bottom of the pit. Grav had been able to halt the quicksand, solidifying it easily and killing any inside.

"Pretty sure I killed around twenty?" Balmur winked at Yohsuke from where he cleaned his weapons. Sorrow he left alone, the blade craved blood, and as soon as it touched it, it sucked it into the blade like a straw.

"Those are rookie numbers," Muu scoffed, Yoh rolled his eyes.

"I am certain Fainnir's quicksand has more than thirty-five kobolds in there," Maebe observed out loud as she stepped closer to me. "I think he wins by default. And you, my love, are absolutely terrifying."

I grinned at her, some of the dried blood caked in my fur cracking as I did. "Thanks."

Shadows passed over my body, and the blood and sweat left with them. "Being clean is nice too, but still very frightening." Maebe turned to the others and did the same for them. Her intervention was appreciated.

"The loot has been a little garbage," James said, grunting as he rifled through our findings. All the coinage we found; we gave to Fainnir because he would need it more than us. The weapons were shitty at best, and the ore, judging from what Jaken and Balmur saw, was very low quality.

And I hadn't seen anything of value up top or down here, but Balmur and I made our way back up the levels and looked around while the others did a report with Fainnir, letting him know how things went and what they thought. It was nice. Balmur and I were about done with the third floor when something caught his eye.

"That section of stone look weird to you?" He pointed toward a section of the wall that looked like stone to me. It matched the stuff around it too. I shook my head, and he paced closer to it with a confused look on his face. "It does look weird, here check this out."

I looked at the portion of the wall he touched and noticed an indent and hole. "Door?"

He nodded, and I relayed our find to the others, they sent James and Muu up, and the others stayed below just in case.

Once our paladin and fighter arrived, Balmur worked on unlocking the door. It took him a couple moments, but eventually, he made it in. The small room held food, and a large supply of mediocre ore that Muu and Jaken gathered for inventory.

Jaken sighed. "Just copper and iron, but we can give it all to Rowland or something." Jaken turned and looked askance at us. "Onward to the boss room?"

We made our way down to the bottom once more and gathered together to give the food to Yohsuke.

"Anyone need to prep anything? Fainnir?" I glanced around and no one made a move to stop, so I shrugged. Bea was busy munching on something, I stopped and looked, and it was an arm. "That's fucking gross, dude. You have food with us, why would you do that? There's venom in there."

Hungry. Her mental shrug prompted Kayda to poke her head over my shoulder.

Food? She looked down at the arm that Bea now pulled away like a dog with a bone and sniffed. *Yuck.*

"Finally, some sense!" I threw my hands up and walked on, the two of them following as they would.

The boss door was gigantic, easily more than twenty-five feet tall and thirty feet wide. The doors were metallic and had a large circular glyph in the center.

"Something is wrong," Maebe warned as she stepped ahead of us.

"What is it?" Fainnir's voice quavered lightly.

Maebe touched the glyph lightly, it glowed for a second, and she whipped her hand away. "This isn't designed to keep things out, but to keep something in. Whatever is inside that room will be coming out here to fight us."

I looked around more than I would like to have admitted than I did before. There were two altars on each side of the door, both of them loaded with items and sacrifices of food. A small kobold's corpse laid on top of one pile split open and spread apart like some kind of kobold baked potato.

Oh god, I can't believe I just thought that.

"So, what do you suggest we do?" Yoh stepped closer to the door.

"Prepare," I said with a grunt. The others looked at me. "Look, whatever comes out of there is likely going to be huge, we need to be ready. I want Bokaj, and Fainnir up on the second level raining down spells, Grav can be down here to help the melee fighters. Yoh and I are going to provide support from down here, Bea will do what she can to run distraction and Jaken and Muu know what to do. I trust Balmur and James to know where and how they will be most effective."

"What would you have of me, my King?" The Fae Queen's hips swayed as she walked toward me, firelight playing in her deep-green eyes.

"Can you open that door?" She nodded. "Then I need you to open it and let us work. With how high the levels of the kobolds were, it wouldn't surprise me if the boss is even higher leveled than the norm. If you feel we'll be overwhelmed, step in."

She smiled and kissed my cheek. "As my King wishes."

Heat rushed to my cheeks as the others rolled their eyes and turned to their own tasks.

"See something, say something—no one be a hero," I said, my voice a rusty growl. "Call it out loud if you have to, I don't give a shit, but we *will* communicate through this. Fainnir, if you need us, yell. And I swear to you, if you do something crazy, I'll have more than just words for you, do you understand?"

"Yes!" Fainnir's jaw set in a determined manner, and he sprinted up toward the second level.

Good shit, you do know that he's going to try some stuff, right? Bokaj lifted an eyebrow as he walked by me. I nodded, and he smiled.

I was hoping he would surprise me.

I waited until everyone was ready, then nodded to Maebe. She lifted a hand, said a word, and her fingers shifted. The temperature in the room dropped wildly, and I had to fight not to shiver, then the cold sucked in toward her all at once, and a large shard of pure ice floated above her hand. She lazily threw her hand forward, and the ice shard sailed through the air into the crease between the doors and dented it open, then burst into a thousand tiny shards that blew the door wide.

A set of glowing blood-red eyes opened, then a pair of golden-hued eyes and another lavender-colored pair glared out at us and stepped forward from the darkness. A dragon's head, copper scales glowing in the firelight with slitted-red eyes, stood tall in the center of the creature's body. The head on the left shoulder looked more like a ram's with lavender eyes, and the final head was that of a man with a bald head and bland features except for his golden eyes.

As the lion-like body cleared the broken door, so too did the tail, a large snake's head rose from the shadows behind it and hissed at us with irises of a cornflower blue. The fur looked mangy in places, and the back legs had to be the goat portion of the creature.

"A Chimera?" Balmur groaned.

"Yeah seriously, what the fuck are we going to do with this thing?" Muu snorted. "It's gonna look at us really hard."

Yohsuke whistled. "Shut your sucks and get ready for a brawl. Each of those eyes communicated better and more naturally than we do, and chimeras are magical creatures. This thing is going to have magic, buckle down!"

Dungeon-born Chimera Level 35

This is some bullshit, I growled at the others. *How is it so much stronger?*

"Don't know, don't care—kill it!" Yohsuke barked, and the show was on.

Jaken and Muu both roared in unison as they dashed forward, weapons drawn and an aura of enmity grabbing red around each.

"You eight-eyed freak of nature, I bet your mother only talks to you on Halloween!" Muu cried, and the creature roared at him.

Jaken let his dancing sword and shield do their work as he took out his holy sword and swung at the creature's heads.

Fainnir shot shards of earth down at the creature, and Grav fought desperately to keep the tail's attention so it wouldn't attack the dwarf.

Get that tail! I ordered, and Bokaj rained down unholy hell on the thrashing snake-like appendage. It hissed and thrashed, damage appearing above its head—making us aware of more bad news.

They each have health bars! Balmur cried, moving from a shadow off to my right into line with the chimera's stomach, where he stabbed brutally with both of his weapons, but he didn't seem to be doing much there. It roared and stamped the ground near his position, but Balmur moved easily enough, a cloven hoof leaving a mark on the floor.

"I'll be charging a spell, give me a moment." Immediately I activated the ability and held a fireball, adding more mana and manipulating the spell so that it would do what I wanted. I only held it for ten seconds, the full cost of the spell 457 MP, but a javelin of pure flame streaked toward the chimera's chest.

"Ahhhhhhhh!" The human head screeched, and the spell seemed to redirect toward Bokaj's position.

"Bokaj lookout!" The spell crashed into the floor, and the archer fell even as I called out. Tmont soared through the air after her falling master, letting the elf grasp the loose fur near the nape of her neck so that she could haul him from the chimera's reaching, salivating maw. He still took a healthy chunk of damage from the fall and some of the rubble smacking into him, but it wasn't immediately life-threatening.

"No more big spells like that," James called. "Looks like the head has more magic capability than we could have thought."

"Kill it!" Bokaj roared as soon as he could stand. His bow was up, and arrows flew forth at increasing speed and volume.

"You gonna get in there, Zeke?" Yoh hollered as he took his astral adaptor in hand.

"Yeah, give me a second." I focused myself and cast Aspect of the Ursolon, then pulled out Storm Caller, leaning the weapon against my body as I put Magus Bane onto the latches of my armored back. This was going to be fun, and I'd be switching between the two weapons when I needed to.

Glancing about, I found a target—the snake tail. Or the freaky-looking human head.

I took Storm Caller and whipped the weapon toward the human face, but the chimera's dragon head shifted over to it protectively, and the dragon just roared at it, taking the attack to the scales of its throat as if it were nothing. I had not expected that the nearly 4% of the head's health bar that it took away was alright, but I'd need to change tactics to get to my real targets.

I called the weapon back to me, the bolt of lightning striking my palm and solidifying into my great axe once more. This time, I aimed my weapon above the chimera, and called Bea, *I need a distraction but don't get too close.*

The adolescent raptor barked three times and booked it straight at the chimera's legs, crying out in challenge. Muu's short spear blurred into the creature's chest three times, and finally, the dragon's eyes glowed deeply and its chest expanded widely.

"Breath weapon!" Jaken and I shouted in unison, I thrust my arms forward, summoning Void Shield in front of Muu and Bea to stop the flames. 203 MP and counting as the thing exhaled, and kept going, and going. It finally stopped after I had expended 398 MP total. The fucker was getting on my nerves, making me dip into Mage's Well so early into the fight and with very little mana left.

Time to go old school.

Magus Bane felt good in my hands as I marched forward, activating Charge once I was in range and slammed the invisible blade into the Chimera's leg, draining a small chunk of HP and stealing forty-seven mana. It roared and tried to bat at me, then the ram's lavender eyes ignited, wreathed in electricity. A pulse of static charge filled the air around me, the fur on my body rising to stand up on end.

Kayda! I roared mentally and felt her presence even as I called to her, she was there duking it out with the snake, but her own electrical field had begun to meld and spark against the chimera's, almost canceling it. The sensation of building electrical energy continued to rise, and the scent of ozone with it. That gave me an idea, but it was unlikely if that human head had anything to do with it.

Focus on the human head and make sure it doesn't see me. The others didn't acknowledge my order so much as they went ape shit on the chosen target. The beast cried out in pain and anger.

If our casters were to stand a decent chance, I had to hope that each of these heads had some kind of off switch, or an elemental difference. Meaning that the ram's head was probably highly resistant to lightning damage, but that another might not be.

As soon as Kayda's warning came, I cast Water Sphere on the human head from beneath it at the same time as the goat cast its spell and Kayda loosed her own. The electrical current passed me and zipped straight at the water with Kayda's added lightning, and the water rippled, but the current fried everything inside. The head tried to shriek in agony, but it merely took in water, the other heads struck at the spell, but the damage was done. The majority of the human head's HP was gone, and Muu and Jaken had decided to capitalize on it.

"Guuuuragh!" Muu grunted and launched his ice lance at the globe of water, freezing it solid while Jaken hopped off his hovering shield like a springboard and shattered the sphere with the pommel of his sword, the head shattering with it.

"Yeah!" Fainnir howled in triumph, just in time for the snake's mouth to snap forward and grasp Jaken by his leg, swinging him toward the dragon's maw and the ram's waiting horns. A length of shadow snapped out from my left and wrapped around Jaken's left arm as a trio of arrows sprouted from the snake's eye. The snake released Jaken, and the shadow pulled him clear of the chimera.

The beast roared in rage, and a claw whipped out and smacked me from my spot as an observer, sending me flying into James. "*Oof!*"

The two of us careened into the far wall, his health taking the brunt of the damage, but I still lost 35% of my HP, the gash on my chest smarting something fierce. I hated to do it, but I cast Void's Respite on myself, then covered myself in shadows so that I would get the full benefit of the spell. It's not cheating if you're smart enough to do it.

James flashed with golden energy, and his health was topped off once more. "This thing is pretty fucking bonkers, man. I don't know if we want to keep going down the dungeon if shits gonna be broken like this, you know?"

"I feel it." I spat, watching the others' assault on the chimera.

Before, it had been content to wallop us at its leisure where it had stopped upon exiting its chamber. Now, it seemed to have decided that moving was going to be better for it because it did, and it was *fast.*

The chimera bounded from its spot, batting Jaken aside with a paw and bounced off the wall to our left before colliding with Muu. The two of them crashed to the ground, the fighter roaring in outrage and the dragon head slamming into him like a pecking bird with a worm.

"Get. Off. ME!" He growled futilely, taking his shield and sticking it against the chimera's clawed paw and pulling the trigger on the two-fold weapon. A blade with green venom pouring from it erupted from the portion above his wrist, and the monster howled angrily but didn't budge.

The ram's eyes glowed again, and Kayda screeched as she rocketed across the air above. *Uncle Goblin!*

The storm roc crashed into the ram's head hard enough to knock it off Muu and buffeted the chimera with her wings before sending cold lightning crashing into the dragon's left eye.

Hot blood spattered the ground in front of me, and I took Magus Bane in hand, ready to intercede when I heard a cry.

My eyes darted to the second floor, where Fainnir desperately fought off a kobold that had feigned death well enough it had fooled us. Then I saw another one off to my right on this floor. Then four more.

The dungeon was actively spawning them!

"We got company!" I roared, putting the axe down long enough to whip Storm Caller at the closest kobolds. I put Magus Bane on my back and bolted toward Jaken. "Jaken, need a boost!"

"Got it." The paladin whistled, and his shield came to his arm, he grasped it and as I jumped onto it in fox form, he launched me into the air where I shifted into my eagle form. I beat my wings, shooting toward the struggling duo, Grav having joined in the fight to assist in defending his master.

The kobold's pick swung to and fro, slowly chipping into the elementals stone body. I careened into the fight as the little bastard tried to juke around Grav and get to Fainnir before he could cast another spell. My claws spread as I swooped down and picked the scaly thing up by his head and shoulder, his limbs tried to beat at my claws, but he seemed to realize that I literally held his life in my hands.

Well, feet.

I lifted him higher until I could see everything happening below us. My friends had begun fighting the kobolds, specifically Bokaj and James, who could assist each other and dispatch them swiftly.

Muu was standing once more and had taken his hammer out to play, working on trying to pulverize the chimera's limbs as Jaken gained his attention and sliced at the draconian-lead head. It looked to be close to about 70% health, but they were working on it.

Yohsuke stood off to the side of the fight, hurling shadow magic at the snake tail, the hissing monstrosity's life ebbing further and further. Balmur had opted to go to Fainnir and assist him how he could when his hands moved and the two men's figures faded slightly, likely having disappeared from sight to anyone else.

Bea scrambled between the chimera's legs, much too fast to hit, but she had taken a little bit of a beating. Kayda still harried the heads as best as she could, the ram's head suddenly jutting forward to collide with her chest, knocking her on her back, a clawed paw smashing into her taking 15% of her health.

You bastard! I mentally roared and took my frustration out on the creature in my claws, tossing him to the side nearest the chimera's chamber and shifting into my fox-man form. I fell as I took Magus Bane in both hands and set myself up for this attack. The others did an amazing job running interference until I was about twenty feet above the chimera, where I used the axe to roll into a front flip, then activated Cleave and Epicenter simultaneously. The weight of the great axe in my hands quadrupled, and I knew I was leading this strike in the right direction.

"Fuck. *You!*" The blade slammed home next to the chimera's spine, the back half of the body crumpling, and a large chunk of its overall health plummeting by 25% as blood flecked my face from the impact. I noted a symbol under the health bar that I was well acquainted with—it was paralyzed. The chimera tried to stand but listed to the side, stepping off of Kayda's body, golden energy covering her as Jaken held out his hand in her direction.

The time limit on my aspect spell held, and I knew I had about four more minutes. Time to make them count.

A hissing sound drew my attention, and that familiar sense of precognition made the fur on the back of my neck stand. I shifted into my fox form, wind from the snake head's passing ruffling my fur, I shifted into my Terran Gorilla form, and hefted Magus Bane into its disgusting, scaled throat with a whoop of rage.

More hot blood splattered against me, and the snake tried to whip back around, but I sliced it again at the same time that Yohsuke joined me, stabbing his Astral Blade into the throat and using my back to leap up, deepening the wound until he found a large artery.

"Move!" Balmur shouted from above us.

I got my happy ass the hell out of Dodge in time to hear a cacophonous boom above us. I turned hard enough that my momentum tripped me, and I fell onto my back, this twenty-foot-long stalactite plummeting toward the chimera and me.

"The man said move!" Muu's grunted and his voice strained as he grabbed me by the scruff of the neck, so I shifted to fox-man form, and he hauled me out of the line of fire. The world tilted, and gravity shifted as we lifted into the air, his jump carrying us into the space above the group with ease.

A loud crashing squelch and a bleating roar from both heads signaled the gruesome environmental weapon had found its mark. I craned my neck to see the stalactite had penetrated the thing's right shoulder and pinned it to the ground.

"No better time than now!" Yoh hollered, rushing forward. "Stick to the sides!"

"Muu, throw me at it." I growled. We had cleared the distance to the nearest wall with ease.

"Fastball special coming up." He chuckled and I shifted into my fox form. As soon as his feet touched the wall, he shoved himself back toward the chimera and threw me as hard as he could.

The wind screeched in my ears, my eyes slitted to protect them, and as soon as I was near the dragon head, I shifted into my Belgar form and rammed my horn into the side of its face. The crunch of breaking bones and the warmth of the blood running down my face from it let me know I had done well.

I shifted into a fox and fell in time to just barely miss the paw that slapped into the creature's head where I had been.

I landed in fox-man form and slammed my axe into the other paw where Jaken and James pummeled it. It roared again, then cackling growing steadily louder, and the chimera fell under the immense weight of Muu's aerial assault.

Blood and bile frothed from its wheezing jaws, both heads fading. *Thud.* A crash and another howl of manic laughter came from Muu as he slammed back into it again. The creature expired then and there.

More than a dozen Kobolds came from the entry to the next chamber.

"We can take them!" Jaken snarled, preparing himself for the brawl.

Another dozen flooded in behind them carrying bows with nocked arrows dripping a thick, oily-looking liquid.

Okay, maybe we don't try to. That shit looks dangerous. Bokaj sent with a growling tone from where he stood in the shadows. *I'll give you guys cover fire; we need to figure out how to get the hell out of here.*

Do we want to get out of here? I asked as arrows sprang from the archers' arrows. I cast Void Shield, blocking the majority of them so that Bokaj could fire on them, and the rest of us wouldn't be skewered. *Yeah, we want to get out.*

The sound of an explosion rocked us, Yohsuke grinning as I turned. "Star Burst."

Jaken called his sword and shield to him with a shrill whistle, the weapons taking arrows as they returned. "Let's get to getting then. Balmur and Fainnir!"

They materialized next to him, making him jump. "You called?"

"Yeah, let's go." Jaken looked back to the rest of us. "Zeke, Yoh, you mind clearing us a path?"

"I'm about tapped." I growled, even with the mana I had managed to steal from the chimera I had about 200 MP on my own and the dregs in my ring.

"I can clear us a path, get ready." Yohsuke rolled up his sleeves, flames crackling on his hands. I turned toward the kobolds and the yawning entrance to the chimera's room when four more sets of differently colored eyes opened inside it.

"Back the way we came!" James barked as Yoh cast his spell with a gasp.

Fuck it. I summoned my mana, adding another 100 MP to my casting with Elemental Tinkering and sent an empowered Fireball at the ceiling above the door, leaving my mana at nothing. The blast shook the room, and rubble plummeted from above.

"Let's go, Fainnir." Balmur snatched the kid up by the shoulder and dragged him. He seemed to be in complete shock.

Kayda fluttered down onto my shoulder in her parrot form. The rubble covered the majority of the doorway.

Suddenly, ice and shadows crashed onto the kobolds from all sides and froze them solid before the shadows gobbled them up.

"If you plan to flee, there is no need for me to not assist you," Maebe's cool voice greeted us from the entry to the room. "That will only anger the dungeon more, we must flee to the Great Below from here if we are to have a chance at survival."

"Okay, but how?" Bokaj sounded out of breath from firing arrows, for once.

Maebe pointed to Fainnir. "His elementals will be able to create a path for us."

"I don't know if they can do that." Fainnir sounded uncertain.

"Grav dig. Shield." The large elemental grumbled, loping toward the wall east of us. He began punching the wall and moving the stone aside, but it resisted him a little.

"Did you level up Fainnir?" I asked hurriedly, keeping an eye on the chimera door.

"Once, but that won't be enough to help us through." He already had his status screen open.

Then we need more firepower. I thought to myself. *Better now than never. Gorumbal? Can you hear me?*

I could feel a shifting in the earth around me, as if it came closer, *I hear you, friend Zeke.*

We could use some help here. I know we haven't been able to complete the quest for you all yet, but if we're going to make it out of here, we could use a down payment.

There was a pause. As if he considered my proposal. A thunderous roar echoed across the pit from us, and a silver dragon's head burst through the rubble, more kobolds with it. These ones beefier than the last.

Gorumbal, my friend, I bind myself with my word to you, on my strength and titles, that I will do what was asked of me. If we fall here, we all fall. Please, give us the power to protect Fainnir.

The pressure around us grew, and my mind fogged over as that pressure centered on me.

I take you at your word, friend Zeke. Gorumbal's rumbling, grating voice echoed through my head. *Take this power and protect your charge. Prove yourself adept, and I may allow you to keep it. Do not crumble under the pressure, friend Zeke.*

The world swam in my vision, and suddenly, the earth around me cleared into more focus than it ever had been before.

ABILITIES UNLOCKED

Elemental Tinkering (Earth) – Earth now heeds your command unlike it ever has before, and new spells can be created and discovered within the proper elemental realm. Be warned that mana is consumed at a higher rate while tinkering with or discovering a new spell.

I blinked, and the closeness faded, as did Gorumbal's attention.

Mana potions! I dug through my own stores, downing all of the mana potions I could to fill both my ring and my reserves.

"Keep it distracted," I ordered the others. "Mae, you too, but don't kill it, that could make things more difficult. Fainnir, come here."

The dwarf sidled up to me, his wide eyes glued to the new chimera's dragon head my friends were attempting to distract.

"Hey, *eyes*!" My snarled order at him brought his attention to me, but he was scared. "I need you to focus on making a spell that will allow you to move the earth, like creating a path. Like you might wade through a stack of leathers waiting to be sold. You're just shoving them aside to get to the good stuff."

He nodded and closed his eyes, trying to do what I had told him. "Find us a weak spot in the stone, Grav."

The elemental disappeared before I did the same as Fainnir. I focused my intent and will using the earth mana that I now had at my disposal and dug deep. It was hard. Really hard. Earth was so new to me, but it was also as natural as taking muddy dirt and shoving it aside to look for worms.

Finally, the spell clicked in my mind after spending 523 MP on it.

Stone's Path – Caster molds the earth around them,

forcing the very flesh of the world to part for their steps. Cost: 20 MP per 15 foot by 15 foot by 15-foot section of stone moved. Duration: 1-hour (or until dismissed) Range: 15 feet. Cooldown: None.

If I had read that correctly, that meant I could move a lot of stone, more than six hundred feet if my Math for Marines course had done anything for me. Even more, if I used the ring. But I'd save that for later if I could.

I glanced at Fainnir, who still focused, sweat beading on his brow and his face. I silently said a prayer for him, hoping Fainne or Radiance could hear us in here.

I stepped over next to where Grav was now beating on the wall and touched the stone. I could almost feel the pulse of the world beneath it, and it made me wonder if this was how Fainnir felt all the time. I cast the spell, and fifteen cubic feet of stone slammed out of the way toward my feet. The hole it left was a little more than seven feet wide at the entrance, and a just over eight feet tall.

"Oh, that's too cool." Muu's voice behind me made me flinch. I glanced back to see the others backing up toward the space, and I could also see why. More kobolds clambered over the stones, some of them advancing on us, others helping to dig the second chimera out of the chamber. A second head cleared the debris, the slavering, baying hound-like face with black fur and green eyes. It barked, and a blast of energy swept our way, tossing Yohsuke and James toward the wall.

Maebe cast a shield of ice in time to save the others and Fainnir, but those two slapped into the wall like rag dolls and fell unconscious, their health bars' halved instantly.

"Muu, get them," Jaken called, and the other man sprinted to the prone figures, hefting them with ease. "Zeke, let's get out of here!"

"Grab Fainnir, I think he's still trying to get the spell made," James called to Jaken, and the paladin gathered the dwarf into his arms.

Kayda was on my shoulder, and the others had entered into

the hall I had made. But I couldn't help the thought that I was forgetting something.

Bea! I glanced toward the fallen chimera's chest, and sure enough, there was a small hole. "Fuck!"

Kayda, don't get too close, but I need you to shock the ever-living hell out of that other chimera, okay? She took off without a thought and soared toward our pursuers and screeched. "Bokaj, cover me!"

"Got you. Balmur, get his six." Bokaj grunted, and his bow slung arrows through the air with ease.

I didn't bother looking back, I just moved toward my raptor. Oh... she and I would have words about this.

"Bea!" The sloshing, squelching movement inside the chimera's chest paused for a split second then began anew in an even more wild and fervent frenzy. "You selfish little *shit*!"

I heard her clicking inside the body and took my clawed metal hand and tore the my way into the corpse as best as I could, the scent of copper almost overwhelming.

This time, rather than going after her myself, I was going to send my shadows in. I gathered them around my feet, and they slithered into the gore with my awareness as well. The inside of this creature was a disgusting jumbled mess and massive. The musculature so much denser and more disturbing than what I could ever imagine.

I took anatomy in high school, and I was okay at it. Just okay. Loved the teacher though, great guy. This would make him freak the fuck out, though.

I focused on the task at hand and not what was inside this thing and finally found what Bea was chomping at the bit to get. Once I had it, I snatched it free and brought it to my hand. Bea stopped moving, the instant wash of rage in her mind traveling through our bond as she searched for what was missing.

Get your ass out here, and we can get to it later! She scrambled out of the corpse, blood all over her and clawed at my hand with her teeth bared at me. I slipped the crystal into my inventory and tapped her head as she snapped at me, making her get into the collar. She didn't want to, but I forced her to obey with the sheer weight of my own rage.

Yeah, she was definitely my familiar if we both reached for anger so readily. I turned, finding my friends closer to the corpse, and Jaken dragging a bloodied Kayda toward our makeshift exit as he pumped healing energy into her. "We gotta go!"

Maebe was all that stood between us, the chimera, and his horde of kobolds. The nebulous energy of snow and shadow keeping them at bay long enough for us to sweep past. "All of you run!" She grunted and a blast of flame beat against the energy she held. "I will push them back once more before I join you."

"Go for it!" I screamed, more used to stress than a lot of the people I knew but seeing Kayda like that and not having known she was so injured made the tunnel vision I was trying to fight settle around my vision. *Get your fucking head in the game, Marine! Freak the hell out later.*

A burst of mana washed over us, and Maebe was suddenly running next to and then passing me easily.

I blinked at my surroundings and growled low in my chest as I sprinted toward the exit, Bokaj taking the rear so he could cover our retreat. "Where's Fainnir?"

"Up front, soon as he was near the wall, he opened his eyes and set to work. Kid's a monster, but he won't last much longer." Jaken planted a foot in a kobold's chest as it made it past Bokaj's barrage. The creature screeched and fell, shadows eating at its head.

Maebe spoke from the entrance. "Get to the front and lead us from there. Bokaj, Jaken go. I will be the rear guard."

I nodded once and beat feet to the front where Fainnir panted and gulped down a mana potion. Then I noticed the blood pouring from his nose and cast Regrowth to help a little.

"I got it kiddo, take a moment." I touched the wall, willing the path to angle down, hoping to reach the Great Below soon. "I need you to send either Grav or Pebble into the earth around us so that they can tell us how far we need to go and which direction."

Fainnir glanced at Grav and blinked. "Pebble, I need you."

Pebble popped out of the ground where the other elemental had disappeared and instantly melted into the ground. I glanced at Fainnir in alarm, but he pointed away toward our path. I got busy, the sound of battle reaching us from the front as we moved.

Well, the sound of Maebe stacking bodies so high that the kobolds couldn't get through gave us a little bit of breathing room. Even if it did smell like death, it was appreciated.

Pebble guided us down to the point where, after a few hours, we were able to make it to a natural cavern. Not the Great Below that I was aware of, but hey, it was a start. I made sure Kayda was good as we went, her parrot-sized body resting on my shoulder.

Once we were in the area, I had everyone guard their eyes and cast Exposing Flames. As the light radiated through the area like sunlight, I added mana to it.

Something shifted in the far corner of the room, and everyone just turned and blasted the absolute hell out of it. We watched, exhausted, starving, and angry as the creature fell to the ground dead. Some kind of beast with tentacles and craggy, stone-covered skin. I didn't even know what level it was, but as I cast Life Sense, I could tell it was gone. And the miserable amount of experience it gave us was telling, too.

The area was filled with mounds of stone, bones, and nothing that looked to be of any material value, though we took some bones just in case. The gamer in us really called for it.

"I have an idea that will help make this all a lot easier if you have the time and brain function to enchant later." Balmur patted me on the shoulder, his soft smile and tired eyes making me laugh at the attempted joke.

"You got it bud, just let me nap for forever." I yawned; the headache that comes with too much mana use almost blinding me.

Cool hands slid over my temples. "Let me help soothe that, my love." I smiled despite the pain. I'd never get used to Maebe calling me that.

What about the others? I glanced around and checked on them. Each of them looked to have stopped and taken out their bedrolls. Except for Yoh and James, who rested on a blanket that Muu had laid out. They had woken up briefly, but Jaken had mumbled that they should rest more in case there were head injuries.

It had been a while since my first aid training, and even I wasn't sure if that was a good idea, but if someone with access to a goddess who allowed them to heal people said it was okay —who was I to argue?

Fainnir was passed out on the floor close to Muu, who had fallen asleep sitting up. Conserving mana had been an instinctive idea for all of us it seemed. Though our, "Oh shit" buttons like Summon Celestial or Jaken's big heal could have helped. We just hated to use them if mana was needed because they took everything.

"All of you will rest, and I will keep watch," Maebe ordered gently as the cold from her hands radiated into my skin and soothed the ache more and more. "I am proud of your work leading our friends today, Zeke. You did well, given the circumstances. Rest."

The cool touch of her hands kneading my flesh numbed my mind enough that I was finally able to fall into a fitful slumber.

CHAPTER NINETEEN

"..u must awaken." Maebe's voice entered my dreams as she shook me. "Zeke, wake up!"

I came to, looking for danger and found my friends waking up. I blinked at Maebe, her concerned glances around the room made me panic even more.

"What's wrong." I yawned despite the fear.

"Something is amiss." Her eyebrows arched inward, and her frown was pronounced. "I can't tell what it is, but it feels almost as though there is an awareness in the darkness that is foreign to me and the void. And there is something large very close to us."

"It smells like acid in here." Yohsuke groaned like he tasted bile.

The scent hit my nose, faint at first, but building. Shit. "Maebe, can you cover us all in shadow?"

"Yes, gather close." A flood of viscous liquid secreted from the walls.

"Ice too," Bokaj grumbled as the liquid rose from the ground beneath us. The noxious fumes gathering and building.

A sheen of ice formed over the acid, and we made our way to the wall.

"Let's blast through this." Muu growled with his short spear out and at the ready.

I agreed and closed my eyes, reaching for the shadows, flames, and earth at my disposal and poured my mana into the spell. I wasn't sure it would work, but I wanted the fuck out of here in the worst way. I spiraled the magic like a drill and shoved it savagely into the wall in front of us, a rumbling screech shook us, and my mana depleted rapidly as it dipped in.

Once it was through and my mana close to bottoming, I stopped the spell. "Yohsuke, Balmur, use the shadows to tear the lining apart so we can bounce!"

"On it," Balmur snarled, his hands up with shadows wreathing around them violently.

"Got you!" Yohsuke stood with his eyes closed.

"Now!" Maebe groaned as her arms spread out as if to keep us from being crushed.

The two of them grunted and growled as they cupped their hands and tore at the edges of the hole I had made. It seemed like we would be crushed by the pressure of it as we eked our way through the hole in the side of whatever creature this was. Slowly, so painfully slow, we made out out into cool air and then we were falling. Falling for so long. What felt like an eternity and then we came to a screeching, bone-rattling halt in water that froze instantly on contact with Maebe's magic.

"We need to get out of here." I cast Life Sense, a large blip of crimson red appeared over top of us, even as Bokaj muttered those words.

Pebble sank into the ground and popped out again. "North, forty feet then down at a slight angle. Go!"

He was gone again, and we ran, the ball of ice and shadows spinning around us like a hamster wheel.

"What the hell was that thing?" Muu gasped as a slithering sound crashed into existence around us. I could just make out a large tentacle.

"The mother of whatever we killed?" Yohsuke guessed. "Less jabber-jawing and more hustle!"

As soon as we reached the wall, ten feet of stone peeled aside thanks to Fainnir, and I began to work the next. We alternated as we went, Maebe and the others fighting to cover our escape.

"Fuck this place!" Jaken roared, an almost blinding light flashed against the stone ahead of us as he sent some kind of spell at the creature.

"Move, move, move!" The words left me in a rush as I forced the others to pass me.

A somewhat bleeding and mangled tentacle came close to grasping me, but I managed to dismiss the section of stone it entered and crushed it. The creature screeching in pain and outrage that prey had escaped.

"We need to move, air won't last," my warning made me break out in a sweat. I hated confined spaces like this. Claustrophobia has plagued me my whole life, and here I was, under thousands of tons of earth and stone.

"Zeke, chill, you're hyperventilating." Yohsuke's voice sounded so far away.

Maebe's cool hand found mine and dragged me closer to reality. Fainnir had lengthened our escape route significantly in our time away, so I did the next section. On we went for another ten minutes, the air growing more and more humid and uncomfortable. Dots swam in my vision, and I was worried we wouldn't make it when Fainnir broke through into fresh air. Well, oxygenated air at least.

The sudden rush of oxygen into our bodies was almost like getting a buzz. It felt good, but suddenly the room spun, and all I could think of was resting.

How were we supposed to fight the minions and generals of War, if the dungeons and nature gave us such a huge problem?

"None." James panted, caught his breath a bit, and continued haltingly, "Of that... was in... my books."

"They probably didn't survive," Balmur grumbled, and he was decidedly less breathless than the rest of us, but he had been held captive by demons and our enemy. Who knew what he had been through?

We needed to rest. Really rest.

"What was it you had in mind, Balmur?" I yawned tiredly. My mana was recovering quickly enough, and if it would help, it would be worth the mana headache.

He handed me a small item made of platinum that had been hammered into a round shape with a beautifully cut diamond set inside, kind of like a doorknob with a lock at the center. There was an engraving already set into it. Complex lines and symbols with what looked like simple and compli- cated-looking runes in different places.

It was foreign, and yet everything I thought enchanting could be. What with the level of complication I had expected from all my gaming and reading this looked to be exactly what I had expected to learn my first day training to enchant things.

"What the hell is this?" I looked over it some more, but I couldn't figure out what it was supposed to do.

"It's a component necessary for a spell I learned." He took me through the different symbols and runes. "These are spatial glyphs designed to create, maintain, and control an extra- dimensional space. These lines are the dimension limiters and boundaries, and then the diamond acts as the focal point and 'locking mechanism' for the doorway. I didn't have time to finish it until a little bit ago before we turned out to be in a creature's stomach."

"Damn, Balmur, that's in-depth." I raised my eyebrows and whistled at his explanation. "What do you need me to do?"

"I need you to add a component that you are familiar with to give it structure inside, and to feed it the proper amount of mana." Balmur clapped. "Otherwise, the rest is up to you. I don't know much about enchanting really, but Nic said that if I give it to an enchanter, they would know what to do."

"I mean, in theory, I do." I scratched my head; I didn't really want to bother the other enchanters. "I can give it a shot, sure. If it doesn't work, I'll just repay you for the components."

He just nodded and sat back before I waved him closer. "I'll need you to tell me about the spell. It'll help me with my intent and will."

"Well, that doorknob will open the way for us to enter an extra-dimensional space. The inside will be pretty much whatever we need. If I were to add more components to it, I could make it nicer, and I might eventually, but I think for now, being out of here would suffice."

It was hard to argue with that logic. I gave the item another once over, handing Balmur a mana potion to feed me if I needed it, then closed my eyes.

The engravings were there. The intent was there as well, I just had to tell my mana what I wanted it to do. I took out a small sack of my desired component and kept focusing. I wanted this item to open the door to whatever spell Balmur had in mind. Keeping that in mind, I fed mana into the item, ensuring that each of the runes, symbols, and border lines were filled as much as was needed. A little over halfway through, I dipped into Mage's Well as I sprinkled the fairy iron dust over the item. A hundred mana and closing in on the end, I tilted my head back and opened my mouth.

Balmur poured the mana potion into my mouth. I held the position. Another potion. Both of them had given me about 50 MP each and I still needed more. Another potion. Another. Finally, it was done. Jesus.

Maybe it was time to up my intelligence again?

"Here you go, man. And sorry about using your potions." I grumbled and rubbed my aching head.

"It's going to be worth it; I think. Let's give it a try." He looked out into the yawning darkness beneath us. "Looks like the floor is a good ten stories down. Think we could figure out a way down there?"

Maebe stepped forward, her shadows surrounding us all, and I felt a shift in the world around me, and then we stopped. She glanced at Balmur and nodded once. "Do what you must. I must rest soon."

I stepped over to her, pulling her against me so that she could begin to wind down. Her body felt feverish almost. Cold and hot all at once. Her skin clammy and moist. What the hell was going on?

Balmur looked wildly around the large cavern we had appeared in and finally found a stone wall. He pressed the doorknob into the stone and turned it like one might open a door, and a seam appeared in the stone, large enough for people to walk through.

"Come on!" He called back excitedly and whipped open the door, warm light spilling into the space before us all.

I didn't need to be told twice. I had lifted Maebe up into my arms so that I could carry her inside almost as soon as the door opened. She felt so faint against me, and she didn't struggle.

The inside of the spell was simple, almost like a home with an unfinished interior made of green walls. Couches and cushions sat around low tables made of wood a shade of brown so deep, they looked black.

As soon as Balmur was through the door, he shut it, and it sealed shut with the knob on the inside, he then spoke out loud, "I require enough rooms for all present, fully furnished, and customizable to the individuals' needs within reason for the spell."

The rest of us blinked at him, thinking, 'what the—'then it happened. A small pop like a balloon exploding, and doors appeared around the room. Enough for each of us to have our own, but Maebe and I would be sharing. I needed to take care of her.

I rushed her into the room closest to us on the right, having to actually open the door with the handle because I didn't want to just break in the door. The room had been fully furnished with a single person bed, a small nightstand, and a pot for the business.

"I need a larger bed, with the moon and stars above us." It was wishful thinking, but I had to try.

The bed grew larger until I felt it was good, and the room seemed to just *know* when I wanted it to stop. Pillows appeared on it to make up for the space and a down comforter. I lay Maebe on it, pulling the blanket back and putting her underneath.

I had been about to call for Jaken when a popping sound caught my attention, and a tap on my door grabbed my attention. I turned to find the paladin standing in the doorway. "Let me take a look at her."

I nodded and stood aside as he went through the process of checking her out. To do so, he had to pull the blanket back and look her over. He lifted her arms, her hair, and even her shirt. I knew that this was all professional, and I wanted to help how I could, so I stayed quiet.

"Found it." He pulled her boot off and took out a knife, cutting her breeches away so that he could get to her left leg.

He lifted it, and she didn't even so much as wince, she was so delirious with fever.

"Can we get some cool water and towels in here?" Jaken called. Another popping sound, and a matronly woman in green bustled into the room, her features almost unfinished, but she carried a bucket of water and linens for us to use. She patted Jaken on the shoulder to let him know she was there, then he grabbed the linens and soaked them in the water before cleaning Maebe's forehead and leaving a cool one in place to help the fever.

"I don't know what the hell this is, but it looks bad." Jaken swore under his breath. "We need to get whatever the hell that is, out of her."

I looked at where he pointed and to what could have easily been a gash in her leg, except for the small tentacles wriggling outside and just beneath the skin.

I held Purify for as long as I could, using Vulpine Cunning to halve the cost of the spell and blasted the parasite with it. I thought it moved a little slower, but it didn't stop.

"Do we call for divine intervention here?" I asked, worry edging my voice.

"Do we risk it?" Jaken scratched his head. "Yeah sure, they could possibly heal it, or they could be warriors who answer and just amputate her leg, and we would be stuck with the aftermath of that."

Fuck. That left me with little choice. We needed an actual healer. Someone possibly loyal to Maebe, who could help her. Cost be damned.

Time to use the Calling. "Jaken, thank you, buddy. I appreciate you being so ready to help. I need you to step out for a moment."

He eyed me as if I were daft for a moment before he nodded, "You call me if you need me. I'll be up."

I watched him go, and he shut the door softly behind him. I waited until my mana was full once more before I uttered under my breath, "Milnolian."

This time, it only took all of my mana and 300 MP from Mage's Well before his voice greeted me. "Majesty."

"I'm sorry Servant, but I don't have time for niceties."

His eyes flitted to Maebe's sweating form on the bed and then flicked back to me, the golden slits narrowing.

"What would you have of me?" His form, that of a large black cat blurred, and a handsome elven man made of pure darkness stood before me.

"I need you to go to the Fae Realm and bring me the strongest healer the Unseelie have." The golden eyes widened significantly.

"And what price are you willing to pay?" Servant's voice was almost too quiet.

"I don't know, but I know that I need to be careful." I growled and shut my eyes. "Bring them to me, by order of the King, and they can barter with me themselves."

"As you wish, your Majesty." The elven form bowed and stepped back, fading from sight.

There I waited, doing my best to take care of Maebe how I

could for more than half an hour when I felt a tug on my mana. Then a larger pull. All of my reserves, and then some to the point where my health dropped down to five points and I lay bleeding and foaming from the mouth on the ground.

"You never said he was so weak," a wizened voice spoke to Servant.

"He has had his moments, and not everyone can withstand the price of summoning you even second hand, Ancient One." Servant's smooth voice held an edge of bitterness to it.

"Shut up." An odd warmth covered my skin, and my health bar popped back up almost instantaneously. I had to fight the urge to nap as whatever it was blanketed me in heavy drowsiness. "You need to sleep, young King. Healer's orders."

I was almost out when Servant whispered, "I will watch over her. Rest."

Darkness washed over me, and I could feel that I had one of those, "I can feel myself snoring, but I can't really do anything about it, so I'll just stay napping," naps. You know the kind. After what felt like only ten minutes of that, I woke up refreshed, although my throat felt a little thick from all the snoring.

"Finally, the Bandersnatch awakens," a gruff voice greeted me from a rocking chair next to the bed. "Look alive, young king, we have a bargain to strike."

I sat up, blearily looking around, noting that Servant lay next to Maebe on the bed in his cat form. I looked to the figure in the chair, the blurry person coming into clarity as a medium-sized person with fur covering his body, stubby limbs with a snout like a bear's but not a bear's. I thought I could recall having read about a creature like this once, but the name eluded me.

"What would you have of me, other than Maebe's life, power, my life, my power, her crown, mine, or anything to do with any of my friends." I finished my spiel and the figure chuckled.

"You were right," the figure said. "He is learning. No, I have no interest in those things. I like having the Lady Darkest as our Queen of the Unseelie, thank you. And rule has never really been of all that much interest to me. No, I want something else."

"No games," I ordered. "Tell me what you want, and I will tell you whether I can give it or no."

The figure smiled, canines flashing. "I want an apprentice. Someone to pass my vast knowledge on to."

"We can probably do that." I frowned, that seemed almost too easy. There had to be a catch, so I voiced my worry. "What's your play, though? What do you get out of it?"

"The passing on of my profession to someone who should prove to be even stronger than those before them, even me." The healer's grin seemed to grow ever wider.

"Why not take your pick then?" I shrugged. "A bunch of children were just taken to the Fae Realm from the Prime. One of them should suffice, right?"

He shook his head. "No, they could not handle my strength. What I want is the ability to choose who I want when the time comes. You can tell the queen when she awakens, she will likely not care. She may worry, certainly, but I have served her line since well before her mother's time as Queen. She knows that I hold the hope of the Unseelie within my old, withered heart."

I glanced over to Servant, who said, "He tells no lies."

"Your services are appreciated, Healer." I stood and moved a bit to work the stiffness out of my joints. The healer watched, unworried while I stretched. "If you mean no ill will, then I don't see the harm in allowing you this boon as payment for saving the ruler of the realm."

"I want your word," he stated icily. "I know you to be Fae enough that your word holds weight. Swear it so as King, and I will tell you more of what ailed our Queen and how best to assist her further."

"I, as King of the Unseelie Fae, swear that when the time comes for you to choose a successor, you may choose who you please so long as it is in the best interests of the Unseelie Court and will not be a detriment to the realm or my Queen." I grinned, noting the marked look of recognition in his eyes.

A weight settled over my chest, but no notification came to me. Weird. Then the weight was gone, and a slow grin spread over the healer's face once more.

"It is done, then. Thank you, Majesty." He stood and pulled out a jar filled with a slithering mass of tentacles and spines near the base of each of them. "This was inside her, poisoning her, and siphoning away her strength and magic. It will take her time to recover all of her strength, but it was before the point where she could have lost any levels, so she was blessed you caught it before then."

"And how do I assist her further?" I raised an eyebrow as I turned my attention to Maebe, where she meditated in the bed, almost like she was asleep.

"Short of allowing her to return home for a time, longer periods inside this space will assist her. It's not quite the Fae Realm, but it is partially of it thanks to the metal, and it doesn't have the...*ordered* nature of the Prime Realm." He blinked up at me, his weird, furry face taking on a look of disgust at the word, then shook his head. "This place will help until she can go home. Use it often."

He walked toward the edge of the room where the wall met the floor before turning back, "Your friends came for you, and I looked them over. None of them were affected by this thing, but know that there could be more. If you want to get it out of them, or anyone else for that matter, you must cut it out, then purify the wound with fire. It can latch onto you, but it cannot burrow without an opening. Something cut her leg so that it could get in."

I took the news stoically, trying not to let my worries and fears gather on my face. "Thank you, Healer."

"Do not call on me again unless she is dying, and even then, be prepared for a steep price—my King." The creature faded from sight, the cold black eyes seeming to linger even as the rest was gone.

"I despise that old fool," Servant grumbled, making me look at him. "I have known him far too long, and you did well to control things the way you did, though it may have seemed a little inevitable that he would get his way."

"Thank you," I replied simply, taking the healer's spot in the rocking chair.

"You may call on me more, my King," Milnolian offered, and when I looked at him, his teeth shone in the sparse light of the room. "I will not take as much from you knowing that you mean well and that you can be trusted. It is not a full trust yet. I may never see you as I do my Queen, but I like you."

"Look at the two of you getting along," Maebe observed softly. Her green eyes stared straight ahead. "What was the price of my good health?"

"An apprentice of his choice, your Majesty," The panther answered before I could. "The King did well in your stead. Not quite so good as you, but passable."

"I think I'll take that back-handed compliment, Servant." A wry grin graced my lips, and my hand found Maebe's. "How do you feel, my love?"

She turned her head, her normally deep-black skin looking clammy and thin somehow. "Like shit."

"You kiss me with that mouth?" I raised an eyebrow at her playfully, and she didn't quite seem to get it. "I'm teasing. Hold still."

I went through the process of casting every healing spell in my arsenal on her as I pulled shadows from all around us over her like an umbrella. Regrowth, Mass Regrowth, Renewing Flames, Void's Respite, and Heal. My mana took a hit, but it was okay. She breathed a little easier, and she rested more comfortably where she lay back in the bed.

Finally, I called to Jaken through our earrings, *Hey, she's doing a lot better, but we need to keep an eye out for those little parasites.*

We know, the brownie told us. He responded sleepily. *All of us will be trying to get some sleep, and then planning when we wake up. I suggest you take advantage.*

"So, he was a brownie?" I wondered aloud as I turned back to Maebe. "I admit, I don't know much about them."

Servant opened an eye and rolled it toward me, the golden slit widening slightly. "Generally helpful creatures who usually enjoy cleaning, but his power makes him much more astute and less content to simply clean."

"What is his power?" My heart beat a little less steadily, wondering what fate I had just consigned someone to.

Maebe responded, "No one knows. But he is the strongest healer I have ever known. And he's dangerous."

"I gathered as much if he could make me sleep the way he did." I rubbed my head, suddenly exhausted once more. I looked longingly at the bed. "You feeling up to company?"

"Always." Her soft smile was comforting. I disrobed and passed shadows over my body, then stopped cold. A shiver ran down my back like something was looking for me. I glanced back, finding nothing.

"What is wrong?" Servant asked, his head suddenly up and on the alert, nostrils flaring.

"I keep feeling something as if it's trying to get my attention, but I can't quite place it." It was starting to freak me out, which was making me angry.

I am not certain what it is, but it is time, friend Zeke. Gorumbal interrupted the bitterness in my heart at my inability to figure out what was going on.

I sighed, but a smile spread across my face as I responded out loud, "Thank you, Gorumbal, for allowing me to sample your strength and giving us the hope we needed to get out of that dungeon."

His rumbling presence eased on my mind, an avalanche-like sound of crashing, skittered through my being, and my body grew heavier. *My children and I expected great things—we were not displeased. How did you say it? A sample was what you had, and you used it well. If you can resolve this quest for us, that power is yours. Good luck, friend Zeke.*

His presence left, and I felt alone before Servant stood next to me, his elven form surprising me, but his arm around my body helped me to stay on my feet.

"Your scent has changed." His features looked puzzled. This close, he was handsome, but the features seemed a little fuzzy. "You no longer smell like freshly tilled earth."

"What do I shmell like now?" The world swam a bit, and I leaned a little more heavily on him.

"Like a bonfire on a crisp moonlit night, the moon shining in the sky." I blinked at his answer, and he tilted his head. "The night and scent of ash make sense to you, yes?"

"You're fuzzy." My eyelids could have been tied to millstones for all I knew at that moment.

Weightlessness, then warmth and the scent of cool night air. Hands on my skin and gentle whispers of affection spoken against my forehead.

———

I woke up to find Servant sleeping on the floor in front of the doorway, and Maebe watching me with a small smile on her lips. She looked much better than she had before. Her normally immaculate colorful hair a bit mussed from the night.

"How are you feeling?" I brushed a finger through her hair, sweeping it behind her long right ear.

"Well, since the last time that you asked me, I feel much better." Her smile shifted into a grin at my confusion. "You asked me any time I moved, though I don't think you recall it, do you?"

"I don't." I stretched, the aching of my muscles finally abating a bit. I stood and stretched some more, bending and sweeping to and fro to adjust my bones and muscles further. "Thank you for watching over us, Servant."

"Well, when someone tosses and turns as much as you do,

my King, it seems appropriate, though tiring." His baleful eyes shifted to Maebe. "How you deal with that, Majesty is beyond me. But you made your choice."

"How long do you plan to stay?" She asked, likely choosing to ignore his sass.

He stood and stretched himself out, wicked claws extending from his front paws. "I will return home. And remember, my King, you can summon me at any time. I will not tax your strength so much anymore."

Before I could say anything, his body faded from the room.

"I am glad to see that he likes you." I could hear the contentment in Maebe's voice. "While you slept, he told me everything. Thank you."

"You're my wife, Mae." I turned to see her standing, stepping closer to me. "It's my duty to protect you, not just as your husband and someone who loves you, but for our people."

She paused. "I do so love when you call them our people."

"Well, they are." My palms massaged my temples, my stomach roaring at me angrily. "Let's go get something to eat before my stomach decides to really riot."

"Let us." Her small hand wound its way into mine and tugged me back before I could reach the door. "You should dress first."

I blinked at her, then looked down. Yup. I was naked. Thank the gods for her. As I pulled my clothes on, I had to ask, "Was what I did okay?"

"The old man can be trusted in the manner that a tree can." She sighed, seeming a little worried. "He thinks of the long game, longer even than most true immortals. His strength is unfathomable, and his is a might that my mother and I are grateful to have among the Unseelie. An apprentice to one so strong would not be an unwelcome thing, especially if they prove to be as loyal as he is and less fickle about the use of his powers."

That put me a little more at ease as I pulled my shirt over my head and laced my boots.

We dressed for travel underground in dark clothes meant to help us blend in a little, then stepped out into the common area. For once, we seemed to be the first ones there.

Then Yoh's door opened, and the scent of cooking food wafted out, his pleasant smile was a nice surprise though. "Dude, I have a stove. This shit is awesome."

I laughed and thought of a table. The one in the center of the room elongating on its own and stopping when it was done, having grown until we could all sit on the cushioned chairs that a green man in a butler outfit brought out and set up silently.

"Those guys can be a little creepy, but they're a part of the spell, so no worries." Balmur joined us in the room, his cloak hiding the rest of his body from view. "I'm glad you're feeling better, Maebe."

She smiled and nodded in return. The others came out as they would, Muu bringing up the rear of the pack looking refreshed but tired. We ate breakfast, all kinds of eggs, toast, bacon, and some chorizo. Amazing. Maebe loved the chorizo and ended up snagging some from my plate when I wasn't looking.

Bea and Kayda ate off in another room with Tmont, the sounds of Bea and Kayda planning a coup were adorable. No, no, you heard me right. I could feel through our connections that the two of them were plotting on me. They wanted me to give one of them that crystal that Bea had alerted me to. Tmont seemed less interested, something about her not needing to really change any more than she had already to prove that she was worthy of Bokaj.

Let them plot. I can take it.

"So, do we know where we're going?" Yosuke asked softly once most of us had finished eating. The servants had come to take most of our plates so they could be cleaned and brought all of us fresh water.

"Not really." James sighed, his book came out of his inventory, and I found myself eyeing it critically. Seemed normal. "It's not like the drow are going to advertise themselves. They're perfectly adapted to living down here in this area. Their cities and everything will be perfectly hidden and well protected.

"Then how do we find them?" Bokaj smacked the table, making Fainnir jump. "Sorry, man."

"We can have Pebble look," Fainnir offered with what seemed like little hope that anyone would take it seriously.

"Can he look that far quickly?" Muu asked, still shoveling food into his face.

"He can go pretty far, looking for signs of life and stuff." The young dwarf shrugged. "I know that the stone in this area isn't all that good for mining and that they would likely set up their cities in an area of the Great Below with a high concentration of water and good metal veins."

A few of us nodded, Jaken breaking the silence, "That's so astute, and we can train on our way there."

"Let's make that happen, then." Balmur clapped his hands. "We have a few more hours in here before the spell fades. Let's try and devise a way to make this happen in the easiest way possible."

"Sounds good." I stood from the table and walked toward our room, I needed to think something through. Something about what Servant had said was bothering me, then I realized something, "How long have we been in here?"

"Roughly sixteen hours, give or take an hour." Balmur looked over the room. "It'll last up to twenty-four hours depending on how much we manipulate the inside. Then it takes about eight or so hours to cooldown. Again, based on our consumption."

I nodded and walked toward our room once more with Maebe joining me, quiet at first as I sat in the center of the room on the floor and closed my eyes. Finally, as I went through my third breathing cycle, she spoke, "What is it that you mean to do?"

I let myself drift back to where I could answer her, "I smell like a bonfire at night under the bright moon and stars. Servant had said something to that effect to me. And I can't help but wonder what it means. Thinking about the powers I have at my disposal; I can tinker with fire and shadows. Servant said, 'when he first got here, I smelled of freshly tilled earth'—what if he could smell the elemental blessings on me?"

"Then, his nose is much stronger than I have given it credit for in the past." I could hear a thoughtful tone in her voice. "But why does this seem to concern you so?"

"Because the 'under bright moon and stars' bit doesn't belong. I can't tinker with light." My confusion continued to make me rise to the surface of my mediation, so I took a moment to relax and try to center myself until I could continue. "I've spoken to each of the other elements, but never this one. I think I should try."

"Good luck," she said softly, and I breathed myself into a state of calm and inner focus.

I was deeper, I think than I had been when I reached out to the elements with Elder Leo before in the monastery. But I focused anyway.

Warmth radiating from the sun as rays of light shone into my back yard, where I happily read a book. The light playing in the breeze, dodging the branches and boughs of the trees at the park where I played. The bright spot reflecting off the water below me when I had flown with squadrons of Marines over the oceans off the Californian coast. Lightning shattering the sky, brightening the clouds during a storm, and the small beam of brilliance in my hand as a kid, using a flashlight to navigate the darkness.

I had known light my whole life. It allowed me to see. It kept us warm and, at times, gave us a sense of security. It played tricks on the blacktop and in the deserts and even more wild, if focused, it could destroy things.

Inside my mind's eye, a small ball of dull gray light pulsed with my heartbeat. The more examples of light I saw, experienced, and reasoned with, the brighter and stronger the light became until it was uncomfortably bright.

At last. Warmth flooded me, and the light dulled until a

single mote of it floated in the darkness of my mind. The light whispering voice sounded equally surprised and frustrated.

"I'm sorry I didn't know that I needed to reach out." I felt a little more bashful than sarcastic. This touch against my being felt familiar. The times I seemed to just miraculously know danger was imminent, this sensation was it. It had been the Light's touch.

You are so used to the Elemental Primordials coming to you with their issues, or you to them, now, that you neglected to properly connect with me. Her voice paused. *I am not angry, I am relieved. You are close. I am not at full strength down here, but you are closer to the place you seek than you know. I know your task, and I know that you must be careful. Do not fade, new light.*

Her presence was gone instantly, and I opened my eyes as a burning itch took over my chest where my tattoo was with all the elemental blessings, then it spread to the rest of my body. I turned my face down, then to my arms as the flecks of white all over my fur changed hue from straight white to a more golden hue.

"Well, damn." I unbuttoned my shirt and saw that the formerly white ink that had made up the mostly finished pentagram on my pec was now golden-white as well.

"That is different." Maebe knelt down next to me and ran her hand over my fur. "You feel warmer than usual as well…as if you've been in the sunlight."

That seemed to make sense, though such a huge outward change had not been expected.

"Is it bad?" I raised my eyebrows and glanced at her nervously.

"No. Now, as you had been before and continue to be, you are almost my opposite. I am the Dark and Cold, you are the Light and Warmth." Her eyes lit up mischievously. "Something like this would not change my feelings toward you, my love."

"Thank you." She leaned back as the words left my lips. "For loving me."

"Thank you for being the only person I felt I could for the

longest time." Her nose crinkled as she kissed me, I took my human form to make it a little more convenient, and she observed my skin some more. "You really are hot, Zeke."

George Takei, take us out, buddy.

"Oh my."

CHAPTER TWENTY

Pebble scouted ahead for the second time that day. It had taken him the better part of four hours searching after we had left Balmur's Happy Home spell. He had named it that because it was supposed to keep us happy while inside.

When he came back, he pointed us south of our current position, so on we moved from there, carefully moving through the darkness without light. It was annoying, but it had to be done because who knew what could be hunting naive creatures that needed light down here.

"Fainnir, I wanted to let you know that you're the only one with earth magic right now unless I shapeshift into an earth elemental. Okay?" he looked stricken, so I waved off his concern. "Don't worry, I'm not in trouble or anything, but I had to uphold my bargain. I'll still be able to lead you through making spells. Okay?"

"Alright." He scratched his head in thought. "How come ye look so different?"

"I partnered with another Primordial Elemental, and she gave me a makeover." A wry grin spread on my face at my own humor. I was getting used to it.

"I see." He held his own hand up and admired the metals that banded and flowed around his own flesh. "I like it."

I ruffled his hair, noting that he seemed to be looking a little scruffier in the beard department with a few more hairs sprouting on his chin.

We walked in relative silence to avoid detection, but the entire time we moved, I had Fainnir pushing his awareness into the ground around us. We were trying to see what he could sense and using Pebble to verify if he was doing it or not. He was right on what was around us about a fourth of the time now and that he was able to keep his awareness in the earth on the move was impressive.

I found myself reaching into the void around us with my own awareness. The shadows here felt so much denser than I'd ever felt anywhere other than when training with Maebe. I focused myself and pulled everything in the area toward us, spinning it around above us, the miasma of shadows giving us cover from anything that could be watching from above. Even with so much room above us, I began to sweat with the knowledge that the flesh of the planet was so far above us. All that weight ready to crash down at any time.

I closed my eyes for a moment and decided to soldier on regardless. My friends needed me here with them, not worried about something that might not happen. It was hard work, the mana drain steady enough that I could only manage it for ten minutes before I had to stop.

"That is a good idea, but maybe you limit it to a single location and a thick surface that you keep fixed to a point?" Maebe suggested helpfully.

I waited until my mana was good while Balmur and Yohsuke took turns doing the same with the shadows. Their control varied, but it was good to see how each of them managed the strain. Yohsuke dealt with a lot of power, and his control needed to be fine-tuned to handle the demonic nature of some of his powers, otherwise, they could consume him.

Balmur just had a love of magic that made his control something fun and compelling, and his ability to work on things like that was nothing short of inspiring.

Once it was my turn again, I focused on doing the work without the use of my hands. It was harder, sure, but it was an interesting way of trying to manage my magic's impact on the world around me.

Muu worked with Fainnir on refining his body positioning when we rested for the evening inside the Happy Home. They worked through motions like chopping, deflecting, parrying, and slicing foes down. Fainnir had been so excited to be doing well, that he had accidentally walloped the helpful fighter in the head with the side of his axe at a kind word.

"That was no axe-ident," Muu grumbled as he walked away, rubbing the side of his head.

"He should've whacked you harder for that attempt at a pun." Jaken grinned at Muu and cast a healing spell on him.

"No one axed you," the fighter grinned, the rest of us groaning at his sense of humor.

"Fainnir, two hundred chops, then two hundred slices—horizontal and diagonal—while you cast your Earth Shard with the other hand." Fainnir looked both excited and a little afraid at the same time when I issued my orders. "You run out of mana, you swing harder, understand?"

"For his crimes against our brains, Muu can join him and correct his form." Yohsuke grinned at the cursing dragon-kin. "Hey, someone's head had to be on the chopping block."

Balmur and James both guffawed at the joke while I rolled my eyes. We had another day or two at a good clip before we would reach what Pebble assured us was civilized space. How civilized, we would see, but for now, we had a heading, and that was better than nothing.

The tunnels we worked our way through currently had been burrowed wide, at least as wide as a four-lane highway. Enough so that the chimera we'd fought would fit comfortably standing.

We hadn't found any life forms in our time here, strangely. I had expected the Great Below to be teeming with monsters and things that preyed on the sightless in the heavy shadows and rocky caverns.

Is anyone else slightly alarmed that we haven't found any creatures that go bump in the dark? Bokaj whispered through our minds, as though something out there might hear him.

I glanced at the others, well, in the direction I knew them to be thanks to my almost constant casting of Life Sense. The more familiar I was with the spell, the more I could glean from my surroundings. It was still really hard to see, but Pebble gave us directions as we went to keep us out of danger as best as he could.

Yeah, a little, but that's to be expected. After the shit we went through to get here, relaxing can be a little hard, James responded though he sounded a little more wary about the situation than he seemed to want to let on.

"There is something up ahead," Pebble stated softly. "I can feel the change in the earth and stone. I am unfamiliar with this."

That's no good, I thought to myself, but whispered, "We go cautious and slow. Heads on a swivel."

Our path went on for another mile or so, then around a bend in the stoney cavern wall came a dull light off in the distance.

"Think tha' be it?" Fainnir's harsh whisper almost made me jump out of my skin.

"Not so loud!" Yohsuke said in a soft hiss, authority dripping from his tone. "I'm not sure. Drow don't need light to see in the darkness. They see in a sort of infrared vision that lets them view heat signatures if what James had learned about them is true."

That tracked with what I knew at home, though things had been different in small ways here before, so it wouldn't surprise me if our intel was wrong.

From there on, we relied solely on hand and arm signals to communicate with Fainnir thanks to his dwarven heritage lending him almost perfect sight in our current locale, and our earrings with each other. We approached the light cautiously, but as we did, heat began to build in the area with the growing dim glow.

Lava flows carved through the earthen ground in lazy, molten rivers flowing over the side of a cliff face that could have gone to the center of Brindolla for all I knew. The heat was ridiculous in the room, almost rivaling the hells, and being this close made all of us a little uncomfortable except for Balmur.

We could clearly see the other side of the room. Our destination looked to be a large opening in the far wall leading into a dimly lit space, but there appeared to be multiple exits and entrances to the room.

"Straight ahead but be cautious." It was difficult to tell what sort of emotion—if any—the little creature felt with his almost-blank face, but Pebble's warning seemed to be deeply ingrained in him. "What could be solid stone one moment, can be magma the next. I do not know much else, other than earth elementals should stay clear of lava and volcanoes, so I will be leaving you to navigate this place at your risk."

Fainnir nodded, understanding and Pebble tapped him on the shoulder. "Be safe." Then sank into the ground.

"How do we wanna do this?" Muu voice nervously quavered, his eyes sliding along the different lava paths while the rest of us thought.

"I can turn into a flame elemental and just cross." I shrugged. "Not to mention, I still have the blessings from when I still had Coal. Fire isn't all that bad to me anymore. If you want to follow me with the Mobile Spring Rod and let us try to stay close together, that's fine."

"Why don't we just have Maebe freeze the lava? Or zip us across with her shadow magic?" Bokaj seemed confused.

"Because she just got over being bodily invaded by a parasite that put her damned near out of commission and the last time we met with another Elven Queen, she had to fight them." Yohsuke explained in a biting tone. "We need to try and figure shit out without relying on her too much. I love having her here, and all, as annoying as her and Zeke can be together, but she's not gonna fix shit for us. We can do this."

The others nodded, Jaken stepped over and frowned. "Give me the rod."

I smacked Muu as his head lifted quickly. "Cool it, you fifth-grade class clown."

He grumbled angrily and threw his hands up.

I passed Jaken the rod, and the heat died down to a much more manageable level. "Let's go. All of you stay near me, and we will see if we can make it across in one piece. Zeke, save your elemental form for now."

I gave him a thumbs up, and we cautiously made our way forward. The first quarter of the way into the room was alright. The ground beneath us was more solid than not, and we only had to dodge a building bubble of liquid magma a couple times.

When we reached the center of the room, it was as if the heat was magnified twenty-fold. Sweat poured from each of us, even with the rod, and every step taxed us more and more.

In the center, something in me cracked, and I whipped my head to Jaken. "Throw the rod away, *now!*"

Jaken didn't hesitate and tossed it away from him. Unfortunately, he had thrown it straight ahead so he could pull his shield up in time to take the damage. *Boom!* The rod itself exploded, the gem at the top of it had been overpowered by the heat in here and had turned it into a bomb.

"We got company!" Bokaj almost shouted.

I turned to our left and rear, finding more than a dozen large, bat-like creatures flapping into the room and looking in our direction.

We gotta go! James's panicked voice flooded our heads.

The way forward is straight fucking lava, man! Yohsuke shot back. *We need to go around.*

No, we don't. Thinking quickly, I offered a suggestion. *We gotta move fast. All three of us are going to pull the shadows to us and form a walkway above the lava to make a break for it.*

They didn't have time to argue, a ringing in our ears almost made my knees buckle, Muu's arm flashed, and the ringing stopped. "Now!"

Balmur, Yoh, and I held out our arms and tore the shadows from everywhere around us, my reach farther than theirs only because I was so used to doing this. We pressed and compounded the void energy into a bridge and planted it over the lava before anchoring it to the stone on the other side. It had cost me 603 MP to do so, but it looked sturdy, and we were out of time.

"Go!" I snatched up Fainnir together with Muu, and we hauled him to safety, sprinting over the naked river of bubbling, angry-looking lava below us. A sizzling globule of the magma splattered against my metallic arm where it met my flesh, and even with the fire resistance I naturally had, thanks to Heart Flame, it still burnt like a motherfucker.

"They're closing in!" Bokaj warned, the whistling of arrows piercing the air behind me punctuation to his warning.

"Keep running!" Yoh shouted, tossing a ball of black and gray energy into the air behind us, another explosion five seconds after that blew our hearing a bit, but another screech of pain brought a grim smile to my face.

Fifty feet closer to safety. More arrows flew from Bokaj's bow.

Forty feet, the heat still hadn't abated, and spots grew in my vision from the heat and exertion acting against me.

Thirty feet, the same ringing that had almost felled us earlier tore into my ears, making me stumble, so I let go of Fainnir as I fell. I felt fingers on my clothes, then heard a curse, tearing and another screech. I tried to force myself forward over the lava as far out as I could and shifted into my fire elemental form just as my body should have struck the lava.

The lava pressed against the flames that my body consisted of like water might against my real body. Focusing, I forced myself above the lava, mana trickling from my MP bar as I glided across it. One of the creatures strayed too close to me, so I reached out and grasped its wing, dragging it into the lava.

Vampire Bat level 35

Its health shot down as it struggled, my strength clearly higher than its, the screeching noise not affecting me as much since I didn't really have eardrums for the sound to reverberate off of. It struggled mightily, but I forced it under the lava, killing it and moving toward my friends. They'd made it to the other side of the room and fought the four remaining creatures.

One of them had arrows sprouting from its chest from Bokaj, and Balmur had his holy daggers out and had somehow managed to climb onto one's back. He drove a dagger into the throat, the gurgling growl sending flecks of blood everywhere, then dug a trench of gore down another's back and wing, before another of the creatures swooped down, grabbed him by the throat and lifted him off.

The injured bat flew headfirst into Jaken's shield, Righteous Brand flashing in the glow of the lava and beheading the creature. Another managed to flank Yohsuke and pulled him into the air as he swiped and snarled at the bastard. I saw the creature's head dip the same time Yoh's flesh turned an angry red color, his Infernal Body spell activating in a flash of light.

The vampire bat's head shook, and Yohsuke roared in anger before Kayda touched the creature and froze it solid, before enlarging enough to take him to safety.

I caught the ledge of an embankment next to the lava river they battled over and watched in horror as more motion came into the cave we had been heading toward.

Arrows crossed the distance, eaten by shadows, and clattering against Jaken and Muu's armor.

Drow elves had arrived in all-black attire, silken-looking threads covering their bodies, no doubt made of spider silk.

"We have come to speak with your Queen," Maebe called to them, their forward motion unceasing.

Two of the bats were left, one of them struggling to try and make off with Fainnir, but the dwarf had summoned Grav, who had him in his massive arms as the vampire bats flapped toward the lava.

Fainnir's axe sliced out and slid through a wing, then he cast Earth Shard and pierced its eye with a gout of black ichor that splattered the ground and Fainnir's clothes.

The other bat went toward the fallen Yohsuke, his health just under 70%, lifting him away from his weapon and digging its claws into his body. It made to fly off with a triumphant hiss, an arrow striking it but doing little. Then, Yoh's fist slammed into its mouth, and both hands clamped it shut.

Thwumph! Its head exploded in a shower of gray matter with enough concussive force that Yohsuke plummeted toward the lava, nuking more than a quarter of his health in the process.

Kayda! I howled at myself, uncertain if my elemental mind would be able to get my desire for her to catch him across to her.

A blur of green soared through the air, Muu reaching out and catching Yohsuke with enough force that his momentum carried them upward. Wings of almost solid green venom spread from his shoulders and fanned out, using the heat from the magma below to glide toward us. Jaken sent his shield out to meet the two of them, and Muu bounced off it to safely land next to me.

I dropped my flame elemental form instantly, and cast Void's Respite as the others poured healing spells into him. They didn't seem to be doing the best on him, but he was no longer at less than half health.

He was covered in blood and gore; Infernal Body having worn off. It was all over him, wet and black liquid and bits on his face, in his hair. And he was unconscious, blood coagulating on his neck still, after having been bitten.

"Muu, stand guard over him, we need to speak to these guys." I nodded to him as I passed him where he stood in front of where Yoh lay on the ground.

Maebe had stepped forward, and I joined her, the others falling back behind us except for Fainnir. The young dwarf stood at my left with his axe drawn and a look of pure, unadulterated hatred devouring his features.

"Fainnir, you're family to me, buddy." I turned so that only he would hear me as I whispered the rest, "But if you fuck this up because you think you can take them, I will beat your ass myself once all of them are dead. Calm down."

To his credit, he took a deep breath, like he had when we began meditating, and slowly let it go. He stepped back with the others and Balmur stepped up next to me, tapping his ears.

I cast Languages, so I can understand them and translate for you. I nodded once to him at his explanation and then looked to our guests. Or were we theirs?

They motioned to each other with their hands, complicated series of flashes that reminded me of sign language, but the intensity of the conversation and the complexity of it eluded me to no end. I had no clue what was being said—neither did Balmur.

The one who looked to have spoken the least stepped forward, his white hair was cropped short to his head, almost in a military-type fade, with his angular elven features making him look severe as he spoke in an almost inaudible voice. Black eyes watched us from around him, making his blue ones seem out of place.

"He wants to know what we are doing here so close to their tunnels," Balmur translated, the speaker tilted his head, and another drow stepped forward and whispered into his ear.

He motioned for us to continue, pointing from us to the one who spoke to him, then to Balmur. We had a way to communicate.

"We are here to see your ruler," Maebe spoke, and the others looked confused. "I am Queen Maebe of the Unseelie Fae, and this is my husband."

They seemed wary, Maebe took the hint and brought a globe of darkness into one hand, and ice into the other before smiling sweetly.

"Do you dare doubt?" They shook their heads, and the leader spoke again, motioning toward us.

"Your consort and the other male slaves, what of them?"

Balmur frowned at the name, but James sent a telepathic explanation.

Males in their society are seen as lesser because their women are stronger, he tapped a book in his hand. *All the lore in this world and ours points to that being the same.*

"They are my knights. Servants of my will and my court," Maebe explained away with a wave. "They are mine."

"Why would you want to see our Queen?" He motioned to the area around us. "We are far from the Fae, and she rules here. What could you gain?"

"What could she lose by allowing a visiting queen to meet her in her domain, to bask in her glory, and share knowledge?" Balmur offered slyly. "Queen Maebe has come to usher in a new era of prosperity for her people. Maybe that prosperity is shared with your people. But it needs your Queen's support, of course. If you would turn us away, we can leave, and she can decide what to do with you from there."

They didn't really seem fazed until Balmur muttered something in a guttural language that I didn't understand. The one who translated for them stiffened, his eyes wide as he repeated what had been said.

"Stop!" The drow spoke louder as if shouting, Balmur echoing him to us. "If you did well enough to come this far, we will allow you to follow us to our city. What the Queen chooses to do is her choice, but your concubine and the other males should learn their place."

I could feel the anger seeping from the men behind me, but held a hand up to wave it away, *it's their culture guys. They don't mean it necessarily in a bad way. Though we should stick close to each other.*

Why? I could almost hear the audible gulp from Muu.

They may try to take you and add you to their slaves, or worse—their beds. James whispered through our heads. *And trust me, you don't want to end up on one of their ladies' menu.*

"Shit." A groan behind me made me still and I turned to

see Yohsuke sitting up with a hand to his neck. "What the fuck was that?"

"I could ask you the same thing." Balmur looked him over with Jaken. The drow stepped around us to get a better view, their hands flashing to each other. "Those things seemed hell-bent on you, and when they surrounded us, you went down like a sack of potatoes. What the fuck?"

"Some sort of echolocation that they use as an attack?" He grumbled and held his head. "My bell is still fucking ringing."

"He was bitten," Balmur translated for one of the drow, a look of concern on his dwarven features. "Before the bite perverts him and he kills you all, you must end him."

That resonated with me more than a little. "No."

Yohsuke seemed confused, then a look of acceptance passed over his features as he read something, "Got a notification."

We blinked at him and waited, finally he spoke through our earrings, *It says that I can be cured, but that it's hard. And reading some of the stat boosts I'd get, I don't know that turning would be a bad thing.*

What's the downside? Bokaj asked softly. Yohsuke looked at him in askance. *We all know there's a downside. Zeke went furry for a bit, well furrier, and lost his shit a lot before he was able to fully take control and not kill someone. Or at least have us not worry about it. What would yours be?*

He shrugged, then seemed to be reading, *Hunger seems to be the worst of it, knowing that I'm a little resistant to traditional healing magic, and then there's the sunlight. I have less of an allergic reaction to silver than Zeke does, but that's because it's a type of holy metal.*

We can try and find ways around that, I offered. They had tried to do those things for me when I was learning.

"Why are you not killing him?" Balmur angrily translated for the drow once more. They seemed genuinely confused. "He will turn. He will need to feed. Those creatures you fought are just minions, little more than shadows of their master. They are nothing more than cannon fodder and hunters at their master's beck and call."

"Does that mean that he will turn into one of them?" James

tried not to sound like a dick, but I could tell he was ready to scrap.

Balmur waited while the drow conferred with each other, finally deciding to answer. "We don't know. There are others among our kind who would know more, but all know that those bitten feel the call of the one who made them."

I pointed to the rapidly decaying bodies. "The one who made him died. Does that count for anything?"

They shook their heads, the speaker stating, "The bite belongs to the master."

"Well, Zeke was able to kill Pastella and take control of his own line," Maebe began, she leaned down to offer a hand to Yohsuke. "We will do the same for you, my friend."

"We must go," the drow urged, their weapons bared as the others looked around. "We have wasted enough time here as it is, and there are always others."

I pressed my awareness into the darkness that I had seen the ones we'd fought exit from, stretching my shadow thin and calling more to it as it went. There was definitely something there. Many.

"Let's move," I whispered to the others, and we were on our way into the darkness the drow had separated themselves from during our fight.

We moved as fast as we could behind them, their maneuvering in the darkness better even than ours likely would have been in broad daylight on the surface.

It felt like forever moving at their pace, but we kept up as they bounded over rocks, shelves of stone, and around corners. They stopped to let us recover as they could, warily watching their surroundings, their suspicion making me cast Life Sense.

There were blips on the map in my head, the gray ones that matched the drow within the spell's radius. Then, as I pressed my awareness into the shadows around us, I discovered more drow who seemed to be staying more than a hundred feet away around us.

There are more drow around us, I can feel at least twenty, I warned the others.

Balmur tapped the translator for the drow, his smack audible, making all of us stiffen in the near silence around us and pointed to his ear. They both cast their spells, and he mumbled to him. The drow motioned that he should calm down and muttered back.

This is their main hunting party. They were the scouting party sent to check on the noise that had been in the chamber we were in, they keep their distance in hopes that we attract something they can take back to their people.

I rolled my eyes. We spent several more hours moving toward the city before the drow halted us, Balmur told us, "They're stopping to rest. We have eight hours."

I don't think we should use the spell for the night, man. Yohsuke stopped Balmur as he rifled through his inventory. *We can save that as a means to hide if shit goes south. No need for them to know about it.*

It's going to suck, but okay. Good idea. Balmur stretched and pulled out his bedroll, casting his dome so that it surrounded him, Muu and Bokaj. They were our snorers, and the dome would dull the sound a little.

"My lady wife, would you like to create a barrier of shadow to cover all of us?" I glanced her way, and she smiled. The darkness around us came alive, motion everywhere as she funneled it into her body, her skin darkening completely, then a soft thrum of power played along my skin as she pressed that darkness outward in all directions covering not just us, but the elves that had refused to come much closer.

"How is that, my lord husband?" She raised an eyebrow, her green eyes glowing even in the darkness.

"They want to know what that was." Balmur poked his head out of his dome. "I told them it was you making a barrier, but they don't believe that anyone but their Queen has that much control over the darkness."

Several of the drow that had remained hidden came

forward with weapons drawn, looking around angrily. One of them was a woman, and she was physically larger and stronger looking than the males who accompanied her.

The way she strode forward left no doubts about who was in charge, her bare shoulders powerfully muscled, and the small globe of darkness in her palm meant she had access to magic as well. Her broad, severe-looking face was calm, yet somehow still appraising as her eyes wandered over my body. I took it, no need to worry, really.

Drow Hunt Leader Level 40

"Who did this?" She asked, her accent thick, but her attempt to speak the common tongue, not unnoticed.

Maebe stepped forward. "I did."

"This is pretender magic." The drow snarled, her features screwing up.

"You guys gonna get your girl here, or is my wife going to have to stomp her skull in?" I blinked tiredly at the drow, the translator gasping audibly at what I had said before passing the message along to those closest to him. Their weapons pointed my way, and I smiled.

The drowess ignored me, her eyes on Maebe. "This magic is pretender magic, and does not belong in our Queen's domain. Take down."

"If you want your people to be exposed to the cavern we're in, by all means," Maebe snapped her fingers, the click making the drow flinch as the barrier flashed past all of them until only the three of us were in it. "There. But you should know, child."

Maebe stepped closer slowly, her hips swaying with her movements almost as if to provoke the person in front of her. She waited until she stood directly in front of the other woman, then levitated until she was eye to eye with her to speak, "The realm of shadows is *mine.*"

Maebe reached out with her left hand and plucked the soft-ball-sized globe of darkness from the other woman's hand and smirked. "Cute."

The drow leader looked ready to throw a punch, but I

stepped closer. "I wouldn't do that if I were you. I've seen her freeze people for less. And if you hit her, I'll kill you myself. Now, so we can leave this unpleasantness behind, how long have those vampires been around? They recent here?"

She glanced at me, her red irises captivating for a second before she narrowed her eyes. "Males seen, not heard."

She stuck out a hand, and a whip of shadow leapt from it, my awareness tipping me off to the motion as the thing cracked the air in front of my face. I reached up with my own left hand and snatched the darkness from her grasp, making her gasp in outrage.

"Males should not raise hand to woman!" She stalked closer slowly. "Males not to touch the shadows!"

I rolled my eyes at her, Maebe smirked and let the ball of darkness go before spreading the shadow barrier out until all of the drow were inside once more. Maebe pointed to the drow translator and pointed to her side. Her motion left no room for any kind of disobedience.

"You will be my mouthpiece," she explained to him, his hands signing her words to the others. "Your leader has insulted me by accusing me, the Queen of the Dark Frost, of being a pretender. If I were not here to speak with your Queen as a potential ally, I would kill her, and a war unlike anything you have ever experienced or read of would ensue. I would swallow your people like a plague and take what I wanted from the corpses and frozen wastes that your lands would be. But I am forgiving. I would propose a little contest. My husband, whom she has also insulted, is King of the Unseelie, and by all rights, my equal. If she can wrest the shadows from his hands without bleeding, I will settle for you simply taking us to your Queen, and I will praise you all as friends."

The motioning didn't stop for a moment, but the drowess raised her head, "I not lose, no need to speak more."

"This is not for you." Maebe smiled sweetly. She turned to the others. "When she loses, I will kill her, and those of you who raise your arms to me, or mine, will all die horribly. The survivors will take us to the city, and I will not turn my ire on your people or Queen. Do we have an agreement?"

The others quickly put their weapons into their sheathes, eyes on their leader.

"I not lose. If I win, I beat male for insolence, and you no use pretender magic again." She seemed to take joy in the little addition that she had. "Unless afraid?"

Maebe's smile was even more unnerving. "I so swear it."

The shadows danced once more around us, and the leader panned through her notifications.

I looked to Maebe, stricken. But she only nodded to me once and stated, "You have one minute."

QUEST ALERT!

Shadow Boxing — Queen Maebe has offered a contest with simple rules, you are to hold a ball of shadows in your hands while the other participant tries to take them from you, or makes you lose your grasp of them without them being bled within the time limit. Should they fail to take the shadows, or be bled, you win! Should they succeed, you lose.

Success: Queen Maebe exacts her vengeance on the opponent and may continue using Shadow Magic.

Failure: You receive a beating from the winner, and Queen Maebe loses access to her Shadow Magic.

Do you accept? Yes? / No?

I sighed softly, allowing my jitters to siphon from my body into the nether. Opening my eyes, I called the shadows to my hands, packing them tightly until the ball was roughly the size of a basketball in my hands.

The leader hissed as I did so, and Maebe laughed softly. "The count begins…now!"

A small clock counting down from sixty seconds appeared in the left bottom corner of my vision, and I grinned. The drow reached out, a little over a foot away from the ball of void energy in my hands and grasped at the air. I felt her will barrel its way toward the shadows in my grasp and held firm. Nothing happened, and her former look of cocky anger transitioned to disbelief, then rage. She stalked forward until she almost touched the shadows.

57, 56, 55, 54. Nothing happened still, and she drew her weapon, aiming it at my heart. 52, 51, 50. She tried to strike at me, the blade sliding off my right arm as I twisted my body to avoid the strike.

Nothing had been stated about her trying to make me lose focus and having the shadows disperse. 48, 47.

I laughed, enraging her further. Maebe had trained me well, taking the shadows from me all the time. Forcing me to move and control them with nothing but pure will and tenacity. The strikes came and kept coming. Do I want to say that I didn't take a single cut? Sure. But that's not what happened. The little cuts and slashes I took stung, but the look on her face as I continued to dance away from her, drawing more shadows to me was worth it. She had lost, and the rest of this was for show.

Plus, how many people could say they'd fought a drow and walked away?

40, 39, 38, 37. She snarled, her blade flashing forward at the shadows held in my hands as if she meant to cleave it in two. I let the blade pass through the outside of it and into the center, then solidified it with my will, jerking it aside so, the blade snapped in half.

While she was distracted with what had happened, I hopped into the air, spun and snapped my right leg back in a vicious spinning back kick that I had learned when I was a teenager in taekwondo. My booted foot slammed into her solar plexus knocking the wind from her and forcing her to bend a little toward the ground.

In a move that I thought would make James proud, I shot my foot forward in a front kick that knocked her onto her ass with a thud. Several of the male drow drew arrows, but they held their hands as my opponent hissed at them.

29, 28, 27. I stalked forward, gathering shadows around her throat like a hand, and using them to lift her body into the air. I pulled a blade of pure shadows from the ball in my hands with my right hand and stalked forward. She had insulted my love. Me. Her existence was an affront to the dwarves who her people had attacked.

Would I feel bad for her death? No. I was the predator here, now.

I slid the blade across her forearm, blood dribbling from the wound and dripping to the ground.

"With all of you as witnesses, you see that my husband has won." Maebe stepped forward so that she stood in front of the drow. "Well, are there any of you who would seek to try and stop me? None of you who would try to save your mistress?"

None of them moved, so I stepped forward. "None of you who would seek to betray us and kill us when you think it convenient?"

Some of them looked uncomfortable as the translator signed that question to them, one of the drow tried to slink away. James walked out of the shadows behind him with his fists clenched.

"Speak." He growled menacingly.

"He wants to go home; he is tired of this charade with pretenders," Balmur spoke up from my left.

Shadows solidified around his throat, and his head slumped from his shoulders. I turned to see Maebe's hands moving up and down the captive drowess's arms.

"I told you what would happen," she whispered, shadows slithering up from the ground. "Now, this 'pretender's' magic will consume you."

They did just that, slithering up her body like ooze that pulled her into it, and then she was gone in seconds.

"All of you will be here when we wake, or more of you will die," Maebe ordered, the translator's fingers flying through motions. "And I will take it as an affront from your Queen. I tire of playing these games with you. Sleep well."

With that, the majority of them sat down facing outward,

inside the shadow barrier and began to meditate. Some of them looked up into the air, others out into the darkness.

Maebe touched my shoulder. "You did well. Thank you."

I nodded once. "That was a lot of pressure, dearest."

"And look at the diamond it created." her smile widened. "I know that seeing this side of me can be alarming and that it's not always the most presentable side—"

I held a hand up to stop her, "Don't apologize. You likely just kept us from being murdered, and now they're probably so terrified of you that you've earned their respect. Hell, that may be the only time."

She stayed quiet for a moment, her gaze searching mine in the darkness. It was easier to see her this close. "I understand that we are the predators. I understand that you have to solidify your strength, and there are certain ways that you have to handle things like insults and slights against you. They're against not just you, but our people. They have to be crushed."

Her hand found its way to my chest. "Some of that lovely naivety I found cute has been replaced by a small amount of jaded wisdom, my love. You are proving to be a fine King."

I lifted her hand and ducked my head so that I could kiss it. "Thank you."

"Thank you for trying." Her words quieted, and we laid down for a rest. Here in the darkness with so many potential enemies around, it was a little more difficult to sleep, but having her there with me and Kayda resting at my back helped greatly.

CHAPTER TWENTY-ONE

Our speed through the last portion of the outer tunnels and caves had been slower due to a large number of creatures that inhabited them.

Goblins and other goblinoid slaves that the drow kept for the city littered the area, and the hunting party took great pride in moving around and through them as if they weren't there. Unseen and uncaring. That meant lashings verbal and physical for any of the unlucky creatures who got in their way.

The city itself was supposed to take up an entire cavern itself, from what the books James had scrounged up said. But there was little else after that to describe them, and the drow had been rightfully tight-lipped after that contest. We had run into more patrolling drow, and other kinds of creatures that looked like stone, like the small one we had killed in the stomach before.

Around a bend, the drow froze in place, globes of darkness springing up around each of them. Maebe conjured one around us, as a large, deeper shadow passed in front of the tunnel before us. It moved slowly, slithering in great heaves of its body as the sound of crushing and cracking stone split the air.

Ten minutes later, it was gone, and the drow sprinted forward with everything they had. Gone was the silence. Gone was the reservation and stealth. They hauled ass, and we hauled ass with them.

It took another ten minutes of sprinting forward for us to see the large room that the drow had been leading us toward. An expanse that made the previous places we had been feel almost cluttered and closed off. The ceiling of the room was thousands of feet up and covered in glowing colorful crystals shining with magical light of differing spectrums.

The translator rushed to us; his voice raised to a normal volume for us as the sound was almost deafening. More voices rang out, crashing stone and metal tearing buffeted us violently.

Balmur spoke, his tone hurried, "The city is under attack by great worms. They eat the stone and are attracted to noise, but this has never happened before. You must leave."

Then he was on his way back to the others, their cries and lamenting turning to rage and whoops of war. They rushed forward, their weapons drawn, and began hacking at the nearest perceived enemy.

"The fuck are we supposed to do?" Muu groaned incredulously. "Yoh's been bitten by goddamn vampire bats, and now this?"

"We will assist them how we can," Maebe stated coldly, then turned back. "If all of you are willing. I will not force you to do this."

"It's experience." Balmur cracked his neck and cast a challenging glare at the others. "I'm in. I know that these guys are dicks, but that's not to say that there can't be something salvaged here, right?"

"If Balmur's in, I am, too," Bokaj added with a heavy sigh. "But how the hell do we fight these things?"

"I don't know, but we can't forget that there's a good chance that a minion or a general is here somewhere," Yohsuke reminded us with a hand on his astral adaptor. "We need to stick close together. And use our surroundings to our advantage."

"Dude, I don't think you heard the part where they *eat stone*." Muu thrust his head forward and motioned toward the worms rising in the distance. "Because they do."

"Yeah, and we have a fuck ton of magic on our side." James smacked his arm gently. "We can use that to our advantage. I say we have our casters start the show. Between Maebe, Zeke, Balmur, Yoh, and Fainnir, we can do this, right?"

"Well, I can help to enlarge some of the magic that they use," Balmur shrugged. "And all of us have Shadow Magic. What if those of us who have Shadow Magic summon a bunch of the shadows in the area to us for Maebe to direct and use?"

"What will the rest of us do?" Jaken had his shield and sword drawn as he cast his gaze about. Goblins flooded the area, fleeing from the threat and dying in droves under the weight of the massive earth eaters. They were too far away to see their level, but being the size of a small skyscraper had to lend some serious strength, right?

Here was hoping that they were bigger than their level, or we were fucked.

"You guys and Fainnir can keep the goblins from swarming us and by being a distraction." I motioned to one of the little things that had wandered too close and tried to lash out at Fainnir. Grav's arms exploded from the earth and pulled it, screaming down to its doom. "We will do what we can, but we need all of you to keep us safe."

"You got it." Jaken thumped his shield with his sword and pointed to four different locations.

Muu to the east side, Jaken north, James south, and Fainnir to our western flank with Bokaj to keep him from being overrun.

Kayda grew to her full size, and stood behind her Uncle Goblin, stubbornly watching his six, and I allowed Bea out of my collar with a warning and a promise.

"If you are good, and stay close, I will give you that crystal that you want so badly." She cocked her head to the side and sent me an image of it, drool pooling in her mouth. "Yes, that one. But you have to protect us and stay close. Do you understand?"

Want, her mind butted against mine, and I gruffly snatched her up by the back of her skull, forcing her to look into my eyes.

"You will earn it, and only by doing what I say," I said, then growled at her. "Do you understand?"

Kill. She gave the affirmative and squawked once. She would listen. For now.

I let her go, and she bumped my leg affectionately before turning her back and watching for prey to come too close.

"You done fucking about?" Yohsuke raised an eyebrow. I flipped him the bird, and he grinned. "Good. Head in the game. Maebe, take the center. Balmur, you're in front of her, I'm back left, and Zeke is back right. Grab as much shadow as you can and pull it to Maebe. We all good?"

Everyone nodded, the light in the place making it so much easier to see, and the plan began.

Gathering the shadows in the cavern was much easier than it should have been. The area was steeped in them, and they seemed to be almost as magically charged as pure mana, but I paid it no mind. Once we had gathered enough shadow energy, a ball of it roughly the size of the boulder from Indiana Jones, Maebe took full control of it and weaponized it. She compacted it, lengthening it into a spear with a tip of frost so cold that I could see my breath from forty feet beneath it.

"Ready Balmur?" She motioned to the other man politely.

The newbie wizard raised his hands and began weaving through a series of complicated gestures, muttering arcane words until he snapped his fingers, and the spear grew slightly larger.

Balmur's chest heaved as he dropped to a knee and consumed a couple mana potions. We had a decent stock, but we would likely need to restock once this fight was over. If we made it.

Maebe lined up her shot, held her hands up, and spun the spear like a drill. It blurred a second later, streaking forward with a cannonball-explosion-like burst of speed, the frost leaving a winter's trail behind it when it struck its target.

A rumbling, ear-piercing screech of pain and anguish crashed into us, and the worm crashed to the ground, drow and other creatures clambering all over it like ants on a fallen foe, ready to take it back to the nest.

"Again, let's go," Yohsuke said, his voice a sharp bark of tension.

We gathered more shadows, the ease of it still startling, but I ignored it and pressed on.

The others kept the goblins away from us, their weapons bloodied, but they seemed to be doing well. Bea had dragged a goblin's leg to me as a present, like a cat with a bird, and then ran off to kill another that had come too close to James.

We fired off three more rounds of icy shadow-spears before a large inky-black glob of energy swirled into the air and split into six swords. Each glowed with spectral-purple energy from tip to pommel as they tipped toward the remaining worms and slashed forward, their tips crashing and splitting the worms in two in some cases.

The last worm fell, crashing to the ground with a screech that cut short when the sword slammed home into its head.

"That will likely be the Queen and her priestesses," James whispered in awe.

Screams and shouts came from the city for another ten to twenty minutes as we rested where we were under the cover of a shadow dome that we erected together. We were tired. It had taken us a good three minutes to gather enough shadow for that final spear. We had gone to the point where Balmur's nose had bled, and Jaken had to heal him to keep us going.

Yoh wasn't looking too hot either, his gray skin seemed more pale than normal, and he was sweating profusely.

The others sat with us, covered in goblin blood and gore. James had fallen prey to a larger goblinoid who had smacked him hard enough to blacken his eye with a sucker punch. Luckily Fainnir had been there to use his axe and slice cleanly through the bastard's leg, giving Bokaj and Bea enough time to step in.

Muu's short spear had shattered when he had attempted to throw it through one of the worms as it slithered too close. He'd been supremely angry about that, but we promised him a new one, and it placated him a little.

Fainnir, the poor kid, had been blindsided by so many goblins after saving James that Bokaj had to have Tmont drag him out of the pile by his cloak as he swung and cursed wildly. He was still shaken from it but seemed to be recovering well.

The tide of goblins had stemmed closer to the fall of the fourth worm, as they had been either crushed or were well into the tunnels outside the city.

With the calm, my gaze fell on the city. Ruined as it was, it likely would have been breathtaking if we had come upon it before the attack. Speaking of attacks, I opened my status screen and notifications.

I had received a whopping 33,600 EXP from the fight, the majority of it coming from the worms, but the others had slain a mountain of goblins that added to the experience we had to sacrifice to each other and Maebe.

That had been enough to send me over to level 39. So close to the second twenty level milestone, I could taste it. Most of the others had gained a level as well. Yohsuke, Jaken, and Bokaj made it to level 39 with me. James to level 38 with Balmur almost making it to level 41. Our pets had leveled up, too. Tmont and Kayda had both made it to level 24 with a good chunk of experience toward the next level.

Hell, Fainnir had leapt up by eighteen levels, putting him up to level 27! He told us that his strength and constitution had been bumped up by six points each naturally, and his dexterity, intelligence, and wisdom all by three points respectively as well. That left him thirty-six points to use to better himself.

"How should I go about it?" He looked to the rest of us

with a look of gleeful excitement plastered on his face. "Never had this many points!"

"Well, what do you feel like you use the most?" Muu finished tinkering with his own stats. "For me, it's my strength, constitution, and dexterity."

The young dwarf thought for a moment, "It would be all five of me abilities but for charisma. I do nae—not, thank ye Pebble—plan to go into merchant work, so I feel that one a waste."

"Then focus your stats in those areas where you think they will do the best work for you," Yohsuke advised tiredly. He looked a little pale, but that had been a lot of magic we had worked with.

Fainnir nodded and set to work, finally coming to a decision he was proud of. None of us pried, he took his privacy seriously and I had no doubt that he would reveal his hand soon.

Kayda's three natural points went directly into intelligence for some reason, making it twenty-two in total. As I thought on it, she had been helping to reign in Bea a lot, I guess, so that had to help. I added one to wisdom, taking it to fifteen, then added two to strength and constitution. That brought each respective stat to twenty-seven and thirty-three with the final four going into dexterity for a total of thirty-three.

Bea had leveled up like crazy, making it to level 17! And was almost on the cusp of Level 18. That meant that she had gained ten natural points and thirty points for me to spend on top of that! Holy hell. This had to have been how Muu felt with all those points to spend on weapon skills. Jesus.

Her ten natural points had gone several different directions. Two to intelligence, strength, and wisdom. And four points to dexterity. That was incredible, but I wanted to make sure I knew what she wanted.

"Bea, you have a lot of points to spend on your levels, how do you want to grow?" She seemed perplexed for a moment until I showed her how I went through Kayda's leveling up and the last time she had leveled up.

Faster. Smarter. She rubbed her bloodied muzzle against my hand.

"Okay, but I have to make sure that you won't die in one hit, okay? So, I need to make sure your health goes up, alright?" She nuzzled my hand and leaned against me.

Okay, so I threw an even ten into the stats that she wanted me to, and to her constitution as well, somewhat against my better judgment, but hey—maybe she would listen if I did, right?

Name: Bea Arthur
Race: Gust Raptor (Hatchling)
Level: 17
Strength: 12
Dexterity: 29
Constitution: 21
Intelligence: 22
Wisdom: 6
Charisma: 3
Unspent Attribute Points: 0

That was much better, and I had to admit, I could feel her getting smarter as I added the points.

Tell me why I felt that was dangerous.

Father, Her voice interrupted my anxiety over the potential mistake. I glanced down at her, her eyes seeming just a tad sharper than normal, she seemed a little healthier and much lither than she had been before.

Father, I was good. I would like my reward now, please. She chirped at my hand and bumped me with her clawed hands as if she were trying to shove me into moving faster.

"You did earn it." I glanced about, making sure the coast was clear so that I could reward her.

A large host of drow broke through the city walls with weapons in hand, a good majority of them being women.

"Soon, dear heart." I could feel her indignation, but I

tugged her muzzle toward the procession. "We have to wait until it's safe for you to eat it, and that means that we need to have privacy. I will reward you, I promised. Just not when I would give it to you."

She snorted and touched the collar at my throat, filtering into it on her own, disgust invading my mind as she left. The little shit had stormed out on me!

What the hell had I just done to myself?

Maebe collected herself, smoothing her hair back away from her face, but doing little else to hide her involvement in the fray, before she dropped the dome of shadows that protected us from sight.

"Well met, welcoming party to a visiting Queen." Maebe's voice was friendly, but cold as she greeted the horde before us. "Would that we could have met under better circumstances, but I will happily cede that your city is safe in no small part thanks to myself and my Knights of the Unseelie Fae."

"Yes, your unneeded aid was much appreciated, and I assume I have the *honor* of addressing her Grace, the Lady of the Unseelie Darkness and Cold?" The lead woman said, then almost spat. Her features were dark, muscular and covered in fine ceremonial garb. The black silk covering her but clinging to her shapely figure at every curve with every motion of her hands. "I am Felis Sca'Urdentir, highest priestess to our Lady of the Web."

"Well met." Maebe nodded once in return.

"What can we do for you?" Felis seemed on edge.

"I came to introduce myself to your Queen and to speak with her regarding a matter of the highest importance." Maebe raised her head at the taller woman, almost daring her to say something off.

"I am certain that to you, it is, but the Spider Queen has other matters to attend at the moment, so I am afraid that I must bid you return another day." Felis' smile was almost weaponized and seething.

"No." Maebe sighed theatrically. "That will not do. We were

beset upon by vampires on our way here and unfortunately, one of your people gravely insulted my husband and me. I will see the Queen. Now."

Felis looked ready to start a fight she wasn't sure she could win, and I tried to focus on their levels, but they looked hazy. Unfocused, and that was just way too little to go on if we were going to duke it out with these guys.

"Let them pass, Felis," A soft voice spoke from behind the large woman.

Her eyes widened as if panicked, and she hurried to the side while taking a knee. The other drow with her took a knee on the side as well.

A small woman, her legs replaced by that of a sedan-sized, spindly-legged spider body scuttled gracefully through the crowd of drow. She was beautiful, in a weird almost-Burtonesque kind of way. Her elven ears peeked up through her closely cut white ringlets on the side of her head. Her button nose drew your gaze to both her bright pink eyes and her artfully thin set of lips that only partially hid dainty fangs. She wore only a set of heavy jewelry with glyphs and runes engraved in them that almost radiated with magic the closer she moved, that covered most of her lithe, athletic humanoid upper body.

"I am she who you seek, I am called many things, but you may call me Lilith." Her voice was cultured, almost sounded English to me, but it was hard not to stare in horror. "You bring many males with you, where are your protectors, Queen Maebe?"

"I need none—they are with me because I deem their presence worthy for travel." Not a lie, but ouch. Then again, giving any kind of weakness to a spider was asking for trouble, right? "I have come to speak with you and have found insult, then battle—how is the state of affairs among the drow?"

"Until recently, things were as they ought to be, but there are many who would see our empire fall to nothing but dust and memory." The Spider Queen's shoulder lifted and dropped in a demure shrug. "But do tell me, how is it that the Queen of another realm of darkness has come to be among mine and why she has come."

"Is there a more appropriate place to speak of such matters?" Maebe inquired, a hand slowly motioning to the tense group kneeling nearby.

"There is, please join me, and Felis?" The high priestess lifted her head, adoration, and fear apparent in her gaze. "Come to me, child."

The drow priestess stood and mechanically made her way over to stand before her goddess and Queen.

"You did well," I heard Lilith whisper softly, then she raised her voice slightly. "Your post was gained in the fall of another, was it not?"

"Yes, my Lady of the Web." Felis knelt before her queen and dipped her head. "Marinellith fell some years ago during my training, and I was the strongest of our faith to ascend to your side. Assisting you has given me much."

"So it seems," Lilith observed. Her body shifted, the spider portion almost turning back on itself so that it could expel a rope of matte-black silk that hit the woman in the face.

Her front-most legs grasped the struggling high priestess and twisted her until the webbing covered her head and shoulders before lifting her bodily from the ground and twisting her faster. Seconds later, she was a struggling cocoon, gasps, and groans escaped as she fought to escape.

"Let her folly serve as a reminder to the rest of you—you serve beneath me and never at my side." She didn't even bother to narrow her eyes or physically show the threat as she raised her voice to carry over the crowd. "I make my own decisions, and for any of you to attempt to decide for me means you do not fear me. Ambition is needed, rewarded, and if left unchecked, a warrant for death. Go. Repair my city and our fortifications. Do not fail me."

The crowd stood and rushed away, the drow elves carefully avoiding each other as they went to see to the repairs of the city and whatever other goals they thought might assist in their queen's orders.

"Follow me." Lilith made to turn, then stopped. "My guard are busy, can I trust your knights to see us to safety should another attack arise?"

"You may," Maebe replied with a cool, but amicable tone. "What do you intend for her?"

Lilith bared her fangs in a sadistic smile that made the fur on the back of my neck rise.

"She will be a sacrifice to my continued good health and strength." She blinked, the sickening smile sliding further across her face. "As many have before her."

"Then, if you would, please allow me to carry her for you," I offered, thinking to help strengthen her goodwill toward Maebe if I could.

Lilith scuttled closer, her head poking closer to me with an openly curious look on her face. I could see through her glamour this close, her features decidedly more spider-like from a foot or two away. The outline of closed eyes around the two she had open, the slight shift in what looked to be hairs all over her humanoid body that matched the ones on her bulbous spider body.

"I take it this one is your, what was the term you used, 'husband,' that you seem to be so proud of?" A thrill screeched through my body as the word evoked a threat of some sort, I wasn't aware of why. Like the primal fear that some people who hate creepy crawly things get when confronted by one, and here that one was.

"Yes, he is mine." The inflection on her claim to me did not go unnoticed by the Spider Queen, and her sickening smile lessened slightly. "And I mentioned him only once."

"You took great umbrage against Zeboya for insulting him." Our blank looks must have given her more information than we had, as her smile widened again. "I have made it a habit to scry on my hunting parties to ensure their work is up to my standards and that I am aware of the happenings of my realm. It can be dull, at times, but I knew the moment you were within sight of my people who had stepped into my web."

So, she had seen everything, and as she continued to stare at me, the shadows around us deepened.

"You were well within your rights as Queen, and your contest had been fair," Lilith stated as she leaned back. "It angers me that one of my own lost to a male, but he seems to be a prize in his own right."

"Thank you," I offered, attempting to sound unaffected by her proximity, but my voice wavered a bit.

She capitalized on it, moving closer still, several of her other eyes opening. "It surprises me that you would keep one with the sight as a pet, let alone as your partner, Maebe. Especially based on the stories told of you and your realm."

"My Zeke is special, what more can I say, other than that he is *full* of surprises?" Maebe glanced at me, lovingly with a smile and then back at Lilith. "He and his friends have surprised me many times over, and continue to do so. My enemies, as well."

"Duly noted," she muttered, her gaze landing on the others, then she turned her back slowly to make her way into the city, calling over her shoulder, "Welcome to my domain, the city of nightmares and ambition—Milsolinium'achbenir."

I lifted the now-tame, probably unconscious sacrifice from the ground, and we followed after her.

That had been a mouthful, but then again, the city was a sight to behold. Even as destroyed as it was, the buildings left standing alluded to structures of horrid and strangely beautiful design of palatial proportions. The compounds they were situated in had what looked like some sort of fungal grass of deep brown coloring. The rest of the buildings and walls were designed in ebon stone and metallic swirling patterns.

The dim light above us shifted coloring to a lighter blue, almost like the sky, and I found that a little unsettling despite the familiarity, considering our surroundings. It was an hour walk down the main thoroughfare because people avoided our host like the plague except for the bravest female souls, but even they watched from a respectful distance in silence.

Goblins, hobgoblins, and these tall wooly creatures with long, strong arms lifted rubble searching for what they could. Males in black armor with shaved heads patrolled on lizards almost as large as motorcycles and twice as long snout to tail. They carried multiple weapons, but the most popular one seemed to be the spear. Wicked looking with exaggeratedly long slicing edges that looked sword-like in quality.

They all averted their gaze as Lilith strutted by without so much as a glance.

At the end of our trek, we came to a tall, gated entryway with a gigantic spider-person statue situated over top of it that held a set of swords, one in each hand. The statue looked to be made of black metal that ate the light around it, even with the carved tattoos along the surface that had been filled with crystal that matched the ceiling of the expansive cavern.

Drow guards with bodies similar to their queen's stood guard at the gate, but they didn't seem quite so intelligent as their Queen. Muscular and dangerous looking, to be certain, but not as cunning if I had to wager.

I was hoping that I'd wagered correctly because the claim could be our lives if this went poorly.

The gates swung open with a wave of the Spider Queen's hands, and in we went. The black wrought metal barriers clicking closed softly after the last of us entered the area.

Her compound was gorgeous, if not terrifyingly so. Spun threads of black wire covered the top of it in an almost invisible dome, the light from above passing through despite the block-age. Dozens more of the same kinds of guards crawled over the top of it, as if it were nothing to do so, and regarded the Queen with respectful nods. Large spiders the size of luxury all-terrain vehicles scurried about the grounds like attack dogs that didn't dare come too close to their master.

"Welcome to my humble home," Lilith said, in a purring tone. I turned in time to catch her watching our reactions.

Lock it down. I ordered the others, and she smiled even more.

"Please, follow me." She led us through a set of doors with symbols of spiders, webs, and sacrifices on them, darkened hallways, then onto a set of stairs that led up in a widely turning rise.

As you went up, there was a barred door and a moderately lit interior with some sort of captive creature or person on every landing

"Queen Lilith, your H-Highness," Bokaj stuttered as he tried to make sense of the creatures we climbed by. "Who or what are all of these things?"

"The creatures and people toward the bottom of the tower are those who displeased me and who might survive long enough to earn their freedom," Lilith explained as she took the stairs slower and slower so that we could see each of her prizes. "As we climb, the crimes against my people and me grow ever more heinous and unforgivable." She stopped at one of the barred doors, seeming to relish the creature inside for a moment then spoke again, "Or they just happen to be my favorite toys."

We stopped by a doorway and inside this one was a small drow boy, a shaggy mop of white hair covered his face where he looked out at us with golden eyes, his body emaciated and scarred from some of the beatings he had likely taken.

Him. A new but familiar voice touched my mind, warmth radiating from it. Light in my mind as the feminine voice of the Light Primordial filled my thoughts with her will, *He is mine.*

Fuck, I growled to myself, the light recoiling a little bit from my anger. *I'm not mad at you, but fuck. This could be bad, trying to get the kid out of here.*

He is mine. Do what you must, and your reward will be great. Because there is more than just your life at stake if our power cannot touch this world.

Her presence left me then, and I had to hurry up the stairs after the others, but had I thrown some travel rations into the room with the kid before I did.

Good news and bad news guys, I tried not to sound too cynical as I mentally called to the others.

Let me guess, we gotta spring the kid from his cell? Jaken answered knowingly.

Beat me to it. Yohsuke grumped, speaking with fatigue. I glanced his way, and he was having trouble keeping up with the others, sweating profusely. His body had a small tremor as I grabbed his arm to help him.

And I'm not feeling too fuckin' hot either, he admitted, the others glancing back to him with worry on their features. *Turn around you stupid bastards! You'll gimme away.*

The others did as they were told, and we continued on, passing other abominable and loathsome creatures as we rose. Another ten minutes of upward movement, and we came to a landing with a larger set of bars and sets of glowing eyes glaring out at us. Then we were back on our way up the tower with intermittent landings scattered here and there. Eventually, breathless and irritated, we came to a stopping point.

There was a larger landing with another set of stairs, but there were several barred openings on this one. I was in the back with Yohsuke attempting to keep him good, but it was getting a little worse.

I think I just found another reason how this gets better, and worse, Muu said with a growl. *I think I just found Gerty.*

CHAPTER TWENTY-TWO

Sure enough, as we walked by the bars on our way into the room the queen entered, there was a well-muscled dwarven woman who sat at the back of her area with a spiteful, hate-filled glare on her face.

Keep Fainnir away from that door. James ordered as we strode by into the room from the stairs. Muu grasped the dwarfs arm and hauled him bodily into the room as the doors closed behind us.

The room was intimate with gaudy baubles and shiny objects that filled every corner of it like a nest. I set the sacrifice on a table where Lilith motioned and left her there.

"Do you require refreshment, or should we skip straight to business?" She eyed all of us and sighed, "I would offer you time to freshen up, but it seems you have much you wish to discuss and I find my humors less inclined to wait."

Maebe looked to us as Lilith eyed her morsel on the table, and we all shook our heads.

"Business before pleasure it is." Lilith turned, strode from her meal and sat on a cushion on a pedestal where she eyed us. "Please, be seated."

We looked down to find small chairs had appeared behind

each of us. Yoh all but fell into his, his eyes unfocused and nearly rolled into the back of his head.

I tried to pump healing energy into him, but it wasn't taking.

"He was the one bitten?" Lilith asked, her head cocked to the side. "I can save him from the undeath that you have seen for a price."

"What is your price?" Maebe asked without hesitation.

"I know that you will not abdicate your throne or part with your power, so I will ask a favor." Lilith steepled her hands in front of her chest, pointing with her eyes narrowed at Yohsuke. "His safety from undead servitude, for a simple favor. I want the Vampire Lord, who I believe has orchestrated these attacks, slain, or brought to me. Do this, and I will save him."

Maebe raised her chin. "You are right in those things, but it makes no sense for a Vampire Lord to orchestrate a large-scale attack like that and not send his children when he has a steady food source."

White foam flecked with blood formed at the corner of Yohsuke's mouth and he began convulsing, his whole body fighting whatever took place inside.

"I can concede that notion, but your time is running out— will you kill the Vampire Lord?" Lilith held out a small bottle of red liquid, her pink gaze blazing as she stared at Maebe.

"Yes, anything after that will be negotiated." Maebe struck the deal, and Lilith tossed the bottle to me as she scurried forward.

"Lift his shirt away," Lilith ordered, her hand flashed once, and a large, slimy creature appeared in her grasp. She placed it over his heart with a look of disgust on her face and it pulsed wildly. "This will take some time."

"What is it doing?" I asked cautiously, she did seem to recognize that I was interested, but her kind didn't care for males.

"Draining his infected blood." Her eyes never left his body as she watched her work. "The problem with being bitten by the bitten is that the bite infects with the intent to turn one into a servant. If a true vampire is to be created, the trading of blood is required."

"You seem to know an awful lot about vampirism," James observed a little more coldly than I would have liked.

Lilith snapped her fingers toward the wall next to her cushioned pedestal, and a large shelf of books appeared. "When one has an enemy, immense study of their biology, creation, and workings within most societies are what lead to well-informed decisions. Some of those being how best to bring on their destruction or manipulation. I am quite adept."

"As you seem to have no issue letting us know," Maebe challenged, a knowing tone entering her voice. "You tried to trick us. Me."

"I did, but you were smart enough to see through the falsehood." Lilith smiled at Maebe, and it looked to be genuine. "A trait that most of the Fae are well known for."

"Why would you willingly risk my anger?" Maebe seemed to be genuinely confused as she looked at the other queen in shock.

"Because I have the upper hand in this negotiation, and in the superiority of force," Lilith's honesty was stated as if it were the most obvious thing in the world and she explained it to a child. "I could have this room flooded in shadow so swiftly that only you and Zeke could hope to respond before the others were stilled. I could have dozens of my personal arachnid guard here in seconds after that to subdue and take you captive, and I could spend delicious weeks carving my way into the minds of your Knights until they beg to serve me."

Maebe's body went rigid with fury, her fists clenched, and if I hadn't been so worried about my brother, I'd have been excited to see her wipe the floor with this uppity bitch's face, but Lilith wasn't done.

"Or I could make it look like a poorly disguised trick to fool you so that you would agree to what I really wanted with there being minimal risk to me, my throne, my people, and to any sort of relations we might have in the future." Lilith blinked at Maebe, who visibly calmed herself, which was so unlike her. "I hadn't expected this to work so smoothly, but then again, I hadn't seen all of the attack on your party to plan for this."

"And what is in the vial?" Maebe's voice was carefully neutral.

"A Vampire Lord's blood," Lilith responded with a grin. "A group of adventurers had been traveling in my realm and come across one on the surface. I think they meant to make a home in the Great Below, or at least a lair, but my people found them first."

"And it's not the same as the line we will be hunting?" Muu wondered loudly with Fainnir held firmly in front of him.

"Not to my knowledge, but I am not certain." Lilith stepped back to her spot and glanced at Maebe. "This certainly played better into my hand than I had expected."

Maebe eyed her steadily, not saying anything, content to just watch her until Lilith sighed heavily. "My people are seen as evil; we embrace it because the blood of the spider courses through our very beings. We are seen as evil—never stupid or incapable. But is it truly so bad that we take care of ourselves first and foremost? That we take what we want because we are strong enough, or brave enough to do so? Our peoples are not that different, Maebe."

"Were it because o' brav'ry tha' ye attacked an' killed me pa's clan?!" Fainnir had finally snapped, tears of impotent rage poured from his eyes as he stared at the queen in outrage. "Were it purely fer sport tha' ye slew me kin under Djurn Forge? When ye left dozens o' me brothers an' sisters o' the Way litterin' the bowels of the earth as ye fled like cowards?!"

Lilith blinked at the young dwarf, and I sighed, prepping myself for a fight. I felt my friends around me stiffening and preparing themselves as well, even as Fainnir strained against Muu's grasp in futility.

"Yes, and stupidity on my general's part, which she paid for with her life." Fainnir was so shocked by her answer that he stood there with his mouth agape. "We had heard tapping, mining above us for centuries and never paid it any mind. To be honest, we had thought it the deep dwarves or some other burrowing creatures that we could enslave and use to our own ends. Imagine our surprise when my incursion force bursts into a city full of some of the fiercest fighters to ever thwart my people? They killed several of my driders, did you know that?"

Lilith snapped her fingers three times, and one of the hulking spider-drow warriors known as a drider hauled in a whirlwind of curses and hatred. A female dwarf who could only be Gerty. She moved too much to get a good look at her, but her fighting spirit was enough to cement that thought in my mind.

Fainnir swore under his breath and strained harder against Muu's grasp, to the point where we were likely to have to knock him unconscious to get him to calm down.

"This was the one who led the attack against my people, killing scores of them." Lilith walked over and tapped the stout woman on the head, and she stilled, as if in a trance. "Not once have I ever harmed a hair on her head without provocation, do you know why?"

"Why?" Fainnir sobbed, his voice hoarse as he fought.

"Respect." Lilith pointed at Fainnir, almost making him stop in his tracks. "She was a worthy opponent, and not only did she successfully lead her warriors against mine, but she fought on the front lines. What I wouldn't give to have a hundred drow just like her. Her ferocious tenacity and willingness to destroy in blind obedience to her people was so inspiring that I had to have her brought back here so that I could meet her."

"Give her back," Balmur whispered, tears in his eyes, his teeth gritted against the memories plaguing his mind.

"I will sweeten the deal, then." Lilith pointed to the vial in my hands, then Gerty. "Both of these to you if you will kill the Vampire Lord and his minions. The vial is obviously a down payment, but the dwarf once the job is done. What say you?"

"Fine." Balmur, James, Fainnir, and Muu barked in unison

as if she was going to change her mind. And I couldn't help feeling like she had been playing us here, too.

"What's in it for you?" I asked, airing my suspicion.

Lilith smiled at me. "Brave Zeke, I get to sleep well, knowing that a scourge of my people is gone." When I didn't blink or give any sign that my question had been answered, she pouted and continued, "This creature has taken dozens of my drow, slaves, and even some of my driders as victims over the past several months with increasing rates of disappearance. That is part of why I scry on my patrols now, so I know that they will return."

"This creature's death will spell the end of his line and those he has turned with him. Those of his brood who are strong enough to sustain themselves after he is gone will be close to him. Once he is dead, they may try to flee, so it is crucial that they all be slain so that my people are safe."

She eyed me, and I nodded once, somewhat satisfied. "And why are you giving her back?"

"The stubborn one?" Lilith snorted, definitely not queen-like, and pointed to Gerty. "She has grown to be boring. I respect her too much to harm her, but I cannot trust her not to try to kill me or some of my people if I allow her to leave on her own."

"So really, we're just doing you a bunch of favors." Jaken frowned, then sighed and kicked on his surfer-like charm. "I'm okay with that."

"Where do we go to try and kill this thing?" Bokaj motioned, his map now out in front of him.

"I will have a guide take you to the place where my patrols have been attacked most often." Lilith stood next to her sacrifice, her fingers trailing down the black threads wrapped around it longingly.

"What was the deal with the kid down near the bottom of the cells?" Jaken asked slyly. "What did he do?"

"He was born." The queen frowned; her fangs disappeared with the expression. "His matron mother thought him a worthy sacrifice to me as a guard, but he has not the will to kill. He is soft and worthless."

"I wouldn't say that." I smiled, sensing Jaken's motives. Lilith turned her gaze my way. "He's small, seems young, and is likely a virgin, right?" She nodded slowly. "Seems like perfect vampire bait."

"You would use a child of the drow as bait for the vampires?" Lilith's voice was deadpan as she reiterated what I had said.

"You have him locked up, and you said it yourself; the lower they are on the stairs, the more likely they can prove to be of use to you and your people." Jaken shrugged. "What better way to prove your worth than to assist the hunters in catching what stalks your family?"

"What're ye sayin'?" Fainnir cried in disbelief. "He's a wee lad with nae a hair on his chin! He'd die in a fight!"

Here's hoping Fainnir is as righteous as I think, I thought.

"Then we would know where the enemy is, kid." I shot an angry glare his way, shutting him up. "It's a sacrifice that sometimes we have to make. If we go into this area like we're hunting, it could tip off our prey. We need a reason to be there and something to lure them out, or they keep doing what they're doing."

"A guide and a lamb to the slaughter..." Lilith mused, her fingers tapping her chin. "Fine. I can approve of this. If he survives this, then he may prove useful. If not, then it is of no consequence so long as the goal is accomplished. But be warned —should you fail and these drow die without success, any of the survivors of your group are mine, and do not think of leaving. If you do, my people will hunt for you, possibly starting at this dwarven city you seem to hold dear."

QUEST ALERT

Drowning in vampires – Queen Lilith has given you a quest to kill the Vampire Lord as well as his strongest minions plaguing her people here in the Great Below. A

guide (to be determined) and the bait will be provided to aid in your success.

Reward: Vial of Vampire Lord blood (received) and possession of the dwarf who led the attack on the drow in Djurn Forge.

Failure: Failure to kill the Vampire Lord and all of his strongest minions will result in loss of your freedom should you survive. Leaving the Great Below (unless in pursuit of the Vampire Lord) will cause the drow to hunt for you in the shadows, beginning in Djurn Forge.

This quest has already been accepted.

Oh, goody. And here I thought our word was our bond only. Cool. Awesome. Fuck.

But this was working out, and that was all that mattered. We just had to make sure that the kid would be safe long enough for us to give him the power of the Light Primordial and then get him to safety. And, you know, kill a powerful vampire. Maybe not in that order, but it was the general plan.

"It is nearing time." Lilith nodded toward the leach on Yohsuke's chest, the thing was massive now, Yoh's body pale and looking almost lifeless.

Yoh, I don't know if you can hear me, but if we're going to save you, you have to drink this blood. I steeled myself above his head. *It's going to make you a vampire, you cool with that?*

Lilith took the leech off of my friend's body, the teeth having left perfect circular indents where they had latched into the skin. I reached out and took the thing into my hands and scorched it with Black Flames, the screech deafening, but the look of awe on Lilith's face was worth it.

Noooooooooo—shut the fuck up and give me the blood already you wet-dog-smelling fuck! Yohsuke snickered at me as I unstoppered the vial and stuffed it into his fucking gullet, unceremoniously dumping the contents into his gob.

No, I wasn't hoping he drowned, I just hoped it tasted like piss. Fucking asshole.

The red liquid filtered into his mouth, his throat worked, then froze as his body fought swallowing.

"Nope. You need it to live, motherfucker—swallow." I clamped my metallic hand around his mouth and jaws, careful not to block his nose, then his Adam's apple bobbed, and it was gone.

The convulsions and shaking stopped, his body stilled, and his chest slowly stilled as well.

"Is he going to be okay?" Muu asked quietly.

"The change is different for every person, and we shall see how he adapts to his." Lilith raised her eyebrows and shrugged. "It will likely take him more time to recover, and I can tell that all of you are tired. I will have lodging arranged for you so that you can rest and recover your faculties."

She raised a hand, snapped three times, and a scantily clad male drow came through the door, his head bowed subserviently. "Yes, Highness."

"Prepare the guest hall," Lilith ordered dismissively, then added, "Have it done in half an hour. Go."

The other drow fled from the room in great haste, and the door clicked shut behind him.

"Can you tell us anything about this Vampire Lord?" Bokaj motioned to James who took out his notebook and a quill.

"Only that I am not the one to ask." Lilith smiled at him in return, before continuing, "From what I can scry, these creatures come from the area where you will be attempting to bait them and track from there, but I have yet to see any of the more powerful types of undead that I suspect to be responsible."

"If you have known of this for months, as you say, why have you not done something about them sooner?" Maebe raised the question politely. "You could have sent any one of your priestesses, or powerful mages, to investigate the area."

"Because when I did that very thing, they were the ones abducted." Lilith waved her hand as if to perish the thought. "I sent two parties to search, and both failed. This way, I lose minimal assets and stand to gain the most. By the way, this important information you wished to share—what was it?"

Maebe collected herself before speaking, "I have plans to establish my presence in this realm, more so than as just a myth. I have already spoken with the high elves, and those of the kingdom of humanity." Lilith's eyes widened at the mention of the other races, but she stayed silent while the other royal explained more. "For too long, my people have grown stagnant in the Fae realm, constantly at war with the Seelie. Here in the Prime Realm, my power, my people, have a chance to flourish and grow. To become more in tune with those who could become more sympathetic to our cause."

"And while you grow in strength here, your people gain much in the Fae realm as well," Lilith completed the idea out loud. Maebe affirmed her guess with a simple nod. "And my people gain…what? A potential ally? If I were to accept some sort of treaty with you, allowing your people to be among my kind, what do you offer us?"

Maebe must have paused in thought for a moment too long for Lilith's liking, because she moved the thought in another direction. "If I were to accept this and go to war with the surface realm, would you support my cause? If I decided that the dwarves of Djurn Forge would be better suited toiling under my rule, would you send forces into the mountains?"

Fainnir made to shout something, but Balmur cast his dome spell around himself, Muu, Yohsuke, and Fainnir before the young dwarf could spout off at the mouth.

"While I like you, and find you fascinating, I need to think of my people." Lilith raised her chin. "I welcome your people among my own should they wish to visit and lobby for succor or aid from time to time, but I can offer no more aid than neutrality."

Maebe inclined her head in respect. "I thank you for your consideration. How long have you known of my designs, and how many of the Seelie are among you?"

Lilith smiled, her fangs flashing in the light of the room.

"Several weeks, and only three. If it gives you any pleasure, I swear to you here and now that I had the same sort of discussion and findings with their envoy, though you coming personally means that I like you a little more."

"I appreciate your honesty." Maebe regarded more of her surroundings, steel seeping into her spine as she did. "Forgive me, but how long have you been, Queen?"

"A century or so," Lilith replied as if the question meant little to her.

"Ah, so you mean to usher in a new era for your people as well." Maebe nodded knowingly as Lilith turned her gaze on Maebe.

"My mother fell swiftly, as is the way of things, and I have seen my people through much, and will do so for much more—one hundred and fifty years really isn't much by other elves' standards, but it is a healthy amount to us."

They both looked like they were about to delve into a likely brutal conversation, so I inserted myself into it, hoping to defuse the situation.

"Queen Lilith, your people are known for their near-perfect Darkvision, so good in fact that they can see better than almost all of the creatures below the ground." She smiled at my flattery. "With that being the case, why do you have crystals that give off light as you do?"

She blinked, tapping her spidery legs on the ground in thought before explaining, "Those are crystals of condensed mana, highly volatile if misused, but capable of augmenting and permeating the area with magic. I understand that some among you are shadow users?"—I nodded, and so did Maebe—"Then I take it you felt more magic than normal inside the shadows here while working with them?"

"Yes, I had wondered about that, but had attributed it to the more pure darkness." I frowned in thought. Had that been it? The crystal above was augmenting the magic here with stronger mana? Or just more of it?

"Never forget, Zekiel, that the darkest shadows are always

next to the light," Lilith stated cryptically with a grin on her face.

That was fair. We needed to get our mitts on some of that crystal. If nothing more than as materials for items. I wondered how much we could make when there was a knock on the door.

The same drow as before entered the room with a low bow. "The rooms are ready, your Highness."

"Wait outside." Lilith watched the drow leave the room and motioned to the door. "I will have all of you brought food if you have need, and I swear to you that it will not be poisoned or of lesser quality in any way, shape, or form within my realm of understanding."

"Thank you, we may be obliged to take it." I nodded my head to her in deference, and she watched calmly as we left the room. As the door closed, leaving the Queen and her drider with Gerty alone, I watched the queen stalking toward the table and the figure still on it, then the door shut.

The drow servant bowed and silently brought us down the stairs. I watched for the drow boy again on our way down, but his back was very carefully turned to the bars.

We moved on in silence, leaving the area and heading to the right once we were back outside, a building growing from the silken threads as we crossed between the large-spider infested grounds.

This area had been left under guard, three hulking driders sporting spears watched us as we walked through them without so much as a grunt.

He led us to the rooms that they had prepared, and it had seemed that the staff had anticipated Lilith's promise of food because there were plates of meats, breads, cheeses, and fruits on the small tables inside.

That night or was it day? We all slept as best as we could, as swiftly as we could.

Or rather, I would have loved to if Kayda hadn't so lovingly reminded me of my promise to her little sister. I pulled out the crystal, hiding it in a ball of shadows in my hand, before summoning the grumpy lizard shit so she could stare at me balefully in the eyes.

"I made you a promise." I dismissed the shadows around the crystal so that she could see it. Her eyes widened, and she chirruped softly, whistling and wagging her tail. "Are you sure that you want this?"

Her head bobbed up and down excitedly, so I tossed her the crystal with a tired sigh. She caught it easily, tilting her head back so that the rough stone would slide down her throat a little easier. She swallowed a few times, choked, then stomped her foot as she worked the item down her long neck. She smacked her lips contentedly, at the same time a look of panic came over her face, and a notification popped up in front of my eyes.

ALERT!

Your familiar has found and consumed a monster crystal. This has resulted in there being a mutation to her abilities.

Chimerical Imbalance – 25% resistance to all hostile magic, thickened hide bestowing +10 to natural defenses, and the skill Serpent's Gaze that will ensnare a creature with low intelligence or charisma for 15 seconds once daily.

Warning: Like the chimera, the consumer of this crystal will never be alone in their own head. Upon the rising of the sun, the personality of the familiar may change dramatically - 40% chance.

Do you accept? Yes? / No?

"Are you okay with that?" I glanced at her, and she seemed to be having trouble deciding on if she wanted to puke or not, but I felt an affirmation in her mind coming across mine.

I selected yes and watched her for any kind of outward sign that she was changing. There didn't seem to be anything right yet, so Maebe and I laid down for the night and let the girls sleep as they would.

I didn't dream here, and I wondered if it was from lack of light, the exhaustion, or the mental wear from not knowing what day it was. Either way, the blessed freedom from the existence I knew for what felt like mere moments was amazing.

I awoke to a rustling sound, waking to find Maybe sitting in the bed facing Kayda and Bea.

"What's wrong, babe?" I sat up and immediately saw what she had been staring at.

Bea had mutated during the night, and she was definitely much different. For one, she was larger now, almost what I would have assumed to have been adult-sized. What I hoped to have been adult-sized because she was just about taller than me now. Along her gray-scaled body, you could see that there were rougher-looking scales that had grown in. A growth of copper scales had sprouted from her neck near her shoulders that looked like a necklace, it spread down her chest a little bit then stopped. She still had the green wind-like coloration on her scales, but it was so much brighter than it had been before.

Atop her head, she had a small set of horns that raised out of the top near her ear holes that looked almost like a dragon's horns. Her brown eye—wait, eye?

"What the fuck?" I clambered out of the bed to get closer to her, where she watched me. I stepped next to her, and she dipped her head down toward me. Her right eye was her normal brown coloring, but her left eye shone lavender.

Like the ram's head. I lifted my hands to smooth them over her head comfortingly, and she nuzzled my shoulder affectionately.

"What in the actual hell is going on?" I looked into her eyes, and she cocked her head.

I am only giving affection, is that okay? Her voice seemed more subdued and controlled than it might normally be. Less of her eager self and more loving. Her gaze was almost more intense than normal, too.

Maebe moved to my side, her hands reaching toward the raptor's face. Bea shifted slightly and ran her face across the woman's hands like some kind of great-scaled cat.

Love you both, her thoughts projected to me.

"This is...cool, but weird." I rifled through her stats and searched for anything that could tell me what she had going on with her but found nothing. Nada. Zip. Goose eggs.

In case you didn't know—those mean I found jack shit. Which pissed me off even more.

Was it so bad that she was going through this? I couldn't tell you. But that lavender eye staring at me didn't seem like her.

You worry. She tilted her head, and Kayda shuffled over to investigate. *Why? I love you all the time.*

"I worry because I don't know that this is truly you, or if you're under some kind of effect." I paused, trying to gather my thoughts so I could explain to her what I was thinking and feeling, but she already knew.

Memories flooded into my mind. The sight of me staring down at her held in the crook of my arms with love and affection on my face. Of telling her about the people I cared about. The first time I introduced her to Kayda. How I defended her.

The first memories of me yelling at her as she played, the feelings that she had attached to them—she thought I had just been worried for her safety when I was equally angry she wouldn't listen to me. Shame crushed my soul.

My own memories of her being put into the collar because I didn't want to have to try to contain and control her with her curious nature and desire to run free shattered my heart. I was the worst kind of partner she could have ever ended up with. And here she was innocently trying to show me why she loved me. I was a terrible person.

Maebe looked at me with concern on her face, worry forcing her eyebrows to knit together. "I can feel your hurt. What is wrong?"

"She sees the same memories through love and adoration, where I remember how I felt." Tears of disgust and anger built in my eyes. "I've been terrible to her."

"You have much to contend with." Maebe tried to comfort me, but I could see that slight tension in her gaze that meant she had seen it too and was trying to hide her thoughts. "There would have come a time when it would have been easier to train her. When she would be large enough to defend herself."

I sighed defeatedly, suddenly mentally drained. "You knew, and you still said nothing."

"I knew and I understood," she corrected gently. "At least how best that I could. Kayda and Bea are not like our subjects. They are not human or humanoid. They are beasts. Animals. Their minds are their own, and they are only as capable as nature will allow them to be and as their training and lifestyle will facilitate. You had Kayda from birth, and she is a creature of myth forced to grow as swiftly as you did. She had to learn very early on to care not just for herself, but for you and the party as well because if she did not, you could have died for it. Now that you are so much stronger, the threats that you face are much grander, yes, but you can take care of yourself, and Bea has had a much more sheltered upbringing than Kayda. You provided a better life for her. Not to say that either of them is less for having been brought up the way they have, but they are both vastly different, and you have done what you could given the circumstances."

I stayed quiet. Her speech had been just that, a speech. Could it have helped? Sure. But it didn't. It did give some insight, but what I decided to do then was different.

"Bea, if you want to stay with me, I will keep you, but I've been terrible." I put my forehead against the side of her head and sent her the memories, thoughts, and feelings I had for her. Everything I had been thinking every time we had interacted.

She was hurt at some of them, certainly. I could feel her confusion as she processed what she was seeing. What I had wanted her to know.

"If you want to leave, I understand." I nodded, taking my forehead from hers so I could move to the bed and sit while she digested everything.

Bea looked up, taking her head from Maebe's hands, then looked over to Kayda. I felt their minds shut off from mine, iron-clad doors slamming shut so hard that I couldn't feel either of them as they spoke. I gave them their privacy, not casting Nature's Voice so that their thoughts were their own.

Maebe sat next to me, her hand finding its way into my own. "If you ever feel like I could be doing something better, or differently, please say something."

She closed her eyes and her mouth moved, then the darkness around us shot toward us and solidified.

"I know that you wish for that earnestly, and that is truly endearing, but your actions carry weight and you will not always have someone to tell you if they are the right things." She let go of my hand so that she could dig into her inventory as she spoke. "You made a decision when you felt my life was in danger. You made a decision that affected *all* of our people for one person. Your decision to have her contained until there was time for her to mature and be less of a burden—"

"She's not a burden," I interjected, and the interruption made her pause and eye me, a little of her queen showing.

She continued, "Until she was mature and less of a *handful* to you, was sound. Not just for your own sanity, but for her safety and the rest of the group's as well. When she runs ahead, or springs on something, or acts out and doesn't listen, that distracts the whole party. And then you have to chase her and force her to submit. All you did was cut out the middling portion of that. Contained, you knew where she was and that she was safe. You could focus."

I nodded but stayed quiet because I could sense a "but" coming.

"But you could also have been working with her more. And the monster crystals were unexpected because we did not keep them if we found them. We could have put them into jewelry or sold them." She seemed to be searching for something, then smiled. "She has grown so swiftly, that I had not had the chance to address this with you—again—because the circumstances surrounding your decision were sound."

I deflated. It would really only matter what Bea thought, anyway.

"But I will give you the respect of my telling you when I think the situation could change enough to allow you some frivolity." Her eyes were forward when she said that, my glance her way making me discover her playful smile. She looked at me then, her green eyes flashing mischievously. "I will stand with you. I trust your judgment, for that is something I took into account when I followed my heart to you. When I bound myself to you. No matter what happens now, I am here for you."

I kissed her hand and motioned to the darkness, my will tearing it apart so that the shadows returned to their rightful places.

Kayda and Bea stared at us, their minds still shut off from mine, watching us. Kayda lifted a wing and used it to bump Bea forward encouragingly.

She stumbled forward, whipping her head around and hissing reproachfully at her sister, then regarded me.

Her barrier lifted, and her mind brushed against mine tentatively.

"What have you decided, dear?"

I wish to stay. I smiled despite myself. *I want to have the chance to prove that I can be a part of this family and not be a nuisance to you.*

"You aren't a nuisance little one—you just get excited, right?" I reached out and ran my hand over her scales. Her clicks of satisfaction making me laugh, it was nice knowing she could fully express herself now, though it made me wonder how much she had grown mentally.

Excited or not, I will do better. Her gaze found mine. *Sister was right. I have done much that she did not. And more than she has in many ways. I am sorry. And I can feel your regret. I know you will do better.*

"I will," I stated. "We all will. We're a family, and we have each other's back. Kayda, come here. Let's all get a hug going."

They all gathered around, Maebe and I wrapped our arms around Bea, while Kayda wrapped her wings around us. It was a good hug.

You all awake? Yoh filtered into my mind. *I made food.*

Yeah, give us a second, and we'll be out. How're you feeling? I tried to hide the worry in my tone but couldn't.

Well, I'm not alive so… he let it off there, and I bolted for the door immediately with Maebe hot on my tail.

I opened the door to see the others grinning at us like idiots, Yoh said, "See? Told you he'd come running."

"You bastard!" I snarled vehemently and whipped my fist in the direction of his voice. A dark blue blur, and suddenly, he stood in front of me with his shit-eating grin firmly in place.

He looked a little more pale than normal, his canine teeth were slightly longer and more sharply pointed, and his eyes seemed to have a bit more pull to them than before.

"Don't look me directly in the eyes," he warned, averting his gaze slightly. "It's not really that great, but if we didn't have these rings on, I'd probably be able to lure you with my eyes, and I don't want any of y'all."

"So, how's life as a vampire?" I laughed and smacked his shoulder.

"Well, for one, I can't taste any of the food that I make," his face was angry as he stated it. "It tastes like shit and makes me gag. But good news is that Muu is happy to taste test for me, and I can keep leveling my skill if I have someone to taste test it."

"Have you…you know…" I failed to try and find the right word, wondering if that was a touchy subject.

"Yeah, man, I fed." His features softened a little. "I'm good for a little while between feedings. I sleep differently now. So, I may have to carry a coffin with me. Think I might have to have you guys enchant a coffin for me so I can have it. Also, can't come into anywhere I'm not invited. So, I wanted to try something. Balmur, could you summon the Happy House? I want to see if it will let me in without being invited."

"It's a twenty-four-hour cast, so it may not be a good idea to waste it for just that." Yohsuke seemed disappointed, but let it slide.

"Well, here's breakfast. What say we go nail that bastard's

coffin shut and give him a sun-lit salute?" Muu clapped his hands and grinned at the rest of us as we tucked into our food. Fainnir hadn't decided to join us, and after yesterday, I could understand why.

Kayda chose that moment to flutter out of the room in her parrot-sized form, hunting for food, with Bea scrabbling out of the room behind her.

"Woah!" Bokaj whispered, then raised his voice. "Is that what happened when she ate those crystals?"

I nodded, and he snapped his fingers, "Shit. Should've seen if Tmont could've found any."

"The point was to level the ones who needed it." Jaken raised a hand to calm the ice elf a little. "It worked. Granted, it was a little rough at the end there. And the monster crystals only seemed to come from within the dungeon. Maybe we can find another one somewhere and go on our down time?"

"That would be cool," James bit into his toast excitedly as he looked at the rest of us. "So, what's up with the kid, Zeke? I know you have a plan for him and that he's important, but how are we going to convince Lilith to let us keep him?"

"You say that like he's a puppy," Balmur said, then snorted. "Besides, I'm pretty sure Zeke might have thought of a way to help us keep him alive."

I eyed him, and he continued through our earrings, *We need to be very careful about what we say in this place. Ears everywhere, and there's no telling if she can scry on us or not.*

What the hell is scrying? Muu glanced about. *The context of it was kind of odd to me.*

It allows her to focus on a thing, person, or place and watch it like we did with TVs. It's how she stays aware of things in her realm, and she has probably been spying on us this whole time. Balmur explained. *So, we need a way to keep her sight off us.*

Won't that piss her off? James sounded like he wanted to remain cautious.

You heard her the last time we were with her, her people are her main concern. So, if she can't see us, oh well. We just have to play it smart.

Bokaj grinned, then looked over at me. *And if we can try having you make us something that will keep her from being able to spy on us... well, how could she be mad at us for wanting to protect our privacy?*

The old, "If you can do it, why can't they" argument could work too, right? Yohsuke raised an eyebrow, nodded sagely, and leaned back. *If this Vampire Lord we're supposed to hunt has the same kind of magic that she does, or at least the same kinds of spells, it may work to keep Lilith off our backs. I can support that position. My magic is closer to infernal than ever, so I have more of an attunement to that. I'm not sure if my vampirism affects my magical disposition, though. We will have to see.*

Sounds like a plan to me, I want each of you to give me a platinum coin, I have an idea. They each put a hand into their inventories, and I took out three of mine, so I could make one for me, then looked over at Kayda and Bea, who teased Tmont as she tried to eat. I also needed to make one for Fainnir, the kid, and Tmont. Not to mention Gerty. This was an expensive task.

Going to need Muu and Jaken to make collars for the familiars so that I can add it to them as well, just to be safe. Both of them nodded and began their work with measuring and designing straps that could work for each of the familiars.

I turned my attention to the coins. I would have to be precise and crafty.

"Mae, will you put a barrier around us? As thick as you can make it?" She nodded at my request and closed her eyes. She splayed her fingers out, her hands lifting from her sides to grasp and *pulled* with her will. A dome of icy void energy solidified around us.

"I thought that mixing my control over the cold into the barrier would assist in hiding us a little better." She seemed less and less certain of her words as they left her mouth, a small line of strain showing that the spell was fatiguing her a little. "I cannot know for how long it will keep her out—if at all."

"It has to bother you that she has some sort of ability with Shadow Magic," I observed as I worked.

The engraving I had in mind was simple and easily done, so my attention could be divided a little for this portion. Between coins, I glanced up at her to find her looking particularly pensive.

"Penny for your thoughts?" She glanced over at me, my voice seeming to shock her from the thoughts in her head.

"I do not know what a 'penny' is, but I assume it is a small monetary sum from where you hail?" My smile gave her the answer she needed, so she gave me mine. "My thoughts are expensive; you couldn't afford them."

I snorted, and she chuckled at my finding her funny, then she answered, "Yes, I do find it vexing that the drow seem to have an innate control over what I do, but their level of control and mastery is not mine, and I am the chosen champion of the Void. While it might be concerning for some, it is but a minor annoyance for me."

I finished engraving another coin, passing the symbol straight through the center, carefully carving it out before grabbing another.

"And that annoyance makes you think…what, exactly?" I pressed my mana forth and smiled at my work. "Do you feel a kindred spirit in Lilith? Do you hate her for turning you and your people down? Do you wish ill on them?"

"She did the smart thing." Maebe actually grinned, her smile turning into a smirk. "If she were to join me and mine, she would have been hunted by the Seelie. If she had chosen them over me, then they would have had to die as well. Neutrality was the only way her people could prosper best. Though her using us makes me wonder if she had tried the same of the Seelie first and they failed. No matter. We will move on."

I finished another coin and set it onto the handkerchief in front of me.

"Tell me, husband, do you agree with my analysis?" I paused, looking back at her to find her sitting before me with her eyes staring into mine.

"I do, but I also believe that the Fae in all their iterations are fickle and unpredictable creatures." Her face was a mask of perfect neutrality as I made my remarks. "Like you, for example. I never thought you would propose to me. Never in my wildest dreams. Titania has been playing her games and was knowingly, or unwittingly, supporting War by having his minion among her advisors and used the Wild Hunt to hunt down things for fun. Servant? *Just* decided that he liked me and chose not to almost kill me when summoned. That healer, whatever the fuck he was, has his own plots and plans."

"It makes sense to me that she would too, and if she does—I know for damned sure you do." She smiled proudly for a moment before I continued, "Then there's this new King of the Seelie sending his minions into this realm to try and kidnap people? Just to try and thwart you? All of you are nuts. The Fae, all of them, are the way they are, and that will not change. You may sway her eventually, but it will take time and something extreme."

She nodded slowly. "An apt assessment, my king. You are learning, and I am proud of you for it." She lifted a hand and caressed my cheek. "Does it bother you that I can be fickle and ever-changing at times? Does it bother you when I revert to my training as royalty? When I need to be harsh?"

"Not nearly so jarring as it used to be." I shrugged, finishing yet another coin and collecting the next. "I'll be honest, the first time we met, you were terrifying, and you kept proving yourself to be. But those times we would speak earnestly and honestly gave me glimpses into the depth of you, surrounded by this façade of cold, calculating cruelty, showed me there was more. Something I wanted to find, because I could feel a loneliness in you that seemed to mirror my own. That could very well have been me projecting onto you, and I apologize if it sounds that way. I mean no disrespect."

"I know, and in some ways, I was. At the time I do not think that I realized how true that was until all of you were gone." She picked up a coin, eyeing it in the dim glow of my mana. "I found myself wondering if you were well. How your fight had fared. If you had all survived. At first, I attributed it to my drive for this endeavor to succeed. But then we spoke again, and I knew it was that I wanted to see you again. To be there for my friend. My friends."

"I'm glad that we found each other." I smiled at her, finishing the last coin.

"I am glad I did not kill you." She leaned closer to kiss me on my nose. The contact made me laugh, and she shoved me playfully. "We have much to do, King of the Unseelie. Attend your craft."

"Yes, your Majesty." I winked at her roguishly and snorted at her when she tried to do it back, her eyelid flickering and a look of concern passing over her features.

I dove into myself, the depths of my magic and thought about what I wanted the coins to do. The goal that was their design.

I would need to bring quite a few different ideals into this. First, to stop the scrying in a way that would make it look not only necessary but be painful, just to slide the point home. And since the drow were cool with the shadows and darkness, a little light was in order.

I felt a spell like the one I had created in the dungeon, Exposing Flames, was the opposite of what I needed for this. I needed light so bright it would obscure things.

I focused on that part of me that communed with the elementals and reached to the light. *Can you hear me?*

I am with you always mote, you have found my champion, why have you not obtained him for me? Her tone was more curious than angry, and I could navigate that one.

Because if I took him now, many lives would be in danger. Light formed behind my eyes as I finished that, so I continued quickly, *I have a plan to acquire him, though, so that I can bring him into your embrace. But I need assistance to do it, first. He needs something to obscure him, and us with him, so that he is hidden from a spell called Scrying. Can I use your light?*

The bright light behind my eyes ebbed and flowed around my mind, then blinked out.

You have the ability to create one *spell so that you might bring my champion to me. Use it wisely. There will be more to come upon completion of your task.*

The Light Primoidial's voice faded from my mind, the warmth of her presence still lingering as I set to work.

Focus. Intent. Build these things together to make a source of light so bright that it burned.

Man, I can be really dense, can't I?

I focused on bringing light and flame together and making them bind and become one around Purify like it was a small ball of holy energy that would radiate throughout it.

I drained everything I had into the spell, then dipped into Mage's Well, stopping at 1,245 MP. But it was worth it.

Solar Flare – The caster summons a miniature sun to blind and torment their foes with radiant flames for a short time. Cost: 300 MP. Range: 200 ft radius. Duration: 30 Seconds. Cooldown: 1 minute.

That would do us well, though it would likely kill Yohsuke if he was in the blast radius of it. I'd have to enchant his cloak for him to try and protect him from the sun and my magic.

I wiped some of the sweat from my brow and focused on feeling the ambient mana in the air around me, what thickened the shadows around us, and pulled it inward.

This was the first time I had done so, but the idea was fairly common in a lot of the books I'd read and games I had played. I had secretly tried it before above ground but never had any success. Meditation seemed to help a little bit, but here? Here I could pull the mana in faster, if only minutely.

Once the ring and I were topped off, I began to apply my intent and focus to the coins with that spell in mind to assist, then cast the spell on it to add strength. Total, each coin cost 1,000 MP, and the component I used to fill them was powdered diamond.

I had carved an eye into the middle of each of them with a crystal ball in the center that had an X going through it so that it all stayed together. The intent was obviously to cause pain or extreme discomfort to those who tried to spy on us using Scrying magics. It could even blind them. Hopefully.

It took a while for each coin, and I was intent on ensuring each one was perfect, my focus slipping near the end of them, so I had to sacrifice a coin of my own to redo it. Once they had been finished, I poked my head out of the dome and tossed one to each of my friends so they could admire my handy-work.

Anti-eye coin

When the bearer of this coin is spied upon by magical means, such as Scrying, Farsighted, and other Divination-type magics, the caster is accosted by a magical counter in the form of a sun-like obstruction that blocks the vision. This item may sap mana from the bearer if the caster is persistent.

Coin enchanted by Adept Enchanter Zekiel Erebos.

It was nice to get that one out of me, though there was no telling how much of a mana drain it would be. I had also gained a level putting me up to Level 46 Enchanting. More than halfway to master, woo!

"Nice, man!" Yohsuke smiled. "And I didn't catch fire when you threw it at me, so there's that."

"I will glare at you and your dickish behavior later, gimme your cloak, I need to enchant it." He seemed to hesitate for a moment, "What, you got a better one?"

"No, but how are we going to test it?"

"That's a good idea, slowly at first?" I shrugged. "Maebe and I can pack some serious magic into it if needed. The design is going to be for it to make shadows that keep you safe from the sun while the hood is up."

He seemed to think about it for a moment, then nodded. "That would be useful, especially since I almost always have my hood up, anyway. Thanks, man."

"Yeah, yeah, quit your blubbering," I teased him, and he started forward. "Bye!"

I pulled myself through the dome where Maebe and I set to work and then failed. Miserably. The quality of the cloak was nice, but it had seen a lot of action, and it was highly damaged from the fighting we had been doing lately.

I rummaged through my inventory to no avail, and so did Maebe. I poked my head back out into the room with the others. "Anybody have a cloak with good quality that is not too damaged?"

The others looked through their inventories and didn't find anything of use. Most of them just had rain gear, and that was it.

"How about you enchant an item to shape the darkness like a cloak to the wearer?" Balmur asked helpfully. "Like a necklace or something?"

"If I were higher level, I'd try it." I shrugged. "Even with Maebe wrangling the shadows, I would probably have to have you feed it a steady stream of mana for it to work, and that would be a terrible idea in a fight. We'll have to see if we can either find something or buy something from around here."

"What about if we get into a fight, and someone starts slinging daylight?" Bokaj nodded as if he knew what I had done. "Don't look at me all confused, I know the things you can do, and this coin is way too specific. You have a vampire nuke, and you could use it to kill a good majority of them and our friend."

"We don't know if it will work exactly like the sun, and if it comes to that, then I'll put his ass in my collar for safety," I said, in a growling tone while I checked the familiar's new collars out. They were simple designs with pouches sewn in for the coins to rest in.

"We could try it, right?" Muu took a drink from his canteen.

"In a confined space like this, it would likely nuke us all." I shrugged, then shook my head. "Better not try it until we know we need it. We have holy weapons and abilities we can use if needs be."

The others nodded, and I went to go check on Fainnir. His door was unlocked, but I knocked anyway. When there was no answer, I walked into the room, fearing the worst only to find him meditating.

"You okay, Fainnir?" I asked softly as his breathing continued.

Softly, he responded, "Aye."

"You want to talk about what's bothering you?" I sat down in front of him on the floor in a room that mirrored my own. A simple bed, no furniture, and a decent amount of space.

"Ye be bargaining' with the enemy o' our people." He didn't open his eyes, as if his meditation was all that kept him calm. "Ye did naw strike her down where she stood—ye offered aid and alliance."

"We did." I allowed with a nod, my heart thumping in my chest in the silence almost deafeningly loud. "And you heard the consequences of any hostility we may have offered. Any betrayal. So much as a sneeze in the wrong tone could have spelled disaster for the city of Djurn Forge and all of our people. Sometimes it's best to deal with the enemy you can see so that they remain seen."

"That made no sense." Yohsuke stepped into the room and sat next to me. "Sometimes, keeping your friends close and your enemies closer works better in that instance, I think."

Fainnir opened his eyes and narrowed them at Yohsuke, the newly-reborn vampire held his hands up as if to ward off something.

"It's my fault, I'll take that blame, but Zeke and Maebe were doing what they felt was best for all of us." Yohsuke pulled a small plate out from behind us and offered it to the dwarf. "If she had agreed to ally with the Fae, then your people would have been safe from her. At least knowing that she's neutral makes us aware that she could be a threat, and we can keep an eye on her—oh, that's what you meant by that? It's still weird—but that's not all."

Fainnir regarded the food for a moment before his stomach began to growl, then lifted it onto his lap. "What else is there?"

"Now we know that there aren't any more drow plans to

fuck with your home since they had royally screwed up their invasion force before." Yoh smiled, and I couldn't help my grin. "Not only that, but we can take a war hero home—isn't that something that you want?"

He nodded, chewing thoughtfully. "The boy, the drow one, why were ye so keen to get him and use him as bait? Made it seem like ye were bad folk, and I be know'n yer nae."

I held out the coin I had for him, hoping we had been unseen by anyone scrying in the area or on us before I answered.

"Because he's important to our cause, like you," I answered, honestly. "He belongs to the Light Primordial as you do to the Earth. This is our attempt to bring him into our protection so that our goals are closer to being accomplished."

"Offering him a chance to 'prove' himself leaned toward what she would want of her people, the males especially," Yohsuke explained further, adding to my thoughts. "We play to our strengths, and sometimes that requires a little bit of subterfuge to get what we want. It's no different from a black-smith peddling his wares to a customer who knows little of his craft. You haggle, and you up the ante by telling them what they want to hear sometimes. Do you understand, now?"

Fainnir seemed to think on it a bit more, longer than I would have liked, so I added, "We would no sooner see him harmed than we would you. He isn't you, and from what we've heard, he's not like some of the other drow either. We're doing our best."

"I understand that ye meant no harm," he started and paused, his eyes closed in thought, tighter and tighter until I saw a tear run down his cheek. "They killed me people, and here we are. No blood shed in their honor. Not a single drop. Here we are trying to save one of them to give them power that they don't even know to want."

"You didn't either, Fainnir, but you're here with that same sort of power." I prodded him in his chest. "Power just as unearned as his will be. You are a conduit to something greater than yourself, and he can be, too. You can be greater than you ever dreamed, and you could lead your people to do great things. And he might be able to as well. You don't know. Neither do we. But the Light Primordial wants what she wants, and I am going to give it to her as best I can because it helps us all."

"I understand a little more," he stated solemnly, "I don't get it all, because I lack the mind for it, but I thank ye for tryin' to help me understand. I will trust that ye know what yer doin' and support ye. I'll be askin' questions, though, and if we get the opportunity to avenge our kin, I trust ye'll nae hold me back?"

"If we have to dig in, we'll be waist-deep with you." I grinned wolfishly, and Yohsuke punched a fist into his hand. The message got across. "We will be leaving soon to set our trap and then get back to the surface, okay?"

"I'll be ready." He closed his eyes and began to breathe deeply again.

Yohsuke and I stepped out of the room, I glanced at him, taking his fangs in one more time. "Thanks, man, you sure you're okay?"

"I mean, I'm alright." He shrugged, thinking for a bit. "It's no longer temporary, but it just adds to my strength and dexterity. I'm pretty sure it also makes me much better with some of my draining spells. And there are things I can do as a vampire, like shapeshift into fog and a bat! Dude, we can shapeshift into things and work together!"

"We can be the monster squad." I grinned at him, and we clasped hands, teeth flashing in the dimly lit room.

"Yeah, yeah, monster mash-looking fuckers," Bokaj said, then grunted. "Rub your monster-y-ness all up in our faces, why don't you?"

I rolled my eyes, and we finished eating and preparing how we could. We had undead and a Vampire Lord to hunt down.

CHAPTER TWENTY-THREE

"The Queen wished me to inform you that she is focused on other matters of greater importance to the drow and that I am at your full disposal until such a time as your quest is completed, I die, or we all perish."

I glanced at the others as we regarded the male drow before us. A spindly thing, with long limbs and lithe muscles, his white hair styled into a mohawk almost a foot tall. His eyes were gray and blue swirls that seemed to glow eerily as he looked over all of us. His nose was a little long, eyebrows a little high, and his thin face made the mohawk almost comical, but I wasn't one to judge, normally. His robes of black had other colors sewn in, likely showing his rank in their culture.

"I am called, Xaenth, and I am the current Umber Wizard's aid." He bowed respectfully as we stood outside Lilith's doors. "I will be your guide for this quest. Our young morsel will join us shortly. Is there anything we need to do before leaving, or are we clear to set off?"

I reached into my pocket and pulled out the extra coin I had made as an afterthought, then tossed it to him. His eyes grew wide as he looked back at me, but I stopped him from refusing with a raised hand and my prepared explanation.

"We have reason to believe that whoever is abducting your people could also have the ability to view others from afar, this will help us stalk them." I nodded to my own coin that I held up in my hand, the diamond refracting a little of the now-green light filtering into the windows from the larger cavern outside. "Each of us has one, and now you and the bait will, too."

He seemed distrustful of it for a moment, but I pocketed mine and he did the same. We walked down the spiral staircase until we reached where the kid should have been, but the little cage was empty.

"He is likely at the bottom of the stairs awaiting us with a guard." Xaenth shrugged, and we continued down the stairs, a little faster. That kid was our current ticket to more power. He'd better be okay.

I heard a cry of pain as we neared the bottom of the steps and flitted down in the air as an owl, not caring that we were in someone else's territory.

I came to the bottom, finding nothing, then banked and hurtled outside to see a raised spear shaft and the drow boy laying on his back with his hands held up to defend himself.

I shifted into my fox-man form in time to catch the spear shaft on my metallic arm and growled angrily at the drider guard in front of me. "What the hell are you doing?"

It hissed at me, speaking softer than I could understand, then raised the spear as if to strike me, too.

"Halt!" Xaenth shouted as he cleared the doorway. The drider regarded him with indifference, before turning back to his business with me.

"Finish that strike you half-spider freak." My blood boiled, but I still kept my cool, this was just a pre-fight surge of adrenaline that I welcomed. "I'll rip one of those legs off and shove it where the silk comes from."

"That will hardly be necessary, master druid, I will take care of this." The drow guide lifted a hand, and shadows leapt to do his bidding, wrapping around each of the drider's legs and lifting it twenty feet into the air. "I speak, you listen. I am the word of the Queen while she is busy, and if you harm her guests, or the chances of this mission by being a brute, then she will see you and your brothers dead. And she will be far, *far* less merciful about it than I would. Am I clear?"

The drider glared at him, the spear still gripped in both hands, but it seemed to say something that satisfied Xaenth. He lowered his hand, and the shadows slowly brought the creature to the ground where it walked away upon release, clearly getting the fuck out of Dodge.

I turned to the boy, bruises all over his body, we were in the dark, so I cast Void's Respite over him, then Renewing Flames. His bruises disappeared swiftly, and he stared up at me, open-mouthed.

"You okay, kid?" I offered him my hand, and he just stared at it for a moment in wonder.

Seems a little slow, if you ask me. Bokaj grunted, and I shot him a glare.

I leaned down and lifted the young drow to his feet. He squirmed at my touch, and I wondered if he had been beaten further, poor kid.

Maebe came over and put a hand on his shoulder, speaking softly, "All of these men are here to protect you, you are safe now. And any who would see you suffer or harm you from here on will incur my wrath. I am a Queen, little one, and my word is law."

His eyes grew impossibly large, and he nodded his head quietly.

"Tell us, child, what is your name?" Maebe's head tilted to the side, her soft smile and welcoming gaze almost making the kid forget the rest of us, until Xaenth wandered over to stand behind her.

The boy looked up, the easy wonder in his large eyes draining into fear and distrust. "Dirt."

The drow mage snorted, and I glanced his direction. He

raised an eyebrow. "Dirt is a name given to the weakest of a drow family. Like a title. And his family would clearly not suffer his presence hence their attempting to give him as a sacrifice to the Queen. No wonder she didn't take him."

Then he looked over at Yohsuke. "I am surprised you don't know all of this as well, Dirt that you are by birth and that alone. Your gray skin is telling. You should educate the people you ally yourself with, mongrel."

I had to fight the urge to not say some stupid shit, and I *know* Maebe did as well because her jaw was ticking as she spoke sweetly to the boy, "Come then, sweet child, I will walk with you and keep you safe for now."

She held her hand out and he took it. She pulled bits of food out of her inventory, and he took them from her to devour ravenously.

"Plumping up the bait?" Xaenth nodded with approval, then looked over at Yohsuke, who looked like he was counting to some ridiculously high number. "Excellent idea, Queen Maebe. Did I upset the garbage?"

I glanced at him, he was close enough that I should be able to see his level, but it was hidden from sight. "Look, Xaenth, I know that power is a lot of what matters to all of you, but you ain't exactly the top of the food chain, either. Where we're heading is dangerous, and there's a lot at stake, so if you want to make enemies and be a dick now—go ahead. But I'll thank you to remember that when shit gets real."

"I am aware of my lot in life, druid." Xaenth blinked as we moved forward down the street. "Aware as I am, I am also one of the most formidable drow in this city, who can handle himself and knows when to keep an eye at his back. Drow life is hard, and one never sees the knife they never expect—so always expect it. If you betray my Queen, she will know. And if you betray me, you all die."

"No one here is speaking of betrayal," I shot back, obviously minding my volume. "What I *am* speaking about is loyalty. It was cool of you to step in back there, and I appreciate that.

But if you keep being rude to a kid in front of a queen who cares deeply for children, that appreciation I feel toward you means nothing. We might need you for now, but she will kill you if you keep this shit up. And if you keep treating my brother like shit, I'll kill you myself to save him the trouble. You've been warned." I raised my voice slightly, "Everyone huddle up, I want to get this shit over with."

The others gathered around us, I already had Bea in the collar—she had volunteered to be in there for now—so there were only twelve of us including the two drow and the familiars without Bea. When everyone was touching, I focused on the cavern outside the magma chamber that we had been in when we entered the fiery area. It had been where Lilith had said her patrols had been going, that, and the surrounding areas when they disappeared. I held the location in mind and cast Teleport.

We landed in the darkness a heartbeat later, everyone groaning slightly, but surprisingly, no one vomited. Kudos to the passengers.

"This was the location of the attack?" Xaenth asked softly, and a few of us nodded. "You're lucky the drow can see heat signatures, or no one would know that you had nodded. Take me to the other room then."

I counted to five, then responded softly, "We're going to wait half an hour before we move on. It's the cooldown for my tele-port spell, it's going to be our contingency exit plan."

"Clever, very well then." Xaenth shrugged and moved to stand a little closer to the wall so that it was at his back.

I cast Life Sense and pressed my awareness into the shad-ows. There appeared to be nothing in the area that came up on my radar, but then again, we had come out here to hunt the undead. I was really going to need to come up with a way to sense the dead.

I closed my eyes, and the wait was on. Once I knew the cooldown had expired, I was up on my feet, and we gathered to roll out.

Xaenth led us into the cavern with all of the lava flows, we pointed toward where we had seen the vampire bats coming from and he nodded. "As I feared, that is where they had been coming from for our parties, as well. Come."

We traversed the lava room easily enough, if not a little more uncomfortably than last time without the mobile spring rod. I would have to make another and find a way to power it since I wasn't entirely sure why that one had become unstable.

Once we crossed the lava, Muu carrying the kid because he wore no shoes, we entered another cavern. This one was different, almost like a tunnel that led us onward. I pressed my awareness into the shadows around us and felt nothing other than spots of dampness on the floor that smelled like pennies. I stepped closer and took a knee next to the largest pool to confirm my initial thought.

Guard up, there's a scent of blood in this place. I warned the others through our earrings.

I can't smell anything over your oppressive stank. Yohsuke growled with his hand to his nose.

Shit, does that mean they can smell Zeke because he's a werewolf? Balmur's curiosity carrying in his voice, despite the major blow to our cover that I was.

I'm not really sure, it could be that it's worse since I'm standing a foot away from him, but if I can smell him, maybe he can smell me? The question confused me a little bit.

Yoh, are you suggesting I take a whiff of your vampire undeath in an attempt to hunt down others of your kind? I raised an eyebrow as I asked the question rhetorically. I knew the answer was yes.

Yeah, get in there and get a sniffle of them pits. Bokaj snorted, making James and Jaken chuckle quietly.

"We're going to try something, so don't freak out," I warned Xaenth, who seemed nonplussed. I stepped over to Maebe and touched her shoulder. "I'm going to take my werewolf form, keep the kid quiet for me? I'm going to attempt to track them that way."

"I think he will be brave enough to stay quiet, will you not, little one?" Maebe looked down toward the boy in the fading orange light of the lava behind us, and he nodded bravely. "He will be with me. Be safe, my love."

I told Kayda to go and keep Jaken company as I walked toward the front of the group with Yohsuke. I focused my will on bringing the beast forward, taking the werewolf from within me, and bringing it to be me. I was the wolf.

I felt the change take place, easier than before, less conflicted than I had ever felt in the time since I had received the bite.

The shadows in the tunnel seemed a little less oppressive than they had before, my sense of smell taking over for some of the deficiency of my sight. I stepped toward Yohsuke, who stood still as I leaned down to take a huge huff of his scent in. Then promptly sneezed on his chest and face.

"Oh, you *bastard*!" He swore intensely in a low whisper. "I'll fucking kick your ass."

"You smell terrible," I growled softly. His scent was that of everything around me dying, like a skunk puréed with rotten sage, pumice, mouse droppings in kitty litter, and vomit all rolled into one. It was everything I could do not to throw up then and there.

I turned away hurriedly and began to pace for the scent. Eventually, I found one, gagging violently because this one was somehow even worse than Yohsuke's. I held a hand up and motioned for everyone to follow me as I moved forward.

I could almost see the scent I was tracking further into the tunnel. It wasn't a meandering scent or even a linear one. It was all throughout the air, and since the creatures could fly, that made sense. It was more than a little disturbing, but it was true.

We followed the scent slowly, ensuring that nothing would come attack us from the depths of the void as we followed. I had to stop and rest after a while, all of us having a bite to eat except for Yohsuke, who kept watch for us.

While we sat and ate, a thought occurred to me. "Milnolian."

The whispered word drained 159 MP from my mana, and

the creature's golden eyes opened before me, his typical panther form stalking from the shadows.

"My King?" He inclined his head respectfully.

"I have a task for you, someone to protect for a while, can you do that?" He lifted his nose into the air, inhaling deeply.

"Children." He blinked and cocked his head. "Show them to me."

"One of them is strong enough to stand a chance, but I'll introduce them both to you." I used the shadows around me to get Maebe's attention and whispered, "Maebe, bring the boy here."

She stepped closer with the drow in tow, I hated to call him Dirt, that seemed rude. Custom or not.

Send Fainnir to me. I ordered the others.

What do you say….? Muu retorted, and I cast a baleful glare in his direction, knowing he couldn't see me.

Send. Him. To. Me. Now! I snarled in return.

Sounds like someone needs a tummy rub and his favorite squeaky toy. Bokaj chortled, and I heard someone snort out loud. All of us froze.

When nothing came hauling ass at us out of the darkness, we sighed in relief, and Fainnir made his way to me.

When both of them were there, I made the introductions. "Boys, this is Servant. He's a Fae creature who I have asked to protect you while we fight. There's no knowing what lies in store for the party, and we don't want to risk you guys. So, Fainnir is going to assist in protecting you, young one, and Servant will protect you both."

Fainnir looked like he was about to say something against it but took in the sight before him. The scared drow child, the watching Fae, and two of several people he looked up to.

"I'll protect him, an' I'll get us information we can use." He snapped his fingers and muttered something under his breath. Pebble shot from out of the ground.

"Fainnir," The Elemental greeted warmly.

"Pebble, my friend." Fainnir gave the Elemental a hug and

clapped him on the shoulder. "I be needin' a favor. Go to the end o' our path here an' see what ye can find. Return when you know what lays ahead, mind ye stay deep enough that ye can't be sensed by magic, aye?"

"Your dialect," the elemental tutted, but he nodded once and sank into the ground.

Fainnir smiled at us, then turned to the boy. "I don't doubt ye know my kind and yer's don't be getting' along, aye?"

The drow nodded, and Fainnir continued, "Good. I don't know, ye. But I can tell tha' yer different, and I'll not be callin' ye names, be they given or not. Yer me ward, now." Servant sat next to the small drow and huffed slightly. "*Our* ward. And me ward's gotta be havin' a proper name."

He seemed to think for a moment, scratching his head and coming up blank. He blinked up at Maebe, "Don't suppose ye be knowin' any strong elven names, Auntie? I can only think of dwarven names."

"Your heart is in the right place, Fainnir—you sweet boy— but I think a name from you would mean more." Maebe patted his head affectionately. Servants golden eyes blinked lazily at the exchange.

"Hmm." Fainnir looked about. "Oh! Jafrik Darkskin, that'll be a good one. Fine dwarven name, that."

"Ya-frick?" The newly named drow child tested the sounds by saying the name how it sounded.

"Aye, I'll learn ye to scribble it too, but that'll be later." Fainnir seemed to grow steadily more awkward as our gazes continued to rest on him, his cheeks reddening. "So, stay safe, and we can learn it."

Fainnir made to move away, but Jafrik's hand whipped out and tugged on the dwarf's sleeve. When Fainnir glanced back, Jafrik whispered, "Thank you."

Fainnir frowned to himself and nodded before he turned and walked off. Once he had walked off to a good distance, Fainnir sat down and sat like he had when he was meditating.

"You do seem to attract the oddest creatures, Majesty,"

Servant observed softly, startling me and making Jafrik turn to stare at the Fae creature dumbfounded. "Yes, I speak. I do many things, but I will protect you so long as my King requires. Stay near to me, child."

"We're moving out." I kissed Maebe on the cheek, and she touched mine with her hand. "Let's get this underway, then."

"Be strong and swift, my King." Her proud smile made me grin boyishly as I summoned the werewolf within me to the surface. We moved further on into the tunnel from there, the scent leading the way.

———

Hold up! Balmur called to us all. I froze where I was. *Pebble returned just now, and it seems to him like this is a feeder tunnel to a larger one up ahead that leads into a small cavern with a densely built structure of mostly metal.*

We'd only been traveling for about fifteen minutes by this point, and knowing that we were closer now was a relief. *Does he know what kind of metal?*

Steel. The simple reply almost made me curse out loud.

Steel was an alloy with iron, and iron was poisonous to the Fae. That meant Maebe would be staying outside with Servant. And the boys, because there was no way we would be taking them into there with us with so many variables.

We stop and plan before we get to the main tunnel then, and so close to the base, there's bound to be traps. Yohsuke sighed. *That's some shit, man. Steel. Fuck.*

I heard Fainnir grumbling. "I'd be havin' patrols all up and down this tunnel if'n it were me runnin' thin's." Pebble smacked his arm and motioned broadly, and the dwarf just shook his head. "It's true, an' you know it. Minin' tunnels at the bottoms of our shafts are trapped up to the beard, and we've seen not one guard? Lazy, it is."

That was a fair bit of reasoning... the place was probably

trapped to shit then. That or the vampires weren't worried about being found. Either way, that wasn't good.

We gathered around each other, and Balmur had Pebble explain his findings.

Maebe wasn't pleased in the slightest, and the boys either.

"Ye can't leave us behind!" Fainnir insisted emphatically. "What if ye need us?"

"Then we will have to do without." Muu shrugged, and put a hand on his shoulder. "You're the man of the house now, Fainnir."

"Dude, so not the time for that kind of speech." James threw his hands into the air.

"Hey, focus up," Jaken said to the two of them. His arms crossed over his chest as he thought. "They'll know we're here as soon as Zeke is in the cavern if they don't already. But what we do need is eyes on the outside. Fainnir and Jafrik will stay with Maebe and Servant so that they can keep anything outside from coming inside. Jafrik, you know how to fight?"

The drow shook his head. Bokaj stepped over and looked him over before taking him to the side of the group and speaking to him alone for a bit.

"Maebe, you gonna be okay out here on your own with them?" I watched her as she thought.

"I have to be. Going into that place would leave me vulnerable." She lifted her head. "Nothing will happen to the boys, and nothing will come in after you."

"Thank you, baby." I butted my head against the top of hers affectionately.

"Yes, yes, you cuddly fox." She sighed dramatically, casting her eyes up at me. "But you had all *better* be safe in there."

"We'll try to be." Balmur smiled at her from where he stepped out of the shadows. "The drow is going in with us, and then from there, we hunt. But to get in there, we still have the rest of this tunnel and the main one. My thinking is that there are going to be traps. So, I'll be up front with you checking for them while we move forward. We ready?"

I assumed my werewolf form. "Let's hit it."

We worked our way slowly down the tunnel, not really finding anything at first, but then we began to see claw marks in the ground. Piles of freshly dug earth covered the sides and center of the tunnel as we moved further. Occasionally, Balmur would call a halt so that we could look for trips and triggers.

On this most recent stop, we found a wire trap.

"This isn't good." His voice sounded a little strained as he looked the thing over. "No good at all. Fuck."

"What?" I leaned over it a little, my balance a little more precarious than I would have expected it to be on flat earth. A sense of vertigo fell over me, and I pitched forward, almost ramming into the wire.

Balmur was swift and clapped a hand onto the scruff of my neck, hauling me away from the trap and flinging me backward.

I landed a foot and a half from the line. "I know that wasn't on purpose," he stated, "but we need to be careful because I think this area is covered in inconvenient enchantments and traps."

"What kind?" Jaken asked, as he came up to our rear.

"Nasty ones, there's a cord right in front of Zeke's left foot, four inches from the floor that looks like a tripwire." He pointed to a small mote that looked more like dust than wire, then to something else four feet ahead. "Pressure mine, and some kind of log trap. Then there is the enchantment trap that I can just make out as a rune on the wall. I'd have to get a little closer to study it."

Before I could even ask, he picked up some dust and blew it onto the wire and frowned. Three more became visible within three feet.

"Getting through here is going to take time." Balmur sighed. He followed the line of the wire toward the tunnel wall off to the right of us.

"Why don't we just have Zeke fly over and ferry us in his collar?" James spoke softly, carefully so as not to be heard from too far off.

"The rune traps." Balmur motioned carefully forward. "My mentor taught me all about them, and they can be nasty little things. There's no telling what they're meant to do, and I'm not going to risk having this whole section of tunnel coming down on us because we were in a rush. Chill, and let me work."

So, we did. He seemed to find the mechanism for the first trap easily. Putting a small copper coin on the trigger to act as a shim so it wouldn't strike a pan that it was connected to, then checked the other end before he cut the wire. It was slow-moving, sure, but his attention to the details saved us.

"See this one here?" He pointed to the last wire.

I shook my head, and he just rolled his eyes as he traced it with his hand. As he followed it, he traced it over to the hidden mechanism that looked to be a pulley, then up toward the side of the tunnel wall. He motioned for Muu to come over, and the dragon-kin lifted him so that he could collect a small vial hidden behind a hanging stone.

He put it into my hand.

Undead's Lament

Liquid contents of this vial take on a gaseous form and spreads into a large area. The contents infect those who inhale it with a plague that will render them mindless over time. Their flesh falling from the bones and rotting forever alive.

One use.

Ooooh no. That would be terrible.

"Yeah, you take your time, and the next fuck who says anything about speedrunning this place—I wallop with my axe."

The others looked skeptically at me, but I passed the vial around, and it quelled their discomfort with the pace real fast.

It took us a good fifteen minutes to get to the first rune, and even then, Balmur had no idea what it did.

Normally, I would have to touch something to look at the enchantment. But I wanted to try to do something with my growing magical senses. I pressed my awareness forward through the darkness and tried to explore what the rune did or held in store for the activation.

I didn't get a status for it, or any normal explanation, but I did get a general feel for it.

Anyone alive who walked through the range of that rune set off an alarm that the caster would hear. Other than that, there was no way for me to break it, but there would be a way to get rid of it. If Yoh were strong enough, he could take my axe and do the dirty work himself, but his low strength might just as easily cause him to fall into another trap and screw us over.

A heavy sigh escaped me as I looked to my friends, "This could get fucked up, but there's no way I can touch that thing to disarm it, and I can't dispel magic." I brought Magus Bane out into my hands from my inventory, hefting the comfortable weight. "But I've got my personal eraser right here. Stand back."

The others backed a little farther down the tunnel toward where we had come from, and I turned my weapon until the hammer portion of the weapon was forward. I set my feet wide, bent my knees, and pulled the axe back like a major-league batter before swinging it forward toward the outer circle of the runic symbol. Then stopped abruptly. Shit. That wasn't a good idea.

The sound of stone being hit by metal would reverberate throughout the tunnel and give us away. So, I kept my wide stance and softly tapped the rune with the hammer head just enough that a small bit of stone fell away. When I checked the rune again, I could somehow tell that it was just ruined enough to allow us to move through without giving the alarm. But I wasn't sure if it would raise the alarm if destroyed either. We had to move.

"There could be kickback from that, they may know we're here anyhow, let's go," I warned and shouldered Magus Bane.

Balmur stepped in front of us, and we moved forward again slowly, half an hour in, Yohsuke perked up. We had almost made it through the majority of the traps too, damn.

You guys hear that? I couldn't really hear anything, *sounds coming from our route ahead.*

Hide! He hissed to us and waved us to the side. I threw up a thin veil of shadows, and Maebe threw a wall of deep shadow up in front that hid us as we stood near a tunnel wall.

Four figures approaching, and what looks like mist, he explained as it was too difficult for us to see right that moment. *Vampire bats, levels in the low thirties. Can't make anything on the mist.*

It was quiet for a moment, then Yoh spoke out loud, "So this is where I had to come to learn more about myself?"

A moment of silence again. "Yeah, they all died terribly, but that's because they attacked us."

What the hell is happening out there? James asked Yohsuke quietly.

They're grilling me, shut up a minute.

"Yeah, that's because there is one." Yohsuke sounded tired. The scent of rotten garbage floated and sifted through the shadows. "Well, if you're going to be like that, hell no, I don't want to join you. I don't care if your master is displeased about my not being a pawn."

Hissing sounds, and a snarl sounded from the other side of the shadows just before Maebe, and I dropped our cover, and the fight was on.

Three vampire bats flapped at Yohsuke's back, trying to flank and lift him up, the fourth held by the throat as the spell blade growled and sliced into it like it was a kabob. The thing's health was draining swiftly, ebbing from 70% to 65% and by more and more as Yoh held on.

James crashed into one of the vampires trying to lift his friend from behind in a flurry of punches and kicks with his flaming weapons slashing and puncturing. His victim screeched and fell onto an Earthen Spike summoned by Fainnir.

Jaken sprinted forward toward the mist with Righteous Brand raised to strike, but Balmur tackled him onto the ground at the same time as a spike erupted from the ceiling scoring the earth where they had just been.

"Don't do that!" Balmur snarled impatiently, then rolled off the paladin's chest into the shadows, before launching himself out from beneath one of the vampire bats and coming out slashing like he was some kind of chef's nightmare.

Arrows bounced off the tunnel walls as Jafrik attempted to hit a target, anything really, but he just kept shaking too much.

Me? I summoned Falfyre. The holy blade appeared in my grasp as the mana cost drained away, and I stabbed forward. The vampire bat in Yohsuke's grasp caught fire as soon as the sword slashed through his back, the scent of ash spreading. The other vampire bats screeched at me, the vibrations coalescing on me, bringing me to my knees, my eardrums pounding furiously. I let the blade go, covered my ears, and willed it to shoot forward into the farthest one.

It died, and the other two tried to flee, but Bokaj whipped arrows into their wings with silver coins attached to them. Once they fell, Jaken and I fell on them with holy vengeance.

They were dust by the time we finished, several of the traps behind them having been triggered in their attempt to run from us.

"Where the fuck is Muu?" James asked as we looked around. It was a solid question; I couldn't see him.

"He is standing over his kill." Maebe pointed down the tunnel to where the mist had been floating away. "When Jaken tried to go by foot, he jumped after the mist and threw his holy spear. The holy weapon must have struck true because it pinned the vampire to the stone."

I narrowed my eyes and tried to see him, but I couldn't. "We gotta get to him, let's go."

Balmur led the charge to him. By charge, I mean trudge. We had to stop and wait for him to disarm the traps and for me to kill the runes. Then I heard grunting and soft cursing.

I cast my awareness forward and felt a wall of shadows in front of us about thirty feet out. I shredded it with my will and exposed Muu standing over a corpse with its fangs bared. It looked to be human, with red hair, glowing black eyes, and pale skin. Claws reached out toward our friend and tried to knock the spear out of his hand.

Muu fought desperately to keep the vampire pinned where it was as his ring glowed blue like a beacon, his eyes closed tightly while he muttered.

"Balmur, go," I ordered softly, and the rogue nodded once. I took a breath and threw Falfyre forward, spending the necessary couple points of mana a second to keep the weapon under control. Once Balmur stepped from Muu's shadow, he spoke softly, too low for me to hear at this distance and jabbed forward with his holy daggers.

The vampire spat and tried to fight back, but Falfyre slid straight into its open mouth, the body crumbling to ash a second later.

Good job, bud, I told him softly through our earrings. *Stay there, let Balmur work his way back to us, and we can move on.*

It took about ten more minutes for him to work his way back to us, but it was worth it.

"I hadn't expected that to work." Muu shuddered. "I could feel him trying to weasel his way into my head. Don't look in their eyes."

"Dude, I told you that." Yohsuke pinched his shoulder lightly.

"And I forgot!" He hissed back. "Never again."

A shiver ran down my spine, and I refocused on what lay ahead. There were fewer traps now, but they were much deadlier. One of them had activated a secondary trigger when the first had been disabled that shot an arrow toward Balmur. He dodged it easily but hadn't bothered to redirect the shot. The arrow almost pegged Jafrik in the head, but Maebe snatched the boy out of the way.

The arrowhead collided with the stone behind them and splattered a solution onto it. It sizzled, and noxious fumes exuded from the spot. I summoned shadows to swallow the fumes making it so we could breathe. We took our time from there on, investigating each trap a bit more thoroughly than before, thanks to that last one.

It was slow going, working our way closer to the main tunnel, but worthwhile. There was nothing else to slow us down, and we made it to the other larger tunnel that connected us to the larger cavern.

The walls here appeared to be covered in dust and spores that looked unnatural, like spider eggs.

Uh, you guys seeing all this? Jaken whispered through our heads. *Those look like spider eggs to you?*

Cool shadows swept out from behind us, I turned to see Maebe grimace. The shadows swept over the walls, and where they went, the eggs disappeared.

It's a good thing she married you because she could have killed us all. Muu observed with a pat on my shoulder and grim smile.

I nodded back, watching before us warily.

If they sent scouts and don't hear back, they may suspect something is up. James warned from where he snuck through the tunnel.

It was twice as large as the previous one and had veins of marble and other different kinds of stone in the walls.

"May be a good time to have Pebble do a sweep of the area, Fainnir." I ducked down to speak to Fainnir, who eyed the stone around us suspiciously.

"No, Pebble is on another mission righ' now." He held out a hand and knocked on the stone. A large figure stepped out of it, twelve feet tall and more human-looking in shape than anything he had summoned before stood before us. "This be Gem, she's here to see us there safely. Doesn't talk much, but she's smart."

I looked at him pointedly, and he sort of bowed his head bashfully. "While the rest of ye were workin' this mornin' and havin' yer talks and breakfast, I was summoning her. I'm strong enough now to control her and one other, weaker elemental. She be of the Sword caste of elementals."

He looked up at the large elemental, who patted his head

gently. She looked to be made of the surrounding stone, but there were precious gems, veins of platinum, silver, and mithril as well as veins of precious and semi-precious stones in her body, even some sharper-looking ones sticking from her hands like fingers. Her eyes looked like brightly polished coins of onyx, and her mouth was small compared to her brothers'.

"Good job," I whispered hoarsely, the elemental regarding me curiously, before patting me on the head. It was like when you see a child very obviously petting a dog way too hard, but the dog loves the child and seems to know they don't mean any harm by it, and they're happy anyway. Picture that with a grown-ass man and a giant baby. With sharp fingers and little strength control. "Ouch! Shit, man."

"Friend," she grumbled at me, her small mouth quirking up at the sides oddly in a smile.

I nodded and tried to smile back at the unnerving creature before turning back to the others and motioning that we should move.

While we crept forward, I asked Fainnir, "What's Pebble doing?"

"Scouting the way," he replied mysteriously, and I grabbed his shoulder softly to stop him. He sighed. "Donae worry. This trust thin' goes both ways, you reckon?"

I should have said he hadn't earned it yet, but the truth was that he had. He'd been working hard to try and help us as he could with our direction.

"Okay." I thumped his arm, and we set off again. "But if you have new abilities like this, you need to say something, okay? What is it that you have planned?"

He shook his head before replying, "Hopefully somethin' tha' we won't be needin'. If what I learned 'bout vampires be true from the legends o' the elder dwarves what schooled us, the less information I share, the better."

I looked at him oddly, then remembered Muu's reaction to the vampire earlier. "They can weasel information out of people if they ensnare them with their gaze?" He nodded and I closed my eyes in thought. Shit. "There's not enough time for me to make a ring of mental protection for you, so we need to keep you safe."

He nodded and pointed forward, the others having made it a little further from us and looked to be closing on the mouth to the place we were headed to.

We crept forward slowly, our eyes falling on a dimly lit chasm with our goal rising from the gloom on the other side. There were no bridges we could see on this side. Dim light filtered from crystals similar to those of the ones over the drow city somewhere above us.

Amber light made the place look like some sort of boss castle in a video game.

It looked like a castle, like a proper castle, but made entirely of steel. How, I couldn't tell you, but the walls looked to be riveted together, that or they had been welded. Maybe some kind of ancient society that had the metallurgical skills necessary to do this had abandoned it? Maybe it was all some sort of spell. There was a single large tower that rose higher than the light allowed us to see, and some of the other details were fuzzy from this distance.

I took a deep breath and gagged immediately, bile rising into my throat. It *reeked* in here.

Shut up. Yohsuke side-eyed me, then shook his head. *How are we getting across?*

I shrugged, before analyzing things closer. A fifty-foot expanse of ground with white bone and smatterings of crimson littered all over it preceded the chasm, and from where I stood, it looked to be about eighty to a hundred feet wide.

Some of us could fly, and I could ferry people over and have Kayda do so as well, but it was a matter of us being safe enough to do so. If we were to build a shadow bridge like we did in the lava chamber, we would be easy pickings if anyone was watching for us. Who knew if they didn't have something waiting in the deeper shadows above the light, and I was too far away to really sense anything with any certainty.

Can't you just mist yourself over it? Muu asked quietly.

Yeah, you're one of them now. James shrugged and motioned forward.

"If all of you are attempting to choose how you get across," Xaenth drawled softly. "I may be of assistance."

"Mae and the boys, you guys want to be here on this side, or over on the other side near us?" Jaken motioned to the entry-way, then the other side of the chasm as he spoke.

The boys looked to Maebe, who seemed uncertain, then decided. "Here. The other side is much too close for me to retain my strength near so much of the fell metal."

Servant slunk from the entry to stand next to the boys, "I will watch their backs. All of you go."

We stepped closer to the drow mage, and his arms waved in the air, radiating pulses of darkness and pale light flickered from his palms. A small circle of dull-glowing light surrounded our feet, his eyes flickered white and black and he snapped his fingers, then the world around us blurred.

We were in motion, but not. Then we stopped on the other side of the chasm in the blink of an eye.

"The hell was that?!" Balmur whispered fiercely.

"A simple transport spell, called Locomotion," Xaenth explained patiently. "Takes a group of people close together and moves them a short distance, merely up to three hundred feet from the origin of the casting."

"I need to learn that," Balmur said, his voice a bitter grumble.

"It is something that must be studied deeply, but you are welcome to attempt it someday." The drow smiled as if at a child, then regarded the others we had left behind. "Tell me, though, if he was to be bait, why does Dirt wait in safety?"

"Think of how potent his virgin blood is," Yohsuke answered, a look of longing crossing his features, his eyes closed and nose to the imaginary wind. "One whiff and the lesser vampires will come running."

"Flapping," Bokaj stated.

"Dude, hardly the time to correct the man's English," Muu said, then snorted derisively.

"No." The ranger lifted his bow with an arrow nocked and pulled taut. "*Flapping!*"

I could hear it now, the sound of wings that grew steadily louder until it was almost deafening. Glaring above us, several hundred screeching bats separated from the ceiling and plummeted through the light, the shadows twisting and growing in the dim glow. The small creatures fluttered and flapped like a hurricane of fangs and flesh moving across the chasm toward the small group.

Gem exploded from the earth and swatted dozens of the creatures onto the ground beneath her stomping feet.

"We need to get in there before they're any more aware of our presence than they might be, already," Yohsuke's voice cut through my worry. "Maebe and Fainnir have that. Let's go."

We pressed ourselves against the steel wall of the fortress and moved as swiftly as we could without attracting unwanted attention. Once we reached the doors, I groaned softly.

The door was covered in sigils, runes, and circles that glowed sickly green, deep purple, and shadowy in the light.

I pressed my awareness against it and knew that the door could withstand all of us, casting our strongest spells at it simultaneously and still come out unfazed.

"I cannot dispel this quickly." Xaenth frowned as he poured over the door from a reasonable distance. "And, there appears to be a blowback trigger on it."

I wanted to choke him the hell out for not volunteering earlier to help with the traps, but we had other, bigger concerns.

The bats used echolocation in all directions, screeching and calling into the nether. We had run out of time. Either we waited to see if something opened up, tried to find another door, or we went in like badasses.

"Cover me," I shouted at the others and focused my mind on my claw and began to funnel flame-aspected mana into it at a slow and steady pace.

The others moved to stand close to my back but gave me enough room to work. I stayed closer to the door than I wanted to, but it was a necessary evil as I dug my burning diamondhard claw into the steel surrounding the door. It didn't take at first, but I funneled more mana into it and persisted, working my way through the steel around it. It was thicker than I thought, and I almost summoned Falfyre to assist, but this way would work.

I began funneling mana into my other claws and dug in with a grunt of effort, the steel melting and clearing faster and faster, and I increased the mana I was using.

It took about two minutes of constant funneling, and by the time I was finished, the bats were falling faster. The bad news was that larger specimens had detached from the ceiling and began to fly over the chasm, toward us, and toward my wife and the kids.

My mana was about half full at that moment, so I decided to trust my friends and focus on getting us inside.

"Let me get a couple shots off, and we will see about getting all the way in there." Bokaj took a deep breath, and before he fired, I cast one of the few buffs I had, Star Blade. It wasn't purely for melee weapons, it was any weapon really, and at a measly 25 MP, I kicked myself for not having cast it earlier. It lasted for an hour, which seemed a little broken, but hey—I ain't gonna complain.

Starry mana infused with Bokaj's bow and his arrows streaked into the air like shooting stars, catching some of the larger bats in the wings, and they screeched horribly as they burst into flame.

Yeah, Celestial spells do some serious holy damage sometimes.

The larger bats began to fall into the gaping maw of the chasm below them, the void gobbling them up, but not their echoing cries of anguish. As two more echoing cries sounded, my claws penetrated the wall fully, and I made the hole wider with more ease than I'd had earlier.

"Go on." Bokaj fired another arrow, then I stepped through our newly made hole with Balmur just in front of me.

The rest of the group filed in without touching the still slightly molten, but as I crossed the threshold Yohsuke gasped.

I turned to find him standing outside the door with a look of confusion on his face. "The hell are you waiting for?"

"An invitation, you asshat!" He snarled back, he tapped the empty air before him, and it seemed to be solid. "You know, for a nerd who knows as much lore as you do, you seem to know precious little about vampires. They have someone alive in there who lives in this place."

"I invite you in," I tried, and it didn't work at all. "Go help Maebe and the boys stay alive, and I'll get ahold of you when we find the person who can invite you in."

"Okay." He nodded and turned to sprint away. I heard him filling the others in mentally.

This is some bullshit. Muu grumbled loudly. *We have a vampire and a werewolf, what's next? Sasquatch?*

Dude, you're literally a humanoid dragon, James shot back. *Get your scaly ass in gear, and let's get this over with!*

Looking around, I saw the entryway down here was only that, an entryway. We came out next to a closet that held skeletal remains in it, some bones crushed to dust, others splintered, with few whole bones left and a coat that held nothing of interest. The rest of this lower portion was just a hall to the stairs. No other doors, nothing. I thought I saw a flicker of movement above us up the stairs and glanced back at the others who nodded that they were ready, Bokaj still looking outside for a moment.

I sprinted up the stairs in front of me two at a time and came to the second floor with my friends. The area looked to be some sort of nightmare dining room with a large crystal-covered chandelier glowing above a long table. The gray walls were splattered with crimson. Goblets of blood, plates of gore, and organs, with fine golden forks and knives laid out most perfectly for some kind of fancy dinner. The only thing ruining what could have been a perfectly fucked up civilized moment were the bodies that hung from meat hooks instead of sitting in chairs around the sides of the room. Some were human, some drow, and other creatures I didn't readily recognize, but the majority of them looked to be goblins. The small corpses seeming to float.

"This is hardly pleasant." Xaenth sniffed and held a kerchief to his nose with disdain in his gaze.

The worst part of all of it was that there was someone seated at the head of the table with a hooded figure behind them. She sat with her legs draped over the side of the chair as if lounging, with a goblet of crimson liquid held in her hand.

"Rude of you to break into someone's home, uninvited as you are," she observed before raising the glass to her lips.

Her drow features were elegant and beautiful, less Amazonian than the other female drow elves I had seen so far. Her figure was much more athletic in her simple pale dress. Her eyes glowed scarlet as she watched us all with mild curiosity, the slight impression of blood left behind on her lips disappeared with a slow, lazy flick of her tongue. Dainty fangs peeked out from behind her lips as they quirked into a smile.

"I see you have brought a few friends and a dog?" Her eyebrows raised, and her voice dripped with sarcasm, "Well, I always did want another pet, though mother never did care for animals and beasts. That was why she always seemed to have such a soft spot for my cold-hearted, psychotic little sister. Oh well. She is dead now, and the latter sits on a throne built of lies."

"What do you mean?" Bokaj asked, stepping forward slightly. As he did, the chandelier dimmed, and the darkness above deepened considerably.

"Meaning that she takes credit for things that had been orchestrated by someone else, but dead men can keep all sorts of wonderful secrets." She smiled fully then. "I wonder if any of you would be willing to be turned here and now? Save me some time? My benefactor has an interest in you all as well, though why I do not know. All she wants is either your demise or your cooperation."

"It was you." Jaken frowned, then blinked at her. "You were the one who sent that invasion force to Djurn Forge, and who are you talking about? Is the figure behind you this benefactor?"

The woman said nothing, gave away nothing with her pleasantly blank face, but the figure laughed, creepily. "I take it that you haven't liked my meddling? Good. You will all die here; my minion will see to that. And this world will be ours. And then we come for yours, and all the people you protect will fall."

I ground my teeth as the figure stepped forward and faded before I could even cast a single spell, fuck. *So, she is a minion then, and that must have been the general we thought was here.* The others had to have heard me, but they stayed quiet while Jaken finished his thoughts.

"You did that, and then while you were overseeing it, she killed your mother and cast you out," Jaken continued on. I watched as he began to deduce more and more, but the shadows above us deepened further still. There was something up there. "And that's why she sent us here—to kill you and tie up the loose ends. But with a benefactor... why would you need to do all this? As a minion, your job is to create chaos, right?"

"Very clever, Holy One." She purred as she slowly clapped her hands softly. "Though you do realize that, even if you were to make it out of this place alive, she will likely kill you all for making the connections that you have. Seeing as though she seems to want to 'tie up loose ends,' and such. My benefactor gave me this place, and with it, the ability to raise the dead and make them the *un*dead. She was quite gracious, even gave me a taste of her power, though that she calls me minion irks me, and you will not do so either. No matter."

Righteous Brand flew from Jaken's fist, piercing her heart. The goblet falling from her hand as she had been swirling it.

The paladin stood up straight with a grim expression on his face, but the body in the chair began to change.

"You honestly did not think I would be here to greet my beloved little sister's pet assassins personally, did you?" Her disembodied voice sounded sarcastic and surprised. "Here I had been thinking you smart enough to have figured that out, my lady truly does give you all too much credit."

The shadows deepened once more, and glowing eyes opened within them.

"No, I have my sights set on something much better," she said happily. "Something made slightly less...well-defended by an attack that had been too fortuitously devastating to pass up. But do not worry, I'm certain you'll find your current hosts' much better company than I. You see, dinner is *served*."

Her haughty laugh echoed throughout the room while seven hulking figures dropped from the darkness above the chandelier, their twisted bodies grotesque and oddly shaped. They looked to be large, wingless vampire bats, but their musculature was insane and would have likely made the hulk fit right in. Large, clawed hands balled into half fists then spread wide as they crouched as if to spring at us.

Time to get the fuck out of here, she's going for the city! Balmur called to all of us and we began to back away.

Xaenth, who had been behind us, spoke out loud, "Well, this is an unfortunate turn of events." His fists began to glow with a sickly light as he looked from the hulking vampires to us. "I thought she would at least wait to watch as I killed you for her."

"Mother fucker!" I snarled aloud as the light left his hand but bounced off of Balmur's dome spell.

Balmur burst from the shadows at the drow elf's feet at the same time three arrows burst from Xaenth's chest. One more bounced off of a barrier he erected before him, but Balmur stabbed Sorrow into the traitorous mage's spine, the hand dropping to his side.

I bounded forward and kicked him at the vampires that had

charged, and he hit one, the beast stopping to put the limp body to its mouth before savaging the throat and tearing it out to chew on.

"Let's move!" Jaken shouted as an aura of red radiated from his body, his sword, and shield in his hands.

"What about Righteous Brand?" Muu called as he stabbed at one of the vampires with his holy spear.

"I'll have another made; we need to leave!" He said as two of them crashed into his shield and I had to steady him with my hands on his back. "Zeke, fry them, and let's get out of here."

"Balmur, cover the door in shadows so the light won't escape!" I called, and he shouted back.

"Done!"

I nodded and focused my mind, then cast Solar Flare into the back of the room just next to the wall. A miniature sun burst into existence there, and the light from it scorched the wall and everything in the immediate vicinity. I tried to pull some of the shadows up in front of us to assist in keeping us from getting the brunt of the attack, but it still hurt like crazy. I was down to a little less than half health, and the others, but for Muu and Jaken, had fared a little worse.

The hulking vampires screamed and roared, thrashing in the light, attempting to get to cover, one of them upended the table to try and get something between it and the offending spell. Its life ebbed as the table burned, and Bokaj's silver-coin arrows pierced it, knocking it onto its back into the light of the spell, where it screamed once more and fell dead in a pile of ash and dust. One of the others had managed to get around us by jumping over the balcony, crushing the stairway a bit, but having fallen prone.

Muu stabbed it several times in quick, shallow strikes with the holy damage carrying it to its final death. The other hulking vampires had followed us to the stairway where Balmur and Bokaj did their best to harry them where they could, how they could. Jaken began attempting to heal the others, and I ensured that nothing was following us as we came through the hole in the wall.

"Don't touch the door!" James reminded us as we came closer to it. The larger bat creatures continued to screech from outside, and now that they were away from the Solar Flare, the hulking vampires grew a little braver. One grabbed Jaken's shield in his hands and began to twist, the metal groaning in protest. Gnashing teeth and fangs reached over it as the paladin's sword began glowing a deep gold.

"In Her name, and by Her strength, I cast you from my sight!" Jaken roared as he brought the radiant weapon back, then stabbed it forward. "Smite!"

The vampire screamed pitiably and died in a flash of radiant energy like an explosion. The others kept their distance after that, the four who still lived, but they were badly hurt, around 40% health at best.

We gotta kill these things. James head-butted one who had come too close to him, trying to get a good grasp of him to bite. *Any more of that smiting left Jaken?*

Cooldown, and the mana cost isn't pleasant. Jaken huffed as the vampire behind the one he had killed lumbered forward. *Keeping these things funneled like this is cool and all, but they keep trying to go through my damned shield. Let's get moving!*

We took the lot of them back toward the door, Balmur guiding us as we fell back into the open. Once we reached the doorway, an idea hit me.

Let's see if we can get them to touch the door! I called to the others. They agreed, and we lured the creatures out, a little of the light from my still burning spell highlighting them from behind. *Step aside and out of the way as soon as you can, give me at least fifty feet just in case it doesn't work.*

I'd had a bit of time since I'd worked through the wall and cast my heavier spell, and I was feeling better about casting this spell if needed. Once the vampires were dead, we could get a couple minutes to recover. My friends scrambled out of the doorway behind me, and a clawed hand wrapped around the back of my neck and froze, getting ready to dish out the worst beating I could, then the hand lifted and pulled me *away* from the door and the approaching vampires.

"Don't worry little fella, I got you," Muu whispered behind me, the adrenal dump I had experienced making me angrier at him than I truly was at that moment.

The vampires had made it to the door, and Jaken beat his sword against his bent and dented shield, another burst of red aura filtering from his body. They looked like they might jump the door, but the lead one stepped right onto it, and nothing happened. Shit!

I cast Phoenix Burst immediately, the small ball of burning radiant flame careening into the lead vampire and engulfing him as the ball spread over fifty feet and blasted purifying flames over them. Bokaj's arrows rained into the doorway once the flames had died down, and I saw another beam of red zip into the door before detonating, and another gout of burning flame erupted.

The vampires inside were well beyond fried and ash, they had to be, but the absence of the light gave me pause. I needed to be sure. I poked my head inside the room doorway, taking in the sight of the singed, still burning floorboards and stairs. No more vampires.

"What the hell are we supposed to do now?" Jaken sat on the ground for a moment to rest and check on his shield. He must have decided it was beyond repair, the clawed rents in it, the dents, and the beginnings of a tear in the top being too much because he threw it over the ledge of the chasm. We waited in silence, but nothing came for a long time. Then a distant, echoing thud.

"We kill her, then make sure that we get the fuck out of dodge so they can't come after us." Yohsuke stated as he stepped from the side of the wall. "James told me everything that was happening in real-time while all of you were in there. Maebe and the boys are okay over there, so let's start getting you guys across."

"I'll jump across, see you guys over there." Muu marched over to the wall behind us, took a runner's stance with his head down, then pushed himself forward as hard as he could. Once he came close to the ledge, he leapt with all his strength and sailed through the air with his legs and arms windmilling as he did. He easily cleared the distance and landed about twenty feet from the far wall near the entrance to this place.

Balmur just shook his head and looked to me. "You want to polymorph someone, and I can do the other?"

"Since when do you have polymorph?" I asked incredulously.

"It was in the book that I was studying, once I understood the spell, I could cast it to a lesser degree." He shrugged and tapped the book in the breast portion of his armor. "Granted, I can only do creatures I've seen before, and it only lasts for fifteen minutes, but that's plenty of time, right?"

I nodded and looked to Jaken. "I'll turn you into a sugar glider, then throw you over there, okay?"

He nodded, and I cast the spell. His body disappeared in a puff of white smoke, and on the stone ground rustled a small, brown-furred critter with huge eyes and skin flaps meant to help him glide.

I bent to pick him up, and noted mist had gathered where Yohsuke had been, then he was back. "Nope, that won't work."

"Can you turn into a bat?" Bokaj asked curiously, the rest of us looking at him oddly. "What? Homeboy is on some Dracula shit now, and that's a pretty common thing in a lot of stories, right?"

"I guess I could try. There's a status screen for vampirism, but it's kind of grayed out."

"Do you need to feed?" I asked quietly. He glanced up at me, a strange look passing over his face, then gave a nod.

"I don't think you want my blood, but is there anyone else willing to donate?" I looked over at the others, and they seemed a little wary. "Guys, it doesn't have to be him actually biting you. You can just bleed into a cup, and then he can drink it."

"I'll help." Balmur sighed, glancing over at me. "You heal me after?"

I nodded, and Yohsuke pulled out a cup and handed it over. Balmur took one of his other daggers and slid it over his wrist with little more than a hiss of pain like he'd gotten a paper cut. Crimson droplets dribbled into the cup, then more as Bokaj stepped over and did the same.

"We can all help share the load." Once they were both done, I cast Renewing Flames on each and their wounds knit cleanly back together.

Yohsuke took the cup from me, sniffed it before shrugging and upending the glass into his gullet. He drank deeply, a little color returning to his body as he did so. His eyes closed, and he seemed to just still for a moment before they reopened, slightly darker than before, but still orange.

"Thanks, guys." He shook out his shoulders and had shadows come and clean the cup out for him before putting it into his inventory. He appeared to try and do something but seemed confused. "I'm activating the skill, but it's not working."

"Did you try envisioning the animal you want to become?" I asked sincerely. "I have to do it every time I shapeshift. Try to see the bat in your mind first, then activate it."

He closed his eyes, his brows knitting together in concentration. He took a deep breath, then a poof of smoke, and a bat fluttered in the air where he had been. His flight was a little more harrowing than I would have liked, but he eventually made it across the chasm safely.

I glanced down at Jaken, his little brown eyes staring up at me in fear.

"Let's practice your gliding first, okay?" I lifted him and tossed him to Balmur. It took a couple passes for him to get it down, but by the time he was ready, I warmed up to the idea of throwing one of my best friends over a chasm that could easily mean his doom.

I picked him up and rocked my arm down low, then rotated like a pitcher and whipped my arm up and over with a good follow-through. Jaken's sugar glider form passed through the air without incident, but he couldn't seem to stick the landing as he hit the ground harder than we had expected he might and rolled until he lost his form and crashed into Muu with a resounding crack.

Kayda flew over with Tmont in one of her claws in her smaller cat form, and Balmur had turned Bokaj into a corgi who also dangled from Kayda's delicately clenched talons.

"Our turn, how do you want to do this?" I clapped my hands and looked over at Balmur who eyed the distance.

"I think I can shadow step it now, with our blessing from the shadow elemental, I have a much farther range. I just haven't really had the chance to try it out yet." He frowned, then shook his head. "Better not push our limits over a chasm, right? I'll wait here, and you can ferry me."

It was a swift flight to cross the distance over the chasm, and by the time I made it there, Kayda had already gone back for the Azer dwarf.

Once the two of them landed, Balmur having patted her in gratitude, Kayda looked to me, *Do we go to fight, now?*

"I think that's something we need to discuss," I informed her, then looked at my friends. "We've very obviously been set up, and we also know that whoever that vampire chick was, she was a minion likely working for a general. We haven't seen the two of them working together before, it's kind of been loners here and there. You think they're starting to organize?"

"Makes sense." Yohsuke sighed, rubbing his neck. "They want us to back off, then they start to organize and actively try to cause as much chaos and strife as possible. Not to mention that once we kill Lilith's sister, we're likely on the hit list. What's the point in trying to do that?"

"Keeping Djurn Forge safe?" Muu spread his hands wide, then pointed at Fainnir, who seemed lost in thought and staring off into the stone in the distance. "See? He's already fucked up about it!"

"So, then we kill her and the major baddies, then we grab

Gerty and beat feet," Bokaj suggested softly, then seemed to decide that was best. "There's no way we can go up against that many drow and vampires at the same time. And since the vampires took the fight to the drow, they may decide they just don't need us, and then try to kill us on sight anyway. So, we need to do this right. I have a plan, so hear me out."

CHAPTER TWENTY-FOUR

"This is fucking nuts; you know that, right?" Muu tried desperately not to look as scared as his complaining made him out to be.

The plan was simple enough; we had an extraction team ready to go in and get Gerty while the assault team created both a distraction and an attack meant to...well assault.

The teams broke down as follows: the assault team would consist of me, Balmur and Yohsuke. The extraction team would consist of Muu, James, Jaken, Bokaj, and Fainnir. Servant, Maebe, and Jafrik would go with them to wait at our rendezvous point, which was where the extraction point would be at Lilith's palace. It would be easier for us to get there than it would be for the extractors to get back to the entry to the city. Plus, teleporting made anywhere a viable extraction point.

We were hoping that in the confusion of fighting, we would be able to either blend in or be overlooked. But that would mainly depend on how well we did this.

I opted to let Bea out of the collar for this one. Her dizzying speed could prove useful to the extractors. I told her she had to listen to what the others told her to do, and she nodded before licking my ear.

"We all remember our roles?" Bokaj stared at all of us, and we nodded. "Alright, let's hop to it."

We had already teleported back to the city's entryway, the one to the cavern, not the gate. Then waited for the cooldown to end before the mission truly began because that was going to be our escape card. While I wanted to make a weapon for Gerty and to be sure we were good for the fight, our planning had to come first, and we would make do. We could hear muted fighting in the distance, watching as flying figures and blasts of flame and magic shot into the sky at what I assumed to be the vampire bats that darted down and lifted figures from the ground.

There was no telling if someone would catch sight of me while I was enchanting and send forces here to fight us. Another loud gout of flame breached the second of silence.

It was looking bad out there. I looked up at Kayda. "You ready, sweetie?"

We hunt! Her feathers fluttered as she spread her wings and lifted from the ground with Balmur on her back. Yohsuke and I took off behind her, me as an owl and Yohsuke as the bat held in Balmur's left hand.

Our goal was to get to the crystals up at the top of the cavern and create just a smidgeon of mayhem.

We had done well the first couple minutes to avoid some of the flying vampire bats, but spells still flew like mortar fire and surface to air missiles all around us. Dodging them took everything we had, and even then, some of the bursting eldritch and shadow spells swatted the storm roc a bit, damaging her little by little.

I willed her to fly higher, dipping down to take the brunt of a spell that looked like some sort of pure ball of magic the size of a baseball. It hurt, dipping me down by a quarter of my health, but we made it to our destination and hid in a cluster of the crystals for cover.

I landed on Kayda's back as she flapped her powerful wings carefully to keep us hovering.

We're in position for Operation Disco Ball, Balmur reported through our earrings, then out loud, he said, "I love him to death, but between Bokaj and Muu trying to name things, this gets weird, you know?"

I nodded my owl head, and we waited for a moment longer, then Jaken reported, *We're outside the Spider Queen's palace now. The majority of the vampires are out in the open, but the worst ones seem to be over here. Whatever you guys have planned; you may want to get on it so we can get in there after Gerty.*

Let's get to it, Zeke, Balmur whispered fiercely. We had one go at this, and it would leave both of us dangerously close to tapped even after I used my ace in the hole. 1,400 MP at my disposal and I was about to burn through all but two hundred of it for a single spell. Balmur would be spending at least 376 MP from what he had explained about his half of the spell.

I shifted into my fox-man form, tapped Yoh in his bat form still cradled against Balmur, and he filtered into my collar for safety. Then Kayda descended, from where we were, slowly as I charged Solar flare and activated Vulpine Casting, a once-daily ability that halves the mana cost of a spell. Twenty seconds in, I was ready with a glowing metallic palm. We were well below the crystals now, and Balmur muttered and motioned before nodding at me as he touched my hand. I focused on the point I wanted the spell to originate from, then blasted it. A miniature sun dawned into being in the center of the crystals, refracting light blazed all over and screaming began in earnest.

Balmur had done to my spell what he had to Fainnir's in the dungeon, amplifying it and making it larger with his knowledge of magical laws, conversion, and relativity. It wasn't by much, but it helped.

Who knew what would be attracted by this much noise— but we wouldn't be here to find out.

I rolled off of Kayda's back and shifted into my eagle form immediately, my feathers whistling a little as we soared toward the palace of web and lies. I glanced down and saw vampires bubbling and bursting into flames when they touched direct light from it. Drow elves held their faces in their hands and hid their eyes from the harsh light of the spell.

Heat radiated out of it in waves, and concentrated beams of light flared down, as if from a magnifying glass. Kayda and I dodged them as we came upon them, but that didn't mean we didn't bully some of the vampires into them how we could. Shoving them, leading them—we drew them to the light like moths to the flame.

A moment later, we were in sight of the huge mass of webs and stone that was the Queen's palace, the roof of spires barely jutting out from above it. I caught a glimmer of something below us, just inside.

My friends looked to be fighting the drider guards and the vampire invaders in the shadowed cover of the webs. The fight seemed to be going poorly, as it was a free for all. Drider and drow fought vampire and our party members alike in a melee that made my adrenaline spike harder than ever. I screeched, and both Kayda and I dropped toward the fray.

A crack of booming thunder echoed above as lightning rent the air before us, striking one of the driders in the chest where he stood in front of Fainnir and James.

"Bout time!" The dwarf called with a smile drenched in blood. He was covered in it, but his health seemed to be fine. "Come on; the fight's almost won!"

I had no idea what he meant, but it would be a good idea to start to beat some ass. First, it would be a better idea to try and recover some of my mana. I shifted into my fox man form as I landed, then took out Magus Bane and looked around for a good opponent.

Driders and drow elves tried to fight the same hulking vampires that we had been battling at the steel fort, and there was no shortage on either side of free bodies.

"Where is the Queen and the Vampire Lord?" I called over the din of the fighting.

Yohsuke filtered from my collar and flitted by me, stepping in front of a hulking vampire and shouting, "Fuck you!"

A spear of hellish, sulfur-smelling flames soared from his grasp and caught it in the chest as Muu sailed onto its back and stabbed his spear into the back of its neck where its black blood drained with its HP bar.

Muu pointed toward the steps where the two women seemed to be duking it out ferociously. Larger drider guards standing with the Spider Queen as she swung a rapier against her undead sister.

We get Gerty yet? Balmur spoke through our earrings as he tore into a vampire bat who had come too close to him. His holy crystal weapons flashing in the darkness and severing the creature's wings.

We couldn't get into the place; it was too heavily guarded by the drow, and then the vampires came in en masse. James huffed as he punched a drow spellcaster in the face, a blast of his ki shattering their focus and dropping them to the ground where they floundered like a fish out of water. *I think Maebe mentioned something about going in after her.*

Shit, let's get moving then boys. I growled as I set my sights on the front lines of the battle, the vampires ganging up on the drow and lifting them into the sky more often than they had been before. They began sinking their teeth into their prey's necks, draining their life force, and bolstering their own in the process.

"We need to keep that from happening too much more," Yohsuke called out, taking his Astral Blade and cutting into one of the hulking vampire's legs as it clutched at a drider it had been trying to drain. Jaken leapt forward with his greatsword out and severed the foul creature's arm with a mighty cleave and then kicked it as hard as he could in the chest. The thing rocked back but managed to grasp his leg with its remaining hand, dragging Jaken along with him.

James and Balmur were on top of the beast in the blink of an eye with their fists and weapons flashing dangerously.

"Where's Bokaj?" Balmur called once the beast was dead.

The others glanced around in a panic, then, *Where the hell are you, Bokaj?*

The ranger answered Yohsuke tersely, *Inside!* Then seemed to find a little more time to fully answer, *Lilith set the creatures in the cages free and we're fighting our way up. Maebe is killing them quickly, but there are things that are immune to shadow in here, and she's getting tired!*

Muu was next to me in a heartbeat. "Think we should make our own door?"

"What do you have in mind?" I raised an eyebrow as dread gripped my heart.

"I'm going to jump with you in hand as high as I can, then throw you at the wall. You go belgar and have Kayda keep me from touching the webs." He put his spear into his inventory, then pulled out his hammer and affixed it to his belt with a strap. "Once you get inside, I can try and get the others up to you as fast as possible, but it'll take a second unless you take one of them in the collar?"

Jaken stepped forward and touched the collar and filtered into it, answering my unasked question for me.

"Let's drop my fat ass on them." I sighed and filled Kayda in swiftly, she understood, and another bolt of cold lightning crashed into a battling set of drow and vampire bats.

Gem lumbered over with Fainnir at her feet with his axe swinging and a savage smile on his lips as he cast a stone shard that pierced a drow warrior's eye where he fought his way forward. I had to admit I was proud of how far he had come. Something about fighting the enemies of his people seemed to drain the meekness from him. Made him stronger and more willing to lead and hunt them down.

I shifted into my fox form, and Muu snatched me up by the scruff of my neck, shaving a couple points off my health bar with his claws, but I didn't care. A heartbeat later, Muu's powerful legs sent us soaring into the air, the wind making my fur ripple and my eyes water slightly.

"Get ready!" He pulled me back, and I straightened my

body like a furry arrow, and he *hurled* me at the top of the tower as hard as he could. I tried my best to strobe my eyes, the stone and webbing looming ever closer, ever faster, until finally —*NOW!*

I shifted into my massive belgar form, my body hardening, and the horn jutting from my face. This was going to hurt.

CRASH! The stone and mortar before me collapsed inward, and dust rose around me. I shifted back swiftly, and Jaken filtered out of the collar at a thought.

"Let's get to them." His grim countenance shifted to irritation as he put his greatsword away so he could grab his dancing sword. The place was too small for his larger weapon, even though it was large enough for driders to pass through comfortably.

"You go ahead, I'll grab Gerty, and we can put the moves on getting the hell back to the party and out of here." He nodded at me and turned to move down the stairwell as he bellowed, "I hate being separated from you, asshats!"

"Stay safe, brother," I muttered to his back, and turned toward my route. Motion caught my eye, and James sailed into the room, crashing into an empty cage and then bounding over.

"Hey, which way to the ass-kicking?" He hit me with a huge grin. I pointed down the stairs, and he took off without a second thought to me or what I was doing, his weapons blazing.

My friends, I shook my head and bounded up the steps as swiftly as I could. Once I reached the last floor before Lilith's room, Gerty's open cage came into view; as well as the drider and pale drow man duking it out with her. The drow had to be a vampire, as his snarling open mouth held fangs that he tried to sink into either opponent when they weren't focusing on him.

But Gerty was my prize here, and she looked to be barely hanging in there. I focused my will and summoned Falfyre, the blazing holy sword filling me with warmth and light, then bolted forward with a roaring cry, "For clan Mugfist!"

I heard her cry in return, her fist raised and new energy

flooding her as I whipped the weapon through the vampire's arm, and it hissed in return.

"Yer nae a dwarf!" She howled, her eyes moist with tears and pain.

"No, but I'm clan, and I'm here for you on Farnik, and your kids' behalf," I said, then grunted as the drider stabbed a spear toward me and almost spiked me to the floor. I managed to just get out of the way, a line of agony burning across the outside of my right quadricep. "Now, let's kill these things and get you to my friends."

She took me at my word, but the vampire struck out and sliced her across the shoulder, dragging his hand down to her elbow with blood trailing behind.

She growled fiercely, the arm limp and the muscle torn. The vampire licked the blood from his clawed hands, and his eyes glowed red a second. His cut limb quivered, and I stepped in. I threw Falfyre at him while he was distracted and cast Lighting Bolt into the drider next to me, his health dropped past 50%, then I cast Renewing Flames on Gerty.

Footsteps behind me drew my attention, and I turned in time to see Tmont slinking up the steps next to Bokaj, bloodied, and limping.

I cast Heal on him, and he nodded at me in thanks, then loosed two arrows at the drider that sprouted from its eyes and made it cry out in agony.

"Let's go," Bokaj said with a huff, then Tmont knocked me aside in time to help me avoid a clawed hand through my throat. "Good girl!"

I turned and called the holy sword to me as the bastard tried to slam his pallid, dark-skinned hand through my body again. I caught his hand just in time to have Falfyre slice through his head, stopping just beneath the eyes, then slamming into the chest cavity from behind like some kind of invisible sword master had taken the sword in hand.

The vampire dropped to the ground in a pile of ashes, and

Bokaj with Tmont and Gerty had put the finishing touches on the drider.

"Gerty, this is Bokaj and his kitty, Tmont, they're with me." She eyed both of them silently, not fully trusting me. "Gerty, the Way is long and winding, but I need you to walk with me so that Farnik and the clan can know peace at last. Come *on*."

She nodded once and joined the three of us in running breakneck down the stairs. Maebe saw us and turned with Jafrik in tow to head back down the stairs. I heard Kayda screeching outside, her keening call one of rage and triumph. I touched her mind and looked through her eyes. The battle still raged below with Bea running from each of my friends, luring wounded creatures to them and Kayda shelling out damage where she could with her Lightning Ball and Lightning Bolts.

I saw one of the hulking vampires frozen solid shattering as it had dropped from eighty feet in the sky, the ice shards piercing enemies nearby. A ground splintering explosion echoed around us; I had to grab the window ledge to my left to stay standing and motion outside drew my attention. Lilith and the Vampire Lord minion cast huge lines of shadow at each other, another line of crimson crashing into the tower and rocking it, some stone falling onto the ground and crushing one of the large spiders in the area.

Then I saw Maebe descending slowly to the ground on a circle of darkness. As she lowered herself, she motioned with her right hand and three spears of bright blue ice formed before screeching through the air like mortar fire at the Vampire Lord's feet, flinging her back. Lilith sent a wave of darkness at Maebe, and the fight was on.

"Come on now!" Gerty yanked on my hand. "This place might be fallin' over with all that magic they swing!"

It was a few more bouts of us sprinting down the blood-soaked stairs as creatures of all shapes and sizes littered the landings with blood and gore spattered and frozen in places. I almost slipped and brained myself when another attack shook the tower, but Gerty snatched me up by my armor and hauled me to my feet with a grunt of effort.

I nodded my thanks to her, and we cleared the rest of the tower, the doorway to the outer courtyard splintered and bowed inward toward us. It had been long enough that my light spell had faded already, but that didn't seem to matter much in here.

And as we reached the ground floor, my heart sank. The dead drow and vampire-bitten driders rose from the ground slowly as if reanimated. They had been turned, and they would be ravenous.

We need to get the hell out of Dodge; there's no way we can brute force our way through all of these assholes. James panted as he landed just after axe-kicking a drow warrior in the top of the head. *Not unless Zeke can cast that spell again.*

I was about to suggest we all get together and teleport away, quest be damned, but a long, loud, and trumpeting burst of sound came from outside the webbing that made Fainnir leap up and down in joy. I turned to look at Gerty, and her face looked haunted. As if she had heard the call of a ghost.

"They came!" Fainnir howled in delight. "They made it!"

"What did you do, kid?!" Jaken shouted the question as the young vampires surged forward toward us. Our group consolidated close together to resist the wave of new undead.

"They be here," Gerty whispered hoarsely, forcing my attention back to her. "The dwarves be here."

A roar unlike anything I had ever heard in my life rose, and I glimpsed motion outside the barrier.

"WHERE BE THE BASTARDS WHAT STOLE ME WIFE?!" A voice I instantly knew was Farnik's, bellowed over the combined rage of gods-knew-how-many dwarves.

I heard, "Stop them!" From two women and caught Lilith and her sister giving orders.

"Well boys," Muu took up his hammer and handed it to Gerty with a wink and, "I'll be needing this back, so don't lose it, 'kay?" She nodded, and he turned his grin on us. "Let's not leave the family to fend for themselves. Let's open the *fucking door!*"

My face nearly split in two as chills ran down my spine. "Then let's open a path, brother. Hop on my back, and let's go."

I shifted into my belgar form and felt a light thud on my back before, "Yeehaw! Mugfist! To meeee!"

Muu's shout rent the air, and I charged forward toward the dead, past a blurry form of Fainnir and heard him whooping and hollering as we sped through dozens of vampire driders, drow and the still-persisting vampire bats and hulking vampires. These I mowed over like a man on a mission, even managing to gore one of them through the mouth with my horn as it had tried to bite me.

"And there aren't any windshield wipers on this damned thing?" Muu cackled and saw a bright blur pass by my face, and the vampire was gone. "Woah, boy—woah!"

I put the brakes on and the weight on my back left, then shifted into my fox form and rolled end over end before leaping onto a drow's shoulder and shifting into my Ursolon form. My crushing bulk brought the woman low; I used her fall and my momentum to crush her skull and turned to see what was coming next with an earth-shattering roar of challenge.

Dwarves bearing clan Mugfist's symbol on their plate armor flooded the entrance to Lilith's webbed courtyard led by Farnik and Brawnwynn. Pebble pointed toward Fainnir; then the gargantuan dwarf Granite's bulk sprang toward a drider vampire with twin battle axes held in his powerful hands, foam, and spittle flying from his mouth and a wild look on his face.

The drider vampire fell, several legs chopped from the lumbering form as Granite snarled and savaged it with one axe, then threw the weapon in his left hand into a drow twenty feet ahead of him before sprinting forward to drive his knee into the skull of a drow vampire. He grabbed his axe from the first fallen foe, and his other weapon fell in a frantic rhythm until the other was dead.

Now I could see where Fainnir wanted to be with his skills. If Fainnir could cast in a frenzy like that? He'd be damned near unstoppable.

"Kill'em all lads!" Farnik hollered, and more than thirty-five dwarves pressed forward with everything they had. Axes rose and fell with a fervor I had never seen, and their voices raised in a dwarven song of battle that seemed to only add to their thirst for blood. Farnik was the worst of them, his chops precise and deadly with little more energy expended than one might use to wave away a fly.

A group of newly turned vampires bounded my way, their slavering mouths opened impossibly wide at the prospect of food, and I readied myself to take them when a cold mist roiled from our left by the tower and froze their legs solid. Their momentum carried them forward into a sword of pure shadow that whipped by taking them all apart with a hiss.

The queens worked frantically now, Maebe shoving her fist into Lilith's large abdomen as the Vampire Lord tried to claw at her back with hazy red energy around her hands. Her look of glee turned to rage as Lilith backhanded her, breaking her neck, it looked like, and throwing her aside. The broken bones snapped back into place, and the lead vampire growled and shot an arrow of crimson energy at them both. Maebe dove aside, the energy splitting a drow, who had been dumb enough to wander too close, in half, and the other went wide into the webbing where Lilith had been.

Hands grasped at my arm, and I snarled, shoving the male drow that had crawled over to me, his severed lower body pulled behind him by little more than sinew and bone which hadn't been fully chopped through. His seeking fangs gouged my leg, pain flaring from the wound. I expected to see him healing, but instead, he started to vomit violently before dying.

Vampires and lycans don't mix! I growled at myself, feeling like a dumbass for not having thought of it sooner. I shifted into my fox-man form, checking on my friends.

Yohsuke had joined the fight with Balmur and James, all of

whom moved in a tight circle toward the dwarven fighters as swiftly as they could.

Fainnir had joined Pebble, Gem greeting him and simultaneously crushing a drider's leg with her great foot. Maebe had dragged Jafrik to her side, and the two of them moved toward the dwarves and looked to be closing in on Fainnir's side.

Dwarves hooted and hollered, drawing my attention. I glanced that way to see Farnik split a drider vampire's skull nearly in half, then launch himself off its falling corpse into the air where he crashed down on a vampire bat and severed its wings midflight. It crashed into the ground twenty feet from the drider, and as if in some sappy romance movie, time seemed to slow.

He had found her. And Gerty had found him. Covered in gore and blood as he was, she froze and called wordlessly to him even as drow went to attack each of them. She ducked a flashing sword and elbowed the attacker in the knee, using it as a platform to step on as she took a sharp rock and slammed it home two, three times in his throat. She took the sword from his failing grasp and used it to sever the head from the shoulders and hopped off the knee. She still had Muu's hammer in hand but seemed to like brutal killing more.

Husband and wife moved toward each other at an all-out sprint featuring the brutal death of any who got in their way. Brawnwynn tackled a hulking vampire, and six dwarves followed him as it had tried to grapple his father from behind on his mad dash to get to his Gerty. My heart sang as they reached each other, lips moving and tears flowing, but there were other problems, and I dragged my eyes away from the scene.

Jaken and Bokaj looked to be having the worst time of it as more of the undead seemed to want to fuck with the paladin in the group. I'd be going to them.

I'll be going on in my werewolf form, so don't attack me! Everyone was too busy to really respond, but they all yelled or shouted unintelligible things to let me know they were good.

Time to play, I whispered through my mind and called to the beast within me. It didn't come at first, but I dragged and fought to make the transformation come.

You thought yourself rid of me; the werewolf's voice whispered through my mind. *You thought yourself predator enough to consume me, well. See how you like being consumed. You may not die from vampire bites, but your friends can. Your mate can. Those children can.*

I blinked and found myself staring at the eyes of the wolf in the shadows inside me. There was no longer a throne, just a pit of darkness.

I could keep you here forever, you know. It growled, almost as if it were Pastella incarnate.

"You wanna play fuck games? "I raised my eyebrows and my voice together. "Fine. Let's play."

The two of us crashed into each other and dragged one another to the ground in the pit, the glowing red eyes before me filled with rage and hatred.

"All of this is mine—you are mine!" I socked him in the jaw and beat his head off the ground, a mire of thick liquid surrounding us. It was red and black, like defiled blood.

So, you think, the wolf laughed and clawed at my chest. *I have lived within you longer than it seems you have. And I know the darkness that dwells here, I welcome it.*

The liquid grasped at my limbs, not wanting to let go of me, and the wolf took his sweet time rocketing closed fists into my stomach and chest, knocking my breath out as the attacks rained down.

"I'll beat myself up, thanks." I spat in his face and yanked at my limbs, finding them loose enough that I could get a good punch in, but he simply ducked and pressed the arm back into the liquid.

Where it touched, it burned slightly, but it felt familiar. So familiar.

Once you are consumed by your rage, you will no longer be able to resist me and my reasoning; his snarling visage crept ever closer. *I will devour you, and we will reign supreme.*

So, this was my rage, and he felt that it was his because he understood it better? I almost laughed, but as I struggled against it, I couldn't bring my rage to my call. It fought me. Why?

You accept it, but you lock it away, the one force that makes you danger-ous. The wolf stuck a clawed hand against my throat and pressed as hard as he could.

Lock it away; I got angry all the time. People here and at home seemed to have this way of pissing me off that only added to my unending rage and anger. It was almost...primal.

As my understanding of the emotion within me, and its place in my world and power met with one another, I finally knew what I had to do.

"You're right, Wolfy." I sighed, the liquid rising until it reached inside my ears and slowly worked toward my mind through my ear canals. "I lock it away because I want to fight smarter, but sometimes, you just gotta let loose. Like Maebe said, I have to let it out somehow."

He seemed to take the admission of his being right as a sign of sure victory, though I couldn't hear him anymore, I could still see him laughing and howling into the nether that was this pit within me.

I summoned the shadows around us to me, *within me*, and then called to my most feared and well-known emotion. That sense of dreaded purpose within me. The rage that had allowed me to shove my fist through a struggling wolf-man's chest to clutch his heart as a show of strength to his friend. That hatred that had honed my senses before when my friends were in danger—as they were this very moment.

I willed it all into me, the feeling of it siphoning into my body, my soul, making me feel both whole and somehow unclean. Unworthy. But I could dwell on that later when things had calmed down.

If this was my strength, then I would claim this force within me and use it for good. I would make my presence as a primal warrior known to the world, rage, and all. Starting with this part of myself that sought to claim what was mine.

The liquid around me swirled and sank into my skin, covering me and somehow just seeping in where it touched my fur and flesh.

Fear consumed the wolf before me. "I have to thank you, Wolfy. I'd not have unlocked this part of myself without some serious therapy and maybe a little booze, but you managed it in such a short time of being stupid. You should really watch monologues; they've ended a few villainous wins prematurely."

He tried to grasp my throat harder, his hips covering my own so he could try to control me. I snickered and lifted my hips up and toward my head, grabbing his chest and sweeping his arms away from my body at the same time. His momentum brought me up into a mounted position, and I used the confusion to summon my beastly werewolf form into being.

I stared down, the red and black liquids still swirled around us and seeped into where it met my legs.

I slammed my fist into his throat, stopping him from having a chance to plead with me. "Now, I'm going to do what I failed to do before and consume *you*."

He clawed at me, but I was stronger now. So much stronger. This was *my* rage, my body, mine to control and do with as I would.

I opened my jaws slowly, then struck like an alligator for the throat, and consumed the beast within me. His strength became mine. His power flooded me, and unlike before, I could feel that it was mine at long last.

With the grim deed done, I opened my eyes and found my friends surrounding me with their backs out.

"What the hell is wrong with him?!" Muu shouted as he stabbed at a hulking vampire. "And why do these things keep getting back up?"

"Zeke!" Yohsuke howled, next to my ear, making me flinch and blink. "Finally!"

"The dwarves need some help, and the queens are all

duking it out," James explained hurriedly, before a flash of cold and darkness burst from our right, the same time as a red slash carved a diagonal line into Lilith's tower, cutting it there. The only reason it didn't plummet to the ground, were the webs holding it in place.

Jaken roared, and a red aura surrounded his body, his great sword planted into the ground. He lifted his longsword and spat, "Dance!" The blade lifted and swung toward some of the drow that had surrounded our position.

Maebe threw a volley of frozen meteors down onto where the other two women fought hand to hand, splitting the ground in twain. Then the projectiles burst, sending shards of ice into the immediate vicinity.

"Balmur, I need you to ensure that the boys are protected, Yoh, you too," I ordered and the two of them moved away. "Jaken, I need you and Muu to get to the dwarves and keep them healed and up, so we don't have to worry about any more vampires."

"What are we doing then?" James looked around as the others moved away. "I'm assuming you have a plan for Bokaj and me. too?"

"Yeah, you and I are going to be playing duck, duck, goose with the queens, and Bokaj is going to make it rain," I said, then growled as I looked up to the sky where Kayda circled. "Kayda, you keep the guys safe. Bea? Come here, baby."

The tug on her mind brought the swift raptor over to me, her brown and lavender eyes searching mine. "I need a favor."

She nodded her head, and I hopped onto her back, my legs molding to the sides of her body easily enough. "I'll see you boys over th—"

Bea jolted forward, wind stealing the words from my mouth as she pushed herself on faster. The queens moved and cast spells at each other with devastating effect to the ground and the world around them. Shadows wove and slashed through the air and defended against blasts of crimson energy, met by ice and cold bursts that attacked and defended simultaneously.

Lilith looked to be drained, one of her legs crushed and hanging limply on her bulbous spider body, but she wove her spells as swiftly as she could. The vampire lady, whose name we hadn't even gotten to learn, levitated, her eyes glowing with a crimson energy like that out of an eldritch nightmare. Her hands moved, summoning a sign in front of her that ate the darkness at the same time as the general's cloaked figure stepped from the darkness and seemed to fuse with her.

Maebe was cut, her left arm bleeding a little bit as she moved her hand through the air, frost forming around her good hand and shooting forward in blistering cold cones of ice that shot forward at both women.

Break off before you get too close, I'm gonna jump for it, then you go and help the others out where you safely can. I patted her side lovingly, *I love you.*

I focused and jumped as I said that last bit, sailing through the air as Bea broke away from the fighting, battling to remain upright against my pushing away from her, and responded, *Love you too.*

I shifted midair into my werewolf form and tackled the distracted vampire leader to the ground with a grunt and gasp of surprise on her part.

As I went to slash at her throat with my claws, she managed to grasp my wrists and shoved up so that she flipped me, and I landed on my back.

"You truly are an annoyance, assassin." She hissed, her face contorted in rage, her glowing red eyes bleeding into the whites. "You dare to interfere and not just die? My lord War will have this world and all others!"

As she spoke and we struggled, I could see her name above her head, and it gave me a little hope.

Marizan level 75

"I always was one to try and steal the last dance," I said back in the snarkiest tone I could manage given the vast differ-ence in our levels. I knew that James and Bokaj were coming, I just didn't know how soon and the fact that her level was visible now meant I was in deep shit.

She pressed her hands up in front of her, palms out and fingers curled toward me like claws. She whipped them downward diagonally, and a stream of red energy scythed toward me only to be stopped by a small mountain of ice.

Maebe growled and raised her hand, then pressed forward to shoot an ice spike of some kind from it, but the vampire just bounded over it to try and land on me with her fangs bared.

An arrow sliced the tip of her nose, and a ball of golden energy smacked her in her hip, throwing her off course slightly.

Ebony energy shot from the ground in front of me and caught her on the chin like a fist, rocking her head back.

I rolled to miss another strike from a similar spell, then bounded forward on all fours. My limbs pumped powerfully as arrows with silver flashed dangerously close to her and I. The nearness screwing with my concentration, but it was bearable.

She took one of the arrows in her shoulder before she stood, trying to dig it out, but then James was on top of her. His fists collided with her face, narrowly avoiding her fangs as his golden ki snapped into her body with devastating precision.

Her health bar fell steadily, but not nearly enough to be indicative of the level of ass-whooping she had taken before and what we were dishing out. She had to be a higher level, losing a single percent of health even with the silver in her shoulder and both of us wailing on her.

Lightning smashed into her from James' fists as he hit her with both at the same time, then a bolt of freezing lightning pierced the ground between her feet and hit her at the same time. The electricity ripped through her body, stopping her long enough to allow me to dig my claws into her chest, hoping to find her heart and pull it out.

She wrapped her hands around my wrists once more, and cried out as she ripped the bloodied and blackened limbs from her chest and lifted me bodily off the ground. She grunted deeply, then swung me bodily, and I felt a body against my legs and a stream of labored obscenities.

She's not taking any damage you guys, Bokaj warned. *And more vampires of higher quality have shown up. Five of the dwarves are down, and I don't know what else is coming.*

We needed to end this shit. And the only way was looking rough.

Yohsuke, I'm probably going to have to cast Solar Flare, hide. I sent him mentally as I tried to stand up.

But I couldn't. I looked up and saw the evil bitch holding my hand with hers, and a sickening smile spreading across her face.

"I don't need to bite you and ingest your blood, wolf," her voice touched my mind as her gaze met mine. "I can steal your mana too, and only by touch."

My health and mana dropped slowly at first, then faster and faster. As I neared the 30% mark, a scaled figure appeared above her, digging claws and teeth into what it could.

Bea had come back to save me.

Tmont, her tail lashing out like a scorpion, jabbing what she could reach savagely. A blur of brown streaked through the air above me and crashed into the woman's chest with a squelch that dropped her to her knees. A shaft of blackened wood that looked to have been burnt and slightly eroded stuck out of her clothes. She touched it, slight embers of light flame spread over her flesh.

"Pie!" Adrenaline poured into my brain as I heard Maebe savagely snarl our safe word for stupid actions a heartbeat before a second blur of black swiped through the Vampire Lords neck and the head dropped off to the left of me, seeming to still be looking around for an explanation of what happened.

I glanced up at my wife, her chest heaving, blood dribbling from a cut on her head, her chest, her arm, and shoulder. She looked at me, her eyes still a little wild. "Are you alright?"

"Funny that you think you're done with me." I blinked and turned to look down at Marizan's head, her eyes stared up at us.

"This is merely an inconvenience, and I have other plans in motion, already. I am so much more than my brothers, and when I return to my full glory, this world is ours."

I took Magus Bane and put it on my shoulder, "You won't get the chance. We're coming, and you're done here." I lifted Magus Bane and cleaved the laughing head in half.

I heard the cheering from both sides and clapping from where Lilith had been. Maebe turned, Morningstar in her left hand and her right lifted to prepare a spell, but Lilith spoke loudly, "Well done, you've done your duty."

"And no thanks to you," My Queen retorted angrily. James helped me to stand, passed me some medium mana potions as Bokaj crept forward. "You planned to try and kill us from the start, didn't you?"

"I did not," Lilith insisted, though her voice was hardly contrite as she walked forward. The drow who had survived the onslaught flocked to her, casters in the front and warriors to the sides at the flanks.

I heard movement behind us, turning to see my friends and the dwarves marching toward us. Farnik and Gerty held hands, but each carried an axe in their free hand, and now she wore mithril plate armor like the others. Good.

Granite limped forward with his son at his side, supporting his father as they stoically took in the scene, blood leaked from one leg. Jaken hit Granite with a healing spell that seemed to help him be able to walk on his own again.

The party looked bloodied and seemed to be recovering well enough, Yohsuke's clothes were a little shredded, but he seemed minutely beaten, and his wounds sealed slowly on their own. He lifted his arm and wiped crimson from his lips, managing to spread and smudge it a bit, but continued forward.

"Then, you will see that our quest is completed, and we will be on our way." Maebe sheathed her weapon but didn't put it away as she watched Lilith for some kind of reaction.

"It seems that all of her line are dead, those here." She shrugged. "But how can I be certain that all of them are dead?"

"You can't," Yohsuke muttered, attracting attention to him. When we glanced at him, he shook his head. "They never stay in one place, and they never have their entire group together, though we burned their place down thanks to Zeke's spell."

He stopped when he stood next to Maebe and me, "But you knew that we wouldn't get the whole line, didn't you? That's why you worded the quest that way. So, we would fail it, or be beholden to you."

"Why would I desire anything of the sort?" Lilith did her best to flutter her eyes at us innocently, but the smug look on her face said it all. Blood seeped from several wounds along her body, and another leg dangled from the rear of her bulbous body. She had really fallen from the major player that she'd been when we got here.

Fighting can do that.

"Because you wanted to have another reason not to be indebted to me, or my people, which I can respect." Maebe seemed comfortable enough that she put Morningstar away in her inventory. "But what will not be tolerated is an abuse of my time and efforts. That quest was nigh impossible without the proper intelligence, you withheld valuable information, and upon our arrival here, your people attacked us."

"Only because it looked as if you had failed in your mission to them, and because my sister told me that you had been swayed to join her." Lilith waved a hand, and her people nodded, but Maebe stilled.

The Fae Queen took a single step forward, and regarded the other woman oddly, her head tilting to one side. "Do you swear to that?"

Lilith seemed confused, before she nodded and stated, "My sister told me that you had been swayed to her cause, I swear it."

Maebe laughed out loud, clapping her hands, causing the few around her to lean back as if struck, except for me. Granite's voice drifted over, the deep tone scraping against my hearing, "Think she's gone daft?"

"No, I've been lied to." Maebe sounded absolutely delighted. "Oh, this is delicious. She thinks she needs to lie so that her people will support her willingly, but in doing so, she's given something up."

Lilith seemed confused until realization dawned on her, and Maebe continued, "You had been so fun to play the game with, my dear sweet child, but now I have won. And for your lies against me and mine, I will collect what is mine for twice the lies of thine."

Maebe's hand shot out, and purple flowing magic spread like thick smoke and wrapped around the liar lifting her into the air.

"For your lies and wicked thoughts, I will take what I please. Two lies, two thefts—this is the way." Maebe smiled sweetly, the drow around their Queen began to beat on the smoke. Their fists hit the magic, and it shot them back onto their backs and rendered them still. "First, I take your power as my own, not your throne, but your *personal* power. And second, I take what was owed, and the child who acted as bait that you intended die, regardless of the outcome."

As she opened her mouth to speak for herself in outrage, the smoke poured into her. It filtered into her body until it was completely gone, and she landed on her spidery legs as if a marionette with invisible strings moving her limbs.

After a long moment, the smoke poured out of her, green now, and spun toward Maebe. The Fae opened her mouth expectantly as the gaseous magic shifted toward her, seeking entry. She inhaled, her green eyes flaring with bright light and her head rocking back before she closed them and swallowed.

A contented sigh escaped her lips. She raised her hand, and wiped away the blood on her forehead and the wound was gone.

"Before we wear out our welcome, I will make one thing perfectly clear," Maebe spoke slowly and enunciated perfectly. "The dwarves of Djurn Forge are mine to protect now, as they are kin and clan to my husband. An attack on them is an attack on me, and I will respond not in kind but with *reverence* to the detail at which I could lay waste to those who touch what is mine. Not a threat, but an oath. One I intend to see through. Our quest with you is done, despite your attempt to control us. Failed or not, I assume you know the consequences of lying to a Fae, now, and those are not what I would bring against an enemy."

The drow stood silently, but Farnik spoke up, his voice thick but unwavering, "I found me and mine, and much blood was shed today. I'll see me kin home to their burial grounds, and me wife to me clan, but if ye e'er set foot in dwarven halls, me clan will nae rest until yer all with the stone. This, I swears on me life, and me beard to grow."

He spat on the ground, and so did every dwarf with him, even Granite and Fainnir, then they turned their backs and walked away. I made sure to eye each of the drow who watched us, Lilith looked weak, and she may have been almost about to be set upon by a pack of lions for all we knew, but our business here was done, and that was good.

We walked away, with Kayda watching our backs we didn't need to worry about an attack. But that didn't mean violence wasn't about to ensue. More than a dozen female drow spellcasters set upon the fallen queen as we walked away. Her enraged shouting and angry casting making the fur on the back of my neck stand.

On our way to the gates, the dwarves stopped and grabbed their fallen, not a tear shed, but for the stoic words of the tales of glory to be sung in the halls this night.

Once we reached the entry point the dwarves had created, they stopped and turned to us.

Farnik and Granite both stepped out, the latter clapping Farnik on the back. "Ye always were bet'er with yer words, lad."

"Aye." Farnik chewed his lip, stubble growing on his chin. It looked better after he had shaved it all off, but it had paid a debt and cleared a clan's name, so I wouldn't give him too much shit. "I were gonna give ye a piece o' me mind for not bringin'

Balmur to us sooner, but he gave us a good reason, so I let it be. But then Fainnir summoned us with his elemental, and when we heard ye were with the drow, we come runnin'.."

He looked back and reached out for his wife and son, who hugged each other close but stepped forward.

"Ye did the clan proud, lads." Farnik sighed. "Did us all a great favor, ye did. And we be in yer debt—you put your hand down boy, or I'll wallop ye right on tha' scaly head o' yers!"

Muu looked abashed and thoroughly cowed as he put his hand down, and the dwarf continued, "Come celebrate with yer kin, tha' be an order from yer clan head as all of ye be clan now. That means yerself too, Highness."

Maebe nodded her head once with a genuine smile. "I would be delighted to join you."

"I can't teleport all of us and all of you." I frowned. I had notifications from after all the fighting, but unless I leveled up a royal shit ton, I wouldn't be able to carry almost thirty people to wherever we were going.

"That's a'right lad. We're gonna go home how we came, and we'll be obstructing the path as we go, though young Fainnir is welcome among us to assist if he be willin'?" Farnik looked to the earth mage, who nodded excitedly. "We'll be seein' ye soon lads, Highness. The hammer falls."

"And rises again." Jaken reached out and pulled the stout man into a fierce hug and gave each of the others a slap on the back.

We had a raucous goodbye from there, then waited until they were on their way, and Fainnir sealed the stone behind them. I turned, watching as several drow lifted the former Queen's body, the legs curled in and carried it toward the tower doors. A single female drow swayed forward after them, all of us forgotten, and the survivors of the fight hardly seemed willing to stand against us. Not without support of numbers against the people who had destroyed their former leader.

I glanced over toward where Maebe stood next to Jafrik and watched as Servant separated himself from the boy's shadow.

His jaws were covered in gore, and he seemed pleased as he nodded to Mae, then me and faded into thin air. He'd likely spent the fight killing anything that had ventured too close to the boy.

Bea butted her head against my chest, drawing my attention, and Kayda landed next to me, and the others gathered around. It was time to get the fuck out of this hell hole. Then I paused.

"I don't know if it's daylight or not outside." I looked at Yohsuke, and he shrugged. "Don't vampires know that kind of shit?"

"Well, I've been stuck underground, so I don't really have a concept to go on for it." he raised his fist and flipped me the bird tiredly. "We need to get me a coffin when I'm up there too. It's required, I think."

"We can work on that." Jaken nodded placatingly to Yoh. "I think he should be in the collar for now, though, just to be safe."

I agreed and had him switch with Bea. She was happy to be out and to get to experience everything that was about to occur as she bumped her head against me, then Kayda affectionately.

I closed my eyes and picked where we would go, Sunrise, if it was close enough. It was, thankfully, and then I cast Teleport with my friends all grasping hands.

CHAPTER TWENTY-FIVE

We opened our eyes to starlit skies and twilight as the eastern sky lit orange and pink, signaling the dawn of a new day, and the next leg of our journey. We would have to discuss it, but I thought it was time we visited the other continents to check for the other generals and maybe minions. We had slain one minion and found out that the others of War's vanguard were beginning to work together. Which was chilling, to say the least.

We would also need to check in with the King and his people to see how Lindyburg had come along. If they fought back or not, or if they had managed to get her out of power peaceably.

I felt warmth along my back and mind, *Have my champion stand in my sight, little mote, and I will bring my love to him.*

I opened my eyes and motioned to the others to step back. "Jafrik, the Light Elemental Primordial wants to give you a gift, and for that, she needs you to be in the light."

"It's so bright up here," he complained as he hid beside Maebe. "And open, you can see forever, how do you do it?"

I couldn't help the smile on my face, the poor boy really had no idea.

Maebe knelt down next to him, "Jafrik, look at me." He opened his eyes a little. "Do you see these specks of white against my skin? They are the stars, as I am a celestial Fae. When you look up into the night sky, I want you to think of me and know that I will always care for you and protect you how I can, sweet child. But another offers you her love—love I cannot hope to give you. Reach out to her, and she will be with you as surely as I am in the night."

He seemed scared as she backed away, but I took his hand with a reassuring smile and walked with him into the town square. Together, we watched as the sun rose, and as it did, I felt the warmth of it hit my chest and the top of his head.

I glanced down and watched with fascination as where the light touched, the purple-Black coloration of his skin dyed golden in the light. His hair stayed white, but there appeared to be streaks of orange and purple in it, like that of the growing dawn.

This is my love, as the darkness has claimed the queen, so shall I claim a king. The two of you are opposites, but this new one will be mine and only mine. The drow have their darkness, and so too do the Unseelie Fae, but he shall have the sun.

My fur stood on end as the warmth from the light changed to burning heat, the golden motes of light on my fur bursting with coronas of light soft rings surrounding them.

I clenched my hand, but Jafrik began to laugh as the light fully doused him. He was changed wholly, and he looked happy about it.

"What is he?" Muu sounded like he was in shock.

Jafrik smiled up at me, then turned to Maebe. "I'm a Dawn Elf now, and I'm not alone anymore!"

Not alone? I thought to myself, rubbing my throbbing chest.

He is not. The light whispered. *He is the first. There were others born throughout the world this very day. I create a race of people to help defend this world as the other elementals have chosen theirs.*

"Where can we find them?" I asked the warmth retreating from my mind.

There is no need, they come to Sunrise.

After our initial shock at the transformation, we headed toward the tavern. People had begun setting up stalls and booths in the center of the village for the day.

Some stopped and said hello, but the majority stared in open amazement at Jafrik. The boy skipped happily alongside Maebe, who watched the boy with curious wonder on her face.

"So, there are more people like him coming here?" Jaken called over my shoulder. "Where do we put them all?"

"I don't know, but I don't think it will be immediately," I answered honestly with a shrug. "All we can do is pass word and oof!"

A large blur of green collided with my chest and waist knocking me prone into the ground, with Kayda squawking angrily above us and Bea growling with her teeth bared at the supposed threat.

"Where have you *been?*" Vrawn's worried features fretted over me as she looked me over. "Why haven't you contacted me? What has been going on? Why *haven't you contacted me?!*"

"Hello Vrawn, Bea, easy she's okay." I waved the still distrusting gust raptor away, and she only stopped growling. "We've been very busy, and if you'll listen, I'll be more than happy to sit and talk you through everything that has happened."

"You had damned well better." A tear fell from her eye as she leaned down and stared at me, hurt, and disappointment in her gaze. I tried to kiss her cheek softly, but she dodged it, and she helped me to my feet before turning from me completely.

She stepped to Maebe, who had come to her side and greeted her with a fierce hug. "I have missed you, as well. Please, tell me that I will be coming with you when you leave next to make up for this. I was worried out of my mind."

Maebe's eyebrows raised in surprise, and I found my own

raised in return. She looked askance at me and based on my own thoughts I shrugged and nodded. If I said no, she would likely try to kill me, and as I looked at her now, I realized that I had fucked up. I would likely be paying for this for a while.

"Yes, but you will need to pull your weight, and the guard should be forewarned of your absence." Maebe patted her shoulder and kissed where she could on the larger woman's arm. "Come, we are all exhausted. We should rest and eat."

"And go through our notifications," James spoke up. "There are a lot."

"Oh, boy!" Jaken snorted, but he did sound excited.

"Let's go," I ordered, and we moved along.

Once we arrived in the tavern, we covered the windows, and I let Yohsuke out of the collar, careful to sit far enough from the door that the light of day wouldn't affect him.

Once we had our food, Willem joined us, and we explained everything as it had happened. While the others spoke, I went through my notifications.

QUEST FAILED!

Drowning in vampires – Queen Lilith has given you a quest to kill the Vampire Lord plaguing her people here in the Great Below as well as his strongest minions. A guide (to be determined) and the bait will be provided to aid in your success.

Failure: You managed to kill the Vampire Lord but not all of her strongest minions resulting in loss of your freedom should you survive. You have also left the Great Below (not in pursuit of the Vampire Lord), causing the drow to hunt for you in the shadows, beginning in Djurn Forge.

ALERT!

The quest giver who could hold you responsible was found and tried by Fae magic, and had her strength taken as recompense for lying. The quest giver is dead and can no longer follow through with the reward or failure.

I blinked and saw that some of the others had been doing the same digging into their notifications as I had. They looked concerned, but I felt relieved that it was over. At least for now.

QUEST ALERT!

SECRET QUEST COMPLETED!

A Hurty for Gerty – The dwarves of Djurn Forge lost a great deal the day their home had been raided by the incursion force of the drow elves. Not much could aid them in the healing process, but you managed to find one of their heroes, Gerty.

Reward: 5,000 EXP and all dwarves of Djurn Forge now see your party as friends and will openly assist you in any way they can. You are clan, and to all who know you, dwarves.

SOCIAL STATUS CHANGE!

Your party's social standing among the dwarves has so greatly changed that no dwarf in the city of Djurn Forge would ever think to not sing your praises. From this point forward, your status will hold the title of Honorary Dwarf. If you have not a clan, any would be happy to adopt you. Some would likely fight over you.

All dwarves of Brindolla can see this title, and their reactions may prove friendly. Or not. Dwarves can be fickle like that.

You and your party are now loathed by the drow. Any who meet you will likely try to kill you. Good luck!

I heard Yohsuke snort, then muttered, "Call *me* Dirt. I'll kill them all."

CONGRATULATIONS!

You have reached a milestone in your advancement and have unlocked the following abilities.

Limitations on shapeshifting abilities have been lifted once more. Newest limitation is set to legendary creatures.

What in the Hells is a legendary creature? I muttered to myself. *Like a god? Something uber rare?*

"I'm sorry to interrupt the conversation." Maebe and Vrawn had been discussing things that had happened with the children while we were gone. "But what the hell is a legendary creature?"

Both of them looked at each other, then pointed to Kayda, who preened herself haughtily.

"So, you know I just unlocked the ability to shapeshift into mythical creatures." I lead them on hopefully.

"Meaning that a dragon like Winterheart would be a legendary creature based on his age, and power alone," Maebe informed me, my chest deflating a little. "However, a dragon Ampharia's age? Not outside the realm of possibility."

"Oh, my *gods!*" Muu squealed, "does this mean Zeke gets to become a *dragon?!*"

"It sounds like it could be possible." Vrawn yawned and stretched, the line of her body arching as she did so. "Finish leveling up and whatnot so that we can go to bed, dear. We have much to discuss, and it starts with the rings on your fingers."

I blushed and did as I was told, Maebe smiling as she spoke softly to Vrawn for me.

I looked at my status page and whistled, we had done enough damage that I had gone up to level 42. I put five points each into intelligence and wisdom. One to constitution, and two to strength and dexterity.

Kayda had leveled up by four, bringing her to level 28, and Bea by six, bringing her to level 23.

Their natural points had gone toward strengthening their wisdom stats for some reason, raising Kayda's to nineteen and Bea's to twelve.

They both had a decent amount of points to spend, but I would let them tell me how they wanted to spend them after we slept.

No? You want to know now? Jeez, needy much? Fine, fine.

I opened my bond to both of them tiredly and asked, "You both leveled up a lot, how would you like to spend your points?"

Kayda responded first, *faster and stronger, so I can carry someone.*

I nodded and started spending her twelve points. I put three into strength, six into constitution, and the last three into dexterity to help her stay swift.

No spells this time for her, which was odd, but to be expected for being the only one of her kind in existence, right?

Faster Bea seemed to be searching herself for a moment, then gazed at Vrawn, *Faster and stronger.*

I blinked at her and did as she asked, this time sinking eight of her eighteen points into strength. The remaining ten, I split between her dexterity and constitution as well.

Bea didn't learn anything either, and that was a little concerning. Had mutating stunted her natural growth?

Both of them seemed to grow a little heavier, their muscles defining and lengthening a bit more. It was odd, but they seemed happy enough.

Another notification caught my eye, and I opened it up. It was for me, not my girls, and I gasped in surprise.

You have unlocked another tail, as a potentially nine-tailed Kitsune, this tail has been earned for a specific personal milestone. As such, it confers a specific ability.

ABILITY UNLOCKED

Hunter's Will – Your desire to control and take back what is yours has gifted you with greater control over yourself.

While in your natural animal form, you may cast minor spells with a cost of no more than 100 MP.

That was *incredible*! I almost howled with delight.

The conversation at the table brought me back to my senses, though, "… I think we need to go overseas next."

James concluded his thought, and the others frowned, but I added, "I do too. They're aware of our movements here, and they could have hidden out there. Can we hold this discussion until tomorrow?"

Jaken eyed me pointedly, then assented likely with my statement and James' with a nod and a gesture of his hand. "We have been getting lucky, though that last one was a shit show only finding a minion, and learning that a general is pulling strings somewhere we can't see. I think, at the very least, we should go over to the continent of beasts and check things out."

"How're we going to get there?" Yohsuke slapped his hands on the table in irritation. "Zeke can't teleport us there, and in case you didn't notice, I'm a damned vampire. He can't fly us, so we have to take a ship, right?"

"Elder Leo gave us a lead to follow when we went to get Fainnir," James explained. "I vote we go party with the dwarves, then make our way to the coast and get to the next continent. To start hunting there."

I looked around at them all. Beaten and bruised, stronger sure, but my friends looked tired. Their gear was busted, armor shredded, and some even had weapons missing. We needed to get our shit back together and get on. And we would do that. Even if I was a little worried about them being able to come after us like this.

We had our heading, we had each other, and we had a whole lot more asses to kick. We weren't out of the fight by any means, so we'd do what we could.

"Party with the dwarves, set out to the high seas, and keep an eye out for demons?" I posed to the others, grins spreading along their faces. "Sounds like Storm Company is about to pick up piracy, boys!"

A raucous cheer erupted around the table as the others thumped the table, loudly making jokes about booty that neither Maebe nor Willem understood. But that was alright.

Because what's a tale without some treasure and a touch of high-seas hijinks?

AUTHOR'S NOTE

Wow guys,

What a wild ride it's been right? Who would have expected all
that stuff, right? I know, some of it had me scared too, but the
boys and I managed. Thanks for coming on this crazy
adventure with us, and who knows how long it'll last, but for
those of you who have stuck with us this far—you fucking rock.

I hope you'll stick around for the long haul. We love you.

Sincerely,
Zeke.

ABOUT CHRISTOPHER JOHNS

Christopher Johns is a former photojournalist for the United States Marine Corps with published works telling hundreds of other peoples' stories through word, photo, and even video.

But throughout that time, his editors and superiors had always said that his love of reading fantasy and about worlds of fantastic beauty and horrible power bled into his work. That meant he should write a book.

Well, ta-da!

Chris has been an avid devourer of fantasy and science fiction for more than twenty years and looks forward to sharing that love with his son, his loving fiancée and almost anyone he could ever hope to meet.

Connect with Chris:
Twitter.com/jonsyjohns
Facebook.com/AxeDruidAuthor
Patreon.com/StormCompanyandBeyond

ABOUT MOUNTAINDALE PRESS

Dakota and Danielle Krout, a husband and wife team, strive to create as well as publish excellent fantasy and science fiction novels. Self-publishing *The Divine Dungeon: Dungeon Born* in 2016 transformed their careers from Dakota's military and programming background and Danielle's Ph.D. in pharmacology to President and CEO, respectively, of a small press. Their goal is to share their success with other authors and provide captivating fiction to readers with the purpose of solidifying Mountaindale Press as the place 'Where Fantasy Transforms Reality.'

Connect with Mountaindale Press:
MountaindalePress.com
Facebook.com/MountaindalePress
Twitter.com/_Mountaindale
Instagram.com/MountaindalePress

MOUNTAINDALE PRESS TITLES

GameLit and LitRPG

The Completionist Chronicles,
The Divine Dungeon, and
Full Murderhobo by Dakota Krout

King's League by Jason Anspach and J.N. Chaney

A Touch of Power by Jay Boyce

Red Mage by Xander Boyce

Space Seasons by Dawn Chapman

Ether Collapse and
Ether Flows by Ryan DeBruyn

Bloodgames by Christian J. Gilliland

Wolfman Warlock by James Hunter and Dakota Krout

Axe Druid and
Mephisto's Magic Online by Christopher Johns

Skeleton in Space by Andries Louws

Chronicles of Ethan by John L. Monk

Pixel Dust by David Petrie

Henchman by Carl Stubblefield

Artorian's Archives by Dennis Vanderkerken and Dakota Krout

APPENDIX

THE GOOD

Zekiel Erebos (Zee-key-uhl Air-uh-bows) – Marine who loves gaming as a civilian with his buddies who are still in. Class: Druid. Race: Kitsune, has a tail.

Yohsuke (Yo-s'kay) – Zeke's best bud/brother from the Marine Corps. Overlord, yeah, you read that right. Class: Spell blade. Race: Abomination (halfbreed drow and high elf)

Jaken Warmecht (Jay-ken) – Zeke's friend who typically needs help catching up in the games the group places together. Class: Paladin of Radiance. Race: Fae-Orc.

Bokaj (Bow-ka-jh) – A friend from the gym who loves video games and is in a pretty wicked band! Class: Ranger. Race: Ice Elf.

Tmont (Tee-M-on-t) – A panther with a taste for tails who happens to not just be a walking bag of assholes but is also Bokaj's pet. Mainly that first one, though.

Balmur (Ball-mer) – Bokaj's best friend, and another good buddy of Zeke's who loves to game! Class: Rogue. Race: Azer Dwarf (Fire dwarf) HIS BEARD IS A FLAME!

James Bautista (Really?) – Another Marine that Yohsuke and Zeke know and game with often. Class: Monk. Race: Dragon Elf.

Muu Ankiman (Moo Ahn-key-men) – Dragon beast-kin with green scales and Zeke's roommate on Earth. Liiiiittle crazy, but he's okay. Class: Fighter. Race: Dragon-kin (it's shorter!)

Kayda (Kay-duh) – A pretty little bird with a shitty past, and hopefully, a bright future. Recently turned into a Storm Roc. Very protective of a certain flame wolf.

Coal – A flame wolf that Zeke was taking care of for a bit on behalf of the Primordial Flame Elemental. He has a good temperament, a little heated at times, but he's a cool pup.

Sir Willem Dillon – Owner of the tavern in Sunrise Village (the starter town) and Paladin of Radiance. The first guy the group meets and doesn't try to kill. (Or do they? MUAHAHAHA— No, really, do they?) Jaken's trainer.

Dinnia (Dih-nee-uh) – An elven druid who takes pity on poor Zeke and brings him into Mother Nature's good graces. Zeke's trainer.

Sharo (shah-row) – Another panther who assists his partner in crime Dinnia in training her student. Not a walking back of assholes.

Kyra – Queen of the bears and good friend of Dinnia's. We like her.

Marin (mare-in) – We, uh... we don't talk about her. 10 out of 10, though. Kickass dire bear.

Rowland – Blacksmith in Sunrise, who decides he likes the travelers, especially the one with the tail—no bias.

Maebe (may-buh—soft buh—if she hears you talking shit, I'm not responsible, yeah?) – Unseelie Queen of Winter and Darkness, who somehow gets thrown into the mix. Also, Zeke's girlfriend. I know, right?

Thogan (ThO-gun) – Champion of the Unseelie Fae, and a rather clingy dwarf with a rough complexion.

Titania – Queen of the Seelie Fae, who has a predisposition of being a raging bitch to anyone and everyone she doesn't like. Like outsiders.

Craglim (Crag-limb) – Rowland's cousin. Racist piece of shit—but he's a good fighter.

Zhavron (Zah-vrun) – Orc fighter with a sordid past. Muu's trainer in all things fighting. A little intense at times.

Pharazulla (Far-uh-zu-la) – A bard of some renown, though a bit of a stuck-up asshole.

Vrawn – A lovely orcish woman with a soft spot for our local druid. She's built like a busty, brick shit house.

Sam – Mayor of Sunrise village. A fair man whose bear-kin wife and half bear-kin children believe in him wholeheartedly. Prefers to hunt for the village rather than govern.

The villagers of Sunrise – Great people who recently went through a lot of bullshit. Go easy on 'em, yeah?

Set – A decent little Fae-orc kid, duped into hunting a Belgar.

Ampharia (Am-far-ee-uh) – An elder green dragon friend of Mother Nature's who comes to Muu with her blessing and teaches him how to fight dragons.

Natholdi, Granite, and son (Nath-ol-dee) – A good, humble dwarven family that both Muu and Zeke love dearly. Newest additions to the Light Hand Clan.

Farnik Mugfist (Far-nick) – Leader of the Mugfist clan and good friend to the party. Loves a good cup of mead and song.

Shellica Light Hand (Shell-ih-cuh) – Leader of the Light hand clan and a Grand Master Enchanter. Crazy as shit with a diabolical wit. Zeke's trainer, unfortunately.

Silvannas (Sill-vahn-us) – Queen of the High Elves on the prime plane of existence. Sort of a role model to Maebe.

Questis (Quest-ihs) – A high elf Druid enchanter who has a soft spot for kitties and bait. Pretty awesome guy. Seriously loves cats, though.

Fern (Like the plant) – A sabertooth cat that has a *serious* god complex. Loves to be fed and worshipped. Gives his druid Questis hell all the time.

Telfino (Tell-fee-no) – Son of Queen Silvannas, and inheritor of the throne. He's a good kid with a seriously strong class.

Manly Warbottom – A rascal bounty hunter halfling with a weird motley crew of badasses. Good lady, likes money. A lot.

Braves of the Thorn – Manly's peeps and party, consisting of Dawn, Nick, Nic, Bonnie, and Manly's best buddy Humphrey. Quality people.

Milnolian (Mill-Gnoll-Ian) – Goes by Servant, but he's a loyal servant of Maebe's who she passed to him as a gift.

Eiran'a (Ee-rahn-ah) – Maebe's momma and a *highly* skilled ice mage. She doesn't really care for the loving protagonist, but hey —beggars and choosers, am I right?

Westwind Royalty – The royal family of Zephyth, good people with a lovely daughter. Aboye (A-boy-Eh), the king, and Chareen (Shareen) his wife.

Villeroa Westwind (Vill-er-oah) – Princess and water mage, with her elemental friend.

Zygnal (Zig-nahl) – Water Elemental assigned to protect and help train Villeroa.

Jafrik (Ya-frick) – A Drow boy chosen by the Primordial Light Elemental to become the first of a new race, the dawn elves.

THE BAD

War – Galactic conquerer who probably suffers from only child syndrome. Probably needs a hug, or he will keep trying to take over the universe.

Minions of War – Not the lovable minions everyone loves. You know, not the yellow ones, or that fish from that one Will Ferrell animated movie. These guys seek to undermine the strength of the gods by eroding the world around them slowly. And serve the other assholes in this list.

The Generals – A Number of War's better warriors capable of taking out the strongest people open the planet—and together they did. Dick move.

Rowan – I'm not gonna say much about this guy—read the book, then you'll know what a dickbag he is. Haha, was—sonofabitch is dead now.

Pastella (Pahs-tell-uh) – Crazy elven woman with a taste for torture and violence.

Tarron Dillingsley (Tair-run Dill-night-slee) – Gnomish enchanter who—let's face it shall we?—sucks as a teacher for various reasons and lest we forget, the asshole in charge of the Children of Brindolla.

Children of Brindolla – A group of misguided citizens who believe they are the only ones who can truly save their world. They found themselves on the receiving end of an ass-kicking— but was that all of them?

Decay – A greater Fiend who held his own against the party and Maebe. Fell due to a brilliant plan and a little bit of finesse. Okay, the plan was half-cocked, and the finesse resulted in some bullshit—happy now?

Spiders – just a bunch of overgrown pests that needed an ass-kicking. Nightmare fuel FOREVER.

Lothir (Low-theer) – Big ol' wanna-be snake goddess who has a village of elves, orcs, and Fae-orcs under her command and demands sacrifices to restore and keep her beauty. All of that means that she's coo coo for Cocoa Puffs.

Melvaren (Mel-vah-ren) – General who took claim over Balmur and tortured him in the Hells for his entire tenure there. We killed the shit out of him. But not before he whipped our asses. Still dead though.

Archemillian (Ark-em-illion) – The demon who Yohsuke

summoned and gets his warlock powers from. Has a huge hard-on for souls, but he helped us this once. Didn't mean he was a fucking good guy, though.

Riktolth (Rick-talth) – The great black dragon who killed a mother red in a bid to die in combat. Yeah, you guessed it. We kicked his ass.

Governess Belltree – The lady leader of Lindyburg with a *serious* distaste for magic. Like genocide level crazy.

Lilith – Drow queen and crazy manipulative, also a spider lady —creepy as hell.

Vampire Lord – Vampires, right? Yeah, she was on some serious minion shit, but had beef with her sister that saw her die.

Xaenth (Shane-th) – Drow guide and a general dickhead.

AND THE UGLY

Insane Wolves – Think crazy wolves, but you know, crazier and angrier for some reason. Due to proximity to a minion of War, the minds of these animals have eroded to nothing but the drive to kill and eat anything that is not them, or another wolf.

Undead creatures – As you can imagine, due to proximity to a minion of War, these poor bastards rose from the dead in order to protect their alien masters. Even the stronger versions are worthy of a small bit of sympathy—they sure as hell didn't get any, but they were worthy of it.

Bone Dragon – I mean, pretty self-explanatory, right? It's a bone dragon! No skin, no muscle—all bleached bones and hate for the living.

General of War (Blight) – The asshole who did some truly terrible things, sent us on a supposedly one-way trip to the Fae Realm, and got his ASS kicked. Yeah. That guy.

Ursolon – Think of a giant, striped bear with an anger management issue the size of North Dakota. Yeah. Now go fight one.

Werewolves – The hero's in some tales—but not this one. Oh no. These guys suck, big time! Hairy, needy pieces of crap.

Alpha Werewolf – The jerk in charge of the the other jerks above. Bigger, badder, stronger, and usually way more cunning and ruthless.

The Wild Hunt – A flock of assholes (read demons) who patrol the realm of the Fae and take out anything they believe doesn't belong there.

Order of the Prime – A bunch of human wizards bent on controlling the elements and restoring mankind to their rightful place as rulers. Some real xenophobic asshats, these ones.

Spiders – Oh, I mentioned these already? Because there were a lot of them. With fangs. And all the feet. Seriously, I need to book an appointment for therapy now.

Belgar – A rhino-like Fae creature with a surprising sense of honor and code that it lives by. Big as shit, and it will run anyone in its way through.

Dofilnarr (Dough-fill-nar) – A Fae creature thought to have been hunted to extinction that takes the forms and abilities of creatures it touches while in its base state. Highly vulnerable to Fae Iron.

Vampire bats – Ugly bastards that looked like man-bats that did a number on the party.

Hulking vampires – Vampires on steroids that would make Dr. Banner feel normal.

Dungeon baddies – Doing what they were designed to do, right?

And other random jerks too unimportant for now to mention— they know who they are. Bunch of assholes.

www.ingramcontent.com/pod-product-compliance
Lightning Source LLC
Chambersburg PA
CBHW030739030726
47497CB00001B/44